G. P. Putnam's Sons
Publishers Since 1838
200 Madison Avenue
New York, NY 10016

First Omnibus Edition 1989

Library of Congress Cataloging-in-Publication Data

Christie, Agatha, 1890-1976.
Three puzzles for Poirot.

Contents: Third girl—Poirot loses a client—
Funerals are fatal.
1. Poirot, Hercule (Fictitious character)—Fiction.
2. Detective and mystery stories, English. I. Title.
PR6005.H66A6 1989 823'.912 89-10152
ISBN 0-399-13496-4

Printed in the United States of America
1 2 3 4 5 6 7 8 9 10

Agatha Christie

Three Puzzles for Poirot

Including

Third Girl

Poirot Loses a Client

Funerals Are Fatal

G. P. PUTNAM'S SONS NEW YORK

Three Puzzles for Poirot

Contents

Third Girl

TO NORA BLACKBOROW

I

HERCULE POIROT was sitting at the breakfast table. At his right hand was a steaming cup of chocolate. He had always had a sweet tooth. To accompany the chocolate was a brioche. It went agreeably with chocolate. He nodded his approval. This was from the fourth shop he had tried. It was a Danish *patisserie* but infinitely superior to the so-called French one nearby. That had been nothing less than a fraud.

He was satisfied gastronomically. His stomach was at peace. His mind also was at peace, perhaps somewhat too much so. He had finished his *magnum opus*, an analysis of great writers of detective fiction. He had dared to speak scathingly of Edgar Allan Poe, he had complained of the lack of method or order in the romantic outpourings of Wilkie Collins, had lauded to the skies two American authors who were practically unknown, and had in various other ways given honor where honor was due and sternly withheld it where he considered it was not. He had seen the volume through the press, had looked upon the results and, apart from a really incredible number of printer's errors, pronounced that it was good. He had enjoyed this literary achievement and enjoyed the vast amount of reading he had had to do, had enjoyed snorting with disgust as he flung a book across the floor (though always remembering to rise, pick it up and dispose of it tidily in the waste-paper basket) and had enjoyed appreciatively nodding his head on the rare occasions when such approval was justified.

And now? He had had a pleasant interlude of relaxation, very necessary after his intellectual labor. But one could not relax forever, one had to go on to the next thing. Unfortunately he had no idea what the next thing might be. Some further literary accomplishment? He thought not. Do a thing well, then leave it alone. That was his maxim. The truth of the matter was, he was bored. All this strenuous mental activity in which he had been indulging—there had been too much of it. It had got him into bad habits, it had made him restless.

Vexatious! He shook his head and took another sip of chocolate.

The door opened and his well-trained servant, George, entered. His manner was deferential and slightly apologetic. He coughed and murmured, "A—" he paused—"a—young lady has called."

Poirot looked at him with surprise and mild distaste.

"I do not see people at this hour," he said reprovingly.

"No, sir," agreed George.

Master and servant looked at each other. Communication was sometimes fraught with difficulties for them. By inflection or innuendo or a certain choice of words George would signify that there was something that might be elicited if the right question was asked. Poirot considered what the right question in this case might be.

"She is good-looking, this young lady?" he inquired carefully.

"In my view—no, sir, but there is no accounting for tastes."

Poirot considered this reply. He remembered the slight pause that George had made before the phrase—young lady. George was a delicate social recorder. He had been uncertain of the visitor's status but had given her the benefit of the doubt.

"You are of the opinion that she is a young lady rather than, let us say, a young person?"

"I think so, sir, though it is not always easy to tell nowadays." George spoke with genuine regret.

"Did she give a reason for wishing to see me?"

"She said"—George pronounced the words with some reluctance, apologizing for them in advance, as it were—"that she wanted to consult you about a murder she might have committed."

Hercule Poirot stared. His eyebrows rose. "*Might* have committed? Does she not *know*?"

"That is what she said, sir."

"Unsatisfactory, but possibly interesting," said Poirot.

"It might—have been a joke, sir," said George dubiously.

"Anything is possible, I suppose," conceded Poirot, "but one would hardly think—" He lifted his cup. "Show her in after five minutes."

"Yes, sir." George withdrew.

Poirot finished the last sip of chocolate. He pushed aside his cup and rose to his feet. He walked to the fireplace and adjusted his mustaches carefully in the mirror over the chimney piece. Satisfied, he returned to his chair and awaited the arrival of his visitor. He did not know exactly what to expect. . . .

He had hoped perhaps for something nearer to his own estimate of female attraction. The outworn phrase "beauty in distress" had occurred to him. He was disappointed when George returned, ushering in the visitor; inwardly he shook his head and sighed. Here was no beauty—and no noticeable distress either. Mild perplexity would seem nearer the mark.

"Pah!" thought Poirot disgustedly. "These girls! Do they not even try to make something of themselves? Well-made-up, attractively dressed, hair that has been arranged by a good hairdresser, then perhaps she might pass. But now!"

His visitor was a girl of perhaps twenty-odd. Long straggly hair of indeterminate color strayed over her shoulders. Her eyes, which were large, bore a vacant expression and were of a greenish blue. She wore what were presumably the chosen clothes of her generation—black high leather boots, white open-work woolen stockings of doubtful cleanliness, a skimpy skirt, and a long and sloppy pullover of heavy wool. Anyone of Poirot's age and generation would have had only one desire—to drop the girl into a bath as soon as possible. He had often felt this same reaction walking along the streets. There were hundreds of girls looking exactly the same. They all looked dirty. And yet—a contradiction in terms—this one had the look of having been recently drowned and pulled out of a river. Such girls, he reflected, were not perhaps really dirty. They merely took enormous care and pains to look so.

He rose with his usual politeness, shook hands, drew out a chair.

"You demanded to see me, mademoiselle? Sit down, I pray of you."

"Oh," said the girl in a slightly breathless voice. She stared at him.

"Eh bien?" said Poirot.

She hesitated. "I think I'd—rather stand." The large eyes continued to stare doubtfully.

"As you please." Poirot resumed his seat and looked at her. He waited. The girl shuffled her feet. She looked down on them, then up again at Poirot.

"You—you are Hercule Poirot?"

"Assuredly. In what way can I be of use to you?"

"Oh, well, it's rather difficult. I mean—"

Poirot felt that she might need perhaps a little assistance. He said helpfully, "My manservant told me that you wanted to consult me because you thought you 'might have committed a murder.' Is that correct?"

The girl nodded. "That's right."

"Surely that is not a matter that admits of any doubt. You must know yourself whether you have committed a murder or not."

"Well, I don't know quite how to put it. I mean—"

"Come now," said Poirot kindly. "Sit down. Relax the muscles. Tell me all about it."

"I don't think—oh, dear, I don't know how to—You see, it's all so difficult. I've—I've changed my mind. I don't want to be rude but—well, I think I'd better go."

"Come now. Courage."

"No, I can't. I thought I could come and—and ask you, ask you what I ought to do—but I can't, you see. It's all so different from—"

"From what?"

"I'm awfully sorry and I really don't want to be rude, but—"

She breathed an enormous sigh, looked at Poirot, looked away, and suddenly blurted out, "You're too old. Nobody told me you were so old. I really don't want to be rude, but—there it is. You're too old. I'm really very sorry."

She turned abruptly and blundered out of the room, rather like a desperate moth in lamplight.

Poirot, his mouth open, heard the bang of the front door.

He ejaculated: *"Nom d'un nom d'un nom . . ."*

2

THE TELEPHONE RANG.

Hercule Poirot did not even seem aware of the fact.

It rang with shrill and insistent persistence.

George entered the room and stepped toward it, turning a questioning glance toward Poirot.

Poirot gestured with his hand.

"Leave it," he said.

George obeyed, leaving the room again. The telephone continued to ring. The shrill irritating noise continued. Suddenly it stopped. After a minute or two, however, it commenced to ring again.

"Ah, *Sapristi!* That must be a woman—undoubtedly a woman."

He sighed, rose to his feet and came to the instrument.

He picked up the receiver. " 'Allo," he said.

"Are you—is that Monsieur Poirot?"

"I, myself."

"It's Mrs. Oliver—your voice sounds different. I didn't recognize it at first."

"*Bonjour*, madame—you are well, I hope?"

"Oh, I'm all right." Ariadne Oliver's voice came through in its usual cheerful accents. The well-known detective story writer and Hercule Poirot were on friendly terms.

"It's rather early to ring you up, but I want to ask you a favor."

"Yes?"

"It is the annual dinner of our detective authors' club; I wondered if you would come and be our guest speaker this year. It would be very, very sweet of you if you would."

"When is this?"

"Next month—the twenty-third."

A deep sigh came over the telephone.

"Alas! I am too old."

"Too old? What on earth do you mean? You're not old at all."

"You think not?"

"Of course not. You'll be wonderful. You can tell us lots of lovely stories about real crimes."

"And who will want to listen?"

"Everyone. They—Monsieur Poirot, is there anything the matter? Has something happened? You sound upset."

"Yes, I am upset. My feelings—ah, well, no matter."

"But tell me about it."

"Why should I make a fuss?"

"Why shouldn't you? You'd better come and tell me all about it. When will you come? This afternoon. Come and have tea with me."

"Afternoon tea, I do not drink it."

"Then you can have coffee."

"It is not the time of day I usually drink coffee."

"Chocolate? With whipped cream on top? Or a tisane. You love sipping tisanes. Or lemonade. Or orangeade. Or would you like decaffeinated coffee if I can get it—"

"*Ah ça, non, par exemple!* It is an abomination."

"One of those sirops you like so much. I know, I've got half a bottle of Ribena in the cupboard."

"What is Ribena?"

"Black currant flavor."

"Indeed, one has to hand it to you! You really do try, madame. I am touched by your solicitude. I will accept with pleasure to drink a cup of chocolate this afternoon."

"Good. And then you'll tell me all about what's upset you."

She rang off.

II

Poirot considered for a moment. Then he dialed a number. Presently he said: "Mr. Goby? Hercule Poirot here. Are you very fully occupied at this moment?"

"Middling," said the voice of Mr. Goby. "Middling to fair. But to oblige you, Monsieur Poirot, if you're in a hurry, as you usually are—well, I wouldn't say that my young men couldn't manage mostly what's on hand at present. Of course, good boys aren't as easy to get as they used to be. Think too much of themselves nowadays. Think they know it all before they've started to learn. But there! Can't expect old heads on young shoulders. I'll be pleased to put myself at your disposal, Monsieur Poirot. Maybe I can put one or two of the better lads on the job. I suppose it's the usual—collecting information?"

He nodded his head and listened while Poirot went into details of exactly what he wanted done. When he had finished with Mr. Goby, Poirot rang up Scotland Yard, where in due course he got through to a friend of his. When he in turn had listened to Poirot's requirements, he replied,

"Don't want much, do you? Any murder, anywhere. Time, place and victim unknown. Sounds a bit of a wildgoose chase, if you ask me, old boy." He added disapprovingly, "You don't seem really to know anything!"

III

At 4:15 that afternoon Poirot sat in Mrs. Oliver's drawing room sipping appreciatively at a large cup of chocolate topped with foaming whipped cream, which his hostess had just placed on a small table beside him. She added a small plate full of *langue de chats* biscuits.

"*Chère* madame, what kindness." He looked over his cup with faint surprise at Mrs. Oliver's coiffure and also at her new wallpaper. Both were new to him. The last time he had seen Mrs. Oliver, her hair style had been plain and severe. It now displayed a richness of coils and twists arranged in intricate patterns all over her head. Its prolific luxury was, he suspected, largely artificial. He debated in his mind how many switches of hair might unexpectedly fall off if Mrs. Oliver was to get suddenly excited, as was her wont. As for the wallpaper . . .

"These cherries—they are new?" He waved a teaspoon. It was, he felt, rather like being in a cherry orchard.

"Are there too many of them, do you think?" said Mrs. Oliver. "So hard to tell beforehand with wallpaper. Do you think my old one was better?''

Poirot cast his mind back dimly to what he seemed to remember as large quantities of bright-colored tropical birds in a forest. He felt inclined to remark *''Plus ça change, plus c'est la même chose,''* but restrained himself.

''And now,'' said Mrs. Oliver, as her guest finally replaced his cup on its saucer and sat back with a sigh of satisfaction, wiping remnants of foaming cream from his mustache, ''what *is* all this about?''

''That I can tell you very simply. This morning a girl came to see me. I suggested she might make an appointment. One has one's routine, you comprehend. She sent back word that she wanted to see me at once because she thought she might have committed a murder.''

''What an odd thing to say. Didn't she know?''

''Precisely! *C'est inouï!* so I instructed George to show her in. She stood there! She refused to sit down. She just stood there staring at me. She seemed quite half-witted. I tried to encourage her. Then suddenly she said that she'd changed her mind. She said she didn't want to be rude but that—(what do you think?)—but that I was too old. . . .''

Mrs. Oliver hastened to utter soothing words. ''Oh, well, girls are like that. Anyone over thirty-five they think is half dead. They've no sense, girls, you must realize that.''

''It wounded me,'' said Hercule Poirot.

''Well, I shouldn't worry about it, if I were you. Of course it was a very rude thing to say.''

''That does not matter. And it is not only *my* feelings. I am worried. Yes, I am worried.''

''Well, I should forget all about it if I were you,'' advised Mrs. Oliver comfortably.

''You do not understand. I am worried about this girl. She came to me for help. Then she decided that I was too old. Too old to be of any use to her. She was wrong, of course, that goes without saying, and then she just ran away. But I tell you that girl needs help.''

''I don't suppose she does really,'' said Mrs. Oliver soothingly. ''Girls make a fuss about things.''

''No. You are wrong. She needs help.''

''You don't think she really has committed a murder?''

''Why not? She said she had.''

''Yes, but—'' Mrs. Oliver stopped. ''She said she *might* have,'' she said slowly. ''But what can she possibly mean by that?''

''Exactly. It does not make sense.''

''Who did she murder or did she think she murdered?''

Poirot shrugged his shoulders.

"And why did she murder someone?"

Again Poirot shrugged his shoulders.

"Of course, it could be all sorts of things." Mrs. Oliver began to brighten as she set her ever prolific imagination to work. "She could have run over someone in her car and not stopped. She could have been assaulted by a man on a cliff and struggled with him and managed to push him over. She could have given someone the wrong medicine by mistake. She could have gone to one of those purple pill parties and had a fight with someone. She could have come to and found she had stabbed someone. She—"

"*Assez*, madame, *assez!*"

But Mrs. Oliver was well away.

"She might have been a nurse in the operating theater and administered the wrong anesthetic or—" she broke off, suddenly anxious for clearer details. "What did she look like?"

Poirot considered for a moment.

"An Ophelia devoid of physical attraction."

"Oh, dear," said Mrs. Oliver. "I can almost see her when you say that. How queer."

"She is not competent," said Poirot. "That is how I see her. She is not one who can cope with difficulties. She is not one of those who can see beforehand the dangers that must come. She is one of whom others will look around and say, 'We want a victim. That one will do.' "

But Mrs. Oliver was no longer listening. She was clutching her rich coils of hair with both hands in a gesture with which Poirot was familiar.

"Wait," she cried in a kind of agony. "Wait!"

Poirot waited, his eyebrows raised.

"You didn't tell me her name," said Mrs. Oliver.

"She did not give it. Unfortunate, I agree with you."

"Wait!" implored Mrs. Oliver, again with the same agony. She relaxed her grip on her head and uttered a deep sigh. Hair detached itself from its bonds and tumbled over her shoulders, a super imperial coil of hair detached itself completely and fell on the floor. Poirot picked it up and put it discreetly on the table.

"Now then," said Mrs. Oliver, suddenly restored to calm. She pushed in a hairpin or two and nodded her head while she thought.

"Who told this girl about you, Monsieur Poirot?"

"No one, so far as I know. Naturally, she had heard about me, no doubt."

Mrs. Oliver thought that "naturally" was not the word at all. What was natural was that Poirot himself was sure that everyone had always heard of him. Actually large numbers of people would only look at you blankly if the name of Hercule Poirot was mentioned, especially the younger generation. "But how am I going to put that to him?" thought Mrs. Oliver, "in such a way that it won't hurt his feelings?"

"I think you're wrong," she said. "Girls—well, girls and young men—they don't know very much about detectives and things like that. They don't hear about them."

"Everyone must have heard about Hercule Poirot," said Poirot superbly.

It was an article of belief for Hercule Poirot.

"But they are all so badly educated nowadays," said Mrs. Oliver. "Really, the only people whose names they know are pop singers, or Groups, or disk jockeys—that sort of thing. If you need someone special, I mean a doctor or a detective or a dentist—well, then, I mean you would ask someone—ask who's the right person to go to? And then the other person says—'My dear, you must go to that absolutely wonderful man in Queen Anne's Street, twists your legs three times round your head and you're cured,' or 'All my diamonds were stolen, and Henry would have been furious, so I couldn't go to the police, but there's a simply uncanny detective, most discreet, and he got them back for me and Henry never knew a thing.' That's the way it happens all the time. *Someone* sent that girl to you."

"I doubt it very much."

"You wouldn't know until you were told. And you're going to be told now. It's only just come to me. *I* sent that girl to you."

Poirot stared. "You? But why did you not say so at once?"

"Because it's only just come to me—when you spoke about Ophelia—long, wet-looking hair, and rather plain. It seemed a description of someone I'd actually seen. Quite lately. And then it came to me who it was."

"Who is she?"

"I don't actually know her name, but I can easily find out. We were talking—about private detectives and private eyes—and I spoke about you and some of the amazing things you had done."

"And you gave her my address?"

"No, of course I didn't. I'd no idea she wanted a detective or anything like that. I thought we were just talking. But I'd mentioned the name several times, and of course it would be easy to look you up in the telephone book and just come along."

"Were you talking about murder?"

"Not that I can remember. I don't even know how we came to be talking about detectives—unless, yes, perhaps it was she who started the subject . . ."

"Tell me then, tell me all you can—even if you do not know her name, tell me all you know about her."

"Well, it was last weekend. I was staying with the Lorrimers. They don't come into it except that they took me over to some friends of theirs for drinks. There were several people there—and I didn't enjoy myself much because, as you know, I don't really like drink, and so people have to find a soft drink for me, which is rather a bore for them. And then people say things to me—you know—how much they like my books, and how they've been longing to meet me—and it all makes me feel hot and bothered and rather silly. But I manage to cope more or less. And they say how much they love my awful detective Sven Hjerson. If they knew how *I* hated him! But my publisher always says I'm not to say so. Anyway, I suppose the talk about detectives in real life grew out of all that, and I talked a bit about you, and this girl was standing around listening. When you said an unattractive Ophelia, it clicked somehow. I thought, 'Now who does that remind me of?' And then it came to me: 'Of course. The girl at the party that day.' I rather think she belonged there unless I'm confusing her with some other girl."

Poirot sighed. With Mrs. Oliver one always needed a lot of patience.

"Who were these people with whom you went to have drinks?"

"Trefusis, I think, unless it was Treherne. That sort of name—he's a tycoon. Rich. Something in the City, but he's spent most of his life in South Africa—"

"He has a wife?"

"Yes. Very good-looking woman. Much younger than he is. Lots of golden hair. Second wife. The daughter was the first wife's daughter. Then there was an uncle of incredible antiquity. Rather deaf. He's frightfully distinguished—strings of letters after his name. An admiral or an air marshal or something. He's an astronomer, too, I think. Anyway, he's got a kind of big telescope sticking out of the roof. Though I suppose that might be just a hobby. There was a foreign girl there, too, who sort of trots about after the old boy. Goes up to London with him, I believe, and sees he doesn't get run over. Rather pretty, she was."

Poirot sorted out the information Mrs. Oliver had supplied him with, feeling rather like a human computer.

"There lives then in the house Mr. and Mrs. Trefusis—"

"It's not Trefusis. I remember now—It's Restarick."

"That is not at all the same type of name."

"Yes, it is. It's a Cornish name, isn't it?"

"There lives there, then, Mr. and Mrs. Restarick, the distinguished elderly uncle. Is his name Restarick, too?"

"It's Sir Roderick something."

"And there is the *au pair* girl, or whatever she is, and a daughter—any more children?"

"I don't think so—but I don't really know. The daughter doesn't live at home, by the way. She was only down for the weekend. Doesn't get on with the stepmother, I expect. She's got a job in London, and she's picked up with a boy friend they don't much like, so I understand."

"You seem to know quite a lot about the family."

"Oh, well, one picks things up. The Lorrimers are great talkers. Always chattering about someone or other. One hears a lot of gossip about the people all around. Sometimes, though, one gets them mixed up. I probably have. I wish I could remember that girl's Christian name. Something connected with a song . . . Thora? *Speak to me, Thora.* Thora, Thora. Something like that, or Myra? Myra, *oh, Myra, my love is all for thee.* Something like that. I *dreamt I dwelt in marble halls.* Norma? Or do I mean Maritana? Norma—Norma Restarick. That's right, I'm sure." She added inconsequently, "She's a third girl."

"I thought you said you thought she was an only child."

"So she is—or I think so."

"Then what do you mean by saying she is the third girl?"

"Good gracious, don't you know what a third girl is? Don't you read *The Times*?"

"I read the births, deaths, and marriages. And such articles as I find of interest."

"No, I mean the front advertisement page. Only it isn't in the front now. So I'm thinking of taking some other paper. But I'll show you."

She went to a side table and snatched up *The Times*, turned the pages over and brought it to him. "Here you are—look. 'THIRD GIRL *for comfortable second-floor flat, own room, central heating, Earl's Court.' 'Third girl wanted to share flat. 5 gns. week, own room.' '4th girl wanted. Regent's Park. Own room.'* It's the way girls like living now. Better than P.G.s or a hostel. The main girl takes a furnished flat, and then shares out the rent. Second girl is usually a friend. Then they find a third girl by advertising, if they don't know one. And, as you see, very often they manage to squeeze in a fourth girl. First girl takes the best room, second girl pays rather less, third girl less still and is stuck in a cat-hole. They fix it among themselves which one has the flat to herself which night a week—or something like that. It works reasonably well."

"And where does this girl whose name might just possibly be Norma live in London?"

"As I've told you, I don't really know anything about her."

"But you could find out?"

"Oh, yes, I expect that would be quite easy."

"You are sure there was no talk, no mention of an unexpected death?"

"Do you mean a death in London—or at the Restaricks' home?"

"Either."

"I don't think so. Shall I see what I can rake up?"

Mrs. Oliver's eyes sparkled with excitement. She was by now entering into the spirit of the thing.

"That would be very kind."

"I'll ring up the Lorrimers. Actually now would be quite a good time." She went toward the telephone. "I shall have to think of reasons and things—perhaps invent things?"

She looked toward Poirot rather doubtfully.

"But naturally. That is understood. You are a woman of imagination—you will have no difficulty. But—not too fantastic, you understand. Moderation."

Mrs. Oliver flashed him an understanding glance.

She dialed and asked for the number she wanted. Turning her head, she hissed: "Have you got a pencil and paper—or a notebook—something to write down names or addresses or places?"

Poirot had already his notebook arranged by his elbow and nodded his head reassuringly.

Mrs. Oliver turned back to the receiver she held and launched herself into speech. Poirot listened attentively to one side of a telephone conversation.

"Hallo. Can I speak to—Oh, it's you, Naomi. Ariadne Oliver here. Oh, yes—well, it was rather a crowd. . . . Oh, you mean the old boy? . . . No, you know I don't. . . . Practically blind? . . . I thought he was going up to London with the little foreign girl. . . . Yes, it must be rather worrying for them sometimes—but she seems to manage him quite well. . . . One of the things I rang up for was to ask you what the girl's address was—No, the Restarick girl, I mean—somewhere in South Ken, isn't it? Or was it Knightsbridge? Well, I promised her a book and I wrote down the address, but of course I've lost it as usual. I can't even remember her name. Is it Thora or Norma? . . . Yes, I thought it was Norma. . . . Wait a minute, I'll get a pencil. . . . Yes, I'm ready . . . Sixty-seven Borodene Mansions. . . . I know—that great block that looks rather like Wormwood Scrubs prison . . . Yes, I believe the flats are very comfortable, with central heating and everything. . . . Who are the other two girls she lives with? . . . Friends of hers? . . . or advertisements? . . . Claudia Reece-Holland . . . her father's the M.P., is he? Who's the other one? . . . No, I suppose you wouldn't know—she's quite nice, too, I suppose. . . . What do they all do? They always seem to be secretaries, don't they? . . . Oh, the other girl's an interior decorator—you think—or to do with an art gallery—No, Naomi, of course I don't really want to know—one just wonders—what do all the girls do nowadays?—Well, it's useful for me to know because of my books—one wants to keep up to date. . . . What was it you told me about some boy friend . . . Yes, but one's so helpless, isn't one? I mean girls do just exactly as they like . . . Does he look very awful? Is he the unshaven dirty kind?—Oh, that kind—Brocade waistcoats, and long curling chestnut hair—lying on his shoulders—yes, so hard to tell whether they're girls or boys, isn't it?—Yes, they do look like Vandykes sometimes if they're good-looking. . . . What did you say? That Andrew Restarick simply hates him? . . . Yes, men usually do. . . . Mary Restarick? . . . Well, I suppose you do usually have rows with a stepmother. I expect she was quite thankful when the girl got a job in London. What do you mean about people saying things? . . . Why, couldn't they find out what was the matter with her? . . . Who said? . . . Yes, but what did they hush up? . . . Oh—a nurse?—talked to the Jenners' governess? Do you mean her husband? Oh, I see—The doctors couldn't find out. . . . No, but people are so ill-natured. I do agree with you. These things are usually quite untrue. . . . Oh, gastric, was it? . . . But how ridiculous. Do you mean people said what's his name—Andrew—You mean it would be easy with all those weed killers about—Yes, but why? . . . I mean, it's not a case of some wife he's hated for years—she's the second wife—and much younger than he is and good-looking. . . . Yes, I suppose that could be—but why should the foreign girl want to either? . . . You mean she might have resented things that Mrs. Restarick said to her. . . . She's quite an attractive little thing—I suppose Andrew might have taken a fancy to her—nothing serious, of course—but it might have annoyed Mary, and then she might have pitched into the girl and—"

Out of the corner of her eye, Mrs. Oliver perceived Poirot signaling wildly to her.

"Just a moment, darling," said Mrs. Oliver into the telephone. "It's the baker." Poirot looked affronted. "Hang on."

She laid down the receiver, hurried across the room, and backed Poirot into a breakfast nook.

"Yes," she demanded breathlessly.

"A baker," said Poirot with scorn. "Me!"

"Well, I had to think of something quickly. What were you signaling about? Did you understand what she—"

Poirot cut her short.

"You shall tell me presently. I know enough. What I want you to do is, with your rapid powers of improvisation, to arrange some plausible pretext for me to visit the Restaricks—an old friend of yours, shortly to be in the neighborhood. Perhaps you could say—"

"Leave it to me. I'll think of something. Shall you give a false name?"

"Certainly not. Let us at least try to keep it simple."

Mrs. Oliver nodded and hurried back to the abandoned telephone.

"Naomi? I can't remember what we were saying. Why does something always come to interrupt just when one has settled down to a nice gossip? I can't even remember now what I rang you up for to begin with—Oh, yes—that child Thora's address—Norma, I mean—and you gave it to me. But there was something else I wanted to—oh, I remember. An old friend of mine. A most fascinating little man. Actually I was talking about him the other day down there. Hercule Poirot his name is. He's going to be staying quite close to the Restaricks and he is most tremendously anxious to meet old Sir Roderick. He knows a lot about him and has a terrific admiration for him, and for some wonderful discovery of his in the war—or some scientific thing he did—anyway, he is very anxious to 'call upon him and present his respects,' that's how he put it. Will that be all right, do you think? Will you warn them? Yes, he'll probably just turn up out of the blue. Tell them to make him tell them some wonderful espionage stories. . . . He—what? Oh! your mowers? Yes, of course you must go. Good-by."

She put back the receiver and sank down in an armchair. "Goodness, how exhausting. Was that all right?"

"Not bad," said Poirot.

"I thought I'd better pin it all to the old boy. Then you'll get to see the lot, which I suppose is what you want. And one can always be vague about scientific subjects if one is a woman, and you can think up something more definite that sounds probable by the time you arrive. Now, do you want to hear what she was telling me?"

"There has been gossip, I gather. About the health of Mrs. Restarick?"

"That's it. It seems she had some kind of mysterious illness—gastric in nature—and the doctors were puzzled. They sent her into hospital and she got quite all right, but there didn't seem any real cause to account for it. And she went home, and it all began to start again—and again the doctors were puzzled. And then people began to talk. A rather irresponsible nurse started it, and her sister told a neighbor, and the neighbor went out on daily work and told someone else, and how queer it all was. And then people began saying that her husband must be trying to poison her. The sort of thing people always say—but in this case it really didn't seem to make sense. And then Naomi and I wondered about the *au pair* girl—at least she isn't exactly an *au pair* girl, she's a kind of secretary companion to the old boy—so really there isn't any kind of reason why she should administer weed killer to Mrs. Restarick."

"I heard you suggesting a few."

"Well, there is usually something possible . . ."

"Murder desired . . ." said Poirot thoughtfully . . . "but not yet committed."

3

MRS. OLIVER drove into the inner court of Borodene Mansions. There were six cars filling the parking space. As Mrs. Oliver hesitated, one of the cars backed out and drove away. Mrs. Oliver hurried neatly into the vacant space.

She descended, banged the door and stood looking up to the sky. It was a recent block, occupying a space left by the havoc of a land mine in the last war. It might, Mrs. Oliver thought, have been lifted *en bloc* from the Great West Road and, first deprived of some such legend as SLYLARK'S FEATHER RAZOR BLADES, have been deposited as a block of flats *in situ*. It looked extremely functional, and whoever had built it had obviously scorned any ornamental additions.

It was a busy time. Cars and people were going in and out of the courtyard as the day's work came to a close.

Mrs. Oliver glanced down at her wrist. Ten minutes to seven. About the right time, as far as she could judge. The kind of time when girls in jobs might be presumed to have returned, either to renew their make-up, change their clothes to tight exotic pants or whatever their particular addiction was, and go out again, or else to settle down to home life and wash their underwear and their stockings. Anyway, quite a sensible time to try. The block was exactly the same on the east and the west, with big swing doors set in the center. Mrs. Oliver chose the left-hand side but immediately found that she was wrong. All this side was numbers from 100 to 200. She crossed over to the other side.

Number 67 was on the sixth floor. Mrs. Oliver pressed the button of the lift. The doors opened like a yawning mouth with a menacing clash. Mrs. Oliver hurried into the yawning cavern. She was always afraid of modern lifts.

Crash. The doors came to again. The lift went up. It stopped almost immediately (that was frightening, too!). Mrs. Oliver scuttled out like a frightened rabbit.

She looked up at the wall and went along the right-hand passage. She came to a door marked 67 in metal numbers affixed to the center of the door. The numeral 7 detached itself and fell on her feet as she arrived.

"This place doesn't like me," said Mrs. Oliver to herself as she winced with pain and picked the number up gingerly and affixed it by its spike to the door again.

She pressed the bell. Perhaps everyone was out.

However, the door opened almost at once. A tall, handsome girl stood in the doorway. She was wearing a dark, well-cut suit with a very short skirt, a white silk shirt, and was very well-shod. She had swept-up dark hair, good but discreet make-up, and for some reason was slightly alarming to Mrs. Oliver.

"Oh," said Mrs. Oliver, galvanizing herself to say the right thing. "Is Miss Restarick in, by any chance?"

"No, I'm sorry, she's out. Can I give her a message?"

Mrs. Oliver said, "Oh" again—before proceeding. She made a play of action by producing a parcel rather untidily done up in brown paper. "I promised her a book," she explained. "One of mine that she hadn't read. I hope I've remembered actually which it was. She won't be in soon, I suppose?"

"I really couldn't say. I don't know what she is doing tonight."

"Oh. Are you Miss Reece-Holland?"

The girl looked slightly surprised.

"Yes, I am."

"I've met your father," said Mrs. Oliver. She went on, "I'm Mrs. Oliver. I write books," she added in the usual guilty style in which she invariably made such an announcement.

"Won't you come in?"

Mrs. Oliver accepted the invitation, and Claudia Reece-Holland led her into a sitting room. All the rooms of the flats were papered the same, with an artificial raw wood pattern. Tenants could then display their modern pictures or apply any forms of decoration they fancied. There was a foundation of modern built-in furniture, cupboard, bookshelves, and so on, a large settee and a pull-out type of table. Personal bits and pieces could be added by the tenants. There were also signs of individuality displayed here by a gigantic Harlequin pasted on one wall, and a stencil of a monkey swinging from branches of palm fronds on another wall.

"I'm sure Norma will be thrilled to get your book, Mrs. Oliver. Won't you have a drink? Sherry? Gin?"

This girl had the brisk manner of a really good secretary.

Mrs. Oliver refused.

"You've got a splendid view up here," she said, looking out of the window and blinking a little as she got the setting sun straight in her eyes.

"Yes. Not so funny when the lift goes out of order."

"I shouldn't have thought that lift would dare to go out of order. It's so—so—robot-like."

"Recently installed, but none the better for that," said Claudia. "It needs frequent adjusting and all that."

Another girl came in, talking as she entered.

"Claudia, have you any idea where I put—"

She stopped, looking at Mrs. Oliver.

Claudia made a quick introduction.

"Frances Cary—Mrs. Oliver. Mrs. *Ariadne* Oliver."

"Oh, how exciting," said Frances.

She was a tall, willowy girl, with long black hair, a heavily made up dead white face, and eyebrows and eyelashes slightly slanted upward—the effect heightened by mascara. She wore tight velvet pants and a heavy sweater. She was a complete contrast to the brisk and efficient Claudia.

"I brought a book I'd promised Norma Restarick," said Mrs. Oliver.

"Oh!—what a pity she's still in the country."

"Hasn't she come back?"

There was quite definitely a pause. Mrs. Oliver thought the two girls exchanged a glance.

"I thought she had a job in London," said Mrs. Oliver, endeavoring to convey innocent surprise.

"Oh, yes," said Claudia. "She's in an interior decorating place. She's sent down with patterns occasionally to places in the country." She smiled. "We live rather separate lives here," she explained. "Come and go as we like—and don't usually bother to leave messages. But I won't forget to give her your book when she does get back."

Nothing could have been easier than the casual explanation.

Mrs. Oliver rose. "Well, thank you very much."

Claudia accompanied her to the door. "I shall tell my father I've met you," she said. "He's a great reader of detective stories."

Closing the door, she went back into the sitting room.

The girl Frances was leaning against the window.

"Sorry," she said. "Did I boob?"

"I'd just said that Norma was out."

Frances shrugged her shoulders.

"I couldn't tell. Claudia, where is that girl? Why didn't she come back on Monday? Where has she gone?"

"I can't imagine."

"She didn't stay on down with her people? That's where she went for the weekend."

"No. I rang up, actually, to find out."

"I suppose it doesn't really matter . . . All the same, she is—well, there's something queer about her."

"She's not really queerer than anyone else." But the opinion sounded uncertain.

"Oh, yes, she is," said Frances. "Sometimes she gives me the shivers. She's not normal, you know."

She laughed suddenly.

"Norma isn't normal! You know she isn't, Claudia, although you won't admit it. Loyalty to your employer, I suppose."

4

HERCULE POIROT walked along the main street of Long Basing. That is, if you can describe as a main street a street that is to all intents and purposes the only street, which was the case in Long Basing. It was one of those villages that exhibit a tendency to length without breadth. It had an impressive church with a tall tower and a yew tree of elderly dignity in its churchyard. It had its full quota of village shops disclosing much variety. It had two antique shops, one mostly consisting of stripped pine chimney pieces, the other disclosing a full house of piled-up ancient maps, a good deal of porcelain, most of it chipped, some worm-eaten old oak chests, shelves of glass, some Victorian silver, all somewhat hampered in display by lack of space. There were two cafés, both rather nasty; there was a basket shop, quite delightful, with a large variety of homemade wares; there was a post office-cum-greengrocer; there was a draper's which dealt largely in millinery, and also a shoe department for children and a large miscellaneous selection of haberdashery of all kinds. There was a stationery and newspaper shop which also dealt in tobacco and sweets. There was a wool shop which was clearly the aristocrat of the place. Two white-haired severe women were in charge of shelves and shelves of knitting materials of every description. Also large quantities of dressmaking patterns and knitting patterns and which branched off into a counter for art needlework. What had lately been the local grocer's had now blossomed into calling itself "a supermarket," complete with stacks of wire baskets and packaged materials of every cereal and cleaning material, all in dazzling paper boxes. And there was a small establishment with one small window with Lillah written across it in fancy letters, a fashion display of one French blouse, labeled "Latest chic," and a navy skirt and a purple-striped jumper labeled "separates." These were displayed by being flung down as by a careless hand in the window.

All of this Poirot observed with a detached interest. Also contained within the limits of the village and facing on the street were several small houses, old-fashioned in style, sometimes retaining Georgian purity, more often showing some signs of Victorian improvement, as a veranda, bow window, or a small conservatory. One or two houses had had a complete face lift and showed signs of claiming to be new and proud of it. There were also some delightful and decrepit old-world cottages, some pretending to be a hundred or so years older than they were, others completely genuine, any added comforts of plumbing or such being carefully hidden from any casual glance.

Poirot walked gently along, digesting all that he saw. If his impatient friend, Mrs. Oliver, had been with him, she would have immediately demanded why he was wasting time, as the house to which he was bound was a quarter of a mile beyond the village limits. Poirot would have told her that he was absorbing the local atmosphere; that these things were sometimes important. At the end of the village there came an abrupt transition. On one side, set back from the road, was a row of newly built council houses, a strip of green in front of them and a gay note set by each house having been given a different-colored front door. Beyond the council houses the sway of fields and hedges resumed its course interspersed now and then by the occasional "desirable residences" of a house agent's list, with their own trees and gardens and a general air of reserve and of keeping themselves to themselves. Ahead of him farther down the road Poirot descried a house, the top story of which displayed an unusual note of bulbous construction. Something had evidently been tacked on up there not so many years ago. This no doubt was the Mecca toward which his feet were bent. He arrived at a gate to which the nameplate Crosshedges was attached. He surveyed the house. It was a conventional house dating perhaps to the beginning of the century. It was neither beautiful nor ugly. Commonplace was perhaps the word to describe it. The garden was more attractive than the house and had obviously been the subject of a great deal of care and attention in its time, though it had been allowed to fall into disarray. It still had smooth green lawns, plenty of flower beds, carefully planted areas of shrubs to display a certain landscape effect. It was all in good order. A gardener was certainly employed in this garden, Poirot reflected. A personal interest was perhaps also taken, since he noted in a corner near the house a woman bending over one of the flower beds, tying up dahlias, he thought. Her head showed as a bright circle of pure gold color. She was tall, slim but square-shouldered. He unlatched the gate, passed through and walked up toward the house. The woman turned her head and then straightened herself, turning toward him inquiringly.

She remained standing, waiting for him to speak, some garden twine hanging from her left hand. She looked, he noted, puzzled.

"Yes?" she said.

Poirot, very foreign, took off his hat with a flourish and bowed. Her eyes rested on his mustaches with a kind of fascination.

"Mrs. Restarick?"

"Yes. I—"

"I hope I do not derange you, madame."

A faint smile touched her lips. "Not at all. Are you—"

"I have permitted myself to pay a visit on you. A friend of mine, Mrs. Ariadne Oliver—"

"Oh, of course. I know who you must be. Monsieur Poiret."

"Monsieur Poir*o*t," he corrected her with an emphasis on the last syllable. "Hercule Poirot, at your service. I was passing through this neighborhood and I ventured to call upon you here in the hope that I might be allowed to pay my respects to Sir Roderick Horsefield."

"Yes. Naomi Lorrimer told us you might turn up."

"I hope it is not inconvenient?"

"Oh, it is not inconvenient at all. Ariadne Oliver was here last weekend. She came over with the Lorrimers. Her books are most amusing, aren't they? But perhaps you don't find detective stories amusing. You are a detective yourself, aren't you—a real one?"

"I am all that there is of the most real," said Hercule Poirot.

He noticed that she repressed a smile. He studied her more closely. She was handsome in a rather artificial fashion. Her golden hair was stiffly arranged. He wondered whether she might not at heart be secretly unsure of herself, whether she were not carefully playing the part of the English lady absorbed in her garden. He wondered a little what her social background might have been.

"You have a very fine garden here," he said.

"You like gardens?"

"Not as the English like gardens. You have for a garden a special talent in England. It means something to you that it does not to us."

"To French people, you mean?"

"I am not French. I am Belgian."

"Oh, yes. I believe that Mrs. Oliver mentioned that you were once with the Belgian police force?"

"That is so. Me, I am an old Belgian police dog." He gave a polite little laugh and said, waving his hands, "But your gardens, you English, I admire. I sit at your feet! The Latin races, they like the formal garden, the gardens of the château, the Château of Versailles in miniature, and also, of course, they invented the *potager*. Very important, the *potager*. Here in England you have the *potager*, but you got it from France and you do not love your *potager* as much as you love your flowers. Hein? That is so?"

"Yes, I think you are right," said Mary Restarick. "Do come into the house. You came to see my uncle."

"I came, as you say, to pay homage to Sir Roderick, but I pay homage to you also, madame. Always I pay homage to beauty when I meet it." He bowed.

She laughed with slight embarrassment. "You mustn't pay me so many compliments."

She led the way through an open French window and he followed her.

"I knew your uncle slightly in nineteen forty-four."

"Poor dear, he's getting quite an old man now. He's very deaf, I'm afraid."

"It was long ago that I encountered him. He will probably have forgotten. It was a matter of espionage and of scientific developments of a certain invention. We owed that invention to the ingenuity of Sir Roderick. He will be willing, I hope, to receive me."

"Oh, I'm sure he'll love it," said Mrs. Restarick. "He has rather a dull life in some ways nowadays. I have to be so much in London—we are looking for a suitable house there." She sighed and said, "Elderly people can be very difficult sometimes."

"I know," said Poirot. "Frequently I, too, am difficult."

She laughed. "Ah, no, Monsieur Poirot, come now, you mustn't pretend you're old."

"Sometimes I am told so," said Poirot. He sighed. "By young girls," he added mournfully.

"That's very unkind of them. It's probably the sort of thing that our daughter would do," she added.

"Ah, you have a daughter?"

"Yes. At least, she is my stepdaughter."

"I shall have much pleasure in meeting her," said Poirot politely.

"Oh, well, I'm afraid she is not here. She's in London. She works there."

"The young girls, they all do jobs nowadays."

"Everybody's supposed to do a job," said Mrs. Restarick vaguely. "Even when they get married, they're always being persuaded back into industry or back into teaching."

"Have they persuaded you, madame, to come back into anything?"

"No. I was brought up in South Africa. I only came here with my husband a short time ago—It's all—rather strange to me still."

She looked round her with what Poirot judged to be an absence of enthusiasm. It was a handsomely furnished room of a conventional type —without personality. Two large portraits hung on the walls—the only personal touch. The first was that of a thin-lipped woman in a gray velvet evening dress. Facing her on the opposite wall was a man of about thirty-odd, with an air of repressed energy about him.

"Your daughter, I suppose, finds it dull in the country?"

"Yes, it is much better for her to be in London. She doesn't like it here." She paused abruptly, and then as though the last words were almost dragged out of her, she said, "—and she doesn't like me."

"Impossible," said Hercule Poirot with Gallic politeness.

"Not at all impossible! Oh, well, I suppose it often happens. I suppose it's hard for girls to accept a stepmother."

"Was your daughter very fond of her own mother?"

"I suppose she must have been. She's a difficult girl. I suppose most girls are."

Poirot sighed and said, "Mothers and fathers have much less control over daughters nowadays. It is not as it used to be in the old good-fashioned days."

"No indeed."

"One dare not say so, madame, but I must confess I regret that they show so very little discrimination in choosing their—how do you say it? —their boy friends?"

"Norma has been a great worry to her father in that way. However, I suppose it is no good complaining. People must make their own experiments. But I must take you up to Uncle Roddy—he has his own rooms upstairs."

She led the way out of the room. Poirot looked back over his shoulder. A dull room, a room without character—except perhaps for the two portraits. By the style of the woman's dress, Poirot judged that they dated from some years back. If that was the first Mrs. Restarick, Poirot did not think that he would have liked her.

He said, "Those are fine portraits, madame."

"Yes. Lansberger did them."

It was the name of a famous and exceedingly expensive fashionable portrait painter of twenty years ago. His meticulous naturalism had now gone out of fashion, and since his death, he was little spoken of. His sitters were sometimes sneeringly spoken of as "clothes props," but Poirot thought they were a good deal more than that. He suspected that there was a carefully concealed mockery behind the smooth exteriors that Lansberger executed so effortlessly.

Mary Restarick said as she went up the stairs ahead of him,

"They have just come out of storage—and been cleaned up and—"

She stopped abruptly—coming to a dead halt, one hand on the stair-rail.

Above her, a figure had just turned the corner of the staircase on its way down. It was a figure that seemed strangely incongruous. It might have been someone in fancy dress, someone who certainly did not match with this house.

He was a figure familiar enough to Poirot in different conditions, a figure often met in the streets of London or even at parties. A representative of the youth of today. He wore a black coat, an elaborate velvet waistcoat, skin-tight pants, and rich curls of chestnut hair hung down on his neck. He looked exotic and rather beautiful, and it needed a few moments to be certain of his sex.

"David!" Mary Restarick spoke sharply. "What on earth are you doing here?"

The young man was by no means taken aback. "Startled you?" he asked. "So sorry."

"What are you doing here—in this house? You—have you come down here with Norma?"

"Norma? No. I hoped to find her here."

"Find her here—what do you mean? She's in London."

"Oh, but, my dear, she isn't. At any rate, she's not at Sixty-seven Borodene Mansions."

"What do you mean, she isn't there?"

"Well, since she didn't come back this weekend, I thought she was probably here with you. I came down to see what she was up to."

"She left here Sunday night as usual." She added in an angry voice, "Why didn't you ring the bell and let us know you were here? What are you doing roaming about the house?"

"Really, darling, you seem to be thinking I'm going to pinch the spoons or something. Surely it's natural to walk into a house in broad daylight. Why ever not?''

''Well, we're old-fashioned and we don't like it.''

''Oh, dear, dear.'' David sighed. ''The fuss everyone makes. Well, my dear, if I'm not going to have a welcome and you don't seem to know where your stepdaughter is, I suppose I'd better be moving along. Shall I turn out my pockets before I go?''

''Don't be absurd, David.''

''Ta-ta, then.'' The young man passed them, waved an airy hand and went on down and out through the open front door.

''Horrible creature,'' said Mary Restarick, with a sharpness of rancor that startled Poirot. ''I can't bear him. I simply can't stand him. Why is England absolutely full of these people nowadays?''

''Ah, madame, do not disquiet yourself. It is all a question of fashion. There have always been fashions. You see less in the country, but in London you meet plenty of them.''

''Dreadful,'' said Mary. ''Absolutely dreadful. Effeminate, exotic.''

''And yet not unlike a Vandyke portrait, do you not think so, madame? In a gold frame, wearing a lace collar, you would not then say he was effeminate or exotic.''

''Daring to come down here like that. Andrew would have been furious. It worries him dreadfully. Daughters can be very worrying. It's not even as though Andrew knew Norma well. He's been abroad since she was a child. He left her entirely to her mother to bring up, and now he finds her a complete puzzle. So do I, for that matter. I can't help feeling that she is a very odd type of girl. One has no kind of authority over them these days. They seem to like the worst type of young men. She's absolutely infatuated with this David Baker. One can't do anything. Andrew forbade him the house, and look, he turns up here, walks in as cool as a cucumber. I think—I almost think I'd better not tell Andrew. I don't want him to be unduly worried. I believe she goes about with this creature in London, and not only with him. There are some much worse ones even. The kind that don't wash, completely unshaven faces and funny sprouting beards and greasy clothes.''

Poirot said cheerfully, ''Alas, madame, you must not distress yourself. The indiscretions of youth pass.''

''I hope so, I'm sure. Norma is a very difficult girl. Sometimes I think she's not right in the head. She's so peculiar. She really looks sometimes as though she isn't all there. These extraordinary dislikes she takes—''

''Dislikes?''

''She hates me. Really hates me. I don't see why it's necessary. I suppose she was very devoted to her mother, but after all, it's only reasonable that her father should marry again, isn't it?''

''Do you think she really hates you?''

''Oh, I know she does. I've had ample proof of it. I can't say how relieved I was when she went off to London. I didn't want to make trouble—'' She stopped suddenly. It was as though for the first time she realized that she was talking to a stranger.

Poirot had the capacity to attract confidences. It was as though when people were talking to him they hardly realized who it was they were talking to. She gave a short laugh now.

''Dear me,'' she said, ''I don't really know why I'm saying all this to you. I expect every family has these problems. Poor stepmothers, we have a hard time of it. Ah, here we are.''

She tapped on a door.

''Come in, come in.''

It was a stentorian roar.

''Here is a visitor to see you, Uncle,'' said Mary Restarick as she walked into the room, Poirot behind her.

A broad-shouldered, square-faced, red-cheeked, irascible-looking elderly man had been pacing the floor. He stumped forward toward them. At the table behind him a girl was sitting sorting letters and papers. Her head was bent over them—a sleek, dark head.

''This is Monsieur Hercule Poirot, Uncle Roddy,'' said Mary Restarick.

Poirot stepped forward gracefully into action and speech. ''Ah, Sir Roderick, it is many years—many years since I have had the pleasure of meeting you. We have to go back so far as the last war. It was, I think, in Normandy the last time. How well I remember, there was there also Colonel Race and there was General Abercromby and there was Air Marshal Sir Edmund Collingsby. What decisions we had to make! And what difficulties we had with security. Ah, nowadays, there is no longer the need for secrecy. I recall the unmasking of that secret agent who succeeded for so long—you remember Captain Henderson.''

''Ah. Captain Henderson indeed. Lord, that damned swine! Unmasked!''

''You may not remember me, Hercule Poirot.''

''Yes, yes, of course I remember you. Ah, it was a close shave that, a close shave. You were the French representative, weren't you? There were one or two of them, one I couldn't get on with—can't remember his name. Ah, well, sit down, sit down. Nothing like having a chat over old days.''

''I feared so much that you might not remember me or my colleague, Monsieur Giraud.''

"Yes, yes, of course I remember both of you. Ah, those were the days, those were the days indeed."

The girl at the table got up. She moved a chair politely toward Poirot.

"That's right, Sonia, that's right," said Sir Roderick. "Let me introduce you," he said, "to my charming little secretary here. Makes a great difference to me. Helps me, you know; files all my work. Don't know how I ever got on without her."

Poirot bowed politely. "*Enchanté*, mademoiselle," he murmured.

The girl murmured something in rejoinder. She was a small creature with black bobbed hair. She looked shy. Her dark blue eyes were usually modestly cast down, but she smiled up sweetly and shyly at her employer. He patted her on the shoulder.

"Don't know what I should do without her," he said. "I don't really."

"Oh, no," the girl protested. "I am not much good really. I cannot type very fast."

"You type quite fast enough, my dear. You're my memory, too. My eyes and my ears and a great many other things."

She smiled again at him.

"One remembers," murmured Poirot, "some of the excellent stories that used to go the round. I don't know if they were exaggerated or not. Now, for instance, the day that someone stole your car and—" he proceeded to follow up the tale.

Sir Roderick was delighted. "Ha, ha, of course now. Yes, indeed, well, bit of exaggeration, I expect. But on the whole, that's how it was. Yes, yes, well, fancy your remembering that, after all this long time. But I could tell you a better one than that now." He launched forth into another tale.

Poirot listened, applauded. Finally he glanced at his watch and rose to his feet.

"But I must detain you no longer," he said. "You are engaged, I can see, in important work. It was just that being in this neighborhood, I could not help paying my respects. Years pass, but you, I see, have lost none of your vigor, of your enjoyment of life."

"Well, well, perhaps you may say so. Anyway, you mustn't pay me too many compliments—but surely you'll stay and have tea. I'm sure Mary will give you some tea." He looked round. "Oh, she's gone away. Nice girl."

"Yes, indeed, and very handsome. I expect she has been a great comfort to you for many years."

"Oh! they've only married recently. She's my nephew's second wife. I'll be frank with you. I've never cared very much for this nephew of mine, Andrew—not a steady chap. Always restless. His elder brother Simon was my favorite. Not that I knew him well, either. As for Andrew, he behaved very badly to his first wife. Went off, you know. Left her high and dry. Went off with a thoroughly bad lot. Everybody knew about her. But he was infatuated with her. The whole thing broke up in a year or two; silly fellow. This girl he's married seems all right. Nothing wrong with her as far as I know. Now Simon was a steady chap—damned dull, though. I can't say I liked it when my sister married into that family. Marrying into trade, you know. Rich, of course, but money isn't everything—we've usually married into the Services. I never saw much of the Restarick lot.''

''They have, I believe, a daughter. A friend of mine met her last week.''

''Oh, Norma. Silly girl. Goes about in dreadful clothes and has picked up with a dreadful young man. Ah, well, they're all alike nowadays. Long-haired young fellows, beatniks, Beatles, all sorts of names they've got. I can't keep up with them. Practically talk a foreign language. Still, nobody cares to hear an old man's criticisms, so there we are. Even Mary—I always thought she was a good, sensible sort, but as far as I can see, she can be thoroughly hysterical in some ways—mainly about her health. Some fuss about going to hospital for observation or something. What about a drink? Whisky? No? Sure you won't stop and have a drop of tea?''

''Thank you, but I am staying with friends.''

''Well, I must say I have enjoyed this chat with you very much. Nice to remember some of the things that happened in the old days. Sonia, dear, perhaps you'll take Monsieur—sorry, what's your name, it's gone again—ah, yes, Poirot. Take him down to Mary, will you?''

''No, no,'' Hercule Poirot hastily waved aside the offer. ''I could not dream of troubling Madame any more. I am quite all right. Quite all right. I can find my way perfectly. It has been a great pleasure to meet you again.''

He left the room.

''Haven't the faintest idea who that chap was,'' said Sir Roderick, after Poirot had gone.

''You do not know who he was?'' Sonia asked, looking at him in a startled manner.

''Personally, I don't remember who half the people are who come up and talk to me nowadays. Of course, I have to make a good shot at it. One learns to get away with that, you know. Same thing at parties. Up comes a chap and says, 'Perhaps you don't remember me. I last saw you in nineteen thirty-nine.' I have to say, 'Of course I remember,' but I don't. It's a handicap being nearly blind and deaf. We got pally with a lot of frogs like that toward the end of the war. Don't remember half of them. Oh, he'd been there, all right. He knew me and I knew a good many of the chaps he talked about. That story about me and the stolen car, that was true enough. Exaggerated a bit, of course; they made a pretty good story of it at the time. Ah, well, I don't think he knew I didn't remember him. Clever chap, I should say, but a thorough frog, isn't he? You know, mincing and dancing and bowing and scraping. Now then, where were we?''

Sonia picked up a letter and handed it to him. She tentatively proffered a pair of spectacles, which he immediately rejected.

''Don't want those damned things—I can see all right.''

He screwed up his eyes and peered down at the letter he was holding. Then he capitulated and thrust it back into her hands.

''Well, perhaps you'd better read it to me.''

She started reading it in her clear soft voice.

5

HERCULE POIROT stood upon the landing for a moment. His head was a little on one side, with a listening air. He could hear nothing from downstairs. He crossed to the landing window and looked out. Mary Restarick was below on the terrace, resuming her gardening work. Poirot nodded his head in satisfaction. He walked gently along the corridor. One by one in turn he opened the doors. A bathroom, a linen cupboard, a double-bedded spare room, an occupied single bedroom, a woman's room, with a double bed (Mary Restarick's?). The next door was that of an adjoining room and was, he guessed, the room belonging to Andrew Restarick. He turned to the other side of the landing. The door he opened first was a single bedroom. It was not, he judged, occupied at the time, but it was a room which possibly was occupied at weekends. There were toilet brushes on the dressing-table. He listened carefully, then tiptoed in. He opened the wardrobe. Yes, there were some clothes hanging up there. Country clothes.

There was a writing table, but there was nothing on it. He opened the desk drawers very softly. There were a few odds and ends, a letter or two, but the letters were trivial and dated some time ago. He shut the desk drawers. He walked downstairs and, going out of the house, bade farewell to his hostess. He refused her offer of tea. He had promised to get back, he said, as he had to catch a train to town very shortly afterward.

"Don't you want a taxi? We could order you one, or I could drive you in the car."

"No, no, madame, you are too kind."

Poirot walked back to the village and turned down the lane by the church. He crossed a little bridge over a stream. Presently he came to where a large car with a chauffeur was waiting discreetly under a beech tree. The chauffeur opened the door of the car, Poirot got inside, sat down and removed his patent-leather shoes, uttering a gasp of relief.

"Now we return to London," he said.

The chauffeur closed the door, returned to his seat and the car purred quietly away. The sight of a young man standing by the roadside furiously thumbing a ride was not an unusual one. Poirot's eyes rested almost indifferently on this member of the fraternity, a brightly dressed young man with long and exotic hair. There were many such, but in the moment of passing him Poirot suddenly sat upright and addressed the driver.

"If you please, stop. Yes, and if you can reverse a little . . . There is someone requesting a lift."

The chauffeur turned an incredulous eye over his shoulder. It was the last remark he would have expected. However, Poirot was gently nodding his head, so he obeyed.

The young man called David advanced to the door. "Thought you weren't going to stop for me," he said cheerfully. "Much obliged, I'm sure."

He got in, removed a small pack from his shoulders and let it slide to the floor, smoothed down his copper brown locks. "So you recognized me," he said.

"You are perhaps somewhat conspicuously dressed."

"Oh, do you think so? Not really. I'm just one of a band of brothers."

"The school of Vandyke. Very dressy."

"Oh. I've never thought of it like that. Yes, there may be something in what you say."

"You should wear a cavalier's hat," said Poirot, "and a lace collar, if I might advise."

"Oh, I don't think we go quite as far as that." The young man laughed. "How Mrs. Restarick dislikes the mere sight of me. Actually, I reciprocate her dislike. I don't care much for Restarick, either. There is something singularly unattractive about successful tycoons, don't you think?"

"It depends on the point of view. You have been paying attentions to the daughter, I understand."

"That is such a nice phrase," said David. "Paying attentions to the daughter. I suppose it might be called that. But there's plenty of fifty-fifty about it, you know. She's paying attention to me, too."

"Where is Mademoiselle now?"

David turned his head rather sharply. "And why do you ask that?"

"I should like to meet her." He shrugged his shoulders.

"I don't believe she'd be your type, you know, any more than I am. Norma's in London."

"But you said to her stepmother—"

"Oh! we don't tell stepmothers everything."

"And where is she in London?"

"She works in an interior decorator's down the King's Road somewhere in Chelsea. Can't remember the name of it for the moment. Susan Phelps, I think."

"But that is not where she lives, I presume. You have her address?"

"Oh, yes, a great block of flats. I don't really understand your interest."

"One is interested in so many things."

"What do you mean?"

"What brought you to that house—(what is its name?—Crosshedges) today? Brought you secretly into the house and up the stairs?"

"I came in the back door, I admit."

"What were you looking for upstairs?"

"That's my business. I don't want to be rude—but aren't you being rather nosy?"

"Yes, I am displaying curiosity. I would like to know exactly where this young lady is."

"I see. Dear Andrew and dear Mary—Lord rot 'em—are employing you, is that it? They are trying to find her?"

"As yet," said Poirot, "I do not think they know that she is missing."

"Someone must be employing you."

"You are exceedingly perceptive," said Poirot. He leaned back.

"I wondered what you were up to," said David. "That's why I hailed you. I hoped you'd stop and give me a bit of dope. She's my girl. You know that, I suppose?"

"I understand that that is supposed to be the idea," said Poirot cautiously. "If so, you should know where she is. Is that not so, Mr.—I am sorry, I do not think I know your name beyond, that is, that your Christian name is David."

"Baker."

"Perhaps, Mr. Baker, you have had a quarrel."

"No, we haven't had a quarrel. Why should you think we had?"

"Miss Norma Restarick left Crosshedges on Sunday evening, or was it Monday morning?"

"It depends. There is an early bus you can take. Gets you to London a little after ten. It would make her a bit late at work, but not too much. Usually she goes back on Sunday night."

"She left there Sunday night, but she has not arrived at Borodene Mansions."

"Apparently not. So Claudia says."

"This Miss Reece-Holland—that is her name, is it not?—was she surprised or worried?"

"Good Lord, no, why should she be? They don't keep tabs on each other all the time, these girls."

"But you thought she was going back there?"

"She didn't go back to work either. They're fed up at the shop, I can tell you."

"Are you worried, Mr. Baker?"

"No. Naturally—I mean, well, I'm damned if I know. I don't see any reason I should be worried, only time's getting on. What is it today—Thursday?"

"She has not quarreled with you?"

"No. We don't quarrel."

"But you are worried about her, Mr. Baker?"

"What business is it of yours?"

"It is no business of mine, but there has, I understand, been trouble at home. She does not like her stepmother."

"Quite right, too. She's a bitch, that woman. Hard as nails. She doesn't like Norma either."

"She has been ill, has she not? She had to go to hospital."

"Who are you talking about—Norma?"

"No, I am not talking about Miss Restarick. I am talking about Mrs. Restarick."

"I believe she did go into a nursing home. No reason she should. Strong as a horse, I'd say."

"And Miss Restarick hates her stepmother."

"She's a bit unbalanced sometimes, Norma. You know, goes off the deep end. I tell you, girls always hate their stepmothers."

"Does that always make stepmothers ill? Ill enough to go to hospital?"

"What the hell are you getting at?"

"Gardening perhaps—or the use of weed killer."

"What do you mean by talking about weed killer? Are you suggesting that Norma—that she'd dream of—that—"

"People talk," said Poirot. "Talk goes round the neighborhood."

"Do you mean that somebody has said that Norma has tried to poison her stepmother? That's ridiculous. It's absolutely absurd."

"It is very unlikely, I agree," said Poirot. "Actually, people have not been saying that."

"Oh. Sorry. I misunderstood. But—what did you mean?"

"My dear young man," said Poirot, "you must realize that there are rumors going about, and rumors are almost always about the same person—a husband."

"What, poor old Andrew? Most unlikely, I should say."

"Yes. Yes, it does not seem to me very likely."

"Well, what were you there for, then? You are a detective, aren't you?"

"Yes."

"Well, then?"

"We are talking at cross purposes," said Poirot. "I did not go down there to inquire into any doubtful or possible case of poisoning. You must forgive me if I cannot answer your questions. It is all very hush-hush, you understand."

"What on earth do you mean by that?"

"I went there," said Poirot, "to see Sir Roderick Horsefield."

"What, that old boy? He's practically gaga, isn't he?"

"He is a man," said Poirot, "who is in possession of a great many secrets. I do not mean that he takes an active part in such things nowadays, but he knows a good deal. He was connected with a great many things in the past war. He knew several people."

"That's all over years ago, though."

"Yes, yes, his part in things is all over years ago. But do you not realize that there are certain things that it might be useful to know?"

"What sort of things?"

"Faces," said Poirot. "A well-known face, perhaps, which Sir Roderick might recognize. A face or a mannerism, a way of talking, a way of walking, a gesture. People do remember, you know. Old people. They remember, not things that have happened last week or last month or last year, but they remember something that happened, say, nearly twenty years ago. And they may remember someone who does not want to be remembered. And they can tell you certain things about a certain man or a certain woman or something they were mixed up in—I am speaking very vaguely, you understand. I went to him for information."

"You went to him for information, did you? That old boy? Gaga. And he gave it to you?"

"Let us say that I am quite satisfied."

David continued to stare at him. "I wonder now," he said, "did you go to see the old boy or did you go to see the little girl, eh? Did you want to know what she was doing in the house? I've wondered once or twice myself. Do you think she took that post there to get a bit of past information out of the old boy?"

"I do not think," said Poirot, "that it will serve any useful purpose to discuss these matters. She seems a very devoted and attentive—what shall I call her—secretary?"

"A mixture of a hospital nurse, a secretary, a companion, an *au pair* girl, an uncle's help? Yes, one could find a good many names for her, couldn't one? He's besotted about her. You noticed that?"

"It is not unnatural under the circumstances," said Poirot primly.

"I can tell you someone who doesn't like her, and that's our Mary."

"And she perhaps does not like Mary Restarick either."

"So that's what you think, is it?" said David. "That Sonia doesn't like Mary Restarick. Perhaps you go as far as thinking that she may have made a few inquiries as to where the weed killer was kept? Bah," he added, "the whole thing's ridiculous. All right. Thanks for the lift. I think I'll get out here."

"Aha. This is where you want to be? We are still a good seven miles out of London."

"I'll get out here. Good-by, Monsieur Poirot."

"Good-by."

Poirot leaned back in his seat as David slammed the door.

II

Mrs. Oliver prowled round her sitting room. She was very restless. An hour ago she had parceled up a typescript that she had just finished correcting. She was about to send it off to her publisher, who was anxiously awaiting it and constantly prodding her about it every three or four days.

"There you are," said Mrs. Oliver, addressing the empty air and conjuring up an imaginary publisher. "There you are, and I hope you like it! I don't. I think it's lousy! I don't believe you know whether anything I write is good or bad. Anyway, I warned you. I told you it was frightful. You said, 'Oh! no, no, I don't believe that for a moment.'

"You just wait and see," said Mrs. Oliver vengefully. "You just wait and see."

She opened the door, called to Edith, her maid, gave her the parcel and directed that it should be taken to the post at once.

"And now," said Mrs. Oliver, "what am I going to do with myself?"

She began strolling about again. "Yes," thought Mrs. Oliver, "I wish I had those tropical birds and things back on the wall instead of these idiotic cherries. I used to feel like something in a tropical wood. A lion or a tiger or a leopard or a cheetah! What could I possibly feel like in a cherry orchard except a bird scarer?"

She looked round again. "Cheeping like a bird, that's what I ought to be doing," she said gloomily. "Eating cherries . . . I wish it was the right time of year for cherries. I'd like some cherries. I wonder now—" She went to the telephone. "I will ascertain, madam," said the voice of George in answer to her inquiry. Presently another voice spoke.

"Hercule Poirot, at your service, madame," he said.

"Where've you been?" said Mrs. Oliver. "You've been away all day. I suppose you went down to look up the Restaricks. Is that it? Did you see Sir Roderick? What did you find out?"

"Nothing," said Hercule Poirot.

"How dreadfully dull," said Mrs. Oliver.

"No, I do not think it is really so dull. It is rather astonishing that I have not found out anything."

"Why is it so astonishing? I don't understand."

"Because," said Poirot, "it means either there was nothing to find out, and that, let me tell you, does not accord with the facts; or else something was being very cleverly concealed. That, you see, would be interesting. Mrs. Restarick, by the way, did not know the girl was missing."

"You mean—she has nothing to do with the girl having disappeared?"

"So it seems. I met there the young man."

"You mean the unsatisfactory young man that nobody likes?"

"That is right. The unsatisfactory young man."

"Did you think he was unsatisfactory?"

"From whose point of view?"

"Not from the girl's point of view, I suppose."

"The girl who came to see me I am sure would have been highly delighted with him."

"Did he look very awful?"

"He looked very beautiful," said Hercule Poirot.

"Beautiful?" said Mrs. Oliver. "I don't know that I like beautiful young men."

"Girls do," said Poirot.

"Yes, you're quite right. They like beautiful young men. I don't mean good-looking young men or smart-looking young men or well-dressed or well-washed-looking young men. I mean they either like young men looking as though they were just going on in a Restoration comedy, or else very dirty young men looking as though they were just going to take some awful tramp's job."

"It seemed that he also did not know where the girl is now—"

"Or else he wasn't admitting it."

"Perhaps. He had gone down there. Why? He was actually in the house. He had taken the trouble to walk in without anyone seeing him. Again why? For what reason? Was he looking for the girl? Or was he looking for something else?"

"You think he was looking for something?"

"He was looking for something in the girl's room," said Poirot.

"How do you know? Did you see him there?"

"No, I only saw him coming down the stairs, but I found a very nice little piece of damp mud in Norma's room that could have come from his shoe. It is possible that she herself may have asked him to bring her something from that room—there are a lot of possibilities. There is another girl in that house—and a pretty one—He may have come down there to meet her. Yes—many possibilities."

"What are you going to do next?" demanded Mrs. Oliver.

"Nothing," said Poirot.

"That's very dull," said Mrs. Oliver disapprovingly.

"I am going to receive, perhaps, a little information from those I have employed to find it; though it is quite possible that I shall receive nothing at all."

"But aren't you going to do something?"

"Not till the right moment," said Poirot.

"Well, I shall," said Mrs. Oliver.

"Pray, pray be very careful," he implored her.

"What nonsense! What could happen to me?"

"Where there is murder, anything can happen. I tell that to you. I, Poirot."

6

MR. GOBY sat in a chair. He was a small, shrunken little man, so nondescript as to be practically nonexistent.

He looked attentively at the claw foot of an antique table and addressed his remarks to it. He never addressed anybody direct.

"Glad you got the names for me, Mr. Poirot," he said. "Otherwise, you know, it might have taken a lot of time. As it is, I've got the main facts—and a bit of gossip on the side . . . Always useful, that. I'll begin at Borodene Mansions, shall I?"

Poirot inclined his head graciously.

"Plenty of porters," Mr. Goby informed the clock on the chimney piece. "I started there, used one or two different young men. Expensive, but worth it. Didn't want it thought that there was anyone making any particular inquiries! Shall I use initials or names?"

"Within these walls you can use the names," said Poirot.

"Miss Claudia Reece-Holland spoken of as a very nice young lady. Father an M.P. Ambitious man. Gets himself in the news a lot. She's his only daughter. She does secretarial work. Serious girl. No wild parties, no drink, no beatniks. Shares flat with two others. Number two works for the Wedderburn Gallery in Bond Street. Arty type. Whoops it up a bit with the Chelsea set. Goes around to places arranging exhibitions and art shows.

"The third one is *your* one. Not been there long. General opinion is that she's a bit 'wanting.' Not all there in the top story. But it's all a bit vague. One of the porters is a gossipy type. Buy him a drink or two and you'll be surprised at the things he'll tell you! Who drinks, and who drugs, and who's having trouble with his income tax, and who keeps his cash behind the cistern. Of course, you can't believe it all. Anyway, there was some story about a revolver being fired one night."

"A revolver fired? Was anyone injured?"

"There seems a bit of doubt as to that. His story is he heard a shot fired one night, and he comes out and there was this girl, *your* girl, standing there with a revolver in her hand. She looked sort of dazed. And then one of the other young ladies—or both of them, in fact—they come running along. And Miss Cary (that's the arty one) says, 'Norma, what on earth have you done?' and Miss Reece-Holland, she says sharplike, 'Shut up, can't you, Frances? Don't be a fool,' and she took the revolver away from your girl and says, 'Give me that.' She slams it into her handbag and then she notices this chap Micky, and goes over to him and says, laughing-like, 'That must have startled you, didn't it?' and Micky, he says it gave him quite a turn, and she says, 'You needn't worry. Matter of fact, we'd no idea this thing was loaded. We were just fooling about.' And then she says, 'Anyway, if anybody asks you questions, tell them it is quite all right,' and then she says, 'Come on, Norma,' and took her arm and led her along to the elevator, and they all went up again.

"But Micky said he was a bit doubtful still. He went and had a good look round the courtyard."

Mr. Goby lowered his eyes and quoted from his notebook:

" 'I'll tell you, I found something, I did! I found some wet patches. Sure as anything I did. Drops of blood, they were. I touched them with my finger. I tell you what *I* think. Somebody had been shot—some man as he was running away . . . I went upstairs and I asked if I could speak to Miss Holland. I says to her: "I think there may have been someone shot, miss," I says. "There are some drops of blood in the courtyard." "Good gracious," she says. "How ridiculous. I expect, you know," she says, "it must have been one of the pigeons." And then she says: "I'm sorry if it gave you a turn. Forget about it," and she slipped me a five-pound note. Five-pound note, no less! Well, naturally, I didn't open my mouth after that.'

"And then, after another whisky, he comes out with some more. 'If you ask me, she took a pot shot at that low-class young chap that comes to see her. I think she and he had a row and she did her best to shoot him. That's what I think. But least said, soonest mended, so I'm not repeating it. If anyone asks me anything, I'll say I don't know what they're talking about.' " Mr. Goby paused.

"Interesting," said Poirot.

"Yes, but it's as likely as not that it's a pack of lies. Nobody else seems to know anything about it. There's a story about a gang of young thugs who came barging into the courtyard one night and had a bit of a fight—flick-knives out and all that."

"I see," said Poirot. "Another possible source of blood in the courtyard."

"Maybe the girl did have a row with her young man, threatened to shoot him, perhaps. And Micky overheard it and mixed the whole thing up—especially if there was a car backfiring just then."

"Yes," said Hercule Poirot, and sighed, "that would account for things quite well."

Mr. Goby turned over another leaf of his notebook and selected his confidant. He chose an electric radiator.

"Joshua Restarick Ltd. Family firm. Been going over a hundred years. Well thought of in the City. Always very sound. Nothing spectacular. Founded by Joshua Restarick in eighteen fifty. Launched out after the first war, with greatly increased investments abroad, mostly South Africa, West Africa and Australia. Simon and Andrew Restarick—the last of the Restaricks. Simon, the elder brother, died about a year ago, no children. His wife had died some years previously. Andrew Restarick seems to have been a restless chap. His heart was never really in the business, though everyone says he had plenty of ability. Finally ran off with some woman, leaving his wife and a daughter of five years old. Went to South Africa, Kenya, and various other places. No divorce. His wife died two years ago. Had been an invalid for some time. He traveled about a lot, and wherever he went he seems to have made money. Concessions for minerals mostly. Everything he touched prospered.

"After his brother's death, he seems to have decided it was time to settle down. He'd married again and he thought the right thing to do was to come back and make a home for his daughter. They're living at the moment with his uncle, Sir Roderick Horsefield—uncle by marriage, that is. That's only temporary. His wife's looking at houses all over London. Expense no object. They're rolling in money."

Poirot sighed. "I know," he said. "What you outline to me is a success story! Everyone makes money! Everybody is of good family and highly respected. Their relations are distinguished. They are well thought of in business circles.

"There is only one cloud in the sky. A girl who is said to be 'a bit wanting,' a girl who is mixed up with a dubious boy friend who has been on probation more than once. A girl who may quite possibly have tried to poison her stepmother, and who either suffers from hallucinations, or else has committed a crime! I tell you, none of that accords well with the success story you have brought me."

Mr. Goby shook his head sadly and said rather obscurely: "There's one in every family."

"This Mrs. Restarick is quite a young woman. I presume she is not the woman he originally ran away with?"

"Oh, no, that busted up quite soon. She was a pretty bad lot, by all accounts, and a tartar as well. He was a fool ever to be taken in by her." Mr. Goby shut his notebook and looked inquiringly at Poirot. "Anything more you want me to do?"

"Yes. I want to know a little more about the late Mrs. Andrew Restarick.

She was an invalid, she was frequently in nursing homes. What kind of nursing homes? Mental homes?''

''I take your point, Mr. Poirot.''

''And any history of insanity in the family—on either side?''

''I'll see to it, Mr. Poirot.''

Mr. Goby rose to his feet. ''Then I'll take leave of you, sir. Good night.''

Poirot remained thoughtful after Mr. Goby had left. He raised and lowered his eyebrows. He wondered, he wondered very much.

Then he rang Mrs. Oliver.

''I told you before,'' he said, ''to be careful. I repeat that—Be very careful.''

''Careful of what?'' said Mrs. Oliver.

''Of yourself. I think there might be danger. Danger to anyone who goes poking about where they are not wanted. There is murder in the air—I do not want it to be yours.''

''Have you had the information you said you might have?''

''Yes,'' said Poirot, ''I have had a little information. Mostly rumor and gossip, but it seems something happened at Borodene Mansions.''

''What sort of thing?''

''Blood in the courtyard,'' said Poirot.

''Really!'' said Mrs. Oliver. ''That's just like the title of an old-fashioned detective story. *The Stain on the Staircase*. I mean nowadays you say something more like *She Asked for Death*.''

''Perhaps there may not have been blood in the courtyard. Perhaps it is only what an imaginative Irish porter imagined.''

''Probably an upset milk bottle,'' said Mrs. Oliver. ''He couldn't see it at night. What happened?''

Poirot did not answer directly.

''The girl thought she 'might have committed a murder.' Was that the murder she meant?''

''You mean she did shoot someone?''

''One might presume that she did shoot *at* someone, but for all intents and purposes missed them. A few drops of blood. That was all. No body.''

''Oh, dear,'' said Mrs. Oliver, ''it's all very confused. Surely if anyone could still run out of a courtyard, you wouldn't think you'd killed him, would you?''

''C'est difficile,'' said Poirot, and rang off.

II

"I'm worried," said Claudia Reece-Holland.

She refilled her cup from the coffee percolator. Frances Cary gave an enormous yawn. Both girls were breakfasting in the small kitchen of the flat. Claudia was dressed and ready to start for her day's work. Frances was still in dressing-gown and pajamas. Her black hair fell over one eye.

"I'm worried about Norma," continued Claudia.

Frances yawned.

"I shouldn't worry if I were you. She'll ring up or turn up sooner or later, I suppose."

"Will she? You know, Fran, I can't help wondering—"

"I don't see why," said Frances, pouring herself out more coffee. She sipped it doubtfully. "I mean—Norma's not really our business, is she? I mean, we're not looking after her or spoon-feeding her or anything. She just shares the flat. Why all this motherly solicitude? I certainly wouldn't worry."

"I daresay you wouldn't. You never worry over anything. But it's not the same for you as it is for me."

"Why isn't it the same? You mean because you're the tenant of the flat or something?"

"Well, I'm in rather a special position, as you might say."

Frances gave another enormous yawn.

"I was up too late last night," she said. "At Basil's party. I feel dreadful. Oh, well, I suppose black coffee will be helpful. Have some more before I've drunk it all? Basil would make us try some new pills—Emerald Dreams. I don't think it's really worth trying all these silly things."

"You'll be late at your gallery," said Claudia.

"Oh, well, I don't suppose it matters much. Nobody notices or cares.

"I saw David last night," she added. "He was all dressed up and really looked rather wonderful."

"Now don't say *you're* falling for him, too, Fran. He really is too awful."

"Oh, I know you think so. You're such a conventional type, Claudia."

"Not at all. But I cannot say I care for all your arty set. Trying out all these drugs and passing out or getting fighting mad."

Frances looked amused.

"I'm not a drug fiend, dear—I just like to see what these things are like. And some of the gang are all right. David can paint, you know, if he wants to."

"David doesn't very often want to, though, does he?"

"You've always got your knife into him, Claudia. You hate him coming here to see Norma. And talking of knives . . ."

"Well? Talking of knives?"

"I've been worrying," said Frances slowly, "whether to tell you something or not."

Claudia glanced at her wrist watch.

"I haven't got time now," she said. "You can tell me this evening if you want to tell me something. Anyway, I'm not in the mood. Oh, dear," she sighed, "I wish I knew what to do."

"About Norma?"

"Yes. I'm wondering if her parents ought to know that we don't know where she is . . ."

"That would be very unsporting. Poor Norma, why shouldn't she slope off on her own if she wants to?"

"Well, Norma isn't exactly—" Claudia stopped.

"No, she isn't, is she? *Non compos mentis*. That's what you meant. Have you rung up that terrible place where she works. Homebirds, or whatever it's called? Oh, yes, of course you did. I remember."

"So where is she?" demanded Claudia. "Did David say anything last night?"

"David didn't seem to know. Really, Claudia, I can't see that it matters."

"It matters for me," said Claudia, "because my boss happens to be her father. Sooner or later, if anything peculiar has happened to her, they'll ask me why I didn't mention the fact that she hadn't come home."

"Yes, I suppose they might pitch on you. But there's no real reason, is there, why Norma should have to report to us every time she's going to be away from here for a day or two. Or even a few nights. I mean, she's not a paying guest or anything. You're not in charge of the girl."

"No, but Mr. Restarick did mention he felt glad to know that she had got a room here with us."

"So that entitles you to go and tittle-tattle about her every time she's absent without leave? She's probably got a crush on some new man."

"She's got a crush on David," said Claudia. "Are you sure she isn't holed up at his place?"

"Oh, I shouldn't think so. He doesn't really care for her, you know."

"You'd like to think he doesn't," said Claudia. "You are rather sweet on David yourself."

"Certainly not," said Frances sharply. "Nothing of the kind."

"David's really keen on her," said Claudia. "If not, why did he come round looking for her here the other day?"

"You soon marched him out again," said Frances. "I think," she added, getting up and looking at her face in a rather unflattering small kitchen mirror, "I think it might have been me he really came to see."

"You're too idiotic! He came here looking for Norma."

"That girl's mental," said Frances.

"Sometimes I really think she is!"

"Well, I know she is. Look here, Claudia, I'm going to tell you that something now. You ought to know. I broke the string of my bra the other day and I was in a hurry. I know you don't like anyone fiddling with your things—"

"I certainly don't," said Claudia.

"—but Norma never minds, or doesn't notice. Anyway, I went into her room and I rootled in her drawer and I—well, I found something. A knife."

"A knife!" said Claudia, surprised. "What sort of a knife?"

"You know we had that sort of shindy thing in the courtyard? A group of beats, teen-agers who'd come in here and were having a fight with flick-knives and all that. And Norma came in just after."

"Yes, yes, I remember."

"One of the boys got stabbed, so a reporter told me, and he ran away. Well, the knife in Norma's drawer was a flick-knife. It had got a stain on it—looked like dried blood."

"Frances! You're being absurdly dramatic."

"Perhaps. But I'm sure that's what it was. And what on earth was that doing hidden away in Norma's drawer, I should like to know?"

"I suppose—she might have picked it up."

"What—a souvenir? And hidden it away and never told us?"

"What did you do with it?"

"I put it back," said Frances slowly. "I—I didn't know what else to do . . . I couldn't decide whether to tell you or not. Then yesterday I looked again and it was gone, Claudia. Not a trace of it."

"You think she sent David here to get it?"

"Well, she might have . . . I tell you, Claudia, in future I'm going to keep my door locked at night."

7

MRS. OLIVER woke up dissatisfied. She saw stretching before her a day with nothing to do. Having packed off her completed manuscript with a highly virtuous feeling, work was over. She had now only, as many times before, to relax, to enjoy herself; to lie fallow until the creative urge became active once more. She walked about her flat in a rather aimless fashion, touching things, picking them up, putting them down, looking in the drawers of her desk, realizing that there were plenty of letters there to be dealt with but feeling also that in her present state of virtuous accomplishment, she was certainly not going to deal with anything so tiresome as that now. She wanted something interesting to do. She wanted—what did she want?

She thought about the conversation she had had with Hercule Poirot, the warning he had given her. Ridiculous! After all, why shouldn't she participate in this problem which she was sharing with Poirot? Poirot might choose to sit in a chair, put the tips of his fingers together, and set his gray cells whirring to work while his body reclined comfortably within four walls. That was not the procedure that appealed to Ariadne Oliver. She had said, very forcibly, that she at least was going to do something. She was going to find out more about this mysterious girl. Where was Norma Restarick? What was she doing? What more could she, Ariadne Oliver, find out about her?

Mrs. Oliver prowled about, more and more disconsolate. What could one do? It wasn't very easy to decide. Go somewhere and ask questions? Should she go down to Long Basing? But Poirot had already been there—and found out presumably what there was to be found out. And what excuse could she offer for barging into Sir Roderick Horsefield's house?

She considered another visit to Borodene Mansions. Something still to be found out there, perhaps? She would have to think of another excuse for going there. She wasn't quite sure what excuse she would use but, anyway, that seemed the only possible place where more information could be obtained. What was the time? Ten A.M. There were certain possibilities . . .

On the way there she concocted an excuse. Not a very original excuse. In fact, Mrs. Oliver would have liked to have found something more intriguing, but perhaps, she reflected prudently, it was just as well to keep to something completely everyday and plausible. She arrived at the stately if grim elevation of Borodene Mansions and walked slowly round the courtyard considering it.

A porter was conversing with a furniture van— A milkman, pushing his milk-cart, came to join Mrs. Oliver near the service lift.

He rattled bottles, cheerfully whistling, while Mrs. Oliver continued to stare abstractedly at the furniture van.

"Number Seventy-six moving out," explained the milkman to Mrs. Oliver, mistaking her interest. He transferred a clutch of bottles from his cart to the lift.

"Not that she hasn't moved already, in a manner of speaking," he added, emerging again. He seemed a cheery kind of milkman.

He pointed a thumb upward.

"Pitched herself out of a window—seventh floor—only a week ago, it was. Five o'clock in the morning. Funny time to choose."

Mrs. Oliver didn't think it so funny.

"Why?"

"Why did she do it? Nobody knows. Balance of mind disturbed, they said."

"Was she—young?"

"Nah! Just an old trout. Fifty if she was a day."

Two men struggled in the van with a chest of drawers. It resisted them, and two mahogany drawers crashed to the ground—a loose piece of paper floated toward Mrs. Oliver, who caught it.

"Don't smash everything, Charlie," said the cheerful milkman reprovingly, and went up in the lift with his cargo of bottles.

An altercation broke out between the furniture movers. Mrs. Oliver offered them the piece of paper, but they waved it away.

Making up her mind, Mrs. Oliver entered the building and went up to Number 67. A clank came from inside and presently the door was opened by a middle-aged woman with a mop, who was clearly engaged in household labors.

"Oh," said Mrs. Oliver, using her favorite monosyllable. "Good morning. Is—I wonder—is anyone in?"

"No, I'm afraid not, madam. They're all out. They've gone to work."

"Yes, of course . . . As a matter of fact, when I was here last I left a little diary behind. *So* annoying. It must be in the sitting room somewhere."

"Well, I haven't picked up anything of the kind, madam, as far as I know. Of course I mightn't have known it was yours. Would you like to come in?" She opened the door hospitably, set aside the mop with which she had been treating the kitchen floor, and accompanied Mrs. Oliver into the sitting room.

"Yes," said Mrs. Oliver, determined to establish friendly relations, "yes, I see here—that's the book I left for Miss Restarick, Miss Norma. Is she back from the country yet?"

"I don't think she's living here at the moment. Her bed wasn't slept in. Perhaps she's still down with her people in the country. I know she was going there last weekend."

"Yes, I expect that's it," said Mrs. Oliver. "This was a book I brought her. One of *my* books."

One of Mrs. Oliver's books did not seem to strike any chord of interest in the cleaning woman.

"I was sitting here," went on Mrs. Oliver, patting an armchair, "at least I think so. And then I moved to the window and perhaps to the sofa."

She dug down vehemently behind the cushions of the chair. The cleaning woman obliged by doing the same thing to the sofa cushions.

"You've no idea how maddening it is when one loses something like that," went on Mrs. Oliver chattily. "One has all one's engagements written down there. I'm quite sure I'm lunching with someone very important today, and I can't remember who it was or where the luncheon was to be. Only, of course, it may be *tomorrow*. If so, I'm lunching with someone else *quite* different. Oh, dear."

"Very trying for you, ma'am, I'm sure," said the cleaning woman with sympathy.

"They're such nice flats, these," said Mrs. Oliver, looking round.

"A long way up."

"Well, that gives you a very good view, doesn't it?"

"Yes, but if they face east, you get a lot of cold wind in winter. Comes right through these metal window frames. Some people have had double windows put in. Oh, yes, I wouldn't care for a flat facing this way in winter. No, give me a nice ground-floor flat every time. Much more convenient, too, if you've got children. For prams and all that, you know. Oh, yes, I'm all for the ground floor, I am. Think if there was to be a fire."

"Yes, of course, that would be terrible," said Mrs. Oliver. "I suppose there are fire escapes?"

"You can't always get to a fire door. Terrified of fire, I am. Always have been. And they're ever so expensive, these flats. You wouldn't believe the rents they ask! That's why Miss Holland, she gets two other girls to go in with her."

"Oh, yes, I think I met them both. Miss Cary's an artist, isn't she?"

"Works for an art gallery, she does. Don't work at it very hard, though. She paints a bit—cows and trees that you'd never recognize as being what they're meant to be. An untidy young lady. The state her room is in—you wouldn't believe it! Now Miss Holland, everything is always as neat as a new pin. She was a secretary in the Coal Board at one time, but she's a private secretary in the City now. She likes it better, she says. She's secretary to a very rich gentleman just come back from South America or somewhere like that. He's Miss Norma's father, and it was he who asked Miss Holland to take her as a boarder when the last young lady went off to get married—and she mentioned as she was looking for another girl. Well, she couldn't very well refuse, could she? Not since he was her employer."

"Did she want to refuse?"

The woman sniffed.

"I think she would have—if she'd known."

"Know what?" The question was too direct.

"It's not for me to say anything, I'm sure. It's not my business—"

Mrs. Oliver continued to look mildly inquiring. Mrs. Mop fell.

"It's not that she isn't a nice young lady. Scatty—but then they're nearly all scatty. But I think as a doctor ought to see her. There are times when she doesn't seem to know rightly what she's doing, or where she is. It gives you quite a turn, sometimes—Looks just how my husband's nephew does after he's had a fit. (Terrible fits he has—you wouldn't believe!) Only I've never known her to have fits. Maybe she takes things—a lot do."

"I believe there is a young man her family doesn't approve of."

"Yes, so I've heard. He's come here to call for her once or twice—though I've never seen him. One of these Mods, by all accounts. Miss Holland doesn't like it—but what can you do nowadays? Girls go their own way."

"Sometimes one feels very upset about girls nowadays," said Mrs. Oliver, and tried to look serious and responsible.

"Not brought up right, that's what *I* says."

"I'm afraid not. No, I'm afraid not. One feels really a girl like Norma Restarick would be better at home than coming all alone to London and earning her living as an interior decorator."

"She don't like it at home."

"Really?"

"Got a stepmother. Girls don't like stepmothers. From what I've heard, the stepmother's done her best, tried to pull her up, tried to keep flashy young men out of the house, that sort of thing. She knows girls pick up with the wrong young man and a lot of harm may come of it. Sometimes"— the cleaning woman spoke impressively—"I'm thankful I've never had any daughters."

"Have you got sons?"

"Two boys, we've got. One's doing very well at school, and the other one, he's in a printer's, doing well there, too. Yes, very nice boys they are. Mind you, boys can cause you trouble, too. But girls is more worrying, I think. You feel you ought to be able to do something about them."

"Yes," said Mrs. Oliver thoughtfully, "one does feel that."

She saw signs of the cleaning woman wishing to return to her cleaning.

"It's too bad about my diary," she said. "Well, thank you very much and I hope I haven't wasted your time."

"Well, I hope you'll find it, I'm sure," said the other woman obligingly.

Mrs. Oliver went out of the flat and considered what she should do next. She couldn't think of anything she could do further that day, but a plan for tomorrow began to form in her mind.

When she got home, Mrs. Oliver, in an important way, got out a notebook and jotted down in it various things under the heading "Facts I have learned." On the whole the facts did not amount to very much, but Mrs. Oliver, true to her calling, managed to make the most of them that could be made. Possibly the fact that Claudia Reece-Holland was employed by Norma's father was the most salient fact of any. She had not known that before, she rather doubted if Hercule Poirot had known it either. She thought of ringing him up on the telephone and acquainting him with it, but decided to keep it to herself for the moment because of her plan for the morrow. In fact, Mrs. Oliver felt at this moment less like a detective novelist than like an ardent bloodhound. She was on the trail, nose down on the scent, and tomorrow morning—well, tomorrow morning we would see.

True to her plan, Mrs. Oliver rose early, partook of two cups of tea and a boiled egg and started out on her quest. Once more she arrived in the vicinity of Borodene Mansions. She wondered whether she might be getting a bit well known there, so this time she did not enter the courtyard, but skulked around either one entrance to it or the other, scanning the various people who were turning out into the morning drizzle to trot off on their way to work. They were mostly girls, and looked deceptively alike. How extraordinary human beings were when you considered them like this, emerging purposefully from these large tall buildings—just like anthills, thought Mrs. Oliver. One had never considered an anthill properly, she decided. It always looked so aimless, as one disturbed it with the toe of a shoe. All those little things rushing about with bits of grass in their mouths, streaming along industriously, worried, anxious, looking as though they were running to and fro and going nowhere, but presumably they were just as well organized as these human beings here. That man, for instance, who had just passed her. Scurrying along, muttering to himself. "I wonder what's upsetting *you*," thought Mrs. Oliver. She walked up and down a little more, then she drew back suddenly.

Claudia Reece-Holland came out of the entranceway walking at a brisk, businesslike pace. As before, she looked very well turned out. Mrs. Oliver turned away so that she should not be recognized. Once she had allowed Claudia to get a sufficient distance ahead of her, she wheeled round again and followed in her tracks. Claudia Reece-Holland came to the end of the street and turned right into a main thoroughfare. She came to a bus stop and joined the queue. Mrs. Oliver, still following her, felt a momentary uneasiness. Supposing Claudia should turn round, look at her, recognize her? All Mrs. Oliver could think of was to do several protracted but noiseless blows of the nose. But Claudia Reece-Holland seemed totally absorbed in her own thoughts. She looked at none of her fellow waiters for buses. Mrs. Oliver was about third in the queue behind her. Finally the right bus came and there was a surge forward. Claudia got on the bus and went straight up to the top. Mrs. Oliver got inside and was able to get a seat close to the door as the uncomfortable third person. When the conducter came round for fares, Mrs. Oliver pressed a reckless one and sixpence into his hand. After all, she had no idea by what route the bus went or indeed how far the distance was to what the cleaning woman had described vaguely as "one of those new buildings by St. Paul's." She was on the alert and ready when the venerable dome was at last sighted. Any time now, she thought to herself, and fixed a steady eye on those who descended from the platform above. Ah, yes, there came Claudia, neat and chic in her smart suit. She got off the bus. Mrs. Oliver followed her in due course and kept at a nicely calculated distance.

"Very interesting," thought Mrs. Oliver. "Here I am actually trailing someone! Just like in my books. And, what's more, I must be doing it very well, because she hasn't the least idea."

Claudia Reece-Holland, indeed, looked very much absorbed in her own thoughts. "That's a very capable-looking girl," thought Mrs. Oliver, as indeed she had thought before. "If I was thinking of having a go at guessing a murderer, a good capable murderer, I'd choose someone very like her."

Unfortunately, nobody had been murdered yet, that is to say, unless the girl Norma had been entirely right in her assumption that she herself had committed a murder.

This part of London seemed to have suffered or profited from a large amount of building in the recent years. Enormous skyscrapers, most of which Mrs. Oliver thought very hideous, mounted to the sky with a square matchbox-like air.

Claudia turned into a building. "Now I shall find out exactly," thought

Mrs. Oliver, and turned into it after her. Four lifts appeared to be all going up and down with frantic haste. This, Mrs. Oliver thought, was going to be more difficult. However, they were of a very large size and by getting into Claudia's one at the last minute, Mrs. Oliver was able to interpose large masses of tall men between herself and the figure she was following. Claudia's destination turned out to be the fourth floor. She went along a corridor and Mrs. Oliver, lingering behind two of her tall men, noted the door where she went in. Three doors from the end of the corridor. Mrs. Oliver arrived at the same door in due course and was able to read the legend on it. "Joshua Restarick Ltd." was the legend it bore.

Having got as far as that, Mrs. Oliver felt as though she did not quite know what to do next. She had found Norma's father's place of business and the place where Claudia worked, but now, slightly disabused, she felt that this was not so much of a discovery as it might have been. Frankly, did it help? Probably it didn't.

She waited around a few minutes, walking from one end to the other of the corridor, looking to see if anybody else interesting went in at the door of Restarick Enterprises. Two or three girls did, but they did not look particularly interesting. Mrs. Oliver went down again in the lift and walked rather disconsolately out of the building. She couldn't quite think what to do next. She took a walk round the adjacent streets, she meditated a visit to St. Paul's.

"I might go up in the Whispering Gallery and whisper," thought Mrs. Oliver. "I wonder now how the Whispering Gallery would do for the scene of a murder?

"No," she decided, "too profane, I'm afraid. No, I don't think that would be quite nice." She walked thoughtfully toward the Mermaid Theatre. That, she thought, had far more possibilities.

She walked back in the direction of the various new buildings. Then, feeling the lack of a more substantial breakfast than she had had, she turned into a local café. It was moderately well filled with people having extra-late breakfast or else early "elevenses." Mrs. Oliver, looking round vaguely for a suitable table, gave a gasp. At a table near the wall the girl Norma was sitting, and opposite her was sitting a young man with lavish chestnut hair curled on his shoulders, wearing a red velvet waistcoat and a very fancy jacket.

"David," said Mrs. Oliver under her breath. "It must be David." He and the girl Norma were talking excitedly together.

Mrs. Oliver considered a plan of campaign, made up her mind and, nodding her head in satisfaction, crossed the floor of the café to a discreet door marked "Ladies."

Mrs. Oliver was not quite sure whether Norma was likely to recognize her or not. It was not always the vaguest-looking people who proved the vaguest in fact. At the moment Norma did not look as though she was likely to look at anybody but David, but who knows?

"I expect I can do something to myself anyway," thought Mrs. Oliver. She looked at herself in a small fly-blown mirror provided by the café's management, studying particularly what she considered to be the focal point of a woman's appearance, her hair. No one knew this better than Mrs. Oliver, owing to the innumerable times that she had changed her mode of hairdressing and had failed to be recognized by her friends in consequence. Giving her head an appraising eye, she started work. Out came the pins, she took off several coils of hair, wrapped them up in her handkerchief and stuffed them into her handbag, parted her hair in the middle, combed it sternly back from her face and rolled it up into a modest bun at the back of her neck. She also took out a pair of spectacles and put them on her nose. There was a really earnest look about her now! "Almost intellectual," Mrs. Oliver thought approvingly. She altered the shape of her mouth by an application of lipstick and emerged once more into the café, moving carefully, since the spectacles were only for reading and in consequence the landscape was blurred. She crossed the café and made her way to an empty table next to that occupied by Norma and David. She sat down so that she was facing David. Norma, on the near side, sat with her back to her. Norma, therefore, would not see her unless she turned her head right around. The waitress drifted up. Mrs. Oliver ordered a cup of coffee and a Bath bun and settled down to be inconspicuous.

Norma and David did not even notice her. They were deeply in the middle of a passionate discussion. It took Mrs. Oliver just a minute or two to tune in to them.

". . . But you only fancy these things," David was saying. "You imagine them. They're all utter, utter nonsense, my dear girl."

"I don't know. I can't tell." Norma's voice had a queer lack of resonance in it.

Mrs. Oliver could not hear her as well as she heard David, since Norma's back was turned to her, but the dullness of the girl's tone struck her disagreeably. There was something wrong here, she thought. Very wrong. She remembered the story as Poirot had first told it to her. *"She thinks she may have committed a murder."* What was the matter with the girl? Hallucinations? Was her mind really slightly affected, or was it no more and no less than truth, and in consequence the girl had suffered a bad shock?

"If you ask me, it's all fuss on Mary's part! She's a thoroughly stupid woman anyway, and she imagines she has illnesses and all that sort of thing."

"She was ill."

"All right then, she was ill. Any sensible woman would get the doctor to give her some antibiotic or other, and not get het up."

"She thought *I* did it to her. My father thinks so too."

"I tell you, Norma, you imagine all these things."

"You just say that to me, David. You say it to me to cheer me up. Supposing I did give her the stuff?"

"What do you mean, suppose? You must know whether you did or you didn't. You can't be so idiotic, Norma."

"I don't know."

"You keep saying that. You keep coming back to that and saying it again and again. 'I don't know.' 'I don't know.' "

"You don't understand. You don't understand in the least what hate is. I hated her from the first moment I saw her."

"I know. You told me that."

"That's the queer part of it. I told you that, and yet I don't even *remember* telling you that. D'you see? Every now and then I—I tell people things. I tell people things that I want to do, or that I have done or that I'm going to do. But I don't even remember telling them the things. It's as though I was *thinking* all these things in my mind, and sometimes they come out in the open and I say them to people. I did say them to you, didn't I?"

"Well—I mean—look here, don't let's harp back to that."

"But I did say it to you? Didn't I?"

"All right, all right! One says things like that. 'I hate her and I'd like to kill her. I think I'll poison her!' But that's only kid stuff, if you know what I mean, as though you weren't quite grown up. It's a very natural thing. Children say it a lot. 'I hate so and so. I'll cut off his head!' Kids say it at school. About some teacher they particularly dislike."

"You think it was just that? But—that sounds as though I wasn't grown up."

"Well, you're not, in some ways. If you'd just pull yourself together, realize how silly it all is. What can it matter if you do hate her? You've got away from home and don't have to live with her."

"Why shouldn't I live in my own home—with my own father?" said Norma. "It's not fair. It's not fair. First he went away and left my mother, and now, just when he's coming back to me, he goes and marries Mary. Of course I hate her and she hates me, too. I used to think about killing her, used to think of ways of doing it. I used to enjoy thinking like that. But then—when she *really* got ill . . ."

David said uneasily: "You don't think you're a witch or anything, do you? You don't make figures in wax and stick pins into them or do that sort of thing?"

"Oh, no. That would be silly. What I did was real. Quite real."

"Look here, Norma, what do you mean when you say it was real?"

"The bottle was there, in my drawer. Yes, I opened the drawer and found it."

"What bottle?"

"*The Dragon Exterminator. Selective weed killer*. That's what it was labeled. Stuff in a dark green bottle and you were supposed to spray it on things. And it had labels with *Caution* and *Poison*, too."

"Did you buy it? Or did you just find it?"

"I don't know where I got it, but it was there, in my drawer, and it was half empty."

"And then you—you—remembered—"

"Yes," said Norma. "Yes. . . ." Her voice was vague, almost dreamy. "Yes . . . I think it was then it all came back to me. You think so too, don't you, David?"

"I don't know what to make of you, Norma. I really don't. I think in a way you're making it all up, you're telling it to yourself."

"But she went to hospital, for observation, they said, they were puzzled. Then they said they couldn't find anything wrong, so she came home—and then she got ill again, and I began to be frightened. My father began looking at me in a queer sort of way, and then the doctor came and they talked together, shut up in Father's study. I went round outside and crept up to the window and I tried to listen. I wanted to hear what they were saying. They were planning together—to send me away to a place where I'd be shut up! A place where I'd have a 'course of treatment'—or something. They thought, you see, that I was crazy, and I was frightened . . . Because—because I wasn't sure what I'd done or what I hadn't done."

"Is that when you ran away?"

"No—that was later—"

"Tell me."

"I don't want to talk about it any more."

"You'll have to let them know sooner or later where you are—"

"I won't! I hate them. I hate my father as much as I hate Mary. I wish they were dead. I wish they were both dead. Then—then I think I'd be happy again."

"Don't get all het up! Look here, Norma—" he paused in an embarrassed manner—"I'm not very set on marriage and all that rubbish . . . I mean I didn't think I'd ever do anything of that kind—oh, well, not for years. One doesn't want to tie oneself up—but I think it's the best thing we could do, you know. Get married. At a registry office or something. You'll have to say you're over twenty-one. Roll up your hair, put on some spectacles or something. Make you look a bit older. Once we're married, your father can't do a thing! He can't send you away to what you call a 'place.' He'll be powerless."

"I hate him."

"You seem to hate everybody."

"Only my father and Mary."

"Well, after all, it's quite natural for a man to marry again."

"Look what he did to my mother."

"All that must have been a long time ago?"

"Yes. I was only a child, but I remember. He went away and left us. He sent me presents at Christmas—but he never came himself. I wouldn't even have known him if I'd met him in the street by the time he did come back. He didn't mean anything to me by then. I think he got my mother shut up, too. She used to go away when she was ill. I don't know where. I don't know what was the matter with her. Sometimes I wonder . . . I wonder, David. I think, you know, there's something wrong in my head, and someday it will make me do something really bad. Like the knife."

"What knife?"

"It doesn't matter. Just a knife."

"Well, can't you tell me what you're talking about?"

"I think it had bloodstains on it—it was hidden there . . . under my stockings."

"Do you remember hiding a knife there?"

"I think so. But I can't remember what I'd done with it *before* that. I can't remember where I'd *been* . . . There is a whole hour gone out of that evening. A whole hour I didn't know where I'd been. I'd been somewhere and done something."

"Hush!" He hissed it quickly as the waitress approached their table. "You'll be all right. I'll look after you. Let's have something more," he said to the waitress in a loud voice, picking up the menu—"Two baked beans on toast."

8

HERCULE POIROT was dictating to his secretary, Miss Lemon.

"And while I much appreciate the honor you have done me, I must regretfully inform you that . . ."

The telephone rang. Miss Lemon stretched out a hand for it. "Yes? Who did you say?" She put her hand over the receiver and said to Poirot, "Mrs. Oliver."

"Ah . . . Mrs. Oliver," said Poirot. He did not particularly want to be interrupted at this moment, but he took the receiver from Miss Lemon. " 'Allo," he said, "Hercule Poirot speaks."

"Oh, Monsieur Poirot, I'm so glad I got you! I've found her for you!"

"I beg your pardon?"

"I've found her for you. Your girl! You know, the one who's committed a murder or thinks she has. She's talking about it too, a good deal. I think she is off her head. But never mind that now. Do you want to come and get her?"

"Where are you, *chère* madame?"

"Somewhere between St. Paul's and the Mermaid Theatre and all that. Calthorpe Street," said Mrs. Oliver, suddenly looking out of the telephone box in which she was standing. "Do you think you can get here quickly? They're in a restaurant."

"They?"

"Oh, she and what I suppose is the unsuitable boy friend. He is rather nice really, and he seems very fond of her. I can't think why. People are odd. Well, I don't want to talk, because I want to get back again. I followed them, you see. I came into the restaurant and saw them there."

"Aha? You have been very clever, madame."

"No, I haven't really. It was a pure accident. I mean, I walked into a small café place and there the girl was, just sitting there."

"Ah. You had the good fortune then. That is just as important."

"And I've been sitting at the next table to them, only she's got her back to me. And anyway I don't suppose she'd recognize me. I've done things to my hair. Anyway, they've been talking as though they were alone in the world, and when they ordered another course—baked beans—(I can't bear baked beans, it always seems to me so funny that people should)—"

"Never mind the baked beans. Go on. You left them and came out to telephone. Is that right?"

"Yes. Because the baked beans gave me time. And I shall go back now. Or I might hang about outside. Anyway, try and get here quickly."

"What is the name of this café?"

"The Merry Shamrock—but it doesn't look very merry. In fact, it looks rather sordid, but the coffee is quite good."

"Say no more. Go back. In due course, I will arrive."

"Splendid," said Mrs. Oliver, and rang off.

II

Miss Lemon, always efficient, had preceded him to the street and was waiting by a taxi. She asked no questions and displayed no curiosity. She did not tell Poirot how she would occupy her time while he was away. She did not need to tell him. She always knew what she was going to do and she was always right in what she did.

Poirot duly arrived at the corner of Calthorpe Street. He descended, paid the taxi, and looked around him. He saw The Merry Shamrock, but he saw no one in its vicinity who looked at all like Mrs. Oliver, however well disguised. He walked to the end of the street and back. No Mrs. Oliver. So either the couple in which they were interested had left the café and Mrs. Oliver had gone on a shadowing expedition, or else—To answer "or else," he went to the café door. One could not see the inside very well from the outside, on account of steam, so he pushed the door gently open and entered. His eyes swept round it.

He saw at once the girl who had come to visit him at the breakfast table. She was sitting by herself at a table against the wall. She was smoking a cigarette and staring in front of her. She seemed to be lost in thought. No, Poirot thought, hardly that. There did not seem to be any thought there. She was lost in a kind of oblivion. She was somewhere else.

He crossed the room quietly and sat down in the chair opposite her. She looked up then, and he was at least gratified to see that he was recognized.

"So we meet again, mademoiselle," he said pleasantly. "I see you recognize me."

"Yes. Yes, I do."

"It is always gratifying to be recognized by a young lady one has only met once and for a very short time."

She continued to look at him without speaking.

"And how did you know me, may I ask? What made you recognize me?"

"Your mustache," said Norma immediately. "It couldn't be anyone else."

He was gratified by that observation and stroked it with the pride and vanity that he was apt to display on these occasions.

"Ah, yes, very true. Yes, there are not many mustaches such as mine. It is a fine one, hein?"

"Yes—well, yes—I suppose it is."

"Ah, you are perhaps not a connoisseur of mustaches, but I can tell you, Miss Restarick—Miss Norma Restarick, is it not?—that it is a very fine mustache."

He had dwelt deliberately upon her name. She had at first looked so oblivious to everything around her, so far away, that he wondered if she would notice. She did. It startled her.

"How did you know my name?" she said.

"True, you did not give your name to my servant when you came to see me that morning."

"How did you know it? How did you get to know it? Who told you?"

He saw the alarm, the fear.

"A friend told me," he said. "One's friends can be very useful."

"Who was it?"

"Mademoiselle, you like keeping your little secrets from me. I, too, have a preference for keeping my little secrets from you."

"I don't see how you could know who I was."

"I am Hercule Poirot," said Poirot with his usual magnificence. Then he left the initiative to her, merely sitting there smiling gently at her.

"I—" she began, then stopped. "Would—" Again she stopped.

"We did not get very far that morning, I know," said Hercule Poirot. "Only so far as your telling me that you had committed a murder."

"Oh, *that*!"

"Yes, mademoiselle, *that*."

"But—I didn't mean it, of course. I didn't mean anything like that. I mean, it was just a joke."

"*Vraiment?* You came to see me rather early in the morning, at breakfast time. You said it was urgent. The urgency was because you might have committed a murder. That is your idea of a joke, eh?"

A waitress who had been hovering, looking at Poirot with a fixed attention, suddenly came up to him and proffered him what appeared to be a paper boat such as is made for children to sail in a bath.

"This for you?" she said. "Mr. Porritt? A lady left it."

"Ah, yes," said Poirot. "And how did you know who I was?"

"The lady said I'd know by your mustache. Said I wouldn't have seen a mustache like that before. And it's true enough,'' she added, gazing at it.

''Well, thank you very much.''

Poirot took the boat from her, untwisted it and smoothed it out; he read some hastily penciled words: ''He's just going. She's staying behind, so I'm going to leave her for you, and follow him.'' It was signed Ariadne.

''Ah, yes,'' said Hercule Poirot, folding it and slipping it into his pocket. ''What were we talking about? Your sense of humor, I think, Miss Restarick.''

''Do you know just my name or—or do you know everything about me?''

''I know a few things about you. You are Miss Norma Restarick, your address in London is Sixty-seven Borodene Mansions. Your home address is Crosshedges, Long Basing. You live there with a father, a stepmother, a great-uncle and—ah, yes, an *au pair* girl. You see, I am quite well informed.''

''You've been having me followed.''

''No, no,'' said Poirot. ''Not at all. As to that, I give you my word of honor.''

''But you are not police, are you? You didn't say you were.''

''I am not police, no.''

Her suspicion and defiance broke down.

''I don't know what to do,'' she said.

''I am not urging you to employ me,'' said Poirot. ''For that you have said already that I am too old. Possibly you are right. But since I know who you are and something about you, there is no reason we should not discuss together in a friendly fashion the troubles that afflict you. The old, you must remember, though considered incapable of action, have nevertheless a good fund of experience on which to draw.''

Norma continued to look at him doubtfully, that wide-eyed stare that had disquieted Poirot before. But she was in a sense trapped, and she had at this particular moment, or so Poirot judged, a wish to talk about things. For some reason, Poirot had always been a person it was easy to talk to.

''They think I'm crazy,'' she said bluntly. ''And—and I rather think I'm crazy, too. Mad.''

''That is most interesting,'' said Hercule Poirot cheerfully. ''There are many different names for these things. Very grand names. Names rolled out happily by psychiatrists, psychologists and others. But when you say crazy, that describes very well what the general appearance may be to ordinary, everyday people. *Eh bien*, then, you are crazy, or you appear crazy or you think you are crazy, and possibly you *may* be crazy. But all the same, that is not to say the condition is serious. It is a thing that people suffer from a good deal, and it is usually easily cured with the proper treatment. It comes about because people have had too much mental strain, too much worry, have studied too much for examinations, have dwelt too much perhaps on their emotions, have too much religion or have a lamentable lack of religion, or have good reasons for hating their fathers or their mothers! Or, of course, it can be as simple as having an unfortunate love affair."

"I've got a stepmother. I hate her and I rather think I hate my father, too. That seems rather a lot, doesn't it?"

"It is more usual to hate one or the other," said Poirot. "You were, I suppose, very fond of your own mother. Is she divorced or dead?"

"Dead. She died two or three years ago."

"And you cared for her very much?"

"Yes. I suppose I did. I mean of course I did. She was an invalid, you know, and she had to go to nursing homes a good deal."

"And your father?"

"Father had gone abroad a long time before that. He went to South America when I was about five or six. I think he wanted Mother to divorce him, but she wouldn't. He went to South America and was mixed up with mines or something like that. Anyway, he used to write to me at Christmas and send me a Christmas present or arrange for one to come to me. That was about all. So he didn't really seem very real to me. He came home about a year ago because he had to wind up my uncle's affairs and all that sort of financial thing. And when he came home he—he brought his new wife with him."

"And you resented the fact?"

"Yes, I did."

"But your mother was dead by then. It is not unusual, you know, for a man to marry again. Especially when he and his wife have been estranged for many years. This wife he brought, was she the same lady he had wished to marry previously, when he asked your mother for a divorce?"

"Oh, no, this one is quite young. And she's very good-looking and she acts as though she just owns my father!"

She went on after a pause—in a different rather childish voice. "I thought perhaps when he came home this time he would be fond of *me* and take notice of *me* and—but she won't let him. She's *against* me. She's crowded me out."

"But that does not matter at all at the age you are. It is a good thing. You do not need anyone to look after you now. You can stand on your own feet, you can enjoy life, you can choose your own friends—"

"You wouldn't think so, the way they go on at home! Well, I mean to choose my own friends."

"Most girls nowadays have to endure criticism about their friends," said Poirot.

"It was all so different," said Norma. "My father isn't at all like I remember him when I was five years old. He used to play with me, all the time, and be so gay. He's not gay now. He's worried and rather fierce and—oh, quite different."

"That must be nearly fifteen years ago, I presume. People change."

"But ought people to change so much?"

"Has he changed in appearance?"

"Oh, no, no, not that. Oh, no! If you look at his picture just over his chair, although it's of him when he was much younger, it's exactly like him now. But it isn't at all the way I remembered him."

"But you know, my dear," said Poirot gently, "people are never like what you remember them. You make them, as the years go by, more and more the way you wish them to be, and as you think you remember them. If you want to remember them as agreeable and gay and handsome, you make them far more so than they actually were."

"Do you think so? Do you really think so?" She paused and then said abruptly, "But why do you think I want to kill people?" The question came out quite naturally. It was there between them. They had, Poirot felt, got at last to a crucial moment.

"That may be quite an interesting question," said Poirot, "and there may be quite an interesting reason. The person who can probably tell you the answer to that will be a doctor. The kind of doctor who *knows*."

She reacted quickly.

"I won't go to a doctor. I won't go *near* a doctor! They wanted to send me to a doctor, and then I'll be shut up in one of those loony places and they won't let me out again. I'm not going to do anything like that." She was struggling now to rise to her feet.

"It is not I who can send you to one! You need not be alarmed. You could go to a doctor entirely on your own behalf, if you liked. You can go and say to him the things you have been saying to me, and you may ask him *why*, and he will perhaps tell you the cause."

"That's what David says. That's what David says I should do, but I don't think—I don't think he understands. I'd have to tell a doctor that I—I might have tried to do things . . ."

"What makes you think you have?"

"Because I don't always remember what I've done—or where I've been. I lose an hour of time—two hours—and I can't remember. I was in a corridor once—a corridor outside a door, her door. I'd something in my hand—I don't know how I got it. She came walking along toward me—But when she got near me, her face changed. It wasn't her at all. She'd changed into somebody else."

"You are remembering, perhaps, a nightmare. There people do change into somebody else."

"It wasn't a nightmare. I picked up the revolver—It was lying there at my feet—"

"In a corridor?"

"No, in the courtyard. She came and took it away from me."

"Who did?"

"Claudia. She took me upstairs and gave me some bitter stuff to drink."

"Where was your stepmother then?"

"She was there, too—No, she wasn't. She was at Crosshedges. Or in the hospital. That's where they found out she was being poisoned—and that it was me."

"It need not have been you—It could have been someone else."

"Who else could it have been?"

"Perhaps—her husband."

"Father? Why on earth should Father want to poison Mary? He's devoted to her. He's silly about her!"

"There are others in the house, are there not?"

"Old Uncle Roderick? Nonsense!"

"One does not know," said Poirot, "he might be mentally afflicted. He might think it was his duty to poison a woman who might be a beautiful spy. Something like that."

"That would be very interesting," said Norma, momentarily diverted, and speaking in a perfectly natural manner. "Uncle Roderick *was* mixed up a good deal with spies and things in the last war. Who else is there? Sonia? I suppose she might be a beautiful spy, but she's not quite my idea of one."

"No, and there does not seem very much reason why she should wish to poison your stepmother. I suppose there might be servants, gardeners?"

"No, they just come in for the day. I don't think—well, they wouldn't be the kind of people to have any *reason*."

"She might have done it herself."

"Committed suicide, do you mean? Like the other one?"

"It is a possibility."

"I can't imagine Mary committing suicide. She's far too sensible. And why should she want to?"

"Yes, you feel that if she did, she would put her head in the gas oven, or she would lie on a bed nicely arranged and take an overdose of sleeping draft. Is that right?"

"Well, it would have been more natural. So you see," said Norma earnestly, "it must have been me."

"Aha," said Poirot, "that interests me. You would almost, it would seem, prefer that it should be you. You are attracted to the idea that it was your hand who slipped the fatal dose of this, that or the other. Yes, you like the idea."

"How dare you say such a thing! How can you?"

"Because I think it is true," said Poirot. "Why does the thought that you may have committed murder excite you, please you?"

"It's not true."

"I wonder," said Poirot.

She scooped up her bag and began feeling in it with shaking fingers.

"I'm not going to stop here and have you say these things to me." She signaled to the waitress, who came, scribbled on a pad of paper, detached it and laid it down by Norma's plate.

"Permit me," said Hercule Poirot.

He removed the slip of paper deftly and prepared to draw his notecase from his pocket. The girl snatched it back again.

"No, I won't let you pay for me."

"As you please," said Poirot.

He had seen what he wanted to see. The bill was for two. It would seem therefore that David of the fine feathers had no objection to having his bills paid by an infatuated girl.

"So it is you who entertain a friend to elevenses, I see."

"How did you know that I was with anyone?"

"I tell you, I know a good deal."

She placed coins on the table and rose. "I'm going now," she said, "and I forbid you to follow me."

"I doubt if I could," said Poirot. "You must remember my advanced age. If you were to run down the street, I should certainly not be able to follow you."

She got up and went toward the door.

"Do you hear? You are not to follow me."

"You permit me at least to open the door for you." He did so with something of a flourish. "*Au revoir*, mademoiselle."

She threw a suspicious glance at him and walked away down the street with a rapid step, turning her head back over her shoulder from time to time. Poirot remained by the door watching her, but made no attempt to gain the pavement or to catch her up. When she was out of sight, he turned back into the café.

"And what the devil does all that mean?" said Poirot to himself.

The waitress was advancing upon him, displeasure on her face. Poirot regained his seat at the table and placated her by ordering a cup of coffee. "There is something here very curious," he murmured to himself. "Yes, something very curious indeed."

A cup of pale beige fluid was placed in front of him. He took a sip of it and made a grimace.

He wondered where Mrs. Oliver was at this moment.

9

MRS. OLIVER was seated in a bus. She was slightly out of breath though full of the zest of the chase. What she called in her own mind the Peacock had led a somewhat brisk pace. Mrs. Oliver was not a rapid walker. Going along the Embankment, she followed him at a distance of some twenty yards or so. At Charing Cross he got into the underground. Mrs. Oliver also got into the underground. At Sloane Square he got out, so did Mrs. Oliver. She waited in a bus queue some three or four people behind him. He got on a bus and so did she. He got out at World's End, so did Mrs. Oliver. He plunged into a bewildering maze of streets between King's Road and the river. He turned into what seemed a builder's yard. Mrs. Oliver stood in the shadow of a doorway and watched. He turned into an alleyway, Mrs. Oliver gave him a moment or two and then followed—he was nowhere to be seen. Mrs. Oliver reconnoitered her general surroundings. The whole place appeared somewhat decrepit. She wandered farther down the alleyway. Other alleyways led off from it—some of them cul-de-sacs. She had completely lost her sense of direction when she once more came to the builder's yard and a voice spoke behind her, startling her considerably. It said, politely, "I hope I didn't walk too fast for you."

She turned sharply. Suddenly what had recently been almost fun, a chase undertaken lightheartedly and in the best of spirits, now was that no longer. What she felt now was a sudden unexpected throb of fear. Yes, she was afraid. The atmosphere had suddenly become tinged with menace. Yet the voice was pleasant, polite; but behind it she knew there was anger—the sudden kind of anger that recalled to her in a confused fashion all the things one read in newspapers: Elderly women attacked by gangs of young men—young men who were ruthless, cruel, who were driven by hate and the desire to do harm. This was the young man whom she had been following. He had known she was there, had given her the slip and had then followed her into this alleyway, and he stood there now barring her way out. As is the precarious fashion of London, one moment you are among people all around you and the next moment there is nobody in sight. There must be people in the next street, someone in the houses near, but nearer than that is a masterful figure, a figure with strong cruel hands. She felt sure that in this moment he was thinking of using those hands . . . The Peacock. A proud peacock. In his velvets, his tight, elegant black trousers, speaking in that quiet, ironical, amused voice that held behind it anger. Mrs. Oliver took three big gasps. Then, in a lightning moment of decision, she put up a quickly imagined defense. Firmly and immediately she sat down on a dustbin which was against the wall quite close to her.

"Goodness, how you startled me," she said. "I'd no idea you were there. I hope you're not annoyed."

"So you were following me?"

"Yes, I'm afraid I was. I expect it must have been rather annoying to you. You see I thought it would be such an excellent opportunity. I'm sure you're frightfully angry but you needn't be, you know. Not really. You see—" Mrs. Oliver settled herself more firmly on the dustbin—"you see, I write books. I write detective stories and I've really been very worried this morning. In fact I went into a café to have a cup of coffee just to try and think things out. I'd just got to the point in my book where I was following somebody. I mean my hero was following someone and I thought to myself, 'Really, I know very little about following people.' I mean, I'm always using the phrase in a book and I've read a lot of books where people do follow other people, and I wondered if it was as easy as it seems to be in some people's books or if it was as almost entirely impossible as it seemed in other people's books. So I thought, 'Well, really, the only thing was to try it out myself'—because until you try things out yourself, you can't really tell what it's like. I mean you don't know what you feel like, or whether you get worried at losing a person. As it happened, I just looked up and you were sitting at the next table to me in the café and I thought you'd be—I hope you won't be annoyed again—but I thought you'd be an especially good person to follow."

He was still staring at her with those strange, cold blue eyes, yet she felt somehow that the tension had left them.

"Why was I an especially good person to follow?"

"Well, you were so decorative," explained Mrs. Oliver. "They are really very attractive clothes—almost Regency, you know, and I thought, well, I might take advantage of your being fairly easy to distinguish from other people. So you see, when you went out of the café, I went out, too. And it's not really easy at all." She looked up at him. "Do you mind telling me if you knew I was there all the time?"

"Not at once, no."

"I see," said Mrs. Oliver thoughtfully. "But, of course, I'm not as distinctive as you are. I mean you wouldn't be able to tell me very easily from a lot of other elderly women. I don't stand out very much, do I?"

"Do you write books that are published? Have I ever come across them?"

"Well, I don't know. You may have. I've written forty-three by now. My name's Oliver."

"Ariadne Oliver?"

"So you do know my name," said Mrs. Oliver. "Well, that's rather gratifying, of course, though I daresay you wouldn't like my books very much. You probably would find them rather old-fashioned—not violent enough."

"You didn't know me personally beforehand?"

Mrs. Oliver shook her head. "No, I'm sure I don't—didn't, I mean."

"What about the girl I was with?"

"You mean the one you were having—baked beans, was it—with in the café? No, I don't think so. Of course I only saw the back of her head. She looked to me—well, I mean girls do look rather alike, don't they?"

"She knew you," said the boy suddenly. His tone in a moment had a sudden acid sharpness. "She mentioned once that she'd met you not long ago. About a week ago, I believe."

"Where? Was it at a party? I suppose I might have met her. What's her name? Perhaps I'd know that."

She thought he was in two moods whether to mention the name or not, but he decided to and he watched her face very keenly as he did so.

"Her name's Norma Restarick."

"Norma Restarick. Oh, of course, yes, it was at a party in the country. A place called—wait a minute—Long Norton, was it? I don't remember the name of the house. I went there with some friends. I don't think I would have recognized her anyway, though I believe she did say something about my books. I even promised I'd give her one. It's very odd, isn't it, that I should make up my mind and actually choose to follow a person who was sitting with somebody I more or less knew. Very odd. I don't think I could put anything like that in my book. It would look rather too much of a coincidence, don't you think?"

Mrs. Oliver rose from her seat.

"Good gracious, what have I been sitting on? A dustbin! Really! Not a very nice dustbin, either." She sniffed. "What is this place I've got to?"

David was looking at her. She felt suddenly that she was completely mistaken in everything she had previously thought. "Absurd of me," thought Mrs. Oliver, "absurd of me. Thinking that he was dangerous, that he might do something to me." He was smiling at her with an extraordinary charm. He moved his head slightly and his chestnut ringlets moved on his shoulders. What fantastic creatures there were in the way of young men nowadays!

"The least I can do," he said, "is to show you, I think, where you've been brought to, just by following me. Come on, up these stairs." He indicated a ramshackle outside staircase running up to what seemed to be a loft.

"Up those stairs?" Mrs. Oliver was not so certain about this. Perhaps he was trying to lure her up there with his charm, and he would then knock her on the head. "It's no good, Ariadne," said Mrs. Oliver to herself, "you've got yourself into this spot, and now you've got to go on with it and find out what you can find out."

"Do you think they'll stand my weight?" she said. "They look frightfully rickety."

"They're quite all right. I'll go up first," he said, "and show you the way."

Mrs. Oliver mounted the ladderlike stairs behind him. It was no good. She was, deep down, still frightened. Frightened, not so much of the Peacock, as frightened of where the Peacock might be taking her. Well, she'd know very soon. He pushed open the door at the top and went into a room. It was a large, bare room and it was an artist's studio, an improvised kind of one. A few mattresses lay here and there on the floor, there were canvases stacked against the wall, a couple of easels. There was a pervading smell of paint. There were two people in the room, a bearded young man was standing at an easel, painting. He turned his head as they entered.

"Hallo, David," he said, "bringing us company?"

He was, Mrs. Oliver thought, quite the dirtiest-looking young man she'd ever seen. Oily black hair hung in a kind of circular bob down the back of his neck and over his eyes in front. His face apart from the beard was unshaven, and his clothes seemed mainly composed of greasy black leather and high boots. Mrs. Oliver's glance went beyond him to a girl who was acting as a model. She was on a wooden chair on a dais, half flung across it, her head back and her dark hair drooping down from it. Mrs. Oliver recognized her at once. It was the second one of the three girls in Borodene

Mansions. Mrs. Oliver couldn't remember her last name, but she remembered her first one. It was the highly decorative and languid-looking girl called Frances.

"Meet Peter," said David, indicating the somewhat revolting-looking artist. "One of our budding geniuses. And Frances, who is posing as a desperate girl demanding abortion."

"Shut up, you ape," said Peter.

"I believe I know you, don't I?" said Mrs. Oliver cheerfully, without any air of conscious certainty. "I'm sure I've met you somewhere! Somewhere quite lately, too."

"You're Mrs. Oliver, aren't you?" said Frances.

"That's what she said she was," said David. "True, too, is it?"

"Now, where did I meet you?" continued Mrs. Oliver. "Some party, was it? No. Let me think. I know. It was Borodene Mansions."

Frances was sitting up now in her chair and speaking in weary but elegant tones. Peter uttered a loud and miserable groan.

"Now you've ruined the pose! Do you have to have all this wriggling about? Can't you keep still?"

"No, I couldn't any longer. It was an awful pose. I've got the most frightful crick in my shoulder."

"I've been making experiments in following people," said Mrs. Oliver. "It's much more difficult than I thought. Is this an artist's studio?" she added, looking around her brightly.

"That's what they're like nowadays, a kind of loft—and lucky if you don't fall through the floor," said Peter.

"It's got all you need," said David. "It's got a north light and plenty of room and a pad to sleep on, and a fourth share in the loo downstairs —and what they call cooking facilities. And it's got a bottle or two," he added. Turning to Mrs. Oliver, but in an entirely different tone, one of utter politeness, he said, "And can we offer you a drink?"

"I don't drink," said Mrs. Oliver.

"The lady doesn't drink," said David. "Who would have thought it!"

"That's rather rude, but you're quite right," said Mrs. Oliver. "Most people come up to me and say, 'I always thought you drank like a fish.' "

She opened her handbag—and immediately three coils of gray hair fell on the floor. David picked them up and handed them to her.

"Oh! thank you." Mrs. Oliver took them. "I hadn't time this morning. I wonder if I've got any more hairpins." She delved in her bag and started attaching the coils to her head.

Peter roared with laughter. "Bully for you," he said.

"How extraordinary," Mrs. Oliver thought to herself, "that I should ever have had this silly idea that I was in danger. *Danger*—from *these* people? No matter what they look like, they're really very nice and friendly. It's quite true what people always say to me. I've far too much imagination.''

Presently she said she must be going, and David, with Regency gallantry, helped her down the rickety steps and gave her definite directions as to how to rejoin the King's Road in the quickest way.

''And then,'' he said, ''you can get a bus—or a taxi if you want it.''

''A taxi,'' said Mrs. Oliver. ''My feet are absolutely dead. The sooner I fall into a taxi, the better. Thank you,'' she added, ''for being so very nice about my following you in what must have seemed a very peculiar way. Though after all, I don't suppose private detectives, or private eyes or whatever they call them, would look anything at all like me.''

''Perhaps not,'' said David gravely. ''Left here—and then right, and then left again until you see the river and go toward it, and then sharp right and straight on.''

Curiously enough, as she walked across the shabby yard, the same feeling of unease and suspense came over her. ''I mustn't let my imagination go again.'' She looked back at the steps and the window of the studio. The figure of David still stood looking after her. ''Three perfectly nice young people,'' said Mrs. Oliver to herself. ''Perfectly nice and very kind. Left here, and then right. Just because they look rather peculiar, one goes and has silly ideas about their being dangerous. Was it right again? or left? Left, I think. Oh, goodness, my feet. It's going to rain, too.'' The walk seemed endless and the King's Road incredibly far away. She could hardly hear the traffic now—And where on earth was the river? She began to suspect that she had followed the directions wrong.

''Oh, well,'' thought Mrs. Oliver, ''I'm bound to get somewhere soon—the river, or Putney or Wandsworth or somewhere!'' She asked her way to the King's Road from a passing man who said he was a foreigner and didn't speak English.

Mrs. Oliver turned another corner wearily, and there ahead of her was the gleam of the water. She hurried toward it down a narrow passageway, heard a footstep behind her, half turned, when she was struck from behind and the world went up in sparks.

10

A VOICE SAID: "Drink this."

Norma was shivering. Her eyes had a dazed look. She shrank back a little in the chair. The command was repeated. "Drink this." This time she drank obediently, then choked a little.

"It's—it's very strong," she gasped.

"It'll put you right. You'll feel better in a minute. Just sit still and wait."

The sickness and the giddiness which had been confusing her passed off. A little color came into her cheeks, and the shivering diminished. For the first time she looked around her, noting her surroundings. She had been obsessed by a feeling of fear and horror, but now things seemed to be returning to normal. It was a medium-sized room and it was furnished in a way that seemed faintly familiar. A desk, a couch, an armchair and an ordinary chair, a stethoscope on a side table and some machine that she thought had to do with eyes. Then her attention went from the general to the particular. The man who had told her to drink.

She saw a man of perhaps thirty-odd with red hair and a rather attractively ugly face, the kind of face that is craggy but interesting. He nodded at her in a reassuring fashion.

"Beginning to get your bearings?"

"I—I think so. I—did you—what happened?"

"Don't you remember?"

"The traffic. I—it came at me—it—" She looked at him. "I was run over."

"Oh, no, you weren't run over." He shook his head. "I saw to that."

"You?"

"Well, there you were in the middle of the road, a car bearing down on you, and I just managed to snatch you out of its way. What were you thinking of to go running into the traffic like that?"

"I can't remember. I—yes, I suppose I must have been thinking of something else."

"A Jaguar was coming pretty fast, and there was a bus bearing down on the other side of the road. The car wasn't trying to run you down or anything like that, was it?"

"I—no, no, I'm sure it wasn't. I mean, I—"

"Well, I wondered—It just might have been something else, mightn't it?"

"What do you mean?"

"Well, it could have been deliberate, you know."

"What do you mean by deliberate?"

"Actually I just wondered whether you were trying to get yourself killed?" He added casually, "Were you?"

"I—no—well—no, of course not."

"Damn silly way to do it, if so." His tone changed slightly. "Come now, you must remember something about it."

She began shivering again. "I thought—I thought it would be all over. I thought—"

"So you were trying to kill yourself, weren't you? What's the matter? You can tell me. Boy friend? That can make one feel pretty bad. Besides, there's always the hopeful thought that if you kill yourself, you make him sorry—but one should never trust to that. People don't like feeling sorry or feeling anything is their fault. All the boy friend will probably say is, 'I always thought she was unbalanced. It's really all for the best.' Just remember that next time you have an urge to charge Jaguars. Even Jaguars have feelings to be considered. Was that the trouble? Boy friend walk out on you?"

"No," said Norma. "Oh, no. It was quite the opposite." She added suddenly, "He wanted to marry me."

"That's no reason for throwing yourself down in front of a Jaguar."

"Yes, it is. I did it because—" She stopped.

"You'd better tell me about it, hadn't you?"

"How did I get here?" asked Norma.

"I brought you here in a taxi. You didn't seem injured—a few bruises, I expect. You merely looked shaken to death, and in a state of shock. I asked you your address, but you looked at me as though you didn't know what I was talking about. A crowd was about to collect. So I hailed a taxi and brought you here."

"Is this a—a doctor's surgery?"

"This is a doctor's consulting room and I'm the doctor. Stillingfleet my name is."

"I don't want to see a doctor! I don't want to talk to a doctor! I don't—"

"Calm down, calm down. You've been talking to a doctor for the last ten minutes. What's the matter with doctors, anyway?"

"I'm afraid. I'm afraid a doctor would say—"

"Come now, my dear girl, you're not consulting me professionally.

Regard me as a mere outsider who's been enough of a busybody to save you from being killed or what is far more likely, having a broken arm or a fractured leg or a head injury or something extremely unpleasant which might incapacitate you for life. There are other disadvantages. Formerly, if you deliberately tried to commit suicide, you could be had up in Court. You still can if it's a suicide pact. There now, you can't say I haven't been frank. You could oblige now by being frank with me and telling me why on earth you're afraid of doctors. What's a doctor ever done to you?"

"Nothing. Nothing has been done to me. But I'm afraid that they might—"

"Might what?"

"Shut me up."

Dr. Stillingfleet raised his sandy eyebrows and looked at her.

"Well, well," he said. "You seem to have some very curious ideas about doctors. Why should I want to shut you up? Would you like a cup of tea?" he added, "or would you prefer a purple heart or a tranquilizer? That's the kind of thing people of your age go in for. Done a bit yourself in that line, haven't you?"

She shook her head. "Not—not really."

"I don't believe you. Anyway, why the alarm and despondency? You're not really mental, are you? I shouldn't have said so. Doctors aren't at all anxious to have people shut up. Mental homes are far too full already. Difficult to squeeze in another body. In fact, lately they've been letting a good many people out—in desperation—pushing them out, you might say—who jolly well ought to have been kept in. Everything's so overcrowded in this country.

"Well," he went on, "what are your tastes? Something out of my drug cupboard or a good solid old-fashioned English cup of tea?"

"I—I'd like some tea," said Norma.

"Indian or China? That's the thing to ask, isn't it? Mind you, I'm not sure if I've got any China."

"I like Indian better."

"Good."

He went to the door, opened it and shouted, "Annie. Pot of tea for two."

He came back and sat down and said, "Now you get this quite clear, young lady. What's your name, by the way?"

"Norma Res—" She stopped.

"Yes?"

"Norma West."

"Well, Miss West, let's get this clear. I'm not treating you, you're not consulting me. You are the victim of a street accident—that is the way we'll put it and that is the way I suppose you meant it to appear, which would have been pretty hard on the fellow in the Jaguar."

"I thought of throwing myself off a bridge first."

"Did you? You wouldn't have found that so easy. People who build bridges are rather careful nowadays. I mean you'd have had to climb up onto the parapet and it's not so easy. Somebody stops you. Well, to continue with my dissertation, I brought you home, as you were in too much of a state of shock to tell me your address. What is it, by the way?"

"I haven't got an address. I—I don't live anywhere."

"Interesting," said Dr. Stillingfleet. "What the police call 'of no fixed abode.' What do you do—sit out on the Embankment all night?"

She looked at him suspiciously.

"I could have reported the accident to the police, but there was no obligation upon me to do so. I preferred to take the view that in a state of maiden meditation you were crossing the street before looking left first."

"You're not at all like my idea of a doctor," said Norma.

"Really? Well, I've been getting gradually disillusioned in my profession in this country. In fact, I'm giving up my practice here and I'm going to Australia in about a fortnight. So you're quite safe from me, and you can if you like tell me how you see pink elephants walking out of the wall, how you think the trees are leaning out their branches to wrap round and strangle you, how you think you know just when the devil looks out of people's eyes, or any other cheerful fantasy, and I shan't do a thing about it! You look sane enough, if I may say so."

"I don't think I am."

"Well, you may be right," said Dr. Stillingfleet handsomely. "Let's hear what your reasons are."

"I do things and don't remember about them. I tell people things about what I've done but I don't remember telling them . . ."

"It sounds as though you have a bad memory."

"You don't understand. They're all—wicked things."

"Religious mania? Now that would be very interesting."

"It's not religious. It's just—just *hate*."

There was a tap at the door and an elderly woman came in with a tea tray. She put it down on the desk and went out again.

"Sugar?" said Dr. Stillingfleet.

"Yes, please."

"Sensible girl. Sugar is very good for you when you've had a shock." He poured out two cups of tea, set hers at her side and placed the sugar bowl beside it. "Now then." He sat down. "What were we talking about? Oh, yes, hate."

"It is possible, isn't it, that you could hate someone so much that you really want to kill them?"

"Oh, yes," said Stillingfleet cheerfully still. "Perfectly possible. In fact, most natural. But even if you really want to do it, you can't always screw yourself up to the point, you know. The human being is equipped with a natural braking system and it applies the brakes for you just at the right moment."

"You make it sound so ordinary," said Norma. There was a distinct overtone of annoyance in her voice.

"Oh, well, it is quite natural. Children feel like it almost every day. Lose their tempers, say to their mothers or their fathers, 'You're wicked, I hate you, I wish you were dead.' Mothers, being sometimes sensible people, don't usually pay any attention. When you grow up, you still hate people, but you can't take quite so much trouble wanting to kill them by then. Or if you still do—well, then you go to prison. That is, if you actually brought yourself to do such a messy and difficult job. You aren't putting all this on, are you, by the way?" he asked casually.

"Of course not." Norma sat up straight. Her eyes flashed with anger. "Of course not. Do you think I would say such awful things if they weren't true?"

"Well, again," said Dr. Stillingfleet, "people do. They say all sorts of awful things about themselves and enjoy saying them." He took her empty cup from her. "Now then," he said, "you'd better tell me all about everything. Who you hate, why you hate them, what you'd like to do to them."

"Love can turn to hate."

"Sounds like a melodramatic ballad. But remember hate can turn to love, too. It works both ways. And you say it's not a boy friend. *He was your man and he did you wrong*. None of that stuff, eh?"

"No, no. Nothing like that. It's—it's my stepmother."

"The cruel stepmother motif. But that's nonsense. At your age you can get away from a stepmother. What has she done to you beside marrying your father? Do you hate him too, or are you so devoted to him that you don't want to share him?"

"It's not like that at all. Not at all. I used to love him once. I loved him dearly. He was—he was—I thought he was wonderful."

"Now then," said Dr. Stillingfleet, "listen to me. I'm going to suggest something. You see that door?"

Norma turned her head and looked in a puzzled fashion at the door.

"Perfectly ordinary door, isn't it? Not locked. Opens and shuts in the ordinary way. Go on, try it for yourself. You saw my housekeeper come in and go out through it, didn't you? No illusions. Come on. Get up. Do what I tell you."

Norma rose from her chair and rather hesitatingly went to the door and opened it. She stood in the aperture, her head turned toward him inquiringly.

"Right. What do you see? A perfectly ordinary hallway, wants redecorating, but it's not worth having it done when I'm just off to Australia. Now go to the front door, open it, also no tricks about it. Go outside and down to the pavement and that will show you that you are perfectly free with no attempts to shut you up in any way. After that when you have satisfied yourself that you could walk out of this place at any minute you like, come back, sit in that comfortable chair over there and tell me all about yourself. After which I will give you my valuable advice. You needn't take it," he added consolingly. "People seldom do take advice, but you might as well have it. See? Agreed?"

Norma got up slowly, she went a little shakily out of the room, out into—as the doctor had described—the perfectly ordinary hallway, opened the front door with a simple catch, down four steps and stood on the pavement in a street of decorous but rather uninteresting houses. She stood there a moment, unaware that she was being watched through a lace blind by Dr. Stillingfleet himself. She stood there for about two minutes, then with a slightly more resolute bearing she turned, went up the steps again, shut the front door and came back into the room.

"All right?" said Dr. Stillingfleet. "Satisfy you there's nothing up my sleeve? All clear and above board."

The girl nodded.

"Right. Sit down there. Make yourself comfortable. Do you smoke?"

"Well, I—"

"Only reefers—something of that kind? Never mind, you needn't tell me."

"Of course, I don't take anything of that kind."

"I shouldn't have said there was any 'of course' about it, but one must believe what the patient tells one. All right. Now tell me all about yourself."

"I—I don't know. There's nothing to tell really. Don't you want me to lie down on a couch?"

"Oh, you mean your memory of dreams and all that stuff? No, not particularly. I just like to get a background. You know. You were born, you lived in the country or the town, you have brothers and sisters or you're an only child, and so on. When your own mother died, were you very upset by her death?"

"Of course I was." Norma sounded indignant.

"You're much too fond of saying of course, Miss West. By the way, West isn't really your name, is it? Oh, never mind, I don't want to know any other one. Call yourself West or East or North or anything you like. Anyway, what went on after your mother died?"

"She was an invalid for a long time before she died. In nursing homes a good deal. I stayed with an aunt, rather an old aunt, down in Devonshire. She wasn't really an aunt, she was Mother's first cousin. And then my father came home just about six months ago. It—it was wonderful." Her face lighted up suddenly. She was unaware of the quick, shrewd glance the apparently casual young man shot at her. "I could hardly remember him, you know. He must have gone away when I was about five. I didn't really think I'd ever see him again. Mother didn't very often talk about him. I think at first she hoped that he'd give up this other woman and come back."

"Other woman?"

"Yes. He went away with someone. She was a very bad woman, Mother said. Mother talked about her very bitterly and very bitterly about Father, too, but I used to think that perhaps—perhaps Father wasn't as bad as she thought, that it was all this woman's fault."

"Did they marry?"

"No. Mother said she would never divorce Father. She was a—is it an Anglican?—very High Church, you know. Rather like a Roman Catholic. She didn't believe in divorce."

"Did they go on living together? What was the woman's name, or is that a secret too?"

"I don't remember her last name." Norma shook her head. "No, I don't think they lived together long, but I don't know much about it all, you see. They went to South Africa, but I think they quarreled and parted quite soon, because that's when Mother said she hoped Father might come back again. But he didn't. He didn't write even. Not even to me. But he sent me things at Christmas. Presents always."

"He was fond of you?"

"I don't know. How could I tell? Nobody ever spoke about him. Only Uncle Simon—his brother, you know. He was in business in the City and he was very angry that Father had chucked up everything. He said he had always been the same, could never settle to anything, but he said he wasn't a bad chap really. He said he was just weak. I didn't often see Uncle

Simon. It was always Mother's friends. Most of them were dreadfully dull. My whole life has been very dull.

"Oh, it seemed so wonderful that Father was really coming home. I tried to remember him better. You know, things he had said, games he had played with me. He used to make me laugh a lot. I tried to see if I couldn't find some old snapshots or photographs of him. They seem all to have been thrown away. I think Mother must have torn them all up."

"She had remained vindictive, then."

"I think it was really Louise she was vindictive against."

"Louise?"

He saw a slight stiffening on the girl's part.

"I don't remember—I told you—I don't remember any names."

"Never mind. You're talking about the woman your father ran away with. Is that it?"

"Yes. Mother said she drank too much and took drugs and would come to a bad end."

"But you don't know whether she did?"

"I don't know anything." Her emotion was rising. "I wish you wouldn't ask me questions! I don't know anything about her! I never heard of her again! I'd forgotten her until you spoke about her. I tell you I don't know anything."

"Well, well," said Dr. Stillingfleet. "Don't get so agitated. You don't need to bother about past history. Let's think about the future. What are you going to do next?"

Norma gave a deep sigh.

"I don't know. I've nowhere to go. I can't—it's much better—I'm sure it's much better to—to end it all—only—"

"Only you can't make the attempt a second time, is that it? It would be very foolish if you did, I can tell you that, my girl. All right, you've nowhere to go, no one to trust; got any money?"

"Yes, I've got a banking account, and Father pays so much into it every quarter, but I'm not sure . . . I think perhaps, by now, they might be looking for me. I don't want to be found."

"You needn't be. I'll fix that up for you all right. Place called Kenway Court. Not as fine as it sounds. It's a kind of convalescent nursing home where people go for a rest cure. It's got no doctors or couches, and you won't be shut up there, I can promise you. You can walk out any time you like. You can have breakfast in bed, stay in bed all day if you like. Have a good rest and I'll come down one day and talk to you and we'll solve a few problems together. Will that suit you? Are you willing?"

Norma looked at him. She sat, without expression, staring at him; slowly she nodded her head.

II

Later that evening, Dr. Stillingfleet made a telephone call.

"Quite a good operation kidnap," he said. "She's down at Kenway Court. Came like a lamb. Can't tell you much yet. The girl's full of drugs. I'd say she'd been taking purple hearts, and dream bombs, and probably L.S.D. She's been all hopped up for some time. She says no, but I wouldn't trust much to what she says."

He listened for a moment. "Don't ask me! One will have to go carefully there. She gets the wind up easily . . . Yes, she's scared of something, or she's pretending to be scared of something . . .

"I don't know yet. I can't tell. Remember, people who take drugs are tricky. You can't believe what they say always. We haven't rushed things, and I don't want to startle her . . .

"A father complex as a child. I'd say didn't care much for her mother, who sounds a grim woman, by all accounts—the self-righteous martyr type. I'd say Father was a gay one and couldn't quite stand the grimness of married life—Know of anyone called Louise? . . . The name seemed to frighten her—She was the girl's first hate, I should say. She took Father away at the time the child was five. Children don't understand very much at that age, but they're very quick to feel resentment of the person they feel was responsible. She didn't see Father again until apparently a few months ago. I'd say she'd had sentimental dreams of being her father's companion and the apple of his eye. She got disillusioned, apparently. Father came back with a wife, a new, young, attractive wife. She's not called Louise, is she? . . . Oh, well, I only asked. I'm giving you roughly the picture, the general picture, that is."

The voice at the other end of the wire said sharply, "What is that you say? Say it again."

"I said I'm giving you roughly the picture."

There was a pause.

"By the way, here's one little fact might interest you. The girl made a rather ham-handed attempt to commit suicide. Does that startle you? . . .

"Oh, it doesn't . . . No, she didn't swallow the aspirin bottle or put her head in the gas oven. She rushed into the traffic in the path of a Jaguar going faster than it should have done . . . I can tell you I only got to her just in time . . . Yes, I'd say it was a genuine impulse . . . She admitted it. Usual classic phrase—she 'wanted to get out of it all.' "

He listened to a rapid flow of words, then he said: ''I don't know. At this stage, I can't be sure—The picture presented is clear. A nervy girl, neurotic and in an overwrought state from taking drugs of too many kinds. No, I couldn't tell you definitely what kind. There are dozens of these things going about, all producing slightly different effects. There can be confusion, loss of memory, aggression, bewilderment, or sheer fuzzle-headedness! The difficulty is to tell what the real reactions are as opposed to the reactions produced by drugs. There are two choices, you see. Either this is a girl who is playing herself up, depicting herself as neurotic and nervy and claiming suicidal tendencies. It could be actually so. Or it could be a whole pack of lies. I wouldn't put it past her to be putting up this story for some obscure reason of her own—wanting to give an entirely false impression of herself. If so, she's doing it very cleverly. Every now and then, there seems something not quite right in the picture she's giving. Is she a very clever little actress, acting a part? Or is she a genuine semimoronic suicidal victim? She could be either . . . What did you say? . . . Oh, the Jaguar! . . . Yes, it was being driven far too fast. You think it mightn't have been an attempt at suicide? That the Jaguar was deliberately meaning to run her down?''

He thought for a minute or two. ''I can't say,'' he said slowly. ''It just could be so. Yes, it could be so, but I hadn't thought of it that way. The trouble is, everything's possible, isn't it? Anyway, I'm going to get more out of her shortly. I've got her in a position where she's semi-willing to trust me, so long as I don't go too far too quickly and make her suspicious. She'll become more trusting soon and tell me more, and if she's a genuine case, she'll pour out her whole story to me—force it on me in the end. At the moment she's frightened of something . . .

''If, of course, she's leading me up the garden path, we'll have to find out the reason why. She's at Kenway Court and I think she'll stay there. I'd suggest that you keep someone with an eye on it for a day or so, and if she does attempt to leave, someone she doesn't know by sight had better follow her.''

II

ANDREW RESTARICK was writing a check—he made a slight grimace as he did so.

His office was large and handsomely furnished in typical conventional tycoon fashion. The furnishing and fittings had been Simon Restarick's, and Andrew Restarick had accepted them without interest and had made few changes except for removing a couple of pictures and replacing them by his own portrait, which he had brought up from the country, and a water color of Table Mountain.

Andrew Restarick was a man of middle age, beginning to put on flesh, yet strangely little changed from the man some fifteen years younger in the picture hanging above him. There was the same jutting-out chin, the lips firmly pressed together, and the slightly raised quizzical eyebrows. Not a very noticeable man—an ordinary type and at the moment not a very happy man. His secretary entered the room—she advanced toward his desk as he looked up.

"A Monsieur Hercule Poirot is here. He insists that he has an appointment with you—but I can find no trace of one."

"A Monsieur Hercule Poirot?" The name seemed vaguely familiar, but he could not remember in what context. He shook his head. "I can't remember anything about him—though I seem to have heard the name. What does he look like?"

"A very small man—foreign—French, I should say—with an enormous mustache—"

"Of course! I remember Mary describing him. He came to see old Roddy. But what's all this about an appointment with me?"

"He says you wrote him a letter."

"Can't remember it—even if I did. Perhaps Mary—Oh, well, never mind—bring him in. I suppose I'd better see what this is all about."

A moment or two later Claudia Reece-Holland returned, ushering with her a small man with an egg-shaped head, large mustaches, pointed patent-leather shoes and a general air of complacency which accorded very well with the description he had had from his wife.

"Monsieur Hercule Poirot," said Claudia Reece-Holland.

She went out again as Hercule Poirot advanced toward the desk. Restarick rose.

"Monsieur Restarick? I am Hercule Poirot, at your service."

"Oh, yes. My wife mentioned that you'd called upon us or rather called upon my uncle. What can I do for you?"

"I have presented myself in answer to your letter."

"What letter? I did not write to you, Monsieur Poirot."

Poirot stared at him. Then he drew from his pocket a letter, unfolded it, glanced at it and handed it across the desk with a bow.

"See for yourself, monsieur."

Restarick stared at it. It was typewritten on his own office stationery. His signature was written in ink at the bottom.

Dear Monsieur Poirot,

I should be very glad if you could call upon me at the above address at your earliest convenience. I understand from what my wife tells me and also from what I have learned by making various inquiries in London, that you are a man to be trusted when you agree to accept a mission that demands discretion.

Yours truly,
Andrew Restarick

He said sharply: "When did you receive this?"

"This morning. I had no matters of moment on my hands, so I came along here."

"This is an extraordinary thing, Monsieur Poirot. That letter was not written by me."

"Not written by you?"

"No. My signature is quite different—look for yourself." He cast out a hand as though looking for some example of his handwriting, and without conscious thought turned the check book on which he had just written his signature so that Poirot could see it. "You see? The signature on the letter is not in the least like mine."

"But that is extraordinary," said Poirot. "Absolutely extraordinary. Who could have written this letter?"

"That's just what I'm asking myself."

"It could not—excuse me—have been your wife?"

"No, no. Mary would never do a thing like that. And, anyway, why should she sign it with my name? Oh, no, she would have told me if she'd done such a thing, prepared me for your visit."

"Then you have no idea why anyone might have sent this letter?"

"No, indeed."

"Have you no knowledge, Mr. Restarick, as to what the matter might be on which in this letter you apparently want to engage me?"

"How could I have an idea?"

"Excuse me," said Poirot, "you have not yet completely read this letter. You will notice at the bottom of the first page, after the signature, there is a small postscript."

Restarick turned the letter over. At the top of the next page the typewriting continued.

The matter on which I wish to consult you concerns my daughter, Norma.

Restarick's manner changed. His face darkened.

"So that's it! But who could know—who could possibly meddle in this matter? Who knows about it?"

"Could it be a way of urging you to consult me? Some well-meaning friend? You have really *no* idea who the writer may have been?"

"I've no idea whatever."

"And you are not in trouble over a daughter of yours—a daughter named Norma?"

Restarick said slowly: "I have a daughter named Norma. My only daughter." His voice changed slightly as he said the last words.

"And she is in trouble, difficulty of some kind?"

"Not that I know of." But he hesitated slightly as he spoke the words.

Poirot leaned forward.

"I don't think that is exactly right, Mr. Restarick. I think there *is* some trouble or difficulty concerning your daughter."

"Why should you think that? Has someone spoken to you on this subject?"

"I was going entirely by your intonation, monsieur. Many people," added Hercule Poirot, "are in trouble over daughters at the present date. They have a genius, young ladies, for getting into various kinds of trouble and difficulty. It is possible that the same obtains here."

Restarick was silent for some few moments, drumming with his fingers on the desk.

"Yes, I am worried about Norma," he said at last. "She is a difficult girl. Neurotic, inclined to be hysterical. I—unfortunately I don't know her very well."

"Trouble, no doubt, over a young man?"

"In a way, yes, but that is not entirely what is worrying me. I think—" He looked appraisingly at Poirot. "Am I to take it that you are a man of discretion?"

"I should be very little good in my profession if I were not."

"It is a case, you see, of wanting my daughter found."

"Ah?"

"She came home last weekend as she usually does to our house in the country. She went back on Sunday night ostensibly to the flat which she occupies in common with two other girls, but I now find that she did not go there. She must have gone—somewhere else."

"In fact, she has disappeared?"

"It sounds too much of a melodramatic statement, but it does amount to that. I expect there's a perfectly natural explanation, but—well, I suppose any father would be worried. She hasn't rung up, you see, or given any explanation to the girls with whom she shares her flat."

"They too are worried?"

"No, I should not say so. I think—well, I think they take such things easily enough. Girls are very independent. More so than when I left England fifteen years ago."

"What about the young man of whom you say you do not approve? Can she have gone away with him?"

"I devoutly hope not. It's possible, but I don't—my wife doesn't think so. You saw him, I believe, the day you came to our house to call on my uncle—"

"Ah, yes, I think I know the young man of whom you speak. A very handsome young man but not, if I may say so, a man of whom a father would approve. I noticed that your wife was not pleased, either."

"My wife is quite certain that he came to the house that day hoping to escape observation."

"He knows, perhaps, that he is not welcome there?"

"He knows, all right," said Restarick grimly.

"Do you not then think that it is only too likely your daughter may have joined him?"

"I don't know what to think. I didn't—at first."

"You have been to the police?"

"No."

"In the case of anyone who is missing, it is usually much better to go to the police. They too are discreet and they have many means at their disposal which persons like myself have not."

"I don't want to go to the police. It's my daughter, man, you understand? My daughter. If she's chosen to—to go away for a short time and not let us know, well, that's up to her. There's no reason to believe that she's in any danger or anything like that. I—I just want to know for my own satisfaction where she is."

"Is it possible, Mr. Restarick—I hope I am not unduly presuming, that that is not the only thing that is worrying you about your daughter?"

"Why should you think there was anything else?"

"Because the mere fact that a girl is absent for a few days without telling her parents, or the friends with whom she is living, where she is going is not particularly unusual nowadays. It is that, taken in conjunction with something else, I think, which has caused you this alarm."

"Well, perhaps you're right. It's—" He looked doubtfully at Poirot. "It is very hard to speak of these things to strangers."

"Not really," said Poirot. "It is infinitely easier to speak to strangers of such things than it would be to speak of them to friends or acquaintances. Surely you must agree to that?"

"Perhaps. Perhaps. I can see what you mean. Well, I will admit I am upset about my girl. You see she—she's not quite like other girls, and there's been something already that has definitely worried me—worried us both."

Poirot said: "Your daughter, perhaps, is at that difficult age of young girlhood, an emotional adolescence when, quite frankly, they are capable of performing actions for which they are hardly to be held responsible. Do not take it amiss if I venture to make a surmise. Your daughter perhaps resents having a stepmother?"

"That is unfortunately true. And yet she has no reason to do so, Monsieur Poirot. It is not as though my first wife and I had recently parted. The parting took place many years ago." He paused and then said, "I might as well speak frankly to you. After all, there has been no concealment about the matter. My first wife and I drifted apart. I need not mince matters. I had met someone else, someone with whom I was quite infatuated. I left England and went to South Africa with the other woman. My wife did not approve of divorce and I did not ask her for one. I made suitable financial provision for my wife and for the child—she was only five years old at the time—"

He paused and then went on: "Looking back, I can see that I had been dissatisfied with life for some time. I'd been yearning to travel. At that period of my life I hated being tied down to an office desk. My brother reproached me several times with not taking more interest in the family business, now that I had come in with him. He said that I was not pulling my weight. But I didn't want that sort of life. I was restless. I wanted an adventurous life. I wanted to see the world and wild places . . ."

He broke off abruptly.

"Anyway—you don't want to hear the story of my life. I went to South Africa and Louise went with me. It wasn't a success. I'll admit that straight away. I was in love with her, but we quarreled incessantly. She hated life in South Africa. She wanted to get back to London and Paris—all the sophisticated places. We parted only about a year after we arrived there."

He sighed.

"Perhaps I ought to have gone back then, back to the tame life that I disliked the idea of so much. But I didn't. I don't know whether my wife would have had me back or not. Probably she would have considered it her duty to do so. She was a great woman for doing her duty."

Poirot noted the slight bitterness that ran through that sentence.

"But I ought to have thought more about Norma, I suppose. Well, there it was. The child was safely with her mother. Financial arrangements had been made. I wrote to her occasionally and sent her presents, but I never once thought of going back to England and seeing her. That was not entirely blameworthy on my part. I had adopted a different way of life and I thought it would be merely unsettling for the child to have a father who came and went and perhaps disturbed her own peace of mind. Anyway, let's say I thought I was acting for the best."

Restarick's words came fast now. It was as though he was feeling a definite solace in being able to pour out his story to a sympathetic listener. It was a reaction that Poirot had often noticed before and he encouraged it.

"You never wished to come home on your own account?"

Restarick shook his head very definitely. "No. You see, I was living the kind of life I liked, the kind of life I was meant for. I went from South Africa to East Africa. I was doing very well financially; everything I touched seemed to prosper; projects with which I was associated, occasionally with other people, sometimes on my own, all went well. I used to go off into the bush and trek. That was the life I'd always wanted. I am by nature an out-of-door man. Perhaps that's why when I was married to my first wife I felt trapped, held down. No, I enjoyed my freedom and I'd no wish to go back to the conventional type of life that I'd led here."

"But you did come back in the end?"

Restarick sighed. "Yes. I did come back. Ah, well, one grows old, I suppose. Also, another man and I had made a very good strike. We'd secured a concession which might have very important consequences. It would need negotiation in London. There I could have depended on my brother to act, but my brother died. I was still a partner in the firm. I could return if I chose and see to things myself. It was the first time I had thought of doing so. Of returning, I mean, to City life."

"Perhaps your wife—your second wife—"

"Yes, you may have something there. I had been married to Mary just a month or two when my brother died. Mary was born in South Africa, but she had been to England several times and she liked the life there. She liked particularly the idea of having an English garden!

"And I? Well, for the first time perhaps I felt I would like life in England, too. And I thought of Norma as well. Her mother had died two years earlier. I talked to Mary about it all, and she was quite willing to help me make a home for my daughter. The prospects all seemed good and so—'' he smiled—''and so I came home.''

Poirot looked at the portrait that hung behind Restarick's head. It was in a better light here than it had been at the house in the country. It showed very plainly the man who was sitting at the desk; there were the distinctive features, the obstinacy of the chin, the quizzical eyebrows, the poise of the head, but the portrait had one thing that the man sitting in the chair beneath it lacked: Youth!

Another thought occurred to Poirot. Why had Andrew Restarick moved the portrait from the country to his London office? The two portraits of him and his wife had been companion portraits done at the same time and by that particular fashionable artist of the day whose specialty was portrait painting. It would have been more natural, Poirot thought, to have left them together, as they had been meant to be originally. But Restarick had moved one portrait, his own, to his office. Was it a kind of vanity on his part—a wish to display himself as a City man, as someone important to the City? Yet he was a man who had spent his time in wild places, who professed to prefer wild places. Or did he perhaps do it in order to keep before his mind himself in his City personality? Did he feel the need of reinforcement?

''Or, of course,'' thought Poirot, ''it could be simple vanity!''

''Even I myself,'' said Poirot to himself, in an unusual fit of modesty, ''even I myself am capable of vanity on occasions.''

The short silence, of which both men had seemed unaware, was broken. Restarick spoke apologetically.

''You must forgive me, Monsieur Poirot. I seem to have been boring you with the story of my life.''

''There is nothing to excuse, Mr. Restarick. You have been talking really only of your life as it may have affected that of your daughter. You are much disquieted about your daughter. But I do not think that you have yet told me the real reason. You want her found, you say?''

''Yes, I want her found.''

''You want her found, yes, but do you want her found by me? Ah, do not hesitate. *La politesse*—it is very necessary in life, but it is not necessary here. Listen. I tell you, if you want your daughter found, I advise you, I—Hercule Poirot—to go to the police, for they have the facilities. And from my own knowledge they can be discreet.''

''I won't go to the police unless—well, unless I get very desperate.''

''You would rather go to a private agent?''

''Yes. But you see, I don't know anything about private agents. I don't know who—who can be trusted. I don't know who—''

"And what do you know about me?"

"I do know something about you. I know, for instance, that you held a responsible position in Intelligence during the war, since, in fact, my own uncle vouches for you. That is an admitted fact."

The faintly cynical expression on Poirot's face was not perceived by Restarick. The admitted fact was, as Poirot was well aware, a complete illusion—although Restarick must have known how undependable Sir Roderick was in the matter of memory and eyesight—he had swallowed Poirot's own account of himself hook, line and sinker. Poirot did not disillusion him. It merely confirmed him in his long-held belief that you should never believe anything anyone said without first checking it. *Suspect everybody,* had been for many years, if not his whole life, one of his first axioms.

"Let me reassure you," said Poirot. "I have been throughout my career exceptionally successful. I have been indeed in many ways unequaled."

Restarick looked less reassured by this than he might have been! Indeed, to an Englishman, a man who praised himself in such terms aroused some misgivings.

He said: "What do you feel yourself, Monsieur Poirot? Have you confidence that you can find my daughter?"

"Probably not as quickly as the police could do, but yes. I shall find her."

"And—and if you do—"

"But if you wish me to find her, Mr. Restarick, you must tell me all the circumstances."

"But I have told them to you. The time, the place, where she ought to be. I can give you a list of her friends . . ."

Poirot was making some violent shakings of his head. "No, no, I suggest you tell me the truth."

"Do you suggest I haven't told you the truth?"

"You have not told me all of it. Of that I am assured. What are you afraid of? What are the unknown facts—the facts that I have to know if I am to have success. Your daughter dislikes her stepmother. That is plain. There is nothing strange about that. It is a very natural reaction. You must remember that she may have secretly idealized you for many, many years. That is quite possible in the case of a broken marriage, where a child has had a severe blow in her affections. Yes, yes, I know what I am talking about. You say a child forgets. That is true. Your daughter could have forgotten you in the sense that when she saw you again she might not remember your face or your voice. She would make her own image of you. You went away. She wanted you to come back. Her mother, no doubt, discouraged her from talking about you, and therefore she thought about you perhaps all the more. You *mattered* to her all the more. And because she could not talk about you to her own mother, she had what is a very natural reaction with a child—the blaming of the parent who remains for the absence of the parent who has gone. She said to herself something in the nature of 'Father was fond of me. It's Mother he didn't like,' and from that was born a kind of idealization, a kind of secret liaison between you and her. What had happened was not her father's fault. She will not believe it!

"Oh, yes, that often happens, I assure you. I know something of the psychology. So when she learns that you are coming home, that you and she will be reunited, many memories that she has pushed aside and not thought of for years return. Her father is coming back! He and she will be happy together! She hardly realizes the stepmother, perhaps, until she sees her. And then she is violently jealous. It is most natural, I assure you. She is violently jealous partly because your wife is a good-looking woman, sophisticated, and well poised, which is a thing girls often resent because they frequently lack confidence in themselves. She herself is possibly gauche, with perhaps an inferiority complex. So when she sees her competent and good-looking stepmother, quite possibly she hates her; but hates her as an adolescent girl who is still half a child might do."

"Well—" Restarick hesitated. "That *is* more or less what the doctor said when we consulted him. I mean—"

"Aha," said Poirot, "so you consulted a doctor? You must have had some reason, it is not so, for calling in a doctor?"

"Nothing really."

"Ah, no, you cannot say that to Hercule Poirot. It was not nothing. It was something serious and you had better tell me, because if I know just what has been in this girl's mind, I shall make more progress. Things will go quicker."

Restarick was silent for several moments, then he made up his mind.

"This is in absolute confidence, Monsieur Poirot? I can rely on you—I have your assurance as to that?"

"By all means. What was the trouble?"

"I cannot be—be sure."

"Your daughter entered into some action against your wife? Something more than being merely childishly rude or saying unpleasant things. It was something worse than that—something more serious. Did she perhaps attack her physically?"

"No, it was not an attack—not a physical attack, but—nothing was proved."

"No, no. We will admit that."

"My wife became far from well—" He hesitated.

"Ah," said Poirot. "Yes, I see . . . And what was the nature of her illness? Digestive, possibly? A form of enteritis?"

"You're quick, Monsieur Poirot. You're very quick. Yes, it was digestive. This complaint of my wife's was puzzling, because she had always had excellent health. Finally they sent her to the hospital for 'observation,' as they call it. A checkup."

"And the result?"

"I don't think they were completely satisfied. She appeared to regain her health completely and was sent home in due course. But the trouble recurred. We went carefully over the meals she had, the cooking. She seemed to be suffering from a form of intestinal poisoning for which there appeared to be no cause. A further step was taken, tests were made of the dishes she ate. By taking samples of everything, it was definitely proved that a certain substance had been administered in various dishes. In each case it was a dish of which only my wife had partaken."

"In plain language, somebody was giving her arsenic. Is that right?"

"Quite right. In small doses which would in the end have a cumulative effect."

"You suspected your daughter?"

"No."

"I think you did. Who else could have done it? You suspected your daughter."

Restarick gave a deep sigh.

"Frankly, yes."

II

When Poirot arrived home, George was awaiting him.

"A woman named Edith rang up, sir—"

"Edith?" Poirot frowned.

"She is, I gather, in the service of Mrs. Oliver. She asked me to inform you that Mrs. Oliver is in St. Giles' Hospital."

"What has happened to her?"

"I understand she has been—er—coshed." George did not add the latter part of the message, which had been: "—and you tell him it's been all his fault."

Poirot clicked his tongue. "I warned her. I was uneasy last night when I rang her up, and there was no answer. *Les Femmes!*"

12

"LET'S BUY a peacock," said Mrs. Oliver suddenly and unexpectedly. She did not open her eyes as she made this remark, and her voice was weak though full of indignation.

Three people brought startled eyes to bear upon her. She made a further statement.

"Hit on the head."

She opened badly focused eyes and endeavored to make out where she was.

The first thing she saw was a face entirely strange to her—a young man who was writing in a notebook. He held the pencil poised in his hand.

"Policeman," said Mrs. Oliver decisively.

"I beg your pardon, madam?"

"I said you were a policeman," said Mrs. Oliver. "Am I right?"

"Yes, madam."

"Criminal assault," said Mrs. Oliver and closed her eyes in a satisfied manner. When she opened them again, she took in her surroundings more fully. She was in a bed, one of those rather high, hygienic-looking hospital beds, she decided—the kind that you shoot up and down and around and about. She was not in her own home. She looked round and decided on her environment.

"Hospital, or could be nursing home," she said.

A sister was standing with an air of authority at the door, and a nurse was standing by her bed. She identified a fourth figure. "Nobody," said Mrs. Oliver, "could mistake those mustaches. What are you doing here, Monsieur Poirot?"

Hercule Poirot advanced toward the bed. "I told you to be careful, madame," he said.

"Anyone might lose their way," said Mrs. Oliver, somewhat obscurely, and added, "My head aches."

"With good cause. As you surmise, you were hit on the head."

"Yes. By the Peacock."

The policeman stirred uneasily, then said, "Excuse me, madam, you say you were assaulted by a peacock?"

"Of course. I'd had an uneasy feeling for some time—you know, atmosphere." Mrs. Oliver tried to wave her hand in an appropriate gesture to describe atmosphere, and winced. "Ouch," she said, "I'd better not try that again."

"My patient must not get overexcited," said the sister with disapproval.

"Can you tell me where this assault occurred?"

"I haven't the faintest idea. I'd lost my way. I was coming from a kind of studio. Very badly kept. Dirty. The other young man hadn't shaved for days. A greasy leather jacket."

"Is this the man who assaulted you?"

"No, it's another one."

"If you could just tell me—"

"I am telling you, aren't I? I'd followed him, you see, all the way from the café—only I'm not very good at following people. No practice. It's much more difficult than you'd think."

Her eyes focused on the policeman. "But I suppose you know all about that. You have courses—in following people, I mean? Oh, never mind, it doesn't matter. You see," she said, speaking with sudden rapidity, "it's quite simple. I had got off at World's End, I think it was, and naturally I thought he had stayed with the others—or gone the other way. But instead, he came up behind me."

"Who was this?"

"The Peacock," said Mrs. Oliver, "and he startled me, you see. It does startle you when you find things are the wrong way round. I mean he following you instead of you following him—only it was earlier—and I had a sort of uneasy feeling. In fact, you know, I was afraid. I don't know why. He spoke quite politely, but I was afraid. Anyway, there it was and he said, 'Come up and see the studio,' and so I came up rather a rickety staircase. A kind of ladder staircase and there was this other young man —the dirty young man—and he was painting a picture, and the girl was acting as model. She was quite clean. Rather pretty, really. And so there we were and they were quite nice and polite, and then I said I must be getting home, and they told me the right way to get back to the King's Road. But they can't really have told me the right way. Of course I might have made a mistake. You know, when people tell you second left and third right, well, you sometimes do it the wrong way round. At least I do. Anyway, I got into a rather peculiar slummy part quite close to the river. The afraid feeling had gone away by then. I must have been quite off my guard when the Peacock hit me."

"I think she's delirious," said the nurse in an explanatory voice.

"No, I'm not," said Mrs. Oliver. "I know what I'm talking about."

The nurse opened her mouth, caught the sister's admonitory eye and shut it again quickly.

"Velvets and satins and long curly hair," said Mrs. Oliver.

"A peacock in satin? A real peacock, madame. You thought you saw a peacock near the river in Chelsea?"

"A real peacock?" said Mrs. Oliver. "Of course not. How silly. What would a real peacock be doing down on Chelsea Embankment?"

Nobody appeared to have an answer to this question.

"He struts," said Mrs. Oliver, "that's why I nicknamed him a peacock. Shows off, you know. Vain, I should think. Proud of his looks. Perhaps a lot of other things as well." She looked at Poirot. "David something. You know who I mean."

"You say this young man of the name of David assaulted you by striking you on the head?"

"Yes, I do."

Hercule Poirot spoke. "You saw him?"

"I didn't see him," said Mrs. Oliver. "I didn't know anything about it. I just thought I heard something behind me, and before I could turn my head to look—it all happened! Just as if a ton of bricks or something fell on me. I think I'll go to sleep now," she added.

She moved her head slightly, made a grimace of pain, and relapsed into what appeared to be a perfectly satisfactory unconsciousness.

13

POIROT SELDOM used the key to his flat. Instead, in an old-fashioned manner, he pressed the bell and waited for that admirable factotum, George, to open the door. On this occasion, however, after his visit to the hospital, the door was opened to him by Miss Lemon.

"You've got two visitors," said Miss Lemon, pitching her voice in an admirable tone, not as carrying as a whisper but a good many notes lower than her usual pitch. "One's Mr. Goby and the other is an old gentleman called Sir Roderick Horsefield. I don't know which you want to see first."

"Sir Roderick Horsefield," mused Poirot. He considered this with his head on one side, looking rather like a robin while he decided how this latest development was likely to affect the general picture. Mr. Goby, however, materialized with his usual suddenness from the small room which was sacred to Miss Lemon's typewriting and where she had evidently kept him in storage.

Poirot removed his overcoat. Miss Lemon hung it up on the hall-stand, and Mr. Goby, as was his fashion, addressed the back of Miss Lemon's head.

"I'll have a cup of tea in the kitchen with George," said Mr. Goby. "My time is my own. I'll keep."

He disappeared obligingly into the kitchen. Poirot went into his sitting room, where Sir Roderick was pacing up and down, full of vitality.

"Run you down, my boy," he said genially. "Wonderful thing, the telephone."

"You remembered my name? I am gratified."

"Well, I didn't exactly remember your name," said Sir Roderick. "Names, you know, have never been my strong point. Never forget a face," he ended proudly. "No. I rang up Scotland Yard."

"Oh!" Poirot looked faintly startled, though reflecting that that was not the sort of thing that Sir Roderick would do.

"Asked me who I wanted to speak to. I said, put me on to the top. That's the thing to do in life, my boy. Never accept second in charge. No good. Go to the top, that's what I say. I said who I was, mind you. Said I wanted to speak to the top brass, and I got on to it in the end. Very civil fellow. Told him I wanted the address of a chap in Allied Intelligence who was out with me at a certain place in France at a certain date. The chap seemed a bit at sea, so I said: 'You know who I mean.' A Frenchman, I said, or a Belgian. Belgian, weren't you? I said: 'He's got a Christian name something like Achilles. It's not Achilles,' I said, 'but it's *like* Achilles. Little chap,' I said, 'big mustaches.' And then he seemed to catch on, and he said you'd be in the telephone book, he thought. I said that's all right, but I said: 'He won't be listed under Achilles or Hercules (as he said it was), will he? and I can't remember his second name.' So then he gave it me. Very civil sort of fellow. Very civil, I must say."

"I am delighted to see you," said Poirot, sparing a hurried thought for what might be said to him later by Sir Roderick's telephone acquaintance. Fortunately it was not likely to have been quite the top brass. It was presumably someone with whom he was already acquainted, and whose job it was to produce civility on tap for distinguished persons of a bygone day.

"Anyway," said Sir Roderick, "I got here."

"I am delighted. Let me offer you some refreshment. Tea, a grenadine, a whisky and soda, some *sirop de cassis*—"

"Good Lord, no," said Sir Roderick, alarmed at the mention of *sirop de cassis*. "I'll take whisky for choice. Not that I'm allowed it," he added, "but doctors are all fools, as we know. All they care for is stopping you having anything you've a fancy for."

Poirot rang for George and gave him the proper instructions. The whisky and the siphon were placed at Sir Roderick's elbow and George withdrew.

"Now," said Poirot, "what can I do for you?"

"Got a job for you, old boy."

After the lapse of time, he seemed even more convinced of the close liaison between him and Poirot in the past, which was as well, thought Poirot, since it would produce an even greater dependence on his, Poirot's, capabilities by Sir Roderick's nephew.

"Papers," said Sir Roderick, dropping his voice. "Lost some papers and I've got to find 'em, see? So I thought what with my eyes not being as good as they were, and the memory being a trifle off key sometimes, I'd better go to someone in the know. See? You came along in the nick of time the other day, just in time to be useful, because I've got to cough 'em up, you understand."

"It sounds most interesting," said Poirot. "What are these papers, if I may ask?"

"Well, I suppose if you're going to find them, you'll have to ask, won't you? Mind you, they're very secret and confidential. Top secret—or they were once. And it seems as though they are going to be again. An interchange of letters, it was. Not of any particular importance at the time—or it was thought they were of no importance; but then, of course, politics change. You know the way it is. They go round and face the other way. You know how it was when the war broke out. None of us knew whether we were on our head or on our heels. One war we're pals with the Italians, next war we're enemies. I don't know which of them all was the worst. First war the Japanese were our dear allies, and the next war there they are blowing up Pearl Harbor! Never knew where you were! Start one way with the Russians, and finish the opposite way. I tell you, Poirot, nothing's more difficult nowadays than the question of allies. They can change overnight."

"And you have lost some papers," said Poirot, recalling the old man to the subject of his visit.

"Yes. I've got a lot of papers, you know, and I've dug 'em out lately. I had 'em put away safely. In a bank, as a matter of fact, but I got 'em all out and I began sorting through them because I thought why not write my memoirs. All the chaps are doing it nowadays. We've had Montgomery and Alanbrooke and Auchinleck all shooting their mouths off in print, mostly saying what they thought of the other generals. We've even had old Moran, a respectable physician, blabbing about his important patient. Don't know what things will come to next! Anyway, there it is, and I thought I'd be quite interested myself in telling a few facts about some people I knew! Why shouldn't I have a go as well as everyone else? I was in it all."

"I am sure it could be a matter of much interest to people," said Poirot.

"Ah-ha, yes! One knew a lot of people in the news. Everyone looked at them with awe. They didn't know they were complete fools, but I knew. My goodness, the mistakes some of those brass-hats made—you'd be surprised. So I got out my papers, and I had the little girl help me sort 'em out. Nice little girl, that, and quite bright. Doesn't know English very well, but apart from that, she's very bright and helpful. I'd salted away a lot of stuff, but everything was in a bit of a muddle. The point of the whole thing is, the papers I wanted weren't there."

"Weren't there?"

"No. We thought we'd given it a miss by mistake to begin with, but we went over it again and I can tell you, Poirot, a lot of stuff seemed to me to have been pinched. Some of it wasn't important. Actually, the stuff I was looking for wasn't particularly important—I mean, nobody had thought it was, otherwise I suppose I shouldn't have been allowed to keep it. But anyway, these particular letters weren't there."

"I wish, of course, to be discreet," said Poirot, "but can you tell me at all the nature of these letters you refer to?"

"Don't know that I can, old boy. The nearest I can go is of somebody who's shooting off his mouth nowadays about what he did and what he said in the past. But he's not speaking the truth, and these letters just show exactly how much of a liar he is! Mind you, I don't suppose they'd be published now. We'll just send him nice copies of them, and tell him this is exactly what he did say at the time, and that we've got it in writing. I shouldn't be surprised if—well, things went a bit differently after that. See? I hardly need ask that, need I? You're familiar with all that kind of talky-talky."

"You're quite right, Sir Roderick. I know exactly the kind of thing you mean, but you see also that it is not easy to help you recover something if one does not know what that something is, and where it is likely to be now."

"First things first: I want to know who pinched 'em, because you see that's the important point. There may be more top secret stuff in my little collection, and I want to know who's tampering with it."

"Have you any ideas yourself?"

"You think I ought to have, heh?"

"Well, it would seem that the principal possibility—"

"I know. You want me to say it's the little girl. Well, I don't think it is the little girl. She says she didn't, and I believe her. Understand?"

"Yes," said Poirot with a slight sigh, "I understand."

"For one thing she's too young. She wouldn't know these things were important. It's before her time."

"Someone else might have instructed her as to that," Poirot pointed out.

"Yes, yes, that's true enough. But it's too obvious as well."

Poirot sighed. He doubted if it was any use insisting in view of Sir Roderick's obvious partiality. "Who else had access?"

"Andrew and Mary, of course, but I doubt if Andrew would even be interested in such things. Anyway, he's always been a very decent boy. Always was. Not that I've ever known him very well. Used to come for the holidays once or twice with his brother and that's about all. Of course, he ditched his wife and went off with an attractive bit of goods to South Africa, but that might happen to any man, especially with a wife like Grace. Not that I ever saw much of her, either. Kind of woman who looked down her nose and was full of good works. Anyway, you can't imagine a chap like Andrew being a spy. As for Mary, she seems all right. Never looks at anything but a rosebush, as far as I can make out. There's a gardener, but he's eighty-three and has lived in the village all his life, and there are a couple of women always dodging about the house making a noise with Hoovers, but I can't see them in the role of spies either. So you see, it's got to be an outsider. Of course Mary wears a wig," went on Sir Roderick rather inconsequently. "I mean it might make you think she was a spy because she wore a wig, but that's not the case. She lost her hair in a fever when she was eighteen. Pretty bad luck for a young woman. I'd no idea she wore a wig to begin with, but a rosebush caught in her hair one day and whisked it sideways. Yes, very bad luck."

"I thought there was something a little odd about the way she had arranged her hair," said Poirot.

"Anyway, the best secret agents never wear wigs," Sir Roderick informed him. "Poor devils have to go to plastic surgeons and get their faces altered. But someone's been mucking about with my private papers."

"You don't think that you may perhaps have placed them in some different container—in a drawer or a different file? When did you see them last?"

"I handled these things about a year ago. I remember I thought then they'd make rather good copy, and I noted those particular letters. Now they're gone. Somebody's taken them."

"You do not suspect your nephew Andrew, his wife or the domestic staff. What about the daughter?"

"Norma? Well, Norma's a bit off her onion, I'd say. I mean she might be one of those kleptomaniacs who take people's things without knowing they're taking them, but I don't see her fumbling about among my papers."

"Then what do you think?"

"Well, you've been in the house. You saw what the house is like. Anyone can walk in and out any time they like. We don't lock our doors. We never have."

"Do you lock the door of your own room—if you go up to London, for instance?"

"I never thought of it as necessary. I do now, of course, but what's the use of that? Too late. Anyway, I've only an ordinary key, fits any of the doors. Someone must have come in from outside. Why, nowadays that's how all the burglaries take place. People walk in in the middle of the day, stump up the stairs, go into any room they like, rifle the jewel box, go out again, and nobody sees them or cares who they are. They probably look like mods or rockers or beatniks or whatever they call these chaps nowadays with the long hair and the dirty nails. I've seen more than one of them prowling about. One doesn't like to say, 'Who the devil are you?' You never know which sex they are, which is embarrassing. The place crawls with them. I suppose they're Norma's friends. Wouldn't have been allowed in in the old days. But you turn them out of the house, and then you find out it's Viscount Endersleigh or Lady Charlotte Majoribanks. Don't know where you are nowadays." He paused. "If anyone can get to the bottom of it, you can, Poirot." He swallowed the last mouthful of whisky and got up.

"Well, that's that. It's up to you. You'll take it on, won't you?"

"I will do my best," said Poirot.

The front-door bell rang.

"That's the little girl," said Sir Roderick. "Punctual to the minute. Wonderful, isn't it? Couldn't go about London without her, you know. Blind as a bat. Can't see to cross the road."

"Can you not have glasses?"

"I've got some somewhere, but they're always falling off my nose or else I lose them. Besides, I don't like glasses. I've never had glasses. When I was sixty-five, I could see to read without glasses and that's pretty good."

"Nothing," said Hercule Poirot, "lasts for ever."

George ushered in Sonia. She was looking extremely pretty. Her slightly shy manner became her very well, Poirot thought. He moved forward with Gallic *empressement*.

"*Enchanté*, mademoiselle," he said, bowing over her hand.

"I'm not late, am I, Sir Roderick?" she said, looking past him. "I have not kept you waiting? Please, I hope not."

"Exact to the minute, little girl," said Sir Roderick. "All shipshape and Bristol fashion," he added.

Sonia looked slightly perplexed.

"Made a good tea, I hope," Sir Roderick went on. "I told you, you know, to have a good tea, buy yourself some buns or éclairs or whatever it is young ladies like nowadays, eh? You obeyed orders, I hope."

"No, not exactly. I took the time to buy a pair of shoes. Look, they are pretty, are they not?" She stuck out a foot.

It was certainly a very pretty foot. Sir Roderick beamed at it.

"Well, we must go and catch our train," he said. "I may be old-fashioned, but I'm all for trains. Start on time and get there on time, or they should do. But these cars, they get in a queue in the rush hour and you may idle the time away for about an hour and a half more than you need. Cars! Pah!"

"Shall I ask Georges to get you a taxi?" asked Hercule Poirot. "It will be no trouble, I assure you."

"I have a taxi already waiting," said Sonia.

"There you are," said Sir Roderick, "you see, she thinks of everything." He patted her on the shoulder. She looked at him in a way that Hercule Poirot fully appreciated.

Poirot accompanied them to the hall door and took a polite leave of them. Mr. Goby had come out of the kitchen and was standing in the hall giving, it could be said, an excellent performance of a man who had come to see about the gas.

George shut the hall door as soon as they had disappeared into the lift, and turned to meet Poirot's gaze.

"And what is your opinion of that young lady, Georges, may I ask?" said Poirot. It was sometimes his habit to seek information from George. On certain points he always said George was infallible.

"Well, sir," said George, "if I might put it that way, if you'll allow me, I would say he'd got it badly, sir. All over her as you might say."

"I think you are right," said Hercule Poirot.

"It's not unusual, of course, with gentlemen of that age. I remember Lord Mountbryan. He'd had a lot of experience in his life, and you'd say he was as fly as anyone. But you'd be surprised. A young woman as came to give him massage. You'd be surprised at what he gave her. An evening frock and a pretty bracelet. Forget-me-nots, it was. Turquoise and diamonds. Not *too* expensive, but costing quite a pretty penny, all the same.

Then a fur wrap—not mink, Russian ermine, and a petit point evening bag. After that her brother got into trouble, debt or something, though whether she ever had a brother, I sometimes wondered. Lord Mountbryan gave her the money to square it—she was so upset about it! All platonic, mind you, too. Gentlemen seem to lose their sense that way when they get to that age. It's the clinging ones they go for, not the bold type."

"I have no doubt that you are quite right, Georges," said Poirot. "It is all the same not a complete answer to my question. I asked what you thought of the young lady."

"Oh, the young lady . . . Well, sir, I wouldn't like to say definitely, but she's quite a definite type. There's never anything that you could put your finger on. But they know what they're doing, I'd say."

Poirot entered his sitting room and Mr. Goby followed him, obeying Poirot's gesture. Mr. Goby sat down on an upright chair in his usual attitude—knees together, toes turned in. He took a rather dog-eared little notebook from his pocket, opened it carefully and then proceeded to survey the soda water siphon severely.

"Re the backgrounds you asked me to look up.

"Restarick family, perfectly respectable and of good standing. No scandal. The father, James Patrick Restarick, said to be a sharp man over a bargain. Business has been in the family three generations. Grandfather founded it, father enlarged it, Simon Restarick kept it going. Simon Restarick had coronary trouble two years ago, health declined. Died of coronary thrombosis about a year ago.

"Younger brother Andrew Restarick came into the business soon after he came down from Oxford, married Miss Grace Baldwin. One daughter, Norma. Left his wife and went out to South Africa. A Miss Birell went with him. No divorce proceedings. Mrs. Andrew Restarick died two and a half years ago. Had been an invalid for some time. Miss Norma Restarick was a boarder at Meadowfield Girls' School. Nothing against her."

Allowing his eyes to sweep across Hercule Poirot's face, Mr. Goby observed, "In fact, everything about the family seems quite O.K. and according to Hoyle."

"No black sheep, no mental instability?"

"It doesn't appear so."

"Disappointing," said Poirot.

Mr. Goby let this pass. He cleared his throat, licked his finger, and turned over a leaf of his little book.

"David Baker. Unsatisfactory record. Been on probation twice. Police are inclined to be interested in him. He's been on the fringe of several rather dubious affairs, thought to have been concerned in an important art robbery, but no proof. He's one of the arty lot. No particular means of subsistence, but he does quite well. Prefers girls with money. Not above living on some of the girls who are keen on him. Not above being paid off by their fathers either. Thorough bad lot, if you ask me, but enough brains to keep himself out of trouble."

Mr. Goby shot a sudden glance at Poirot.

"You met him?"

"Yes," said Poirot.

"What conclusions did you form, if I may ask?"

"The same as you," said Poirot. "A gaudy creature," he added thoughtfully.

"Appeals to women," said Mr. Goby. "Trouble is nowadays they won't look twice at a nice hard-working lad. They prefer the bad lots—the scroungers. They usually say, 'He hasn't had a chance, poor boy.' "

"Strutting about like peacocks," said Poirot.

"Well, you might put it like that," said Mr. Goby rather doubtfully.

"Do you think he'd use a cosh on anyone?"

Mr. Goby thought, then very slowly shook his head at the electric fire.

"Nobody's accused him of anything like that. I don't say he'd be past it, but I wouldn't say it was his line. He is a smooth-spoken type, not one for the rough stuff."

"No," said Poirot, "no, I should not have thought so. He could be bought off? That was your opinion?"

"He'd drop any girl like a hot coal if it was made worth his while."

Poirot nodded. He was remembering something: Andrew Restarick turning a check toward him so that he could read the signature on it. It was not only the signature that Poirot had read—it was the person to whom the check was made out. It had been made out to David Baker and it was for a large sum. Would David Baker demur at taking such a check? Poirot wondered. He thought not on the whole. Mr. Goby clearly was of that opinion. Undesirable young men had been bought off in any time or age, so had undesirable young women. Sons had sworn and daughters had wept, but money was money. To Norma, David had been urging marriage. Was he sincere? Could it be that he really cared for Norma? If so, he would not be so easily paid off. He had sounded genuine enough. Norma, no doubt, believed him genuine. Andrew Restarick and Mr. Goby and Hercule Poirot thought differently. They were very much more likely to be right.

Mr. Goby cleared his throat and went on.

"Miss Claudia Reece-Holland? She's all right. Nothing against her. Nothing dubious, that is. Father a Member of Parliament, well off. No scandals. Not like some M.P.s we've heard about. Educated Roedean,

Lady Margaret Hall, came down and did a secretarial course. First secretary to a doctor in Harley Street, then went to the Coal Board. First-class secretary. Has been secretary to Mr. Restarick for the last two months. No special attachments, just what you'd call minor boy friends. Eligible and useful if she wants a date. Nothing to show there's anything between her and Restarick. I shouldn't say there is, myself. Has had a flat in Borodene Mansions for the last three years. Quite a high rent there. She usually has two other girls sharing it, no special friends. They come and go. Young lady, Frances Cary, the second girl, has been there some time. Was at R.A.D.A. for a time, then went to the Slade. Works for the Wedderburn Gallery—well-known place in Bond Street. Specializes in arranging art shows in Manchester, Birmingham, sometimes abroad. Goes to Switzerland and Portugal. Arty type and has a lot of friends among artists and actors.''

He paused, cleared his throat and gave a brief look at the little notebook.

''Haven't been able to get much from South Africa yet. Don't suppose I shall. Restarick moved about a lot. Kenya, Uganda, Gold Coast, South America for a while. He just moved about. Restless chap. Nobody seems to have known him particularly well. He'd got plenty of money of his own to go where he liked. He made money, too, quite a lot of it. Liked going to out-of-the-way places. Everyone who came across him seems to have liked him. Just seems as though he was a born wanderer. He never kept in touch with anyone. Three times I believe he was reported dead—gone off into the bush and not turned up again—but he always did in the end. Five or six months and he'd pop up in some entirely different place or country.

''Then last year his brother in London died suddenly. They had a bit of trouble in tracing him. His brother's death seemed to give him a shock. Perhaps he'd had enough, and perhaps he'd met the right woman at last. Good bit younger than him, she was, and a teacher, they say. The steady kind. Anyway, he seems to have made up his mind then and there to chuck wandering about and come home to England. Besides being a very rich man himself, he's his brother's heir.''

''A success story and an unhappy girl,'' said Poirot. ''I wish I knew more about her. You have ascertained for me all that you could, the facts I needed. The people who surrounded that girl, who might have influenced her, who perhaps did influence her. I wanted to know something about her father, her stepmother, the boy she is in love with, the people she lived with and worked for in London. You are sure that in connection with this girl there have been no deaths? That is important—''

''Not a smell of one,'' said Mr. Goby. ''She worked for a firm called

Homebirds—on the verge of bankruptcy, and they didn't pay her much. Stepmother was in hospital for observation recently—in the country, that was. A lot of rumors flying about, but they didn't seem to come to anything."

"She did not die," said Poirot. "What I need," he added in a bloodthirsty manner, "is a death."

Mr. Goby said he was sorry about that and rose to his feet. "Will there be anything more you are wanting at present?"

"Not in the nature of information."

"Very good, sir." As he replaced his notebook in his pocket, Mr. Goby said: "You'll excuse me, sir, if I'm speaking out of turn, but that young lady you had here just now—"

"Yes, what about her?"

"Well, of course it's—I don't suppose it's anything to do with this, but I thought I might just mention it to you, sir—"

"Please do. You have seen her before, I gather?"

"Yes. Couple of months ago."

"Where did you see her?"

"Kew Gardens."

"Kew Gardens?" Poirot looked slightly surprised.

"I wasn't following her. I was following someone else, the person who met her."

"And who was that?"

"I don't suppose as it matters mentioning it to you, sir. It was one of the junior attachés of the Herzegovinian Embassy."

Poirot raised his eyebrows. "That is interesting. Yes, very interesting. Kew Gardens," he mused. "A pleasant place for a rendezvous. Very pleasant."

"I thought so at the time."

"They talked together?"

"No, sir, you wouldn't have said they knew each other. The young lady had a book with her. She sat down on a seat. She read the book for a little, then she laid it down beside her. Then my bloke came and sat there on the seat also. They didn't speak—only the young lady got up and wandered away. He just sat there and presently he gets up and walks off. He takes with him the book that the young lady has left behind. That's all, sir."

"Yes," said Poirot. "It is very interesting."

Mr. Goby looked at the bookcase and said Good night to it. He went.

Poirot gave an exasperated sigh.

"Enfin," he said, "it is too much! There is far too much. Now we have espionage and counterespionage. All I am seeking is one perfectly simple

murder. I begin to suspect that that murder only occurred in a drug addict's brain!"

14

"CHÈRE MADAME." Poirot bowed and presented Mrs. Oliver with a bouquet very stylized, a posy in the Victorian manner.

"Monsieur Poirot! Well, really, that is very nice of you, and it's very like you, somehow. All my flowers are always so untidy." She looked toward a vase of rather temperamental-looking chrysanthemums, then back to the prim circle of rosebuds. "And how nice of you to come and see me."

"I come, madame, to offer you my felicitations on your recovery."

"Yes," said Mrs. Oliver, "I suppose I am all right again." She shook her head to and fro rather gingerly. "I get headaches, though," she said. "Quite bad headaches."

"You remember, madame, that I warned you not to do anything dangerous."

"Not to stick my neck out, in fact. That I suppose is just what I did do." She added, "I felt something evil was about. I was frightened, too, and I told myself I was a fool to be frightened, because what was I frightened of? I mean, it was London. Right in the middle of London. People all about. I mean—how could I be frightened? It wasn't like a lonely wood or anything."

Poirot looked at her thoughtfully. He wondered, had Mrs. Oliver really felt this nervous fear, had she really suspected the presence of evil, the sinister feeling that something or someone wished her ill, or had she read it into the whole thing afterward? He knew only too well how easily that could be done. Countless clients had spoken in much the same words that Mrs. Oliver had just used. "I knew something was wrong. I could feel evil. I knew something was going to happen" and actually they had not felt anything of the kind. What kind of person was Mrs. Oliver?

He looked at her consideringly. Mrs. Oliver in her own opinion was famous for her intuition. One intuition succeeded another with remarkable rapidity, and Mrs. Oliver always claimed the right to justify the particular intuition which turned out to be right!

And yet one shared very often with animals the uneasiness of a dog or a cat before a thunderstorm, the knowledge that there is something wrong, although one does not know what it is that is wrong.

"When did it come upon you, this fear?"

"When I left the main road," said Mrs. Oliver. "Up till then it was all ordinary and quite exciting and—yes, I was enjoying myself, though vexed at finding how difficult it was to trail anybody."

She paused, considering. "Just like a game. Then suddenly it didn't seem so much like a game, because they were queer little streets and rather sort of broken-down places, and sheds and open spaces being cleared for building—oh, I don't know, I can't explain it. But it was all different. Like a dream, really. You know how dreams are. They start with one thing, a party or something, and then suddenly you find you're in a jungle or somewhere quite different—and it's all sinister."

"A jungle?" said Poirot. "Yes, it is interesting you should put it like that. So it felt to you as though you were in a jungle and you were afraid of a peacock?"

"I don't know that I was especially afraid of him. After all, a peacock isn't a dangerous sort of animal. It's—well, I mean I thought of him as a peacock because I thought of him as a decorative creature. A peacock is very decorative, isn't it? And this awful boy is decorative, too."

"You didn't have any idea anyone was following you before you were hit?"

"No. No, I'd no idea—but I think he directed me wrong, all the same."

Poirot nodded thoughtfully.

"But, of course, it must have been the Peacock who hit me," said Mrs. Oliver. "Who else? The dirty boy in the greasy clothes? He smelt nasty, but he wasn't sinister. And it could hardly be that limp Frances something—she was draped over a packing case with long black hair streaming all over the place. She reminded me of some actress or other."

"You say she was acting as a model?"

"Yes. Not for the Peacock. For the dirty boy. I can't remember if you've seen her or not."

"I have not yet had that pleasure—if it is a pleasure."

"Well, she's quite nice-looking in an untidy, arty sort of way. Very much made up. Dead white and lots of mascara and the usual kind of limp hair hanging over her face. Works in an art gallery, so I suppose it's quite natural that she should be all among the beatniks, acting as a model. How these girls can! I suppose she might have fallen for the Peacock. But it's probably the dirty one. All the same, I don't see her coshing me on the head somehow."

"I had another possibility in mind, madame. Someone may have noticed you following David—and in turn followed you."

"Someone saw *me* trailing David, and then they trailed *me*?"

"Or someone may have been already in the mews or the yard, keeping perhaps an eye on the same people that you were observing."

"That's an idea, of course," said Mrs. Oliver. "I wonder who they could be?"

Poirot gave an exasperated sigh. "Ah, it is there. It is difficult—too difficult. Too many people, too many things. I cannot see anything clearly. I see only a girl who said that she may have committed a murder! That is all that I have to go on, and you see even there there are difficulties."

"What do you mean by difficulties?"

"Reflect," said Poirot.

Reflection had never been Mrs. Oliver's strong point.

"You always mix me up," she complained.

"I am talking about a murder, but what murder?"

"The murder of the stepmother, I suppose."

"But the stepmother is not murdered. She is alive."

"You really are the most maddening man," said Mrs. Oliver.

Poirot sat up in his chair. He brought the tips of his fingers together and prepared—or so Mrs. Oliver suspected—to enjoy himself.

"You refuse to reflect," he said. "But to get anywhere, we must reflect."

"I don't want to reflect. What I want to know is what you've been doing about everything while I've been in the hospital? You must have done something. What have you done?"

Poirot ignored this question.

"We must begin at the beginning. One day you rang me up. I was in distress. Yes, I admit it, I was in distress. Something extremely painful had been said to me. You, madame, were kindness itself. You cheered me, you encouraged me. You gave me a delicious *tasse de chocolat*. And what is more, you not only offered to help me, but you did help me. You helped me to find a girl who had come to me and said that she thought she might have committed a murder! Let us ask ourselves, madame, what about this murder? Who has been murdered? Where have they been murdered? Why have they been murdered?"

"Oh, do stop," said Mrs. Oliver. "You're making my head ache again, and that's bad for me."

Poirot paid no attention to this plea. "Have we got a murder at all? You say—the stepmother—but I reply that the stepmother is not dead—so as yet we have no murder. But there ought to have been a murder. So me, I inquire first of all, who is dead? Somebody comes to me and mentions a murder. A murder that has been committed somewhere and somehow. But I cannot find that murder, and what you are about to say once again, that the attempted murder of Mary Restarick will do very well, does not satisfy Hercule Poirot."

"I really can't think what more you want," said Mrs. Oliver.

"I want a murder," said Hercule Poirot.

"It sounds very bloodthirsty when you say it like that!"

"I look for a murder and I cannot find a murder. It is exasperating—so I ask you to reflect with me."

"I've got a splendid idea," said Mrs. Oliver. "Suppose Andrew Restarick murdered his first wife before he went off in a hurry to South Africa. Had you thought of that possibility?"

"I certainly did not think of any such thing," said Poirot indignantly.

"Well, I've thought of it," said Mrs. Oliver. "It's very interesting. He was in love with this other woman, and he wanted like Crippen to go off with her, and so he murdered the first one and nobody ever suspected."

Poirot drew a long, exasperated sigh. "But his wife did not die until eleven or twelve years after he'd left this country for South Africa, and his child could not have been concerned in the murder of her own mother at the age of five years old."

"She could have given her mother the wrong medicine or perhaps Restarick just said that she died. After all, we don't know that she's dead."

"I do," said Hercule Poirot. "I have made inquiries. The first Mrs. Restarick died on the fourteenth of April nineteen sixty-three."

"How can you know these things?"

"Because I have employed someone to check the facts. I beg of you, madame, do not jump to impossible conclusions in this rash way."

"I thought I was being rather clever," said Mrs. Oliver obstinately. "If I was making it happen in a book, that's how *I* would arrange it. And I'd make the child have done it. Not meaning to, but just by her father telling her to give her mother a drink made of pounded up box hedge."

"Nom d'un nom d'un nom!" said Poirot.

"All right," said Mrs. Oliver. "You tell it your way."

"Alas, I have nothing to tell. I look for a murder and I do not find one."

"Not after Mary Restarick is ill and goes to hospital and gets better and comes back and is ill again, and if they looked they'd probably find arsenic or something hidden away by Norma somewhere."

"That is exactly what they did find."

"Well, really, Monsieur Poirot, what more do you want?"

"I want you to pay some attention to the meaning of language. That girl said to me the same thing as she had said to my manservant, Georges. She did not say on either occasion, 'I have tried to kill someone' or 'I have tried to kill my stepmother.' She spoke each time of a deed that had been done, something that had already happened. Definitely happened. In the past tense."

"I give up," said Mrs. Oliver. "You just won't believe that Norma tried to kill her stepmother."

"Yes, I believe it is perfectly possible that Norma may have tried to kill her stepmother. I think it is probably what happened—it is in accord psychologically with her distraught frame of mind. But it is not proved. Anyone, remember, could have hidden a preparation of arsenic among Norma's things. It could even have been put there by the husband."

"You always seem to think that husbands are the ones who kill their wives," said Mrs. Oliver.

"A husband is usually the most likely person," said Hercule Poirot, "so one considers him first. It could have been the girl, Norma, or it could have been one of the servants, or it could have been the *au pair* girl, or it could have been old Sir Roderick. Or it could have been Mrs. Restarick herself."

"Nonsense. Why?"

"There could be reasons. Rather far-fetched reasons, but not beyond the bounds of belief."

"Really, Monsieur Poirot, you can't suspect everybody."

"*Mais oui,* that is just what I can do. I suspect everybody. First I suspect, then I look for reasons."

"And what reason would that poor foreign child have?"

"It might depend on what she is doing in that house, and what her reasons are for coming to England and a good deal more beside."

"You're really crazy."

"Or it could have been the boy David. Your Peacock."

"Much too far-fetched. David wasn't there. He's never been near the house."

"Oh, yes, he has. He was wandering about its corridors the day I went there."

"But not putting poison in Norma's room."

"How do you know?"

"But she and that awful boy are in love with each other."

"They appear to be so, I admit."

"You always want to make everything difficult," complained Mrs. Oliver.

"Not at all. Things have been made difficult for me. I need information and there is only one person who can give me information. And she has disappeared."

"You mean Norma."

"Yes, I mean Norma."

"But she hasn't disappeared. We found her, you and I."

"She walked out of that café and once more she has disappeared."

"And you let her go?" Mrs. Oliver's voice quivered with reproach.

"Alas!"

"You let her go? You didn't even try to find her again?"

"I did not say I had not tried to find her."

"But so far you have not succeeded. Monsieur Poirot, I really am disappointed with you."

"There is a pattern," said Hercule Poirot almost dreamily. "Yes, there is a pattern. But because there is one factor missing, the pattern does not make sense. You see that, don't you?"

"No," said Mrs. Oliver, whose head was aching.

Poirot continued to talk more to himself than his listener—if Mrs. Oliver could be said to be listening. She was highly indignant with Poirot, and she thought to herself that the Restarick girl had been quite right and that Poirot was too old! There, she herself had found the girl for him, had telephoned him so that he might arrive in time, had gone off herself to shadow the other half of the couple. She had left the girl to Poirot, and what had Poirot done—lost her! In fact she could not really see that Poirot had done anything at all of any use at any time whatever. She was disappointed in him. When he stopped talking, she would tell him so again.

Poirot was quietly and methodically outlining what he called "the pattern."

"It interlocks. Yes, it interlocks and that is why it is difficult. One thing relates to another and then you find that it relates to something else that seems outside the pattern. But it is not outside the pattern. And so it brings more people again into a ring of suspicion. Suspicion of what? There again one does not know. We have first the girl and through all the maze of conflicting patterns I have to search the answer to the most poignant of questions. Is the girl a victim, is she in danger? Or is the girl very astute? Is the girl creating the impression she wants to create for her own purposes? It can be taken either way. I need something still. Some one sure pointer, and it is there somewhere. I am sure it is there somewhere."

Mrs. Oliver was rummaging in her handbag.

"I can't think why I can never find my aspirin when I want it," she said in a vexed voice.

"We have one set of relationships that hook up. The father, the daughter, the stepmother. Their lives are interrelated. We have the elderly uncle, somewhat gaga, with whom they live. We have the girl Sonia. She is linked with the uncle. She works for him. She has pretty manners, pretty ways. He is delighted with her. He is, shall we say, a little soft about her. But what is her role in the household?''

''Wants to learn English, I suppose,'' said Mrs. Oliver.

''She meets one of the members of the Herzegovinian Embassy—in Kew Gardens. She meets him there, but she does not speak to him. She leaves behind her a book and he takes it away—''

''What is all this?'' said Mrs. Oliver.

''Has this anything to do with the other pattern? We do not as yet know. It seems unlikely, but it may not be unlikely. Had Mary Restarick unwittingly stumbled upon something which might be dangerous to the girl?''

''Don't tell me all this has something to do with espionage or something.''

''I am not telling you. I am wondering.''

''You said yourself that old Sir Roderick was gaga.''

''It is not a question of whether he is gaga or not. He was a person of some importance during the war. Important papers passed through his hands. Important letters can have been written to him. Letters which he was at perfect liberty to have kept once they had lost their importance.''

''You're talking of the war, and that was ages ago.''

''Quite so. But the past is not always done with, because it is ages ago. New alliances are made. Public speeches are made repudiating this, denying that, telling various lies about something else. And suppose there exist still certain letters or documents that will change the picture of a certain personality. I am not telling you anything, you understand. I am only making assumptions—assumptions such as I have known to be true in the past. It might be of the utmost importance that some letters or papers should be destroyed, or else passed to some foreign government. Who better to undertake that task than a charming young lady who assists and aids an elderly notability to collect material for his memoirs? Everyone is writing their memoirs nowadays. One cannot stop them from doing so! Suppose that the stepmother gets a little something in her food on the day that the helpful secretary plus *au pair* girl is doing the cooking? And suppose it is she who arranges that suspicion should fall on Norma?''

''What a mind you have,'' said Mrs. Oliver. ''Tortuous, that's what I call it. I mean, *all* these things can't have happened.''

''That is just it. There are too many patterns. Which is the right one? The girl Norma leaves home, goes to London. She is, as you have instructed me, a third girl sharing a flat with two other girls. There again you may have a pattern. The two girls are strangers to her. But then what do I learn? Claudia Reece-Holland is private secretary to Norma Restarick's father.

Here again we have a link. Is that mere chance? Or could there be a pattern of some kind behind it? The other girl, you tell me, acts as a model and is acquainted with the boy you call 'the Peacock,' with whom Norma is in love. Again a link. More links. And what is David—the Peacock—doing in all this? Is he in love with Norma? It would seem so. Her parents dislike it, as is only probable and natural."

"It's odd about Claudia Reece-Holland being Restarick's secretary," said Mrs. Oliver thoughtfully. "I should judge she was unusually efficient at anything she undertook. Perhaps it was she who pushed the woman out of the window on the seventh floor."

Poirot turned slowly toward her.

"What are you saying?" he demanded. "What are you saying?"

"Just someone in the flats—I don't even know her name, but she fell out of a window or threw herself out of a window on the seventh floor and killed herself."

Poirot's voice rose high and stern.

"And you never told me?" he said accusingly.

Mrs. Oliver stared at him in surprise.

"I don't know what you mean."

"What I mean? I ask you to tell me of a death. That is what I mean. *A death*. And you say there are no deaths. You can think only of an attempted poisoning. And yet here is a death. A death at—what is the name of those mansions?"

"Borodene Mansions."

"Yes, yes. And when did it happen?"

"This suicide? Or whatever it was? I think—yes—I think it was about a week before I went there."

"Perfect! How did you hear about it?"

"A milkman told me."

"A milkman, *bon Dieu!*"

"He was just being chatty," said Mrs. Oliver. "It sounded rather sad. It was in the daytime—very early in the morning, I think."

"What was her name?"

"I've no idea. I don't think he mentioned it."

"Young, middle-aged, old?"

Mrs. Oliver considered. "Well, he didn't say her exact age. Fifty-ish, I think, was what he said."

"I wonder now. Anyone the three girls knew?"

"How can I tell? Nobody has said anything about it."

"And you never thought of telling me."

"Well, really, Monsieur Poirot, I cannot see that it has anything to do with all this. Well, I suppose it may have—but nobody seems to have said so, or thought of it."

"But, yes, there is the link. There is this girl Norma, and she lives in those flats, and one day somebody commits suicide (for that, I gather, was the general impression). That is, somebody throws herself or falls out of a seventh-floor high window and is killed. And then? Some days later this girl Norma, after having heard you talk about me at a party, comes to call upon me and she says to me that she is afraid that she may have committed a murder. Do you not see? A death—and not many days later someone who thinks she may have committed a murder. Yes, this must be the murder."

Mrs. Oliver wanted to say "nonsense," but she did not quite dare to do so. Nevertheless, she thought it.

"This then must be the one piece of knowledge that had not yet come to me. This ought to tie up the whole thing! Yes, yes, I do not see yet how, but it must be so. I must think. That is what I must do. I must go home and think until slowly the pieces fit together—because this will be the key piece that ties them all together. . . . Yes. At last. At last I shall see my way."

He rose to his feet and said, "*Adieu, chère* madame," and hurried from the room. Mrs. Oliver at last relieved her feelings.

"Nonsense," she said to the empty room. "Absolute nonsense. I wonder if four would be too many aspirins to take?"

15

AT HERCULE POIROT'S elbow was a tisane prepared for him by George. He sipped at it and thought. He thought in a certain way peculiar to himself. It was the technique of a man who selected thoughts as one might select pieces of a jigsaw puzzle. In due course they would be reassembled together so as to make a clear and coherent picture. At the moment the important thing was the selection, the separation. He sipped his tisane, put down the cup, rested his hands on the arms of his chair and let various pieces of his puzzle come one by one into his mind. Once he recognized them all, he would select. Pieces of sky, pieces of green bank, perhaps striped pieces like those of a tiger. . . .

The painfulness of his own feet in patent-leather shoes. He started there. Walking along a road set on this path by his good friend, Mrs. Oliver. A stepmother. He saw himself with his hand on a gate. A woman who turned, a woman bending her head cutting out the weak growth of a rose, turning and looking at him? What was there for him there? Nothing. A golden head, a golden head bright as a cornfield, with twists and loops of hair slightly reminiscent of Mrs. Oliver's own in shape. He smiled a little. But Mary Restarick's hair was more tidily arranged than Mrs. Oliver's ever was. A golden frame for her face that seemed just a little too large for her. He remembered that old Sir Roderick had said that she had to wear a wig because of an illness. Sad for so young a woman. There was, when he came to think of it, something unusually heavy about her head. Far too static, too perfectly arranged. He considered Mary Restarick's wig—if it was a wig—for he was by no means sure that he could depend on Sir Roderick. He examined the possibilities of the wig in case they should be of significance. He reviewed the conversation they had had. Had they said anything important? He thought not. He remembered the room into which they had gone. A characterless room recently inhabited in someone else's house. Two pictures on the wall, the picture of a woman in a dove-gray dress. Thin mouth, lips set closely together. Hair that was grayish brown. The first Mrs. Restarick. She looked as though she might have been older than her husband. His picture was on the opposite wall, facing her. Good portraits, both of them. Lansberger had been a good portrait painter. His mind dwelt on the portrait of the husband. He had not seen it so well that first day as he had later in Restarick's office. . . .

Andrew Restarick and Claudia Reece-Holland. Was there anything there? Was their association more than a merely secretarial one? It need not be. Here was a man who had come back to this country after years of absence, who had no near friends or relatives, who was perplexed and troubled over his daughter's character and conduct. It was probably natural enough that he should turn to his recently acquired eminently competent secretary and ask her to suggest somewhere for his daughter to live in London. It would be a favor on her part to provide that accommodation, since she was looking for a Third Girl. Third girl . . . The phrase that he had acquired from Mrs. Oliver always seemed to be coming to his mind —as though it had a second significance, which for some reason he could not see.

His manservant, George, entered the room, closing the door discreetly behind him.

"A young lady is here, sir. The young lady who came the other day."

The words came too aptly with what Poirot was thinking. He sat up in a startled fashion.

"The young lady who came at breakfast time?"

"Oh, no, sir. I mean the young lady who came with Sir Roderick Horsefield."

"Ah, indeed."

Poirot raised his eyebrows. "Bring her in. Where is she?"

"I showed her into Miss Lemon's room, sir."

"Ah. Yes, bring her in."

Sonia did not wait for George to announce her. She came into the room ahead of him with a quick and rather aggressive step.

"It has been difficult for me to get away, but I have come to tell you that I did not take those papers. I did not steal anything. You understand?"

"Has anybody said that you had?" Poirot asked. "Sit down, mademoiselle."

"I do not want to sit down. I have very little time. I just came to tell you that it is absolutely untrue. I am very honest and I do what I am told."

"I take your point. I have already taken it. Your statement is that you have not removed any papers, information, letters, documents of any kind from Sir Roderick Horsefield's house? That is so, is it not?"

"Yes, and I've come to tell you it is so. *He* believes me. *He* knows that I would not do such a thing."

"Very well then. That is a statement and I note it."

"Do you think you are going to find those papers?"

"I have other inquiries in hand," said Poirot. "Sir Roderick's papers will have to take their turn."

"He is worried. He is very worried. There is something that I cannot say to him. I will say it to you. He loses things. Things are not put away where he thinks they are. He puts them in—how do you say it?—in funny places. Oh, I know. You suspect me. Everyone suspects me because I am foreign. Because I come from a foreign country and so they think—they think I steal secret papers like in one of your silly English spy stories. I am not like that. I am an intellectual."

"Aha," said Poirot. "It is always nice to know." He added: "Is there anything else you wish to tell me?"

"Why should I?"

"One never knows."

"What are these other cases you speak of?"

"Ah, I do not want to detain you. It is your day out, perhaps."

"Yes. I have one day a week when I can do what I like. I can come to London. I can go to the British Museum."

"Ah, yes, and to the Victoria and Albert also, no doubt."

"That is so."

"And to the National Gallery and see the pictures. And on a fine day you can go to Kensington Gardens, or perhaps as far as Kew Gardens."

She stiffened. She shot him an angry, questioning glance.

"Why do you say Kew Gardens?"

"Because there are some very fine plants and shrubs and trees there. Ah! You should not miss Kew Gardens. The admission fee is very small. A penny, I think, or twopence. And for that you can go and see tropical trees, or you can sit on a seat and read a book." He smiled at her disarmingly and was interested to notice that her uneasiness was increased. "But I must not detain you, mademoiselle. You have perhaps friends to visit at one of the embassies, maybe."

"Why do you say that?"

"No particular reason. You are, as you say, a foreigner and it is quite possible you may have friends connected with your own embassy here."

"Someone has told you things. Someone has made accusations against me! I tell you he is a silly old man who mislays things. That is all! And he knows nothing of importance. He has no secret papers or documents. He never has had."

"Ah, but you are not quite thinking of what you are saying. Time passes, you know. He was once an important man who did know important secrets."

"You are trying to frighten me."

"No, no. I am not being so melodramatic as that."

"Mrs. Restarick. It is Mrs. Restarick who has been telling you things. She does not like me."

"She has not said so to me."

"Well, I do not like her. She is the kind of woman I mistrust. I think she has secrets."

"Indeed?"

"Yes, I think she has secrets from her husband. I think she goes up to London or to other places to meet other men. To meet, at any rate, one other man."

"Indeed," said Poirot, "that is very interesting. You think she goes to meet another man?"

"Yes, I do. She goes up to London very often and I do not think she always tells her husband, or she says it is shopping or things she has to buy. All those sort of things. He is busy in the office and he does not think of why his wife comes up. She is more in London than she is in the country. And yet she pretends to like gardening so much."

"You have no idea who this man is whom she meets?"

"How should I know? I do not follow her. Mr. Restarick is not a suspicious man. He believes what his wife tells him. He thinks perhaps about business all the time. And, too, I think he is worried about his daughter."

"Yes," said Poirot, "he is certainly worried about his daughter. How much do you know about the daughter? How well do you know her?"

"I do not know her very well. If you ask what I *think*—well, I tell you! I think she is mad."

"You think she is mad? Why?"

"She says odd things sometimes. She sees things that are not there."

"Sees things that are not there?"

"People that are not there. Sometimes she is very excited and other times she seems as though she is in a dream. You speak to her and she does not hear what you say to her. She does not answer. I think there are people who she would like to have dead."

"You mean Mrs. Restarick?"

"*And* her father. She looks at him as though she hates him."

"Because they are both trying to prevent her marrying a young man of her choice?"

"Yes. They do not want that to happen. They are quite right, of course, but it makes her angry. Someday," added Sonia, nodding her head cheerfully, "I think she will kill herself. I hope she will do nothing so foolish, but that is the thing one does when one is much in love." She shrugged her shoulders. "Well—I go now."

"Just tell me one thing. Does Mrs. Restarick wear a wig?"

"A wig? How should I know?" She considered for a moment. "She might, yes," she admitted. "It is useful for traveling. Also it is fashionable. I wear a wig myself sometimes. A *green* one! Or I did." She added again, "I go now," and went.

16

"TODAY I HAVE much to do," Hercule Poirot announced as he rose from the breakfast table next morning and joined Miss Lemon. "Inquiries to make. You have made the necessary researches for me, the appointments, the necessary contacts?"

"Certainly," said Miss Lemon. "It is all here." She handed him a small briefcase. Poirot took a quick glance at its contents and nodded his head.

"I can always rely on you, Miss Lemon," he said. *"C'est fantastique."*

"Really, Monsieur Poirot, I cannot see anything fantastic about it. You gave me instructions and I carried them out. Naturally."

"Pah, it is not so natural as that," said Poirot. "Do I not give instructions often to the gas men, the electricians, the man who comes to repair things, and do they always carry out my instructions? Very, very seldom."

He went into the hall.

"My slightly heavier overcoat, Georges. I think the autumn chill is setting in."

He popped his head back in his secretary's room. "By the way, what did you think of that young woman who came yesterday?"

Miss Lemon, arrested as she was about to plunge her fingers on the typewriter, said briefly, "Foreign."

"Yes, yes."

"Obviously foreign."

"You do not think anything more about her than that?"

Miss Lemon considered. "I had no means of judging her capability in any way." She added rather doubtfully, "She seemed upset about something."

"Yes. She is suspected, you see, of stealing! Not money, but papers, from her employer."

"Dear, dear," said Miss Lemon. "Important papers?"

"It seems highly probable. It is equally probable, though, that he has not lost anything at all."

"Oh, well," said Miss Lemon, giving her employer a special look that she always gave and which announced that she wished to get rid of him so that she could get on with proper fervor with her work. "Well, I always say that it's better to know where you are when you are employing someone, and buy British."

Hercule Poirot went out. His first visit was to Borodene Mansions. He took a taxi. Alighting at the courtyard, he cast his eyes around. A uniformed porter was standing in one of the doorways whistling a somewhat doleful melody. As Poirot advanced upon him, he said: "Yes, sir?"

"I wondered," said Poirot, "if you can tell me anything about a very sad occurrence that took place here recently."

"Sad occurrence?" said the porter. "Nothing that I know of."

"A lady who threw herself, or shall we say fell from one of the upper stories, and was killed."

"Oh, *that*. I don't know anything about that because I've only been here a week, you see. Hi, Joe."

A porter emerging from the opposite side of the block came over.

"You'd know about the lady as fell from the seventh. About a month ago, was it?"

"Not quite as much as that," said Joe. He was an elderly, slow-speaking man. "Nasty business it was."

"She was killed instantly?"

"Yes."

"What was her name? It may, you understand, have been a relative of mine," Poirot explained. He was not a man who had any scruples about departing from the truth.

"Indeed, sir. Very sorry to hear it. She was a Mrs. Charpentier."

"She had been in the flat some time?"

"Well, let me see now. About a year—a year and a half perhaps. No, I think it must have been about two years. Number Seventy-six, seventh floor."

"That is the top floor?"

"Yes, sir. A Mrs. Charpentier."

Poirot did not press for any other descriptive information since he might be presumed to know such things about his own relative. Instead he asked: "Did it cause much excitement, much questioning? What time of day was it?"

"Five or six o'clock in the morning, I think. No warning or anything. Just down she came. In spite of being so early, we got a crowd almost at once, pushing through the railing over there. You know what people are."

"And the police, of course."

"Oh, yes, the police came quite quickly. And a doctor and an ambulance. All the usual," said the porter rather in the weary tone of one who had had people throwing themselves out of a seventh-story window once or twice every month.

"And I suppose people came down from the flats when they heard what had happened."

"Oh, there wasn't so many coming from the flats because, for one thing, with the noise of traffic and everything around here, most of them didn't know about it. Someone or other said she gave a bit of a scream as she came down, but not so that it caused any real commotion. It was only people in the street, passing by, who saw it happen. And then, of course, they craned their necks over the railings, and other people saw them craning and joined them. You know what an accident is!"

Poirot assured him he knew what an accident was.

"She lived alone?" he said, making it only half a question.

"That's right."

"But she had friends, I suppose, among the other flat dwellers?"

Joe shrugged and shook his head. "May have done. I couldn't say. Never saw her in the restaurant much with any of our lot. She had outside friends to dinner here sometimes. No, I wouldn't say she was specially pally with anybody here. You'd do best," said Joe, getting slightly restive, "to go and have a chat with Mr. McFarlane, who's in charge here, if you want to know about her."

"Ah, I thank you. Yes, that is what I mean to do."

"His office is in that block over there, sir. On the ground floor. You'll see it marked up on the door."

Poirot went as directed. He detached from his briefcase the top letter with which Miss Lemon had supplied him, and which was marked "Mr. McFarlane." Mr. McFarlane turned out to be a good-looking, shrewd-looking man of about forty-five. Poirot handed him the letter. He opened and read it.

"Ah, yes," he said, "I see."

He laid it down on the desk and looked at Poirot.

"The owners have instructed me to give you all the help I can about the sad death of Mrs. Louise Charpentier. Now what do you want to know exactly, Monsieur"—he glanced at the letter again—"Monsieur Poirot?"

"This is, of course, all quite confidential," said Poirot. "Her relatives have been communicated with by the police and by a solicitor, but they were anxious, as I was coming to England, that I should get a few more personal facts, if you understand me. It is distressing when one can get only official reports."

"Yes, quite so. Yes, I quite understand that it must be. Well, I'll tell you anything I can."

"How long had she been here and how did she come to take the flat?"

"She'd been here—I can look it up exactly—about two years. There was a vacant tenancy and I imagine that the lady who was leaving, being an acquaintance of hers, told her in advance that she was giving it up. That was a Mrs. Wilder. Worked for the B.B.C. Had been in London for some time, but was going to Canada. Very nice lady—I don't think she knew the deceased well at all. Just happened to mention she was giving up the flat. Mrs. Charpentier liked the flat."

"You found her a suitable tenant?" There was a very faint hesitation before Mr. McFarlane answered.

"She was a satisfactory tenant, yes."

"You need not mind telling me," said Hercule Poirot. "There were wild parties, eh? A little too—shall we say—gay in her entertaining?"

Mr. McFarlane stopped being so discreet.

"There were a few complaints from time to time, but mostly from elderly people."

Hercule Poirot made a significant gesture.

"A bit too fond of the bottle, yes, sir—and in with quite a gay lot. It made for a bit of trouble now and again."

"And she was fond of the gentlemen?"

"Well, I wouldn't like to go as far as *that*."

"No, no, but one understands."

"Of course she wasn't so young."

"Appearances are very often deceptive. How old would you have said she was?"

"It's difficult to say. Forty—forty-five." He added, "Her health wasn't good, you know."

"So I understand."

"She drank too much—no doubt about it. And then she'd get very depressed. Nervous about herself. Always going to doctors, I believe, and not believing what they told her. Ladies do get it into their heads—especially about that time of life—she thought that she had cancer. Was quite sure of it. The doctor reassured her, but she didn't believe him. He said at the inquest that there was nothing really wrong with her. Oh, well, one hears of things like that every day. She got all worked up and one fine day—" He nodded.

"It is very sad," said Poirot. "Did she have any special friends among the residents of the flats?"

"Not that I know of. This place, you see, isn't what I call the matey kind. They're mostly people in business, in jobs."

"I was thinking possibly of Miss Claudia Reece-Holland. I wondered if they had known each other."

"Miss Reece-Holland? No, I don't think so. Oh, I mean they were probably acquaintances, talked when they went up in the lift together, that sort of thing. But I don't think there was much social contact of any kind. You see, they would be in a different generation. I mean—" Mr. McFarlane seemed a little flustered. Poirot wondered why.

He said, "One of the other girls who share Miss Holland's flat knew Mrs. Charpentier, I believe—Miss Norma Restarick."

"Did she? I wouldn't know—she's only come here quite recently. I hardly know her by sight. Rather a frightened-looking young lady. Not long out of school, I'd say." He added, "Is there anything more I can do for you, sir?"

"No, thank you. You've been most kind. I wonder if possibly I could see the flat. Just in order to be able to say—" Poirot paused, not particularizing what he wanted to be able to say.

"Well, now, let me see. A Mr. Travers has got it now. He's in the City all day. Yes, come up with me if you like, sir."

They went up to the seventh floor. As Mr. McFarlane introduced his key, one of the numbers fell from the door and narrowly avoided Poirot's patent-leather shoe. He hopped nimbly and then bent to pick it up. He replaced the spike which fixed it on the door very carefully.

"These numbers are loose," he said.

"I'm very sorry, sir. I'll make a note of it. Yes, they wear loose from time to time. Well, here we are."

Poirot went into the living room. At the moment it had little personality. The walls were papered with a paper resembling grained wood. It had conventional comfortable furniture, the only personal touch was a television set and a certain number of books.

"All the flats are partly furnished, you see," said Mr. McFarlane. "The tenants don't need to bring anything of their own, unless they want to. We cater very largely for people who come and go."

"And the decorations are all the same?"

"Not entirely. People seem to like this raw wood effect. Good background for pictures. The only things that are different are on the one wall facing the door. We have a whole set of frescoes which people can choose from.

"We have a set of ten," said Mr. McFarlane with some pride. "There is the Japanese one—very artistic, don't you think? And there is an English garden one; a very striking one of birds; one of trees, a Harlequin one, a rather interesting abstract effect—lines and cubes, in vividly contrasting colors, that sort of thing. They're all designs by good artists. Our furniture is all the same. Two choices of colors or, of course, people can add what they like of their own. But they don't usually bother."

"Most of them are not, as you might say, homemakers," Poirot suggested.

"No, rather the bird of passage type, or busy people who want solid comfort, good plumbing and all that but aren't particularly interested in decoration, though we've had one or two of the do-it-yourself type, which isn't really satisfactory from our point of view. We've had to put a clause in the lease saying they've got to put things back as they found them—or pay for that being done."

They seemed to be getting rather far away from the subject of Mrs. Charpentier's death. Poirot approached the window.

"It was from here?" he murmured delicately.

"Yes. That's the window. The left-hand one. It has a balcony."

Poirot looked out down below.

"Seven floors," he said. "A long way."

"Yes, death was instantaneous, I am glad to say. Of course, it might have been an accident."

Poirot shook his head.

"You cannot seriously suggest that, Mr. McFarlane. It must have been deliberate."

"Well, one always likes to suggest an easier possibility. She wasn't a happy woman, I'm afraid."

"Thank you," said Poirot, "for your great courtesy. I shall be able to give her relations in France a very clear picture."

His own picture of what had occurred was not as clear as he would have liked. So far there had been nothing to support his theory that the death of Louise Charpentier had been important. He repeated the Christian name thoughtfully. Louise . . . Why had the name Louise some haunting memory about it? He shook his head. He thanked Mr. McFarlane and left.

17

CHIEF INSPECTOR NEELE was sitting behind his desk looking very official and formal. He greeted Poirot politely and motioned him to a chair. As soon as the young man who had introduced Poirot to the presence had left, Chief Inspector Neele's manner changed.

"And what are you after now, you secretive old devil?" he said.

"As to that," said Poirot, "you already know."

"Oh, yes, I've rustled up some stuff, but I don't think there's much for you from that particular hole."

"Why call it a hole?"

"Because you're so exactly like a good mouser. A cat sitting over a hole waiting for the mouse to come out. Well, if you ask me, there isn't any mouse in this particular hole. Mind you, I don't say that you couldn't unearth some dubious transactions. You know these financiers. I dare say there's a lot of hoky-poky business, and all that, about minerals and concessions and oil and all those things. But Joshua Restarick Ltd. has got a good reputation. Family business—or used to be—but you can't call it that now. Simon Restarick hadn't any children, and his brother Andrew Restarick only has this daughter. There was an old aunt on the mother's side. Andrew Restarick's daughter lived with her after she left school and her own mother died. The aunt died of a stroke about six months ago. Mildly potty, I believe—belonged to a few rather peculiar religious societies. No harm in them. Simon Restarick was a perfectly plain type of shrewd businessman and had a social wife. They were married rather late in life.''

''And Andrew?''

''Andrew seems to have suffered from wanderlust. Nothing known against him. Never stayed anywhere long, wandered about South Africa, South America, Kenya and a good many other places. His brother pressed him to come back more than once, but he wasn't having any. He didn't like London or business, but he seems to have had the Restarick family flair for making money. He went after mineral deposits, things like that. He wasn't an elephant hunter or an archaeologist or a plant man or any of those things. All his deals were business deals and they always turned out well.''

''So he also in his way is conventional?''

''Yes, that about covers it. I don't know what made him come back to England after his brother died. Possibly a new wife—he's married again. Good-looking woman a good deal younger than he is. At the moment they're living with old Sir Roderick Horsefield, whose sister had married Andrew Restarick's uncle. But I imagine that's only temporary. Is any of this news to you? Or do you know it all already?''

''I've heard most of it,'' said Poirot. ''Is there any insanity in the family on either side?''

''Shouldn't think so, apart from old Auntie and her fancy religions. And that's not unusual in a woman who lives alone.''

''So all you can tell me really is that there is a lot of money,'' said Poirot.

''Lots of money,'' said Chief Inspector Neele. ''And all quite respectable. Some of it, mark you, Andrew Restarick brought into the firm. South African concessions, mines, mineral deposits. I'd say that by the time these were developed, or placed on the market, there'd be a very large sum of money indeed.''

''And who will inherit it?'' said Poirot.

''That depends on how Andrew Restarick leaves it. It's up to him, but I'd say that there's no one obvious, except his wife and his daughter.''

''So they both stand to inherit a very large amount of money one day?''

''I should say so. I expect there are a good many family trusts and things like that. All the usual City gambits.''

''There is, for instance, no other woman in whom he might be interested?''

''Nothing known of such a thing. I shouldn't think it likely. He's got a good-looking new wife.''

''A young man,'' said Poirot thoughtfully, ''could easily learn all this?''

"You mean and marry the daughter? There's nothing to stop him, even if she was made a ward of Court or something like that. Of course her father could then disinherit her if he wanted to."

Poirot looked down at a neatly written list in his hand.

"What about the Wedderburn Gallery?"

"I wondered how you'd got on to that. Were you consulted by a client about a forgery?"

"Do they deal in forgeries?"

"People don't deal in forgeries," said Chief Inspector Neele reprovingly. "There *was* a rather unpleasant business. A millionaire from Texas over here buying pictures, and paying incredible sums for them. They sold him a Renoir and a Van Gogh. The Renoir was a small head of a girl and there was some query about it. There seemed no reason to believe that the Wedderburn Gallery had not bought it in the first place in all good faith. There was a case about it. A great many art experts came and gave their verdicts. In fact, as usual, in the end they all seemed to contradict each other. The gallery offered to take it back, in any case. However, the millionaire didn't change his mind, since the latest fashionable expert swore that it was perfectly genuine. So he stuck to it. All the same, there's been a bit of suspicion hanging round the gallery ever since."

Poirot looked again at his list.

"And what about Mr. David Baker? Have you looked him up for me?"

"Oh, he's one of the usual mob. Riffraff—go about in gangs and break up night clubs. Live on purple hearts—heroin—coke—Girls go mad about them. He's the kind they moan over, saying his life has been so hard and he's such a wonderful genius. His painting is not appreciated. Nothing but good old sex, if you ask me."

Poirot consulted his list again.

"Do you know anything about Mr. Reece-Holland, M.P.?"

"Doing quite well politically. Got the gift of the gab, all right. One or two slightly peculiar transactions in the City, but he's wriggled out of them quite neatly. I'd say he was a slippery one. He's made quite a good deal of money off and on by rather doubtful means."

Poirot came to his last point.

"What about Sir Roderick Horsefield?"

"Nice old boy, but gaga. What a nose you have, Poirot; get it into everything, don't you? Yes, there's been a lot of trouble in the Special Branch. It's this craze for memoirs. Nobody knows what indiscreet revelations are going to be made next. All the old boys, service and otherwise, are racing hard to bring out their own particular brand of what they remember of the indiscretions of others! Usually it doesn't much matter, but sometimes—well, you know, Cabinets change their policies and you don't want to affront someone's susceptibilities or give the wrong publicity, so we have to try and muffle the old boys. Some of them are not too easy. But you'll have to go to the Special Branch if you want to nose into any of that. I shouldn't think there was much wrong. The trouble is they don't destroy the papers they should. They keep the lot. However, I don't think there is much in that, but we have evidence that a certain Power is nosing around."

Poirot gave a deep sigh.

"Haven't I helped?" asked the Chief Inspector.

"I am very glad to get the real lowdown from official quarters. But, no, I don't think there is much help in what you have told me." He sighed and then said, "What would be your opinion if someone said to you casually that a woman—a young attractive woman—wore a wig?"

"Nothing in that," said Chief Inspector Neele, and added, with slight asperity, "my wife wears a wig when we're traveling any time. It saves a lot of trouble."

"I beg your pardon," said Hercule Poirot.

As the two men bade each other good-by, the Chief Inspector asked: "You got all the dope, I suppose, on that suicide case you were asking about in the flats? I had it sent round to you."

"Yes, thank you. The official facts, at least. A bare record."

"There was something you were talking about just now that brought it back to my mind. I'll think of it in a moment. It was the usual, rather sad story. Gay woman, fond of men, enough money to live upon, no particular worries, drank too much and went down the hill. And then she gets what I call the health bug. You know, they're convinced they have cancer or something in that line. They consult a doctor and he tells them they're all right, and they go home and don't believe him. If you ask me, it's usually because they find they're no longer as attractive as they used to be to men. That's what's really depressing them. Yes, it happens all the time. They're lonely, I suppose, poor devils. Mrs. Charpentier was just one of them. I don't suppose that any—" he stopped. "Oh, yes, of course, I remember. You were asking about one of our M.P.s., Reece-Holland. He's a fairly gay one himself in a discreet way. Anyway, Louise Charpentier was his mistress at one time. That's all."

"Was it a serious liaison?"

"Oh, I shouldn't say so particularly. They went to some rather questionable clubs together and things like that. You know, we keep a discreet eye on things of that kind. But there was never anything in the press about them. Nothing of that kind."

"I see."

"But it lasted for a certain time. They were seen together, off and on for about six months, but I don't think she was the only one and I don't think he was the only one either. So you can't make anything of that, can you?"

"I do not think so," said Poirot.

"But all the same," he said to himself as he went down the stairs, "all the same, it is a link. It explains the embarrassment of Mr. McFarlane. It is a link, a tiny link, a link between Emlyn Reece-Holland, M.P., and Louise Charpentier." It didn't mean anything, probably. Why should it? But yet—"I know too much," said Poirot angrily to himself. "I know too much. I know a little about everything and everyone, but I cannot get my pattern. Half these facts are irrelevant. I want a pattern. A pattern. My kingdom for a pattern," he said aloud.

"I beg your pardon, sir," said the lift boy, turning a startled head.

"It is nothing," said Poirot.

18

POIROT PAUSED at the doorway of the Wedderburn Gallery to inspect a picture which depicted three aggressive-looking cows with vastly elongated bodies overshadowed by a colossal and complicated design of windmills. The two seemed to have nothing to do with each other or the very curious purple coloring.

"Interesting, isn't it?" said a soft purring voice.

A middle-aged man who at first sight seemed to have shown a smile which exhibited an almost excessive number of beautiful white teeth was at his elbow.

"Such freshness."

He had large, white, plump hands which he waved as though he was using them in an arabesque.

"Clever exhibition. Closed last week. Claude Raphael show opened the day before yesterday. It's going to do well. Very well indeed."

"Ah," said Poirot, and was led through gray velvet curtains into a long room.

Poirot made a few cautious if doubtful remarks. The plump man took him in hand in a practiced manner. Here was someone, he obviously felt, who must not be frightened away. He was a very experienced man in the art of salesmanship. You felt at once that you were welcome to be in his gallery all day if you liked without making a purchase. Sheerly, solely looking at these delightful pictures—though when you entered the gallery you might not have thought that they were delightful. But by the time you went out, you were convinced that delightful was exactly the word to describe them. After receiving some useful artistic instruction, and making a few of the amateur's stock remarks such as "I rather like that one," Mr. Boscombe responded encouragingly by some such phrase as:

"Now that's very interesting that you should say that. It shows, if I may say so, great perspicacity. Of course you know it isn't the ordinary reaction. Most people prefer something—well, shall I say slightly *obvious* like that"—he pointed to a blue and green striped effect arranged in one corner of the canvas—"but this, yes, you've spotted the quality of the thing. I'd say myself—of course, it's only my personal opinion—that that's one of Raphael's masterpieces."

Poirot and he looked together with both their heads on one side at an orange lopsided diamond with two human eyes depending from it by what looked like a spidery thread. Pleasant relations established and time obviously being infinite, Poirot remarked: "I think a Miss Frances Cary works for you, does she not?"

"Ah, yes. Frances. Clever girl that. Very artistic and very competent, too. Just come back from Portugal, where she's been arranging an art show for us. Very successful. Quite a good artist herself, but not I should say really creative, if you understand me. She is better on the business side. I think she recognizes that herself."

"I understand that she is a good patron of the arts?"

"Oh, yes. She's interested in *Les Jeunes*. Encourages talent, persuaded me to give a show for a little group of young artists last spring. It was quite successful—the press noticed it—all in a small way, you understand. Yes, she has her protégés."

"I am, you understand, somewhat old-fashioned. Some of these young men—*vraiment!*" Poirot's hands went up.

"Ah," said Mr. Boscombe indulgently, "you mustn't go by their appearance. It's just a fashion, you know. Beards and jeans or brocades and hair. Just a passing phase."

"David someone," said Poirot. "I forget his last name. Miss Cary seemed to think highly of him."

"Sure you don't mean Peter Cardiff? He's her present protégé. Mind you, I'm not quite so sure about him as she is. He's really not so much *avant-garde* as he is—well, positively reactionary. Quite—quite—Burne-Jones sometimes! Still, one never knows. You do get these reactions. She acts as his model occasionally.''

''David Baker—that was the name I was trying to remember,'' said Poirot.

''He is not bad,'' said Mr. Boscombe without enthusiasm. ''Not much originality, in my opinion. He was one of the group of artists I mentioned, but he didn't make any particular impression. A good painter, mind, but not striking. Derivative!''

Poirot went home. Miss Lemon presented him with letters to sign, and departed with them duly signed. George served him with an *omelette fines herbes* garnished, as you might say, with a discreetly sympathetic manner. After lunch, as Poirot was settling himself in his square-backed armchair with his coffee at his elbow, the telephone rang.

''Mrs. Oliver, sir,'' said George, lifting the telephone and placing it at his elbow.

Poirot picked up the receiver reluctantly. He did not want to talk to Mrs. Oliver. He felt that she would urge upon him something which he did not want to do.

''Monsieur Poirot?''

''C'est moi.''

''Well, what are you doing? What have you done?''

''I am sitting in this chair,'' said Poirot. ''Thinking,'' he added.

''Is that all?'' said Mrs. Oliver.

''It is the important thing,'' said Poirot. ''Whether I shall have success in it or not I do not know.''

''But you must find that girl. She's probably been kidnaped.''

''It would certainly seem so,'' said Poirot. ''And I have a letter here which came by the midday post from her father, urging me to come and see him and tell him what progress I have made.''

''Well, what progress *have* you made?''

''At the moment,'' said Poirot reluctantly, ''none.''

''Really, Monsieur Poirot, you really must take a grip on yourself.''

''You, too!''

''What do you mean, me, too?''

''Urging me on.''

''Why don't you go down to that place in Chelsea where I was hit on the head.''

''And get myself hit on the head also?''

''I simply don't understand you,'' said Mrs. Oliver. ''*I* gave you a clue by finding the girl in the café. You said so.''

"I know, I know."

"And then you go and lose her!"

"I know, I know."

"What about that woman who threw herself out of a window. Haven't you got anything out of that?"

"I have made inquiries, yes."

"Well?"

"Nothing. The woman is one of many. They are attractive when young, they have affairs, they are passionate, they have still more affairs, they get less attractive, they are unhappy and drink too much, they think they have cancer or some fatal disease and so at last in despair and loneliness they throw themselves out of a window!"

"You said her death was important—that it meant something."

"It ought to have done."

"Really!" At a loss for further comment, Mrs. Oliver rang off.

Poirot leaned back in his armchair, as far as he could lean back since it was of an upright nature, waved to George to remove the coffeepot and also the telephone, and proceeded to reflect upon what he did or did not know. To clarify his thoughts, he spoke out loud. He recalled three philosophic questions.

"What do I know? What can I hope? What ought I to do?"

He was not sure that he got them in the right order or indeed if they were quite the right questions, but he reflected upon them.

"Perhaps I am too old," said Hercule Poirot, at the bottom depths of despair. "What do I know?"

Upon reflection he thought that he knew too much! He laid that question aside for the moment.

"What can I hope?" Well, one could always hope. He could hope that those excellent brains of his, so much better than anybody else's, would come up sooner or later with an answer to a problem which he felt uneasily that he did not really understand.

"What ought I to do?" Well, that was very definite. What he ought to do was to go and call upon Mr. Andrew Restarick, who was obviously distraught about his daughter, and who would no doubt blame Poirot for not having by now delivered the daughter in person. Poirot could understand that, and sympathized with his point of view, but disliked having to present himself in such a very unfavorable light. The only other thing he could do was to telephone to a certain number and ask what developments there had been.

But before he did that, he would go back to the question he had laid aside.

"What do I know?"

He knew that the Wedderburn Gallery was under suspicion—so far it had kept on the right side of the law, but it would not hesitate at swindling ignorant millionaires by selling them dubious pictures.

He recalled Mr. Boscombe with his plump white hands and his plentiful teeth, and decided that he did not like him. He was the kind of man who was almost certainly up to dirty work, though he would no doubt protect himself remarkably well. That was a fact that might come into use because it might connect up with David Baker. Then there was David Baker himself, the Peacock. What did he know about him? He had met him, he had conversed with him, and he had formed certain opinions about him. He would do a crooked deal of any kind for money, he would marry a rich heiress for her money and not for love, he might perhaps be bought off. Yes, he probably could be bought off. Andrew Restarick certainly believed so, and he was probably right. Unless—

He considered Andrew Restarick, thinking more of the picture on the wall hanging above him than of the man himself. He remembered the strong features, the jutting-out chin, the air of resolution, of decision. Then he thought of Mrs. Andrew Restarick, deceased. The bitter lines of her mouth. . . . Perhaps he would go down to Crosshedges again and look at that portrait, so as to see it more clearly because there might be a clue to Norma in that. Norma—no, he must not think of Norma yet. What else was there?

There was Mary Restarick, whom the girl Sonia said must have a lover because she went up to London so often. He considered that point but he did not think that Sonia was right. He thought Mrs. Restarick was much more likely to go to London in order to look at possible properties to buy, luxury flats, houses in Mayfair, decorators, all the things that money in the metropolis could buy.

Money . . . It seemed to him that all the points that had been passing through his mind came to this in the end. Money. The importance of money. There was a great deal of money in this case. Somehow, in some way that was not obvious, money counted. Money played its part. So far there had been nothing to justify his belief that the tragic death of Mrs. Charpentier had been the work of Norma. No sign of evidence, no motive; yet it seemed to him that there *was* an undeniable link. The girl had said that she "might have committed a murder." A death had taken place only a day or two previously—a death that had occurred in the building where she lived. Surely it would be too much of a coincidence that that death should not be connected in any way? He thought again of the mysterious illness which had affected Mary Restarick. An occurrence so simple as to be classic in its outline. A poison case where the poisoner was—must be—one of the household. Had Mary Restarick poisoned herself, had her husband tried to poison her, had the girl Sonia administered poison? Or had Norma been the culprit? Everything pointed, Hercule Poirot had to confess, to Norma as being the logical person.

"Tout de même," said Poirot, "since I cannot find anything, *eh bien*, then the logic falls out of the window."

He sighed, rose to his feet and told George to fetch him a taxi. He must keep his appointment with Andrew Restarick.

19

CLAUDIA REEÇE-HOLLAND was not in the office today. Instead, a middle-aged woman received Poirot. She said that Mr. Restarick was waiting for him and ushered him into Restarick's room.

"Well?" Restarick hardly waited until he had come through the door. "Well, what about my daughter?"

Poirot spread out his hands.

"As yet—nothing."

"But look here, man, there must be something—some clue. A girl can't just disappear into thin air."

"Girls have done it before now and will do it again."

"Did you understand that no expense was to be spared, none whatever? I—I can't go on like this."

He seemed completely on edge by this time. He looked thinner, and his red-rimmed eyes spoke of sleepless nights.

"I know what your anxiety must be, but I assure you that I have done everything possible to trace her. These things, alas, cannot be hurried."

"She may have lost her memory or—or she may—I mean, she might be sick. Ill."

Poirot thought he knew what the broken form of the sentence meant. Restarick had been about to say, "She may perhaps be dead."

He sat down the other side of the desk and said: "Believe me, I appreciate your anxiety and I have to say to you once again that the results would be a lot quicker if you consulted the police."

"No!" The word broke out explosively.

"They have greater facilities, more lines of inquiry. I assure you it is not only a question of money. Money cannot give you the same result as a highly efficient organization can do."

"Man, it's no use your talking in that soothing way. Norma is my daughter—my only daughter, the only flesh and blood I've got."

"Are you sure that you have told me everything—everything possible—about your daughter?"

"What more can I tell you?"

"That is for you to say, not me. Have there been, for instance, any incidents in the past?"

"Such as? What do you mean, man?"

"Any definite history of mental instability."

"You think that—that—"

"How do I know? How can I know?"

"And how do I know?" said Restarick, suddenly bitter. "What do I know of her? All these years. Grace was a bitter woman. A woman who did not easily forgive or forget. Sometimes I feel—I feel that she was the wrong person to have brought Norma up."

He got up, walked up and down the room and then sat down again.

"Of course, I shouldn't have left my wife. I know that. I left her to bring up the child. But then at the time I suppose I made excuses for myself. Grace was a woman of excellent character devoted to Norma. A thoroughly good guardian for her. But was she? Was she really? Some of the letters Grace wrote to me were as though they breathed anger and revenge. Well, I suppose that's natural enough. But I was away all those years. I should have come back, come back more often and found out how the child was getting on. I suppose I had a bad conscience. Oh, it's no good making excuses now."

He turned his head sharply.

"Yes. I did think when I saw her again that Norma's whole attitude was neurotic, undisciplined. I hoped she and Mary would—would get on better after a little while, but I have to admit that I don't feel the girl was entirely normal. I felt it would be better for her to have a job in London and come home for weekends, but not to be forced into Mary's company the whole time. Oh, I suppose I've made a mess of everything. But where is she, Monsieur Poirot? Where is she? Do you think she may have lost her memory? One hears of such things."

"Yes," said Poirot, "that is a possibility. In her state, she may be wandering about quite unaware of who she is. Or she may have had an accident. That is less likely. I can assure you that I have made all inquiries in hospitals and other places."

"You don't think she is—you don't think she's dead?"

"She would be easier to find dead than alive, I can assure you. Please calm yourself, Mr. Restarick. Remember, she may have friends of whom you know nothing. Friends in any part of England, friends whom she has known while living with her mother, or with her aunt, or friends who were friends of school friends of hers. All these things take time to sort out. It may be—you must prepare yourself—that she is with a boy friend of some kind."

"David Baker? If I thought that—"

"She is not with David Baker. That," said Poirot dryly, "I ascertained first of all."

"How do I know what friends she has?" He sighed. "If I find her, *when* I find her—I'd rather put it that way—I'm going to take her out of all this."

"Out of all what?"

"Out of this country. I have been miserable, Monsieur Poirot, miserable ever since I returned here. I always hated City life. The boring round of office routine, continual consultations with lawyers and financiers. The life I liked was always the same. Traveling, moving about from place to place, going to wild and inaccessible places. That's the life for me. I should never have left it. I should have sent for Norma to come out to me and, as I say, when I find her, that's what I'm going to do. Already I'm being approached with various take-over bids. Well, they can have the whole caboodle on very advantageous terms. I'll take the cash and go back to a country that means something, that's real."

"Aha! And what will your wife say to that?"

"Mary? She's used to that life. That's where she comes from."

"To *les femmes* with plenty of money," said Poirot, "London can be very attractive."

"She'll see it my way."

The telephone rang on his desk. He picked it up.

"Yes? Oh. From Manchester? Yes. If it's Claudia Reece-Holland, put her through."

He waited a minute.

"Hallo, Claudia. Yes. Speak up—it's a very bad line. I can't hear you. They agreed? . . . Ah, pity . . . No, I think you did very well . . . Right . . . All right, then. Take the evening train back. We'll discuss it further tomorrow morning."

He replaced the telephone on its rest.

"That's a competent girl," he said.

"Miss Reece-Holland?"

"Yes. Unusually competent. Takes a lot of bother off my shoulders. I gave her pretty well *carte blanche* to put through this deal in Manchester on her own terms. I really felt I couldn't concentrate. And she's done exceedingly well. She's as good as a man in some ways.''

He looked at Poirot, suddenly bringing himself back to the present.

''Ah, yes, Monsieur Poirot. Well, I'm afraid I've rather lost my grip. Do you need more money for expenses?''

''No, monsieur. I assure you that I will do my utmost to restore your daughter sound and well. I have taken all possible precautions for her safety.''

He went out through the outer office. When he reached the street, he looked up at the sky.

''A definite answer to one question,'' he said; ''that is what I need.''

20

HERCULE POIROT looked up at the façade of the dignified Georgian house in what had been until recently a quiet street in an old-fashioned market town. Progress was rapidly overtaking it, but the new supermarket, the Gifte Shoppe, Margery's Boutique, Peg's Café, and a palatial new bank had all chosen sites in Croft Road and not encroached on the narrow High Street.

The brass knocker on the door was brightly polished, Poirot noted with approval. He pressed the bell at the side.

It was opened almost at once by a tall, distinguished-looking woman with upswept gray hair and an energetic manner.

''Monsieur Poirot? You are very punctual. Come in.''

''Miss Battersby?''

''Certainly.'' She held back the door. Poirot entered. She deposited his hat on the hall-stand and led the way to a pleasant room overlooking a narrow walled garden.

She waved toward a chair and sat down herself in an attitude of expectation. It was clear that Miss Battersby was not one to lose time in conventional utterances.

''You are, I think, the former principal of Meadowfield School?''

''Yes. I retired a year ago. I understand you wished to see me on the subject of Norma Restarick, a former pupil.''

''That is right.''

"In your letter," said Miss Battersby, "you gave me no further details." She added, "I may say that I know who you are, Monsieur Poirot. I should therefore like a little more information before I proceed further. Are you, for instance, thinking of employing Norma Restarick?"

"That is not my intention, no."

"Knowing what your profession is, you understand why I should want further details. Have you, for instance, an introduction to me from any of Norma's relations?"

"Again, no," said Hercule Poirot. "I will explain myself further."

"Thank you."

"In actual fact, I am employed by Miss Restarick's father, Andrew Restarick."

"Ah. He has recently returned to England, I believe, after many years' absence."

"That is so."

"But you do not bring me a letter of introduction from him?"

"I did not ask him for one."

Miss Battersby looked at him inquiringly.

"He might have insisted on coming with me," said Hercule Poirot. "That would have hampered me in asking you the questions that I wish to ask, because it is likely that the answers to them might cause him pain and distress. There is no reason why he should be caused further distress than he is already suffering at this moment."

"Has anything happened to Norma?"

"I hope not. . . . There is, however, a possibility of that. You remember the girl, Miss Battersby?"

"I remember all my pupils. I have an excellent memory. Meadowfield, in any case, is not a very large school. Two hundred girls, no more."

"Why have you resigned from it, Miss Battersby?"

"Really, Monsieur Poirot, I cannot see that that is any of your business."

"No, I am merely expressing my quite natural curiosity."

"I am seventy. Is that not a reason?"

"Not in your case, I should say. You appear to me to be in full vigor and energy, fully capable of continuing your headmistresship for a good many years to come."

"Times change, Monsieur Poirot. One does not always like the way they are changing. I will satisfy your curiosity. I found I was having less and less patience with parents. Their aims for their daughters are short-sighted and quite frankly stupid."

Miss Battersby was, as Poirot knew from looking up her qualifications, a very well-known mathematician.

"Do not think that I lead an idle life," said Miss Battersby. "I lead a life where the work is far more congenial to me. I coach senior students. And now, please, may I know the reason for your interest in the girl Norma Restarick?"

"There is some occasion for anxiety. She has, to put it baldly, disappeared."

Miss Battersby continued to look quite unconcerned.

"Indeed? When you say 'disappeared,' I presume you mean that she has left home without telling her parents where she was going. Oh, I believe her mother is dead, so without telling her father where she was going. That is really not at all uncommon nowadays, Monsieur Poirot. Mr. Restarick has not consulted the police?"

"He is adamant on that subject. He refuses definitely."

"I can assure you that I have no knowledge as to where the girl is. I have heard nothing from her. Indeed, I have had no news from her since she left Meadowfield. So I fear I cannot help you in any way."

"It is not precisely that kind of information that I want. I want to know what kind of a girl she is—how you would describe her. Not her personal appearance. I do not mean that. I mean as to her personality and characteristics."

"Norma, at school, was a perfectly ordinary girl. Not scholastically brilliant, but her work was adequate."

"Not a neurotic type?"

Miss Battersby considered. Then she said slowly: "No, I would not say so. Not more, that is, than might be expected, considering her home circumstances."

"You mean her invalid mother?"

"Yes. She came from a broken home. The father, to whom I think she was very devoted, left home suddenly with another woman—a fact which her mother quite naturally resented. She probably upset her daughter more than she need have done by voicing her resentment without restraint."

"Perhaps it may be more to the point if I ask you your opinion of the late Mrs. Restarick?"

"What you are asking me for is my private opinion?"

"If you do not object?"

"No, I have no hesitation at all in answering your question. Home conditions are very important in a girl's life and I have always studied them as much as I can through the meager information that comes to me. Mrs. Restarick was a worthy and upright woman, I should say. Self-righteous, censorious and handicapped in life by being an extremely stupid one!"

"Ah," said Poirot appreciatively.

"She was also, I would say, a *malade imaginaire*. A type that would exaggerate her ailments. The type of woman who is always in and out of nursing homes. An unfortunate home background for a girl—especially a girl who has no very definite personality of her own. Norma had no marked intellectual ambitions, she had no confidence in herself, she was not a girl to whom I would recommend a career. A nice ordinary job followed by marriage and children was what I would have hoped for her."

"You saw—forgive me for asking—no signs at any time of mental instability?"

"Mental instability?" said Miss Battersby. "Rubbish!"

"So that is what you say. Rubbish! And not neurotic?"

"Any girl, or almost any girl, can be neurotic, especially in adolescence and in her first encounters with the world. She is still immature and needs guidance in her first encounters with sex. Girls are frequently attracted to completely unsuitable, sometimes even dangerous young men. There are, it seems, no parents nowadays, or hardly any, with the strength of character to save them from this, so they often go through a time of hysterical misery and perhaps make an unsuitable marriage which ends not long after in divorce."

"But Norma showed no signs of mental instability?" Poirot persisted with the question.

"She is an emotional but normal girl," said Miss Battersby. "Mental instability! As I said before—rubbish! She's probably run away with some young man to get married, and there's nothing more normal than that!"

21

POIROT SAT IN his big square armchair. His hands rested on the arms, his eyes looked at the chimney piece in front of him without seeing it. By his elbow was a small table and on it, neatly clipped together, were various documents. Reports from Mr. Goby, information obtained from his friend, Chief Inspector Neele, a series of separate pages under the heading of "Hearsay, gossip, rumor" and the sources from which it had been obtained.

At the moment he had no need to consult these documents. He had, in fact, read them through carefully and laid them there in case there was any particular point he wished to refer to once more. He wanted now to assemble together in his mind all that he knew and had learned, because he was convinced that these things must form a pattern. There must be a pattern there. He was considering now from what exact angle to approach it. He was not one to trust in enthusiasm for some particular intuition. He was not an intuitive person—but he did have feelings. The important thing was not the feelings themselves—but what might have caused them. It was the cause that was interesting; the cause was so often not what you thought it was. You had very often to work it out by logic, by sense and by knowledge.

What did he feel about this case—what kind of case was it? Let him start from the general, then proceed to the particular. What were the salient facts of this case?

Money was one of them, he thought, though he did not know how. Somehow or other, money . . . He also thought, increasingly so, that there was evil somewhere. He knew evil. He had met it before. He knew the tang of it, the taste of it, the way it went. The trouble was that here he did not yet know exactly where it *was*. He had taken certain steps to combat evil. He hoped they would be sufficient. Something was happening, something was in progress, that was not yet accomplished. Someone, somewhere, was in danger.

The trouble was that the facts pointed both ways. If the person he *thought* was in danger was really in danger, there seemed so far as he could see no reason *why*. Why should that particular person be in danger? There was no motive. If the person he thought was in danger was *not* in danger, then the whole approach might have to be completely reversed. . . . Everything that pointed one way he must turn around and look at from the completely opposite point of view.

He left that for the moment in the balance, and he came from there to the personalities—to the people. What pattern did they make? What part were they playing?

First—Andrew Restarick. He had accumulated by now a fair amount of information about Andrew Restarick. A general picture of his life before and after going abroad. A restless man, never sticking to one place or purpose long, but generally liked. Nothing of the wastrel about him, nothing shoddy or tricky. Not, perhaps, a strong personality? Weak in many ways?

Poirot frowned, dissatisfied. That picture did not somehow fit the Andrew Restarick that he himself had met. Not weak surely, with that thrust-out chin, the steady eyes, the air of resolution. He had been a successful businessman, too, apparently. Good at his job in the earlier years, and he had put through good deals in South Africa and in South America. He had increased his holdings. It was a success story that he had brought home with him, not one of failure. How then could he be a weak personality? Weak, perhaps, only where women were concerned. He had made a mistake in his marriage—married the wrong woman. . . . Pushed into it perhaps by his family? And then he had met the other woman. Just that one woman? Or had there been several women? It was hard to find a record of that kind after so many years. Certainly he had not been a notoriously unfaithful husband. He had had a normal home, he had been fond, by all accounts, of his small daughter. But then he had come across a woman whom he had cared for enough to leave his home and to leave his country. It had been a real love affair.

But had it, perhaps, matched up with any additional motive? Dislike of office work, the City, the daily routine of London? He thought it might. It matched the pattern. He seemed, too, to have been a solitary type. Everyone had liked him both here and abroad, but there seemed no intimate friends. Indeed, it would have been difficult for him to have intimate friends abroad because he had never stopped in any one spot long enough. He had plunged into some gamble, attempted a coup, had made good, then tired of the thing and gone on somewhere else. Nomadic! A wanderer.

It still did not quite accord with his own picture of the man . . . A *picture*? The word stirred in his mind the memory of the picture that hung in Restarick's office on the wall behind his desk. It had been a portrait of the same man fifteen years ago. How much difference had those fifteen years made in the man sitting there? Surprisingly little, on the whole! More gray in the hair, a heavier set to the shoulders, but the lines of character on the face were much the same. A determined face. A man who knew what he wanted, who meant to get it. A man who would take risks. A man with a certain ruthlessness.

Why, he wondered, had Restarick brought that picture up to London? They had been companion portraits of a husband and wife. Strictly speaking artistically, they should have remained together. Would a psychologist have said that subconsciously Restarick wanted to dissociate himself from his former wife once more, to separate himself from her? Was he then mentally still retreating from her personality although she was dead? An interesting point. . . .

The pictures had presumably come out of storage with various other family articles of furnishing. Mary Restarick had no doubt selected certain personal objects to supplement the furniture of Crosshedges for which Sir Roderick had made room. He wondered whether Mary Restarick, the new wife, had liked hanging up that particular pair of portraits. More natural, perhaps, if she had put the first wife's portrait in an attic! But then he reflected that she would probably not have had an attic to stow away unwanted objects at Crosshedges. Presumably Sir Roderick had made room for a few family things while the returned couple were looking about for a suitable house in London. So it had not mattered much, and it would have been easier to hang both portraits. Besides, Mary Restarick seemed a sensible type of woman—not a jealous or emotional type.

"*Tout de même*," thought Hercule Poirot to himself, "*les femmes*, they are all capable of jealousy, and sometimes the ones you would consider the least likely!"

His thoughts passed to Mary Restarick, and he considered her in turn. It struck him that what was really odd was that he had so few thoughts about her! He had seen her only the once, and she had, somehow or other, not made much impression on him. A certain efficiency, he thought, and also a certain—how could he put it?—artificiality? ("But there, my friend," said Hercule Poirot, again in parenthesis, "there you are considering her wig!")

It was absurd, really, that one should know so little about a woman—a woman who was efficient and who wore a wig, and who was good-looking, and who was sensible, and who could feel anger. Yes, she had been angry when she had found the Peacock Boy wandering uninvited in her house. She had displayed it sharply and unmistakably. And the boy—he had seemed what? Amused, no more. But she had been angry, very angry at finding him there. Well, that was natural enough. He would not be any mother's choice for her daughter—

Poirot stopped short in his thoughts, shaking his head vexedly. Mary Restarick was not Norma's mother. Not for her the agony, the apprehension about a daughter making an unsuitable unhappy marriage or announcing an illegitimate baby with an unsuitable father! What did Mary feel about Norma? Presumably, to begin with, that she was a thoroughly tiresome girl—who had picked up with a young man who was going to be obviously a source of worry and annoyance to Andrew Restarick. But after that? What had she thought and felt about a stepdaughter who was apparently deliberately trying to poison her?

Her attitude seemed to have been the sensible one. She had wanted to get Norma out of the house, herself out of danger; and to co-operate with her husband in suppressing any scandal about what had happened. Norma came down for an occasional weekend to keep up appearances, but her life henceforward was bound to center in London. Even when the Restaricks moved into the house they were looking for, they would not suggest Norma living with them. Most girls, nowadays, lived away from their families. So that problem had been settled.

Except that, for Poirot, the question of who had administered poison to Mary Restarick was very far from settled. Restarick himself believed it was his daughter—

But Poirot wondered. . . .

His mind played with the possibilities of the girl Sonia. What was she doing in that house? Why had she come there? She had Sir Roderick eating out of her hand all right—perhaps she had no wish to go back to her own country? Possibly her designs were purely matrimonial—old men of Sir Roderick's age married pretty young girls every day of the week. In the worldly sense, Sonia could do very well for herself. A secure social position, and widowhood to look forward to, with a settled and sufficient income—or were her aims quite different? Had she gone to Kew Gardens with Sir Roderick's missing papers tucked between the pages of a book?

Had Mary Restarick become suspicious of her—of her activities, of her loyalties, of where she went on her days off, and of whom she met? And had Sonia, then, administered the substances which, in cumulative small doses, would arouse no suspicion of anything but ordinary gastroenteritis?

For the time being, he put the household at Crosshedges out of his mind.

He came, as Norma had come, to London, and proceeded to the consideration of three girls who shared a flat.

Claudia Reece-Holland, Frances Cary, Norma Restarick. Claudia Reece-Holland, daughter of a well-known Member of Parliament, well off, capable, well trained, good-looking, a first-class secretary. Frances Cary, a country solicitor's daughter, artistic, had been to drama school for a short time, then to the Slade, chucked that also, occasionally worked for the Arts Council, now employed by an art gallery. Earned a good salary, was artistic and had bohemian associations. She knew the young man, David Baker, though not apparently more than casually. Perhaps she was in love with him? He was the kind of young man, Poirot thought, disliked generally by parents, members of the Establishment and also the police. Where the attraction lay for well-born girls, Poirot failed to see. But one had to acknowledge it as a fact. What did he himself think of David?

A good-looking boy with the impudent and slightly amused air whom he had first seen in the upper stories of Crosshedges, doing an errand for Norma (or reconnoitering on his own, who should say?). He had seen him again when he gave him a lift in his car. A young man of personality, giving indeed an impression of ability in what he chose to do. And yet there was clearly an unsatisfactory side to him. Poirot picked up one of the papers on the table by his side and studied it. A bad record, though not positively criminal. Small frauds on garages, hooliganism, smashing up things, on probation twice. All those things were the fashion of the day. They did not come under Poirot's category of evil. He had been a promising painter, but had chucked it. He was the kind that did no steady work. He was vain, proud, a peacock in love with his own appearance. Was he anything more than that? Poirot wondered.

He stretched out an arm and picked up a sheet of paper on which was scribbled down the rough topics of the conversation held between Norma and David in the café—that is, as well as Mrs. Oliver could remember them. And how well was that, Poirot thought? He shook his head doubtfully. One never knew quite at what point Mrs. Oliver's imagination would take over! Did the boy care for Norma, really want to marry her? There was no doubt about her feelings for him. He had suggested marrying her. Had Norma got money of her own? She was the daughter of a rich man, but that was not the same thing. Poirot made an exclamation of vexation. He had forgotten to inquire the terms of the late Mrs. Restarick's will. He flipped through the sheets of notes. No, Mr. Goby had not neglected this obvious need. Mrs. Restarick apparently had been well provided for by her husband during her lifetime. She had had, apparently, a small income of her own amounting perhaps to a thousand a year. She had left everything she possessed to her daughter. It would hardly amount, Poirot thought, to a motive for marriage. Probably, as his only child, she would inherit a lot of money at her father's death, but that was not at all the same thing. Her father might leave her very little indeed if he disliked the man she had married.

He would say then, that David did care for her, since he was willing to marry her. And yet—Poirot shook his head. It was about the fifth time he had shaken it. All these things did not tie up, they did not make a satisfactory pattern. He remembered Restarick's desk, and the check he had been writing—apparently to buy off the young man—and the young man, apparently, was quite willing to be bought off! So that again did not tally. The check had certainly been made out to David Baker, and it was for a very large—really a preposterous—sum. It was a sum that might have tempted any impecunious young man of bad character. And yet he had suggested marriage to her only a day before. That, of course, might have been just a move in the game—a move to raise the price he was asking. Poirot remembered Restarick sitting there, his lips hard. He must care a great deal for his daughter to be willing to pay so high a sum; and he must have been afraid, too, that the girl herself was quite determined to marry him.

From thoughts of Restarick, he went on to Claudia. Claudia and Andrew

Restarick. Was it chance, sheer chance, that she had come to be his secretary? There might be a link between them. Claudia. He considered her. Three girls in a flat, Claudia Reece-Holland's flat. She had been the one who had taken the flat originally and shared it first with a friend, a girl she already knew, and then with another girl, the third girl. *The third girl*, thought Poirot. Yes, it always came back to that. The third girl. And that is where he had come in the end. Where he had had to come. Where all this thinking out of patterns had led. To Norma Restarick.

A girl who had come to consult him as he sat at breakfast. A girl whom he had joined at a table in a café where she had recently been eating baked beans with the young man she loved. (He always seemed to see her at mealtimes, he noted!) And what did he think about her? First, what did other people think about her? Restarick cared for her and was desperately anxious about her, desperately frightened for her. He not only suspected—he was quite sure, apparently, that she had tried to poison his recently married wife. He had consulted a doctor about her. Poirot felt he would like dearly to talk to that doctor himself, but he doubted if he would get anywhere. Doctors were very chary of parting with medical information to anyone but a duly accredited person such as the parents. But Poirot could imagine fairly well what the doctor had said. He had been cautious, Poirot thought, as doctors are apt to be. He'd hemmed and hawed and spoken perhaps of medical treatment. He had not stressed too positively a mental angle, but had certainly suggested it or hinted at it. In fact, the doctor probably was privately sure that that was what had happened. But he also knew a good deal about hysterical girls, and that they sometimes did things that were not really the result of mental causes, but merely of temper, jealousy, emotion, and hysteria. He would not be a psychiatrist himself nor a neurologist. He would be a G.P. who took no risks of making accusations about which he could not be sure, but suggested certain things out of caution. A job somewhere or other—a job in London, later perhaps treatment from a specialist?

What did anyone else think of Norma Restarick? Claudia Reece-Holland? He didn't know. Certainly not from the little that he knew about her. She was capable of hiding any secret; she would certainly let nothing escape her which she did not mean to let escape. She had shown no signs of wanting to turn the girl out—which she might have done if she had been afraid of her mental condition. There could not have been much discussion between her and Frances on the subject, since the other girl had so innocently let escape the fact that Norma had not returned to them after her weekend at home. Claudia had been annoyed about that. It was possible that Claudia was more in the pattern than she appeared. She had brains,

Poirot thought, and efficiency. . . . He came back to Norma, came back once again to the third girl. What was her place in the pattern? The place that would pull the whole thing together. Ophelia, he thought? But there were two opinions to that, just as there were two opinions about Norma. Was Ophelia mad or was she pretending madness? Actresses had been variously divided as to how the part should be played—or perhaps, he should say, producers. They were the ones who had the ideas. Was Hamlet mad or sane? Take your choice. Was Ophelia mad or sane?

Restarick would not have used the word "mad" even in his thoughts about his daughter. *Mentally disturbed* was the term that everyone preferred to use. The other word that had been used of Norma had been "batty." "She's a bit batty." "Not quite all there." "A bit wanting, if you know what I mean." Were "daily women" good judges? Poirot thought they might be. There *was* something odd about Norma, certainly, but she might be odd in a different way to what she seemed. He remembered the picture she had made slouching into his room, a girl of today, the modern type looking just as so many other girls looked. Limp hair hanging on her shoulders, the characterless shift dress, a skimpy look about the knees—all to his old-fashioned eyes looking like an adult girl pretending to be a child.

"I'm sorry, you are too old."

Perhaps it was true. He'd looked at her through the eyes of someone old, without admiration, to him just a girl without apparently will to please, without coquetry—a girl without any sense of her own femininity—no charm or mystery or enticement, who had nothing to offer, perhaps, but plain biological sex. So it may be that she was right in her condemnation of him. He could not help her because he did not understand her, because it was not even possible for him to appreciate her. He had done his best for her, but what had that meant up to date? What had he done for her since that one moment of appeal? And in his thoughts the answer came quickly. He had kept her safe. That at least. If, indeed, she needed keeping safe. That was where the whole point lay. Did she need keeping safe? That preposterous confession! Really, not so much a confession as an announcement: "*I think I may have committed a murder.*"

Hold on to that, because that was the crux of the whole thing. That was his métier. To deal with murder, to clear up murder, to prevent murder! To be the good dog who hunts down murder. Murder announced. Murder somewhere. He had looked for it and had not found it. The pattern of arsenic in the soup? A pattern of young hooligans stabbing each other with knives? The ridiculous and sinister phrase, *bloodstains in the courtyard*. A shot fired from a revolver. At whom, and why?

It was not as it ought to be, a form of crime that would fit with the words she had said: "I may have committed a murder." He had stumbled on in the dark, trying to see a pattern of crime, trying to see where the third girl fitted into that pattern, and coming back always to the same urgent need to know what this girl was really like.

And then with a casual phrase, Ariadne Oliver had, as he thought, shown him the light. The supposed suicide of a woman at Borodene Mansions. That would fit. It was where the third girl had her living quarters. It must be the murder that she had meant. Another murder committed about the same time would have been too much of a coincidence! Besides, there was no sign or trace of any other murder that had been committed about then. No other death that could have sent her hot-foot to consult him after listening at a party to the lavish admiration of his own achievements which his friend, Mrs. Oliver, had given to the world. And so, when Mrs. Oliver had informed him in a casual manner of the woman who had thrown herself out of the window, it had seemed to him that at last he had got what he had been looking for.

Here was the clue, the answer to his perplexity. Here he would find what he needed—the why, the when, the where.

"*Quelle déception*," said Hercule Poirot out loud.

He stretched out his hand and sorted out the neatly typed résumé of a woman's life—the bald facts of Mrs. Charpentier's existence. A woman of forty-three of good social position, reported to have been a wild girl—two marriages—two divorces—a woman who liked men. A woman who of late years had drunk more than was good for her. A woman who liked parties. A woman who was now reported to go about with men a good many years younger than herself. Living in a flat alone in Borodene Mansions, Poirot could understand and feel the sort of woman she was, and had been, and he could see why such a woman might wish to throw herself out of a high window one early morning when she awoke to despair.

Because she had cancer or thought she had cancer? But at the inquest, the medical evidence had said very definitely that that was not so.

What he wanted was some kind of link with Norma Restarick. He could not find it. He read through the dry facts again.

Identification had been supplied at the inquest by a solicitor. Louise Carpenter, though she had used a Frenchified form of her surname—Charpentier. Because it went better with her Christian name? Louise? Why was the name Louise familiar? Some casual mention?—a phrase?—his fingers riffled neatly through typewritten pages. Ah! there it was! Just that one reference. The girl for whom Andrew Restarick had left his wife had been a girl named Louise Birell. Someone who had proved to be of little significance in Restarick's later life. They had quarreled and parted after about a year. The same pattern, Poirot thought. The same thing obtaining that had probably obtained all through this particular woman's life. To love a man violently, to break up his home, perhaps, to live with him, and then to quarrel with him and leave him. He felt sure, absolutely sure, that this Louise Charpentier was the same Louise.

Even so, how did it tie up with the girl Norma? Had Restarick and Louise Charpentier come together again when he returned to England? Poirot doubted it. Their lives had parted years ago. That they had by any chance come together again seemed unlikely to the point of impossibility! It had been a brief and in reality unimportant infatuation. His present wife would hardly be jealous enough of her husband's past to wish to push his former mistress out of a window. Ridiculous! The only person so far as he could see who might have been the type to harbor a grudge over many long years, and wish to execute revenge upon the woman who had broken up her home, might have been the first Mrs. Restarick. And that sounded wildly impossible also, and, anyway, the first Mrs. Restarick was dead!

The telephone rang. Poirot did not move. At this particular moment he did not want to be disturbed. He had a feeling of being on a trail of some kind. . . . He wanted to pursue it. . . . The telephone stopped. Good. Miss Lemon would be coping with it.

The door opened and Miss Lemon entered.

"Mrs. Oliver wants to speak to you," she said.

Poirot waved a hand. "Not now, not now, I pray you! I cannot speak to her now."

"She says there is something that she has just thought of—something she forgot to tell you. About a piece of paper—an unfinished letter, which seems to have fallen out of a blotter in a desk in a furniture van. A rather incoherent story," added Miss Lemon, allowing a note of disapproval to enter her voice.

Poirot waved more frantically.

"Not now," he urged. "I beg of you, not *now*."

"I will tell her you are busy."

Miss Lemon retreated.

Peace descended once more upon the room. Poirot felt waves of fatigue creeping over him. Too much thinking. One must relax. Yes, one must relax. One must let tension go—in relaxation the pattern would come. He closed his eyes. There were all the components there. He was sure of that now; there was nothing more he could learn from outside. It must come from inside.

And quite suddenly—just as his eyelids were relaxing in sleep—it came. . . .

It was all there—waiting for him! He would have to work it all out. But he knew now. All the bits were there, disconnected bits and pieces, all fitting in. A wig, a picture, 5 A.M., women and their hair-dos, the Peacock Boy—all leading to the phrase with which it had begun:

Third Girl . . .

"I may have committed a murder . . ." Of course!

A ridiculous nursery rhyme came into his mind. He repeated it aloud.

Rub a dub dub, three men in a tub,
And who do you think they be?
A butcher, a baker, a candlestick maker . . .

Too bad, he couldn't remember the last line.

A baker, yes, and in a far-fetched way, a butcher—

He tried out a feminine parody:

Pat a cake, pat, three girls in a flat,
And who do you think they be?
A Personal Aide and a girl from the Slade
And the Third is a—

Miss Lemon came in.

"Ah—I remember now—'*And they all came out of a weenie* POTATO.' "

Miss Lemon looked at him in anxiety.

"Dr. Stillingfleet insists on speaking to you at once. He says it is urgent."

"Tell Dr. Stillingfleet he can—*Dr. Stillingfleet*, did you say?"

He pushed past her, caught up the receiver. "I am here. Poirot speaking! Something has happened?"

"She's walked out on me."

"What?"

"You heard me. She's walked out. Walked out through the front gate."

"You let her go?"

"What else could I do?"

"You could have stopped her."

"No."

"To let her go was madness."

"No."

"You don't understand."

"That was the arrangement. Free to go at any time."

"You don't understand what may be involved."

"All right then, I don't. But I know what *I*'m doing. And if I don't let her go, all the work I've done on her would go for nothing. And I have worked on her. Your job and my job aren't the same. We're not out for the same thing. I tell you, I was getting somewhere. Getting somewhere, so that I was quite sure she wouldn't walk out on me."

"Ah, yes. And then, *mon ami*, she did."

"Frankly, I can't understand it. I can't see why the setback came."

"Something happened."

"Yes, but what?"

"Somebody she saw, somebody who spoke to her, somebody who found out where she was."

"I don't see how that could have happened. . . . But what you don't seem to see is that she's a free agent. She had to be a free agent."

"Somebody got at her. Somebody found out where she was. Did she get a letter, a telegram, a telephone call?"

"No, nothing of that kind. That I am quite sure of."

"Then how—of course! Newspapers. You have newspapers, I suppose, in that establishment of yours?"

"Certainly. Normal, everyday life, that's what I stand for in my place of business."

"Then that is how they got at her. Normal, everyday life. What papers do you take?"

"Five." He named the five.

"When did she go?"

"This morning. Half-past ten."

"Exactly. After she read the papers. That is good enough to start on. Which paper did she usually read?"

"I don't think she had any special choice. Sometimes one, sometimes another, sometimes the whole lot of them—sometimes only glanced at them."

"Well, I must not waste time talking."

"You think she saw an advertisement. Something of that kind?"

"What other explanation can there be? Good-by, I can say no more now. I have to search. Search for the possible advertisement and then get on quickly."

He replaced the receiver.

"Miss Lemon, bring me our two papers. The *Morning News* and the *Daily Comet*. Send Georges out for all the others."

As he opened out the papers to the Personal advertisements and went carefully down them, he followed his line of thought.

He would be in time. He must be in time . . . There had been one murder already. There would be another one to come. But he, Hercule Poirot, would prevent that. . . . If he was in time. . . . He was Hercule Poirot—the avenger of the innocent. Did he not say (and people laughed when he said it), "I do not approve of murder"? They had thought it an understatement. But it was not an understatement. It was a simple statement of fact without melodrama. He did not approve of murder.

George came in with a sheaf of newspapers.

"There are all this morning's, sir."

Poirot looked at Miss Lemon, who was standing by waiting to be efficient.

"Look through the ones that I have searched in case I have missed anything."

"The Personal column, you mean?"

"Yes. I thought there would be the name David perhaps. A girl's name. Some pet name or nickname. They would not use Norma. An appeal for help, perhaps, or to a meeting."

Miss Lemon took the papers obediently with some distaste. This was not her kind of efficiency, but for the moment he had no other job to give her. He himself spread out the *Morning Chronicle*. That was the biggest field to search. Three columns of it. He bent over the open sheet.

A lady who wanted to dispose of her fur coat . . . Passengers wanted for a car trip abroad . . . Lovely period house for sale . . . Paying guests . . . Backward children . . . Homemade chocolates . . . *"Julia. Shall never forget. Always yours."* That was more the kind of thing. He considered it, but passed on. Louis XVth furniture . . . Middle-aged lady to help run a hotel. . . . *"In desperate trouble. Must see you. Come to flat 4:30 without fail. Our code Goliath."*

He heard the doorbell ring just as he called out: "Georges, a taxi," slipped on his overcoat, and went into the hall just as George was opening the front door and colliding with Mrs. Oliver. All three of them struggled to disentangle themselves in the narrow hall.

22

FRANCES CARY, carrying her overnight bag, walked down Mandeville Road, chattering with the friend she had just met on the corner, toward the bulk of Borodene Mansions.

"Really, Frances, it's like living in a prison block, that building. Wormwood Scrubs or something."

"Nonsense, Eileen. I tell you, they're frightfully comfortable, these flats. I'm very lucky and Claudia is a splendid person to share with—never bothers you. And she's got a wonderful daily. The flat's really very nicely run."

"Are there just the two of you? I forget. I thought you had a third girl?"

"Oh, well, she seems to have walked out on us."

"You mean she doesn't pay her rent?"

"Oh, I think the rent's all right. I think she's probably having some affair with a boy friend."

Eileen lost interest. Boy friends were too much a matter of course.

"Where are you coming back from now?"

"Manchester. Private view was on. Great success."

"Are you really going to Vienna next month?"

"Yes, I think so. It's pretty well fixed up by now. Rather fun."

"Wouldn't it be awful if some of the pictures got stolen?"

"Oh, they're all insured," said Frances. "All the really valuable ones, anyway."

"How did your friend Peter's show go?"

"Not terribly well, I'm afraid. But there was quite a good review by the critic of *The Artist*, and that counts a lot."

Frances turned into Borodene Mansions, and her friend went on her way to her own small mews house farther down the road. Frances said "Good evening" to the porter and went up in the lift to the sixth floor. She walked along the passage, humming a little tune to herself.

She inserted her key in the door of the flat. The light in the hall was not on yet. Claudia was not due back from the office for another hour and a half. But in the sitting room, the door of which was ajar, the light was on.

Frances said aloud: "Light's on. That's funny."

She slipped out of her coat, dropped her overnight bag, pushed the sitting-room door farther open and went in. . . .

Then she stopped dead. Her mouth opened and then shut. She stiffened all over—her eyes staring at the prone figure on the floor; then they rose slowly to the mirror on the wall that reflected back at her her own horror-stricken face . . .

Then she drew a deep breath. The momentary paralysis over, she flung back her head and screamed. Stumbling over her bag on the hall floor and kicking it aside, she ran out of the flat and along the passage and beat frenziedly at the door of the next flat.

An elderly woman opened it.

"What on earth—"

"There's someone dead—someone dead. And I think it's someone I know. . . . David Baker. He's lying there on the floor . . . I think he's stabbed . . . he must have been stabbed. There's blood—blood everywhere."

She began to sob hysterically. Miss Jacobs shook her, steadied her, lowered her onto a sofa and said authoritatively: "Be quiet now. I'll get you some brandy." She shoved a glass into her hand. "Stay there and drink it."

Frances sipped obediently. Miss Jacobs went rapidly out of the door along the passage and through the open door from which the light was pouring out. The living-room door was wide open and Miss Jacobs went straight through it.

She was not the kind of woman who screams. She stood just within the doorway, her lips pursed hard together.

What she was looking at had a nightmarish quality. On the floor lay a handsome young man, his arms flung wide, his chestnut hair falling on his shoulders. He wore a crimson velvet coat, and his white shirt was dappled with blood.

She was aware with a start that there was a second figure with her in the room. A girl was standing pressed back against the wall, the great Harlequin above seeming to be leaping across the painted sky.

The girl had a white woolen shift dress on, and her pale brown hair hung limp on either side of her face. In her hand she was holding a kitchen knife.

Miss Jacobs stared at her and she stared back at Miss Jacobs.

Then she said in a quiet, reflective voice, as though she was answering what someone had said to her: "Yes, I've killed him. . . . The blood got on my hands from the knife . . . I went into the bathroom to wash it off —but you can't really wash things like that off, can you? And then I came back in here to see if it was really true . . . But it is . . . Poor David. . . . But I suppose I had to do it."

Shock forced unlikely words from Miss Jacobs. As she said them, she thought how ridiculous they sounded!

"Indeed? Why did you have to do anything of the kind?"

"I don't know. . . . At least—I suppose I do—really. He was in great trouble. He sent for me—and I came. . . . But I wanted to be free of him. I wanted to get away from him. I didn't really love him."

She laid the knife carefully on the table and sat down on a chair.

"It isn't safe, is it?" she said. "To hate anyone . . . It isn't safe because you never know what you might do . . . Like Louise . . ."

Then she said quietly: "Hadn't you better ring up the police?"

Obediently, Miss Jacobs dialed 999.

II

There were six people now in the room with the Harlequin on the wall. A long time had passed. The police had come and gone.

Andrew Restarick sat like a man stunned. Once or twice he said the same words. "I can't believe it . . ." Telephoned for, he had come from his office, and Claudia Reece-Holland had come with him. In her quiet way, she had been ceaselessly efficient. She had put through telephone calls to lawyers, had rung Crosshedges and two firms of estate agents to try and get in touch with Mary Restarick. She had given Frances Cary a sedative and sent her to lie down.

Hercule Poirot and Mrs. Oliver sat side by side on a sofa. They had arrived together at the same time as the police.

Last of all to arrive, when nearly everyone else had gone, had been a quiet man with gray hair and a gentle manner, Chief Inspector Neele of Scotland Yard, who had greeted Poirot with a slight nod and been introduced to Andrew Restarick. A tall, red-haired young man was standing by the window staring down into the courtyard.

What were they all waiting for? Mrs. Oliver wondered. The body had been removed, the photographers and other police officers had done their work, they themselves, after being herded into Claudia's bedroom, had been re-admitted into the sitting room, where they had been waiting, she supposed, for the Scotland Yard man to arrive.

"If you want me to go"—Mrs. Oliver said to him uncertainly.

"Mrs. Ariadne Oliver, aren't you? No, if you have no objection, I'd rather you remained. I know it hasn't been pleasant—"

"It didn't seem real."

Mrs. Oliver shut her eyes—seeing the whole thing again. The Peacock Boy, so picturesquely dead that he had seemed like a stage figure. And the girl—the girl had been different—not the uncertain Norma from Crosshedges—the unattractive Ophelia, as Poirot had called her—but some quiet figure of tragic dignity—accepting her doom.

Poirot had asked if he might make two telephone calls. One had been to Scotland Yard, and that had been agreed to, after the sergeant had made a preliminary suspicious inquiry on the phone. The sergeant had directed Poirot to the extension in Claudia's bedroom, and he had made his call from there, closing the door behind him.

The sergeant had continued to look doubtful, murmuring to his subordinate: "They say it's all right. Wonder who he is? Odd-looking little bloke."

"Foreign, isn't he? Might be Special Branch?"

"Don't think so. It was Chief Inspector Neele he wanted."

His assistant raised his eyebrows and suppressed a whistle.

After making his calls, Poirot had reopened the door and beckoned Mrs. Oliver from where she was standing uncertainly inside the kitchen, to join him. They had sat down side by side on Claudia Reece-Holland's bed.

"I wish we could *do* something," said Mrs. Oliver—always one for action.

"Patience, *chère* madame."

"Surely you can do something?"

"I have. I have rung up the people it is necessary to ring up. We can do nothing here until the police have finished their preliminary investigations."

"Who did you ring up after the inspector man? Her father? Couldn't he come and bail her out or something?"

"Bail is not likely to be granted where murder is concerned," said Poirot dryly. "The police have already notified her father. They got his number from Miss Cary."

"Where is she?"

"Having hysterics in the flat of a Miss Jacobs next door, I understand. She was the one who discovered the body. It seems to have upset her. She rushed out of here screaming."

"She's the arty one, isn't she? Claudia would have kept her head."

"I agree with you. A very—poised young woman."

"Who did you ring up, then?"

"First, as perhaps you heard, Chief Inspector Neele of Scotland Yard."

"Will this lot like his coming and meddling?"

"He is not coming to meddle. He has of late been making certain inquiries for me, which may throw light on this matter."

"Oh—I see . . . Who else did you ring up?"

"Dr. John Stillingfleet."

"Who's he? To say that poor Norma is potty and can't help killing people?"

"His qualifications would entitle him to give evidence to that effect in court if necessary."

"Does he know anything about her?"

"A good deal, I should say. She has been in his care since the day you found her in the Shamrock café."

"Who sent her there?"

Poirot smiled. "I did. I made certain arrangements by telephone before I came to join you at the café."

"What? All the time I was so disappointed in you and kept urging you to do something—you had done something? And you never told me! Really, Monsieur Poirot! Not a word! How could you be so—so mean?"

"Do not enrage yourself, madame, I beg. What I did, I did for the best."

"People always say that when they have done something particularly maddening. What else did you do?"

"I arranged that my services should be retained by her father, so that I could make the necessary arrangements for her safety."

"Meaning this Dr. Stillingwater?"

"Stilling*fleet*. Yes."

"How on earth did you manage that? I shouldn't have thought for a moment that you would be the kind of person that her father would choose to make all these arrangements. He looks the kind of man who would be very suspicious of foreigners."

"I forced myself upon him—as a conjurer forces a card. I called upon him, purporting to have received a letter from him asking me to do so."

"And did he believe you?"

"Naturally. I showed the letter to him. It was typed on his office stationery and signed with his name—though, as he pointed out to me, the handwriting was not his."

"Do you mean you had actually written that letter yourself?"

"Yes. I judged correctly that it would awaken his curiosity, and that he would want to see me. Having got so far, I trusted to my own talents."

"You told him what you were going to do about this Dr. Stillingfleet?"

"No. I told no one. There was danger, you see."

"Danger to Norma?"

"To Norma, or Norma was dangerous to someone else. From the very beginning there have always been the two possibilities. The facts could be interpreted in either way. The attempted poisoning of Mrs. Restarick was not convincing—it was delayed too long, it was not a serious attempt to kill. Then there was an indeterminate story of a revolver shot fired here in Borodene Mansions—and another tale of flick-knives and bloodstains. Every time these things happen, Norma knows nothing about them, cannot remember, et cetera. She finds arsenic in a drawer—but does not remember putting it there. Claims to have had lapses of memory, to have lost long periods of time when she does not remember what she has been doing. So one has to ask oneself—is what she says *true*, or did she, for some reason of her own, invent it? Is she a potential victim of some monstrous and perhaps crazy plot—or is it she herself who is the moving spirit? Is she painting a picture of herself as a girl suffering from mental instability, or has she murder in mind, with a defense of diminished responsibility?"

"She was different today," said Mrs. Oliver slowly. "Did you notice? Quite different. Not—not scatty any longer."

Poirot nodded.

"Not Ophelia—Iphigenia."

A sound of added commotion outside in the flat diverted the attention of both of them.

"Do you think—" Mrs. Oliver stopped. Poirot had gone to the window and was looking down to the courtyard far below. An ambulance was drawn up there.

"Are they going to take It away?" asked Mrs. Oliver in a shaky voice. And then added in a sudden rush of pity: "Poor Peacock."

"He was hardly a likeable character," said Poirot coldly.

"He was very decorative . . . And so young," said Mrs. Oliver.

"That is sufficient for *les femmes*." Poirot was opening the bedroom door a careful crack as he peered out.

"Excuse me," he said, "if I leave you for a moment."

"Where are you going?" demanded Mrs. Oliver suspiciously.

"I understand that that was not a question considered delicate in this country," said Poirot reproachfully.

"Oh, I beg your pardon."

"And that's not the way to the loo," she breathed *sotto voce* after him, as she too applied an eye to the crack of the door.

She went back to the window to observe what was going on below.

"Mr. Restarick has just driven up in a taxi," she observed when Poirot slipped back quietly into the room a few minutes later, "and Claudia has come with him. Did you manage to get into Norma's room, or wherever you really wanted to go?"

"Norma's room is in the occupation of the police."

"How annoying for you. What are you carrying in that kind of black folder thing you've got in your hand?"

Poirot in his turn asked a question.

"What have you got in that canvas bag with Persian horses on it?"

"My shopping bag? Only a couple of avocado pears, as it happens."

"Then if I may, I will entrust this folder to you. Do not be rough with it or squeeze it, I beg."

"What is it?"

"Something that I hoped to find—and that I have found. Ah, things begin to pass themselves—" He referred to increased sounds of activities.

Poirot's words struck Mrs. Oliver as being much more exactly descriptive than English words would have been. Restarick, his voice loud and angry. Claudia coming in to telephone. A glimpse of a police stenographer on an excursion to the flat next door to take statements from Frances Cary and a mythical person called Miss Jacobs. A coming and going of ordered business, and a final departure of two men with cameras.

Then unexpectedly the sudden incursion into Claudia's bedroom of a tall, loosely jointed young man with red hair.

Without taking any notice of Mrs. Oliver, he spoke to Poirot.

"What's she done? Murder? Who is it? The boy friend?"

"Yes."

"She admits it?"

"It would seem so."

"Not good enough. Did she say so in definite words?"

"I have not heard her do so. I have had no chance of asking her anything myself."

A policeman looked in.

"Dr. Stillingfleet?" he asked. "The police surgeon would like a word with you."

Dr. Stillingfleet nodded and followed him out of the room.

"So that's Dr. Stillingfleet," said Mrs. Oliver. She considered for a moment or two. "Quite something, isn't he?"

23

CHIEF INSPECTOR NEELE drew a sheet of paper toward him, jotted one or two notes on it, and looked around at the other five people in the room. His voice was crisp and formal.

"Miss Jacobs?" he said. He looked toward the policeman who stood by the door. "Sergeant Conolly, I know, has taken her statement. But I'd like to ask her a few questions myself."

Miss Jacobs was ushered into the room a few minutes later. Neele rose courteously to greet her.

"I am Chief Inspector Neele," he said, shaking hands with her. "I am sorry to trouble you for a second time. But this time it is quite informal. I just want to get a clearer picture of exactly what you saw and heard. I'm afraid it may be painful—"

"Painful, no," said Miss Jacobs, accepting the chair he offered her.

"It was a shock, of course. But no emotions were involved." She added: "You seem to have tidied up things."

He presumed she was referring to the removal of the body.

Her eyes, both observant and critical, passed lightly over the assembled people, registering, for Poirot, frank astonishment (What on earth is *this*?), for Mrs. Oliver, mild curiosity; appraisement for the back of Dr. Stillingfleet's red head, neighborly recognition for Claudia, to whom she vouchsafed a slight nod, and finally dawning sympathy for Andrew Restarick.

"You must be the girl's father," she said to him. "There's not much point to condolences from a total stranger. They're better left unsaid. It's a sad world we live in nowadays—or so it seems to me. Girls study too hard, in my opinion."

Then she turned her face composedly toward Neele.

"Yes?"

"I would like you, Miss Jacobs, to tell me in your own words exactly what you saw and heard."

"I expect it will vary from what I said before," said Miss Jacobs unexpectedly. "Things do, you know. One tries to make one's description as accurate as possible, and so one uses more words. I don't think one is any more accurate; I think, unconsciously, one adds things that you think you may have seen or ought to have seen—or heard. But I will do my best.

"It started with screams. I was startled. I thought someone must have been hurt. So I was already coming to the door when someone began beating on it and still screaming. I opened it and saw it was one of my next-door neighbors—the three girls who live in Sixty-seven. I'm afraid I don't know her name, though I know her by sight."

"Frances Cary," said Claudia.

"She was quite incoherent and stammered out something about someone being dead—someone she knew—David Someone—I didn't catch his last name. She was sobbing and shaking all over. I brought her in, gave her some brandy, and went to see for myself."

Everyone felt that throughout life that would be what Miss Jacobs would invariably do.

"You know what I found. Need I describe it?"

"Just briefly, perhaps."

"A young man, one of these modern young men—gaudy clothes and long hair. He was lying on the floor and he was clearly dead. His shirt was stiff with blood."

Stillingfleet stirred. He turned his head and looked keenly at Miss Jacobs.

"Then I became aware that there was a girl in the room. She was holding a kitchen knife. She seemed quite calm and self-possessed—really, most peculiar."

Stillingfleet said: "Did she say anything?"

"She said she had been into the bathroom to wash the blood off her hands—and then she said 'But you can't wash things like that off, can you?' "

"*Out, damned spot*, in fact?"

"I cannot say that she reminded me particularly of Lady Macbeth. She was—how shall I put it?—perfectly composed. She laid the knife down on the table and sat down on a chair."

"What else did she say?" asked Chief Inspector Neele, his eyes dropping to a scrawled note in front of him.

"Something about *hate*. That it wasn't safe to *hate* anybody."

"She said something about 'poor David,' didn't she? Or so you told Sergeant Conolly. And that she wanted to be free of him."

"I'd forgotten that. Yes. She said something about his making her come here—and something about Louise, too."

"What did she say about Louise?" It was Poirot who asked, leaning forward sharply. Miss Jacobs looked at him doubtfully.

"Nothing, really, just mentioned the name. *'Like Louise,'* she said, and then stopped. It was after she had said about its not being safe to hate people . . ."

"And then?"

"Then she told me, quite calmly, I had better ring up the police. Which I did. We just—sat there until they came. . . . I did not think I ought to leave her. We did not say anything. She seemed absorbed in her thoughts, and I—well, frankly, I couldn't think of anything to say."

"You could see, couldn't you, that she was mentally unstable?" said Andrew Restarick. "You could see that she didn't know what she had done or why, poor child?"

He spoke pleadingly—hopefully.

"If it is a sign of mental instability to appear perfectly cool and collected after committing a murder, then I will agree with you."

Miss Jacobs spoke in the voice of one who quite decidedly did not agree.

Stillingfleet said: "Miss Jacobs, did she at any time admit that she had killed him?"

"Oh, yes. I should have mentioned that before—It was the very first thing she did say. As though she was answering some question I had asked her. She said, 'Yes, I've killed him,' and then went on about having washed her hands."

Restarick groaned and buried his face in his hands. Claudia put her hand on his arm.

Poirot said: "Miss Jacobs, you say the girl put down the knife she was carrying on that table. It was quite near you? You saw it clearly? Did it appear to you that the knife also had been washed?"

Miss Jacobs looked hesitantly at Chief Inspector Neele. It was clear that she felt that Poirot struck an alien and unofficial note in this presumably official inquiry.

"Perhaps you would be kind enough to answer that?" said Neele.

"No—I don't think the knife had been washed or wiped in any way. It was stained and discolored with some thick sticky substance."

"Ah," Poirot leaned back in his chair.

"I should have thought you would have known all about the knife yourself," said Miss Jacobs to Neele accusingly. "Didn't your police examine it? It seems to me very lax if they didn't."

"Oh, yes, the police examined it," said Neele. "But we—er—always like to get corroboration."

She darted him a shrewd glance.

"What you really mean, I suppose, is that you like to find out how accurate the observation of your witnesses is. How much they make up, or how much they actually see or think they have seen."

He smiled slightly as he said: "I don't think we need have doubts about you, Miss Jacobs. You will make an excellent witness."

"I shan't enjoy it. But it's the kind of thing one has to go through with, I suppose."

"I'm afraid so. Thank you, Miss Jacobs." He looked round. "No one has any additional questions?"

Poirot indicated that he had. Miss Jacobs paused near the doorway, displeased.

"Yes?" she said.

"About this mention of someone called Louise. Did you know who it was the girl meant?"

"How should I know?"

"Isn't it possible that she might have meant Mrs. Louise Charpentier. You knew Mrs. Charpentier, didn't you?"

"I did not."

"You knew that she recently threw herself out of a window in this block of flats?"

"I knew that, of course. I didn't know her Christian name was Louise, and I was not personally acquainted with her."

"Nor, perhaps, particularly wished to be?"

"I have not said so, since the woman is dead. But I will admit that that is quite true. She was a most undesirable tenant, and I and other residents have frequently complained to the management here."

"Of what exactly?"

"To speak frankly, the woman drank. Her flat was actually on the top floor above mine, and there were continual disorderly parties, with broken glass, furniture knocked over, singing and shouting, a lot of—er—coming and going."

"She was, perhaps, a lonely woman," suggested Poirot.

"That was hardly the impression she conveyed," said Miss Jacobs acidly. "It was put forward at the inquest that she was depressed over the state of her health. Entirely her own imagination. She seems to have had nothing the matter with her."

And having disposed of the late Mrs. Charpentier without sympathy, Miss Jacobs took her departure.

Poirot turned his attention to Andrew Restarick. He asked delicately: "Am I correct in thinking, Mr. Restarick, that you were at one time well acquainted with Mrs. Charpentier?"

Restarick did not answer for a moment or two. Then he sighed deeply and transferred his gaze to Poirot.

"Yes. At one time, many years ago, I knew her very well indeed. . . . Not, I may say, under the name of Charpentier. She was Louise Birell when I knew her."

"You were—er—in love with her!"

"Yes, I was in love with her. . . . Head over ears in love with her! I left my wife on her account. We went to South Africa. After barely a year the whole thing blew up. She returned to England. I never heard from her again. I never even knew what had become of her."

"What about your daughter? Did she, also, know Louise Birell?"

"Not to remember her, surely. A child of five years old!"

"But did she know her?" Poirot persisted.

"Yes," said Restarick slowly. "She knew Louise. That is to say, Louise came to our house. She used to play with the child."

"So it is possible that the girl might remember her, even after a lapse of years?"

"I don't know. I simply don't know. I don't know what she looked like; how much Louise might have changed. I never saw her again, as I told you."

Poirot said gently, "But you heard from her, didn't you, Mr. Restarick? I mean, you have heard from her since your return to England?"

Again there came that pause and the deep unhappy sigh.

"Yes—I heard from her . . ." said Restarick. And then, with sudden curiosity, he asked: "How did you know that, Monsieur Poirot?"

From his pocket, Poirot drew a neatly folded piece of paper. He unfolded it and handed it to Restarick.

The latter looked at it with a faintly puzzled frown.

> Dear Andy,
>
> I see from the papers you're home again. We must meet and compare notes as to what we've both been doing all these years—

It broke off here—and started again.

> Andy—Guess who this is from! Louise. Don't dare to say you've forgotten me!—
>
> Dear Andy,
>
> As you will see by this letterhead, I'm living in the same block of flats as your secretary. What a small world it is! We must meet. Could you come for a drink Monday or Tuesday next week?
>
> Andy darling, I must see you again . . . Nobody has ever mattered to me but you—you haven't really forgotten me, either, have you?

"How did you get this?" asked Restarick of Poirot, tapping it curiously.

"From a friend of mine via a furniture van," said Poirot, with a glance at Mrs. Oliver.

Restarick looked at her without favor.

"I couldn't help it," said Mrs. Oliver, interpreting his look correctly. "I suppose it was her furniture being moved out, and the men let go of a desk, and a drawer fell out and scattered a lot of things, and the wind blew this along the courtyard, so I picked it up and tried to give it back to them, but they were cross and didn't want it, so I just put it in my coat pocket without thinking. And I never even looked at it until this afternoon when I was taking things out of pockets before sending the coat to the cleaners. So it really wasn't my fault."

She paused, slightly out of breath.

"Did she get her letter to you written in the end?" Poirot asked.

"Yes—she did—one of the more formal versions! I didn't answer it. I thought it would be wiser not to do so."

"You didn't want to see her again?"

"She was the last person I wanted to see! She was a particularly difficult woman—always had been. And I'd heard things about her—for one that she had become a heavy drinker. And well—other things."

"Did you keep her letter to you?"

"No, I tore it up!"

Dr. Stillingfleet asked an abrupt question.

"Did your daughter ever speak about her to you?"

Restarick seemed unwilling to answer.

Dr. Stillingfleet urged him: "It might be significant if she did, you know."

"You doctors! Yes, she did mention her once."

"What did she say exactly?"

"She said quite suddenly: 'I saw Louise the other day, Father.' I was startled. I said 'Where did you see her?' And she said 'In the restaurant of our flats.' I was a bit embarrassed. I said: 'I never dreamed you'd remember her.' And she said: 'I've never forgotten. Mother wouldn't have let me forget, even if I wanted to.' "

"Yes," said Dr. Stillingfleet. "Yes, that could certainly be significant."

"And you, mademoiselle," said Poirot, turning suddenly to Claudia. "Did Norma ever speak to you about Louise Carpenter?"

"Yes—it was after the suicide. She said something about her being a wicked woman. She said it in rather a childish way, if you know what I mean."

"You were here in the flats yourself on the night—or more correctly the early morning when Mrs. Carpenter's suicide occurred?"

"I was not here that night, no! I was away from home. I remember arriving back here the next day and hearing about it."

She half turned to Restarick. "You remember? It was the twenty-third. I had gone to Liverpool."

"Yes, of course. You were to represent me at the Hever Trust meeting."

Poirot said: "But Norma slept here that night?"

"Yes." Claudia seemed uncomfortable.

"Claudia?" Restarick laid his hand on her arm. "What *is* it you know about Norma? There's something. Something that you're holding back."

"Nothing! What should I know about her?"

"You think she's off her head, don't you?" said Dr. Stillingfleet in a conversational voice. "And so does the girl with the black hair. And so do *you*," he added, turning suddenly on Restarick. "All of us behaving nicely and avoiding the subject and thinking the same thing! Except, that is, the chief inspector. He's not thinking anything. He's collecting the facts: mad or a murderess. What about you, madam?"

"Me?" Mrs. Oliver jumped. "I—don't know."

"You reserve judgment? I don't blame you. It's difficult. On the whole, most people agree on what they think. They use different terms for it—that's all. Bats in the belfry. Scatty. Wanting in the top story. Off her onion. Mental. Delusions. Does *anyone* think that girl is sane?"

"Miss Battersby," said Poirot.

"Who the devil is Miss Battersby?"

"A schoolmistress."

"If I ever have a daughter, I shall send her to that school. . . . Of course I'm in a different category. I know. I know everything about that girl!"

Norma's father stared at him.

"Who is this man?" he demanded of Neele. "What can he possibly mean by saying that he knows everything about my daughter?"

"I know about her," said Stillingfleet, "because she's been under my professional care for the last ten days."

"Dr. Stillingfleet," said Chief Inspector Neele, "is a highly qualified and reputable psychiatrist."

"And how did she come into your clutches—without someone getting my consent first?"

"Ask Mustaches," said Dr. Stillingfleet, nodding toward Poirot.

"You—you . . ."

Restarick could hardly speak, he was so angry.

Poirot spoke placidly.

"I had your instructions. You wanted care and protection for your daughter when she was found. I found her—and I was able to interest Dr. Stillingfleet in her case. She was in danger, Mr. Restarick, very grave danger."

"She could hardly be in any more danger than she is now! Arrested on a charge of murder!"

"Technically she is not yet charged," murmured Neele.

He went on: "Dr. Stillingfleet, do I understand that you are willing to give your professional opinion as to Miss Restarick's mental condition, and as to how well she knows the nature and meaning of her acts?"

"We can save the M'Naughten act for court," said Stillingfleet. "What you want to know now is, quite simply, if the girl is mad or sane? All right, I'll tell you. That girl is sane—as sane as any one of you sitting here in this room!"

24

THEY STARED AT HIM.

"Didn't expect that, did you?"

Restarick said angrily: "You're wrong. That girl doesn't even know what she's done. She's innocent—completely innocent. She can't be held responsible for what she doesn't know she's done."

"You let *me* talk for a while. I know what I'm talking about. You don't. That girl is sane and responsible for her actions. In a moment or two we'll have her in and let her speak for herself. She's the only one who hasn't had the chance of speaking for herself! Oh, yes, they've got her here still—locked up with a police matron in her bedroom. But before we ask her a question or two, I've got something to say that you'd better hear first.

"When that girl came to me, she was full of drugs."

"And he gave them to her!" shouted Restarick. "That degenerate, miserable boy."

"He started her on them, no doubt."

"Thank God," said Restarick. "Thank God for it."

"What are you thanking God for?"

"I misunderstood you. I thought you were going to throw her to the lions when you kept harping on her being sane. I misjudged you. It was the drugs that did it. Drugs that made her do things she would never have done of her own volition, and left her with no knowledge of having done them."

Stillingfleet raised his voice: "If you let me talk instead of talking so much yourself, and being so sure you know all about everything, we might get on a bit. First of all, she's not an addict. There are no marks of injections. She didn't sniff snow. Someone or other, perhaps the boy, perhaps someone else, was administering drugs to her without her knowledge. Not just a purple heart or two in the modern fashion. A rather interesting medley of drugs—L.S.D. giving vivid dream sequences—nightmares or pleasurable. Hemp distorting the time factor, so that she might believe an experience has lasted an hour instead of a few minutes. And a good many other curious substances that I have no intention of letting any of you know about. Somebody who was clever with drugs played merry hell with that girl. Stimulants, sedatives, they all played their part in controlling her and showing her to herself as a completely different person."

Restarick interrupted: "That's what I say. Norma wasn't responsible! Someone was hypnotizing her to do these things."

"You still haven't got the point! Nobody could make the girl do what she didn't want to do! What they could do was make her think she had done it. Now we'll have her in and make her see what's been happening to her."

He looked inquiringly at Chief Inspector Neele, who nodded.

Stillingfleet spoke over his shoulder to Claudia, as he went out of the sitting room. "Where'd you put that other girl, the one you took away from Jacobs, gave a sedative to? In her room on her bed? Better shake her up a bit and drag her along, somehow. We'll need all the help we can get."

Claudia also went out of the sitting room.

Stillingfleet came back, propelling Norma, and uttering rough encouragement.

"There's a good girl . . . Nobody's going to bite you. Sit there."

She sat obediently. Her docility was still rather frightening.

The policewoman hovered by the door, looking scandalized.

"All I'm asking you to do is to speak the truth. It isn't nearly as difficult as you think."

Claudia came in with Frances Cary. Frances was yawning heavily. Her black hair hung like a curtain hiding half her mouth as she yawned and yawned again.

"You need a pick-me-up," said Stillingfleet to her.

"I wish you'd all let me go to sleep," murmured Frances indistinctly.

"Nobody's going to have a chance of sleep until I've done with them! Now, Norma, you answer my questions—That woman along the passage says you admitted to her that you killed David Baker. Is that right?"

Her docile voice said: "Yes. I killed David."

"Stabbed him?"

"Yes."

"How do you know you did?"

She looked faintly puzzled. "I don't know what you mean. He was there on the floor—dead."

"Where was the knife?"

"I picked it up."

"It had blood on it?"

"Yes. And on his shirt."

"What did it feel like—the blood on the knife? The blood that you got on your hand and had to wash off—Wet? Or more like strawberry jam?"

"It was like strawberry jam—sticky." She shivered. "I had to go and wash it off my hands."

"Very sensible. Well, that ties up everything very nicely. Victim, murderer—you—all complete with the weapon. Do you remember actually doing it?"

"No . . . I don't remember *that* . . . But I must have done it, mustn't I?"

"Don't ask me! I wasn't there. It's you are the one who's saying it. But there was another killing before that, wasn't there? An earlier killing."

"You mean—Louise?"

"Yes. I mean Louise . . . When did you first think of killing her?"

"Years ago. Oh, years ago."

"When you were a child?"

"Yes."

"Had to wait a long time, didn't you?"

"I'd forgotten all about it."

"Until you saw her again and recognized her?"

"Yes."

"When you were a child, you hated her. Why?"

"Because she took Father, my father, away."

"And made your mother unhappy?"

"Mother hated Louise. She said Louise was a really wicked woman."

"Talked to you about her a lot, I suppose?"

"Yes. I wish she hadn't . . . I didn't want to go on hearing about her."

"Monotonous—I know. Hate isn't creative. When you saw her again, did you really want to kill her?"

Norma seemed to consider. A faintly interested look came into her face.

"I didn't, really, you know . . . It seemed all so long ago. I couldn't imagine myself—that's why—"

"Why you weren't sure you had?"

"Yes. I had some quite wild idea that I hadn't killed her at all. That it had been all a dream. That perhaps she really had thrown herself out of the window."

"Well—why not?"

"Because I knew I had done it—I said I had done it."

"You said *you* had done it? Who did you say that to?"

Norma shook her head. "I mustn't . . . It was someone who tried to be kind—to help me. She said she was going to pretend to have known nothing about it." She went on, the words coming fast and excitedly: "I was outside Louise's door, the door of Seventy-six, just coming out of it. I thought I'd been walking in my sleep. They—she—said there had been an accident. Down in the courtyard. She kept telling me it had been nothing to do with me. Nobody would ever know—And I couldn't remember what I had done—but there was stuff in my hand—''

''Stuff? What stuff? Do you mean blood?''

''No, not blood—torn curtain stuff. When I'd pushed her out.''

''You remember pushing her out, do you?''

''No, no. That's what was so awful. I didn't remember anything. That's why I hoped. That's why I went—'' she turned her head toward Poirot —''to him—''

She turned back again to Stillingfleet.

''I *never* remembered the things I'd done, none of them. But I got more and more frightened. Because there used to be quite long times that were blank—quite blank—hours I couldn't account for, or remember where I'd been and what I'd been doing. But I found things—things I must have hidden away myself. Mary was being poisoned by me, they found out she was being poisoned at the hospital. And I found the weed killer I'd hidden away in the drawer. In the flat here there was a flick-knife. And I had a revolver that I didn't even know I'd bought! I did kill people, but I didn't remember killing them, so I'm not really a murderer—I'm just—*mad*! I realized that at last. I'm mad, and I can't help it. People can't blame you if you do things when you are mad. If I could come here and even kill David, it shows I am mad, doesn't it?''

''You'd like to be mad, very much?''

''I—yes, I suppose so.''

''If so, why did you confess to someone that you had killed a woman by pushing her out of the window? Who was it you told?''

Norma turned her head, hesitated. Then raised her hand and pointed.

''I told Claudia.''

''That is absolutely untrue.'' Claudia looked at her scornfully. ''You never said anything of the kind to me!''

''I did. I did.''

''When? Where?''

''I—don't know.''

''She told me that she had confessed it all to you,'' said Frances indistinctly. ''Frankly, I thought she was hysterical and making the whole thing up.''

Stillingfleet looked across at Poirot.

''She could be making it all up,'' he said judicially. ''There is quite a case for that solution. But if so, we would have to find the motive, a strong motive, for her desiring the death of those two people—Louise Carpenter and David Baker. A childish hate? Forgotten and done with years ago? Nonsense. David—just to be 'free of him'? It is not for that that girls kill!

We want better motives than that. A whacking great lot of money—say! —greed!'' He looked round him and his voice changed to a conventional tone.

''We want a little more help. There's still one person missing. Your wife is a long time joining us here, Mr. Restarick?''

''I can't think where Mary can be. I've rung up. Claudia has left messages in every place we can think of. By now she ought to have rung up at least from somewhere.''

''Perhaps we have the wrong idea,'' said Hercule Poirot. ''Perhaps madame is at least partly here already—in a manner of speaking.''

''What on earth do you mean?'' shouted Restarick angrily.

''Might I trouble you, *chère* madame?''

Poirot leaned toward Mrs. Oliver. Mrs. Oliver stared.

''The parcel I entrusted to you—''

''Oh.'' Mrs. Oliver dived into her shopping bag. She handed the black folder to him.

He heard a sharp indrawn breath near him, but did not turn his head.

He shook off the wrappings delicately and held up—a wig of bouffant golden hair.

''Mrs. Restarick is not here,'' he said, ''but her wig is. Interesting.''

''Where the devil did you get that, Poirot?'' asked Neele.

''From the overnight bag of Miss Frances Cary, from which she had as yet no opportunity of removing it. Shall we see how it becomes her?''

With a single deft movement, he swept aside the black hair that masked Frances's face so effectively. Crowned with a golden aureole before she could defend herself, she glared at them.

Mrs. Oliver exclaimed: ''Good gracious—it *is* Mary Restarick.''

Frances was twisting like an angry snake. Restarick jumped from his seat to come to her—but Neele's strong grip restrained him.

''No. We don't want any violence from you. The game's up, you know, Mr. Restarick—or shall I call you Robert Orwell—''

A stream of profanity came from the man's lips. Frances's voice was raised sharply: ''Shut up, you damned fool!'' she said.

Poirot had abandoned his trophy, the wig. He had gone to Norma and taken her hand gently in his.

''Your ordeal is over, my child. The victim will not be sacrificed. You are neither mad, nor have you killed anyone. There are two cruel and heartless creatures who plotted against you, with cunningly administered drugs, with lies, doing their best to drive you either to suicide or to belief in your own guilt and madness.''

Norma was staring with horror at the other plotter.

"My father. My father? He could think of doing that to me? His daughter. My father, who loved me—"

"Not your father, *mon enfant*—a man who came here after your father's death to impersonate him and lay hands on an enormous fortune. Only one person was likely to recognize him—or rather to recognize that this man was not Andrew Restarick—the woman who had been Andrew Restarick's mistress fifteen years ago."

25

FOUR PEOPLE SAT in Poirot's room. Poirot in his square chair was drinking a glass of *sirop de cassis*. Norma and Mrs. Oliver sat on the sofa. Mrs. Oliver was looking particularly festive in unbecoming apple green brocade, surmounted by one of her more painstaking coiffures. Dr. Stillingfleet was sprawled out in a chair with his long legs stretched out so that they seemed to reach half across the room.

"Now then, there are lots of things I want to know," said Mrs. Oliver. Her voice was accusatory.

Poirot hastened to pour oil on troubled waters.

"But, *chère* madame, consider. What I owe to you I can hardly express. All, but *all*, my good ideas were suggested to me by you."

Mrs. Oliver looked at him doubtfully.

"Was it not you who introduced to me the phrase 'Third Girl'? It is there that I started—and there, too, that I ended—at the third girl of three living in a flat. Norma was always technically, I suppose, the Third Girl—but when I looked at things the right way round, it all fell into place. The missing answer, the lost piece of the puzzle, every time it was the same—the third girl.

"It was always, if you comprehend me, the person who was not there. She was a name to me, no more."

"I wonder I never connected her with Mary Restarick," said Mrs. Oliver. "I'd seen Mary Restarick at Crosshedges, talked to her. Of course, the first time I saw Frances Cary, she had black hair hanging all over her face. That would have put anyone off!"

"Again it was you, madame, who drew my attention to how easily a woman's appearance is altered by the way she arranges her hair. Frances Cary, remember, had had dramatic training. She knew all about the art of swift makeup. She could alter her voice at need. As Frances, she had long black hair, framing her face and half hiding it, heavy dead white *maquillage*, dark penciled eyebrows and mascara, with a drawling husky voice. Mary Restarick, with her wig of formally arranged golden hair with crimped waves, her conventional clothes, her slight colonial accent, her brisk way of talking, presented a complete contrast. Yet one felt, from the beginning, that she was not quite real. What kind of woman was she? I did not know.

"I was not clever about her—No. I, Hercule Poirot, was not clever at all."

"Hear, hear," said Dr. Stillingfleet. "First time I've ever heard you say that, Poirot! Wonders will never cease!"

"I don't really see why she wanted two personalities," said Mrs. Oliver. "It seems unnecessarily confusing."

"No. It was very valuable to her. It gave her, you see, a perpetual alibi whenever she wanted it. To think that it was there, all the time, before my eyes, and I did not see it! There was the wig—I kept being subconsciously worried by it, but not seeing why I was worried. Two women—never, at any time, seen together. Their lives so arranged that no one noticed the large gaps in their time schedules when they were unaccounted for. Mary goes often to London to shop, to visit house agents, to depart with a sheaf of orders to view, supposedly to spend her time that way. Frances goes to Birmingham, to Manchester, even flies abroad, frequents Chelsea with her special coterie of arty young men, whom she employs in various capacities which would not be looked on with approval by the law. Special picture frames were designed for the Wedderburn Gallery. Rising young artists had 'shows' there. Their pictures sold quite well, and were shipped abroad or sent on exhibition with their frames stuffed with secret packets of heroin. Art rackets—skillful forgeries of the more obscure old masters— She arranged and organized all these things. David Baker was one of the artists she employed. He had the gift of being a marvelous copyist."

Norma murmured: "Poor David. When I first met him, I thought he was wonderful."

"That picture," said Poirot dreamily. "Always, always, I came back to that in my mind. Why had Restarick brought it up to his office? What special significance did it have for him? *Enfin*, I do not admire myself for being so dense."

"I don't understand about the picture?"

"It was a very clever idea. It served as a kind of certificate of identity.

A pair of portraits, husband and wife, by a celebrated and fashionable portrait painter of his day. David Baker, when they come out of store, replaces Restarick's portrait with one of Orwell, making him about twenty years younger in appearance. Nobody would have dreamed that the portrait was a fake; the style, the brush strokes, the canvas, it was a splendidly convincing bit of work. Restarick hung it over his desk. Anyone who knew Restarick years ago might say: 'I'd hardly have known you!' Or 'You've changed quite a lot,' would look up at the portrait, but would only think that he himself had really forgotten what the other man had looked like!"

"It was a great risk for Restarick—or rather Orwell—to take," said Mrs. Oliver thoughtfully.

"Less than you might think. He was never a *claimant*, you see, in the Tichborne sense. He was only a member of a well-known City firm, returning home after his brother's death to settle up his brother's affairs after having spent some years abroad. He brought with him a young wife, recently acquired abroad, and took up residence with an elderly, half blind but extremely distinguished uncle by marriage, who had never known him well after his schoolboy days, and who accepted him without question. He had no other near relations, except for the daughter whom he had last seen when she was a child of five. When he originally left for South Africa, the office staff had had two very elderly clerks, since deceased. Junior staff never remains anywhere long nowadays. The family lawyer is also dead. You may be sure that the whole position was studied very carefully on the spot by Frances after they had decided on their coup.

"She had met him, it seems, in Kenya about two years ago. They were both crooks, though with entirely different interests. He went in for various shoddy deals as a prospector—Restarick and Orwell went together to prospect for mineral deposits in somewhat wild country. There was a rumor of Restarick's death (probably true), which was later contradicted."

"A lot of money in the gamble, I suspect?" said Stillingfleet.

"An enormous amount of money was involved. A terrific gamble—for a terrific stake. It came off. Andrew Restarick was a very rich man himself and he was his brother's heir. Nobody questioned his identity. And then —things went wrong. Out of the blue, he got a letter from a woman who, if she ever came face to face with him, would know at once that he wasn't Andrew Restarick. And a second piece of bad fortune occurred—David Baker started to blackmail him."

"That might have been expected, I suppose," said Stillingfleet thoughtfully.

"They didn't expect it," said Poirot. "David had never blackmailed before. It was the enormous wealth of this man that went to his head, I expect. The sum he had been paid for faking the portrait seemed to him grossly inadequate. He wanted more. So Restarick wrote him large checks, and pretended that it was on account of his daughter—to prevent her from making an undesirable marriage. Whether he really wanted to marry her, I do not know—he may have done. But to blackmail two people like Orwell and Frances Cary was a dangerous thing to do."

"You mean those two just cold-bloodedly planned to kill two people—quite calmly—just like that?" demanded Mrs. Oliver.

She looked rather sick.

"They might have added you to their list, madame," said Poirot.

"Me? Do you mean that it was one of *them* who hit me on the head? Frances, I suppose? Not the poor Peacock?"

"I do not think it was the Peacock. But you had been already to Borodene Mansions. Now you perhaps follow Frances to Chelsea, or so she thinks, with a rather dubious story to account for yourself. So she slips out and gives you a nice little tap on the head to put paid to your curiosity for a while. You would not listen when I warned you there was danger about."

"I can hardly believe it of her! Lying about in attitudes of a Burne-Jones heroine in that dirty studio that day. But why—" She looked at Norma—then back at Poirot. "They used *her*—deliberately—worked upon her, drugged her, made her believe that she had murdered two people. Why?"

"They wanted a victim . . ." said Poirot.

He rose from his chair and went to Norma.

"Mon enfant, you have been through a terrible ordeal. It is a thing that need never happen to you again. Remember that now you can have confidence in yourself always. To have known, at close quarters, what absolute evil means is to be armored against what life can do to you."

"I suppose you are right," said Norma. "To think you are mad—really to *believe* it, is a frightening thing. . . ." She shivered. "I don't see, even now, why I escaped—why anyone managed to believe that I hadn't killed David—not when even I believed I had killed him?"

"Blood was wrong," said Dr. Stillingfleet in a matter-of-fact tone. "Starting to coagulate. Shirt was 'stiff with it,' as Miss Jacobs said, not wet. You were supposed to have killed him not more than about five minutes before Frances's screaming act."

"How did she—" Mrs. Oliver began to work things out. "She had been to Manchester—"

"She came home by an earlier train, changed into her Mary wig and make-up on the train. Walked into Borodene Mansions and went up in the lift as an unknown blonde. Went into the flat where David was waiting for her, as she had told him to do. He was quite unsuspecting, and she stabbed him. Then she went out again and kept watch until she saw Norma coming. She slipped into a public cloakroom, changed her appearance, and joined a friend at the end of the road and walked with her, said good-by to her at Borodene Mansions, and went up herself and did her stuff—quite enjoying doing it, I expect. By the time the police had been called and got there, she didn't think anyone would suspect the time lag. I must say, Norma, you gave us all a hell of a time that day. Insisting on having killed everyone the way you did!"

"I wanted to confess and get it all over . . . Did you—did you think I might really have done it, then?"

"Me? What do you take me for? I know what my patients will do or won't do. But I thought you were going to make things damned difficult. I didn't know how far Neele was sticking his neck out. Didn't seem proper police procedure to me. Look at the way he gave Poirot here his head."

Poirot smiled.

"Chief Inspector Neele and I have known each other for many years. Besides, he had been making inquiries about certain matters already. You were never really outside Louise's door. Frances changed the numbers. She reversed the six and the seven on your own door. Those numbers were loose, stuck on with spikes. Claudia was away that night. Frances drugged you so that the whole thing was a nightmare dream to you."

"I saw the truth suddenly. The only other person who could have killed Louise was the real 'third girl,' Frances Cary."

"You kept half recognizing her, you know," said Stillingfleet, "when you described to me how one person seemed to turn into another."

Norma looked at him thoughtfully.

"You were very rude to people," she said to Stillingfleet. He looked slightly taken aback.

"Rude?"

"The things you said to everyone. The way you shouted at them."

"Oh, well, yes, perhaps I was . . . I've got in the way of it. People are so damned irritating."

He grinned suddenly at Poirot.

"She's quite a girl, isn't she?"

Mrs. Oliver rose to her feet with a sigh.

"I must go home." She looked at the two men and then at Norma. "What are we going to do with *her*?" she asked.

They both looked startled.

"I know she's staying with me at the moment," she went on. "And she says she's quite happy. But I mean there it is, quite a problem. Lots and lots of money because your father—the real one, I mean—left it all to you. And that will cause complications and begging letters and all that. She could go and live with old Sir Roderick, but that wouldn't be much fun for a girl—he's pretty deaf already as well as blind—and completely selfish. By the way, what about his missing papers, and the girl, and Kew Gardens?"

"They turned up where he thought he'd already looked—Sonia found them," said Norma, and added, "Uncle Roddy and Sonia are getting married—next week—"

"No fool like an old fool," said Stillingfleet.

"Aha!" said Poirot. "So the young lady prefers life in England to being embroiled in *la politique*. She is perhaps wise, that little one."

"So that's that," said Mrs. Oliver with finality. "But to go on about Norma, one has to be practical. One's got to make plans. The girl can't know what she wants to do all by herself. She's waiting for someone to tell her."

She looked at them severely.

Poirot said nothing. He smiled.

"Oh, her?" said Dr. Stillingfleet. "Well, I'll tell you, Norma. I'm flying to Australia Tuesday week. I want to look around first—see if what's been fixed up for me is going to work, and all that. Then I'll cable you and you can join me. Then we get married. You'll have to take my word for it that it's not your money I want. I'm not one of those doctors who want to endow whacking great research establishments and all that. I'm just interested in people. I think, too, that you'd be able to manage me all right. All that about my being rude to people—I hadn't noticed it myself. It's odd, really, when you think of all the mess you've been in—helpless as a fly in treacle—yet it's not going to be me running you, it's going to be you running me."

Norma stood quite still. She looked at John Stillingfleet very carefully, as though she was considering something that she knew from an entirely different point of view.

And then she smiled. It was a very nice smile—like a happy young nannie.

"All right," she said.

She crossed the room to Hercule Poirot.

"*I* was rude, too," she said. "The day I came here when you were having breakfast. I said to you that you were too old to help me. That was a rude thing to say. And it wasn't true . . ."

She put her hands on his shoulders and kissed him.

"You'd better get us a taxi," she said to Stillingfleet.

Dr. Stillingfleet nodded and left the room. Mrs. Oliver collected a handbag and a fur stole and Norma slipped on a coat and followed her to the door.

"*Madame, un petit moment—*"

Mrs. Oliver turned. Poirot had collected from the recesses of the sofa a handsome coil of gray hair.

Mrs. Oliver exclaimed vexedly: "It's just like everything that they make nowadays, no good at all! Hairpins, I mean. They just slip out, and everything falls *off!*"

She went out frowning.

A moment or two later she poked her head around the door again. She spoke in a conspiratorial whisper.

"Just tell me—it's all right, I've sent her on down—did you send that girl to this particular doctor on purpose?"

"Of course I did. His qualifications are—"

"Never mind his qualifications. You know what I mean. He and she—Did you?"

"If you must know, yes."

"I thought so," said Mrs. Oliver. "You do think of things, don't you?"

Poirot Loses a Client

TO

DEAR PETER

most faithful of friends

and dearest of companions,

a dog in a thousand

Contents

I

The Mistress of Littlegreen House

MISS ARUNDELL died on May 1st. Though her illness was short her death did not occasion much surprise in the little country town of Market Basing, where she had lived since she was a girl of sixteen. For Emily Arundell was well over seventy, the last of a family of five, and she had been known to be in delicate health for many years and had indeed nearly died of a similar attack to the one that killed her some eighteen months before.

But though Miss Arundell's death surprised no one, something else did. The provisions of her will gave rise to varying emotions, astonishment, pleasurable excitement, deep condemnation, fury, despair, anger and general gossip. For weeks and even months Market Basing was to talk of nothing else! Every one had their own contribution to make to the subject, from Mr. Jones the grocer who held that "blood was thicker than water" to Mrs. Lamphrey at the post office who repeated *ad nauseam* that "there's something behind it, depend upon it! You mark my words."

What added zest to the speculations on the subject was the fact that the will had been made as lately as April 21st. Add to this the further fact that Emily Arundell's near relations had been staying with her just before that date over Easter Bank Holiday and it will be realized that the most scandalous theories could be propounded, pleasurably relieving the monotony of everyday life in Market Basing.

There was one person who was shrewdly suspected of knowing more about the matter than she was willing to admit. That was Miss Wilhelmina Lawson, Miss Arundell's companion. Miss Lawson, however, professed herself just as much in the dark as every one else. She, too, she declared, had been dumbfounded when the will was read out.

A lot of people, of course, did not believe this. Nevertheless, whether Miss Lawson was or was not as ignorant as she declared herself to be, only one person really knew the true facts. That person was the dead woman herself. Emily Arundell had kept her own counsel as she was in the habit of doing. Even to her lawyer she had said nothing of the motives underlying her action. She was content with making her wishes clear.

In that reticence could be found the keynote of Emily Arundell's character. She was, in every respect, a typical product of her generation. She had both its virtues and its vices. She was autocratic and often overbearing, but she was also intensely warmhearted. Her tongue was sharp but her actions were kind. She was outwardly sentimental but inwardly shrewd. She had a succession of companions whom she bullied unmercifully, but treated with great generosity. She had a great sense of family obligation.

On the Friday before Easter Emily Arundell was standing in the hall of Littlegreen House giving various directions to Miss Lawson.

Emily Arundell had been a handsome girl and she was now a well-preserved, handsome old lady with a straight back and a brisk manner. A faint yellowness in her skin was a warning that she could not eat rich food with impunity.

Miss Arundell was saying:

"Now then, Minnie, where have you put them all?"

"Well, I thought—I hope I've done right—Dr. and Mrs. Tanios in the Oak room and Theresa in the Blue room and Mr. Charles in the Old Nursery—"

Miss Arundell interrupted:

"Theresa can have the Old Nursery and Charles will have the Blue room."

"Oh, yes—I'm sorry—I thought the Old Nursery being rather more inconvenient—"

"It will do very nicely for Theresa."

In Miss Arundell's day, women took second place. Men were the important members of society.

"I'm so sorry the dear little children aren't coming," murmured Miss Lawson sentimentally.

She loved children and was quite incapable of managing them.

"Four visitors will be quite enough," said Miss Arundell. "In any case, Bella spoils her children abominably. They never dream of doing what they are told."

Minnie Lawson murmured:

"Mrs. Tanios is a very devoted mother."

Miss Arundell said with grave approval:

"Bella is a good woman."

Miss Lawson sighed and said:

"It must be very hard for her sometimes—living in an outlandish place like Smyrna."

Emily Arundell replied:

"She has made her bed and she must lie on it."

And having uttered this final Victorian pronouncement she went on:

"I am going to the village now to speak about the orders for the week-end."

"Oh, Miss Arundell, do let me. I mean—"

"Nonsense. I prefer to go myself. Rogers needs a sharp word. The trouble with you is, Minnie, that you're not *emphatic* enough. Bob! Bob! Where *is* the dog?"

A wire-haired terrier came tearing down the stairs. He circled round and round his mistress, uttering short staccato barks of delight and expectation.

Together mistress and dog passed out of the front door and down the short path to the gate.

Miss Lawson stood in the doorway smiling rather foolishly after them, her mouth a little open. Behind her a voice said tartly:

"Them pillowcases you gave me, miss, isn't a pair."

"What? How stupid of me. . . ."

Minnie Lawson plunged once more into household routine.

Emily Arundell, attended by Bob, made a royal progress down the main street of Market Basing.

It was very much of a royal progress. In each shop she entered the proprietor always hurried forward to attend to her.

She was Miss Arundell of Littlegreen House. She was "one of our oldest customers." She was "one of the old school. Not many about like her nowadays."

"Good-morning, miss. What can I have the pleasure of doing for you —Not tender? Well, I'm sorry to hear that. I thought myself it was as nice a little saddle—Yes, of course, Miss Arundell. If you say so, it is so— No, indeed, I wouldn't think of sending Canterbury to *you*, Miss Arundell—Yes, I'll see to it myself, Miss Arundell."

Bob and Spot, the butcher's dog, circled slowly round each other, hackles raised, growling gently. Spot was a stout dog of nondescript breed. He knew that he must not fight with customers' dogs, but he permitted himself to tell them, by subtle indication, just exactly what mincemeat he would make of them were he free to do so.

Bob, a dog of spirit, replied in kind.

Emily Arundell said "Bob!" sharply and passed on.

In the greengrocer's there was a meeting of heavenly bodies. Another old lady, spherical in outline, but equally distinguished by that air of royalty, said:

"Mornin', Emily."

"Good-morning, Caroline."

Caroline Peabody said:

"Expecting any of your young people down?"

"Yes, all of them. Theresa, Charles and Bella."

"So Bella's home, is she? Husband too?"

"Yes."

It was a simple monosyllable, but underlying it was knowledge common to both ladies.

For Bella Winter, Emily Arundell's niece, had married a Greek. And Emily Arundell's people, who were what is known as "all service people," simply did not marry Greeks.

By way of being obscurely comforting (for, of course, such a matter could not be referred to openly) Miss Peabody said:

"Bella's husband's got brains. *And* charming manners!"

"His manners are delightful," agreed Miss Arundell.

Moving out into the street Miss Peabody asked:

"What's this about Theresa being engaged to young Donaldson?"

Miss Arundell shrugged her shoulders.

"Young people are so casual nowadays. I'm afraid it will have to be a rather long engagement—that is, if anything comes of it. He has no money."

"Of course Theresa has her own money," said Miss Peabody.

Miss Arundell said stiffly:

"A man could not possibly wish to live on his wife's money."

Miss Peabody gave a rich, throaty chuckle.

"They don't seem to mind doing it, nowadays. You and I are out of date, Emily. What I can't understand is what the child *sees* in him. Of all the namby-pamby young men!"

"He's a clever doctor, I believe."

"Those pince-nez—and that stiff way of talking! In my young days we'd have called him a poor stick!"

There was a pause while Miss Peabody's memory, diving into the past, conjured up visions of dashing, bewhiskered young men. . . .

She said with a sigh:

"Send that young dog Charles along to see me—if he'll come."

"Of course. I'll tell him."

The two ladies parted.

They had known each other for considerably over fifty years. Miss Peabody knew of certain regrettable lapses in the life of General Arundell, Emily's father. She knew just precisely what a shock Thomas Arundell's marriage had been to his sisters. She had a very shrewd idea of certain troubles connected with the younger generation.

But no word had ever passed between the two ladies on any of these subjects. They were both upholders of family dignity, family solidarity, and complete reticence on family matters.

Miss Arundell walked home, Bob trotting sedately at her heels. To herself, Emily Arundell admitted what she would never have admitted to another human being, her dissatisfaction with the younger generation of her family.

Theresa, for instance. She had no control over Theresa since the latter had come into her own money at the age of twenty-one. Since then the girl had achieved a certain notoriety. Her picture was often in the papers. She belonged to a young, bright, go-ahead set in London—a set that had freak parties and occasionally ended up in the police courts. It was not the kind of notoriety that Emily Arundell approved of for an Arundell. In fact, she disapproved very much of Theresa's way of living. As regards the girl's engagement, her feelings were slightly confused. On the one hand she did not consider an upstart Dr. Donaldson good enough for an Arundell. On the other she was uneasily conscious that Theresa was a most unsuitable wife for a quiet country doctor.

With a sigh her thoughts passed on to Bella. There was no fault to find with Bella. She was a good woman—a devoted wife and mother, quite exemplary in behavior—and extremely dull! But even Bella could not be regarded with complete approval. For Bella had married a foreigner—and not only a foreigner—but a Greek. In Miss Arundell's prejudiced mind a Greek was almost as bad as an Argentine or a Turk. The fact that Dr. Tanios had a charming manner and was said to be extremely able in his profession only prejudiced the old lady slightly more against him. She distrusted charm and easy compliments. For this reason, too, she found it difficult to be fond of the two children. They had both taken after their father in looks—there was really nothing English about them.

And then Charles. . . .

Yes, Charles. . . .

It was no use blinding one's eyes to facts. Charles, charming though he was, was not to be trusted. . . .

Emily Arundell sighed. She felt suddenly tired, old, depressed. . . .

She supposed that she couldn't last much longer. . . .

Her mind reverted to the will she had made some years ago.

Legacies to the servants—to charities—and the main bulk of her considerable fortune to be divided equally between these, her three surviving relations. . . .

It still seemed to her that she had done the right and equitable thing. It just crossed her mind to wonder whether there might not be some way of securing Bella's share of the money so that her husband could not touch it. . . . She must ask Mr. Purvis.

She turned in at the gate of Littlegreen House.

Charles and Theresa Arundell arrived by car—the Tanioses by train.

The brother and sister arrived first. Charles, tall and good-looking with his slightly mocking manner, said:

"Hallo, Aunt Emily, how's the girl? You look fine."

And he kissed her.

Theresa put an indifferent young cheek against her withered one.

"How are you, Aunt Emily?"

Theresa, her aunt thought, was looking far from well. Her face, beneath its plentiful make-up, was slightly haggard and there were lines round her eyes.

They had tea in the drawing-room. Bella Tanios, her hair inclined to straggle in wisps from below the fashionable hat that she wore at the wrong angle, stared at her cousin Theresa with a pathetic eagerness to assimilate and memorize her clothes. It was poor Bella's fate in life to be passionately fond of clothes without having any clothes sense. Theresa's clothes were expensive, slightly bizarre, and she herself had an exquisite figure.

Bella, when she arrived in England from Smyrna, had tried earnestly to copy Theresa's elegance at an inferior price and cut.

Dr. Tanios, who was a big, bearded, jolly-looking man, was talking to Miss Arundell. His voice was warm and full—an attractive voice that charmed a listener almost against his or her will. Almost in spite of herself, it charmed Miss Arundell.

Miss Lawson was fidgeting a good deal. She jumped up and down, handing plates, fussing over the tea table. Charles, whose manners were excellent, rose more than once to help her, but she expressed no gratitude.

When, after tea, the party went out to make a tour of the garden Charles murmured to his sister:

"Lawson doesn't like me. Odd, isn't it?"

Theresa said mockingly:

"Very odd. So there *is* one person who can withstand your fatal fascination?"

Charles grinned—an engaging grin—and said:

"Lucky it's only Lawson. . . ."

In the garden Miss Lawson walked with Mrs. Tanios and asked her questions about the children. Bella Tanios's rather drab face lighted up. She forgot to watch Theresa. She talked eagerly and animatedly. Mary had said such a *quaint* thing on the boat. . . .

She found Minnie Lawson a most sympathetic listener.

Presently a fair-haired young man with a solemn face and pince-nez was shown into the garden from the house. He looked rather embarrassed. Miss Arundell greeted him politely.

Theresa said:

"Hallo, Rex!"

She slipped an arm through his. They wandered away.

Charles made a face. He slipped away to have a word with the gardener, an ally of his from old days.

When Miss Arundell re-entered the house Charles was playing with Bob. The dog stood at the top of the stairs, his ball in his mouth, his tail gently wagging.

"Come on, old man," said Charles.

Bob sank down on his haunches, nosed his ball slowly and slowly nearer the edge. As he finally bunted it over he sprang to his feet in great excitement. The ball bumped slowly down the stairs. Charles caught it and tossed it up to him. Bob caught it neatly in his mouth. The performance was repeated.

"Regular game of his, this," said Charles.

Emily Arundell smiled.

"He'll go on for hours," she said.

She turned into the drawing-room and Charles followed her. Bob gave a disappointed bark.

Glancing through the window, Charles said:

"Look at Theresa and her young man. They *are* an odd couple!"

"You think Theresa is really serious over this?"

"Oh, she's crazy about him!" said Charles with confidence. "Odd taste, but there it is. I think it must be the way he looks at her, as though she were a scientific specimen and not a live woman. That's rather a novelty for Theresa. Pity the fellow's so poor. Theresa's got expensive tastes."

Miss Arundell said drily:

"I've no doubt she can change her way of living—if she wants to! And after all she has her own income."

"Eh? Oh, yes, yes, of course."

Charles shot an almost guilty look at her.

That evening, as the others were assembled in the drawing-room waiting to go in to dinner, there was a scurry and a burst of profanity on the stairs. Charles entered with his face rather red.

"Sorry, Aunt Emily, am I late? That dog of yours nearly made me take the most frightful toss. He'd left that ball of his on the top of the stairs."

"Careless little doggie," cried Miss Lawson, bending down to Bob.

Bob looked at her contemptuously and turned his head away.

"I know," said Miss Arundell. "It's most dangerous. Minnie, fetch the ball and put it away."

Miss Lawson hurried out.

Dr. Tanios monopolized the conversation at the dinner table most of the time. He told amusing stories of his life in Smyrna.

The party went to bed early. Miss Lawson carrying wool, spectacles, a large velvet bag and a book accompanied her employer to her bedroom chattering happily.

"Really *most* amusing, Dr. Tanios. He is such *good* company! Not that I should quite care for that kind of life myself. . . . One would have to boil the water, I expect. . . . And goat's milk, perhaps—such a disagreeable taste—"

Miss Arundell snapped:

"Don't be a fool, Minnie. You told Ellen to call me at half-past six?"

"Oh, yes, Miss Arundell. I said no tea, but don't you think it might be wiser—You know, the vicar at Southbridge—a most conscientious man, told me distinctly that there was no obligation to come fasting—"

Once more Miss Arundell cut her short.

"I've never yet taken anything before Early Service and I'm not going to begin now. *You* can do as you like."

"Oh, no—I didn't mean—I'm sure—"

Miss Lawson was flustered and upset.

"Take Bob's collar off," said Miss Arundell.

The slave hastened to obey.

Still trying to please, she said:

"Such a *pleasant* evening. They all seem so *pleased* to be here."

"Hmph," said Emily Arundell. "All here for what they can get."

"Oh, dear Miss Arundell—"

"My good Minnie, I'm not a fool, whatever else I am! I just wonder which of them will open the subject first."

She was not long left in doubt on that point. She and Miss Lawson returned from attending Early Service just after nine. Dr. and Mrs. Tanios were in the dining-room, but there were no signs of the two Arundells. After breakfast, when the others had left, Miss Arundell sat on, entering up some accounts in a little book.

Charles entered the room about ten.

"Sorry I'm late, Aunt Emily. But Theresa's worse. She's not unclosed an eyelid yet."

"At half-past ten breakfast will be cleared away," said Miss Arundell. "I know it is the fashion not to consider servants nowadays, but that is not the case in *my* house."

"Good. That's the true diehard spirit!"

Charles helped himself to kidneys and sat down beside her.

His grin, as always, was very attractive. Emily Arundell soon found herself smiling indulgently at him. Emboldened by this sign of favour, Charles plunged.

"Look here, Aunt Emily, sorry to bother you, but I'm in the devil of a hole. Can you possibly help me out? A hundred would do it."

His aunt's face was not encouraging. A certain grimness showed itself in her expression.

Emily Arundell was not afraid of speaking her mind. She spoke it.

Miss Lawson bustling across the hall almost collided with Charles as he left the dining-room. She glanced at him curiously. She entered the dining-room to find Miss Arundell sitting very upright with a flushed face.

2

The Relations

CHARLES RAN lightly up the stairs and tapped on his sister's door. Her answering "Come in" came promptly and he entered.

Theresa was sitting up in bed yawning.

Charles took a seat on the bed.

"What a decorative female you are, Theresa," he remarked appreciatively.

Theresa said sharply:

"What's the matter?"

Charles grinned.

"Sharp, aren't you? Well, I stole a march on you, my girl! Thought I'd make my touch before *you* got to work."

"Well?"

Charles spread his hands downwards in negation.

"Nothing doing! Aunt Emily ticked me off good and proper. She intimated that she was under no illusions as to why her affectionate family had gathered round her! And she also intimated that the said affectionate family would be disappointed. Nothing being handed out but affection—and not so much of that."

"You might have waited a bit," said Theresa drily.

Charles grinned again.

"I was afraid you or Tanios might get in ahead of me. I'm sadly afraid,

Theresa my sweet, that there'll be nothing doing this time. Old Emily is by no means a fool."

"I never thought she was."

"I even tried to put the wind up her."

"What d'you mean?" asked his sister sharply.

"Told her she was going about it the right way to get bumped off. After all, she can't take the dibs to heaven with her. Why not loosen up a bit?"

"Charles, you are a fool!"

"No, I'm not. I'm a bit of a psychologist in my way. It's never a bit of good sucking up to the old girl. She much prefers you to stand up to her. And after all, I was only talking sense. We get the money when she dies—she might just as well part with a little beforehand! Otherwise the temptation to help her out of the way might become overwhelming."

"Did she see your point?" asked Theresa, her delicate mouth curling up scornfully.

"I'm not sure. She didn't admit it. Just thanked me rather nastily for my advice and said she was perfectly capable of taking care of herself. 'Well,' I said, 'I've warned you.' 'I'll remember it,' she said."

Theresa said angrily:

"Really, Charles, you are an utter fool."

"Damn it all, Theresa, I was a bit ratty myself! The old girl's rolling—simply rolling. I bet she doesn't spend a tenth part of her income—what has she got to spend it on, anyway? And here we are—young, able to enjoy life—and to spite us she's capable of living to a hundred. . . . I want my fun now. . . . So do you. . . ."

Theresa nodded.

She said in a low, breathless voice:

"They don't understand—old people don't . . . they can't. . . . They don't know what it is to *live!*"

Brother and sister were silent for some minutes.

Charles got up.

"Well, my love, I wish you better success than I've had. But I rather doubt it."

Theresa said:

"I'm rather counting on Rex to do the trick. If I can make old Emily realize how brilliant he is, and how it matters terrifically that he should have his chance and not have to sink into a rut as a general practitioner . . . Oh, Charles, a few thousands of capital just at this minute would make all the difference in the world to our lives!"

"Hope you get it, but I don't think you will. You've got through a bit too much capital in riotous living in your time. I say, Theresa, you don't think the dreary Bella or the dubious Tanios will get anything, do you?"

"I don't see that money would be any good to Bella. She goes about looking like a rag bag and her tastes are purely domestic."

"Oh, well," said Charles vaguely. "I expect she wants things for those unprepossessing children of hers, schools, and plates for their front teeth and music lessons. And anyway it isn't Bella—it's Tanios. I bet *he's* got a nose for money all right! Trust a Greek for that. You know he's got through most of Bella's? Speculated with it and lost it all."

"Do you think he'll get something out of old Emily?"

"He won't if I can prevent him," said Charles grimly.

He left the room and wandered downstairs. Bob was in the hall. He fussed up to Charles agreeably. Dogs liked Charles.

He ran towards the drawing-room door and looked back at Charles.

"What's the matter?" said Charles, strolling after him.

Bob hurried into the drawing-room and sat down expectantly by a small bureau.

Charles strolled over to him.

"What's it all about?"

Bob wagged his tail, looked hard at the drawers of the bureau and uttered an appealing squeak.

"Want something that's in here?"

Charles pulled open the top drawer. His eyebrows rose.

"Dear, dear," he said.

At one side of the drawer was a little pile of treasury notes.

Charles picked up the bundle and counted them. With a grin he removed three one pound notes and two ten shilling ones and put them in his pocket. He replaced the rest of the notes carefully in the drawer where he had found them.

"That was a good idea, Bob," he said. "Your uncle Charles will be able at any rate to cover expenses. A little ready cash always comes in handy."

Bob uttered a faint reproachful bark as Charles shut the drawer.

"Sorry, old man," Charles apologized. He opened the next drawer. Bob's ball was in the corner of it. He took it out.

"Here you are. Enjoy yourself with it."

Bob caught the ball, trotted out of the room and presently bump, bump, bump, was heard down the stairs.

Charles strolled out into the garden. It was a fine sunny morning with a scent of lilac.

Miss Arundell had Dr. Tanios by her side. He was speaking of the advantage of an English education—a good education—for children and how deeply he regretted that he could not afford such a luxury for his own children.

Charles smiled with satisfied malice. He joined in the conversation in a light-hearted manner, turning it adroitly into entirely different channels.

Emily Arundell smiled at him quite amiably. He even fancied that she was amused by his tactics and was subtly encouraging them.

Charles's spirits rose. Perhaps, after all, before he left—

Charles was an incurable optimist.

Dr. Donaldson called for Theresa in his car that afternoon and drove her to Worthem Abbey, one of the local beauty spots. They wandered away from the Abbey itself into the woods.

There Rex Donaldson told Theresa at length about his theories and some of his recent experiments. She understood very little, but listened in a spellbound manner, thinking to herself:

"How clever Rex is—and how absolutely adorable!"

Her fiancé paused once and said rather doubtfully:

"I'm afraid this is dull stuff for you, Theresa."

"Darling, it's too thrilling," said Theresa firmly. "Go on. You take some of the blood of the infected rabbit—"

Dr. Donaldson went on.

Presently Theresa said with a sigh:

"Your work means a terrible lot to you, my sweet."

"Naturally," said Dr. Donaldson.

It did not seem at all natural to Theresa. Very few of her friends did any work at all, and if they did they made extremely heavy weather about it.

She thought, as she had thought once or twice before, how singularly unsuitable it was that she should have fallen in love with Rex Donaldson. Why did these things, these ludicrous and amazing madnesses, happen to one? A profitless question. This had happened to her.

She frowned, wondering at herself. Her crowd had been so gay—so cynical. Love affairs were necessary to life of course, but why take them seriously? One loved and passed on.

But this feeling of hers for Rex Donaldson was different; it went deeper. She felt instinctively that here there would be no passing on. . . . Her need of him was simple and profound. Everything about him fascinated her. His calmness and detachment so different from her own hectic, grasping life, the clear, logical coldness of his scientific mind, and something else, imperfectly understood, a secret force in the man masked by his unassuming slightly pedantic manner, but which she nevertheless felt and sensed instinctively.

In Rex Donaldson there was genius—and the fact that his profession was the main preoccupation of his life and that she was only a part—though a necessary part—of existence to him only heightened his attraction for her. She found herself for the first time in her selfish pleasure-loving life content to take second place. The prospect fascinated her. For Rex she would do anything—anything!

"What a damned nuisance money is," she said petulantly. "If only Aunt Emily were to die we could get married at once, and you could come to London and have a laboratory full of test tubes and guinea pigs, and never bother any more about children with mumps and old ladies with livers."

Donaldson said:

"There's no reason why your aunt shouldn't live for many years to come—if she's careful."

Theresa said despondently:

"I know that. . . ."

In the big double-bedded room with the old-fashioned oak furniture, Dr. Tanios said to his wife:

"I think that I have prepared the ground sufficiently. It is now your turn, my dear."

He was pouring water from the old-fashioned copper can into the rose-patterned china basin.

Bella Tanios sat in front of the dressing-table wondering why, when she combed her hair as Theresa did, it should not look like Theresa's!

There was a moment before she replied. Then she said:

"I don't think I want—to ask Aunt Emily for money."

"It's not for yourself, Bella; it's for the sake of the children. Our investments have been so unlucky."

His back was turned; he did not see the swift glance she gave him—a furtive, shrinking glance.

She said with mild obstinacy:

"All the same, I think I'd rather not. . . . Aunt Emily is rather difficult. She can be generous, but she doesn't like being asked."

Drying his hands, Tanios came across from the washstand.

"Really, Bella, it isn't like you to be so obstinate. After all, what have we come down here for?"

She murmured:

"I didn't—I never meant—it wasn't to ask for money. . . ."

"Yet you agreed that the only hope if we are to educate the children properly is for your aunt to come to the rescue."

Bella Tanios did not answer. She moved uneasily.

But her face bore the mild, mulish look that many clever husbands of stupid wives know to their cost.

She said:

"Perhaps Aunt Emily herself may suggest—"

"It is possible, but I've seen no signs of it so far."

Bella said:

"If we could have brought the children with us. Aunt Emily couldn't have helped loving Mary. And Edward is *so* intelligent."

Tanios said drily:

"I don't think your aunt is a great child lover. It is probably just as well the children aren't here."

"Oh, Jacob, but—"

"Yes, yes, my dear. I know your feelings. But these desiccated English spinsters—bah, they are not human. We want to do the best we can, do we not, for our Mary and our Edward? To help us a little would involve no hardship to Miss Arundell."

Mrs. Tanios turned; there was a flush in her cheeks.

"Oh, please, please, Jacob, not this time. I'm sure it would be unwise. I would so very very much rather not."

Tanios stood close behind her, his arm encircling her shoulders. She trembled a little and then was still—almost rigid.

He said and his voice was still pleasant:

"All the same, Bella, I think—I think you will do what I ask. . . . You usually do, you know—in the end. . . . Yes, I think you will do what I say. . . ."

3

The Accident

IT WAS TUESDAY afternoon. The side door to the garden was open. Miss Arundell stood on the threshold and threw Bob's ball the length of the garden path. The terrier rushed after it.

"Just one more, Bob," said Emily Arundell. "A good one."

Once again the ball sped along the ground, with Bob racing at full speed in pursuit.

Miss Arundell stooped down, picked up the ball from where Bob laid it at her feet and went into the house, Bob following her closely. She shut the side door, went into the drawing-room, Bob still at her heels, and put the ball away in a drawer.

She glanced at the clock on the mantelpiece. It was half-past six.

"A little rest before dinner, I think, Bob."

She ascended the stairs to her bedroom. Bob accompanied her. Lying on the big chintz-covered couch with Bob at her feet, Miss Arundell sighed. She was glad that it was Tuesday and that her guests would be going to-morrow. It was not that this week-end had disclosed anything to her that she had not known before. It was more the fact that it had not permitted her to forget her own knowledge.

She said to herself:

"I'm getting old, I suppose. . . ." And then, with a little shock of surprise: "I *am* old. . . ."

She lay with her eyes closed for half an hour, then the elderly house-parlour-maid, Ellen, brought hot water and she rose and prepared for dinner.

Dr. Donaldson was to dine with them that night. Emily Arundell wished to have an opportunity of studying him at close quarters. It still seemed to her a little incredible that the exotic Theresa should want to marry this rather stiff and pedantic young man. It also seemed a little odd that this stiff and pedantic young man should want to marry Theresa.

She did not feel as the evening progressed that she was getting to know Dr. Donaldson any better. He was very polite, very formal and, to her mind, intensely boring. In her own mind she agreed with Miss Peabody's judgment. The thought flashed across her brain, "Better stuff in our young days."

Dr. Donaldson did not stay late. He rose to go at ten o'clock. After he had taken his departure Emily Arundell herself announced that she was going to bed. She went upstairs and her young relations went up also. They all seemed somewhat subdued to-night. Miss Lawson remained downstairs performing her final duties, letting Bob out for his run, poking down the fire, putting the guard up and rolling back the hearthrug in case of fire.

She arrived rather breathless in her employer's room about five minutes later.

"I think I've got everything," she said, putting down wool, work bag, and a library book. "I do hope the book will be all right. She hadn't got any of the ones on your list, but she said she was sure you'd like this one."

"That girl's a fool," said Emily Arundell. "Her taste in books is the worst I've ever come across."

"Oh, dear. I'm so sorry. Perhaps I ought—"

"Nonsense, it's not your fault," Emily Arundell added kindly. "I hope you enjoyed yourself this afternoon."

Miss Lawson's face lighted up. She looked eager and almost youthful.

"Oh, yes, thank you very much. So *kind* of you to spare me. I had the most interesting time. We had the planchette and really—it wrote the most *interesting* things. There were several messages. . . . Of course it's not *quite* the same thing as the sittings. . . . Julia Tripp has been having a lot of success with the automatic writing. Several messages from Those who have Passed Over. It—it really makes one feel so grateful—that such things should be permitted. . . .''

Miss Arundell said with a slight smile:

''Better not let the vicar hear you.''

''Oh, but indeed, dear Miss Arundell, I am convinced—quite convinced—there can be *nothing* wrong about it. I only wish dear Mr. Lonsdale would *examine* the subject. It seems to me so narrow-minded to condemn a thing that you have not even *investigated*. Both Julia and Isabel Tripp are such truly *spiritual* women.''

''Almost too spiritual to be alive,'' said Miss Arundell.

She did not care much for Julia and Isabel Tripp. She thought their clothes ridiculous, their vegetarian and uncooked fruit meals absurd, and their manner affected. They were women of no traditions, no roots—in fact—no breeding! But she got a certain amount of amusement out of their earnestness and she was at bottom kind-hearted enough not to grudge the pleasure that their friendship obviously gave to poor Minnie.

Poor Minnie! Emily Arundell looked at her companion with mingled affection and contempt. She had had so many of these foolish, middle-aged women to minister to her—all much the same, kind, fussy, subservient and almost entirely mindless.

Really poor Minnie was looking quite excited to-night. Her eyes were shining. She fussed about the room, vaguely touching things here and there without the least idea of what she was doing, her eyes all bright and shining.

She stammered out rather nervously:

''I—I do wish you'd been there. . . . I feel, you know, that you're not quite a believer yet. But to-night there was a message—for E. A., the initials came *quite* definitely. It was from a man who had passed over many years ago—a very good-looking military man—Isabel saw him quite distinctly. It must have been dear General Arundell. Such a beautiful message, so full of love and comfort, and how through patience all could be attained.''

''Those sentiments sound very unlike Papa,'' said Miss Arundell.

''Oh, but our Dear Ones change so—on the other side. Everything is love and understanding. And then the planchette spelt out something about a *key*—I think it was the key of the Boule cabinet—could that be it?''

''The key of the Boule cabinet?'' Emily Arundell's voice sounded sharp and interested.

"I think that was it. I thought perhaps it might be important papers—something of the kind. There was a well-authenticated case where a message came to look in a certain piece of furniture and actually a *will* was discovered there."

"There wasn't a will in the Boule cabinet," said Miss Arundell. She added abruptly: "Go to bed, Minnie. You're tired. So am I. We'll ask the Tripps in for an evening soon."

"Oh, that *will* be nice! Good-night, dear. Sure you've got everything? I hope you haven't been tired with so many people here. I must tell Ellen to air the drawing-room *very well* to-morrow, and shake out the curtains—all this smoking leaves such a smell. I must say I think it's very good of you to let them all smoke in the drawing-room!"

"I must make some concessions to modernity," said Emily Arundell. "Good-night, Minnie."

As the other woman left the room, Emily Arundell wondered if this spiritualistic business was really good for Minnie. Her eyes had been popping out of her head, and she had looked so restless and excited.

Odd about the Boule cabinet, thought Emily Arundell as she got into bed. She smiled grimly as she remembered the scene of long ago. The key that had come to light after Papa's death, and the cascade of empty brandy bottles that had tumbled out when the cabinet had been unlocked! It was little things like that, things that surely neither Minnie Lawson nor Isabel and Julia Tripp could possibly know, which made one wonder whether, after all, there wasn't something in this spiritualistic business. . . .

She felt wakeful lying on her big four-poster bed. Nowadays she found it increasingly difficult to sleep. But she scorned Dr. Grainger's tentative suggestion of a sleeping draught. Sleeping draughts were for weaklings, for people who couldn't bear a finger-ache, or a little toothache, or the tedium of a sleepless night.

Often she would get up and wander noiselessly round the house, picking up a book, fingering an ornament, rearranging a vase of flowers, writing a letter or two. In those midnight hours she had a feeling of the equal liveliness of the house through which she wandered. They were not disagreeable, those nocturnal wanderings. It was as though ghosts walked beside her, the ghosts of her sisters, Arabella, Matilda and Agnes, the ghost of her brother Thomas, the dear fellow, as he was before That Woman got ahold of him! Even the ghost of General Charles Laverton Arundell, that domestic tyrant with the charming manners who shouted and bullied his daughters but who nevertheless was an object of pride to them with his experiences in the Indian Mutiny and his knowledge of the world.

What if there were days when he was "not quite so well" as his daughters put it evasively?

Her mind reverting to her niece's fiancé, Miss Arundell thought, "I don't suppose *he'll* ever take to drink! Calls himself a *man* and drank *barley water* this evening! Barley water! And I opened Papa's special port."

Charles had done justice to the port all right. Oh! if only Charles were to be trusted. If only one didn't know that with him—

Her thoughts broke off. . . . Her mind ranged over the events of the week-end. . . .

Everything seemed vaguely disquieting. . . .

She tried to put worrying thoughts out of her mind.

It was no good.

She raised herself on her elbow, and by the light of the night-light that always burned in a little saucer she looked at the time.

One o'clock and she had never felt less like sleep.

She got out of bed and put on her slippers and her warm dressing-gown. She would go downstairs and just check over the weekly books ready for the paying of them the following morning.

Like a shadow she slipped from her room and along the corridor, where one small electric bulb was allowed to burn all night.

She came to the head of the stairs, stretched out one hand to the baluster rail and then, unaccountably, she stumbled, tried to recover her balance, failed and went headlong down the stairs.

The sound of her fall, the cry she gave, stirred the sleeping house to wakefulness. Doors opened, lights flashed on.

Miss Lawson popped out of her room at the head of the staircase.

Uttering little cries of distress, she pattered down the stairs. One by one the others arrived—Charles, yawning, in a resplendent dressing gown. Theresa, wrapped in dark silk. Bella in a navy-blue kimono, her hair bristling with combs to "set the wave."

Dazed and confused, Emily Arundell lay in a crushed heap. Her shoulder hurt her and her ankle—her whole body was a confused mass of pain. She was conscious of people standing over her, of that fool Minnie Lawson crying and making ineffectual gestures with her hands, of Theresa with a startled look in her dark eyes, of Bella standing with her mouth open looking expectant, of the voice of Charles saying from somewhere—very far away so it seemed:

"It's that damned dog's ball! He must have left it here and she tripped over it. See? Here it is!"

And then she was conscious of authority, putting the others aside, kneeling beside her, touching her with hands that did not fumble but *knew*.

A feeling of relief swept over her. It would be all right now.

Dr. Tanios was saying in firm, reassuring tones:

"No, it's all right. No bones broken. . . . Just badly shaken and bruised—and of course she's had a bad shock. But she's been very lucky that it's no worse."

Then he had cleared the others off a little and picked her up quite easily and carried her up to her bedroom, where he had held her wrist for a minute, counting, then nodded his head, sent Minnie (who was still crying and being generally a nuisance) out of the room to fetch brandy and to heat water for a hot bottle.

Confused, shaken, and racked with pain, she felt acutely grateful to Jacob Tanios in that moment. The relief of feeling oneself in capable hands. He gave you just that feeling of assurance—of confidence—that a doctor ought to give.

There was something—something she couldn't quite get hold of—something vaguely disquieting—but she wouldn't think of it now. She would drink this and go to sleep as they told her.

But surely there was something missing—some one.

Oh, well, she wouldn't think. . . . Her shoulder hurt her. She drank down what she was given.

She heard Dr. Tanios say—and in what a comfortable assured voice: "She'll be all right, now."

She closed her eyes.

She awoke to a sound that she knew—a soft, muffled bark.

She was wide awake in a minute.

Bob—naughty Bob! He was barking outside the front door—his own particular "out all night very ashamed of myself" bark, pitched in a subdued key but repeated hopefully.

Miss Arundell strained her ears. Ah, yes, that was all right. She could hear Minnie going down to let him in. She heard the creak of the opening front door, a confused low murmur—Minnie's futile reproaches—"Oh, you naughty little doggie—a very naughty little Bobsie—" She heard the pantry door open. Bob's bed was under the pantry table.

And at that moment Emily realized what it was she had subconsciously missed at the moment of her accident. It was Bob! All that commotion—her fall, people running—normally Bob would have responded by a crescendo of barking from inside the pantry.

So *that* was what had been worrying her at the back of her mind. But it was explained now—Bob, when he had been let out last night, had shamelessly and deliberately gone off on pleasure bent. From time to time he had these lapses from virtue—though his apologies afterwards were always all that could be desired.

So that was all right. But was it? What else was there worrying her, nagging at the back of her head. Her accident—something to do with her accident.

Ah, yes, somebody had said—Charles—that she had slipped on Bob's ball which he had left on the top of the stairs. . . .

The ball had been there—he had held it up in his hand. . . .

Emily Arundell's head ached. Her shoulder throbbed. Her bruised body suffered. . . .

But in the midst of her suffering her mind was clear and lucid. She was no longer confused by shock. Her memory was perfectly clear.

She went over in her mind all the events from six o'clock yesterday evening. . . . She retraced every step . . . till she came to the moment when she arrived at the stairhead and started to descend the stairs. . . .

A thrill of incredulous horror shot through her. . . .

Surely—surely, she must be mistaken. . . . One often had queer fancies after an event had happened. She tried—earnestly she tried—to recall the slippery roundness of Bob's ball under her foot. . . .

But she could recall nothing of the kind.

Instead—

''Sheer nerves,'' said Emily Arundell. ''Ridiculous fancies.''

But her sensible, shrewd, Victorian mind would not admit that for a moment. There was no foolish optimism about the Victorians. They could believe the worst with the utmost ease.

Emily Arundell believed the worst.

4

Miss Arundell Writes a Letter

IT WAS FRIDAY. The relations had left.

They left on the Wednesday as originally planned. One and all, they had offered to stay on. One and all they had been steadfastly refused. Miss Arundell explained that she preferred to be ''quite quiet.''

During the two days that had elapsed since their departure, Emily Arundell had been alarmingly meditative. Often she did not hear what Minnie Lawson said to her. She would stare at her and curtly order her to begin all over again.

"It's the *shock*, poor dear," said Miss Lawson.

And she added with the kind of gloomy relish in disaster which brightens so many otherwise drab lives:

"I dare say she'll never be quite herself again."

Dr. Grainger, on the other hand, rallied her heartily.

He told her that she'd be downstairs again by the end of the week, that it was a positive disgrace she had no bones broken, and what kind of a patient was she for a struggling medical man. If all his patients were like her, he might as well take down his shingle straight away.

Emily Arundell replied with spirit—she and old Dr. Grainger were allies of long standing. He bullied and she defied—they always got a good deal of pleasure out of each other's company!

But now, after the doctor had stumped away, the old lady lay with a frown on her face, thinking—thinking—responding absent-mindedly to Minnie Lawson's well-meant fussing—and then suddenly coming back to consciousness and rending her with a vitriolic tongue.

"Poor little Bobsie," twittered Miss Lawson, bending over Bob, who had a rug spread on the corner of his mistress's bed. "Wouldn't little Bobsie be unhappy if he knew what he'd done to his poor, poor Missus?"

Miss Arundell snapped:

"Don't be idiotic, Minnie. And where's your English sense of justice? Don't you know that every one in this country is accounted innocent until he or she is proved guilty?"

"Oh, but we do know—"

Emily snapped:

"We don't know anything at all. Do stop fidgeting, Minnie. Pulling this and pulling that. Haven't you any idea how to behave in a sick-room? Go away and send Ellen to me."

Meekly Miss Lawson crept away.

Emily Arundell looked after her with a slight feeling of self-reproach. Maddening as Minnie was, she did her best.

Then the frown settled down again on her face.

She was desperately unhappy. She had all a vigorous strong-minded old lady's dislike of inaction in any given situation. But in this particular situation she could not decide upon her line of action.

There were moments when she distrusted her own faculties, her own memory of events. And there was no one, absolutely no one, in whom she could confide.

Half an hour later, when Miss Lawson tiptoed creakingly into the room, carrying a cup of beef-tea, and then passed irresolute at the view of her employer lying with closed eyes, Emily Arundell suddenly spoke two words with such force and decision that Miss Lawson nearly dropped the cup.

"Mary Fox," said Miss Arundell.

"A box, dear?" said Miss Lawson. "Did you say you wanted a box?"

"You're getting deaf, Minnie. I didn't say anything about a box. I said Mary Fox. The woman I met at Cheltenham last year. She was the sister of one of the Canons of Exeter Cathedral. Give me that cup. You've spilt it into the saucer. And don't tiptoe when you come into a room. You don't know how irritating it is. Now go downstairs and get me the London telephone book."

"Can I find the number for you, dear? Or the address?"

"If I'd wanted you to do that I'd have told you so. Do what I tell you. Bring it here, and put my writing things by the bed."

Miss Lawson obeyed orders.

As she was going out of the room after having done everything required of her, Emily Arundell said unexpectedly:

"You're a good, faithful creature, Minnie. Don't mind my bark. It's a good deal worse than my bite. You're very patient and good to me."

Miss Lawson went out of the room with her face pink and incoherent words burbling from her lips.

Sitting up in bed, Miss Arundell wrote a letter. She wrote it slowly and carefully, with numerous pauses for thought and copious underlining. She crossed and recrossed the page—for she had been brought up in a school that was taught never to waste notepaper. Finally, with a sigh of satisfaction, she signed her name and put it into an envelope. She wrote a name upon the envelope. Then she took a fresh sheet of paper. This time she made a rough draft and after having reread it and made certain alterations and erasures, she wrote out a fair copy. She read the whole thing through very carefully, then satisfied that she had expressed her meaning she enclosed it in an envelope and addressed it to William Purvis, Esq., Messrs. Purvis, Purvis, Charlesworth and Purvis, Solicitors, Harchester.

She took up the first envelope again, which was addressed to M. Hercule Poirot, and opened the telephone directory. Having found the address, she added it.

A tap sounded at the door.

Miss Arundell hastily thrust the letter she had just finished addressing—the letter to Hercule Poirot—inside the flap of her writing-case.

She had no intention of rousing Minnie's curiosity. Minnie was a great deal too inquisitive.

She called "Come in" and lay back on her pillows with a sigh of relief. She had taken steps to deal with the situation.

5

Hercule Poirot Receives a Letter

THE EVENTS which I have just narrated were not, of course, known to me until a long time afterwards. But by questioning various members of the family in detail, I have, I think, set them down accurately enough.

Poirot and I were only drawn into the affair when we received Miss Arundell's letter.

I remember the day well. It was a hot, airless morning towards the end of June.

Poirot had a particular routine when opening his morning correspondence. He picked up each letter, scrutinized it carefully and neatly slit the envelope open with his paper-cutter. Its contents were perused and then placed in one of four piles beyond the chocolate-pot. (Poirot always drank chocolate for breakfast—a revolting habit.) All this with a machine-like regularity!

So much was this the case that the least interruption of the rhythm attracted one's attention.

I was sitting by the window, looking out at the passing traffic. I had recently returned from the Argentine and there was something particularly exciting to me in being once more in the roar of London.

Turning my head, I said with a smile:

"Poirot, I—the humble Watson—am going to hazard a deduction."

"Enchanted, my friend. What is it?"

I struck an attitude and said pompously:

"You have received this morning *one* letter of particular interest!"

"You are indeed the Sherlock Holmes! Yes, you are perfectly right."

I laughed.

"You see, *I know your methods*, Poirot. If you read a letter through twice it must mean that it is of special interest."

"You shall judge for yourself, Hastings."

With a smile my friend tendered me the letter in question.

I took it with no little interest, but immediately made a slight grimace. It was written in one of those old-fashioned spidery handwritings, and it was, moreover, crossed on two pages.

"Must I read this, Poirot?" I complained.

"Ah, no, there is no compulsion. Assuredly not."

"Can't you tell me what it says?"

"I would prefer you to form your own judgment. But do not trouble if it bores you."

"No, no, I want to know what it's all about," I protested.

My friend remarked drily:

"You can hardly do *that*. In effect, the letter says nothing at all."

Taking this as an exaggeration, I plunged without more ado into the letter.

M. Hercule Poirot.

Dear Sir,

After much doubt and indecision, I am writing [the last word was crossed out and the letter went on] I am emboldened to write to you in the hope that you may be able to assist me in a matter of a strictly private nature. [The words *strictly private* were underlined three times.] I may say that your name is not unknown to me. It was mentioned to me by a Miss Fox of Exeter, and although Miss Fox was not herself acquainted with you, she mentioned that her brother-in-law's sister (whose name I cannot, I am sorry to say, recall) had spoken of your kindness and discretion in the highest terms [*highest terms* underlined once]. I did not inquire, of course, as to the nature [*nature* underlined] of the inquiry you had conducted on her behalf, but I understood from Miss Fox that it was of a painful and confidential nature [last four words underlined heavily].

I broke off my difficult task of spelling out the spidery words.

"Poirot," I said. "Must I go on? Does she ever get to the point?"

"Continue, my friend. Patience."

"Patience!" I grumbled. "It's exactly as though a spider had got into an inkpot and were walking over a sheet of notepaper! I remember my great-aunt Mary's writing used to be much the same!"

Once more I plunged into the epistle.

In my present dilemma, it occurs to me that you might undertake the necessary investigations on my behalf. The matter is such, as you will readily understand, as calls for the utmost discretion and I may, in fact—and I need hardly say how sincerely I hope and pray [*pray* underlined twice] that this may be the case—I may, in fact, be completely mistaken. One is apt sometimes to attribute too much significance to facts capable of a natural explanation.

"I haven't left out a sheet?" I murmured in some perplexity.

Poirot chuckled.

"No, no."

"Because this doesn't seem to make sense. What is it she is talking about?"

"Continuez toujours."

"The matter is such, as you will readily understand—*No, I'd got past that. Oh! here we are*. In the circumstances as I am sure you will be the first to appreciate, it is quite impossible for me to consult any one in Market Basing [I glanced back at the heading of the letter. Littlegreen House, Market Basing, Berks], but at the same time you will naturally understand that I feel uneasy [*uneasy* underlined]. During the last few days I have reproached myself with being unduly fanciful [*fanciful* underlined three times] but have only felt increasingly perturbed. I may be attaching undue importance to what is, after all, a trifle [*trifle* underlined twice] but my uneasiness remains. I feel definitely that my mind must be set at rest on the matter. It is actually preying on my mind and affecting my health, and naturally I am in a difficult position as I can say nothing to any one [*nothing to any one* underlined with heavy lines]. In your wisdom you may say, of course, that the whole thing is nothing but a mare's nest. The facts may be capable of a perfectly innocent explanation [*innocent* underlined]. Nevertheless, however trivial it may seem, ever since the incident of the dog's ball, I have felt increasingly doubtful and alarmed. I should therefore welcome your views and counsel on the matter. It would, I feel sure, take a great weight off my mind. Perhaps you would kindly let me know what your fees are and what you advise me to do in the matter?

"I must impress on you again that nobody here knows anything at all. The facts are, I know, very trivial and unimportant, but my health is not too good and my nerves [*nerves* underlined three times] are not what they used to be. Worry of this kind, I am convinced, is very bad for me, and the more I think over the matter, the more I am convinced that I was quite right and no mistake was possible. Of course, I shall not dream of saying anything [underlined] to any one [underlined].

"Hoping to have your advice in the matter at an early date,

"I remain,
"Yours faithfully,
"Emily Arundell."

I turned the letter over and scanned each page closely.

"But, Poirot," I expostulated, "what is it all *about*?"

My friend shrugged his shoulders.

"What, indeed?"

I tapped the sheets with some impatience.

"What a woman! Why can't Mrs.—or Miss Arundell—"

"Miss, I think. It is typically the letter of a spinster."

"Yes," I said. "A real fussy old maid. Why can't she say what she's talking about?"

Poirot sighed.

"As you say—a regrettable failure to employ order and method in the mental processes, and without order and method, Hastings—"

"Quite so," I interrupted hastily. "Little grey cells practically non-existent."

"I would not say that, my friend."

"I would! What's the *sense* of writing a letter like that?"

"Very little—that is true," Poirot admitted.

"A long rigmarole all about nothing," I went on. "Probably some upset to her fat lapdog—an asthmatic pug or a yapping Pekingese!" I looked at my friend curiously. "And yet you read that letter through twice. I do not understand you, Poirot."

Poirot smiled.

"You, Hastings, you would have put it straight in the waste-paper basket?"

"I'm afraid I should." I frowned down on the letter. "I suppose I'm being dense, as usual, but *I* can't see anything of interest in this letter!"

"Yet there is one point in it of great interest—a point that struck me at once."

"Wait," I cried. "Don't tell me. Let me see if I can't discover it for myself."

It was childish of me, perhaps. I examined the letter very thoroughly. Then I shook my head.

"No, I don't see it. The old lady's got the wind up, I realize that—but then, old ladies often do! It may be about nothing—it may conceivably be about something, but I don't see that you can tell that that is so. Unless your instinct—''

Poirot raised an offended hand.

''Instinct! You know how I dislike that word. 'Something seems to tell me'—that is what you infer. *Jamais de la vie!* Me, I *reason*. I employ the little grey cells. There is one interesting point about that letter which you have overlooked utterly, Hastings.''

''Oh, well,'' I said wearily. ''I'll buy it.''

''Buy it? Buy what?''

''An expression. Meaning that I will permit you to enjoy yourself by telling me just where I have been a fool.''

''Not a fool, Hastings, merely unobservant.''

''Well, out with it. What's the interesting point? I suppose, like the 'incident of the dog in the nighttime,' the point *is* that there is no interesting point!''

Poirot disregarded this sally on my part. He said quietly and calmly:

''The interesting point is the *date*.''

''The date?''

I picked up the letter. On the top left-hand corner was written April 17th.

''Yes,'' I said slowly. ''That *is* odd. April 17th.''

''And we are to-day June 28th. *C'est curieux, n'est-ce pas?* Over two months ago.''

I shook my head doubtfully.

''It probably doesn't mean anything. A slip. She meant to put June and wrote April instead.''

''Even then it would be ten or eleven days old—an odd fact. But actually you are in error. Look at the colour of the ink. That letter was written more than ten or eleven days ago. No, April 17th is the date assuredly. But why was the letter not sent?''

I shrugged my shoulders.

''That's easy. The old pussy changed her mind.''

''Then why did she not destroy the letter? Why keep it over two months and post it now?''

I had to admit that that was harder to answer. In fact, I couldn't think of a really satisfactory answer. I merely shook my head and said nothing.

Poirot nodded.

''You see—it is a point! Yes, decidedly a curious point.''

He went over to his writing-table and took up a pen.

''You are answering the letter?'' I asked.

''Oui, mon ami.''

The room was silent except for the scratching of Poirot's pen. It was a hot, airless morning. A smell of dust and tar came in through the window.

Poirot rose from his desk, the completed letter in his hand. He opened a drawer and drew out a little square box. From this he took out a stamp. Moistening this with a little sponge, he prepared to affix it to the letter.

Then suddenly he paused, stamp in hand, shaking his head with vigour.

"*Non*!" he exclaimed. "That is the wrong thing I do." He tore the letter across and threw it into the waste-paper basket.

"Not so must we tackle this matter! We will *go*, my friend."

"You mean to go down to Market Basing?"

"Precisely. Why not? Does not one stifle in London today? Would not the country air be agreeable?"

"Well, if you put it like that," I said. "Shall we go in the car?"

I had acquired a second-hand Austin.

"Excellent. A very pleasant day for motoring. One will hardly need the muffler. A light overcoat, a silk scarf—"

"My dear fellow, you're not going to the North Pole!" I protested.

"One must be careful of catching the chill," said Poirot sententiously.

"On a day like this?"

Disregarding my protests, Poirot proceeded to don a fawn-coloured overcoat and wrap his neck up with a white silk handkerchief. Having carefully placed the wetted stamp face downwards on the blotting-paper to dry, we left the room together.

6

We Go to Littlegreen House

I DONT KNOW what Poirot felt like in his coat and muffler, but I myself felt roasted before we got out of London. An open car in traffic is far from being a refreshing place on a hot summer's day.

Once we were outside London, however, and getting a bit of pace on the Great West Road my spirits rose.

Our drive took us about an hour and a half, and it was close upon twelve o'clock when we came into the little town of Market Basing. Originally on the main road, a modern by-pass now left it some three miles to the north of the main stream of traffic and in consequence it had kept an air of old-fashioned dignity and quietude about it. Its one wide street and ample market square seemed to say, "I was a place of importance once and to any person of sense and breeding I am still the same. Let this modern speeding world dash along their new-fangled road; I was built to endure in a day when solidarity and beauty went hand in hand."

There was a parking area in the middle of the big square, though there were only a few cars occupying it. I duly parked the Austin, Poirot divested himself of his superfluous garments, assured himself that his moustaches were in their proper condition of symmetrical flamboyance, and we were then ready to proceed.

For once in a way our first tentative inquiry did not meet with the usual response, "Sorry, but I'm a stranger in these parts." It would seem indeed probable that there were no strangers in Market Basing! It had that effect! Already, I felt, Poirot and myself (and especially Poirot) were somewhat noticeable. We tended to stick out from the mellow background of an English market town secure in its traditions.

"Littlegreen House?" The man, a burly, ox-eyed fellow looked us over thoughtfully. "You go straight up the High Street and you can't miss it. On your left. There's no name on the gate, but it's the first big house after the bank." He repeated again, "You can't miss it."

His eyes followed us as we started on our course.

"Dear me," I complained. "There is something about this place that makes me feel extremely conspicuous. As for you, Poirot, you look positively exotic."

"You think it is noticed that I am a foreigner—yes?"

"The fact cries aloud to heaven," I assured him.

"And yet my clothes are made by an English tailor," mused Poirot.

"Clothes are not everything," I said. "It cannot be denied, Poirot, that you have a noticeable personality. I have often wondered that it has not hindered you in your career."

Poirot sighed.

"That is because you have the mistaken idea implanted in your head that a detective is necessarily a man who puts on a false beard and hides behind a pillar! The false beard, it is *vieux jeu*, and shadowing is only done by the lowest branch of my profession. The Hercule Poirots, my friend, need only to sit back in a chair and think."

"Which explains why we are walking along this exceedingly hot street on an exceedingly hot morning."

"That is very neatly replied, Hastings. For once, I admit, you have made the score off me."

We found Littlegreen House easily enough, but a shock awaited us—a house-agent's board.

As we were staring at it, a dog's bark attracted my attention.

The bushes were thin at that point and the dog could be easily seen. He was a wire-haired terrier, somewhat shaggy as to coat. His feet were planted wide apart, slightly to one side, and he barked with an obvious enjoyment of his own performance that showed him to be actuated by the most amiable motives.

"Good watchdog, aren't I?" he seemed to be saying. "Don't mind me! This is just my fun! My duty too, of course. Just have to let 'em know there's a dog about the place! Deadly dull morning. Quite a blessing to have something to do. Coming into our place? Hope so. It's durned dull. I could do with a little conversation."

"Hallo, old man," I said, and shoved forward a fist.

Craning his neck through the railings, he sniffed suspiciously, then gently wagged his tail, uttering a few short, staccato barks.

"Not been properly introduced, of course, have to keep this up! But I see you know the proper advances to make."

"Good old boy," I said.

"Wuff," said the terrier amiably.

"Well, Poirot?" I said, desisting from this conversation and turning to my friend.

There was an odd expression on his face—one that I could not quite fathom. A kind of deliberately suppressed excitement seems to describe it best.

"The Incident of the Dog's Ball," he murmured. "Well, at least, we have here a dog."

"Wuff," observed our new friend. Then he sat down, yawned widely and looked at us hopefully.

"What next?" I asked.

The dog seemed to be asking the same question.

"*Parbleu*, to Messrs.—what is it—Messrs. Gabler and Stretcher."

"That does seem indicated," I agreed.

We turned and retraced our steps, our canine acquaintance sending a few disgusted barks after us.

The premises of Messrs. Gabler and Stretcher were situated in the Market Square. We entered a dim outer office where we were received by a young woman with adenoids and a lack-lustre eye.

"Good-morning," said Poirot politely.

The young woman was at the moment speaking into a telephone, but she indicated a chair and Poirot sat down. I found another and brought it forward.

"I couldn't say, I'm sure," said the young woman into the telephone vacantly. "No, I don't know what the rates would be. . . . Pardon? Oh, main water, I think, but, of course, I couldn't be certain. . . . I'm very sorry, I'm sure . . . No, he's out. . . . No, I couldn't say. . . . Yes, of course I'll ask him. . . . Yes . . . 8135? I'm afraid I haven't quite got it. Oh . . . 8935 . . . 39 . . . Oh, 5135. . . . Yes, I'll ask him to ring you . . . after six. . . . Oh, pardon, before six. . . . Thank you so much."

She replaced the receiver, scribbled 5319 on the blottingpad and turned a mildly inquiring but uninterested gaze on Poirot.

Poirot began briskly.

"I observe that there is a house to be sold just on the outskirts of this town. Littlegreen House, I think is the name."

"Pardon?"

"A house to be let or sold," said Poirot slowly and distinctly. "Littlegreen House."

"Oh, Littlegreen House," said the young woman vaguely. "*Littlegreen* House, did you say?"

"That is what I said."

"Littlegreen *House*," said the young woman, making a tremendous mental effort. "Oh, well, I expect Mr. Gabler would know about that."

"Can I see Mr. Gabler?"

"He's out," said the young woman with a kind of faint, anaemic satisfaction as of one who says, "A point to me."

"Do you know when he will be in?"

"I couldn't say, I'm sure," said the young woman.

"You comprehend, I am looking for a house in this neighborhood," said Poirot.

"Oh, yes," said the young woman, uninterested.

"And Littlegreen House seems to me just what I am looking for. Can you give me particulars?"

"Particulars?" The young woman seemed startled.

"Particulars of Littlegreen House."

Unwillingly she opened a drawer and took out an untidy file of papers.

Then she called "John."

A lanky youth sitting in a corner looked up.

"Yes, miss."

"Have we got any particulars of—what did you say?"

"Littlegreen House," said Poirot distinctly.

"You've got a large bill of it here," I remarked, pointing to the wall.

She looked at me coldly. Two to one, she seemed to think, was an unfair way of playing the game. She called up her own reinforcements.

"You don't know anything about Littlegreen House, do you, John?"

"No, miss. Should be in the file."

"I'm sorry," said the young woman without looking so in the least. "I rather fancy we must have sent all the particulars out."

"C'est dommage."

"Pardon?"

"A pity."

"We've a nice bungalow at Hemel End, two bed, one sit."

She spoke without enthusiasm, but with the air of one willing to do her duty by her employer.

"I thank you, no."

"And a semi-detached with small conservatory. I could give you particulars of that."

"No, thank you. I desired to know what rent you were asking for Littlegreen House."

"It's not to be rented," said the young woman, abandoning her position of complete ignorance of anything to do with Littlegreen House in the pleasure of scoring a point. "Only to be sold outright."

"The board says, 'To be Let or Sold.' "

"I couldn't say as to that, but it's for sale only."

At this stage in the battle the door opened and a grey-haired, middle-aged man entered with a rush. His eye, a militant one, swept over us with a gleam. His eyebrows asked a question of his employee.

"This is Mr. Gabler," said the young woman.

Mr. Gabler opened the door of an inner sanctum with a flourish.

"Step in here, gentlemen." He ushered us in, an ample gesture swept us into chairs and he himself was facing us across a flat-topped desk.

"And now what can I do for you?"

Poirot began again perseveringly.

"I desired a few particulars of Littlegreen House—"

He got no further. Mr. Gabler took command.

"Ah! Littlegreen House—*there's* a property! An absolute bargain. Only just come into the market. I can tell you, gentlemen, we don't often get a house of that class going at the price. Taste's swinging round. People are fed up with jerry-building. They went sound stuff. Good, honest building. A beautiful property—character—feeling—Georgian throughout. That's what people want nowadays—there's a feeling for period houses if you understand what I mean. Ah, yes, Littlegreen House won't be long in the market. It'll be snapped up. Snapped up! A member of Parliament came to look at it only last Saturday. Liked it so much he's coming down again this week-end. And there's a stock exchange gentlemen after it too. People want quiet nowadays when they come to the country, want to be well away from main roads. That's all very well for some people, but we attract class here. And that's what that house has got. Class! You've got to admit, they knew how to build for gentlemen in those days. Yes, we shan't have Littlegreen long on our books."

Mr. Gabler, who, it occurred to me, lived up to his name very happily, paused for breath.

"Has it changed hands often in the last few years?" inquired Poirot.

"On the contrary. Been in one family over fifty years. Name of Arundell. Very much respected in the town. Ladies of the old school."

He shot up, opened the door and called:

"Particulars of Littlegreen House, Miss Jenkins. Quickly now."

He returned to the desk.

"I require a house about this distance from London," said Poirot. "In the country, but not in the dead country, if you understand me—"

"Perfectly—perfectly. Too much in the country doesn't do. Servants don't like it for one thing. Here, you have the advantages of the country but not the disadvantages." Miss Jenkins flitted in with a typewritten sheet of paper which she placed in front of her employer, who dismissed her with a nod.

"Here we are," said Mr. Gabler, reading with practised rapidity. "Period house of character: four recep., eight bed and dressing, usual offices, commodious kitchen premises, ample outbuildings, stables, etc. Main water, old-world gardens, inexpensive upkeep, amounting in all to three acres, two summer-houses, etc., etc. Price £2,850 or near offer."

"You can give me an order to view?"

"Certainly, my dear sir." Mr. Gabler began writing in a flourishing fashion. "Your name and address?"

Slightly to my surprise, Poirot gave his name as Mr. Parotti.

"We have one or two other properties on our books which might interest you," Mr. Gabler went on.

Poirot allowed him to add two further additions.

"Littlegreen House can be viewed any time?" he inquired.

"Certainly, my dear sir. There are servants in residence. I might perhaps ring up to make certain. You will be going there immediately? Or after lunch?"

"Perhaps after lunch would be better."

"Certainly—certainly. I'll ring up and tell them to expect you about two o'clock—eh? Is that right?"

"Thank you. Did you say the owner of the house—a Miss Arundell, I think you said?"

"Lawson. Miss Lawson. That is the name of the present owner. Miss Arundell, I am sorry to say, died a short time ago. That is how the place has come into the market. And I can assure you it will be snapped up. Not a doubt of it. Between you and me, just in confidence, if you do think of making an offer I should make it quickly. As I've told you, there are two gentlemen after it already, and I shouldn't be surprised to get an offer for it any day from one or other of them. Each of them knows the other's after it, you see. And there's no doubt that competition spurs a man on. Ha, ha! I shouldn't like you to be disappointed."

"Miss Lawson is anxious to sell, I gather."

Mr. Gabler lowered his voice confidentially.

"That's just it. The place is larger than she wants—one middle-aged lady living by herself. She wants to get rid of this and take a house in London. Quite understandable. That's why the place is going so ridiculously cheap."

"She would be open, perhaps, to an offer?"

"That's the idea, sir. Make an offer and set the ball rolling. But you can take it from me that there will be no difficulty in getting a price very near the figure named. Why, it's ridiculous! To build a house like that nowadays would cost every penny of six thousand, let alone the land value and the valuable frontages."

"Miss Arundell died very suddenly, didn't she?"

"Oh, I wouldn't say that. Anno domini—anno domini. She had passed her three-score years and ten some time ago. And she'd been ailing for a long time. The last of her family—you know something about the family, perhaps?"

"I know some people of the same name who have relations in this part of the world. I fancy it must be the same family."

"Very likely. Four sisters there were. One married fairly late in life and the other three lived on here. Ladies of the old school. Miss Emily was the last of them. Very highly thought of in the town."

He leant forward and handed Poirot the orders.

"You'll drop in again and let me know what you think of it, eh? Of course, it may need a little modernizing here and there. That's only to be expected. But I always say, 'What's a bathroom or two? That's easily done.' "

We took our leave and the last thing we heard was the vacant voice of Miss Jenkins saying:

"Mrs. Samuels rang up, sir. She'd like you to ring her—Holland 5391."

As far as I could remember that was neither the number Miss Jenkins had scribbled on her pad nor the number finally arrived at through the telephone.

I felt convinced that Miss Jenkins was having her revenge for having been forced to find the particulars of Littlegreen House.

7
Lunch at The George

AS WE EMERGED into the market square, I remarked that Mr. Gabler lived up to his name! Poirot assented with a smile.

"He'll be rather disappointed when you don't return," I said. "I think he feels he has as good as sold you that house already."

"Indeed, yes, I fear there is a deception in store for him."

"I suppose we might as well have lunch here before returning to London, or shall we lunch at some more likely spot on our way back?"

"My dear Hastings, I am not proposing to leave Market Basing so quickly. We have not yet accomplished that which we came to do."

I stared.

"Do you mean—but, my dear fellow, that's all a washout. The old lady is dead."

"Exactly."

The tone of that one word made me stare at him harder than ever. It was evident that he had some bee in his bonnet over this incoherent letter.

"But if she's dead, Poirot," I said gently, "what's the use? She can't tell you anything now. Whatever the trouble was, it's over and finished with."

"How lightly and easily you put the matter aside! Let me tell you that *no* matter is finished with until Hercule Poirot ceases to concern himself with it!"

I should have known from experience that to argue with Poirot is quite useless. Unwarily I proceeded:

"But since she is dead—"

"Exactly, Hastings. Exactly—exactly—exactly. . . . You keep repeating the significant point with a magnificently obtuse disregard of its significance. Do you not see the importance of the point? Miss Arundell is *dead*."

"But, my dear Poirot, her death was perfectly natural and ordinary! There wasn't anything odd or unexplained about it. We have old Gabler's word for that."

"We have his word that Littlegreen House is a bargain at £2,850. Do you accept that as gospel also?"

"No, indeed. It struck me that Gabler was all out to get the place sold—it probably needs modernizing from top to toe. I'd swear he—or rather his client—will be willing to accept a very much lower figure than that. These large Georgian houses fronting right on the street must be the devil to get rid of."

"*Eh bien*, then," said Poirot. "Do not say, 'But Gabler says so!' as though he were an inspired prophet who could not lie."

I was about to protest further, but at this minute we passed the threshold of The George and with an emphatic "Chut!" Poirot put a damper on further conversation.

We were directed to the coffee-room, a room of fine proportions, tightly shut windows and an odour of stale food. An elderly waiter attended to us, a slow, heavy-breathing man. We appeared to be the only lunchers. We had some excellent mutton, large slabs of watery cabbage and some dispirited potatoes. Some rather tasteless stewed fruit and custard followed. After gorgonzola and biscuits the waiter brought us two cups of a doubtful fluid called coffee.

At this point Poirot produced his orders to view and invited the waiter's aid.

"Yes, sir, I know where most of these are. Hemel Down is three miles away—on the Much Benham road—quite a little place. Naylor's Farm is about a mile away. There's a kind of lane goes off to it not long after the King's Head. Bissett Grange? No, I've never heard of that. Littlegreen House is just close by, not more than a few minutes' walk."

"Ah, I think I have already seen it from the outside. That is the most possible one, I think. It is in good repair—yes?"

"Oh, yes, sir. It's in good condition—roof and drains and all that. Old-fashioned, of course. It's never been modernized in any way. The gardens are a picture. Very fond of her garden Miss Arundell was."

"It belongs, I see, to a Miss Lawson."

"That's right, sir. Miss Lawson, she was Miss Arundell's companion, and when the old lady died everything was left to her—house and all."

"Indeed? I suppose she had no relations to whom to leave it."

"Well, it was not quite like that, sir. She *had* nieces and nephews living. But, of course, Miss Lawson was with her all the time. And, of course, she was an old lady and—well—that's how it was."

"In any case I suppose there was just the house and not much money?"

I have often had occasion to notice how, where a direct question would fail to elicit a response, a false assumption brings instant information in the form of a contradiction.

"Very far from that, sir. Very far indeed. Every one was surprised at the amount the old lady left. The will was in the paper and the amount and everything. It seems she hadn't lived up to her income for many a long year. Something like three or four hundred thousand pounds she left."

"You astonish me," cried Poirot. "It is like a fairy tale—eh? The poor companion suddenly becomes unbelievably wealthy. Is she still young, this Miss Lawson? Can she enjoy her new-found wealth?"

"Oh, no, sir, she's a middle-aged person, sir."

His enunciation of the word "person" was quite an artistic performance. It was clear that Miss Lawson, ex-companion, had cut no kind of a figure in Market Basing.

"It must have been disappointing for the nephews and nieces," mused Poirot.

"Yes, sir, I believe it came as somewhat of a shock to them. Very unexpected. There's been feeling over it here in Market Basing. There are those who hold it isn't right to leave things away from your own flesh and blood. But, of course, there's others as hold that every one's got a right to do as they like with their own. There's something to be said for both points of view, of course."

"Miss Arundell had lived for many years here, had she not?"

"Yes, sir. She and her sisters and old General Arundell, their father, before them. Not that I remember him, naturally, but I believe he was quite a character. Was in the Indian Mutiny."

"There were several daughters?"

"Three of them that I remember, and I believe there was one that married. Yes, Miss Matilda, Miss Agnes, and Miss Emily. Miss Matilda, she died first, and then Miss Agnes, and finally Miss Emily."

"That was quite recently?"

"Beginning of May—or it may have been the end of April."

"Had she been ill some time?"

"On and off—on and off. She was on the sickly side. Nearly went off a year ago with that there jaundice. Yellow as an orange she was for some time after. Yes, she'd had poor health for the last five years of her life."

"I suppose you have some good doctors down here?"

"Well, there's Dr. Grainger. Been here close on forty years, he has, and folks mostly go to him. He's a bit crotchety and he has his fancies, but he's a good doctor, none better. He's got a young partner, Dr. Donaldson. He's more the new-fangled kind. Some folk prefer him. Then, of course, there's Dr. Harding, but he doesn't do much."

"Dr. Grainger was Miss Arundell's doctor, I suppose?"

"Oh, yes. He'd pulled her through many a bad turn. He's the kind that fair bullies you into living whether you want to or not."

Poirot nodded.

"One should learn a little about a place before one comes to settle in it," he remarked. "A good doctor is one of the most important people."

"That's very true, sir."

Poirot then asked for his bill to which he added a substantial tip.

"Thank you, sir. Thank you very much, sir. I'm sure I hope you'll settle here, sir."

"I hope so too," said Poirot mendaciously.

We set forth from The George.

"Satisfied yet, Poirot?" I asked as we emerged into the street.

"Not in the least, my friend."

He turned in an unexpected direction.

"Where are you off to now, Poirot?"

"The church, my friend. It may be interesting. Some brasses—an old monument."

I shook my head doubtfully.

Poirot's scrutiny of the interior of the church was brief. Though an attractive specimen of what the guidebook calls Early Perp. it had been so conscientiously restored in Victorian vandal days that little of interest remained.

Poirot next wandered seemingly aimlessly about the churchyard reading some of the epitaphs, commenting on the number of deaths in certain families, occasionally exclaiming over the quaintness of a name.

I was not surprised, however, when he finally halted before what I was pretty sure had been his objective from the beginning.

An imposing marble slab bore a partly effaced inscription:

SACRED
TO THE MEMORY OF
JOHN LAVERTON ARUNDELL
GENERAL 24TH SIKHS
WHO FELL ASLEEP IN CHRIST MAY 19, 1888
AGED 69
"FIGHT THE GOOD FIGHT WITH ALL THY MIGHT"

ALSO OF
MATILDA ANN ARUNDELL
DIED MARCH 10, 1912
"I WILL ARISE AND GO UNTO MY FATHER"

ALSO OF
AGNES GEORGINA MARY ARUNDELL

DIED NOVEMBER 20, 1921
"ASK AND YE SHALL RECEIVE"

Then came a brand-new piece of lettering, evidently just done:

ALSO OF
EMILY HARRIET LAVERTON ARUNDELL
DIED MAY 1, 1936
"THY WILL BE DONE"

Poirot stood looking for some time.

He murmured softly:

"May 1st. . . . May 1st. . . . And to-day, June 28th, I receive her letter. You see, do you not, Hastings, that that fact has got to be explained?"

I saw that it had.

That is to say, I saw that Poirot was determined that it should be explained.

8

Interior of Littlegreen House

ON LEAVING the churchyard, Poirot led the way briskly in the direction of Littlegreen House. I gathered that his rôle was still that of the prospective purchaser. Carefully holding the various orders to view in his hand with the Littlegreen House one uppermost, he pushed open the gate and walked up the path to the front door.

On this occasion our friend the terrier was not to be seen, but the sound of barking could be heard inside the house, though at some distance—I guessed in the kitchen quarters.

Presently we heard footsteps crossing the hall and the door was opened by a pleasant-faced woman of between fifty and sixty, clearly the old-fashioned type of servant seldom seen nowadays.

Poirot presented his credentials.

"Yes, sir, the house-agent telephoned. Will you step this way, sir?"

The shutters which I had noticed were closed on our first visit to spy out the land, were now all thrown open in preparation for our visit. Everything, I observed, was spotlessly clean and well kept. Clearly our guide was a thoroughly conscientious woman.

"This is the morning-room, sir."

I glanced round approvingly. A pleasant room with its long windows giving on the street. It was furnished with good, solid, old-fashioned furniture, mostly Victorian, but there was a Chippendale bookcase and a set of attractive Hepplewhite chairs.

Poirot and I behaved in the customary fashion of people being shown over houses. We stood stock still, looking a little ill at ease, murmuring remarks such as: "Very nice." "A very pleasant room." "The morning-room, you say?"

The maid conducted us across the hall and into the corresponding room on the other side. This was much larger.

"The dining-room, sir."

This room was definitely Victorian. A heavy mahogany dining-table, a massive sideboard of almost purplish mahogany with great clusters of carved fruit, solid leather-covered dining-room chairs. On the wall hung what were obviously family portraits.

The terrier had continued to bark in some sequestered spot. Now the sound suddenly increased in volume. With a crescendo of barking he could be heard galloping across the hall.

"*Who's* come into the house? *I'll* tear him limb from limb," was clearly the "burden of his song."

He arrived in the doorway, sniffing violently.

"Oh, Bob, you naughty dog," exclaimed our conductress. "Don't mind him, sir. He won't do you no harm."

Bob, indeed, having discovered the intruders, completely changed his manner. He fussed in and introduced himself to us in an agreeable manner.

"Pleased to meet you, I'm sure," he observed as he sniffed round our ankles. "Excuse the noise, won't you, but I have my job to do. Got to be careful who we let in, you know. But it's a dull life and I'm really quite pleased to see a visitor. Dogs of your own, I fancy?"

This last was addressed to me and I stopped and patted him.

"Nice little fellow," I said to the woman. "Needs plucking a bit, though."

"Yes, sir, he's usually plucked three times a year."

"Is he an old dog?"

"Oh, no, sir. Bob's not more than six. And sometimes he behaves just like a puppy. Gets hold of cook's slippers and prances about with them. And he's very gentle, though you wouldn't believe it to hear the noise he makes sometimes. The only person he goes for is the postman. Downright scared of him, the postman is."

Bob was now investigating the legs of Poirot's trousers. Having learned all he could, he gave vent to a prolonged sniff ("H'm, not too bad, but not really a doggy person") and returned to me, cocking his head on one side and looking at me expectantly.

"I don't know why dogs always go for postmen, I'm sure," continued our guide.

"It's a matter of reasoning," said Poirot. "The dog, he argues from reason. He is intelligent; he makes his deductions according to his point of view. There are people who may enter a house and there are people who may not—that a dog soon learns. *Eh bien*, who is the person who most persistently tries to gain admission, rattling on the door twice or three times a day—and who is never by any chance admitted? The postman. Clearly, then, an undesirable guest from the point of view of the master of the house. He is always sent about his business, but he persistently returns and tries again. Then a dog's duty is clear, to aid in driving this undesirable man away, and to bite him if possible. A most reasonable proceeding."

He beamed on Bob.

"And a most intelligent person, I fancy."

"Oh, he is, sir. He's almost human, Bob is."

She flung open another door.

"The drawing-room, sir."

The drawing-room conjured up memories of the past. A faint fragrance of pot-pourri hung about it. The chintzes were worn, their pattern faded garlands of roses. On the walls were prints and water-colour drawings. There was a good deal of china—fragile shepherds and shepherdesses. There were cushions worked in crewel stitch. There were faded photographs in handsome silver frames. There were many inlaid workboxes and tea caddies. Most fascinating of all to me were two exquisitely cut tissue-paper ladies under glass stands. One with a spinning-wheel, one with a cat on her knee.

The atmosphere of a bygone day, a day of leisure, of refinement, of "ladies and gentlemen," closed round me. This was indeed a "withdrawing-room." Here ladies sat and did their fancy-work, and if a cigarette was ever smoked by a favoured member of the male sex, what a shaking out of curtains and general airing of the room there would be afterwards!

My attention was drawn by Bob. He was sitting in an attitude of rapt attention close beside an elegant little table with two drawers in it.

As he saw that I was noticing him, he gave a short, plaintive yelp, looking from me to the table.

"What does he want?" I asked.

Our interest in Bob was clearly pleasing to the maid who obviously was very fond of him.

"It's his ball, sir. It was always kept in that drawer. That's why he sits there and asks."

Her voice changed. She addressed Bob in a high falsetto.

"It isn't there any longer, beautiful. Bob's ball is in the kitchen. In the kitchen, Bobsie."

Bob shifted his gaze impatiently to Poirot.

"This woman's a fool," he seemed to be saying. "You look a brainy sort of chap. Balls are kept in certain places—this drawer is one of those places. There always has been a ball here. Therefore there should be a ball there now. That's obvious dog-logic, isn't it?"

"It's not there now, boy," I said.

He looked at me doubtfully. Then as we went out of the room he followed slowly in an unconvinced manner.

We were shown various cupboards, a downstairs cloakroom, and a small pantry place, "where the mistress used to do the flowers, sir."

"You were with your mistress a long time?" asked Poirot.

"Twenty-two years, sir."

"You are alone here caretaking?"

"Me and cook, sir."

"She was also a long time with Miss Arundell?"

"Four years, sir. The old cook died."

"Supposing I were to buy the house, would you be prepared to stay on?"

She blushed a little.

"It's very kind of you, sir, I'm sure, but I'm going to retire from service. The mistress left me a nice little sum, you see, and I'm going to my brother. I'm only remaining here as a convenience to Miss Lawson until the place is sold—to look after everything."

Poirot nodded.

In the momentary silence a new sound was heard.

"Bump, bump, BUMP."

A monotonous sound increasing in volume and seeming to descend from above.

"It's Bob, sir." She was smiling. "He's got hold of his ball and he's bumping it down the stairs. It's a little game of his."

As we reached the bottom of the stairs a black rubber ball arrived with a thud on the last step. I caught it and looked up. Bob was lying on the top step, his paws splayed out, his tail gently wagging. I threw it up to him. He caught it neatly, chewed it for a minute or two with evident relish, then laid it between his paws and gently edged it forward with his nose till he finally bunted it over and it bumped once more down the stairs, Bob wagging his tail furiously as he watched its progress.

"He'll stay like that for hours, sir. Regular game of his. He'd go on all day at it. That'll do now, Bob. The gentlemen have got something else to do than play with you."

A dog is a great promoter of friendly intercourse. Our interest and liking for Bob had quite broken down the natural stiffness of the good servant. As we went up to the bedroom floors, our guide was talking quite garrulously as she gave us accounts of Bob's wonderful sagacity. The ball had been left at the foot of the stairs. As we passed him, Bob gave us a look of deep disgust and stalked down in a dignified fashion to retrieve it. As we turned to the right I saw him slowly coming up again with it in his mouth, his gait that of an extremely old man forced by unthinking persons to exert himself unduly.

As we went round the bedrooms, Poirot began gradually to draw our conductress out.

"There were four Miss Arundells lived here, did they not?" he asked.

"Originally, yes, sir, but that was before my time. There was only Miss Agnes and Miss Emily when I came and Miss Agnes died soon afterwards. She was the youngest of the family. It seemed odd she should go before her sister."

"I suppose she was not so strong as her sister?"

"No, sir, it's odd that. My Miss Arundell, Miss Emily, she was always the delicate one. She'd had a lot to do with doctors all her life. Miss Agnes was always strong and robust and yet she went first, and Miss Emily who'd been delicate from a child outlived all the family. Very odd the way things happen."

"Astonishing how often that is the case."

Poirot plunged into (I feel sure) a wholly mendacious story of an invalid uncle which I will not trouble to repeat here. It suffices to say that it had its effect. Discussions of death and such matters do more to unlock the human tongue than any other subject. Poirot was in a position to ask questions that would have been regarded with suspicious hostility twenty minutes earlier.

"Was Miss Arundell's illness a long and painful one?"

"No, I would't say that, sir. She'd been ailing, if you know what I mean, for a long time—ever since two winters before. Very bad she was then—this here jaundice. Yellow in the face they go and the whites of their eyes—"

"Ah, yes, indeed—" (Anecdote of Poirot's cousin who appeared to have been the Yellow Peril in person.)

"That's right—just as you say, sir. Terribly ill she was, poor dear. Couldn't keep anything down. If you ask me, Dr. Grainger hardly thought she'd pull through. But he'd a wonderful way with her—bullying, you know. 'Made up your mind to lie back and order your tombstone?' he'd say. And she'd say, 'I've a bit of fight in me still, Doctor,' and he'd say, 'That's right—that's what I like to hear.' A hospital nurse we had, and she made up her mind that it was all over—even said to the doctor once that she supposed she'd better not worry the old lady too much by forcing her to take food—but the doctor rounded on her. 'Nonsense,' he said. 'Worry her? You've got to bully her into taking nourishment.' Valentine's beef juice at such and such a time, Brand's essence—teaspoonfuls of brandy. And at the end he said something that I've never forgotten. 'You're young, my girl,' he said to her. 'You don't realize what fine fighting material there is in age. It's young people who turn up their toes and die because they're not interested enough to live. You show me any one who's lived to over seventy and you show me a fighter—some one who's got the will to live.' And it's true, sir—we're always saying how wonderful old people are—their vitality and the way they've kept their faculties—but as the doctor put it that's just *why* they've lived so long and got to be so old."

"But it is profound what you say there—very profound! And Miss Arundell was like that? Very alive? Very interested in life?"

"Oh, yes, indeed, sir. Her health was poor, but her brain was as keen as anything. And as I was saying, she got over that illness of hers—surprised the nurse, it did. A stuck-up young thing she was, all starched collars and cuffs and the waiting on she had to have and tea at all hours."

"A fine recovery."

"Yes, indeed, sir. Of course, the mistress had to be very careful as to diet at first, everything boiled and steamed, no grease in the cooking, and she wasn't allowed to eat eggs either. Very monotonous it was for her."

"Still the main thing is she got well."

"Yes, sir. Of course, she had her little turns. What I'd call bilious attacks. She wasn't always very careful about her food after a time—but still they weren't very serious until the last attack."

"Was it like her illness of two years before?"

"Yes, just the same sort of thing, sir. That nasty jaundice—an awful yellow colour again—and the terrible sickness and all the rest of it. Brought it on herself, I'm afraid she did, poor dear. Ate a lot of things she shouldn't have done. That very evening she was took bad she'd had curry for supper and as you know, sir, curry's rich and a bit oily."

"Her illness came on suddenly, did it?"

"Well, it seemed so, sir, but Dr. Grainger, he said it had been working up for some time. A chill—the weather had been very changeable—and too rich feeding."

"Surely her companion—Miss Lawson was her companion, was she not—could have dissuaded her from rich dishes?"

"Oh, I don't think Miss Lawson would have much say. Miss Arundell wasn't one to take orders from any one."

"Had Miss Lawson been with her during her previous illness?"

"No, she came after that. She'd been with her about a year."

"I suppose she'd had companions before that?"

"Oh, quite a number, sir."

"Her companions didn't stay as long as her servants," said Poirot, smiling.

The woman flushed.

"Well, you see, sir, it was different. Miss Arundell didn't get out much and what with one thing and another—" She paused.

Poirot eyed her for a minute, then he said:

"I understand a little the mentality of elderly ladies. They crave, do they not, for novelty. They get, perhaps, to the end of a person."

"Well, now, that's very clever of you, sir. You've hit it exactly. When a new lady came Miss Arundell was always interested to start with—about her life and her childhood and where she'd been and what she thought about things, and then, when she knew all about her, well, she'd get—well, I suppose bored is the real word."

"Exactly. And between you and me, these ladies who go as companions, they are not usually very interesting—very amusing, eh?"

"No, indeed, sir. They're poor-spirited creatures, most of them. Downright foolish, now and then. Miss Arundell soon got through with them, so to speak. And then she'd make a change and have some one else."

"She must have been unusually attached to Miss Lawson, though."

"Oh, I don't think so, sir."

"Miss Lawson was not in any way a remarkable woman?"

"I shouldn't have said so, sir. Quite an ordinary person."

"You liked her, yes?"

The woman shrugged her shoulders slightly.

"There wasn't anything to like or dislike. Fussy she was—a regular old maid and full of this nonsense about spirits."

"*Spirits?*" Poirot looked alert.

"Yes, sir, spirits. Sitting in the dark round a table and dead people came back and spoke to you. Downright irreligious I call it—as if we didn't know departed souls had their rightful place and aren't likely to leave it."

"So Miss Lawson was a spiritualist! Was Miss Arundell a believer too?"

"Miss Lawson would have liked her to be!" snapped the other. There was a spice of satisfied malice in her tone.

"But she wasn't?" Poirot persisted.

"The mistress had too much sense." She snorted. "Mind you, I don't say it didn't *amuse* her. 'I'm willing to be convinced,' she'd say. But she'd often look at Miss Lawson as much as to say, 'My poor dear, what a fool you are to be so taken in!' "

"I comprehend. She did not believe in it, but it was a source of amusement to her."

"That's right, sir. I sometimes wondered if she didn't—well, have a bit of quiet fun, so to speak, pushing the table and that sort of thing. And the others all as serious as death."

"The others?"

"Miss Lawson and the two Miss Tripps."

"Miss Lawson was a very convinced spiritualist?"

"Took it all for gospel, sir."

"And Miss Arundell was very attached to Miss Lawson, of course."

It was the second time Poirot had made this certain remark and he got the same response.

"Well, hardly that, sir."

"But surely," said Poirot, "if she left her everything—She did, did she not?"

The change was immediate. The human being vanished. The correct maid-servant returned. The woman drew herself up and said in a colourless voice that held reproof for familiarity in it:

"The way the mistress left her money is hardly my business, sir."

I felt that Poirot had bungled the job. Having got the woman in a friendly mood, he was now proceeding to throw away his advantage. He was wise enough to make no immediate attempt to recover lost ground. After a common-place remark about the size and number of the bedrooms he went towards the head of the stairs.

Bob had disappeared, but as I came to the stair-head, I stumbled and nearly fell. Catching at the baluster to steady myself I looked down and saw that I had inadvertently placed my foot on Bob's ball which he had left lying on the top of the stairs.

The woman apologized quickly.

"I'm sorry, sir. It's Bob's fault. He leaves his ball there. And you can't see it against the dark carpet. Death of some one some day it'll be. The poor mistress had a nasty fall through it. Might easily have been the death of her."

Poirot stopped suddenly on the stairs.

"She had an accident, you say?"

"Yes, sir. Bob left his ball there, as he often did, and the mistress came out of her room and fell over it and went right down the stairs. Might have been killed."

"Was she much hurt?"

"Not as much as you'd think. Very lucky she was, Dr. Grainger said. Cut her head a little, and strained her back and of course there were bruises and it was a nasty shock. She was in bed for about a week, but it wasn't serious."

"Was this long ago?"

"Just a week or two before she died."

Poirot stopped to recover something he had dropped.

"Pardon—my fountain pen—ah, yes, there it is."

He stood up again.

"He is careless, this Master Bob," he observed.

"Ah, well, he don't know no better, sir," said the woman in an indulgent voice. "Nearly human he may be, but you can't have everything. The mistress, you see, usedn't to sleep well at nights and often she'd get up and wander downstairs and round and about the house."

"She did that often?"

"Most nights. But she wouldn't have Miss Lawson or any one fussing after her."

Poirot had turned into the drawing-room again.

"A beautiful room this," he observed. "I wonder, would there be space in this recess for my bookcase? What do you think, Hastings?"

Quite fogged I remarked cautiously that it would be difficult to say.

"Yes, sizes are so deceptive. Take, I pray you, my little rule and measure the width of it and I will write it down."

Obediently I took the folding rule that Poirot handed me and took various measurements under his direction whilst he wrote on the back of an envelope.

I was just wondering why he adopted such an untidy and uncharacteristic method of making a neat entry in his little pocket-book when he handed the envelope to me, saying:

"That is right, is it not? Perhaps you had better verify it."

There were no figures on the envelope. Instead was written: "When we go upstairs again, pretend to remember an appointment and ask if you can telephone. Let the woman come with you and delay her as long as you can."

"That's all right," I said, pocketing the envelope. "I should say both bookcases would go in perfectly."

"It is as well to be sure, though. I think, if it is not too much trouble, I would like to look at the principal bedroom again. I am not quite sure of the wall space there."

"Certainly, sir. It's no trouble."

We went up again. Poirot measured a portion of wall, and was just commenting aloud on the respective possible positions of bed, wardrobe and writing table when I looked at my watch, gave a somewhat exaggerated start and exclaimed:

"By Jove, do you know it's three o'clock already? What will Anderson think? I ought to telephone to him." I turned to the woman. "I wonder if I might use your telephone if you have one."

"Why, certainly, sir. It's in the little room off the hall. I'll show you."

She bustled down with me, indicating the instrument, and then I got her to help me in finding a number in the telephone directory. In the end I made a call—to a Mr. Anderson in the neighbouring town of Harchester. Fortunately he was out and I was able to leave a message saying it was unimportant and that I would ring up later!

When I emerged Poirot had descended the staircase and was standing in the hall. His eyes had a slightly green tinge. I had no clue to his excitement, but I realized that he *was* excited.

Poirot said:

"That fall from the top of the stairs must have given your mistress a great shock. Did she seem perturbed about Bob and his ball after it?"

"It's funny your saying that, sir. It worried her a lot. Why, just as she was dying, she was delirious and she rambled on a lot about Bob and his ball and something about a picture that was ajar."

"A picture that was ajar," said Poirot thoughtfully.

"Of course, it didn't make sense, sir, but she was rambling, you see."

"One moment—I must just go into the drawing-room once more."

He wandered round the room, examining the ornaments. In especial, one big jar with a lid on it seemed to attract him. It was not, I fancy, a particularly good bit of china. A piece of Victorian humour—it had on it a rather crude picture of a bulldog sitting outside a front door with a mournful expression on its face. Below was written: *Out all night and no key*.

Poirot, whose taste I have always been convinced is hopelessly bourgeois, seemed lost in admiration.

"*Out all night and no key*," he murmured. "It is amusing, that! Is that true of our Master Bob? Does he sometimes stay out all night?"

"Very occasional, sir. Oh, very occasional. He's a very good dog, Bob is."

"I am sure he is. But even the best of dogs—"

"Oh, it's quite true, sir. Once or twice he's gone off and come home perhaps at four in the morning. Then he sits down on the step and barks till he's let in."

"Who lets him in—Miss Lawson?"

"Well, any one who hears him, sir. It was Miss Lawson, sir, last time. It was the night of the mistress's accident. And Bob came home about five. Miss Lawson hurried down to let him in before he could make a noise. She was afraid of waking up the mistress and hadn't told her Bob was missing for fear of worrying her."

"I see. She thought it was better Miss Arundell shouldn't be told?"

"That's what she said, sir. She said, 'He's sure to come back. He always does, but she might worry and that would never do.' So we didn't say anything."

"Was Bob fond of Miss Lawson?"

"Well, he was rather contemptuous of her if you know what I mean, sir. Dogs can be. She was kind to him. Called him a good doggie and a nice doggie, but he used to look at her kind of scornful like and he didn't pay any attention at all to what she told him to do."

Poirot nodded. "I see," he said.

Suddenly he did something which startled me.

He pulled a letter from his pocket—the letter he had received this morning.

"Ellen," he said, "do you know anything about this?"

The change that came over Ellen's face was remarkable.

Her jaw dropped and she stared at Poirot with an almost comical expression of bewilderment.

"Well," she ejaculated. "I never did!"

The observation lacked coherency, perhaps, but it left no doubt of Ellen's meaning.

Gathering her wits about her she said slowly:

"Are you the gentleman that letter was written to, then?"

"I am. I am Hercule Poirot."

Like most people, Ellen had not glanced at the name on the order Poirot had held out to her on his arrival. She nodded her head slowly.

"That was it," she said. "Hercules Poirot." She added an S to the Christian name and sounded the T of the surname.

"My word!" she exclaimed. "Cook *will* be surprised."

Poirot said quickly:

"Would it not be advisable, perhaps, for us to go to the kitchen and there in company with your friend, we could talk the matter over?"

"Well—if you don't mind, sir."

Ellen sounded just a little doubtful. This particular social dilemma was clearly new to her. But Poirot's matter-of-fact manner reassured her and we departed forthwith to the kitchen, Ellen elucidating the situation to a large, pleasant-faced woman who was just lifting a kettle from a gas ring.

"You'll never believe it, Annie. This is actually the gentleman that letter was to. You know, the one I found in the blotter."

"You must remember I am in the dark," said Poirot. "Perhaps you will tell me how the letter came to be posted so late in the day?"

"Well, sir, to tell the truth I didn't know what to do. Neither of us did, did we?"

"Indeed, we didn't," the cook confirmed.

"You see, sir, when Miss Lawson was turning out things after the mistress's death a good lot of things were given away or thrown away. Among them was a little paper-matchie, I think they call it, blotter. Very pretty it was, with a lily of the valley on it. The mistress always used it when she wrote in bed. Well, Miss Lawson didn't want it, so she gave it to me along with a lot of other little odds and ends that had belonged to the mistress. I put it away in a drawer, and it wasn't till yesterday that I took it out. I was going to put some new blotting-paper in it so that it was ready for me to use. There was a sort of pocket inside and I just slipped my hand in it when what should I find but a letter in the mistress's handwriting, tucked away.

"Well, as I say, I didn't know rightly what to do about it. It was the mistress's hand all right, and I saw as she'd written it and slipped it in there waiting to post it the next day and then she'd forgot, which is the kind of thing she did many a time, poor dear. Once it was a dividend warrant to her bank and no one could think where it had got to, and at last it was found pushed right back in the pigeon-holes of the desk."

"Was she untidy?"

"Oh, no, sir, just the opposite. She was always putting things away and clearing them up. That was half the trouble. If she'd left things about it would really have been better. It was their being tidied away and then forgotten that was always happening."

"Things like Bob's ball, for instance?" asked Poirot with a smile.

The sagacious terrier had just trotted in from outdoors and greeted us anew in a very friendly manner.

"Yes, indeed, sir. As soon as Bob finished playing with his ball she'd put it away. But that was all right because it had it's own place—in the drawer I showed you."

"I see. But I interrupted you. Pray go on. You discovered the letter in the blotter?"

"Yes, sir, that was the way of it, and I asked Annie what she thought I'd better do. I didn't like to put it in the fire—and, of course, I couldn't take upon myself to open it, and neither Annie nor I could see that it was any business of Miss Lawson's, so after we'd talked it over a bit, I just put a stamp on it and ran out to the post box and posted it."

Poirot turned slightly to me.

"*Voilà*," he murmured.

I could not help saying maliciously:

"Amazing how simple an explanation can be!"

I thought he looked a little crestfallen and rather wished I hadn't been so quick to try and rub it in.

He turned again to Ellen.

"As my friend says: How simple an example can be! You understand, when I received a letter dated over two months ago I was somewhat surprised."

"Yes, I suppose you must have been, sir. We didn't think of that."

"Also—" Poirot coughed. "I am in a little dilemma. That letter, you see—it was a commission with which Miss Arundell wished to entrust me. A matter of a somewhat private character." He cleared his throat importantly. "Now that Miss Arundell is dead I am in some doubt how to act. Would Miss Arundell have wished me to undertake the commission in these circumstances or not? It is difficult—very difficult."

Both women were looking at him respectfully.

"I shall have, I think, to consult Miss Arundell's lawyer. She had a lawyer, did she not?"

Ellen answered quickly:

"Oh, yes, sir. Mr. Purvis from Harchester."

"He knew all her affairs?"

"I think so, sir. He's done everything for her ever since I can remember. It was him she sent for after the fall she had."

"The fall down the stairs?"

"Yes, sir."

"Now let me see, when was that exactly?"

The cook broke in.

"Day after Bank Holiday it was. I remember that well. I stayed in to oblige on Bank Holiday, seeing she had all those people staying, and I had the day on Wednesday instead."

Poirot had whipped out his pocket almanac.

"Precisely—precisely. Easter Bank Holiday, I see, fell on the thirteenth this year. Then Miss Arundell had her accident on the fourteenth. This letter to me was written three days later. A pity that it was never sent. However, it may still not be too late—" He paused. "I rather fancy that the—er—commission she wished me to perform was connected with one of the—er—guests you mentioned just now."

This remark, which could only have been a pure shot in the dark, met with immediate response. A quick look of intelligence passed across Ellen's face. She turned to the cook who gave her back an answering glance.

"That'll be Mr. Charles," she said.

"If you would tell me just who was there—" Poirot suggested.

"Dr. Tanios and his wife, Miss Bella that was, and Miss Theresa and Mr. Charles."

"They were all nephews and nieces?"

"That's right, sir. Dr. Tanios, of course, is no relation. In fact, he's a foreigner, a Greek or something of the sort, I believe. He married Miss Bella, Miss Arundell's niece, her sister's child. Mr. Charles and Miss Theresa are brother and sister."

"Ah, yes, I see. A family party. And when did they leave?"

"On the Wednesday morning, sir. And Dr. Tanios and Miss Bella came down again the next week-end because they were worried about Miss Arundell."

"And Mr. Charles and Miss Theresa?"

"They came the week-end after. The week-end before she died."

Poirot's curiosity, I felt, was quite insatiable. I could see no point in these continued questions. He got the explanation of his mystery, and in my opinion the sooner he retired with dignity the better.

The thought seemed to go from my brain to his.

"*Eh bien*," he said. "This information you have given me is very helpful. I must consult this Mr. Purvis, I think you said? Thank you very much for all your help."

He stopped and patted Bob.

"*Brave chien, va*! You loved your mistress."

Bob responded amiably to these overtures and hopeful of a little play went and fetched a large piece of coal. For this he was reproved and the coal removed from him. He sent me a glance in search of sympathy.

"These women," it seemed to say. "Generous with the food, but not really sportsmen!"

9

Reconstruction of the Dog's Ball Incident

"WELL, POIROT," I said as the gate of Littlegreen House closed behind us. "You are satisfied now, I hope!"

"Yes, my friend. I am satisfied."

"Thank Heaven for that! All the mysteries explained! The Wicked Companion and the Rich Old Lady myth exploded. The delayed letter and even the famous incident of the dog's ball shown in their true colours. Everything settled satisfactorily and according to Cocker!"

Poirot gave a dry little cough and said:

"I would not use the word *satisfactorily*, Hastings."

"You did a minute ago."

"No, no. I did not say the matter was *satisfactory*. I said that, personally, my curiosity was *satisfied*. I know the truth of the Dog's Ball incident."

"And very simple it was too!"

"Not quite so simple as you think." He nodded his head several times. Then he went on: "You see, I know one little thing which you do not."

"And what is that?" I asked somewhat sceptically.

"*I know that there is a nail driven into the skirting board at the top of the stairs.*"

I stared at him. His face was quite grave.

"Well," I said after a minute or two. "Why shouldn't there be?"

"The question is, Hastings, why should there be."

"How do I know. Some household reason, perhaps. Does it matter?"

"Certainly it matters. And I can think of no household reason for a nail to be driven in at the top of the skirting board in that particular place. It was carefully varnished, too, so as not to show."

"What are you driving at, Poirot? Do *you* know the reason?"

"I can imagine it quite easily. If you wanted to stretch a piece of strong thread or wire across the top of the stairs about a foot from the ground, you could tie it one side to the balusters, but on the inner wall side you would need something like a nail to attach the thread to."

"Poirot!" I cried. "What on earth are you driving at?"

"*Mon cher ami*, I am reconstructing *the incident of the Dog's Ball*! Would you like to hear my reconstruction?"

"Go ahead."

"*Eh bien*, here it is. Some one had noticed the habit Bob had of leaving his ball at the top of the stairs. A dangerous thing to do—it might lead to an accident." Poirot paused a minute, then said in a slightly different tone, "If you wished to kill some one, Hastings, how would you set about it?"

"I—well, really—I don't know. Fake up some *alibi* or something, I suppose."

"A proceeding, I assure you, both difficult and dangerous. But then you are not the type of a cold-blooded cautious murderer. Does it not strike you that the *easiest* way of removing some one you want to remove from your path is to take advantage of *accident*? Accidents are happening all the time. And sometimes—Hastings—*they can be helped to happen*!"

He paused a minute, then went on:

"I think the dog's ball left so fortuitously at the top of the stairs gave our murderer an idea. Miss Arundell was in the habit of coming out of her room in the night and wandering about—her eyesight was not good; it was quite within the bounds of probability that she might stumble over it and fall headlong down those stairs. But a careful murderer does not leave things to chance. A *thread* stretched across the top of the stairs would be a much better way. It would send her pitching head foremost. Then, when the household came rushing out—there, plain to see, is the *cause* of the accident—Bob's *ball*!"

"How horrible!" I cried.

Poirot said gravely:

"Yes, it was horrible. . . . It was also unsuccessful. . . . Miss Arundell was very little hurt, though she might easily have broken her neck. Very disappointing for our unknown friend! But Miss Arundell was a sharp-witted old lady. Every one told her she had slipped on the ball, and there the ball was as evidence, but she herself, recalling the happening, felt that the accident had arisen differently. She had *not* slipped on the ball. And in addition she remembered something else. *She remembered hearing Bob barking for admission at five o'clock the next morning*.

"This, I admit, is something in the way of guess-work, but I believe I am right. *Miss Arundell had put away Bob's ball herself* the evening before in its drawer. After that he went out *and did not return*. In that case *it was not* Bob who put that ball on the top of the stairs."

"That is pure guess-work, Poirot," I objected.

He demurred.

"Not quite, my friend. There are the significant words uttered by Miss Arundell when she was delirious—something about Bob's ball and a 'picture ajar.' You see the point, do you not?"

"Not in the least."

"Curious. I know your language well enough to realize that one does not talk of a picture being *ajar*. A *door* is *ajar*. A picture is *awry*."

"Or simply crooked."

"Or simply crooked, as you say. So I realized at once that Ellen has mistaken the meaning of the words she heard. It is not ajar—but a or the jar that was meant. Now in the drawing-room there is a rather noticeable china jar. There is, I have already observed, a picture of a dog on it. With the remembrance of these delirious ravings in my mind I go up and examine it more closely. I find that it deals with the subject of *a dog who has been out all night*. You see the trend of the feverish woman's thoughts? Bob was like the dog in the picture on the jar—out all night—*so it was not he who left the ball on the stairs*."

I cried out, feeling some admiration in spite of myself.

"You're an ingenious devil, Poirot! How you think of these things beats me!"

"I do not 'think of them.' They are *there*—plain—for any one to see. *Eh bien*, you realize the position? Miss Arundell, lying in bed after her fall, becomes suspicious. That suspicion she feels is perhaps fanciful and absurd, but there it is. *'Since the incident of the Dog's Ball I have been increasingly uneasy.'* And so—and so she writes to me, and by a piece of bad luck her letter does not reach me until over two months have gone by. Tell me, does her letter not fit in *perfectly* with these facts?"

"Yes," I admitted. "It does."

Poirot went on:

"There is another point worthy of consideration. Miss Lawson was exceedingly anxious that the fact of Bob's being out all night should not get to Miss Arundell's ears."

"You think that she—"

"I think that the fact should be noted very carefully."

I turned the thing over in my mind for a minute or two.

"Well," I said at last with a sigh, "it's all very interesting—as a mental exercise, that is. And I take off my hat to you. It's been a masterful piece of reconstruction. It's almost a pity really that the old lady has died."

"A pity—yes. She wrote to me that some one had attempted to murder her (that is what it amounts to, after all) and a very short time after, she was dead."

"Yes," I said, "and it's a grand disappointment to you that she died a natural death, isn't it? Come, admit it."

Poirot shrugged his shoulders.

"Or perhaps you think she was poisoned," I said maliciously.

Poirot shook his head somewhat despondently.

"It certainly seems," he admitted, "as though Miss Arundell died from natural causes."

"And therefore," I said, "we return to London with our tail between our legs."

"*Pardon*, my friend, but we do *not* return to London."

"What do you mean, Poirot?" I cried.

"If you show the dog the rabbit, my friend, does he return to London? No, he goes into the rabbit hole."

"What do you mean?"

"The dog hunts rabbits. Hercule Poirot hunts murderers. We have here a murderer—a murderer whose crime failed, yes, perhaps, but nevertheless a murderer. And I, my friend, am going into the burrow after him—or her as the case may be."

He turned sharply in at the gate.

"Where are you off to, Poirot?"

"Into the burrow, my friend. This is the house of Dr. Grainger who attended Miss Arundell in her last illness."

Dr. Grainger was a man of sixty odd. His face was thin and bony with an aggressive chin, bushy eyebrows, and a pair of very shrewd grey eyes. He looked keenly from me to Poirot.

"Well, what can I do for you?" he asked abruptly.

Poirot swept into speech in the most flamboyant manner.

"I must apologize, Dr. Grainger, for this intrusion. I must confess straightaway that I do not come to consult you professionally."

Dr. Grainger said drily:

"Glad to hear it. You look healthy enough!"

"I must explain the purpose of my visit," went on Poirot. "The truth of the matter is that I am writing a book—the life of the late General Arundell, who I understand lived in Market Basing for some years before his death."

The doctor looked rather surprised.

"Yes, General Arundell lived here till his death. At Littlegreen House—just up the road past the Bank—you've been there perhaps?" Poirot nodded assent. "But you understand that was a good bit before my time. I came here in 1919."

"You knew his daughter, however, the late Miss Arundell?"

"I knew Emily Arundell well."

"You comprehend, it has been a severe blow to me to find that Miss Arundell has recently died."

"End of April."

"So I discovered. I counted, you see, on her giving me various personal details and reminiscences of her father."

"Quite—quite. But I don't see what I can do about it."

Poirot asked:

"General Arundell has no other sons or daughters living?"

"No. All dead, the lot of them."

"How many were there?"

"Five. Four daughters, one son."

"And in the next generation?"

"Charles Arundell and his sister Theresa. You could get on to them. I doubt, though, if it would be much use to you. The young generation doesn't take much interest in its grandfathers. And there's a Mrs. Tanios, but I doubt if you'd get much there either."

"They might have family papers—documents?"

"They might have. Doubt it, though. A lot of stuff was cleared out and burnt after Miss Emily's death, I know."

Poirot uttered a groan of anguish.

Grainger looked at him curiously.

"What's the interest in old Arundell? I never heard he was a big pot in any way?"

"My dear sir." Poirot's eyes gleamed with the excitement of the fanatic. "Is there not a saying that history knows nothing of its greatest men? Recently certain papers have come to light which throw an entirely different light on the whole subject of the Indian Mutiny. There is secret history there. And in that secret history John Arundell played a big part. The whole thing is fascinating—fascinating! And let me tell you, my dear sir, it is of especial interest at the present time. India—the English policy in regard to it—is the burning question of the hour."

"H'm," said the doctor. "I have heard that old General Arundell used to hold forth a good deal on the subject of the Mutiny. As a matter of fact, he was considered a prize bore on the subject."

"Who told you that?"

"A Miss Peabody. You might call on her, by the way. She's our oldest inhabitant—knew the Arundells intimately. And gossip is her chief recreation. She's worth seeing for her own sake—a character."

"Thank you. That is an excellent idea. Perhaps, too, you would give me the address of young Mr. Arundell, the grandson of the late General Arundell."

"Charles? Yes, I can put you on to him. But he's an irreverent young devil. Family history means nothing to him."

"He is quite young?"

"He's what an old fogy like me calls young," said the doctor with a twinkle. "Early thirties. The kind of young man that's born to be in trouble and responsibility to their families. Charm of personality and nothing else. He's been shipped about all over the world and done no good anywhere."

"His aunt was doubtless fond of him?" ventured Poirot. "It is often that way."

"H'm—I don't know. Emily Arundell was no fool. As far as I knew he never succeeded in getting any money out of her. Bit of a tartar that old lady. I liked her. Respected her too. An old soldier every inch of her."

"Was her death sudden?"

"Yes, in a way. Mind you, she'd been in poor health for some years. But she'd pulled through some narrow squeaks."

"There was some story—I apologize for repeating gossip—" Poirot spread out his hands deprecatingly—"that she had quarrelled with her family?"

"She didn't exactly *quarrel* with them," said Dr. Grainger slowly. "No, there was no open quarrel as far as I know."

"I beg your pardon. I am, perhaps, being indiscreet."

"No, no. After all, the information's public property."

"She left her money away from her family, I understand?"

"Yes, left it all to a frightened, fluttering hen of a companion. Odd thing to do. Can't understand it myself. Not like her."

"Ah, well," said Poirot thoughtfully. "One can imagine such a thing happening. An old lady, frail and in ill-health. Very dependent on the person who attends and cares for her. A clever woman with a certain amount of personality could gain a great ascendency that way."

The word "ascendency" seemed to act like a red rag to a bull.

Dr. Grainger snorted out:

"Ascendency? Ascendency? Nothing of the kind! Emily Arundell treated Minnie Lawson worse than a dog. Characteristic of that generation! Anyway, women who earn their living as companions are usually fools. If they've got brains they're earning a better living some other way. Emily Arundell didn't suffer fools gladly. She usually wore out one poor devil a year. Ascendency? Nothing of the sort!"

Poirot hastened off the treacherous ground.

"It is possible, perhaps," he suggested, "that there are old family letters and documents in this Miss—er—Lawson's possession?"

"Might be," agreed Grainger. "Usually are a lot of things tucked away in an old maid's house. I don't suppose Miss Lawson's been through half of it yet."

Poirot rose.

"Thank you very much, Dr. Grainger. You have been most kind."

"Don't thank me," said the doctor. "Sorry I can't do anything helpful. Miss Peabody's your best chance. Lives at Morton Manor—about a mile out."

Poirot was sniffing at a large bouquet of roses on the doctor's table.

"Delicious," he murmured.

"Yes, I suppose so. Can't smell 'em myself. Lost my sense of smell when I had flu four years ago. Nice admission for a doctor, eh? 'Physician, heal thyself.' Damned nuisance. Can't enjoy a smoke as I used to."

"Unfortunate, yes. By the way, you *will* give me young Arundell's address?"

"I can get it for you, yes." He ushered us out into the hall and called, "Donaldson."

"My partner," he explained. "He should have it all right. He's by way of being engaged to Charles's sister, Theresa."

He called again: "Donaldson."

A young man came out from a room at the back of the house. He was of medium height and of rather colourless appearance. His manner was precise. A greater contrast to Dr. Grainger could not be imagined.

The latter explained what he wanted.

Dr. Donaldson's eyes, very pale blue eyes slightly prominent, swept over us, appraisingly. When he spoke it was in a dry, precise manner.

"I don't know exactly where Charles is to be found," he said. "I can give you Miss Theresa Arundell's address. Doubtless she will be able to put you in touch with her brother."

Poirot assured him that that would do perfectly.

The doctor wrote down an address on a page in his notebook, tore it out, and handed it to Poirot.

Poirot thanked him and said good-bye to both doctors. As we went out of the door I was conscious of Dr. Donaldson standing in the hall peering after us with a slightly startled look on his face.

10

Visit to Miss Peabody

"IS IT REALLY necessary to tell such elaborate lies, Poirot?" I asked as we walked away.

Poirot shrugged his shoulders.

"If one is going to tell a lie at all—and I notice, by the way, that your nature is very much averse to lying—now, me, it does not trouble me at all—"

"So I've noticed," I interjected.

"—As I was remarking, *if* one is going to tell a lie at all, it might as well be an artistic lie, a romantic lie, a convincing lie!"

"Do you consider this a convincing lie? Do you think Dr. Donaldson was convinced?"

"That young man is of a sceptical nature," admitted Poirot thoughtfully.

"He looked definitely suspicious to me."

"I do not see why he should be so. Imbeciles are writing the lives of other imbeciles every day. It is, as you say, done."

"First time I've heard you call yourself an imbecile," I said, grinning.

"I can adopt a rôle, I hope, as well as any one," said Poirot coldly. "I am sorry you do not think my little fiction well imagined. I was rather pleased with it myself."

I changed the subject.

"What do we do next?"

"That is easy. We get into your car and pay a visit to Morton Manor."

Morton Manor proved to be an ugly substantial house of the Victorian period. A decrepit butler received us somewhat doubtfully and presently returned to ask if we had an appointment.

"Please tell Miss Peabody that we come from Dr. Grainger," said Poirot.

After a wait of a few minutes, the door opened and a short, fat woman waddled into the room. Her sparse, white hair was neatly parted in the middle. She wore a black velvet dress, the nap of which was completely rubbed off in various places, and some really beautiful fine point lace was fastened at her neck with a large cameo brooch.

She came across the room peering at us short-sightedly. Her first words were somewhat of a surprise.

"Got anything to sell?"

"Nothing, madame," said Poirot.

"Sure?"

"But absolutely."

"No vacuum cleaners?"

"No."

"No stockings?"

"No."

"No rugs?"

"No."

"Oh, well," said Miss Peabody, settling herself in a chair, "I suppose it's all right. You'd better sit down then."

We sat obediently.

"You'll excuse my asking," said Miss Peabody with a trace of apology in her manner. "Got to be careful. You wouldn't believe the people who come along. Servants are no good. They can't tell. Can't blame 'em either. Right voices, right clothes, right names. How are they to tell? Commander Ridgeway, Mr. Scot Edgerton, Captain D'Arcy Fitzherbert. Nice-looking fellows, some of 'em. But before you know where you are they've shoved a cream-making machine under your nose."

Poirot said earnestly:

"I assure you, madame, that we have nothing whatever of that kind."

"Well, you should know," said Miss Peabody.

Poirot plunged into his story. Miss Peabody heard him out without comment, blinking once or twice out of her small eyes. At the end she said:

"Goin' to write a book, eh?"

"Yes."

"In English?"

"Certainly—in English."

"But you're a foreigner. Eh? Come now, you're a foreigner, aren't you?"

"That is true."

She transferred her gaze to me.

"You are his secretary, I suppose?"

"Er—yes," I said doubtfully.

"Can you write decent English?"

"I hope so."

"H'm—where did you go to school?"

"Eton."

"Then you can't."

I was forced to let this sweeping charge against an old and venerable centre of education pass unchallenged as Miss Peabody turned her attention once more to Poirot.

"Goin' to write a life of General Arundell, eh?"

"Yes. You knew him, I think."

"Yes, I knew John Arundell. He drank."

There was a momentary pause. Then Miss Peabody went on musingly:

"Indian Mutiny, eh? Seems a bit like flogging a dead horse to me. But that's your business."

"You know, madame, there is a fashion in these things. At the moment India is the mode."

"Something in that. Things do come round. Look at sleeves."

We maintained a respectful silence.

"Leg o' muttons were always ugly," said Miss Peabody. "But I always looked well in Bishops." She fixed a bright eye on Poirot. "Now then, what do you want to know?"

Poirot spread out his hands.

"Anything! Family history. Gossip. Home life."

"Can't tell you anything about India," said Miss Peabody. "Truth is, I didn't listen. Rather boring these old men and their anecdotes. He was a very stupid man—but I dare say none the worse General for that. I've always heard that intelligence didn't get you far in the army. Pay attention to your Colonel's wife and listen respectfully to your superior officers and you'll get on—that's what my father used to say."

Treating this dictum respectfully, Poirot allowed a moment or two to elapse before he said:

"You knew the Arundell family intimately, did you not?"

"Knew 'em all," said Miss Peabody. "Matilda, she was the eldest. A spotty girl. Used to teach in Sunday School. Was sweet on one of the curates. Then there was Emily. Good seat on a horse, she had. She was the only one who could do anything with her father when he had one of his bouts on. Cartloads of bottles used to be taken out of that house. Buried them at night, they did. Then, let me see, who came next, Arabella or Thomas? Thomas, I think. Always felt sorry for Thomas. One man and four women. Makes a man look a fool. He was a bit of an old woman himself, Thomas was. Nobody thought he'd ever marry. Bit of a shock when he did."

She chuckled—a rich Victorian fruity chuckle.

It was clear that Miss Peabody was enjoying herself. As an audience we were almost forgotten. Miss Peabody was well away in the past.

"Then came Arabella. Plain girl. Face like a scone. She married all right though, even if she were the plainest of the family. Professor at Cambridge. Quite an old man. Must have been sixty if he was a day. He gave a series of lectures here—on the wonders of Modern Chemistry, I think it was. I went to 'em. He mumbled, I remember. Had a beard. Couldn't hear much of what he said. Arabella used to stay behind and ask questions. She wasn't a chicken herself. Must have been getting on for forty. Ah, well, they're both dead now. Quite a happy marriage it was. There's something to be said for marrying a plain woman—you know the worst at once and she's not so likely to be flighty. Then there was Agnes. She was the youngest—the pretty one. Rather gay we used to think her. Almost fast! Odd, you'd think if any of them had married it would have been Agnes, but she didn't. She died not long after the war."

Poirot murmured:

"You said that Mr. Thomas's marriage was rather unexpected."

Again Miss Peabody produced that rich, throaty chuckle.

"Unexpected? I should say it was! Made a nine days' scandal. You'd never have thought it of him—such a quiet, timid, retiring man and devoted to his sisters."

She paused a minute.

"Remember a case that made rather a stir in the late nineties? Mrs. Varley? Supposed to have poisoned her husband with arsenic. Good-looking woman. Made a big to-do, that case. She was acquitted. Well, Thomas Arundell quite lost his head. Used to get all the papers and read about the case and cut out the photographs of Mrs. Varley. And would you believe it, when the trial was over, off he went to London and asked her to marry him? Thomas! Quiet, stay-at-home Thomas! Never can tell with men, can you? They're always liable to break out."

"And what happened?"

"Oh, she married him all right."

"It was a great shock to his sisters?"

"I should think so! They wouldn't receive her. I don't know that I blame them, all things considered. Thomas was mortally offended. He went off to live in the Channel Islands and nobody heard any more of him. Don't know whether his wife poisoned her first husband. She didn't poison Thomas. He survived her by three years. There were two children, boy and girl. Good-looking pair—took after their mother."

"I suppose they came here to their aunt a good deal?"

"Not till after their parents died. They were at school and almost grown-up by then. They used to come for holidays. Emily was alone in the world then and they and Bella Biggs were the only kith and kin she had."

"Biggs?"

"Arabella's daughter. Dull girl—some years older than Theresa. Made a fool of herself, though. Married some foreigner who was over at the University. A Greek doctor. Dreadful-looking man—got rather a charming manner, though, I must admit. Well, I don't suppose poor Bella had many chances. Spent her time helping her father or holding wool for her mother. This fellow was exotic. It appealed to her."

"Has it been a happy marriage?"

Miss Peabody snapped out:

"I wouldn't like to say for certain about *any* marriage! They *seem* quite happy. Two rather yellow-looking children. They live in Smyrna."

"But they are now in England, are they not?"

"Yes, they came over in March. I rather fancy they'll be going back soon."

''Was Miss Emily Arundell fond of her niece?''

''Fond of Bella? Oh, quite. She's a dull woman—wrapped up in her children and that sort of thing.''

''Did she approve of the husband?''

Miss Peabody chuckled.

''She didn't *approve* of him, but I think she rather liked the rascal. He's got brains, you know. If you ask me, he was jockeying her along very nicely. Got a nose for money, that man.''

Poirot coughed.

''I understand Miss Arundell died a rich woman?'' he murmured.

Miss Peabody settled herself more comfortably in her chair.

''Yes, that's what made all the pother! Nobody dreamed she was quite as well off as she was. How it came about was this way. Old General Arundell left quite a nice little income—divided equally among his son and daughters. Some of it was reinvested, and I think every investment has done well. There were some original shares of Mortauld. Now, of course, Thomas and Arabella took their shares with them when they married. The other three sisters lived here, and they didn't spend a tenth part of their joint income, it all went back and was reinvested. When Matilda died she left her money to be divided between Emily and Agnes, and when Agnes died she left hers to Emily. And Emily still went on spending very little. Result, she died a rich woman—and the Lawson woman gets it all!''

Miss Peabody brought out the last sentence as a kind of triumphal climax.

''Did that come as a surprise to you, Miss Peabody?''

''To tell you the truth, it did! Emily had always given out quite openly that at her death her money was to be divided between her nieces and her nephew. And as a matter of fact, that was the way it was in the original will. Legacies to the servants and so on and then to be divided between Theresa, Charles and Bella. My goodness, there *was* a to-do when, after her death, it was found she'd made a new will leaving it all to poor Miss Lawson!''

''Was the will made just before her death?''

Miss Peabody directed a sharp glance at him.

''Thinking of undue influence. No, I'm afraid that's no use. And I shouldn't think poor Lawson had the brains or the nerve to attempt anything of the sort. To tell you the truth, she seemed as much surprised as anybody—or said she was!''

Poirot smiled at the addition.

''The will was made about ten days before her death,'' went on Miss Peabody. ''Lawyer says it's all right. Well—it may be.''

''You mean—'' Poirot leaned forward.

"Hanky-panky, that's what I say," said Miss Peabody. "Something fishy somewhere."

"Just what exactly is your idea?"

"Haven't got one. How should I know where the hanky-panky comes in? I'm not a lawyer. But there's something queer about it, mark my words."

Poirot said slowly:

"Has there been any question of contesting the will?"

"Theresa's taken counsel's opinion, I believe. A lot of good that'll do her! What's a lawyer's opinion nine times out of ten? 'Don't!' Five lawyers advised me once against bringing an action. What did I do? Paid no attention. Won my case too. They had me in the witness box and a clever young whippersnapper from London tried to make me contradict myself. But he didn't manage it. 'You can hardly identify these furs positively, Miss Peabody,' he said. 'There is no furrier's mark on them.'

" 'That may be,' I said. 'But there's a darn on the lining and if any one can do a darn like that nowadays I'll eat my umbrella.' Collapsed utterly, he did."

Miss Peabody chuckled heartily.

"I suppose," said Poirot cautiously, "that—er—feeling—runs rather high between Miss Lawson and members of Miss Arundell's family?"

"What do you expect? You know what human nature is. Always trouble after a death, anyway. A man or woman is hardly cold in their coffin before most of the mourners are scratching each other's eyes out."

Poirot sighed.

"Too true."

"That's human nature," said Miss Peabody tolerantly.

Poirot changed to another subject.

"Is it true that Miss Arundell dabbled in spiritualism?"

Miss Peabody's penetrating eye observed him very acutely.

"If you think," she said, "that the spirit of John Arundell came back and ordered Emily to leave her money to Minnie Lawson and that Emily obeyed, I can tell you that you're very much mistaken. Emily wouldn't be that kind of fool. If you ask me, she found spiritualism one degree better than playing patience or cribbage. Seen the Tripps?"

"No."

"If you had, you'd realize just the sort of silliness it was. Irritating women. Always giving you messages from one or other of your relations—and always totally incongruous ones. They believe it all. So did Minnie Lawson. Oh, well, one way of passing your evenings is as good as another, I suppose."

Poirot tried yet another tack.

"You know young Charles Arundell, I presume? What kind of a person is he?"

"He's no good. Charmin' fellow. Always hard up—always in debt—always returning like a bad penny from all over the world. Knows how to get round women all right." She chuckled. "I've seen too many like him to be taken in! Funny son for Thomas to have had, I must say. He was a staid old fogy if you like. Model of rectitude. Ah, well, bad blood somewhere. Mind you, I *like* the rascal—but he's the kind who would murder his grandmother for a shilling or two quite cheerfully. No moral sense. Odd the way some people seem to be born without it."

"And his sister?"

"Theresa?" Miss Peabody shook her head and said slowly, "I don't know. She's an exotic creature. Not usual. She's engaged to that namby-pamby doctor down here. You've seen him, perhaps?"

"Dr. Donaldson."

"Yes. Clever in his profession, they say. But he's a poor stick in other ways. Not the sort of young man I'd fancy if I were a young girl. Well, Theresa should know her mind. She's had her experiences, I'll be bound."

"Dr. Donaldson did not attend Miss Arundell?"

"He used to when Grainger was away on holiday."

"But not in her last illness?"

"Don't think so."

Poirot said, smiling:

"I gather, Miss Peabody, that you don't think much of him as a doctor?"

"Never said so. As a matter of fact, you're wrong. He's sharp enough, and clever enough in his way—but it's not *my* way. Take an instance. In the old days when a child ate too many green apples it had a bilious attack and the doctor called it a bilious attack and went home and sent you along a few pills from the surgery. Nowadays, you're told the child suffers from pronounced acidosis, that its diet must be supervised and you get the same medicine, only it's in nice little white tablets put up by manufacturing chemists and costs you about three times as much! Donaldson belongs to that school, and, mind you, most young mothers prefer it. It *sounds* better. Not that that young man will be in this place long ministering to measles and bilious attacks. He's got his eye on London. He's ambitious. He means to specialize."

"In any particular line?"

"Serum therapeutics. I think I've got it right. The idea being that you get one of these nasty hypodermic needles stuck into you no matter how well you feel, just in case you should catch something. I don't hold with all these messy injections myself."

"Is Dr. Donaldson experimenting with any particular disease?"

"Don't ask me. All I know is a general practitioner's practice isn't good enough for him. He wants to set up in London. But to do that he's got to have money and he's as poor as a church mouse, whatever a church mouse may be."

Poirot murmured:

"Sad that real ability is so often baulked by lack of money. And yet there are people who do not spend a quarter of their incomes."

"Emily Arundell didn't," said Miss Peabody. "It was quite a surprise to some people when that will was read. The amount, I mean, not the way it was left."

"Was it a surprise, do you think, to the members of her own family?"

"That's telling," said Miss Peabody, screwing up her eyes with a good deal of enjoyment. "I wouldn't say yes, and I wouldn't say no. One of 'em had a pretty shrewd idea."

"Which one?"

"Master Charles. He'd done a bit of calculation on his own account. He's no fool, Charles."

"But a little bit of a rogue, eh?"

"At any rate, he isn't a namby-pamby stick," said Miss Peabody viciously.

She paused a minute and then asked:

"Going to get in touch with him?"

"That was my intention," Poirot went on solemnly. "It seems to me possible that he might have certain family papers relating to his grandfather?"

"More likely to have made a bonfire of them. No respect for his elders, that young man."

"One must try all avenues," said Poirot sententiously.

"So it seems," said Miss Peabody drily.

There was a momentary glint in her blue eyes that seemed to affect Poirot disagreeably. He rose.

"I must not trespass any longer on your time, madame. I am most grateful for what you have been able to tell me."

"I've done my best," said Miss Peabody. "Seem to have got rather a long way from the Indian Mutiny, don't we?"

She shook hands with us both.

"Let me know when the book comes out," was her parting remark. "I shall be *so* interested."

And the last thing we heard as we left the room was a rich, throaty chuckle.

II

Visit to the Misses Tripp

"AND NOW," said Poirot as we re-entered the car, "what do we do next?"

Warned by experience I did not this time suggest a return to town. After all, if Poirot was enjoying himself in his own fashion, why should I object?

I suggested some tea.

"Tea, Hastings? What an idea! Regard the time."

"I have regarded it—looked at it, I mean. It's half-past five. Tea is clearly indicated."

Poirot sighed.

"Always the afternoon tea with you English! No, *mon ami*, no tea for us. In a book of etiquette I read the other day that one must not make the afternoon call after six o'clock. To do so is to commit the solecism. We have, therefore, but half an hour in which to accomplish our purpose."

"How social you are to-day, Poirot! On whom are we calling now?"

"*Les demoiselles* Tripp."

"Are you writing a book on spiritualism now? Or is it still the life of General Arundell?"

"It will be simpler than that, my friend. But we must inquire where these ladies live."

Directions were forthcoming readily enough, but of a somewhat confused nature, involving as they did a series of lanes. The abode of the Misses Tripp turned out to be a picturesque cottage—so extremely old-world and picturesque that it looked as though it might collapse any minute.

A child of fourteen or thereabouts opened the door and with difficulty squeezed herself against the wall sufficiently to allow us to pass inside.

The interior was very rich in old oak beams—there was a big open fireplace and such very small windows that it was difficult to see clearly. All the furniture was of pseudosimplicity—ye olde oake for ye cottage dweller—there was a good deal of fruit in wooden bowls and large numbers of photographs—most of them, I noticed, of the same two people represented in different poses—usually with bunches of flowers clasped to their breasts or clutching large leghorn picture-hats.

The child who had admitted us had murmured something and disappeared, but her voice was clearly audible in an upper story.

"Two gentlemen to see you, miss."

A sort of twitter of female voices arose and presently with a good deal of creaking and rustling a lady descended the staircase and came graciously towards us.

She was nearer fifty than forty, her hair was parted in the middle in Madonna fashion, her eyes were brown and slightly prominent. She wore a sprigged muslin dress that conveyed an odd suggestion of fancy dress.

Poirot stepped forward and started the conversation in his most flourishing manner.

"I must apologize for intruding upon you, mademoiselle, but I am in somewhat of a predicament. I came here to find a certain lady, but she has left Market Basing and I was told that you would certainly have her address."

"Really? Who was that?"

"Miss Lawson."

"Oh, Minnie Lawson. Of *course*! We are the *greatest* friends. Do sit down, Mr.—er—"

"Parotti—my friend, Captain Hastings."

Miss Tripp acknowledged the introductions and began to fuss a little.

"Sit here, won't you—no, please—really, I always prefer an *upright* chair myself. Now, are you sure you are comfortable there? Dear Minnie Lawson—oh, here is my sister."

More creaking and rustling and we were joined by a second lady, dressed in green gingham that would have been suitable for a girl of sixteen.

"My sister Isabel—Mr.—er—Parrot—and—er—Captain Hawkins. Isabel dear, these gentlemen are friends of Minnie Lawson's."

Miss Isabel Tripp was less buxom than her sister. She might indeed have been described as scraggy. She had very fair hair done up into a large quantity of rather messy curls. She cultivated a girlish manner and was easily recognizable as the subject of most of the flower poses in photography. She clasped her hands now in girlish excitement.

"How delightful! Dear Minnie! You have seen her lately?"

"Not for some years," explained Poirot. "We have quite lost touch with each other. I have been travelling. That is why I was so astonished and delighted to hear of the good fortune that had befallen my old friend."

"Yes, indeed. And so *well* deserved! Minnie is such a rare soul. So simple—so earnest."

"Julia," cried Isabel.

"Yes, Isabel?"

"How remarkable. *P*. You remember the planchette distinctly insisted on *P*. last night. A visitor from over the water and the initial *P*."

"So it did," agreed Julia.

Both ladies looked at Poirot in rapt and delighted surprise.

"It never lies," said Miss Julia softly.

"Are you interested at all in the occult, Mr. Parrot?"

"I have little experience, mademoiselle, but—like any one who has travelled much in the East, I am bound to admit that there is much one does not understand and that cannot be explained by natural means."

"So true," said Julia. "Profoundly true."

"The East," murmured Isabel. "The home of mysticism and the occult."

Poirot's travellings in the East, as far as I knew, consisted of one journey to Syria extended to Iraq, and which occupied perhaps a few weeks. To judge by his present conversation one would swear that he had spent most of his life in jungles and bazaars and in intimate converse with fakirs, dervishes, and mahatmas.

As far as I could make out the Misses Tripp were vegetarians, theosophists, British Israelites, Christian Scientists, spiritualists and enthusiastic amateur photographers.

"One sometimes feels," said Julia with a sigh, "that Market Basing is an impossible place to live. There is no beauty here—no *soul*. One must have soul, don't you think so, Captain Hawkins?"

"Quite," I said, slightly embarrassed. "Oh, quite."

"*Without vision the people perish*," quoted Isabel with a sigh. "I have often tried to discuss things with the vicar, but I find him most painfully *narrow*. Don't you think, Mr. Parrot, that any definite creed is bound to be *narrowing*?"

"And everything is so simple, really," put in her sister. "As we knew so well, everything is joy and love!"

"As you say, as you say," said Poirot. "What a pity it seems that misunderstandings and quarrels should arise—especially over money."

"Money is so sordid," sighed Julia.

"I gather that the late Miss Arundell was one of your converts?" said Poirot.

The two sisters looked at each other.

"I wonder," said Isabel.

"We were never quite sure," breathed Julia. "One minute she seemed to be convinced and then she would say something—so—so ribald."

"Ah, but you remember that last manifestation," said Julia. "That was really most remarkable." She turned to Poirot. "It was the night dear Miss Arundell was taken ill. My sister and I went round after dinner and we had a sitting—just the four of us. And you know we saw—we all three saw—*most* distinctly, a kind of *halo* round Miss Arundell's head."

"Comment?"

"Yes. It was a kind of luminous haze." She turned to her sister. "Isn't that how you would describe it, Isabel?"

"Yes. Yes, just that. A luminous haze gradually surrounding Miss Arundell's head—an aureole of faint light. It was a *sign*—we know that now—a sign that she was about to pass over to the other side."

"Remarkable," said Poirot in a suitably impressed voice. "It was dark in the room, yes?"

"Oh, yes, we always get better results in the dark, and it was quite a warm evening, so we didn't even have the fire on."

"A most interesting spirit spoke to us," said Isabel. "Fatima, her name was. She told us she had passed over in the time of the Crusades. She gave us a most beautiful message."

"She actually spoke to you?"

"No, not direct voice. She rapped it out. Love. Hope. Life. Beautiful words."

"And Miss Arundell was actually taken ill at the séance?"

"It was just after. Some sandwiches and port wine were brought in, and dear Miss Arundell said she wouldn't have any as she wasn't feeling very well. That was the beginning of her illness. Mercifully, she did not have to endure much suffering."

"She passed over four days later," said Isabel.

"And we have already had messages from her," said Julia eagerly. "Saying that she is very happy and that everything is beautiful and that she hopes that there is love and peace among all her dear ones."

Poirot coughed.

"That—er—is hardly the case, I fear."

"The relations have behaved *disgracefully* to poor Minnie," said Isabel. Her face flushed with indignation.

"Minnie is the most *unworldly* soul," chimed in Julia.

"People have gone about saying the *unkindest* things—that she *schemed* for this money to be left her!"

"When really it was the *greatest* surprise to her—"

"She could hardly believe her *ears* when the lawyer read the will—"

"She told us so herself. 'Julia,' she said to me. 'My dear, you could have knocked me over with a feather. Just a few bequests to the servants and then Littlegreen House and the residue of my estate to Wilhelmina Lawson.' She was so flabbergasted she could hardly speak. And when she could she asked how much it would be—thinking perhaps it would be a few thousand pounds—and Mr. Purvis, after humming and hawing and talking about confusing things like gross and net personalities, said it would be in the neighborhood of three hundred and seventy-five thousand pounds. Poor Minnie nearly fainted, she told us."

"She had no *idea*," the other sister reiterated. "She never thought of such a thing happening!"

"That is what she told you, yes?"

"Oh, yes, she repeated it several times. And that's what makes it so *wicked* of the Arundell family to go on as they have done—cold-shouldering her and treating her with suspicion. After all, this is a free country—"

"English people seem to labour under that misapprehension," murmured Poirot.

"And I should hope *any one* can leave their money exactly as they choose! *I* think Miss Arundell acted very *wisely*. Obviously she *mistrusted* her own relatives and I dare say she had her reasons."

"Ah?" Poirot leant forward with interest. "Indeed?"

This flattering attention encouraged Isabel to proceed.

"Yes, indeed. Mr. Charles Arundell, her nephew, is a thoroughly bad lot. That's well known! I believe he's even wanted by the police in some foreign country. Not at all a desirable character. As for his sister, well, I've not actually *spoken* to her, but she's a very queer-looking girl. Ultra modern, of course, and terribly made-up. Really, the sight of her mouth made me quite *ill*. It looked like *blood*. And I rather suspect she takes drugs—her manner was so *odd* sometimes. She's by way of being engaged to that nice young Dr. Donaldson, but I fancy even *he* looked a little disgusted sometimes. Of course, she is attractive in her way, but I hope that he will come to his senses in time and marry some nice English girl who is fond of country life and outdoor pursuits."

"And the other relations?"

"Well, there you are again. Very undesirable. Not that I've anything to say against Mrs. Tanios—she's quite a nice woman—but absolutely stupid and completely under her husband's thumb. Of course, he's really a Turk, I believe—rather dreadful for an English girl to marry a *Turk*, I think, don't you? It shows a certain lack of *fastidiousness*. Of course, Mrs. Tanios is a very good mother, though the children are singularly unattractive, poor little things."

"So altogether you think Miss Lawson was a more worthy recipient of Miss Arundell's fortune?"

Julia said serenely:

"Minnie Lawson is a thoroughly *good* woman. And so *unworldly*. It isn't as though she had ever *thought* about money. She was *never* grasping."

"Still, she has never thought of refusing to accept the legacy?"

Isabel drew back a little.

"Oh, well—one would hardly do *that*."

Poirot smiled.

"No, perhaps not. . . ."

"You see, Mr. Parrot," put in Julia, "she regards it as a *trust*—a sacred *trust*."

"And she is quite willing to do something for Mrs. Tanios or for the Tanios children," went on Isabel. "Only she doesn't want *him* to get hold of it."

"She even said she would consider making Theresa an allowance."

"And that, I think, was very generous of her—considering the off-hand way that girl has always treated her."

"Indeed, Mr. Parrot, Minnie is the most *generous* of creatures. But there now, you know her, of course!"

"Yes," said Poirot. "I know her. But I still do not know—her address."

"Of course! How stupid of me! Shall I write it down for you?"

"I can write it down."

Poirot produced the invariable notebook.

"17 Clanroyden Mansions, W.2. Not very far from Whiteleys. You'll give her our love, won't you? We haven't heard from her just lately."

Poirot rose and I followed suit.

"I have to thank you both very much," he declared, "for a most charming talk, as well as for your kindness in supplying me with my friend's address."

"I wonder they didn't give it to you at the house," exclaimed Isabel. "It must be that Ellen! Servants are so *jealous* and so *small-minded*. They used to be quite rude to Minnie sometimes."

Julia shook hands in a *grande dame* manner.

"We have enjoyed your visit," she declared graciously. "I wonder—"

She flashed a glance of inquiry at her sister.

"You would, perhaps—" Isabel flushed a little. "Would you, that is to say, stay and share our evening meal? A very simple one—some shredded, raw vegetables, brown bread and butter, fruit."

"It sounds delicious," Poirot said hastily. "But alas! my friend and I have to return to London."

With renewed handshaking and messages to be delivered to Miss Lawson, we at last made our exit.

12

Poirot Discusses the Case

"THANK GOODNESS, Poirot," I said with fervour, "you got us out of those raw carrots! What awful women!"

"*Pour nous, un bon bifteck*—with the fried potatoes—and a good bottle of wine. What should we have had to drink there, I wonder?"

"Well water, I should think," I replied with a shudder. "Or non-alcoholic cider. It was that kind of place! I bet there's no bath and no sanitation except an earth closet in the garden!"

"Strange how women enjoy living an uncomfortable life," said Poirot thoughtfully. "It is not always poverty, though they are good at making the best of straitened circumstances."

"What orders for the chauffeur now?" I asked as I negotiated the last bend of the winding lanes, and we emerged on the road to Market Basing. "On what local light do we call next? Or do we return to The George and interrogate the asthmatic waiter once more?"

"You will be glad to hear, Hastings, that we have finished with Market Basing—"

"Splendid."

"For the moment only. I shall return!"

"Still on the track of your unsuccessful murderer?"

"Exactly."

"Did you learn anything from the fandango of nonsense we've just been listening to?"

Poirot said precisely:

"There were certain points deserving of attention. The various characters in our drama begin to emerge more clearly. In some ways it resembles, does it not, a novelette of olden days. The humble companion, once despised, is raised to affluence and now plays the part of lady bountiful."

"I should imagine that such a patronage must be very galling to people who regard themselves as the rightful heirs!"

"As you say, Hastings. Yes, that is very true."

We drove on in silence for some minutes. We had passed through Market Basing and were now once more on the main road. I hummed to myself softly the tune of "Little Man, You've Had a Busy Day."

"Enjoyed yourself, Poirot?" I asked at last.

Poirot said coldly:

"I do not know quite what you mean by 'enjoyed yourself,' Hastings."

"Well," I said, "it seemed to me you've been treating yourself to a busman's holiday!"

"You do not think that I am serious?"

"Oh, you're *serious* enough. But this business seems to be of the academic kind. You're tackling it for your own mental satisfaction. What I mean is—it's not *real*."

"*Au contraire*, it is intensely real."

"I express myself badly. What I mean is, if there were a question of *helping* our old lady, of protecting her against further attack—well, there would be some excitement then. But as it is, I can't help feeling that as she is dead, why worry."

"In that case, *mon ami*, one would not investigate a murder case at all!"

"No, no, no. That's quite different. I mean, then you have a *body*. . . . Oh, dash it all!"

"Do not enrage yourself. I comprehend perfectly. You make a distinction between a *body* and a mere *decease*. Supposing, for instance, that Miss Arundell had died with sudden and alarming violence instead of respectably of a long-standing illness—then you would not remain indifferent to my efforts to discover the truth?"

"Of course I wouldn't."

"But all the same, some one did attempt to murder her?"

"Yes, but they didn't *succeed*. That makes all the difference."

"It does not intrigue you at all to know *who* attempted to kill her?"

"Well, yes, it does in a way."

"We have a very restricted circle," said Poirot musingly. "That thread—"

"The thread which you merely deduce from a nail in the skirting-board!" I interrupted. "Why, that nail may have been there for years!"

"No. The varnish was quite fresh."

"Well, I still think there might be all sorts of explanations of it."

"Give me one."

At the moment I could not think of anything sufficiently plausible. Poirot took advantage of my silence to sweep on with his discourse.

"Yes, a restricted circle. That thread could only have been stretched across the top of the stairs after every one had gone to bed. Therefore we have *only the occupants of the house to consider*. That is to say, the guilt lies between seven people. Dr. Tanios. Mrs. Tanios. Theresa Arundell. Charles Arundell. Miss Lawson. Ellen. Cook."

"Surely you can leave the servants out of it."

"They received legacies, *mon cher*. And there *might* have been other reasons—spite—a quarrel—dishonesty—one cannot be *certain*."

"It seems to me very unlikely."

"Unlikely, I agree. But one must take all possibilities into consideration."

"In that case, you must allow for eight people, not seven."

"How so?"

I felt I was about to score a point.

"You must include *Miss Arundell* herself. How do you know she may not have stretched that thread across the stairs in order to trip up some other member of the house-party?"

Poirot shrugged his shoulders.

"It is a *bêtise* you say there, my friend. If Miss Arundell laid a trap, she would be careful not to fall into it herself. It was *she* who fell down the stairs, remember."

I retired crestfallen.

Poirot went on in a thoughtful voice:

"The sequence of events is quite clear—the fall—the letter to me—the visit of the lawyer—but there is one doubtful point. Did Miss Arundell deliberately hold back the letter to me, hesitating to post it? Or did she, once having written it, assume it *was* posted?"

"That we can't possibly tell," I said.

"No. We can only *guess*. Personally, I fancy that she assumed it had been posted. She must have been surprised at getting no reply. . . ."

My thoughts had been busy in another direction.

"Do you think this spiritualistic nonsense counted at all?" I asked. "I mean, do you think, in spite of Miss Peabody's ridiculing of the suggestion, that a command was given at one of these *séances* that she should alter her will and leave her money to the Lawson woman?"

Poirot shook his head doubtfully.

"That does not seem to fit in with the general impression I have formed of Miss Arundell's character."

"The Tripp women say that Miss Lawson was completely taken aback when the will was read," I said thoughtfully.

"That is what she told them, yes," agreed Poirot.

"But you don't believe it?"

"*Mon ami*—you know my suspicious nature! I believe nothing that any one says unless it can be confirmed or corroborated."

"That's right, old boy," I said affectionately. "A thoroughly nice, trustful nature."

" 'He says,' 'she says,' 'they say.' Bah! what does that mean? Nothing at all. It may be absolute truth. It may be useful falsehood. Me, I deal only with *facts*."

"And the facts are?"

"Miss Arundell had a fall. That nobody disputes. The fall was not a natural one—it was contrived."

"The evidence for that being that Hercule Poirot says so!"

"Not at all. There is the evidence of the nail. The evidence of Miss Arundell's letter to me. The evidence of the dog having been out that night. The evidence of Miss Arundell's words about the jar and the picture and Bob's ball. All these things are *facts*."

"And the next fact, please?"

"The next fact is the answer to our usual question. Who benefits by Miss Arundell's death? Answer—Miss Lawson."

"The wicked companion! On the other hand, the others thought they were going to benefit. And at the time of the accident they *would* have benefited."

"Exactly, Hastings. That is why they all lie equally under suspicion. There is also the little fact that Miss Lawson took pains to prevent Miss Arundell learning that Bob had been out all night."

"You call that suspicious?"

"Not at all. I merely note it. It may have been natural concern for the old lady's peace of mind. That is by far the most likely explanation."

I looked at Poirot sideways. He is so confoundedly slippery.

"Miss Peabody expressed the opinion that there was 'hanky-panky' about the will," I said. "What do you suppose she meant by that?"

"It was, I think, her way of expressing various nebulous and unformulated suspicions."

"Undue influence, it seems, can be washed out," I said thoughtfully. "And it certainly looks as though Emily Arundell was much too sensible to believe in any tomfoolery like spiritualism."

"What makes you say that spiritualism is tomfoolery, Hastings?"

I stared at him in astonishment.

"My dear Poirot—those appalling women—"

He smiled.

"I quite agree with your estimate of the Misses Tripp. But the mere fact that the Misses Tripp have adopted with enthusiasm Christian Science, vegetarianism, theosophy and spiritualism does not really constitute a damning indictment of those subjects! Because a foolish woman will tell you a lot of nonsense about a fake scarab which she has bought from a rascally dealer, that does not necessarily bring discredit on the general subject of Egyptology!"

"Do you mean you *believe* in spiritualism, Poirot?"

"I have an open mind on the subject. I have never studied any of its manifestations myself, but it must be accepted that many men of science and learning have pronounced themselves satisfied that there are phenomena which cannot be accounted for by—shall we say the credulity of a Miss Tripp?"

"Then you believe in this rigmarole of an aureole of light surrounding Miss Arundell's head?"

Poirot waved a hand.

"I was speaking generally—rebuking your attitude of quite unreasoning scepticism. I may say that, having formed a certain opinion of Miss Tripp and her sister, I should examine very carefully any fact they presented for my notice. Foolish women, *mon ami*, are foolish women, whether they are talking about spiritualism or politics or the relation of the sexes or the tenets of the Buddhist faith."

"Yet you listened to what they had to say very carefully."

"That has been my task to-day—to listen. To hear what every one has got to tell me about these seven people—and mainly, of course, the five people primarily concerned. Already we know certain aspects of these people. Take Miss Lawson. From the Misses Tripp we learn she was devoted, unselfish, unworldly and altogether a beautiful character. From Miss Peabody we learn that she was credulous, stupid, without the nerve or the brains to attempt anything criminal. From Dr. Grainger we learn that she was downtrodden, that her position was precarious, and that she was a poor 'frightened, fluttering hen,' were, I think, the words he used. From our waiter we learned that Miss Lawson was 'a person,' and from Ellen that Bob, the dog, despised her! Every one, you see, saw her from a slightly different angle. That is the same with the others. Nobody's opinion of Charles Arundell's morals seems to have been high, but nevertheless they vary in their manner of speaking of him. Dr. Grainger calls him indulgently 'an irreverent young devil.' Miss Peabody says he would murder his grandmother for twopence but clearly prefers a rascal to a 'stick.' Miss Tripp hints not only that he would do a criminal action but that he has done one—or more. These sidelights are all very useful and interesting. They lead to the next thing."

"Which is?"

"To see for ourselves, my friend."

13

Theresa Arundell

ON THE FOLLOWING morning we made our way to the address given us by Dr. Donaldson.

I suggested to Poirot that a visit to the lawyer, Mr. Purvis, might be a good thing, but Poirot negatived the idea strongly.

"No, indeed, my friend. What could we say—what reason could we advance for seeking information?"

"You're usually pretty ready with reasons, Poirot! Any old lie would do, wouldn't it?"

"On the contrary, my friend, 'any old lie,' as you put it, would *not* do. Not with a lawyer. We should be—how do you say it?—thrown out with the flea upon the ear."

"Oh, well," I said. "Don't let us risk *that*!"

So, as I have said, we set out for the flat occupied by Theresa Arundell.

The flat in question was situated in a block at Chelsea overlooking the river. It was furnished expensively in the modern style, with gleaming chromium and thick rugs with geometric designs upon them.

We were kept waiting a few minutes and then a girl entered the room and looked at us inquiringly.

Theresa Arundell looked about twenty-eight or nine. She was tall and very slender, and she looked rather like an exaggerated drawing in black and white. Her hair was jet black—her face heavily made-up, dead pale. Her eyebrows, freakishly plucked, gave her an air of mocking irony. Her lips were the only spot of colour, a brilliant gash of scarlet in a white face. She also conveyed the impression—how I do not quite know, for her manner was almost wearily indifferent—of being at least twice as much alive as most people. There hung about her the restrained energy of a whiplash.

With an air of cool inquiry she looked from me to Poirot.

Wearied (I hoped) of deceit, Poirot had on this occasion sent in his own card. She was holding it now in her fingers, twirling it to and fro.

"I suppose," she said, "you're M. Poirot?"

Poirot bowed in his best manner.

"At your service, mademoiselle. You permit me to trespass for a few moments of your valuable time?"

With a faint imitation of Poirot's manner, she replied:

"Enchanted, M. Poirot. Pray sit down."

Poirot sat, rather gingerly, on a low square easy-chair. I took an upright one of webbing and chromium. Theresa sat negligently on a low stool in front of the fireplace. She offered us both cigarettes. We refused and she lighted one herself.

"You know my name perhaps, mademoiselle?"

She nodded.

"Little friend of Scotland Yard. That's right, isn't it?"

Poirot, I think, did not much relish this description. He said with some importance:

"I concern myself with problems of crime, mademoiselle."

"How frightfully thrilling," said Theresa Arundell in a bored voice. "And to think I've lost my autograph book!"

"The matter with which I concern myself is this," continued Poirot. "Yesterday I received a letter from your aunt."

Her eyes—very long, almond-shaped eyes—opened a little. She puffed smoke in a cloud.

"From my *aunt*, M. Poirot?"

"That is what I said, mademoiselle."

She murmured:

"I'm sorry if I'm spoiling sport in any way, but really, you know, there isn't any such person! All my aunts are mercifully dead. The last died two months ago."

"Miss Emily Arundell?"

"Yes, Miss Emily Arundell. You don't receive letters from corpses, do you, M. Poirot?"

"Sometimes I do, mademoiselle."

"How *macabre!*"

But there was a new note in her voice—a note suddenly alert and watchful.

"And what did my aunt say, M. Poirot?"

"That, mademoiselle, I can hardly tell you just at present. It was, you see, a somewhat"—he coughed—"delicate matter."

There was silence for a minute or two. Theresa Arundell smoked. Then she said:

"It all sounds delightfully hush-hush. But where exactly do I come in?"

"I hoped, mademoiselle, that you might consent to answer a few questions."

"Questions? What about?"

"Questions of a family nature."

Again I saw her eyes widen.

"That sounds rather pompous! Supposing you give me a specimen."

"Certainly. Can you tell me the present address of your brother Charles?"

The eyes narrowed again. Her latent energy was less apparent. It was as though she withdrew into a shell.

"I'm afraid I can't. We don't correspond much. I rather think he has left England."

"I see."

Poirot was silent for a minute or two.

"Was that all you wanted to know?"

"Oh, I have other questions. For one—are you satisfied with the way in which your aunt disposed of her fortune? For another—how long have you been engaged to Dr. Donaldson?"

"You do jump about, don't you?"

"*Eh bien?*"

"*Eh bien*—since we are so foreign!—my answer to both those questions is that they are none of your business! *Cą ne vous regarde pas, M. Hercule Poirot.*"

Poirot studied her for a moment or two attentively. Then, with no trace of disappointment, he got up.

"So it is like that! Ah, well, perhaps it is not surprising. Allow me, mademoiselle, to congratulate you upon your French accent. And to wish you a very good morning. Come, Hastings."

We had reached the door when the girl spoke. The simile of a whiplash came again into my mind. She did not move from her position, but the two words were like the flick of a whip.

"Come back!" she said.

Poirot obeyed slowly. He sat down again and looked at her inquiringly.

"Let's stop playing the fool," she said. "It's just possible that you might be useful to me, M. Hercule Poirot."

"Delighted, mademoiselle—and how?"

Between two puffs of cigarette smoke she said very quietly and evenly:

"Tell me how to break that will."

"Surely a lawyer—"

"Yes, a lawyer, perhaps—if I knew the right lawyer. But the only lawyers I know are respectable men! Their advice is that the will holds good in law and that any attempt to contest it will be useless expense."

"But you do not believe them."

"I believe there is always a way to do things—if you don't mind being unscrupulous and are prepared to pay. Well, *I am prepared to pay.*"

''And you take it for granted that I am prepared to be unscrupulous if I am paid?''

''I've found that to be true of most people! I don't see why you should be an exception. People always protest about their honesty and their rectitude to begin with, of course.''

''Just so, that is part of the game, eh? But what, given that I was prepared to be—unscrupulous—do you think I could do?''

''I don't know. But you're a clever man. Every one knows that. You could think out some scheme.''

''Such as?''

Theresa Arundell shrugged her shoulders.

''That's your business. Steal the will and substitute a forgery. . . . Kidnap the Lawson woman and frighten her into saying she bullied Aunt Emily into making it. Produce a later will made on old Emily's deathbed.''

''Your fertile imagination takes my breath away, mademoiselle!''

''Well, what is your answer? I've been frank enough. If it's righteous refusal, there's the door.''

''It is not righteous refusal—yet—'' said Poirot.

Theresa Arundell laughed. She looked at me.

''Your friend,'' she observed, ''looks shocked. Shall we send him out to chase himself round the block?''

Poirot addressed himself to me with some slight irritation.

''Control, I pray of you, your beautiful and upright nature, Hastings. I demand pardon for my friend, mademoiselle. He is, as you have perceived, honest. But he is also faithful. His loyalty to myself is absolute. In any case, let me emphasize this point—'' he looked at her very hard—''whatever we are about to do will be strictly within the law.''

She raised her eyebrows slightly.

''The law,'' said Poirot thoughtfully, ''has a lot of latitude.''

''I see.'' She smiled faintly. ''All right, we'll let that be understood. Do you want to discuss your share of the booty—if there turns out to be any booty?''

''That, also, can be understood. Some nice little pickings—that is all I ask.''

''Done,'' said Theresa.

Poirot leant forward.

''Now listen, mademoiselle, usually—in ninety-nine cases out of a hundred cases, shall we say, I am on the side of the law. The hundredth—well, the hundredth is different. For one thing, it is usually much more lucrative. . . . But it has to be done very quietly, you understand—very, very quietly. My reputation, it must not suffer. I have to be careful.''

Theresa Arundell nodded.

"And I must have *all* the facts of the case! I must have the truth! You comprehend that once one knows the truth it is an easier matter to know just what lies to tell!"

"That seems eminently reasonable."

"Very well then. Now, on what date was this will made?"

"On April 21st."

"And the previous will?"

"Aunt Emily made a will five years ago."

"Its provisions being—?"

"After a legacy to Ellen and one to a former cook, all her property was to be divided between the children of her brother Thomas and the children of her sister Arabella."

"Was this money left in trust?"

"No, it was left to us absolutely."

"Now be careful. Did you all know the provisions of this will?"

"Oh, yes. Charles and I knew—and Bella knew too. Aunt Emily made no secret of it. In fact, if any of us asked for a loan she would usually say, 'You'll have all my money when I'm dead and gone. Be content with that fact.' "

"Would she have refused a loan if there had been a case of illness or any dire necessity?"

"No, I don't think she would," said Theresa slowly.

"But she considered you all had enough to live on?"

"She considered so—yes."

There was bitterness in that voice.

"But you—did not?"

Theresa waited a minute or two before speaking. Then she said:

"My father left us thirty thousand pounds each. The interest on that, safely invested, amounts to about twelve hundred a year. Income-tax takes another wedge off it. A nice little income on which one can manage very prettily. But I—" her voice changed, her slim body straightened, her head went back—all that wonderful aliveness I had sensed in her came to the fore—"but I want something better than that out of life! I want the best! The best food, the best clothes—something with line to it—beauty—not just suitable covering in the prevailing fashion. I want to live and enjoy—to go to the Mediterranean and lie in the warm summer sea—to sit round a table and play with exciting wads of money—to give parties—wild, absurd, extravagant parties—I want everything that's going in this rotten world—and I don't want it some day—I want it now!"

Her voice was wonderfully exciting, warm, exhilarating, intoxicating.

Poirot was studying her intently.

"And you have, I fancy, had it now?"

"Yes, Hercule—I've had it!"

"And how much of the thirty thousand is left?"

She laughed suddenly.

"Two hundred and twenty-one pounds, fourteen and sevenpence. That's the exact balance. So you see, little man, you've got to be paid by results. No results—no fees."

"In that case," said Poirot in a matter-of-fact manner, "there will certainly be results."

"You're a great little man, Hercule. I'm glad we got together."

Poirot went on in a business-like way:

"There are a few things that are actually necessary that I should know. Do you drug?"

"No, never."

"Drink?"

"Quite heavily—but not for the love of it. My crowd drinks and I drink with them, but I could give it up tomorrow."

"That is very satisfactory."

She laughed.

"I shan't give the show away in my cups, Hercule."

Poirot proceeded:

"Love affairs?"

"Plenty in the past."

"And the present?"

"Only Rex."

"That is Dr. Donaldson?"

"Yes."

"He seems, somehow, very alien from the life you mention."

"Oh, he is."

"And yet you care for him. Why, I wonder?"

"Oh, what are reasons? Why did Juliet fall for Romeo?"

"Well, for one thing, with all due deference to Shakespeare, he happened to be the first man she had seen."

Theresa said slowly:

"Rex wasn't the first man I saw—not by a long way." She added in a lower voice, "But I think—I feel—he'll be the last man I'll ever see."

"And he is a poor man, mademoiselle."

She nodded.

"And he, too, needs money?"

"Desperately. Oh, not for the reasons I did. He doesn't want luxury—or beauty—or excitement—or any of these things. He'd wear the same suit until it went into holes—and eat a congealed chop every day for lunch quite happily, and wash in a cracked tin bath. If he had money it would all go on test-tubes and a laboratory and all the rest of it. He's ambitious. His profession means everything to him. It means more to him than—I do."

"He knew that you would come into money when Miss Arundell died?"

"I told him so. Oh! after we were engaged. He isn't really marrying me for my money if that is what you are getting at."

"You are still engaged?"

"Of course we are."

Poirot did not reply. His silence seemed to disquiet her.

"Of course we are," she repeated sharply. And then she added, "You—have you seen him?"

"I saw him yesterday—at Market Basing."

"Why? What did you say to him?"

"I said nothing. I only asked him for your brother's address."

"Charles?" Her voice was sharp again. "What did you want with Charles?"

"Charles? Who wants Charles?"

It was a new voice—a delightful, man's voice.

A bronze-faced young man with an agreeable grin strolled into the room.

"Who is talking about me?" he asked. "I heard my name in the hall, but I didn't eavesdrop. They were very particular about eavesdropping at Borstal. Now then, Theresa my girl, what's all this? Spill the beans."

14

Charles Arundell

I MUST CONFESS that from the moment I set eyes on him I entertained a sneaking liking for Charles Arundell. There was something so debonair and carefree about him. His eyes had an agreeable and humorous twinkle and his grin was one of the most disarming I have ever encountered.

He came across the room and sat down on the arm of one of the massive, upholstered chairs.

"What's it all about, old girl?" he asked.

"This is M. Hercule Poirot, Charles. He is prepared to—er—do some dirty work for us in return for a small consideration."

"I protest," cried Poirot. "*Not* dirty work—shall we say a little harmless deception of some kind—so that the original intention of the testator is carried out? Let us put it that way."

"Put it any way you like," said Charles agreeably. "What made Theresa think of you, I wonder?"

"She did not," said Poirot quickly. "I came here of my own accord."

"Offering your services?"

"Not quite that. I was asking for you. Your sister told me you had gone abroad."

"Theresa," said Charles, "is a very careful sister. She hardly ever makes a mistake. In fact, she's suspicious as the devil."

He smiled at her affectionately, but she did not smile back. She looked worried and thoughtful.

"Surely," said Charles. "We've got things the wrong way round? Isn't M. Poirot famous for tracking down criminals? Surely not for aiding and abetting them?"

"We're not criminals," said Theresa sharply.

"But we're quite willing to be," said Charles affably. "I'd thought of a spot of forgery myself—that's rather my line. I got sent down from Oxford because of a little misunderstanding about a cheque. That was childishly simple, though—merely a question of adding a nought. Then there was another little *fracas* with Aunt Emily and the local bank. Foolish on my part, of course. I ought to have realized the old lady was sharp as needles. However, all these incidents have been very small fry—fivers or tenners—that class. A deathbed will would be admittedly risky. One would have to get hold of the stiff and starched Ellen and—is suborn the word?—anyway, induce her to say she had witnessed it. It would take some doing, I fear. I might even marry her and then she wouldn't be able to give evidence against me afterwards."

He grinned amiably at Poirot.

"I feel sure you've installed a secret dictaphone and Scotland Yard is listening in," he said.

"Your problem interests me," said Poirot with a touch of reproof in his manner. "Naturally I could not connive at anything against the law. But there are more ways than one—" He stopped significantly.

Charles Arundell shrugged his graceful shoulders.

"I've no doubt there's an equal choice of devious ways inside the law," he said agreeably. "You should know."

"By whom was the will witnessed? I mean the one made on April 21st?"

"Purvis brought down his clerk and the second witness was the gardener."

"It was signed then in Mr. Purvis's presence?"

"It was."

"And Mr. Purvis, I fancy, is a man of the highest respectability?"

"Purvis, Purvis, Charlesworth and once more Purvis are just about as respectable and impeccable as the Bank of England," said Charles.

"He didn't like making the will," said Theresa. "In an ultra-correct fashion I believe he even tried to dissuade Aunt Emily from making it."

Charles said sharply:

"Did he tell you that, Theresa?"

"Yes. I went to see him again yesterday."

"It's no good, my sweet—you ought to realize that. Only piles up the six and eightpences."

Theresa shrugged her shoulders.

Poirot said:

"I will ask of you to give me as much information as you can about the last weeks of Miss Arundell's life. Now, to begin with, I understand that you and your brother and also Dr. Tanios and his wife stayed there for Easter?"

"Yes, we did."

"Did anything happen of significance during that weekend?"

"I don't think so."

"Nothing? But I thought—"

Charles broke in.

"What a self-centred creature you are, Theresa. Nothing of significance happened to *you*! Wrapped in love's young dream! Let me tell you, M. Poirot, that Theresa has a blue-eyed boy in Market Basing. One of the local sawbones. She's got rather a faulty sense of proportion in consequence. As a matter of fact, my revered aunt took a header down the stairs and nearly passed out. Wish she had. It would have saved all this fuss."

"She fell down the stairs?"

"Yes, tripped over the dog's ball. Intelligent little brute left it at the top of the stairs and she took a header over it in the night."

"This was—when?"

"Let me see—Tuesday—the evening before we left."

"Your aunt was seriously injured?"

"Unfortunately she didn't fall on her head. If she had we might have pleaded softening of the brain—or whatever it's called scientifically. No, she was hardly hurt at all."

Poirot said drily:

"Very disappointing for you!"

"Eh? Oh, I see what you mean. Yes, as you say, very disappointing. Tough nuts, these old ladies."

"And you all left on the Wednesday morning?"

"That's right."

"That was Wednesday, the fifteenth. When did you next see your aunt?"

"Well, it wasn't the next week-end. It was the week-end after that."

"That would be—let me see—the twenty-fifth, would it not?"

"Yes, I think that was the date."

"And your aunt died—when?"

"The following Friday."

"Having been taken ill on the Monday night?"

"Yes."

"That was the Monday that you left?"

"Yes."

"You did not return during her illness?"

"Not until the Friday. We didn't realize she was really bad."

"You got there in time to see her alive?"

"No, she died before we arrived."

Poirot shifted his glance to Theresa Arundell.

"You accompanied your brother on both these occasions?"

"Yes."

"And nothing was said during that second week-end about a new will having been made?"

"Nothing," said Theresa.

Charles, however, had answered at the same moment.

"Oh, yes," he said. "It was."

He spoke airily as ever, but there was something a little constrained, as though the airiness were more artificial than usual.

"It *was*?" said Poirot.

"Charles!" cried Theresa.

Charles seemed anxious not to meet his sister's eye.

He spoke to her without looking at her.

"Surely you remember, old girl? I told you. Aunt Emily made a kind of ultimatum of it. Sat there like a judge in court. Made a kind of speech. Said she thoroughly disapproved of all her relations—that is to say, of me and Theresa. Bella, she allowed, she had nothing against, but on the other hand she disliked and distrusted her husband. Buy British was ever Aunt Emily's motto. If Bella were to inherit any considerable sum of money she said she was convinced that Tanios would somehow or other get possession of it. Trust a Greek to do that! 'She's safer as she is,' she went on to say. Then she said that neither I nor Theresa were fit people to be trusted with money. We would only gamble and squander it away. Therefore, she finished up, she had made a new will and had left the entire estate to Miss Lawson. 'She is a fool,' said Aunt Emily, 'but she is a faithful soul. And I really believe she is devoted to me. She cannot help her lack of brains. I have thought it fairer to tell you this, Charles, as you may as well realize that it will not be possible for you to raise money on your expectations from me.' Rather a nasty one, that. Just what I'd been trying to do."

"Why didn't you tell me, Charles?" demanded Theresa fiercely.

"Thought I did." Charles avoided her eye.

Poirot asked:

"And what did you say, Mr. Arundell?"

"I?" said Charles airily. "Oh, I just laughed. No good cutting up rough. That's not the way. 'Just as you please, Aunt Emily,' I said. 'Bit of a blow, perhaps, but after all, it's your own money and you can do what you like with it.' "

"And your aunt's reaction to that?"

"Oh, it went down well—very well, indeed. She said, 'Well, I will say you're a sportsman, Charles.' And I said, 'Got to take the rough with the smooth. As a matter of fact, if I've no expectations, what about giving me a tenner now?' And she said I was an impudent boy and actually parted with a fiver."

"You concealed your feelings very cleverly."

"Well, as a matter of fact, I didn't take it very seriously."

"You didn't?"

"No. I thought it was what you might call a gesture on the old bean's part. She wanted to frighten us all. I'd a pretty shrewd suspicion that after a few weeks or perhaps months she'd tear that will up. She was pretty hot on family, Aunt Emily. And, as a matter of fact, I believe that's what she *would* have done if she hadn't died so confoundedly suddenly."

"Ah!" said Poirot. "It is an interesting idea that."

He remained silent for a minute or two, then went on:

"Could any one, Miss Lawson, for instance, have overheard your conversation?"

"Rather. We weren't speaking any too low. As a matter of fact, the Lawson bird was hovering about outside the door when I went out. Been doing a bit of snooping in my opinion."

Poirot turned a thoughtful glance on Theresa.

"And you knew nothing of this?"

Before she could answer, Charles broke in:

"Theresa, old girl, I'm sure I told you—or hinted to you."

There was a queer sort of pause. Charles was looking fixedly at Theresa, and there was an anxiety, a fixity, about his gaze that seemed out of all proportion to the subject matter.

Theresa said slowly:

"If you had told me—I don't think I could have forgotten, do you, M. Poirot?"

Her long, dark eyes turned to him.

Poirot said slowly:

"No, I don't think you could have forgotten, Miss Arundell."

Then he turned sharply to Charles.

"Let me be quite clear on one point. Did Miss Arundell tell you she was about to alter her will, or did she tell you specifically that she *had* altered it?"

Charles said quickly:

"Oh, she was quite definite. As a matter of fact, she showed me the will."

Poirot leaned forward. His eyes opened wide.

"This is very important. You say that Miss Arundell actually showed you the will?"

Charles gave a sudden schoolboy wriggle—a rather disarming action. Poirot's gravity made him quite uncomfortable.

"Yes," he said. "She showed it to me."

"You can swear definitely to that?"

"Of course I can." Charles looked nervously at Poirot. "I don't see what is so significant about that."

There was a sudden brusque movement from Theresa. She had risen and was standing by the mantelpiece. She quickly lit another cigarette.

"And you, mademoiselle?" Poirot whirled suddenly round on her. "Did your aunt say nothing of importance to you during that week-end?"

"I don't think so. She was—quite amiable. That is, as amiable as she usually was. Lectured me a bit about my way of life and all that. But then, she always did. She seemed perhaps a bit more jumpy than usual."

Poirot said, smiling:

"I suppose, mademoiselle, that you were more taken up with your fiancé?"

Theresa said sharply:

"He wasn't there. He was away, he'd gone to some medical congress."

"You had not seen him then since the Easter week-end? Was that the last time you had seen him?"

"Yes—on the evening before we left he came to dinner."

"You had not—excuse me—had any quarrel with him then?"

"Certainly not."

"I only thought, seeing that he was away on your second visit—"

Charles broke in:

"Ah, but you see, that second week-end was rather unpremeditated. We went down on the spur of the moment."

"Really?"

"Oh, let's have the truth," said Theresa wearily. "You see, Bella and her husband were down the week-end before—fussing over Aunt Emily because of her accident. We thought they might steal a march on us—"

"We thought," said Charles with a grin, "that we'd better show a little concern for Aunt Emily's health too. Really, though, the old lady was much too sharp to be taken in by the dutiful attention stunt. She knew very well how much it was worth. No fool, Aunt Emily."

Theresa laughed suddenly.

"It's a pretty story, isn't it? All of us with our tongues hanging out for money."

"Was that the case with your cousin and her husband?"

"Oh, yes, Bella's always hard up. Rather pathetic the way she tries to copy all my clothes at about an eighth of the price. Tanios speculated with her money, I believe. They're hard put to it to make both ends meet. They've got two children and want to educate them in England."

"Can you perhaps give me their address?" said Poirot.

"They're staying at the Durham Hotel in Bloomsbury."

"What is she like, your cousin?"

"Bella? Well, she's a dreary woman. Eh, Charles?"

"Oh, definitely a dreary woman. Rather like an earwig. She's a devoted mother. So are earwigs, I believe."

"And her husband?"

"Tanios? Well, he looks a bit odd, but he's really a thoroughly nice fellow. Clever, amusing and a thoroughly good sport."

"You agree, mademoiselle?"

"Well, I must admit I prefer him to Bella. He's a damned clever doctor, I believe. All the same, I wouldn't trust him very far."

"Theresa," said Charles, "doesn't trust anybody."

He put an arm round her.

"She doesn't trust me."

"Any one who trusted you, my sweet, would be mentally deficient," said Theresa kindly.

The brother and sister moved apart and looked at Poirot.

Poirot bowed and moved to the door.

"I am—as you say—on the job! It is difficult, but Mademoiselle is right. There is always a way. Ah, by the way, this Miss Lawson, is she the kind that might conceivably lose her head under cross-examination in court?"

Charles and Theresa exchanged glances.

"I should say," said Charles, "that a really bullying K.C. could make her say black was white!"

"That," said Poirot, "may be very useful."

He skipped out of the room and I followed him. In the hall he picked up his hat, moved to the front door, opened it and shut it again quickly with a bang. Then he tiptoed to the door of the sitting-room and unblushingly applied his ear to the crack. At whatever school Poirot was educated, there were clearly no unwritten rules about eavesdropping. I was horrified but powerless. I made urgent signs to Poirot, but he took no notice.

And then, clearly, in Theresa Arundell's deep, vibrant voice, there came two words:

"You fool!"

There was the noise of footsteps along the passage and Poirot quickly seized me by the arm, opened the front door and passed through, closing it noiselessly behind him.

15

Miss Lawson

"POIROT," I SAID. "Have we *got* to listen at doors?"

"Calm yourself, my friend. It was only I who listened! It was not you who put your ear to the crack. On the contrary, you stood bolt upright like a soldier."

"But I heard just the same."

"True. Mademoiselle was hardly whispering."

"Because she thought that we had left the flat."

"Yes, we practised a little deception there."

"I don't like that sort of thing."

"Your moral attitude is irreproachable! But let us not repeat ourselves. This conversation has occurred on previous occasions. You are about to say that it is not playing the game. And my reply is that murder is not a game."

"But there is no question of murder here."

"Do not be sure of that."

"The *intention*, yes, perhaps. But after all, murder and *attempted* murder are not the same thing."

"Morally they are exactly the same thing. But what I meant was, are you so sure that it is only *attempted* murder that occupies our attention?"

I stared at him.

"But old Miss Arundell died a perfectly natural death."

"I repeat again—*are you so sure*?"

"Every one says so!"

"Every one? Oh, *là là*!"

"The doctor says so," I pointed out. "Dr. Grainger. He ought to know."

"Yes, he ought to know." Poirot's voice was dissatisfied. "But remember, Hastings, again and again a body is exhumed—and in each case a certificate has been signed in all good faith by the doctor attending the case."

"Yes, but in this case, Miss Arundell died of a longstanding complaint."

"It seems so—yes."

Poirot's voice was still dissatisfied. I looked at him keenly.

"Poirot," I said, "I'll begin a sentence with 'Are you sure!' Are you sure *you* are not being carried away by professional zeal? You *want* it to be murder and so you think it *must* be murder."

The shadow on his brow deepened. He nodded his head slowly.

"It is clever what you say there, Hastings. It is a weak spot on which you put your finger. Murder is my business. I am like a great surgeon who specializes in—say—appendicitis or some rarer operation. A patient comes to him and he regards that patient solely from the standpoint of his own specialized subject. Is there any possible reason for thinking this man suffers from so and so . . . ? Me, I am like that, too. I say to myself always, 'Can this possibly be murder?' And you see, my friend, there is nearly always a possibility."

"I shouldn't say there was much possibility here," I remarked.

"But she died, Hastings! You cannot get away from that fact. She *died*!"

"She was in poor health. She was past seventy. It all seems perfectly natural to me."

"And does it also seem natural to you that Theresa Arundell should call her brother a fool with that degree of intensity?"

"What has that got to do with it?"

"Everything! Tell me, what did you think of that statement of Mr. Charles Arundell's—that his aunt had shown him her new will?"

I looked at Poirot warily.

"What do *you* make of it?" I asked.

Why should Poirot always be the one to ask the questions.

"I call it very interesting—very interesting indeed. So was Miss Theresa

Arundell's reaction to it. Their passage of arms was suggestive—very suggestive."

"H'm," I said in oracular fashion.

"It opens up two distinct lines of inquiry."

"They seem a nice pair of crooks," I remarked. "Ready for anything. The girl's amazingly good-looking. As for young Charles, he's certainly an attractive scoundrel."

Poirot was just hailing a taxi. It drew into the curb and Poirot gave an address to the driver.

"17 Clanroyden Mansions, Bayswater."

"So it's Lawson next," I commented. "And after that—the Tanioses?"

"Quite right, Hastings."

"What rôle are you adopting here?" I inquired as the taxi drew up at Clanroyden Mansions. "The biographer of General Arundell, a prospective tenant of Littlegreen House, or something more subtle still?"

"I shall present myself simply as Hercule Poirot."

"How very disappointing," I gibed.

Poirot merely threw me a glance and paid off the taxi.

No. 17 was on the second floor. A pert-looking maid opened the door and showed us into a room that really struck a ludicrous note after the one we had just left.

Theresa Arundell's flat had been bare to the point of emptiness. Miss Lawson's on the other hand was so crammed with furniture and odds and ends that one could hardly move about without the fear of knocking something over.

The door opened and a rather stout, middle-aged lady came in. Miss Lawson was very much as I had pictured her. She had an eager, rather foolish face, untidy greyish hair and pince-nez perched a little askew on her nose. Her style of conversation was spasmodic and consisted of gasps.

"Good-morning—er—I don't think—"

"Miss Wilhelmina Lawson?"

"Yes—yes—that *is* my name. . . ."

"My name is Poirot—Hercule Poirot. Yesterday I was looking over Littlegreen House."

"Oh, yes?"

Miss Lawson's mouth fell a little wider open and she made some inefficient dabs at her untidy hair.

"Won't you sit down?" She went on. "Sit here, won't you? Oh, dear, I'm afraid that table is in your way. I'm just a little bit crowded here. So difficult! These flats! Just a teeny bit on the small side. But *so* central! And I do like being central. Don't you?"

With a gasp she sat down on an uncomfortable-looking Victorian chair and, her pince-nez still awry, leaned forward breathlessly and looked at Poirot hopefully.

"I went to Littlegreen House in the guise of a purchaser," went on Poirot. "But I should like to say at once—this is in the strictest confidence—"

"Oh, yes," breathed Miss Lawson, apparently pleasurably excited.

"The very strictest confidence," continued Poirot, "that I went there with another object. . . . You may or you may not be aware that shortly before she died Miss Arundell wrote to me—"

He paused and then went on.

"I am a well-known private detective."

A variety of expressions chased themselves over Miss Lawson's slightly flushed countenance. I wondered which one Poirot would single out as relevant to his inquiry. Alarm, excitement, surprise, puzzlement. . . .

"Oh," she said. Then after a pause, "Oh," again.

And then, quite unexpectedly, she asked:

"Was it about the money?"

Poirot, even, was slightly taken aback. He said tentatively:

"You mean the money that was—"

"Yes, yes. The money that was taken from the drawer?"

Poirot said quietly:

"Miss Arundell didn't tell you she had written to me on the subject of that money?"

"No, indeed. I had no idea—Well, really, I must say I'm very surprised—"

"You thought she should not have mentioned it to any one?"

"I certainly didn't think so. You see, she had a very good idea—"

She stopped again. Poirot said quickly:

"She had a very good idea who took it. That is what you would say, is it not?"

Miss Lawson nodded and continued breathlessly:

"And I shouldn't have thought she would have wanted—well, I mean she said—that is, she seemed to feel—"

Again Poirot cut in neatly into the midst of these incoherencies.

"It was a family matter?"

"Exactly."

"But me," said Poirot, "I specialize in family matters. I am, you see, very, very discreet."

Miss Lawson nodded vigorously.

"Oh! of course—that makes a difference. It's not like the *police*."

"No, no. I am not at all like the police. That would not have done at all."

"Oh, no. Dear Miss Arundell was such a *proud* woman. Of course, there had been trouble before with Charles, but it was always hushed up. Once, I believe, he had to go to Australia!"

"Just so," said Poirot. "Now the facts of the case were as follows, were they not? Miss Arundell had a sum of money in a drawer—"

He paused. Miss Lawson hastened to confirm his statement.

"Yes—from the Bank. For the wages, you know, and the books."

"And how much was missing exactly?"

"Four pound notes. No, no, I am wrong, three pound notes and two ten shilling notes. One must be exact, I know, very exact, in such matters." Miss Lawson looked at him earnestly and absent-mindedly knocked her pince-nez a little further awry. Her rather prominent eyes seemed to goggle at him.

"Thank you, Miss Lawson. I see you have an excellent business sense."

Miss Lawson bridled a little and uttered a deprecatory laugh.

"Miss Arundell suspected, no doubt with reason, that her nephew Charles was responsible for this theft," went on Poirot.

"Yes."

"Although there was no particular evidence to show who actually took the money?"

"Oh, but it must have been Charles! Mrs. Tanios wouldn't do such a thing, and her husband was quite a stranger and wouldn't have known where the money was kept—neither of them would. And I don't think Theresa Arundell would dream of such a thing. She's got plenty of money and always so beautifully dressed."

"It might have been one of the servants," Poirot suggested.

Miss Lawson seemed horrified by the idea.

"Oh, no, indeed, neither Ellen nor Annie would have *dreamed* of such a thing. They are both *most* superior women and *absolutely honest* I am sure."

Poirot waited a minute or two. Then he said:

"I wonder if you can give me any idea—I am sure you can, for if any one possessed Miss Arundell's confidence you did—"

Miss Lawson murmured confusedly:

"Oh, I don't know about that, I'm sure—" But she was clearly flattered.

"I feel that you will be able to help me."

"Oh, I'm sure, if I can—anything I can do—"

Poirot went on:

"This is in confidence—"

A sort of owlish expression appeared on Miss Lawson's face. The magical words "in confidence" seemed to be a kind of open sesame.

"Have you any idea of the reason which caused Miss Arundell to alter her will?"

"Her will? Oh—her will?"

Miss Lawson seemed slightly taken aback.

Poirot said, watching her closely:

"It is true, is it not, that she made a new will shortly before her death, leaving all her fortune to you?"

"Yes, but I knew nothing about it. Nothing at all!" Miss Lawson was shrill in protest. "It was the *greatest* surprise to me! A *wonderful* surprise, of course! So *good* of dear Miss Arundell. And she never even gave me a *hint*. Not the smallest hint! I was so taken aback, when Mr. Purvis read it out, I didn't know where to look, or whether to laugh or cry! I assure you, M. Poirot, the *shock* of it—the *shock*, you know. The *kindness*—the wonderful kindness of dear Miss Arundell. Of course, I'd hoped, perhaps, for just a little something—perhaps just a teeny, teeny legacy—though of course, there was no *reason* she should have left me even that. I'd not been with her so very long. But this—it was like—it was like a fairy story! Even now I can't quite believe in it, if you know what I mean. And sometimes—well, sometimes—I don't feel altogether comfortable about it. I mean—well, I mean—"

She knocked off her pince-nez, picked them up, fumbled with them and went on even more incoherently:

"Sometimes I feel that—well, flesh and blood is flesh and blood after all, and I don't feel quite comfortable at Miss Arundell's leaving all her money away from her family. I mean, it doesn't seem *right*, does it? Not *all* of it. Such a *large* fortune, too! Nobody had any *idea*! But—well—it does make one feel uncomfortable—and every one saying things, you know—and I'm sure I've never been an *ill-natured* woman! I mean I wouldn't have dreamed of influencing Miss Arundell in any way! And it's not as though I could, either. Truth to tell, I was always just a teeny weeny bit afraid of her! She was so *sharp*, you know, so inclined to *jump* on you. And quite rude sometimes! 'Don't be a downright fool,' she'd snap. And really, after all, I had my feelings and sometimes I'd feel quite upset. . . . And then to find out that all the time she'd really been fond of me—well, it was very wonderful, wasn't it? Only of course, as I say, there's been a lot of *unkindness*, and really in some ways one feels—I mean, well, it does seem a little *hard*, doesn't it, on some people?"

"You mean that you would prefer to relinquish the money?" asked Poirot.

Just for a moment I fancied a flicker of some quite different expression showed itself in Miss Lawson's dull, pale blue eyes. I imagined that, just for a moment, a shrewd, intelligent woman sat there instead of an amiable, foolish one.

She said with a little laugh:

"Well—of course, there is the other side of it too . . . I mean there are two sides to every question. What I say is, Miss Arundell meant me to have the money. I mean if I didn't take it I should be going against her *wishes*. And that wouldn't be right either, would it?"

"It is a difficult question," said Poirot, shaking his head.

"Yes, indeed, I have worried over it a great deal. Mrs. Tanios—Bella—she is such a nice woman—and those dear little children! I mean, I feel sure Miss Arundell wouldn't have wanted her to—I feel, you see, that dear Miss Arundell intended me to use my *discretion*. She didn't want to leave any money *outright* to Bella because she was afraid that man would get hold of it."

"What man?"

"Her husband. You know, Mr. Poirot, the poor girl is *quite* under his thumb. She does *anything* he tells her. I dare say she'd *murder* some one if he told her to! And she's afraid of him. I'm quite sure she's afraid of him. I've seen her look simply *terrified* once or twice. Now that isn't right, Mr. Poirot—you can't say that's right."

Poirot did not say so. Instead he inquired:

"What sort of man is Dr. Tanios?"

"Well," said Miss Lawson hesitatingly, "he's a very pleasant man."

She stopped doubtfully.

"But you don't trust him?"

"Well—no, I don't. I don't know," went on Miss Lawson doubtfully, "that I'd trust *any* man very much! Such *dreadful* things one hears! And all their *poor* wives go through! It's really terrible! Of course, Dr. Tanios pretends to be very fond of his wife and he's quite charming to her. His manners are really *delightful*. But I don't trust foreigners. They're so *artful*! And I'm quite sure dear Miss Arundell didn't want her money to get into *his* hands!"

"It is hard on Miss Theresa Arundell and Mr. Charles Arundell also to be deprived of their inheritance," Poirot suggested.

A spot of colour came into Miss Lawson's face.

"I think Theresa has quite as much money as is good for her!" she said sharply. "She spends hundreds of pounds on her clothes alone. And her underclothing—it's wicked! When one thinks of so many nice, well-bred girls who have to earn their own living—"

Poirot gently completed the sentence.

"You think it would do no harm for her to earn hers for a bit?"

Miss Lawson looked at him solemnly.

"It might do her a lot of *good*," she said. "It might bring her to her senses. Adversity teaches us many things."

Poirot nodded slowly. He was watching her intently.

"And Charles?"

"Charles doesn't deserve a penny," said Miss Lawson sharply. "If Miss Arundell cut him out of her will, it was for a very good cause—after his wicked threats."

"Threats?" Poirot's eyebrows rose.

"Yes, threats."

"What threats? When did he threaten her?"

"Let me see, it was—yes, of course, it was at Easter. Actually on *Easter Sunday*—which made it even worse!"

"What did he say?"

"He asked her for money and she'd refused to give it him! And then he told her that it wasn't wise of her. He said if she kept up that attitude he would—now what was the phrase—a very vulgar American one—oh, yes, he said he would bump her off!"

"He threatened to bump her off?"

"Yes."

"And what did Miss Arundell say?"

"She said: 'I think you'll find, Charles, that I can look after myself.' "

"You were in the room at the time?"

"Not exactly in the room," said Miss Lawson after a momentary pause.

"Quite, quite," said Poirot hastily. "And Charles, what did he say to that?"

"He said: 'Don't be too sure.' "

Poirot said slowly:

"Did Miss Arundell take this threat seriously?"

"Well, I don't know. . . . She didn't say anything to me about it. . . . But then she wouldn't do that, anyway."

Poirot said quietly:

"You knew, of course, that Miss Arundell was making a new will?"

"No, no. I've told you, it was a complete surprise. I never dreamt—"

Poirot interrupted.

"You did not know the *contents*. But you knew the *fact*—that there *was* a will being made?"

"Well—I suspected—I mean her sending for the lawyer when she was laid up—"

"Exactly. That was after she had a fall, was it not?"

"Yes, Bob—Bob was the dog—he had left his ball at the top of the stairs—and she tripped over it and fell."

"A nasty accident."

"Oh, yes; why, she might easily have broken her leg or her arm. The doctor said so."

"She might quite easily have been killed."

"Yes, indeed."

Her answer seemed quite natural and frank.

Poirot said, smiling:

"I think I saw Master Bob at Littlegreen House."

"Oh, yes, I expect you did. He's a dear little doggie."

Nothing annoys me more than to hear a sporting terrier called a dear little doggie. No wonder, I thought, that Bob despised Miss Lawson and refused to do anything she told him.

"And he is very intelligent?" went on Poirot.

"Oh, yes, very."

"How upset he'd be if he knew he had nearly killed his mistress."

Miss Lawson did not answer. She merely shook her head and sighed.

Poirot asked:

"Do you think it possible that that fall influenced Miss Arundell to remake her will?"

We were getting perilously near the bone here, I thought, but Miss Lawson seemed to find the question quite natural.

"You know," she said, "I shouldn't wonder if you weren't right. It gave her a *shock*—I'm sure of that. Old people never like to think there's any chance of their dying. But an accident like that makes one *think*. Or perhaps she might have had a *premonition* that her death wasn't far off."

Poirot said casually:

"She was in fairly good health, was she not?"

"Oh, yes. Very well, indeed."

"Her illness must have come on very suddenly?"

"Oh, it did. It was quite a shock. We had had some friends that evening—" Miss Lawson paused.

"Your friends, the Misses Tripp. I have met those ladies. They are quite charming."

Miss Lawson's face flushed with pleasure.

"Yes, aren't they? Such *cultured* women! Such wide interests! And so very *spiritual*! They told you, perhaps—about our sittings? I expect you are a sceptic—but indeed, I wish I could tell you the inexpressible joy of getting into touch with those who passed over!"

"I am sure of it. I am sure of it."

"Do you know, M. Poirot, my mother has spoken to me—more than once. It is such a joy to know that one's dear ones are still thinking of one and watching over one."

"Yes, yes, I can well understand that," said Poirot gently. "And was Miss Arundell also a believer?"

Miss Lawson's face clouded over a little.

"She was willing to be convinced," she said doubtfully. "But I do not think she always approached the matter in the right frame of mind. She was sceptical and unbelieving—and once or twice her attitude attracted a most *undesirable* type of spirit! There were some very ribald messages—all due, I am *convinced*, to Miss Arundell's attitude."

"I should think very likely due to Miss Arundell," agreed Poirot.

"But on that last evening—" continued Miss Lawson, "perhaps Isabel and Julia told you?—there were distinct phenomena. Actually the beginning of a materialization. Ectoplasm—you know what ectoplasm is, perhaps?"

"Yes, yes, I am acquainted with its nature."

"It proceeds, you know, from the medium's mouth in the form of a *ribbon* and builds itself up into a *form*. Now I am *convinced*, Mr. Poirot, that *unknown to herself* Miss Arundell was a *medium*. On that evening I distinctly saw a *luminous ribbon* issuing from dear Miss Arundell's mouth! Then her head became enveloped in a luminous mist."

"Most interesting!"

"And then, unfortunately, Miss Arundell was suddenly taken ill and we had to break up the *séance*."

"You sent for the doctor—when?"

"First thing the following morning."

"Did he think the matter grave?"

"Well, he sent in a hospital nurse the following evening but I think he hoped she would pull through."

"The—excuse me—the relatives were not sent for?"

Miss Lawson flushed.

"They were notified as soon as possible—that is to say, when Dr. Grainger pronounced her to be in danger."

"What was the cause of the attack? Something she had eaten?"

"No, I don't think there was anything in particular. Dr. Grainger said she hadn't been quite as careful in diet as she should have been. I think he thought the attack was probably brought on by a chill. The weather had been very treacherous."

"Theresa and Charles Arundell had been down that week-end, had they not?"

Miss Lawson pursed her lips together.

"They had."

"The visit was not a success," Poirot suggested, watching her.

"It was not." She added quite spitefully: "Miss Arundell knew what they'd come for!"

"Which was?" asked Poirot, watching her.

"Money!" snapped Miss Lawson. "And they didn't get it."

"No?" said Poirot.

"And I believe that's what Dr. Tanios was after too," she went on.

"Dr. Tanios. He was not down that same week-end, was he?"

"Yes, he came down on the Sunday. He only stayed about an hour."

"Every one seems to have been after poor Miss Arundell's money," hazarded Poirot.

"I know, it is not very nice to think of, is it?"

"No, indeed," said Poirot. "It must have been a shock to Charles and Theresa Arundell that week-end when they learned that Miss Arundell had definitely disinherited them!"

Miss Lawson stared at him.

Poirot said:

"Is that not so? Did she not specifically inform them of the fact?"

"As to that, I couldn't say. *I* didn't hear anything about it! There wasn't any *fuss*, or anything, as far as I know. Both Charles and his sister seemed to go away *quite* cheerful."

"Ah! possibly I have been misinformed. Miss Arundell actually kept her will in the house, did she not?"

Miss Lawson dropped her pince-nez and stooped to pick them up.

"I really couldn't say. No, I think it was with Mr. Purvis."

"Who was the executor?"

"Mr. Purvis was."

"After the death, did he come over and look through her papers?"

"Yes, he did."

Poirot looked at her keenly and asked her an unexpected question.

"Do you like Mr. Purvis?"

Miss Lawson was flustered.

"Like Mr. Purvis? Well, really, that's difficult to say, isn't it? I mean, I'm sure he's a very *clever* man—that is, a clever lawyer, I mean. But rather a brusque *manner*! I mean, it's not very pleasant always to have some one speaking to you as though—well, really, I can't explain what I mean—he was quite civil and yet at the same time almost *rude*, if you know what I mean."

"A difficult situation for you," said Poirot sympathetically.

"Yes, indeed, it was."

Miss Lawson sighed and shook her head.

Poirot rose to his feet.

"Thank you very much, mademoiselle, for all your kindness and help."

Miss Lawson rose too. She sounded slightly flustered.

"I'm sure there's nothing to thank *me* for—nothing at all! So glad if I've been able to do anything—if there's anything more I *can* do—"

Poirot came back from the door. He lowered his voice.

"I think, Miss Lawson, that there is something you ought to be told. Charles and Theresa Arundell are hoping to upset this will."

A sharp flush of colour came into Miss Lawson's cheek.

"They can't do that," she said sharply. "My lawyer says so."

"Ah," said Poirot. "You have consulted a lawyer, then?"

"Certainly. Why shouldn't I?"

"No reason at all. A very wise proceeding. Good-day to you, mademoiselle."

When we emerged from Clanroyden Mansions into the street Poirot drew a deep breath.

"Hastings, *mon ami*, that woman is either exactly what she seems or else she is a very good actress."

"She doesn't believe Miss Arundell's death was anything but natural. You can see that," I said.

Poirot did not answer. There are moments when he is conveniently deaf. He hailed a taxi.

"Durham Hotel, Bloomsbury," he told the driver.

16

Mrs. Tanios

"GENTLEMAN to see you, madam."

The woman who was sitting writing at one of the tables in the writing-room of the Durham Hotel turned her head and then rose coming towards us uncertainly.

Mrs. Tanios might have been any age over thirty. She was a tall, thin woman with dark hair, rather prominent light "boiled gooseberry" eyes and a worried face. A fashionable hat was perched on her head at an unfashionable angle and she wore a rather depressed-looking cotton frock.

"I don't think—" she began vaguely.

Poirot bowed.

"I have just come from your cousin, Miss Theresa Arundell."

"Oh! from Theresa? Yes?"

"Perhaps I could have a few minutes' private conversation?"

Mrs. Tanios looked about her rather vacantly. Poirot suggested a leather sofa at the far end of the room.

As we made our way there a high voice squeaked out.

"Mother, where are you going?"

"I shall be just over here. Go on with your letter, darling."

The child, a thin, peaky-looking girl of about seven, settled down again to what was evidently a laborious task. Her tongue showed through her parted lips in the effort of composition.

The far end of the room was quite deserted. Mrs. Tanios sat down; we did the same. She looked inquiringly at Poirot.

He began:

"It is in reference to the death of your aunt, the late Miss Emily Arundell."

Was I beginning to fancy things, or did a look of alarm spring up suddenly in those pale, prominent eyes.

"Yes?"

"Miss Arundell," said Poirot, "altered her will a very short time before she died. By the new will everything was left to Miss Wilhelmina Lawson. What I want to know, Mrs. Tanios, is whether you will join with your cousins, Miss Theresa and Mr. Charles Arundell, in trying to contest that will?"

"Oh!" Mrs. Tanios drew a deep breath. "But I don't think that's possible, is it? I mean, my husband consulted a lawyer and he seemed to think that it was better not to attempt it."

"Lawyers, madame, are cautious people. Their advice is usually to avoid litigation at all costs—and no doubt they are usually right. But there are times when it pays to take a risk. I am not a lawyer myself and therefore I look at the matter rather differently. Miss Arundell—Miss Theresa Arundell, I mean—is prepared to fight. What about you?"

"I—Oh! I really don't know." She twisted her fingers nervously together. "I should have to consult my husband."

"Certainly, you must consult your husband before anything definite is undertaken. But what are your *own* feelings in the matter?"

"Well, really, I don't know." Mrs. Tanios looked more worried than ever. "It depends so much on my husband."

"But your *yourself*, what do you think, madame?"

Mrs. Tanios frowned, then she said slowly:

"I don't think I like the idea very much. It seems—it seems rather indecent, doesn't it?"

"Does it, madame?"

"Yes—after all, if Aunt Emily chose to leave her money away from her family, I suppose we must put up with it."

"You do not feel aggrieved in the matter, then?"

"Oh, yes, I do." A quick flush showed in her cheeks. "I think it was most unfair! *Most* unfair! And so unexpected. It was so unlike Aunt Emily. And so very unfair on the children."

"You think it is very unlike Miss Emily Arundell?"

"I think it was extraordinary of her!"

"Then isn't it possible that she was not acting of her own free will? Don't you think that perhaps she was being unduly influenced?"

Mrs. Tanios frowned again. Then she said almost unwillingly:

"The difficult thing is that I can't see Aunt Emily being influenced by *anybody*! She was such a decided old lady."

Poirot nodded approvingly.

"Yes, what you say is true. And Miss Lawson is hardly what one would describe as a strong character."

"No, she's a nice creature, really—rather foolish, perhaps—but very, very kind. That's partly why I feel—"

"Yes, madame?" said Poirot as she paused.

Mrs. Tanios twisted her fingers nervously again as she answered:

"Well, that it would be mean to try and upset the will. I feel certain that it wasn't in any way Miss Lawson's doing—I'm sure she'd be quite incapable of scheming and intriguing—"

"Again, I agree with you, madame."

"And that's why I feel that to go to law would be—well, would be undignified and spiteful, and besides it would be very expensive, wouldn't it?"

"It would be expensive, yes."

"And probably useless, too. But you must speak to my husband about it. He's got a much better head for business than I have."

Poirot waited a minute or two, then he said:

"What reason do you think lay behind the making of that will?"

A quick colour rose in Mrs. Tanios's cheeks as she murmured:

"I haven't the least idea."

"Madame, I have told you I am not a lawyer. But you have not asked me what my profession is."

She looked at him inquiringly.

"I am a detective. And, a short time before she died, Miss Emily Arundell wrote me a letter."

Mrs. Tanios leaned forward; her hands pressed themselves together.

"A letter?" she asked abruptly. "About my husband?"

Poirot watched her for a minute or two, then he said slowly:

"I am afraid I am not at liberty to answer that question."

"Then it *was* about my husband." Her voice rose slightly. "What did she say? I can assure you, Mr.—er—I don't know your name."

"Poirot is my name. Hercule Poirot."

"I can assure you, Mr. Poirot, that if anything was said in that letter against my husband, it was entirely untrue! I know, too, who will have inspired that letter! And that is another reason why I would rather have nothing to do with *any* action undertaken by Theresa and Charles! Theresa has never liked my husband. She has said things! I know she has said things! Aunt Emily was prejudiced against my husband because he was not an Englishman, and she may therefore have believed things that Theresa said about him. But they are *not true*, Mr. Poirot, you can take my word for that!"

"Mother—I've finished my letter."

Mrs. Tanios turned quickly. With an affectionate smile she took the letter the little girl held out to her.

"That's very nice, darling, very nice, indeed. And that's a beautiful drawing of Mickey Mouse."

"What shall I do now, Mother?"

"Would you like to get a nice postcard with a picture on it? Here's the money. You go to the gentleman in the hall and choose one and then you can send it to Selim."

The child moved away. I remembered what Charles Arundell had said. Mrs. Tanios was evidently a devoted wife and mother. She was also, as he had said, a little like an earwig.

"That is your only child, madame?"

"No, I have a little boy also. He is out with his father at the moment."

"They did not accompany you to Littlegreen House on your visits?"

"Oh, yes, sometimes, but you see, my aunt was rather old and children were inclined to worry her. But she was very kind and always sent them out nice presents at Christmas."

"Let me see, when did you last see Miss Emily Arundell?"

"I think it was just about ten days before she died."

"You and your husband and your two cousins were all down there together, were you not?"

"Oh, no, that was the week-end before—at Easter."

"And you and your husband were down there the week-end after Easter as well?"

"Yes."

"And Miss Arundell was in good health and spirits then?"

"Yes, she seemed much as usual."

"She was not ill in bed?"

"She was laid up with a fall she had had, but she came downstairs again while we were there."

"Did she say anything to you about having made a new will?"

"No, nothing at all."

"And her manner to you was quite unchanged?"

A slightly longer pause this time before Mrs. Tanios said:

"Yes."

I feel sure that at that moment Poirot and I had the same conviction.

Mrs. Tanios was lying!

Poirot paused a minute and then said:

"Perhaps I should explain that when I asked if Miss Arundell's manner to you was unchanged, I was not using the 'you' plural. I referred to *you personally*."

Mrs. Tanios replied quickly:

"Oh! I see. Aunt Emily was very nice to me. She gave me a little pearl and diamond brooch and she sent ten shillings to each of the children."

There was no constraint in her manner now. The words came freely with a rush.

"And as regards your husband—was there no change in her manner to him?"

The constraint had returned. Mrs. Tanios did not meet Poirot's eye as she replied:

"No, of course not—why should there be?"

"But since you suggest that your cousin Theresa Arundell might have tried to poison your aunt's mind—"

"She did! I'm sure she did!" Mrs. Tanios leant forward eagerly. "You are quite right. There *was* a change! Aunt Emily was suddenly far more distant to him. And she behaved very oddly. There was a special digestive mixture he recommended—even went to the trouble of getting her some—going to the druggist and having it made up. She thanked him and all that—but rather stiffly, and later I actually saw her pouring the bottle down the sink!"

Her indignation was quite fierce.

Poirot's eyes flickered.

"A very odd procedure," he said. His voice was carefully unexcited.

''I thought it *most* ungrateful,'' said Dr. Tanios's wife hotly.

''As you say, elderly ladies distrust foreigners sometimes,'' said Poirot. ''I am sure they think that English doctors are the only doctors in the world. Insularity accounts for a lot.''

''Yes, I suppose it does.'' Mrs. Tanios looked slightly mollified.

''When do you return to Smyrna, madame?''

''In a few weeks' time. My husband—ah! here is my husband and John with him.''

17

Dr. Tanios

I MUST SAY that my first sight of Dr. Tanios was rather a shock. I had been imbuing him in my mind with all sorts of sinister attributes. I had been picturing to myself a dark bearded foreigner with a swarthy aspect and a sinister cast of countenance.

Instead, I saw a rotund, jolly, brown-haired, brown-eyed man. And though it is true he had a beard, it was a modest brown affair that made him look more like an artist.

He spoke English perfectly. His voice had a pleasant timbre and matched the cheerful good-humour of his face.

''Here we are,'' he said, smiling to his wife. ''John has been passionately thrilled by his first ride in the tube. He has always been in buses until to-day.''

John was not unlike his father in appearance, but both he and his little sister had a definitely foreign-looking appearance and I understood what Miss Peabody had meant when she described them as rather yellow-looking children.

The presence of her husband seemed to make Mrs. Tanios nervous. Stammering a little, she introduced Poirot to him. Me, she ignored.

Dr. Tanios took up the name sharply.

''Poirot? Monsieur Hercule Poirot? But I know that name well! And what brings you to us, M. Poirot?''

''It is the affair of a lady lately deceased. Miss Emily Arundell,'' replied Poirot.

''My wife's aunt? Yes—what of her?''

Poirot said slowly:

"Certain matters have arisen in connection with her death—"

Mrs. Tanios broke in suddenly:

"It's about the will, Jacob. M. Poirot has been conferring with Theresa and Charles."

Some of the tensity went out of Dr. Tanios's attitude. He dropped into a chair.

"Ah, the will! An iniquitous will—but there, it is not my business, I suppose."

Poirot sketched an account of his interview with the two Arundells (hardly a truthful one, I may say) and cautiously hinted at a fighting chance of upsetting the will.

"You interest me, M. Poirot, very much. I may say I am of your opinion. Something could be done. I actually went as far as to consult a lawyer on the subject, but his advice was not encouraging. Therefore—" He shrugged his shoulders.

"Lawyers, as I have told your wife, are cautious people. They do not like taking chances. But me, I am different! And you?"

Dr. Tanios laughed—a rich, rollicking laugh.

"Oh, I'd take a chance all right! Often have, haven't I, Bella, old girl?" He smiled across at her, and she smiled back at him—but in a rather mechanical manner, I thought.

He turned his attention back to Poirot.

"I am not a lawyer," he said. "But in my opinion it is perfectly clear that that will was made when the old lady was not responsible for what she was doing. That Lawson woman is both clever and cunning."

Mrs. Tanios moved uneasily. Poirot looked at her quickly.

"You do not agree, madame?"

She said rather weakly:

"She has always been very kind. I shouldn't call her clever."

"She's been kind to you," said Dr. Tanios, "because she had nothing to fear from you, my dear Bella. You're easily taken in!"

He spoke quite good-humouredly, but his wife flushed.

"With me it was different," he went on. "She didn't like me. And she made no bones about showing it! I'll give you an instance. The old lady had a fall down the stairs when we were staying there. I insisted on coming back the following week-end to see how she was. Miss Lawson did her utmost to prevent us. She didn't succeed, but she was annoyed about it, I could see. The reason was clear. *She wanted the old lady to herself.*"

Again Poirot turned to the wife.

"You agree, madame?"

Her husband did not give her time to answer.

"Bella's too kind-hearted," he said. "You won't get her to impute bad motives to anybody. But I'm quite sure I was right. I'll tell you another thing, M. Poirot. The secret of her ascendency over old Miss Arundell was spiritualism! That's how it was done, depend upon it!"

"You think so?"

"Sure of it, my dear fellow. I've seen a lot of that sort of thing. It gets hold of people. You'd be amazed! Especially any one of Miss Arundell's age. I'd be prepared to bet that that's how the suggestion came. Some spirit—possibly her dead father—ordered her to alter her will and leave her money to the Lawson woman. She was in bad health—credulous—"

There was a very faint movement from Mrs. Tanios. Poirot turned to her.

"You think it possible—yes?"

"Speak up, Bella," said Dr. Tanios. "Tell us your views."

He looked at her encouragingly. Her quick look back at him was an odd one. She hesitated, then said:

"I know so little about these things. I dare say you're right, Jacob."

"Depend upon it I'm all right, eh, M. Poirot?"

Poirot nodded his head.

"It may be—yes." Then he said, "You were down at Market Basing, I think, the week-end before Miss Arundell's death?"

"We were down at Easter and again the week-end after—that is right."

"No, no, I meant the week-end after that—on the *26th*. You were there on the Sunday, I think?"

"Oh, Jacob, were you?" Mrs. Tanios looked at him wide-eyed.

He turned quickly.

"Yes, you remember? I just ran down in the afternoon. I told you about it."

Both Poirot and I were looking at her. Nervously she pushed her hat a little further back on her head.

"Surely you remember, Bella," her husband continued. "What a terrible memory you've got."

"Of course!" she apologized, a thin smile on her face. "It's quite true; I have a shocking memory. And it's nearly two months ago now."

"Miss Theresa Arundell and Mr. Charles Arundell were there then, I believe?" said Poirot.

"They may have been," said Tanios easily. "I didn't see them."

"You were not there very long then?"

"Oh, no—just half an hour or so."

Poirot's inquiring gaze seemed to make him a little uneasy.

"Might as well confess," he said with a twinkle. "I hoped to get a loan—but I didn't get it. I'm afraid my wife's aunt didn't take to me as much as she might. Pity, because I liked her. She was a sporting old lady."

"May I ask you a frank question, Dr. Tanios?"

Was there or was there not a momentary apprehension in Tanios's eye?

"Certainly, M. Poirot."

"What is your opinion of Charles and Theresa Arundell?"

The doctor looked slightly relieved.

"Charles and Theresa?" He looked at his wife with an affectionate smile. "Bella, my dear, I don't suppose you mind my being frank about your family?"

She shook her head, smiling faintly.

"Then it's my opinion they're rotten to the core, both of them! Funnily enough I like Charles the best. He's a rogue, but he's a likable rogue. He's no moral sense, but he can't help that. People are born that way."

"And Theresa?"

He hesitated.

"I don't know. She's an amazingly attractive young woman. But she's quite ruthless, I should say. She'd murder any one in cold blood if it suited her book. At least that's my fancy. You may have heard, perhaps, that her mother was tried for murder."

"And acquitted," said Poirot.

"As you say 'and acquitted,' " said Tanios quickly. "But all the same, it makes one—wonder sometimes."

"You met the young man to whom she is engaged?"

"Donaldson? Yes, he came to supper one night."

"What do you think of him?"

"A very clever fellow. I fancy he'll go far—if he gets the chance. It takes money to specialize."

"You mean that he is clever in his profession?"

"That is what I mean, yes. A first-class brain." He smiled. "Not quite a shining light in society yet. A little precise and prim in manner. He and Theresa make a comic pair. The attraction of opposites. She's a social butterfly and he's a recluse."

The two children were bombarding their mother.

"Mother, can't we go in to lunch? I'm so hungry. We'll be late."

Poirot looked at his watch and gave an exclamation.

"A thousand pardons! I delay your lunch hour."

Glancing at her husband, Mrs. Tanios said uncertainly:

"Perhaps we can offer you—"

Poirot said quickly:

"You are most amiable, madame, but I have a luncheon engagement for which I am already late."

He shook hands with both the护Tanioses and with the children. I did the same.

We delayed for a minute or two in the hall. Poirot wanted to put through a telephone call. I waited for him by the hall porter's desk. I was standing there when I saw Mrs. Tanios come out into the hall and look searchingly around. She had a hunted, harried look. She saw me and came swiftly across to me.

"Your friend—M. Poirot—I suppose he has gone?"

"No, he is in the telephone box."

"Oh."

"You wanted to speak to him?"

She nodded. Her air of nervousness increased.

Poirot came out of the box at that moment and saw us standing together. He came quickly across to us.

"M. Poirot," she began quickly in a low, hurried voice. "There is something that I would like to say—that I *must* tell you—"

"Yes, madame."

"It is important—very important. You see—"

She stopped. Dr. Tanios and the two children had just emerged from the writing-room. He came across and joined us.

"Having a few last words with M. Poirot, Bella?"

His tone was good-humoured, the smile on his face pleasantness itself.

"Yes—" She hesitated, then said, "Well, that is really all, M. Poirot. I just wanted you to tell Theresa that we will back her up in anything she decides to do. I quite see that the family *must* stand together."

She nodded brightly to us, then taking her husband's arm she moved off in the direction of the dining-room.

I caught Poirot by the shoulder.

"That wasn't what she started to say, Poirot!"

He shook his head slowly, watching the retreating couple.

"She changed her mind," I went on.

"Yes, *mon ami*, she changed her mind."

"Why?"

"I wish I knew," he murmured.

"She will tell us some other time," I said hopefully.

"I wonder. I rather fear—she may not. . . ."

18

"A Nigger in the Woodpile"

WE HAD LUNCH at a small restaurant not far away. I was eager to learn what he made of the various members of the Arundell family.

"Well, Poirot?" I asked impatiently.

With a look of reproof Poirot turned his whole attention to the menu. When he had ordered he leaned back in his chair, broke his roll of bread in half and said with a slightly mocking intonation:

"Well, Hastings?"

"What do you think of them now you've seen them all?"

Poirot replied slowly:

"*Ma foi*, I think they are an interesting lot! Really, this case is an enchanting study! It is, how do you say, the box of surprises? Look how each time I say, 'I got a letter from Miss Arundell before she died,' something crops up. From Miss Lawson I learn about the missing money. Mrs. Tanios says at once, 'About my husband?' Why about her husband? Why should Miss Arundell write to me, Hercule Poirot, about Dr. Tanios?"

"That woman has something on her mind," I said.

"Yes, she knows something. But *what*? Miss Peabody tells us that Charles Arundell would murder his grandmother for twopence. Miss Lawson says that Mrs. Tanios would murder any one if her husband told her to do so. Dr. Tanios says that Charles and Theresa are rotten to the core, and he hints that their mother was a murderess and says apparently carelessly that Theresa is capable of murdering any one in cold blood.

"They have a pretty opinion of each other, all these people! Dr. Tanios thinks, or *says* he thinks, that there was undue influence. His wife, before he came in, evidently did *not* think so. She does not want to contest the will at first. Later she veers round. See you, Hastings—it is a pot that boils and seethes and every now and then a significant fact comes to the surface and can be seen. There is *something* in the depths there—yes, there is *something*! I swear it, by my faith as Hercule Poirot, I swear it!"

I was impressed in spite of myself by his earnestness.

After a minute or two I said:

"Perhaps you are right, but it seems so vague—so nebulous."

"But you agree with me that there is *something*?"

"Yes," I said hesitatingly. "I believe I do."

Poirot leaned across the table. His eyes bored into mine.

"Yes—you have changed. You are no longer amused, superior—indulging me in my academic pleasures. But what is it that has convinced you? It is not my excellent reasoning—*non, ce n'est pas ça!* But *something*—something quite independent—has produced an effect on you. Tell me, my friend, what it is that has suddenly induced you to take this matter seriously?"

"I think," I said slowly, "it was Mrs. Tanios. She looked—she looked—*afraid*. . . ."

"Afraid of me?"

"No—no, not of you. It was something else. She spoke so quietly and sensibly to begin with—a natural resentment at the terms of the will, perhaps, but otherwise she seemed so resigned and willing to leave things as they are. It seemed the natural attitude of a well-bred but rather apathetic woman. And then that sudden change—the eagerness with which she came over to Dr. Tanios's point of view. The way she came out into the hall after us—the—almost *furtive* way—"

Poirot nodded encouragingly.

"And another little thing which you may not have noticed—"

"I notice everything!"

"I mean the point about her husband's visit to Littlegreen House on that last Sunday. I could swear she knew nothing of it—that it was the most complete surprise to her—and yet she took her cue so quickly—agreed that he had told her about it and that she had forgotten. I—I didn't like it, Poirot."

"You are quite right, Hastings—it was significant—that."

"It left an ugly impression of—of fear on me."

Poirot nodded his head slowly.

"You felt the same?" I asked.

"Yes—that impression was very definitely in the air." He paused and then went on: "And yet you liked Tanios, did you not? You found him an agreeable man, open-hearted, good-natured, genial. Attractive in spite of your insular prejudice against the Argentines, the Portuguese and the Greeks—a thoroughly congenial personality?"

"Yes," I admitted. "I did."

In the silence that ensued, I watched Poirot. Presently I said:

"What are you thinking of, Poirot?"

"I am reflecting on various people, handsome young Norman Gale, bluff, hearty Evelyn Howard, the pleasant Dr. Sheppard, the quiet, reliable Knighton."

For a moment I did not understand these references to people who had figured in past cases.

"What of them?" I asked.

"They were all delightful personalities. . . ."

"My goodness, Poirot, do you really think Tanios—"

"No, no. Do not jump to conclusions, Hastings. I am only pointing out that one's own personal reactions to people are singularly unsafe guides. One must go not by one's feelings but by facts."

"H'm," I said. "Facts are not our strong suit. No, no, Poirot, don't go over it all again!"

"I will be brief, my friend, do not fear. To begin with, we have quite certainly a case of attempted murder. You admit that, do you not?"

"Yes," I said slowly. "I do."

I had, up to now, been a little sceptical over Poirot's (as I thought) somewhat fanciful reconstruction of the events on the night of Easter Tuesday. I was forced to admit, however, that his deductions were perfectly logical.

"*Très bien*. Now one cannot have attempted murder without a murderer. One of the people present on that evening was a murderer—in intention if not in fact."

"Granted."

"Then that is our starting point—a murderer. We make a few inquiries—we, as you would say—stir the mud—and what do we get—several very interesting accusations uttered apparently casually in the course of conversations."

"You think they were not casual?"

"Impossible to tell at the moment! Miss Lawson's innocent-seeming way of bringing out the fact that Charles threatened his aunt may have been quite innocent or it may not. Dr. Tanios's remarks about Theresa Arundell may have absolutely no malice behind them, but be merely a physician's genuine opinion. Miss Peabody, on the other hand, is probably quite genuine in her opinion of Charles Arundell's proclivities—but it is, after all, merely an opinion. So it goes on. There is a saying, is there not, a nigger in the woodpile. *Eh bien*, that is just what I find here. There is —not a nigger—but a murderer in our woodpile."

"What I'd like to know is what you yourself really think, Poirot."

"Hastings—Hastings—I do not permit myself to 'think'—not, that is, in the sense that you are using the word. At the moment I only make certain reflections."

"Such as?"

"I consider the question of motive. What are the likely *motives* for Miss Arundell's death? Clearly the most obvious one is *gain*. Who would have gained by Miss Arundell's death—if she had died on Easter Tuesday?"

"Every one—with the exception of Miss Lawson."

"Precisely."

"Well, at any rate, one person is automatically cleared."

"Yes," said Poirot thoughtfully. "It would seem so. But the interesting thing is that the person who would have gained nothing if death had occurred on Easter Tuesday gains everything when death occurs two weeks later."

"What are you getting at, Poirot?" I said, slightly puzzled.

"Cause and effect, my friend, cause and effect."

I looked at him doubtfully.

He went on:

"Proceed logically! What exactly happened—after the accident?"

I hate Poirot in this mood. Whatever one says is bound to be wrong! I proceeded with intense caution.

"Miss Arundell was laid up in bed."

"Exactly. With plenty of time to think. What next?"

"She wrote to you."

Poirot nodded.

"Yes, she wrote to me. And the letter was not posted. A thousand pities, that."

"Do you suspect that there was something fishy about that letter not being posted?"

Poirot frowned.

"There, Hastings, I have to confess that I do not know. I think—in view of everything I am almost sure—that the letter was genuinely mislaid. I believe—but I cannot be sure—that the fact that such a letter was written was unsuspected by anybody. Continue—what happened next?"

I reflected.

"The lawyer's visit," I suggested.

"Yes—she sent for her lawyer and in due course he arrived."

"And she made a new will," I continued.

"Precisely. She made a new and very unexpected will. Now, in view of that will we have to consider very carefully a statement made to us by Ellen. Ellen said, if you remember, that Miss Lawson was particularly anxious that the news that Bob had been out all night should not get to Miss Arundell's ears."

"But—oh, I see—no, I don't. Or do I begin to see what you are hinting at? . . ."

"I doubt it!" said Poirot. "But if you do, you realize, I hope, the *supreme importance* of that statement."

He fixed me with a fierce eye.

"Of course. Of course," I said hurriedly.

"And then," continued Poirot, "various other things happen. Charles and Theresa come for the week-end, and Miss Arundell shows the new will to Charles—er—so he *says.*"

"Don't you believe him?"

"I only believe statements that are *checked.* Miss Arundell does not show it to Theresa."

"Because she thought Charles would tell her."

"But he doesn't. *Why* doesn't he?"

"According to Charles himself he *did* tell her."

"Theresa said quite positively that he *didn't*—a very interesting and suggestive little clash. And when we depart she calls him a fool."

"I'm getting fogged, Poirot," I said plaintively.

"Let us return to the sequence of events. Dr. Tanios comes down on Sunday—possibly without the knowledge of his wife."

"I should say certainly without her knowledge."

"Let us say *probably.* To proceed! Charles and Theresa leave on the Monday. Miss Arundell is in good health and spirits. She eats a good dinner and sits in the dark with the Tripps and Miss Lawson. Towards the end of the séance she is taken ill. She retires to bed and dies four days later and Miss Lawson inherits all her money, and Captain Hastings says she died a natural death!"

"Whereas Hercule Poirot says she was given poison in her dinner on no evidence at all!"

"I have *some* evidence, Hastings. Think over our conversation with the Misses Tripp. And also one statement that stood out from Miss Lawson's somewhat rambling conversation."

"Do you mean the fact that she had curry for dinner? Curry would mask the taste of a drug. Is that what you meant?"

Poirot said slowly:

"Yes, the curry has a certain significance, perhaps."

"But," I said, "if what you advance (in defiance of all the medical evidence) is true, only Miss Lawson or one of the maids could have killed her."

"I wonder."

"Or the Tripp women? Nonsense. I can't believe that! All these people are palpably innocent."

Poirot shrugged his shoulders.

"Remember this, Hastings, stupidity—or even silliness, for that matter—can go hand in hand with intense cunning. And do not forget the original attempt at murder. That was not the handiwork of a particularly clever or complex brain. It was a very *simple* little murder, suggested by

Bob and his habit of leaving the ball at the top of the stairs. The thought of putting a thread across the stairs was quite simple and easy—a child could have thought of it!"

I frowned.

"You mean—"

"I mean that what we are seeking to find here is just one thing—the wish to kill. Nothing more than that."

"But the poison must have been a very skilful one to leave no trace," I argued. "Something that the ordinary person would have difficulty in getting hold of. Oh, damn it all, Poirot, I simply can't believe it now. You can't *know*! It's all pure hypothesis."

"You are wrong, my friend. As the result of our various conversations this morning I have now something definite to go upon. Certain faint but unmistakable indications. The only thing is—I am afraid."

"Afraid? Of what?"

He said gravely:

"Of disturbing the dogs that sleep. That is one of your proverbs, is it not? To let the sleeping dogs lie! That is what our murderer does at present—sleeps happily in the sun. . . . Do we not know, you and I, Hastings, how often a murderer, his confidence disturbed, turns and kills a second—or even a *third* time!"

"You are afraid of that happening?"

He nodded.

"Yes. *If* there is a murderer in the woodpile—and I think there is, Hastings. Yes, I think there is. . . ."

19

Visit to Mr. Purvis

POIROT CALLED for his bill and paid it.

"What do we do next?" I asked.

"We are going to do what you suggested earlier in the morning. We are going to Harchester to interview Mr. Purvis. That is why I telephoned from the Durham Hotel."

"You telephoned to Purvis?"

"No, to Theresa Arundell. I asked her to write me a letter of introduction to him. To approach him with any chance of success we must be accredited by the family. She promised to send it round to my flat by hand. It should be awaiting us there now."

We found not only the letter but Charles Arundell who had brought it round in person.

"Nice place you have here, M. Poirot," he remarked, glancing round the sitting-room of the flat.

At that moment my eye was caught by an imperfectly shut drawer in the desk. A small slip of paper was preventing it from shutting.

Now if there was one thing absolutely incredible it was that Poirot should shut a drawer in such a fashion! I looked thoughtfully at Charles. He had been alone in this room awaiting our arrival. I had no doubt that he had been passing the time by snooping among Poirot's papers. What a young crook the fellow was! I felt myself burning with indignation.

Charles himself was in a most cheerful mood.

"Here we are," he remarked, presenting a letter. "All present and correct—and I hope you'll have more luck with old Purvis than we did."

"He held out very little hope, I suppose?"

"Definitely discouraging. . . . In his opinion the Lawson bird had clearly got away with the doings."

"You and your sister have never considered an appeal to the lady's feelings?"

Charles grinned.

"I considered it—yes. But there seemed to be nothing doing. My eloquence was in vain. The pathetic picture of the disinherited black sheep—and a sheep not so black as he was painted (or so I endeavoured to suggest)—failed to move the woman! You know, she definitely seems to dislike me! I don't know why." He laughed. "Most old women fall for me quite easily. They think I've never been properly understood and that I've never had a fair chance!"

"A useful point of view."

"Oh, it's been extremely useful before now. But, as I say, with the Lawson bird, nothing doing. I think she's rather anti-man. Probably used to chain herself to railings and wave a suffragette flag in good old prewar days."

"Ah, well," said Poirot, shaking his head. "If simpler methods fail—"

"We must take to crime," said Charles cheerfully.

"Aha," said Poirot. "Now, speaking of crime, young man, is it true that you threatened your aunt—that you said that you would 'bump her off,' or words to that effect?"

Charles sat down in a chair, stretched his legs out in front of him and stared hard at Poirot.

"Now who told you that?" he said.

"No matter. Is it true?"

"Well, there are elements of truth about it."

"Come, come, let me hear the true story—the *true* story, mind."

"Oh, you can have it, sir. There was nothing melodramatic about it. I'd been attempting a touch—if you gather what I mean."

"I comprehend."

"Well, that didn't go according to plan. Aunt Emily intimated that any efforts to separate her and her money would be quite unavailing! Well, I didn't lose my temper, but I put it to her plainly. 'Now look here, Aunt Emily,' I said, 'you know, you're going about things in such a way that you'll end by getting bumped off!' She said, rather sniffily, what did I mean. 'Just that,' I said. 'Here are your friends and relations all hanging around with their mouths open, all as poor as church mice—whatever church mice may be—all hoping. And what do you do? Sit down on the dibs and refuse to part. That's the way people get themselves murdered. Take it from me, if you're bumped off, you'll only have yourself to blame.'

"She looked at me then, over the top of her spectacles in a way she had. Looked at me rather nastily. 'Oh,' she said drily enough, 'so that's your opinion, is it?' 'It is,' I said. 'You loosen up a bit, that's my advice to you.' 'Thank you, Charles,' she said, 'for your well-meant advice. But I think you'll find I'm well able to take care of myself.' 'Please yourself, Aunt Emily,' I said. I was grinning all over my face—and I fancy she wasn't as grim as she tried to look. 'Don't say I didn't warn you.' 'I'll remember it,' she said."

He paused.

"That's all there was to it."

"And so," said Poirot, "you contented yourself with a few pound notes you found in a drawer."

Charles stared at him, then burst out laughing.

"I take off my hat to you," he said. "You're some sleuth! How did you get hold of *that*?"

"It is true, then?"

"Oh, it's true enough! I was damned hard up. Had to get money somehow. Found a nice little wad of notes in a drawer and helped myself to a few. I was very modest—didn't think my little subtraction would be noticed. Even then, they'd probably think it was the servants."

Poirot said drily:

"It would be very serious for the servants if such an idea had been entertained."

Charles shrugged his shoulders.

"Every one for himself," he murmured.

"And *le diable* takes the hindermost," said Poirot. "That is your creed, is it?"

Charles was looking at him curiously.

"I didn't know the old lady had ever spotted it. How did you come to know about it—and about the bumping-off conversation?"

"Miss Lawson told me."

"The sly old pussy cat!" He looked, I thought, just a shade disturbed. "She doesn't like me and she doesn't like Theresa," he said presently. "You don't think—she's got anything more up her sleeve?"

"What could she have?"

"Oh, I don't know. It's just that she strikes me as a malicious old devil." He paused. "She hates Theresa . . ." he added.

"Did you know, Mr. Arundell, that Dr. Tanios came down to see your aunt on the Sunday before she died?"

"What—on the Sunday that we were there?"

"Yes. You did not see him?"

"No. We were out for a walk in the afternoon. I suppose he must have come then. Funny that Aunt Emily didn't mention his visit. Who told you?"

"Miss Lawson."

"Lawson again? She seems to be a mine of information."

He paused and then said:

"You know, Tanios is a nice fellow. I like him. Such a jolly, smiling chap."

"He has an attractive personality, yes," said Poirot.

Charles rose to his feet.

"If I'd been him I'd have murdered the dreary Bella years ago! Doesn't she strike you as the type of woman who is marked out by fate to be a victim? You know, I should never be surprised if bits of her turned up in a trunk at Margate or somewhere!"

"It is not a pretty action that you attribute there to her husband the good doctor," said Poirot severely.

"No," said Charles meditatively. "And I don't think really that Tanios would hurt a fly. He's much too kind-hearted."

"And what about you? Would you do murder if it were made worth your while?"

Charles laughed—a ringing, genuine laugh.

"Thinking about a spot of blackmail, M. Poirot? Nothing doing. I can assure you that I didn't put"—he stopped suddenly and then went on—"strychnine in Aunt Emily's soup."

With a careless wave of his hand he departed.

"Were you trying to frighten him, Poirot?" I asked. "If so, I don't think you succeeded. He showed no guilty reactions whatsoever."

"No?"

"No. He seemed quite unruffled."

"Curious that pause he made," said Poirot.

"A pause?"

"Yes. A pause before the word strychnine. Almost as though he had been about to say something else and thought better of it."

I shrugged my shoulders.

"He was probably thinking of a good, venomous-sounding poison."

"It is possible. It is possible. But let us set off. We will, I think, stay the night at The George in Market Basing."

Ten minutes later saw us speeding through London, bound once more for the country.

We arrived in Harchester about four o'clock and made our way straight to the offices of Purvis, Purvis, Charlesworth and Purvis.

Mr. Purvis was a big, solidly built man with white hair and a rosy complexion. He had a little the look of a country squire. His manner was courteous but reserved.

He read the letter we had brought and then looked at us across the top of his desk. It was a shrewd look and a somewhat searching one.

"I know you by name, of course, M. Poirot," he said politely. "Miss Arundell and her brother have, I gather, engaged your services in this matter, but exactly in what capacity you propose to be of use to them I am at a loss to imagine."

"Shall we say, Mr. Purvis, a fuller investigation of all the circumstances?"

The lawyer said drily:

"Miss Arundell and her brother have already had my opinion as to the legal position. The circumstances were perfectly clear and admit of no misrepresentation."

"Perfectly, perfectly," said Poirot quickly. "But you will not, I am sure, object to just repeating them so that I can envisage the situation clearly."

The lawyer bowed his head.

"I am at your service."

Poirot began:

"Miss Arundell wrote to you giving you instructions on the seventeenth of April, I believe?"

Mr. Purvis consulted some papers on the table before him.

"Yes, that is correct."

"Can you tell me what she said?"

"She asked me to draw up a will. There were to be legacies to two servants and to three or four charities. The rest of her estate was to pass to Wilhelmina Lawson absolutely."

"You will pardon me, Mr. Purvis, but you were surprised?"

"I will admit that—yes, I was surprised."

"Miss Arundell had made a will previously?"

"Yes, she had made a will five years ago."

"That will, after certain small legacies, left her property to her nephew and nieces?"

"The bulk of her estate was to be divided equally between the children of her brother Thomas and the daughter of Arabella Biggs, her sister."

"What has happened to that will?"

"At Miss Arundell's request I brought it with me when I visited her at Littlegreen House on April 21st."

"I should be much obliged to you, Mr. Purvis, if you would give me a full description of everything that occurred on that occasion."

The lawyer paused for a minute or two. Then he said, very precisely:

"I arrived at Littlegreen House at three o'clock in the afternoon. One of my clerks accompanied me. Miss Arundell received me in the drawing-room."

"How did she look to you?"

"She seemed to me in good health in spite of the fact that she was walking with a stick. That, I understand, was on account of a fall she had recently. Her general health, as I say, seemed good. She struck me as slightly nervous and over-excited in manner."

"Was Miss Lawson with her?"

"She was with her when I arrived. But she left us immediately."

"And then?"

"Miss Arundell asked me if I had done what she had asked me to do, and if I had brought the new will with me for her to sign.

"I said I had done so. I—er—" He hesitated for a minute or two, then went on stiffly: "I may as well say that, as far as it was proper for me to do so, I remonstrated with Miss Arundell. I pointed out to her that this new will might be regarded as grossly unfair to her family who were, after all, her own flesh and blood."

"And her answer?"

"She asked me if the money was or was not her own to do with as she liked. I replied that certainly that was the case. 'Very well then,' she said. I reminded her that she had known this Miss Lawson a very short time, and I asked her if she was quite sure that the injustice she was doing to her own family was legitimate. Her reply was, 'My dear friend, I know perfectly what I am doing.' "

"Her manner was excited, you say."

"I think I can definitely say that it was, but understand me, M. Poirot, she was in full possession of her faculties. She was in every sense of the word fully competent to manage her own affairs. Though my sympathies are entirely with Miss Arundell's family, I should be obliged to maintain that in any court of law."

"That is quite understood. Proceed, I pray of you."

"Miss Arundell read through her existing will. Then she stretched out her hand for the one I had had drawn up. I may say that I would have preferred to submit a draft first, but she had impressed upon me that the will must be brought her ready to sign. That presented no difficulties as its provisions were so simple. She read it through, nodded her head, and said she would sign it straightaway. I felt it my duty to enter one last protest. She heard me out quite patiently, but said that her mind was quite made up. I called in my clerk and he and the gardener acted as witnesses to her signature. The servants, of course, were ineligible owing to the fact that they were beneficiaries under the will."

"And afterwards, did she entrust the will to you for safekeeping?"

"No, she placed it in a drawer of her desk, which drawer she locked."

"What was done with the original will? Did she destroy it?"

"No, she locked it away with the other."

"After her death, where was the will found?"

"In that same drawer. As executor I had her keys and went through her papers and business documents."

"Were both wills in the drawer?"

"Yes, exactly as she had placed them there."

"Did you question her at all as to the motive for this rather surprising action?"

"I did. But I got no satisfactory answer. She merely assured me that 'she knew what she was doing.' "

"Nevertheless you were surprised at the proceeding?"

"Very surprised. Miss Arundell, I should say, had always shown herself to have a strong sense of family feeling."

Poirot was silent a minute, then he asked:

"You did not, I suppose, have any conversation with Miss Lawson on the subject?"

"Certainly not. Such a proceeding would have been highly improper."

Mr. Purvis looked scandalized at the mere suggestion.

"Did Miss Arundell say anything to indicate that Miss Lawson knew that a will was being drawn in her favour?"

"On the contrary. I asked her if Miss Lawson was aware of what was being done, and Miss Arundell snapped out that she knew nothing about it.

"It was advisable, I thought, that Miss Lawson should not be aware of what had happened. I endeavoured to hint as much and Miss Arundell seemed quite of my opinion."

"Just why did you stress that point, Mr. Purvis?"

The old gentleman returned his glance with dignity.

"Such things, in my opinion, are best undiscussed. Also it might have led to future disappointment."

"Ah!" Poirot drew a long breath. "I take it that *you thought it probable that Miss Arundell might change her mind in the near future*?"

The lawyer bowed his head.

"That is so. I fancied that Miss Arundell had had some violent altercation with her family. I thought it probable that when she cooled down she would repent of her rash decision."

"In which case she would have done—what?"

"She would have given me instructions to prepare a new will."

"She might have taken the simpler course of merely destroying the will lately made, in which case the older will would have been good?"

"That is a somewhat debatable point. All earlier wills, you understand, had been definitely revoked by the testator."

"But Miss Arundell would not have had the legal knowledge to appreciate that point. She may have thought that by destroying the later will, the earlier one would stand."

"It is quite possible."

"Actually, if she died intestate, her money would pass to her family?"

"Yes. One half to Mrs. Tanios, one half divisible between Charles and Theresa Arundell. But the fact remains, however, that she did *not* change her mind! She died with her decision unchanged."

"But that," said Poirot, "is where I come in."

The lawyer looked at him inquiringly.

Poirot leaned forward.

"Supposing," he said, "that Miss Arundell, on her deathbed, *wished to destroy that will*. Supposing that she believed that she *had* destroyed it—but that, in reality, she only destroyed the *first* will."

Mr. Purvis shook his head.

"No, *both* wills were intact."

"Then supposing she destroyed a *dummy* will—*under the impression that she was destroying the genuine document*. She was very ill, remember; it would be easy to deceive her."

"You would have to bring evidence to that effect," said the lawyer sharply.

"Oh! undoubtedly—undoubtedly. . . ."

"Is there—may I ask—is there any reason to believe something of the kind happened?"

Poirot drew back a little.

"I should not like to commit myself at this stage—"

"Naturally, naturally," said Mr. Purvis, agreeing with a phrase that was familiar to him.

"But I may say, strictly in confidence, that there are some curious features about this business!"

"Really? You don't say so?"

Mr. Purvis rubbed his hands together with a kind of pleasurable anticipation.

"What I wanted from you and what I have got," continued Poirot, "is your opinion that Miss Arundell would, sooner or later, have changed her mind and relented towards her family."

"That is only my personal opinion, of course," the lawyer pointed out.

"My dear sir, I quite understand. You do not, I believe, act for Miss Lawson?"

"I advised Miss Lawson to consult an independent solicitor," said Mr. Purvis.

His tone was wooden.

Poirot shook hands with him, thanking him for his kindness and the information he had given us.

20

Second Visit to Littlegreen House

ON OUR WAY from Harchester to Market Basing, a matter of some ten miles, we discussed the situation.

"Have you any grounds at all, Poirot, for that suggestion you threw out?"

"You mean that Miss Arundell may have believed that that particular will was destroyed? No, *mon ami*—frankly, no. But it was incumbent upon me—you must perceive that—to make *some* sort of suggestion! Mr. Purvis is a shrewd man. Unless I threw out some hint of the kind I did, he would ask himself what I could be doing in this affair."

"Do you know what you remind me of, Poirot?" I said.

"No, *mon ami*."

"Of a juggler juggling with a lot of different-coloured balls! They are all in the air at once."

"The different-coloured balls are the different lies I tell—eh?"

"That's about the size of it."

"And some day, you think, there will come the grand crash?"

"You can't keep it up for ever," I pointed out.

"That is true. There will come the grand moment when I catch the balls one by one, make my bow, and walk off the stage."

"To the sound of thunderous applause from the audience."

Poirot looked at me rather suspiciously.

"That well may be, yes."

"We didn't learn very much from Mr. Purvis," I remarked, edging away from the danger-point.

"No, except that it confirmed our general ideas."

"And it confirmed Miss Lawson's statement that she knew nothing about the will until after the old lady's death."

"Me, I do not see that it confirmed anything of the sort."

"Purvis advised Miss Arundell not to tell her, and Miss Arundell replied that she had no intention of doing so."

"Yes, that is all very nice and clear. But there are keyholes, my friend, and keys that unlock locked drawers."

"Do you really think that Miss Lawson would eavesdrop and poke and pry around?" I asked, rather shocked.

Poirot smiled.

"Miss Lawson—she is not an old school tie, *mon cher*. We know that she overheard *one* conversation which she was not supposed to have heard—I refer to the one in which Charles and his aunt discussed the question of bumping off miserly relatives."

I admitted the truth of that.

"So you see, Hastings, she may easily have overheard some of the conversation between Mr. Purvis and Miss Arundell. He has a good, resonant voice."

"As for poking and prying," went on Poirot, "more people do it than you would suppose. Timid and easily frightened people such as Miss Lawson often acquire a number of mildly dishonourable habits which are a great solace and recreation to them."

"Really, Poirot!" I protested.

He nodded his head a good many times.

"But yes, it is so, it is so."

We arrived at The George and took a couple of rooms. Then we strolled off in the direction of Littlegreen House.

When we rang the bell, Bob immediately answered the challenge. Dashing across the hall, barking furiously, he flung himself against the front door.

"I'll have your liver and your lights!" he snarled. "I'll tear you limb from limb! I'll teach you to try and get into *this* house! Just wait until I get my teeth into you."

A soothing murmur added itself to the clamour.

"Now then, boy. Now then, there's a good doggie. Come in here."

Bob, dragged by the collar, was immured in the morning-room much against his will.

"Always spoiling a fellow's sport," he grumbled. "First chance I've had of giving any one a really good fright for ever so long. Just aching to get my teeth into a trouser leg. You be careful of yourself without me to protect you."

The door of the morning-room was shut on him, and Ellen drew back bolts and bars and opened the front door.

"Oh, it's you, sir," she exclaimed.

She drew the door right back. A look of highly pleasurable excitement spread over her face.

"Come in, sir, if you please, sir."

We entered the hall. From beneath the door on the left, loud snuffling sounds proceeded, interspersed with growls. Bob was endeavouring to "place" us correctly.

"You can let him out," I suggested.

"I will, sir. He's quite all right, really, but he makes such a noise and rushes at people so it frightens them. He's a splendid watchdog though."

She opened the morning-room door, and Bob shot through like a suddenly projected cannon-ball.

"Who is it? Where are they? Oh, there you are. Dear me, don't I seem to remember—" Sniff—sniff—sniff—prolonged snort. "Of course! We *have* met!"

"Hullo, old man," I said. "How goes it?"

Bob wagged his tail perfunctorily.

"Nicely, thank you. Let me just see—" He resumed his researches. "Been talking to a spaniel lately, I smell. Foolish dogs, I think. What's this? A cat? That is interesting. Wish we had her here. We'd have a rare sport. H'm—not a bad bull-terrier."

Having correctly diagnosed a visit I had lately paid to some doggy friends, he transferred his attentions to Poirot, inhaled a noseful of benzine and walked away reproachfully.

"Bob," I called.

He threw me a look over his shoulder.

"It's all right. I know what I'm doing. I'll be back in a jiffy."

"The house is all shut up. I hope you'll excuse—" Ellen hurried into the morning-room and began to unfasten the shutters.

"Excellent, this is excellent," said Poirot, following her in and sitting down. As I was about to join him, Bob reappeared from some mysterious region, ball in mouth. He dashed up the stairs and sprawled himself on the top step, his ball between his paws. His tail wagged slowly.

"Come on," he said. "Come on. Let's have a game."

My interest in detection momentarily eclipsed, we played for some minutes, then with a feeling of guilt I hurried into the morning-room.

Poirot and Ellen seemed to be well away on the subject of illness and medicines.

"Some little white pills, sir, that's all she used to take. Two or three after every meal. That was Dr. Grainger's orders. Oh, yes, she was very good about it. Tiny little things they were. And then there was some stuff Miss Lawson swore by. Capsules, they were, Dr. Loughbarrow's Liver capsules. You can see advertisements of them on all the hoardings."

"She took those too?"

"Yes. Miss Lawson got her them to begin with, and she thought they did her good."

"Did Dr. Grainger know?"

"Oh, sir, he didn't mind. 'You take 'em if you think they do you good,' he'd say to her. And she said, 'Well, you may laugh, but they *do* do me good. A lot better than any of *your* physic.' And Dr. Grainger, he laughed, and said faith was worth all the drugs ever invented."

"She didn't take anything else?"

"No. Miss Bella's husband, the foreign doctor, he went out and got her a bottle of something, but although she thanked him very politely she poured it away and that I know for a fact! And I think she was right. You don't know where you are with these foreign things."

"Mrs. Tanios saw her pouring it away, didn't she?"

"Yes, and I'm afraid she was rather hurt about it, poor lady. I'm sorry, too, for no doubt it was kindly meant on the doctor's part."

"No doubt. No doubt. I suppose any medicines that were left in the house were thrown away when Miss Arundell died?"

Ellen looked a little surprised at the question.

"Oh, yes, sir. The nurse threw away some and Miss Lawson got rid of all the old lot in the medicine-cupboard in the bathroom."

"Is that where the—er—Dr. Loughbarrow's Liver Capsules were kept?"

"No, they were kept in the corner-cupboard in the dining-room so as to be handy for taking after meals as directed."

"What nurse attended Miss Arundell? Can you give me her name and address?"

Ellen could supply that at once and did.

Poirot continued to ask questions about Miss Arundell's last illness.

Ellen gave details with relish, describing the sickness, the pain, the onset of jaundice, and the final delirium. I don't know whether Poirot got any satisfaction out of the catalogue. He listened patiently enough and occasionally interpolated some pertinent little question, usually about Miss Lawson and the amount of time she spent in the sick-room. He was also exceedingly interested in the diet administered to the ill woman, comparing it with that administered to some dead relative (non-existent) of his own.

Seeing that they were enjoying themselves so much, I stole out in the hall again. Bob had gone to sleep on the landing, his ball lying under his chin.

I whistled to him and he sprang up, alert at once. This time, however, doubtless out of offended dignity, he made a protracted business of despatching the ball down to me, several times catching it back at the last minute.

"Disappointed, aren't you? Well, perhaps I *will* let you have it this time."

When I next went back to the morning-room, Poirot was talking about Dr. Tanios's surprise visit on the Sunday before the old lady's death.

"Yes, sir, Mr. Charles and Miss Theresa were out for a walk. Dr. Tanios wasn't expected, I know. The mistress was lying down and she was very surprised when I told her who it was. 'Dr. Tanios?' she said. 'Is Mrs. Tanios with him?' I told her no, the gentleman had come alone. So she said to tell him she'd be down in a minute."

"Did he stay long?"

"Not above an hour, sir. He didn't look too pleased when he went away."

"Have you any idea of the—er—purpose of his visit?"

"I couldn't say, I'm sure, sir."

"You did not happen to hear anything?"

Ellen's face flushed suddenly.

"No, I did *not*, sir! I've never been one to listen at doors, no matter what *some* people will do—and people who ought to know better!"

"Oh, but you misunderstand me." Poirot was eager, apologetic. "It just occurred to me that perhaps you might have brought in tea while the gentleman was there and if so, you could hardly have helped hearing what he and your mistress were talking about."

Ellen was mollified.

"I'm sorry, sir, I misunderstand you. No, Dr. Tanios didn't stay for tea."

Poirot looked up at her and twinkled a little.

"And if I want to know what he came down for—well, it is possible that Miss Lawson might be in a position to know? Is that it?"

"Well, if she doesn't know, sir, nobody does," said Ellen with a sniff.

"Let me see." Poirot frowned as though trying to remember. "Miss Lawson's bedroom—was it next to Miss Arundell's?"

"No, sir. Miss Lawson's room is right at the top of the staircase. I can show you, sir."

Poirot accepted the offer. As he went up the stairs he kept close to the wall side, and just as he reached the top uttered an exclamation and stooped to his trouser-leg.

"Ah—I have just caught a thread—ah, yes, there is a nail here in the skirting-board."

"Yes, there is, sir. I think it must have worked loose or something. I've caught my dress on it once or twice."

"Has it been like that long?"

"Well, some time, I'm afraid, sir. I noticed it first when the mistress was laid up—after her accident, that was, sir—I tried to pull it out but I couldn't."

"It has had a thread round it some time, I think."

"That's right, sir, there was a little loop of thread, I remember. I can't think what for, I'm sure."

But there was no suspicion in Ellen's voice. To her it was just one of the things that occur in houses and which one does not bother to explain!

Poirot had stepped into the room at the top of the stairs. It was of moderate size. There were two windows directly facing us. There was a dressing-table across one corner and between the windows was a wardrobe with a long mirror. The bed was to the right behind the door facing the windows. On the left-hand wall of the room was a big mahogany chest of drawers and a marble-topped washstand.

Poirot looked round the room thoughtfully and then came out again on the landing. He went along the passage, passing two other bedrooms and then came to the large bed-chamber which had belonged to Emily Arundell.

"The nurse had the little room next door," Ellen explained.

Poirot nodded thoughtfully.

As we descended the stairs, he asked if he might walk round the garden.

"Oh, yes, sir, certainly. It looks lovely just now."

"The gardener is still employed?"

"Angus? Oh, yes, Angus is still here. Miss Lawson wants everything kept nice because she thinks it will sell better that way."

"I think she is wise. To let a place run to seed is not the good policy."

The garden was very peaceful and beautiful. The wide borders were full of lupins and delphiniums and great scarlet poppies. The peonies were in bud. Wandering along, we came presently to a potting-shed where a big, rugged old man was busy. He saluted us respectfully and Poirot engaged him in conversation.

A mention that we had seen Mr. Charles that day thawed the old man and he became quite garrulous.

"Always a one, he was! I've known him come out here with half a gooseberry pie and the cook hunting high and low for it! And he'd go back with such an innocent face that durned if they wouldn't say it must have been the cat, though I've never known a cat eat a gooseberry pie! Oh, he's a one, Mr. Charles is!"

"He was down here in April, wasn't he?"

"Yes, down here two week-ends. Just before the missus died, it was."

"Did you see much of him?"

"A good bit, I did. There wasn't much for a young gentleman to do down here, and that's a fact. Used to stroll up to The George and have one. And then he'd potter round here, asking me questions about one thing and another."

"About flowers?"

"Yes—flowers—and weeds too." The old man chuckled.

"Weeds?"

Poirot's voice held a sudden, tentative note. He turned his head and looked searchingly along the shelves. His eye stopped at a tin.

"Perhaps he wanted to know how you got rid of them?"

"He did that!"

"I suppose this is the stuff you use."

Poirot turned the tin gently round and read the label.

"That's it," said Angus. "Very handy stuff it is."

"Dangerous stuff?"

"Not if you use it right. It's arsenic, of course. Had a bit of a joke about that, Mr. Charles and I did. Said as how when he had a wife and didn't like her, he'd come to me and get a little of that stuff to put her away with! Maybe, I sez, *she*'ll be the one that wants to do away with *you*! Ah, that made him laugh proper, that did! It was a good one, that!"

We laughed as in duty bound. Poirot prised up the lid of the tin.

"Nearly empty," he murmured.

The old man had a look.

"Ay, there's more gone than I thought. No idea I'd used that much. I'll be having to order some more."

"Yes," said Poirot, smiling. "I'm afraid there's hardly enough for you to spare me some for *my* wife!"

We all had another good laugh over this witticism.

"You're not married, I take it, mister?"

"No."

"Ah! it's always them as isn't that can afford to joke about it. Those that isn't married don't know what trouble is!"

"I gather that your wife—?" Poirot paused delicately.

"She's alive all right—very much so."

Angus seemed a little depressed about it.

Complimenting him on his garden, we bade him farewell.

21

The Chemist. The Nurse. The Doctor

THE TIN of weed-killer had started a new train of thought in my mind. It was the first definite suspicious circumstance that I had encountered. Charles's interest in it, the old gardener's obvious surprise at finding the tin almost empty—it all seemed to point in the right direction.

Poirot was, as usual when I am excited, very non-committal.

"Even if some of the weed-killer *has* been taken, there is as yet no evidence that Charles was the person to take it, Hastings."

"But he talked so much to the gardener about it!"

"Not a very wise procedure if he was going to help himself to some."

Then he went on:

"What is the first and simplest poison to come into your mind if you were asked to name one quickly?"

"Arsenic, I suppose."

"Yes. You understand then, that very marked pause before the word strychnine when Charles was talking to us to-day."

"You mean—?"

"That he was about to say 'arsenic in the soup,' and stopped himself."

"Ah!" I said, "and why did he stop himself?"

"Exactly. *Why?* I may say, Hastings, that it was to find the answer to that particular 'why?' which made me go out into the garden in search of any likely source of weed-killer."

"And you found it!"

"And I found it."

I shook my head.

"It begins to look rather bad for young Charles. You had a good talk with Ellen over the old lady's illness. Did her symptoms resemble those of arsenic poisoning?"

Poirot rubbed his nose.

"It is difficult to say. There was abdominal pain—sickness."

"Of course—that's it!"

"H'm, I am not so sure."

"What poison did it resemble?"

"*Eh bien*, my friend, it resembled not so much poison as disease of the liver and death from that cause!"

"Oh, Poirot," I cried. "It *can't* be natural death! It's *got* to be murder!"

"Oh, *là là*, we seem to have changed places, you and I."

He turned abruptly into a druggist's shop. After a long discussion of Poirot's particular internal troubles, he purchased a small box of indigestion lozenges. Then, when his purchase was wrapped up and he was about to leave the shop, his attention was taken by an attractively wrapped package of Dr. Loughbarrow's Liver Capsules.

"Yes, sir, a very good preparation." The druggist was a middle-aged man of a chatty disposition. "You'll find them very efficacious."

"Miss Arundell used to take them, I remember. Miss Emily Arundell."

"Indeed she did, sir. Miss Arundell of Littlegreen House. A fine old lady, one of the old school. I used to serve her."

"Did she take many patent medicines?"

"Not really, sir. Not so many as some elderly ladies I could name. Miss Lawson, now, her companion, the one that's come into all the money—"

Poirot nodded.

"She was a one for this, that, and the other. Pills, lozenges, dyspepsia tablets, digestive mixtures, blood mixtures. Really enjoyed herself among the bottles." He smiled ruefully. "I wish there were more like her. People nowadays don't take to medicines as they used. Still, we sell a lot of toilet preparations to make up for it."

"Did Miss Arundell take these Liver Capsules regularly?"

"Yes, she'd been taking them for three months, I think, before she died."

"A relative of hers, a Dr. Tanios, came in to have a mixture made up one day, didn't he?"

"Yes, of course, the Greek gentleman that married Miss Arundell's niece. Yes, a very interesting mixture it was. One I've not previously become acquainted with."

The man spoke as of a rare botanical trophy.

"It makes a change, sir, when you get something new. Very interesting combination of drugs, I remember. Of course, the gentleman is a doctor. Very nice he was—a pleasant way with him."

"Did his wife do any shopping here?"

"Did she now? I don't recall. Oh, yes, came in for a sleeping-draught—chloral it was, I remember. A double quantity the prescription was for. It's always a little difficult for us with hypnotic drugs. You see, most doctors don't prescribe much at a time."

"Whose prescription was it?"

"Her husband's, I think. Oh, of course, it was quite all *right*—but, you know, we have to be careful nowadays. Perhaps you don't know the fact, but if a doctor makes a mistake in a prescription and we make it up in all good faith and anything goes wrong it's we who have to take the blame—not the doctor."

"That seems very unfair!"

"It's worrying, I'll admit. Ah, well, I can't complain. No trouble has come *my* way—touching wood."

He rapped the counter sharply with his knuckles.

Poirot decided to buy a package of Dr. Loughbarrow's Liver Capsules.

"Thank you, sir. Which size—25, 50, 100?"

"I suppose the larger ones are better value—but still—"

"Have the 50, sir. That's the size Miss Arundell had. Eight and six."

Poirot agreed, paid over eight and six and received the parcel.

Then we left the shop.

"So Mrs. Tanios bought a sleeping-draught," I exclaimed as we got out into the street. "An overdose of that would kill any one, wouldn't it?"

"With the greatest of ease."

"Do you think old Miss Arundell—"

I was remembering Miss Lawson's words, "*I dare say she'd murder some one if he told her to*!"

Poirot shook his head.

"Chloral is a narcotic and a hypnotic. Used to alleviate pain and as a sleeping-draught. It can also become a habit."

"Do you think Mrs. Tanios had acquired the habit?"

Poirot shook his head perplexedly.

"No, I hardly think so. But it is curious. I can think of one explanation. But that would mean—"

He broke off and looked at his watch.

"Come, let us see if we can find this Nurse Carruthers who was with Miss Arundell in her last illness."

Nurse Carruthers proved to be a sensible-looking, middle-aged woman.

Poirot now appeared in yet another rôle and with one more fictitious relative. This time he had an aged mother for whom he was anxious to find a sympathetic hospital nurse.

"You comprehend—I am going to speak to you quite frankly. My mother, she is difficult. We have had some excellent nurses, young women, fully competent, but the very fact that they are young has been against them. My mother dislikes young women, she insults them, she is rude and fractious, she fights against open windows and modern hygiene. It is very difficult."

He sighed mournfully.

"I know," said Nurse Carruthers sympathetically. "It's very trying sometimes. One has to use a lot of tact. It's no use upsetting a patient. Better to give in to them as far as you can. And once they feel you're not trying to force things on them, they very often relax and give in like lambs."

"Ah, I see that you would be ideal in the part. You understand old ladies."

"I've had to do with a few in my time," said Nurse Carruthers with a laugh. "You can do a lot with patience and good humour."

"That is so wise. You nursed Miss Arundell, I believe. Now, she could not have been an easy old lady."

"Oh, I don't know. She was strong-willed, but I didn't find her difficult at all. Of course, I wasn't there any length of time. She died on the fourth day."

"I was talking to her niece, Miss Theresa Arundell, only yesterday."

"Really. Fancy that now! What I always says is—the world's a small place!"

"You know her, I expect?"

"Well, of course, she came down after her aunt's death and she was here for the funeral. And, of course, I've seen her about before when she's been staying down here. A very handsome girl."

"Yes, indeed—but too thin—definitely too thin."

Nurse Carruthers, conscious of her own comfortable plumpness, preened herself slightly.

"Of course," she said, "one shouldn't be *too* thin."

"Poor girl," continued Poirot. "I am sorry for her. *Entre nous*"—he leaned forward confidentially—"her aunt's will was a great blow."

"I suppose it must have been," said Nurse Carruthers. "I know it caused a good deal of *talk*."

"I cannot imagine what induced Miss Arundell to disinherit all her family. It seems an extraordinary procedure."

"Most extraordinary. I agree with you. And, of course, people say there must have been something behind it all."

"Did you ever get any idea of the *reason*? Did old Miss Arundell say anything?"

"No. Not to me—that is."

"But to somebody else?"

"Well, I rather fancy she mentioned *something* to Miss Lawson because I heard Miss Lawson say, 'Yes, dear, but you see it's at the lawyer's.' And Miss Arundell said, 'I'm sure it's in the drawer downstairs.' And Miss Lawson said, 'No, you sent it to Mr. Purvis. Don't you remember?' And then my patient had an attack of nausea again and Miss Lawson went away while I saw to her, but I've often wondered if it was the will they were talking about."

"It certainly seems probable."

Nurse Carruthers went on:

"If so, I expect Miss Arundell was worried and perhaps wanted to alter it—but there, she was so ill, poor dear, after that—that she was past thinking of anything."

"Did Miss Lawson take part in the nursing at all?" asked Poirot.

"Oh, dear no, she was no manner of good! Too fussy, you know. She only irritated my patient."

"Did you, then, do all the nursing yourself? *C'est formidable ça*."

"The maid—what was her name—Ellen, helped me. Ellen was very good. She was used to illness and used to looking after the old lady. We managed pretty well between us. As a matter of fact, Dr. Grainger was sending in a night nurse on the Friday, but Miss Arundell died before the night nurse arrived."

"Perhaps Miss Lawson helped to prepare some of the invalid's food?"

"No, she didn't do anything at all. There wasn't really anything to prepare. I had the Valentine and the brandy—and the Brand's and glucose and all that. All Miss Lawson did was to go about the house crying and getting in every one's way."

The nurse's tone held distinct acrimony.

"I can see," said Poirot, smiling, "that you have not a very high opinion of Miss Lawson's usefulness."

"Companions are usually a poor lot, in my opinion. They're not *trained*, you see, in any way. Just *amateurs*. And usually they're women who wouldn't be any good at anything else.''

''Do you think Miss Lawson was very attached to Miss Arundell?''

''She seemed to be. Very upset and took on terribly when the old lady died. More than the relatives did, in *my* opinion,'' Nurse Carruthers finished with a sniff.

''Perhaps, then,'' said Poirot, nodding his head sagely, ''Miss Arundell knew what she was doing when she left her money as she did.''

''She was a very shrewd old lady,'' said the nurse. ''There wasn't much *she* didn't take in and know about, I must say!''

''Did she mention the dog, Bob, at all?''

''It's funny you should say that! She talked about him a lot—when she was delirious. Something about his ball and a fall she'd had. A nice dog, Bob was—I'm very fond of dogs. Poor fellow, he was very miserable when she died. Wonderful, aren't they? Quite human.''

And on the note of the humanity of dogs, we parted.

''There is one who has clearly no suspicions,'' remarked Poirot after we had left.

He sounded slightly discouraged.

We had a bad dinner at The George—Poirot groaning a good deal, especially over the soup.

''And it is so easy, Hastings, to make good soup. *Le pot au feu*—''

I avoided a disquisition on cookery with some difficulty.

After dinner we had a surprise.

We were sitting in the ''lounge'' which we had to ourselves. There had been one other man at dinner—a commercial traveller by his appearance —but he had gone out. I was just idly turning over the pages of an antiquated *Stock-Breeder's Gazette* or some such periodical when I suddenly heard Poirot's name being mentioned.

The voice in question was somewhere outside.

''Where is he? In here? Right—I can find him.''

The door was flung violently open, and Dr. Grainger, his face rather red, his eyebrows working irritably, strode into the room. He paused to close the door and then advanced upon us in no uncertain fashion.

''Oh, here you are! Now then, M. Hercule Poirot, what the devil do you mean by coming round to see me and telling me a pack of lies?''

''One of the juggler's balls?'' I murmured maliciously.

Poirot said in his oiliest voice:

''My dear doctor, you must allow me to explain—''

''Allow you? Allow you? Damn it, I'll *force* you to explain! You're a detective, that's what you are! A nosing, prying detective! Coming round to me and feeding me up with a pack of lies about writing old General Arundell's biography! More fool me to be taken in by such a damn fool story."

"Who told you of my identity?" asked Poirot.

"Who told me? Miss Peabody told me. *She* saw through you all right!"

"Miss Peabody—yes." Poirot sounded reflective. "I rather thought—"

Dr. Grainger cut in angrily.

"Now then, sir, I'm waiting for your explanation!"

"Certainly. My explanation is very simple. *Attempted murder.*"

"What? What's that?"

Poirot said quietly:

"Miss Arundell had a fall, did she not? A fall down the stairs shortly before her death?"

"Yes, what of it? She slipped on that damned dog's ball."

Poirot shook his head.

"No, Doctor, *she did not.* A *thread* was fastened across the top of the stairs so as to trip her up."

Dr. Grainger stared.

"Then why didn't she tell me so?" he demanded. "Never said a word to me about it."

"That is perhaps understandable—if it were *a member of her own family* who placed that thread there!"

"H'm—I see." Grainger cast a sharp glance at Poirot, then threw himself into a chair. "Well?" he said. "How did you come to be mixed up in this affair?"

"Miss Arundell wrote to me, stressing the utmost secrecy. Unfortunately the letter was delayed."

Poirot proceeded to give certain carefully edited details and explained the finding of the nail driven into the skirting-board.

The doctor listened with a grave face. His anger had abated.

"You can comprehend my position was a difficult one," Poirot finished. "I was employed, you see, by a dead woman. But I counted the obligation none the less strong for that."

Dr. Grainger's brows were drawn together in thought.

"And you've no idea who it was stretched that thread across the head of the stairs?" he asked.

"I have no *evidence* as to who it was. I will not say I have no *idea.*"

"It's a nasty story," said Grainger, his face grim.

"Yes. You can understand, can you not, that to begin with I was uncertain whether there had or had not been a sequel?"

"Eh? What's that?"

"To all intents and purposes Miss Arundell died a natural death, but could one be sure of that? There had been *one* attempt on her life. How could I be sure that there had not been a second? And this time a successful one!"

Grainger nodded thoughtfully.

"I suppose you are *sure*, Dr. Grainger—please do not get angry—that Miss Arundell's death *was* a natural one? I have come across certain evidence to-day—"

He detailed the conversation he had had with old Angus, Charles Arundell's interest in the weed-killer, and finally the old man's surprise at the emptiness of the tin.

Grainger listened with keen attention. When Poirot had finished he said quietly:

"I see your point. Many a case of arsenical poisoning has been diagnosed as acute gastric enteritis and a certificate given—especially when there are no suspicious contributing circumstances. In any case, arsenical poisoning presents certain difficulties—it has so many different forms. It may be acute, subacute, nervous or chronic. There may be vomiting and abdominal pain—these symptoms may be entirely absent—the person may fall suddenly to the ground and expire shortly afterwards—there may be narcotism and paralysis. The symptoms vary widely."

Poirot said:

"*Eh bien*, taking the facts into account, what is your opinion?"

Dr. Grainger was silent for a minute or two. Then he said slowly:

"Taking everything into account, and without any bias whatever, I am of the opinion that no form of arsenical poisoning could account for the symptoms in Miss Arundell's case. She died, I am quite convinced, of yellow atrophy of the liver. I have, as you know, attended her for many years, and she has suffered previously from attacks similar to that which caused her death. That is my considered opinion, M. Poirot."

And there, perforce, the matter had to rest.

It seemed rather an anti-climax when somewhat apologetically, Poirot produced the package of Liver Capsules he had brought at the druggist's.

"Miss Arundell took these, I believe?" he said. "I suppose they could not be injurious in any way?"

"That stuff? No harm in it. *Aloes—podophyllin*—all quite mild and harmless," said Grainger. "She liked trying the stuff. I didn't mind."

He got up.

"You dispensed certain medicines for her yourself?" asked Poirot.

"Yes—a mild liver pill to be taken after food." His eyes twinkled. "She could have taken a boxful without hurting herself. I'm not given to poisoning my patients, M. Poirot."

Then, with a smile, he shook hands with us both and departed.

Poirot undid the package he had purchased at the druggist's. The medicament consisted of transparent capsules, three quarters full of a dark brown powder.

"They look like a seasick remedy I once took," I remarked.

Poirot opened a capsule, examined its contents and tasted it gingerly with his tongue. He made a grimace.

"Well," I said, throwing myself back in my chair and yawning. "Everything seems harmless enough. Dr. Loughbarrow's specialities, and Dr. Grainger's pills! And Dr. Grainger seems definitely to negative the arsenic theory. Are you convinced at last, my stubborn Poirot."

"It is true that I am pig-headed—that is your expression, I think? Yes, definitely I have the head of the pig," said my friend meditatively.

"Then, in spite of having the druggist, the nurse and the doctor against you, you still think that Miss Arundell was murdered?"

Poirot said quietly:

"That is what I believe. No—more than believe. I am *sure* of it, Hastings."

"There's one way of proving it, I suppose," I said slowly. "Exhumation."

Poirot nodded.

"Is that the next step?"

"My friend, I have to go carefully."

"Why?"

"Because," his voice dropped, "I am afraid of a second tragedy."

"You mean—?"

"I am afraid, Hastings, I am afraid. Let us leave it at that."

22

The Woman on the Stairs

ON THE FOLLOWING morning a note arrived by hand. It was in a rather weak, uncertain handwriting slanting very much uphill.

Dear M. Poirot,

I hear from Ellen that you were at Littlegreen House yesterday. I shall be much obliged if you could call and see me sometime to-day.

Yours truly,
Wilhelmina Lawson.

"So *she's* down here," I remarked.

"Yes."

"Why has she come, I wonder?"

Poirot smiled.

"I do not suppose there is any sinister reason. After all, the house belongs to her."

"Yes, that's true, of course. You know, Poirot, that's the worst of this game of ours. Every single little thing that any one does is open to the most sinister constructions."

"It is true that I myself have enjoined upon you the motto, 'suspect every one.' "

"Are you still in that state yourself?"

"No—for me it has boiled down to this. I suspect one particular person."

"Which one?"

"Since, at the moment, it is only suspicion and there is no definite proof, I think I must leave you to draw your own deductions, Hastings. And do not neglect the psychology—that is important. The character of the murder—implying as it does a certain temperament in the murderer—that is an essential clue to the crime."

"I can't consider the character of the murderer if I don't know who the murderer is!"

"No, no, you have not paid attention to what I have just said. If you reflect sufficiently on the character—the necessary character of the *murder—then* you will realize *who* the murderer is!"

"Do you really know, Poirot?" I asked curiously.

"I cannot say I *know* because I have no proofs. That is why I cannot say more at the present. But I am quite sure—yes, my friend, in my own mind I am very sure."

"Well," I said, laughing, "mind he doesn't get *you*! That *would* be a tragedy!"

Poirot started a little. He did not take the matter as a joke. Instead he murmured: "You are right. I must be careful—extremely careful."

"You ought to wear a coat of chain mail," I said chaffingly. "And employ a taster in case of poison! In fact, you ought to have a regular band of gunmen to protect you!"

"*Merci*, Hastings, I shall rely on my wits."

He then wrote a note to Miss Lawson saying that he would call at Littlegreen House at eleven o'clock.

After that we breakfasted and then strolled out into the Square. It was about a quarter past ten and a hot sleepy morning.

I was looking into the window of the antique shop at a very nice set of Hepplewhite chairs when I received a highly painful lunge in the ribs, and a sharp, penetrating voice said: "Hi!"

I spun round indignantly to find myself face to face with Miss Peabody. In her hand (the instrument of her assault upon me) was a large and powerful umbrella with a spiked point.

Apparently completely callous to the severe pain she had inflicted, she observed in a satisfied voice:

"Ha! Thought it was you. Don't often make a mistake."

I said rather coldly:

"Er—good-morning. Can I do anything for you?"

"You can tell me how that friend of yours is getting on with his book—*Life of General Arundell*?"

"He hasn't actually started to write it yet," I said.

Miss Peabody indulged in a little silent but apparently satisfying laughter. She shook like a jelly. Recovering from that attack, she remarked:

"No, I don't suppose he will be starting to write it."

I said, smiling:

"So you saw through our little fiction?"

"What d'you take me for—a fool?" asked Miss Peabody. "I saw soon enough what your downy friend was after! Wanted me to talk! Well, *I* didn't mind. I like talking. Hard to get any one to listen nowadays. Quite enjoyed myself that afternoon."

She cocked a shrewd eye at me.

"What's it all about, eh? What's it all about?"

I was hesitating what exactly to reply when Poirot joined us. He bowed with *empressement* to Miss Peabody.

"Good-morning, mademoiselle. Enchanted to encounter you."

"Good-mornin'," said Miss Peabody. "What are you this morning, Parotti or Poirot—eh?"

"It was very clever of you to pierce my disguise so rapidly," said Poirot, smiling.

"Wasn't much disguise to pierce! Not many like you about, are there? Don't know if that's a good thing or a bad one. Difficult to say."

"I prefer, mademoiselle, to be unique."

"You've got your wish, I should say," said Miss Peabody drily. "Now then, Mr. Poirot, I gave you all the gossip you wanted the other day. Now it's my turn to ask questions. What's it all about? Eh? What's it all about?"

"Are you not asking a question to which you already know the answer?"

"I wonder." She shot a sharp glance at him. "Something fishy about that will? Or is it something else? Going to dig Emily up? Is that it?"

Poirot did not answer.

Miss Peabody nodded her head slowly and thoughtfully as though she had received a reply.

"Often wondered," she said inconsequently, "what it would feel like. . . . Readin' the papers you know—wondered if any one would ever be dug up in Market Basing. . . . Didn't think it would be Emily Arundell. . . ."

She gave him a sudden, piercing look.

"She wouldn't have liked it, you know. I suppose you've thought of that—hey?"

"Yes, I have thought of it."

"I suppose you would do—you're not a fool! Don't think you're particularly officious either."

Poirot bowed.

"Thank you, mademoiselle."

"And that's more than most people would say—looking at your moustache. Why d'you have a moustache like that? D'you like it?"

I turned away convulsed with laughter.

"In England the cult of the moustache is lamentably neglected," said Poirot. His hand surreptitiously caressed the hirsute adornment.

"Oh, I see! Funny," said Miss Peabody. "Knew a woman once who had a goitre and was proud of it! Wouldn't believe that, but it's true! Well, what I say is, it's lucky when you're pleased with what the Lord has given you. It's usually the other way about."

She shook her head and sighed.

"Never thought there would be a murder in this out-of-the-world spot." Again she shot a sudden, piercing look at Poirot. "Which of 'em did it?"

"Am I to shout that to you here in the street?"

"Probably means you don't know. Or do you? Oh, well—bad blood—bad blood. I'd like to know whether that Varley woman poisoned her husband or not. Makes a difference."

"You believe in heredity?"

Miss Peabody said suddenly:

"I'd rather it was Tanios. An outsider! But wishes ain't horses, worse luck. Well, I'll be getting along. I can see you're not goin' to tell me anything. . . . Who are you actin' for, by the way?"

Poirot said gravely:

"I am acting for the dead, mademoiselle."

I am sorry to say that Miss Peabody received this remark with a sudden shriek of laughter. Quickly subduing her mirth she said:

"Excuse me. It sounded like Isabel Tripp—that's all! What an awful woman! Julia's worse, I think. So painfully girlish. Never did like mutton-dressed lamb fashion. Well, good-bye. Seen Dr. Grainger at all?"

"Mademoiselle, I have the bone to pick with you. You betrayed my secret."

Miss Peabody indulged in her peculiar throaty chuckle.

"Men are simple! He'd swallowed that preposterous tissue of lies you told him. Wasn't he mad when I told him? Went away snorting with rage! He's looking for you."

"He found me last night."

"Oh! I wish I'd been there."

"I wish you had, mademoiselle," said Poirot gallantly.

Miss Peabody laughed and prepared to waddle away. She addressed me over her shoulder.

"Good-bye, young man. Don't you go buying those chairs. They're a fake."

She moved off, chuckling.

"That," said Poirot, "is a very clever old woman."

"Even although she did not admire your moustaches?"

"Taste is one thing," said Poirot coldly. "Brains are another."

We passed into the shop and spent a pleasant twenty minutes looking round. We emerged unscathed in pocket and proceeded in the direction of Littlegreen House.

Ellen, rather redder in the face than usual, admitted us and showed us into the drawing-room. Presently footsteps were heard descending the stairs and Miss Lawson came in. She seemed somewhat out of breath and flustered. Her hair was pinned up in a silk handkerchief.

"I hope you'll excuse my coming in like this, M. Poirot. I've been going through some locked-up cupboards—so many things—old people are inclined to *hoard* a little, I'm afraid—dear Miss Arundell was no exception—and one gets so much dust in one's *hair*—astonishing, you know, the things people collect—if you can believe me, two dozen needlebooks—actually, two dozen."

"You mean that Miss Arundell had bought two dozen needlebooks?"

"Yes, and put them away and forgot about them—and, of course, now the needles are all rusty—such a pity. She used to give them to the maids as Christmas presents."

"She was very forgetful—yes?"

"Oh, *very*. Especially in the way of putting things away. Like a dog with a bone, you know. That's what we used to call it between us. 'Now don't go and dog and bone it,' I used to say to her."

She laughed and then producing a small handkerchief from her pocket suddenly began to sniff.

"Oh, dear," she said tearfully. "It seems so dreadful of me to be laughing here."

"You have too much sensibility," said Poirot. "You feel things too much."

"That's what my mother always used to say to me, M. Poirot. 'You take things to heart too much, Mina,' she used to say. It's a great drawback, M. Poirot, to be so sensitive. Especially when one has one's living to get."

"Ah, yes, indeed, but that is all a thing of the past. You are now your own mistress. You can enjoy yourself—travel—you have absolutely no worries or anxieties."

"I suppose that's true," said Miss Lawson rather doubtfully.

"Assuredly it is true. Now talking of Miss Arundell's forgetfulness I see how it was that her letter to me never reached me for so long a time."

He explained the circumstances of the finding of the letter. A red spot showed in Miss Lawson's cheek. She said sharply:

"Ellen should have told *me*! To send that letter off to you without a word was great impertinence! She should have consulted me first. *Great* impertinence, I call it! Not one word did I hear about the whole thing. Disgraceful!"

"Oh, my dear lady, I am sure it was done in all good faith."

"Well, I think it was very *peculiar* myself! *Very* peculiar! Servants really do the oddest things. Ellen should have remembered that I am the mistress of the house now."

She drew herself up importantly.

"Ellen was very devoted to her mistress, was she not?" said Poirot.

"Yes, I dare say, but that makes no difference. I should have been *told*!"

"The important thing is—that I received the letter," said Poirot.

"Oh, I agree that it's no good making a fuss after things have happened, but all the same I think Ellen ought to be told that she mustn't take it upon herself to do things without asking first!"

She stopped, a red spot on each cheekbone.

Poirot was silent for a minute, then he said:

"You wanted to see me to-day? In what way can I be of service to you?"

Miss Lawson's annoyance subsided as promptly as it had arisen. She began to be flustered and incoherent again.

"Well, really—you see, I just *wondered* . . . Well, to tell the truth, M. Poirot, I arrived down here yesterday and, of course, Ellen told me you had been here, and I just wondered—well, as you hadn't *mentioned* to me that you were coming—Well, it seemed rather *odd*—and I couldn't see—"

"You could not see what I was doing down here?" Poirot finished for her.

"I—well—no, that's exactly it. I couldn't."

She looked at him, flushing but inquiring.

"I must make a little confession to you," said Poirot. "I have permitted you to remain under a misapprehension, I am afraid. You assumed that the letter I received from Miss Arundell concerned itself with the question of a small sum of money abstracted by—in all possibility—Mr. Charles Arundell."

Miss Lawson nodded.

"But that, you see, was not the case. . . . In fact, the first I heard of the stolen money was from you. . . . Miss Arundell wrote to me on the subject of her accident."

"Her accident?"

"Yes, she had a fall down the stairs, I understand."

"Oh, quite—quite—" Miss Lawson looked bewildered. She stared vacantly at Poirot. She went on. "But—I'm sorry—I'm sure it's very stupid of me—but why should she write to *you*? I understand—in fact, I think you said so—that you are a detective. You're not a—a doctor, too? Or a faith healer, perhaps?"

"No, I am not a doctor—nor a faith healer. But, like the doctor, I concern myself sometimes with so-called accidental deaths."

"With accidental deaths?"

"With *so-called* accidental deaths, I said. It is true that Miss Arundell did not *die*—but she might have died!"

"Oh, dear me, yes, the doctor said so, but I don't understand—"

Miss Lawson sounded still bewildered.

"The cause of the accident was supposed to be the ball of the little Bob, was it not?"

"Yes, yes, that was it. It was Bob's ball."

"Oh, no, it was not Bob's ball."

"But, excuse me, Mr. Poirot, I saw it there myself—as we all ran down."

"You saw it—yes, perhaps. But *it was not the cause of the accident. The cause of the accident, Miss Lawson, was a dark-coloured thread stretched about a foot above the top of the stairs*!"

"But—but a dog couldn't—"

"Exactly," said Poirot quickly. "A dog could not do that—he is not sufficiently intelligent—or, if you like, he is not sufficiently *evil*. . . . A *human being* put that thread in position. . . ."

Miss Lawson's face had gone deadly white. She raised a shaking hand to her face.

"Oh, Mr. Poirot—I can't believe it—you don't mean—but that is awful—really awful. You mean it was done on *purpose*?"

"Yes, it was done on purpose."

"But that's dreadful. It's almost like—like killing a person."

"If it had succeeded it *would* have been killing a person! In other words—it would have been murder!"

Miss Lawson gave a little shrill cry.

Poirot went on in the same grave tone.

"A nail was driven into the skirting-board so that the thread could be attached. That nail was varnished so as not to show. Tell me, do you ever remember a smell of varnish that you could not account for?"

Miss Lawson gave a cry.

"Oh, how extraordinary! To think of that! Why, of course! And to think I never thought—never dreamed—but then, how could I? And yet it did seem odd to me at the time."

Poirot leant forward.

"So—you can help us, mademoiselle. Once again you can help us. *C'est épatant!*"

"To think that was it! Oh, well, it all fits in."

"Tell me, I pray of you. You smelt varnish—yes?"

"Yes. Of course, I didn't know what it was. I thought—dear me—it is paint—no, it's more like floor stain, and then, of course, I thought I must have *imagined* it."

"When was this?"

"Now let me see—when was it?"

"Was it during that Easter week-end when the house was full of guests?"

"Yes, that was the time—but I'm trying to recall just which day it was. . . . Now, let me see, it wasn't Sunday. No, and it wasn't on Tuesday—that was the night Dr. Donaldson came to dinner. And on the Wednesday they had all left. No, of course, it was the *Monday*—Bank Holiday. I'd been lying awake—rather worried, you know. I always think Bank Holiday is such a worrying day! There had been only just enough cold beef to go round at supper and I was afraid Miss Arundell might be annoyed about it. You see *I'd* ordered the joint on the Saturday, and of course I ought to have said seven pounds but I thought five pounds would do nicely, but Miss Arundell was always so vexed if there was any shortage—she was so hospitable—"

Miss Lawson paused to draw a deep breath and then rushed on.

"And so I was lying awake and wondering whether she'd say anything about it to-morrow, and what with one thing and another I was a long time dropping off—and then just as I was going off something seemed to wake me up—a sort of rap or tap—and I sat up in bed, and then I sniffed. Of course, I'm always terrified of fire—sometimes I think I smell fire two or three times a night—(so awful wouldn't it be if one were *trapped*?). Anyway, there was a smell, and I sniffed hard, but it wasn't smoke or anything like that. And I said to myself it's more like paint or floor stain—but, of course, one wouldn't smell that in the middle of the night. But it was quite strong and I sat up sniffing and sniffing, and then I saw her in the glass—"

"Saw *her*? Saw whom?"

"In my looking-glass, you know, it's really most convenient. I left my door open a little always, so as to hear Miss Arundell if she were to call, and if she went up and down stairs I could see her. The one light was always left switched on in the passage. That's how I came to see her kneeling on the stairs—Theresa, I mean. She was kneeling on about the third step with her head bent down over something and I was just thinking, 'How odd, I wonder if she's *ill*?' when she got up and went away, so I supposed she'd just slipped or something. Or perhaps was stooping to pick something up. But, of course, I never thought about it again one way or another."

"The tap that aroused you would be the tap of the hammer on the nail," mused Poirot.

"Yes, I suppose it would. But oh, M. Poirot, how *dreadful*—how truly dreadful. I've always felt Theresa was, perhaps, a little *wild*, but to do a thing like that—"

"You are sure it was Theresa?"

"Oh, dear me, yes."

"It couldn't have been Mrs. Tanios or one of the maids, for instance?"

"Oh, no, it was Theresa."

Miss Lawson shook her head and murmured to herself, "Oh, dear, oh, dear," several times.

Poirot was staring at her in a way I found it hard to understand.

"Permit me," he said suddenly, "to make an experiment. Let us go upstairs and endeavour to reconstruct this little scene."

"Reconstruct? Oh, really—I don't know—I mean I don't quite see—"

"I will show you," said Poirot, cutting in upon these doubts in an authoritative manner.

Somewhat flustered, Miss Lawson led the way upstairs.

"I hope the room's tidy—so much to do—what with one thing and another—" She tailed off incoherently.

The room was indeed somewhat heavily littered with miscellaneous articles, obviously the result of Miss Lawson's turning out of cupboards. With her usual incoherence Miss Lawson managed to indicate her own position and Poirot was able to verify for himself the fact that a portion of the staircase was reflected in the wall-mirror.

"And now, mademoiselle," he suggested, "if you will be so good as to go out and reproduce the actions that you saw."

Miss Lawson, still murmuring, "Oh, dear—" bustled out to fulfill her part. Poirot acted the part of observer.

The performance concluded, he went out on the landing and asked which electric light had been left switched on.

"This one—this one along here. Just outside Miss Arundell's door."

Poirot reached up, detached the bulb and examined it.

"A forty watt lamp, I see. Not very powerful."

"No, it was just so that the passage shouldn't be quite dark."

Poirot retraced his steps to the top of the stairs.

"You will pardon me, mademoiselle, but with the light being fairly dim and the way that shadow falls it is hardly possible that you can have seen very clearly. Can you be positive it was Miss Theresa Arundell and not just an indeterminate female figure in a dressing gown?"

Miss Lawson was indignant.

"No, indeed, M. Poirot! I'm *perfectly* sure! I know Theresa well enough, I should hope! Oh, it was her all right. Her dark dressing gown and that big shining brooch she wears with the initials—I saw that plainly."

"So that there is no possible doubt. You saw the initials?"

"Yes, T. A. I know the brooch. Theresa often wore it. Oh, yes, I could swear to its being Theresa—and I will swear to it if necessary!"

There was a firmness and decision in those last two sentences that was quite at variance with her usual manner.

Poirot looked at her. Again there was something curious in his glance. It was aloof, appraising—and had also a queer appearance of finality about it.

"You would swear to that, yes?" he said.

"If—if—it's necessary. But I suppose it—will it be necessary?"

Again Poirot turned that appraising glance upon her.

"That will depend on the result of the exhumation," he said.

"Ex-exhumation?"

Poirot put out a restraining hand. In her excitement Miss Lawson very nearly went headlong down the stairs.

"It may possibly be a question of exhumation," he said.

"Oh, but surely—how *very* unpleasant! But I mean, I'm sure the family would oppose the idea very strongly—very strongly indeed."

"Probably they will."

"I'm quite sure they won't hear of such a thing!"

"Ah, but if it is as an order from the Home Office."

"But, M. Poirot—*why*? I mean it's not as though—not as though—"

"Not as though what?"

"Not as though there were anything—*wrong*."

"You think not?"

"No, of course not. Why, there *couldn't* be! I mean the doctor and the nurse and everything—"

"Do not upset yourself," said Poirot calmly and soothingly.

"Oh, but I can't help it! Poor dear Miss Arundell! It's not even as though Theresa had been here in the house when she died."

"No, she left on the Monday before she was taken ill, did she not?"

"Quite early in the morning. So you see, *she* can't have had anything to do with it!"

"Let us hope not," said Poirot.

"Oh, dear." Miss Lawson clasped her hands together. "I've never known *anything* so dreadful as all this! Really, I don't know whether I'm on my head or my heels."

Poirot glanced at his watch.

"We must depart. We are returning to London. And you, mademoiselle, you are remaining down here some little time?"

"No—no . . . I have really no settled plans. Actually I'm going back myself to-day. . . . I only came down just for a night to—to settle things a little."

"I see. Well, good-bye, mademoiselle, and forgive me if I have upset you at all."

"Oh, M. Poirot. *Upset* me? I feel quite *ill!* Oh, dear—oh, dear. It's such a *wicked* world! Such a dreadfully wicked world."

Poirot cut short her lamentations by taking her hand firmly in his.

"Quite so. And you are still ready to swear *that you saw Theresa Arundell kneeling on the stairs on the night of Easter Bank Holiday*?"

"Oh, yes, I can swear to that."

"And you can also swear that you saw a halo of light round Miss Arundell's head during the séance?"

Miss Lawson's mouth fell open.

"Oh, M. Poirot, don't—don't joke about these things."

"I am not joking. I am perfectly serious."

Miss Lawson said with dignity:

"It wasn't exactly a halo. It was more like the beginning of a manifestation. A ribbon of some luminous material. I think it was beginning to form into a face."

"Extremely interesting. *Au revoir*, mademoiselle, and please keep all this to yourself."

"Oh, of course—of course. I shouldn't dream of doing anything else. . . ."

The last we saw of Miss Lawson was her rather sheeplike face gazing after us from the front door step.

23

Dr. Tanios Calls on Us

NO SOONER HAD WE left the house than Poirot's manner changed. His face was grim and set.

"*Dépêchons-nous*, Hastings," he said. "We must get back to London as soon as possible."

"I'm willing." I quickened my pace to suit his. I stole a look at his grave face.

"Who do you suspect, Poirot?" I asked. "I wish you'd tell me. Do you believe it was Theresa Arundell on the stairs or not?"

Poirot did not reply to my question. Instead he asked a question of his own.

"Did it strike you—reflect before you answer—did it strike you that there was something *wrong* with that statement of Miss Lawson's?"

"How do you mean—wrong with it?"

"If I knew that I should not be asking you!"

"Yes, but wrong in what way?"

"That is just it. I cannot be precise. But as she was talking I had, somehow, a feeling of unreality . . . as though there was something—some small point that was wrong—that was, yes, that was the feeling—something that was *impossible*. . . ."

"She seemed quite positive it was Theresa!"

"Yes, yes."

"But after all, the light couldn't have been very good. I don't see how she can be quite so sure."

"No, no, Hastings, you are not helping me. It was some small point—something connected with—yes, I am sure of it—with the bedroom."

"With the bedroom?" I repeated, trying to recall the details of the room. "No," I said at last. "I can't help you."

Poirot shook his head vexedly.

"Why did you bring up that spiritualistic business again?" I asked.

"Because it is important."

"What is important? Miss Lawson's luminous 'ribbon development'?"

"You remember the Misses Tripp's description of the séance?"

"I know they saw a halo round the old lady's head." I laughed in spite of myself. "*I* shouldn't think she was a saint by all accounts! Miss Lawson seems to have been terrified by her. I felt quite sorry for the poor woman when she described how she lay awake, worried to death because she might get into trouble over ordering too small a sirloin of beef."

"Yes, it was an interesting touch that."

"What are we going to do when we get to London?" I asked as we turned into The George and Poirot asked for the bill.

"We must go and see Theresa Arundell immediately."

"And find out the truth? But won't she deny the whole thing anyway?"

"*Mon cher*, it is not a criminal offence to kneel upon a flight of stairs! She may have been picking up a pin to bring her luck—something of that sort!"

"And the smell of varnish?"

We could say no more just then, as the waiter arrived with the bill.

On the way to London we talked very little. I am not fond of talking and driving, and Poirot was so busy protecting his moustaches with his muffler from the disastrous effects of wind and dust that speech was quite beyond him.

We arrived at the flat at about twenty to two.

George, Poirot's immaculate and extremely English manservant, opened the door.

"A Dr. Tanios is waiting to see you, sir. He has been here for half an hour."

"Dr. Tanios? Where is he?"

"In the sitting-room, sir. A lady also called to see you, sir. She seemed very distressed to find you were absent from home. It was before I received your telephone message, sir, so I could not tell her when you would be returning to London."

"Describe this lady."

"She was about five foot seven, sir, with dark hair and light blue eyes. She was wearing a grey coat and skirt and a hat worn very much to the back of the head instead of over the right eye."

"Mrs. Tanios," I ejaculated in a low voice.

"She seemed in a condition of great nervous excitement, sir. Said it was of the utmost importance she should find you quickly."

"What time was this?"

"About half-past ten, sir."

Poirot shook his head as he passed on towards the sitting-room.

"That is the second time I have missed hearing what Mrs. Tanios has to say. What would you say, Hastings? Is there a fate in it?"

"Third time lucky," I said consolingly.

Poirot shook his head doubtfully.

"Will there be a third time? I wonder. Come, let us hear what the husband has to say."

Dr. Tanios was sitting in an armchair reading one of Poirot's books on psychology. He sprang up and greeted us.

"You must forgive this intrusion. I hope you don't mind my forcing my way in and waiting for you like this."

"*Du tout, du tout*. Pray sit down. Permit me to offer you a glass of sherry."

"Thank you. As a matter of fact, I have an excuse. M. Poirot, I am worried, terribly worried, about my wife."

"About your wife? I'm very sorry. What's the matter?"

Tanios said:

"You have seen her perhaps, lately?"

It seemed quite a natural question, but the quick look that accompanied it was not so natural.

Poirot replied in the most matter-of-fact manner.

"No, not since I saw her at the hotel with you yesterday."

"Ah—I thought perhaps she might have called upon you."

Poirot was busy pouring out three glasses of sherry.

He said in a slightly abstracted voice:

"No. Was there any—reason for her calling on me?"

"No, no." Dr. Tanios accepted his sherry. "Thank you. Thank you very much. No, there was no exact *reason*, but, to be frank, I am very much concerned about my wife's state of health."

"Ah, she is not strong?"

"Her bodily health," said Tanios slowly, "is good. I wish I could say the same for her mind."

"Ah?"

"I fear, M. Poirot, that she is on the verge of a complete nervous breakdown."

"My dear Dr. Tanios, I am extremely sorry to hear this."

"This condition has been growing for some time. During the last two months her manner towards me has completely changed. She is nervous, easily startled, and she has the oddest fancies—actually they are more than fancies—they are *delusions*!"

"Really?"

"Yes. She is suffering from what is commonly known as persecution mania—a fairly well-known condition."

Poirot made a sympathetic noise with his tongue.

"You can understand my anxiety!"

"Naturally. Naturally. But what I do not quite understand is why you have come to me. How can I help you?"

Dr. Tanios seemed a little embarrassed.

"It occurred to me that my wife might have—or may yet—come to you with some extraordinary tale. She may conceivably say that she is in danger from me—something of that kind."

"But why should she come to *me*?"

Dr. Tanios smiled—it was a charming smile—genial yet wistful.

"You are a celebrated detective, M. Poirot. I saw—I could see at once—that my wife was very impressed at meeting you yesterday. The mere fact of meeting a detective would make a powerful impression on her in her present state. It seems to me highly probable that she might seek you out and—and—well, confide in you. That is the way these nervous affections go! There is a tendency to turn against those nearest and dearest to you."

"Very distressing."

"Yes, indeed. I am very fond of my wife." There was a rich tenderness in his voice. "I always feel it was so brave of her to marry me—a man of another race—to come out to a far country—to leave all her own friends and surroundings. For the last few days I have been really distraught. . . . I can see only one thing for it. . . ."

"Yes?"

"Perfect rest and quiet—and suitable psychological treatment. There is a splendid home I know of run by a first-class man. I want to take her down there—it is in Norfolk—straightaway. Perfect rest and isolation from outside influence—that is what is needed. I feel convinced that once she has been there a month or two under skilled treatment there will be a change for the better."

"I see," said Poirot.

He uttered the words in a matter-of-fact manner without any clue to the feelings that prompted him.

Tanios again shot a quick glance at him.

"That is why, if she should come to you, I should be obliged if you will let me know at once."

"But certainly. I will telephone you. You are at the Durham Hotel still?"

"Yes. I am going back there now."

"And your wife is not there?"

"She went out directly after breakfast."

"Without telling you where she was going?"

"Without saying a word. That is most unlike her."

"And the children?"

"She took them with her."

"I see."

Tanios got up.

"Thank you so much, M. Poirot. I need hardly say that if she does tell you any high-flown stories of intimidation and persecution, pay no attention to them. It is, unfortunately, a part of her malady."

"Most distressing," said Poirot with sympathy.

"It is indeed. Although one knows, medically speaking, that it is part of a recognized mental disease, yet one cannot help being hurt when a person very near and dear to you turns against you and all their affection changes to dislike."

"You have my deepest sympathy," said Poirot as he shook hands with his guest.

"By the way—" Poirot's voice recalled Tanios just as he was at the door.

"Yes?"

"Do you ever prescribe chloral for your wife?"

Tanios gave a startled movement.

"I—no—at least I may have done. But not lately. She seems to have taken an aversion to any form of sleeping draught."

"Ah! I suppose because she does not trust you?"

"M. Poirot!"

Tanios came striding forward angrily.

"That would be part of the disease," said Poirot smoothly.

Tanios stopped.

"Yes, yes, of course."

"She is probably highly suspicious of anything you give her to eat or drink. Probably suspects you of wanting to poison her?"

"Dear me, M. Poirot, you are quite right. You know something of such cases, then?"

"One comes across them now and then in my profession, naturally. But do not let me detain you. You may find her waiting for you at the hotel."

"True. I hope I shall. I feel terribly anxious."

He hurried out of the room.

Poirot went swiftly to the telephone. He flicked over the pages of the telephone directory and asked for a number.

"'Allo—'allo—is that the Durham Hotel? Can you tell me if Mrs. Tanios is in? What? T-A-N-I-O-S. Yes, that is right. Yes? Yes? Oh, I see."

He replaced the receiver.

"Mrs. Tanios left the hotel this morning early. She returned at eleven, waited in the taxi whilst her luggage was brought down and drove away with it."

"Does Tanios know she took away her luggage?"

"I think not as yet."

"Where has she gone?"

"Impossible to tell."

"Do you think she will come back here?"

"Possibly. I cannot tell."

"Perhaps she will write."

"Perhaps."

"What can we do?"

Poirot shook his head. He looked worried and distressed.

"Nothing at the moment. A hasty lunch and then we will go and see Theresa Arundell."

"Do you believe it *was* her on the stairs?"

"Impossible to tell. One thing I made sure of—Miss Lawson could not have seen her face. She saw a tall figure in a dark dressing gown, that is all."

"And the brooch?"

"My dear friend, a brooch is not part of a person's anatomy! It can be detached from that person. It can be lost—or borrowed—or even stolen."

"In other words, you don't want to believe Theresa Arundell guilty?"

"I want to hear what she has to say on the matter."

"And if Mrs. Tanios comes back?"

"I will arrange for that."

George brought in an omelette.

"Listen, George," said Poirot. "If that lady comes back, you will ask her to wait. If Dr. Tanios comes while she is here, on no account let him in. If he asks if his wife is here, you will tell him she is not. You understand?"

"Perfectly, sir."

Poirot attacked the omelette.

"This business complicates itself," he said. "We must step very carefully. If not—the murderer will strike again."

"If he did you might get him."

"Quite possibly, but I prefer the life of the innocent to the conviction of the guilty. We must go very, very carefully."

24

Theresa's Denial

WE FOUND Theresa Arundell just preparing to go out.

She was looking extraordinarily attractive. A small hat of the most outrageous fashion descended rakishly over one eye. I recognized with momentary amusement that Bella Tanios had worn a cheap imitation of such a hat yesterday and had worn it—as George had put it—on the back of the head instead of over the right eye. I remembered well how she had pushed it further and further back on her untidy hair.

Poirot said politely:

"Can I have just a minute or two, mademoiselle, or will it delay you too much?"

Theresa laughed.

"Oh, it doesn't matter. I'm always three quarters of an hour late for everything. I might just as well make it an hour."

She led him into the sitting-room. To my surprise Dr. Donaldson rose from a chair by the window.

"You've met M. Poirot already, Rex, haven't you?"

"We met at Market Basing," said Donaldson stiffly.

"You were pretending to write the life of my drunken grandfather, I understand," said Theresa. "Rex, my angel, will you leave us?"

"Thank you, Theresa, but I think that from every point of view it would be advisable for me to be present at this interview."

There was a brief duel of eyes. Theresa's were commanding. Donaldson's were impervious. She showed a quick flash of anger.

"All right, stay then, damn you!"

Dr. Donaldson seemed unperturbed.

He seated himself again in the chair by the window, laying down his book on the arm of it. It was a book on the pituitary gland, I noticed.

Theresa sat down on her favourite low stool and looked impatiently at Poirot.

"Well, you've seen Purvis? What about it?"

Poirot said in a non-committal voice:

"There are—possibilities, mademoiselle."

She looked at him thoughtfully. Then she sent a very faint glance in the direction of the doctor. It was, I think, intended as a warning to Poirot.

"But it would be well, I think," went on Poirot, "for me to report later when my plans are more advanced."

A faint smile showed for a minute on Theresa's face.

Poirot continued:

"I have to-day come from Market Basing and while there I have talked to Miss Lawson. Tell me, mademoiselle, did you on the night of April 13th (that was the night of the Easter Bank Holiday) kneel upon the stairs after every one had gone to bed?"

"My dear Hercule Poirot, what an extraordinary question. Why should I?"

"The question, mademoiselle, is not why you *should*, but whether you *did*."

"I'm sure I don't know. I should think it most unlikely."

"You comprehend, mademoiselle, Miss Lawson *says you did*."

Theresa shrugged her attractive shoulders.

"Does it matter?"

"It matters very much."

She stared at him in a perfectly amiable fashion. Poirot stared back.

"Loopy!" said Theresa.

"Pardon?"

"Definitely loopy!" said Theresa. "Don't you think so, Rex?"

Dr. Donaldson coughed.

"Excuse me, M. Poirot, but what is the point of the question?"

My friend spread out his hands.

"It is most simple! Some one drove in a nail in a convenient position at the head of the stairs. The nail was just touched with brown varnish to match the skirting-board."

"Is this a new kind of witchcraft?" asked Theresa.

"No, mademoiselle, it is much more homely and simple than that. On the following evening, the Tuesday, *some one* attached a string or thread from the nail to the balusters with the result that when Miss Arundell came out of her room she caught her foot in it and went headlong down the stairs."

Theresa drew in her breath sharply.

"That was Bob's ball!"

"*Pardon*, it was not."

There was a pause. It was broken by Donaldson, who said in his quiet, precise voice:

"Excuse me, but what evidence have you in support of this statement?"

Poirot said quietly:

"The evidence of the nail, the evidence of Miss Arundell's own written words, and finally the evidence of Miss Lawson's eyes."

Theresa found her voice.

"She says *I* did it, does she?"

Poirot did not answer except by bending his head a little.

"Well, it's a lie! I had nothing to do with it!"

"You were kneeling on the stairs for quite another reason?"

"I wasn't kneeling on the stairs at all!"

"Be careful, mademoiselle."

"I wasn't there! I never came out of my room after I went to bed on any evening I was there."

"Miss Lawson recognized you."

"It was probably Bella Tanios or one of the maids she saw."

"She says it was you."

"She's a damned liar!"

"She recognized your dressing gown and a brooch you wear."

"A brooch—what brooch?"

"A brooch with your initials."

"Oh, I know the one! What a circumstantial liar she is!"

"You still deny that it was you she saw?"

"If it's my word against hers—"

"You are a better liar than she is—eh?"

Theresa said calmly:

"That's probably quite true. But in this case I'm speaking the truth. I wasn't preparing a booby trap, or saying my prayers, or picking up gold or silver, or doing anything at all on the stairs."

"Have you this brooch that was mentioned?"

"Probably. Do you want to see it?"

"If you please, mademoiselle."

Theresa got up and left the room. There was an awkward silence. Dr. Donaldson looked at Poirot much as I imagined he might have looked at an anatomical specimen.

Theresa returned.

"Here it is."

She almost flung the ornament at Poirot. It was a large rather showy chromium or stainless steel brooch with T.A. enclosed in a circle. I had to admit that it was large enough and showy enough to be easily seen in Miss Lawson's mirror.

"I never wear it now. I'm tired of it," said Theresa. "London's been flooded with them. Every little skivvy wears one."

"But it was expensive when you bought it?"

"Oh, yes. They were quite exclusive to begin with."

"When was that?"

"Last Christmas, I think it was. Yes, about then."

"Have you ever lent it to any one?"

"No."

"You had it with you at Littlegreen House?"

"I suppose I did. Yes, I did. I remember."

"Did you leave it about at all? Was it out of your possession while you were there?"

"No, it wasn't. I wore it on a green jumper, I remember. And I wore the same jumper every day."

"And at night?"

"It was still in the jumper."

"And the jumper?"

"Oh, hell, the jumper was sitting on a chair."

"You are sure no one removed the brooch and put it back again the next day?"

"We'll say so in court if you like—if you think that's the best lie to tell! Actually I'm *quite sure* that nothing like that happened! It's a pretty idea that somebody framed me—but I don't think it's true."

Poirot frowned. Then he got up, attached the brooch carefully to his coat lapel and approached a mirror on a table at the other end of the room. He stood in front of it and then moved slowly backward, getting an effect of distance.

Then he uttered a grunt.

"Imbecile that I am! Of course!"

He came back and handed the brooch to Theresa with a bow.

"You are quite right, mademoiselle. The brooch did *not* leave your possession! I have been regrettably dense."

"I do like modesty," said Theresa, pinning the brooch on carelessly.

She looked up at him.

"Anything more? I ought to be going."

"Nothing that cannot be discussed later."

Theresa moved towards the door. Poirot went on in a quiet voice:

"There is a question of exhumation, it is true—"

Theresa stopped dead. The brooch fell from her hand to the ground.

"What's that?"

Poirot said clearly:

"It is possible that the body of Miss Emily Arundell may be exhumed."

Theresa stood still, her hands clenched. She said in a low, angry voice:

"Is this *your* doing? It can't be done without an application from the family!"

"You are wrong, mademoiselle. It can be done on an order from the Home Office."

"My God!" said Theresa.

She turned and walked swiftly up and down.

Donaldson said quietly:

"I really don't see that there is any need to be so upset, Tessa. I dare say that to an outsider the idea is not very pleasant, but—"

She interrupted him.

"Don't be a fool, Rex!"

Poirot asked:

"The idea disturbs you, mademoiselle?"

"Of course it does! It isn't decent. Poor old Aunt Emily. Why the devil *should* she be exhumed?"

"I presume," said Donaldson, "that there is some doubt as to the cause of death?" He looked inquiringly at Poirot. He went on. "I confess that I am surprised. I think that there is no doubt that Miss Arundell died a natural death from a disease of long standing."

"You told me something about a rabbit and liver trouble once," said Theresa. "I've forgotten it now, but you infect a rabbit with blood from a person with yellow atrophy of the liver, and then you inject that rabbit's blood into another rabbit, and then that second rabbit's blood into a person and the person gets a diseased liver. Something like that."

"That was merely an illustration of serum therapeutics," said Donaldson patiently.

"Pity there are so many rabbits in the story!" said Theresa with a reckless laugh. "None of us keep rabbits." She turned on Poirot and her voice altered.

"M. Poirot, is this *true*?" she asked.

"It is true enough, but—there are ways of avoiding such a contingency, mademoiselle."

"Then avoid it!" Her voice sank almost to a whisper. It was urgent, compelling. "Avoid it *at all costs*!"

Poirot rose to his feet.

"Those are your instructions?" His voice was formal.

"Those are my instructions."

"But, Tessa—" Donaldson interrupted.

She whirled round on her fiancé.

"Be quiet! She was *my* aunt, wasn't she? Why should *my* aunt be dug up? Don't you know there will be paragraphs in the papers and gossip and general unpleasantness?" She swung round again on Poirot.

"You must stop it! I give you *carte blanche*. Do anything you like, but *stop it*!"

Poirot bowed formally.

"I will do what I can. *Au revoir, mademoiselle, au revoir, Doctor*."

"Oh, go away!" cried Theresa. "And take St. Leonards with you. I wish I'd never set eyes on either of you."

We left the room. Poirot did not this time deliberately place his ear to the crack, but he dallied—yes, he dallied.

And not in vain. Theresa's voice rose clear and defiant:

"Don't look at me like that, Rex."

And then suddenly, with a break in her voice: "Darling."

Dr. Donaldson's precise voice answered her.

He said very clearly:

"That man means mischief."

Poirot grinned suddenly. He drew me through the front door.

"Come, St. Leonards," he said. "*C'est drôle, ça!*"

Personally I thought the joke a particularly stupid one.

25

I Lie Back and Reflect

NO I THOUGHT, as I hurried after Poirot, there was no doubt about it now. Miss Arundell had been murdered and Theresa knew it. But was she herself the criminal or was there another explanation?

She was afraid—yes. But was she afraid for herself or for some one else? Could that some one be the quiet, precise young doctor with the calm, aloof manner?

Had the old lady died of genuine disease *artificially induced*?

Up to a point it all fitted in—Donaldson's ambitions, his belief that Theresa would inherit money at her aunt's death. Even the fact that he had been at dinner there on the evening of the accident. How easy to leave a convenient window open and return in the dead of night to tie the murderous thread across the staircase. But then, what about the placing of the nail in position?

No, Theresa must have done that. Theresa, his fiancée and accomplice. With the two of them working it together, the whole thing seemed clear enough. In that case it was probably Theresa who had actually placed the thread in position. The *first* crime, the crime that failed, had been *her* work. The second crime, the crime that had succeeded, was Donaldson's more scientific masterpiece.

Yes—it all fitted in.

Yet even now there were loose strands. Why had Theresa blurted out those facts about inducing liver disease in human beings? It was almost as though she did not realize the truth. . . . But in that case—and I felt my mind growing bewildered, and I interrupted my speculations to ask:

"Where are we going, Poirot?"

"Back to my flat. It is possible that we may find Mrs. Tanios there."

My thoughts switched off on a different track.

Mrs. Tanios! That was another mystery! If Donaldson and Theresa were guilty, where did Mrs. Tanios and her smiling husband come in? What did the woman want to tell Poirot and what was Tanios's anxiety to prevent her doing so?

"Poirot," I said humbly, "I'm getting rather muddled. They're not *all* in it, are they?"

"Murder by a syndicate? A family syndicate? No, not this time. There is the mark of one brain and one brain only in this. The psychology is very clear."

"You mean that either Theresa or Donaldson did it—but not *both* of them? Did he get her to hammer that nail in on some entirely innocent pretext, then?"

"My dear friend, from the moment I heard Miss Lawson's story I realized that there were three possibilities: (1) That Miss Lawson was telling the exact truth. (2) That Miss Lawson had invented the story for reasons of her own. (3) That Miss Lawson actually believed her own story, but that her identification rested upon the brooch—and as I have already pointed out to you—a brooch is easily detachable from its owner."

"Yes, but Theresa insists that the brooch did not leave her possession."

"And she is perfectly right. I had overlooked a small but intensely significant fact."

"Very unlike you, Poirot," I said solemnly.

"*N'est-ce pas*? But one has one's lapses."

"Age will tell!"

"Age has nothing to do with it," said Poirot coldly.

"Well, what is the significant fact?" I asked as we turned in at the entrance of the Mansions.

"I will show you."

We had just reached the flat.

George opened the door to us. In reply to Poirot's anxious question he shook his head.

"No, sir, Mrs. Tanios has not called. Neither has she telephoned."

Poirot went into the sitting-room. He paced up and down for a few moments. Then he picked up the telephone. He got first on to the Durham Hotel.

"Yes—yes, please. Ah, Dr. Tanios, this is Hercule Poirot speaking. Your wife has returned? Oh, not returned. Dear me. . . . Taken her luggage you say. . . . And the children. . . . You have no idea where she has gone. . . . Yes, quite. . . . Oh, perfectly. . . . If my professional services are of any use to you? I have a certain experience in these matters. . . . Such things can be done quite discreetly. . . . No, of course not. . . . Yes, of course that is true. . . . Certainly—certainly. I shall respect your wishes in the matter."

He hung up the receiver thoughtfully.

"He does not know where she is," he said thoughtfully. "I think that is quite genuine. The anxiety in his voice is unmistakable. He does not want to go to the police; that is understandable. Yes, I understand that.

He does not want my assistance either. That is, perhaps, not quite so understandable. . . . He wants her found—but he does not want *me* to find her. . . . No, definitely he does not want me to find her. . . . He seems confident that he can manage the matter himself. He does not think she can remain long hidden, for she has very little money with her. Also she has the children. Yes, I fancy he will be able to hunt her down before long. But, I think, Hastings, that we shall be a little quicker than he is. It is important, I think, that we should be."

"Do you think it's true that she is slightly batty?" I asked.

"I think that she is in a highly nervous, overwrought condition."

"But not to such a point that she ought to be in a mental home?"

"That, very definitely, no."

"You know, Poirot, I don't quite understand all this."

"If you will pardon my saying so, Hastings, you do not understand at all!"

"There seem so many—well—side issues."

"Naturally there are side issues. To separate the main issue from the side issues is the first task of the orderly mind."

"Tell me, Poirot, have you realized all along that there were *eight* possible suspects and not seven?"

Poirot replied drily:

"I have taken that fact into consideration from the moment that Theresa Arundell mentioned that the last time she saw Dr. Donaldson was when he dined at Littlegreen House on April 14th."

"I can't quite see—" I broke off.

"What is it you cannot quite see?"

"Well, if Donaldson had planned to do away with Miss Arundell by scientific means—by inoculation, that is to say—I can't see why he resorted to such a clumsy device as a string across the stairs."

"*En vérité*, Hastings, there are moments when I lose patience with you! One method is a highly scientific one needing fully specialized knowledge. That is so, is it not?"

"Yes."

"And the other is a homely simple method—'the kind that mother makes'—as the advertisements say. Is that not right?"

"Yes, exactly."

"Then think, Hastings—*think*. Lie back in your chair, close the eyes, employ the little grey cells."

I obeyed. That is to say, I leant back in the chair and closed my eyes and endeavoured to carry out the third part of Poirot's instructions. The result, however, did not seem to clarify matters much.

I opened my eyes to find Poirot regarding me with the kindly attention a nurse might display towards a childish charge.

"Eh bien?"

I made a desperate attempt to emulate Poirot's manner.

"Well," I said, "it seems to me that the kind of person who laid the original booby-trap is not the kind of person to plan out a scientific murder."

"Exactly."

"And I doubt if a mind trained to scientific complexities would think of anything so childish as the accident plan—it would be altogether too haphazard."

"Very clearly reasoned."

Emboldened, I went on:

"Therefore, the only logical solution seems to be this—the two attempts were planned by two different people. We have here to deal with murder attempted by two entirely different people."

"You do not think that is too much of a coincidence?"

"You said yourself once that one coincidence is nearly always found in a murder-case."

"Yes, that is true. I have to admit it."

"Well, then."

"And who do you suggest for your villains?"

"Donaldson and Theresa Arundell. A doctor is clearly indicated for the final and successful murder. On the other hand, we know that Theresa Arundell is concerned in the first attempt. I think it's possible that they acted quite independently of each other."

"You are so fond of saying 'we know,' Hastings. I can assure you that no matter what *you* know, I do not know that Theresa was implicated."

"But Miss Lawson's story."

"Miss Lawson's story is Miss Lawson's story. Just that."

"But she says—"

"She says—she says. . . . Always you are so ready to take what people say for a proved and accepted fact. Now listen, *mon cher*, I told you at the time, did I not, that something struck me as wrong about Miss Lawson's story?"

"Yes, I remember your saying so. But you couldn't get hold of what it was."

"Well, I have done so now. A little moment and I will show you what I, imbecile that I am, ought to have seen at once."

He went over to the desk and opening a drawer took out a sheet of cardboard. He cut into this with a pair of scissors, motioning to me not to overlook what he was doing.

"Patience, Hastings, in a little moment we will proceed to our experiment."

I averted my eyes obligingly.

In a minute or two Poirot uttered an exclamation of satisfaction. He put away the scissors, dropped the fragments of cardboard into the waste-paper basket and came across the room to me.

"Now, do not look. Continue to avert the eyes while I pin something to the lapel of your coat."

I humoured him. Poirot completed the proceeding to his satisfaction, then, propelling me gently to my feet he drew me across the room, and into the adjoining bedroom.

"Now, Hastings, regard yourself in the glass. You are wearing, are you not, a fashionable brooch with your initials on it—only, *bien entendu*, the brooch is made not of chromium nor stainless steel, nor gold, nor platinum—but of humble cardboard!"

I looked at myself and smiled. Poirot is uncommonly neat with his fingers. I was wearing a very fair representation of Theresa Arundell's brooch—a circle cut out of cardboard and enclosing my initials—A. H.

"*Eh bien*," said Poirot. "You are satisfied? You have there, have you not, a very smart brooch with your initials?"

"A most handsome affair," I agreed.

"It is true that it does not gleam and reflect the light, but all the same you are prepared to admit that that brooch could be seen plainly from some distance away?"

"I've never doubted it."

"Quite so. Doubt is not your strong point. Simple faith is more characteristic of you. And now, Hastings, be so good as to remove your coat."

Wondering a little, I did so. Poirot divested himself of his own coat and slipped on mine, turning away a little as he did so.

"And now," he said. "Regard how the brooch—the brooch with *your* initials—becomes me?"

He whisked round. I stared at him—for the moment uncomprehendingly. Then I saw the point.

"What a blithering fool I am! Of course. It's H. A. in the brooch, not A. H. at all."

Poirot beamed on me, as he reassumed his own clothes and handed me mine.

"Exactly—and now you see what struck me as wrong with Miss Lawson's story. She stated that she had seen Theresa's initials clearly on the brooch she was wearing. But she saw Theresa in the *glass*. So, *if she saw the initials at all*, she must have seen them *reversed*."

"Well," I argued. "Perhaps she did, and realized that they were reversed."

"*Mon cher*, did that occur to you just now? Did you exclaim, 'Ha! Poirot, you've got it wrong—that's H. A. really—not A. H.'? No, you did not. And yet you are a good deal more intelligent, I should say, than Miss Lawson. Do not tell me that a muddle-headed woman like that woke up suddenly, and still half-asleep, realized that A. T. was really T. A. No, that is not at all consistent with the mentality of Miss Lawson."

"She was determined it should be Theresa," I said slowly.

"You are getting nearer, my friend. You remember, I hint to her that she could not really see the face of any one on the stairs, and immediately—what does she do?"

"Remembers Theresa's brooch and lugs that in—forgetting that the mere fact of having seen it in the glass gave her own story the lie."

The telephone bell rang sharply. Poirot crossed to it.

He only spoke a few non-committal words.

"Yes? Yes . . . certainly. Yes, quite convenient. The afternoon, I think. Yes, two o'clock will do admirably."

He replaced the receiver and turned to me with a smile.

"Dr. Donaldson is anxious to have a talk with me. He is coming here to-morrow afternoon at two o'clock. We progress, *mon ami*, we progress."

26

Mrs. Tanios Refuses to Speak

WHEN I CAME round after breakfast the following morning I found Poirot busy at the writing-table.

He raised a hand in salutation, then proceeded with his task. Presently he gathered up the sheets, enclosed them in an envelope and sealed them up carefully.

"Well, old boy, what are you doing?" I asked facetiously. "Writing an account of the case to be placed in safe-keeping in case some one bumps you off during the course of the day?"

"You know, Hastings, you are not so far wrong as you think."

His manner was serious.

"Is our murderer really about to get dangerous?"

"A murderer is always dangerous," said Poirot gravely. "Astonishing how often that fact is overlooked."

"Any news?"

"Dr. Tanios rang up."

"Still no trace of his wife?"

"No."

"Then that's all right."

"I wonder."

"Dash it all, Poirot, you don't think she's been bumped off, do you?"

Poirot shook his head doubtfully.

"I confess," he murmured, "that I should like to know where she is."

"Oh, well," I said. "She'll turn up."

"Your cheerful optimism never fails to delight me, Hastings!"

"My goodness, Poirot, you don't think she'll turn up in parcels or dismembered in a trunk?"

Poirot said slowly:

"I find the anxiety of Dr. Tanios somewhat excessive—but no more of that. The first thing to do is to interview Miss Lawson."

"Are you going to point out that little error over the brooch?"

"Certainly not. That little fact remains up my sleeve until the right moment comes."

"Then what are you going to say to her?"

"That, *mon ami*, you will hear in due course."

"More lies, I suppose?"

"You are really very offensive sometimes, Hastings. Anybody would think I enjoyed telling lies."

"I rather think you do. In fact, I'm sure of it."

"It is true that I sometimes compliment myself upon my ingenuity," Poirot confessed naïvely.

I could not help giving a shout of laughter. Poirot looked at me reproachfully and we set off for Clanroyden Mansions.

We were shown into the same crowded sitting-room and Miss Lawson came bustling in, her manner even more incoherent than usual.

"Oh, dear, M. Poirot, good-morning. Such a to-do—rather untidy, I'm afraid. But then, everything is at sixes and sevens this morning. Ever since Bella arrived—"

"What is that you say? Bella?"

"Yes, Bella Tanios. She turned up half an hour ago—*and* the children—completely exhausted, poor soul! Really, I don't know what to do about it. You see, she's left her husband."

"Left him?"

"So she says. Of course, I've no doubt she's fully *justified*, poor thing."

"She has confided in you?"

"Well—not exactly *that*. In fact, she won't say anything at all. Just repeats that she's left him and that nothing will induce her to go back to him!"

"That is a very serious step to take."

"Of course it is! In fact, if he'd been an Englishman, I would have advised her—but there, he isn't an Englishman. . . . And she looks so peculiar, poor thing, so—well, so *scared*. What can he have been doing to her? I believe Turks are frightfully cruel sometimes."

"Dr. Tanios is a Greek."

"Yes, of course, that's the other way about—I mean, they're usually the ones who get massacred by the Turks—or am I thinking of Armenians? But all the same, I don't like to think of it. I don't think she *ought* to go back to him, do you, M. Poirot? Anyway, I mean, she says she won't. . . . She doesn't even want him to know where she is."

"As bad as that?"

"Yes, you see it's the *children*. She's so afraid he could take them back to Smyrna. Poor soul, she really is in a terrible way. You see, she's got no money—no money at all. She doesn't know where to go or what to do. She wants to try and earn her living, but, really, you know, M. Poirot, that's not so easy as it sounds. I know that. It's not as though she were *trained* for anything."

"When did she leave her husband?"

"Yesterday. She spent last night in a little hotel near Paddington. She came to me because she couldn't think of any one else to go to, poor thing."

"And are you going to help her? That is very good of you."

"Well, you see, M. Poirot, I really feel it's my *duty*. But, of course, it's all very difficult. This is a very small flat and there's no room—and what with one thing and another."

"You could send her to Littlegreen House?"

"I suppose I could—but, you see, her husband might think of that. Just for the moment I've got her rooms at the Wellington Hotel in Queen's Road. She's staying there under the name of Mrs. Peters."

"I see," said Poirot.

He paused for a minute, then said:

"I would like to see Mrs. Tanios. You see, she called at my flat yesterday but I was out."

"Oh, did she? She didn't tell me that. I'll tell her, shall I?"

"If you would be so good."

Miss Lawson hurried out of the room. We could hear her voice.

"Bella—Bella—my dear, will you come and see M. Poirot?"

We did not hear Mrs. Tanios's reply, but a minute or two later she came into the room.

I was really shocked at her appearance. There were dark circles under her eyes and her cheeks were completely destitute of colour, but what struck me far more than this was her obvious air of terror. She started at the least provocation, and she seemed to be continually listening.

Poirot greeted her in his most soothing manner. He came forward, shook hands, arranged a chair for her and handed her a cushion. He treated the pale, frightened woman as though she had been a queen.

"And now, madame, let us have a little chat. You came to see me yesterday, I believe?"

She nodded.

"I regret very much that I was away from home."

"Yes—yes, I wish you had been there."

"You came because you wanted to tell me something?"

"Yes, I—I meant to—"

"*Eh bien*, I am here, at your service."

Mrs. Tanios did not respond. She sat quite still, twisting a ring round and round on her finger.

"Well, madame?"

Slowly, almost reluctantly, she shook her head.

"No," she said. "I daren't."

"You *daren't*, madame?"

"No. I—if he knew—he'd—Oh, something would happen to me!"

"Come, come, madame—that is absurd."

"Oh, but it isn't absurd—it isn't absurd at all. You don't know him. . . ."

"By *him*, you mean your husband, madame?"

"Yes, of course."

Poirot was silent a minute or two, then he said:

"Your husband came to see me yesterday, madame."

A quick look of alarm sprang up in her face.

"Oh, no! You didn't tell him—but of course you didn't! You couldn't. You didn't know where I was. Did he—did he say I was *mad*?"

Poirot answered cautiously.

"He said that you were—highly nervous."

But she shook her head, undeceived.

"No, he said that I was mad—or that I was going mad! He wants to shut me up so that I shan't be able to tell any one ever."

"Tell any one—what?"

But she shook her head. Twisting her fingers nervously round and round, she muttered:

"I'm afraid. . . ."

"But, madame, once you have *told* me—you are *safe*! The secret is out! The fact will protect you automatically."

But she did not reply. She went on twisting—twisting at her ring.

"You must see that yourself," said Poirot gently.

She gave a sort of gasp.

"How am I to know? . . . Oh, dear, it's terrible. He's so *plausible*! And he's a doctor! People will believe him and not me. I know they will. I should myself. Nobody will believe me. How could they?"

"You will not even give me the chance?"

She shot a troubled glance at him.

"How do I know? You may be on his side."

"I am on no one's side, madame. I am—always—on the side of the truth."

"I don't know," said Mrs. Tanios hopelessly. "Oh, I don't know."

She went on, her words gathering volume, tumbling over each other.

"It's been so awful—for years now. I've seen things happening again and again. And I couldn't say anything or do anything. There have been the children. It's been like a long nightmare. And now this. . . . But I won't go back to him. I won't let him have the children! I'll go somewhere where he can't find me. Mina Lawson will help me. She's been so kind—so wonderfully kind. Nobody could have been kinder." She stopped, then shot a quick look at Poirot and asked:

"What did he say about me? Did he say I had delusions?"

"He said, madame, that you had—changed towards him."

She nodded.

"And he said I had delusions. He *did* say that, didn't he?"

"Yes, madame, to be frank, he did."

"That's it, you see. That's what it will sound like. And I've no proof—no real proof."

Poirot leaned back in his chair. When he next spoke it was with an entire change of manner.

He spoke in a matter-of-fact, business-like voice with as little emotion as if he had been discussing some dry matter of business.

"Do you suspect your husband of doing away with Miss Emily Arundell?"

Her answer came quickly—a spontaneous flash.

"I don't suspect—I know."

"Then, madame, it is your duty to speak."

"Ah, but it isn't so easy—no, it isn't so easy."

"How did he kill her?"

"I don't know exactly—but he did kill her."

"But you don't know the method he employed?"

"No—it was something—something he did that last Sunday."

"The Sunday he went down to see her?"

"Yes."

"But you don't know what it was?"

"No."

"Then how, forgive me, madame, can you be so sure?"

"Because he—" She stopped and said slowly, "I *am* sure!"

"*Pardon*, madame, but there is something you are keeping back. Something you have not yet told me?"

"Yes."

"Come, then."

Bella Tanios got up suddenly.

"No. No. I can't do that. The children. Their father. I can't. I simply can't. . . ."

"But, madame—"

"I can't, I tell you."

Her voice rose almost to a scream. The door opened and Miss Lawson came in, her head cocked on one side with a sort of pleasurable excitement.

"May I come in? Have you had your little talk? Bella, my dear, don't you think you ought to have a cup of tea, or some soup, or perhaps a little brandy even?"

Mrs. Tanios shook her head.

"I'm quite all right." She gave a weak smile. "I must be getting back to the children. I have left them to unpack."

"Dear little things," said Miss Lawson. "I'm so fond of children."

Mrs. Tanios turned to her suddenly.

"I don't know what I should do without you," she said. "You—you've been wonderfully kind."

"There, there, my dear, don't cry. Everything's going to be all right. You shall come round and see my lawyer—such a nice man, so sympathetic, and he'll advise you the best way to get a divorce. Divorce is so simple nowadays, isn't it, everybody says so. Oh, dear, there's the bell. I wonder who that is."

She left the room hurriedly. There was a murmur of voices in the hall. Miss Lawson reappeared. She tiptoed in and shut the door carefully behind her. She spoke in an excited whisper, mouthing the words exaggeratedly.

"Oh, dear, Bella, it's your husband. I'm sure I don't know—"

Mrs. Tanios gave one bound towards a door at the other end of the room. Miss Lawson nodded her head violently.

"That's right, dear, go in there, and then you can slip out when I've brought him in here."

Mrs. Tanios whispered:

"Don't say I've been here. Don't say you've seen me."

"No, no, of course I won't."

Mrs. Tanios slipped through the door. Poirot and I followed hastily. We found ourselves in a small dining-room.

Poirot crossed to the door into the hall, opened it a crack and listened. Then he beckoned.

"All is clear. Miss Lawson has taken him into the other room."

We crept through the hall and out by the front door. Poirot drew it to as noiselessly as possible after him.

Mrs. Tanios began to run down the steps, stumbling and clutching at the bannisters. Poirot steadied her with a hand under her arm.

"*Du calme—du calme*. All is well."

We reached the entrance-hall.

"Come with me," said Mrs. Tanios piteously. She looked as though she might be going to faint.

"Certainly I will come," said Poirot reassuringly.

We crossed the road, turned a corner, and found ourselves in the Queen's Road. The Wellington was a small, inconspicuous hotel of the boarding-house variety.

When we were inside, Mrs. Tanios sank down on a plush sofa. Her hand was on her beating heart.

Poirot patted her reassuringly on the shoulder.

"It was the narrow squeak—yes. Now, madame, you are to listen to me very carefully."

"I can't tell you anything more, M. Poirot. It wouldn't be *right*. You—you know what I think—what I believe. You—you must be satisfied with that."

"I asked you to listen, madame. Supposing—this is a supposition only—*that I already know the facts of the case*. Supposing that what you could tell me *I have already guessed*—that would make a difference, would it not?"

She looked at him doubtfully. Her eyes were painful in their intensity.

"Oh, believe me, madame, I am not trying to trap you into saying what you do not wish to. But it *would* make a difference—yes?"

"I—I suppose it would."

"Good. Then let me say this. *I, Hercule Poirot, know the truth*. I am not going to ask you to accept my word for it. Take this." He thrust upon her the bulky envelope I had seen him seal up that morning. "The facts are there. After you have read them, if they satisfy you, ring me up. My number is on the notepaper."

Almost reluctantly she accepted the envelope.

Poirot went on briskly:

"And now, one more point, you must leave this hotel at once."

"But why?"

"You will go to the Coniston Hotel near Euston. Tell no one where you are going."

"But surely—here—Minnie Lawson won't tell my husband where I am."

"You think not?"

"Oh, no—she's entirely on my side."

"Yes, but your husband, madame, is a very clever man. He will not find it difficult to turn a middle-aged lady inside out. It is essential—*essential*, you understand, that your husband should not know where you are."

She nodded dumbly.

Poirot held out a sheet of paper.

"Here is the address. Pack up and drive there with the children as soon as possible. You understand?"

She nodded.

"I understand."

"It is the children you must think of, madame, not yourself. You love your children."

He had touched the right note.

A little colour crept into her cheeks, her head went back. She looked, not a frightened drudge, but an arrogant, almost handsome woman.

"It is arranged, then," said Poirot.

He shook hands and he and I departed. But not far. From the shelter of a convenient café, we sipped coffee and watched the entrance of the hotel. In about five minutes we saw Dr. Tanios walking down the street. He did not even glance up at the Wellington. He passed it, his head bowed in thought, then he turned into the Underground station.

About ten minutes later we saw Mrs. Tanios and the children get into the taxi with their luggage and drive away.

"*Bien*," said Poirot, rising with the check in his hand. "We have done our part. Now it is on the knees of the gods."

27

Visit of Dr. Donaldson

DONALDSON arrived punctually at two o'clock. He was as calm and precise as ever.

The personality of Donaldson had begun to intrigue me. I had started by regarding him as a rather nondescript young man. I had wondered what a vivid, compelling creature like Theresa could see in him. But I now began to realize that Donaldson was anything but negligible. Behind that pedantic manner there was force.

After our preliminary greetings were over, Donaldson said:

"The reason for my visit is this. I am at a loss to understand exactly what your position is in this matter, M. Poirot."

Poirot replied guardedly:

"You know my profession, I think?"

"Certainly. I may say that I have taken the trouble to make inquiries about you."

"You are a careful man, Doctor."

Donaldson said drily:

"I like to be sure of my facts."

"You have the scientific mind!"

"I may say that all reports on you are the same. You are obviously a very clever man in your profession. You have also the reputation of being a scrupulous and honest one."

"You are too flattering," murmured Poirot.

"That is why I am at a loss to explain your connection with this affair."

"And yet it is so simple!"

"Hardly that," said Donaldson. "You first present yourself as a writer of biographies."

"A pardonable deception, do you not think? One cannot go everywhere announcing the fact that one is a detective—though that, too, has its uses sometimes."

"So I should imagine." Again Donaldson's tone was dry. "Your next proceeding," he went on, "was to call on Miss Theresa Arundell and represent to her that her aunt's will might conceivably be set aside."

Poirot merely bowed his head in assent.

"That, of course, was ridiculous." Donaldson's voice was sharp. "You knew perfectly well that that will was valid in law and that nothing could be done about it."

"You think that is the case?"

"I am not a fool, M. Poirot—"

"No, Dr. Donaldson, you are certainly not a fool."

"I know something—not very much, but enough—of the law. That will can certainly not be upset. Why did you pretend it could? Clearly for reasons of your own—reasons which Miss Theresa Arundell did not for a moment grasp."

"You seem very certain of her reactions."

A very faint smile passed across the young man's face.

He said unexpectedly:

"I know a good deal more about Theresa than she suspects. I have no doubt that she and Charles think they have enlisted your aid in some questionable business. Charles is almost completely amoral. Theresa has a bad heredity and her upbringing has been unfortunate."

"It is thus you speak of your fiancée—as though she was a guinea-pig?"

Donaldson peered at him through his pince-nez.

"I see no occasion to blink the truth. I love Theresa Arundell and I love her for what she is and not for any imagined qualities."

"Do you realize that Theresa Arundell is devoted to you and that her wish for money is mainly in order that your ambitions should be gratified?"

"Of course I realize it. I've already told you I'm not a fool. But I have no intention of allowing Theresa to embroil herself in any questionable situation on my account. In many ways Theresa is a child still. I am quite capable of furthering my career by my own efforts. I do not say that a substantial legacy would not have been acceptable. It would have been most acceptable. But it would merely have provided a short cut."

"You have, in fact, full confidence in your own abilities?"

"It probably sounds conceited, but I have," said Donaldson composedly.

"Let us proceed, then. I admit that I gained Miss Theresa's confidence by a trick. I let her think that I would be—shall we say, reasonably dishonest—for money. She believed that without the least difficulty."

"Theresa believes that any one would do anything for money," said the young doctor in the matter-of-fact tone one uses when stating a self-evident truth.

"True. That seems to be her attitude—her brother's also."

"Charles probably *would* do anything for money!"

"You have no illusions, I see, about your future brother-in-law."

"No. I find him quite an interesting study. There is, I think, some deep-seated neurosis—but that is talking shop. To return to what we are discussing. I have asked myself *why* you should act in the way you have done, and I have found only one answer. It is clear that you suspect either Theresa or Charles of having a hand in Miss Arundell's death. No, please don't bother to contradict me! Your mention of exhumation was, I think, a mere device to see what reaction you would get. Have you, in actual fact, taken any steps towards getting a Home Office order for exhumation?"

"I will be quite frank with you. As yet, I have not."

Donaldson nodded.

"So I thought. I suppose you have considered the possibility that Miss Arundell's death may turn out to be from natural causes?"

"I have considered the fact that it may appear to be so—yes."

"But your own mind is made up?"

"Very definitely. If you have a case of—say—tuberculosis that looks like tuberculosis, behaves like tuberculosis, and in which the blood gives a positive reaction—*eh bien*, you consider it *is* tuberculosis, do you not?"

"You look at it that way? I see. Then what exactly are you waiting for?"

"I am waiting for a final piece of evidence."

The telephone bell rang. At a gesture from Poirot I got up and answered it. I recognized the voice.

"Captain Hastings? This is Mrs. Tanios speaking. Will you tell M. Poirot that he is perfectly right. If he will come here to-morrow morning at ten o'clock, I will give him what he wants."

"At ten o'clock to-morrow?"

"Yes."

"Right, I'll tell him."

Poirot's eyes asked a question. I nodded.

He turned to Donaldson. His manner had changed. It was brisk—assured.

"Let me make myself clear," he said. "I have diagnosed this case of mine as a case of murder. It looked like murder, it gave all the characteristic reactions of murder—in fact, it *was* murder! Of that, there is not the least doubt."

"Where then does the doubt—for I perceive there *is* a doubt—lie?"

"The doubt lay in *the identity of the murderer*—but that is a doubt no longer!"

"Really? You know?"

"Let us say that I shall have definite proof in my hands to-morrow."

Dr. Donaldson's eyebrows rose in a slightly ironical fashion.

"Ah," he said. "To-morrow! Sometimes, M. Poirot, to-morrow is a long way off."

"On the contrary," said Poirot, "I always find that it succeeds to-day with monotonous regularity."

Donaldson smiled. He rose.

"I fear I have wasted your time, M. Poirot."

"Not at all. It is always as well to understand each other."

With a slight bow, Dr. Donaldson left the room.

28

Another Victim

THAT IS a clever man," said Poirot thoughtfully.

"It's rather difficult to know what he is driving at."

"Yes. He is a little inhuman. But extremely perceptive."

"That telephone call was from Mrs. Tanios."

"So I gathered."

I repeated the message. Poirot nodded approval.

"Good. All marches well. Twenty-four hours, Hastings, and I think we shall know exactly where we stand."

"I'm still a little fogged. Who exactly do we suspect?"

"I really could not say who *you* suspect, Hastings! Everybody in turn, I should imagine!"

"Sometimes I think you *like* to get me into that state!"

"No, no, I would not amuse myself in such a way."

"I wouldn't put it past you."

Poirot shook his head, but somewhat absently. I studied him.

"Is anything the matter?" I asked.

"My friend, I am always nervous towards the end of a case. If anything should go wrong—"

"Is anything likely to go wrong?"

"I do not think so." He paused, frowning. "I have, I think, provided against every contingency."

"Then, supposing that we forget crime and go to a show?"

"*Ma foi*, Hastings, that is a good idea!"

We passed a very pleasant evening, though I made the slight mistake of taking Poirot to a crook play. There is one piece of advice I offer to all my readers. Never take a soldier to a military play, a sailor to a naval play, a Scotsman to a Scottish play, a detective to a thriller—and an actor to any play whatsoever! The shower of destructive criticism in each case is somewhat devastating. Poirot never ceased to complain of faulty psychology, and the hero detective's lack of order and method nearly drove him demented. We parted that night with Poirot still explaining how the whole business might have been laid bare in the first half of the first act.

"But in that case, Poirot, there would have been no play," I pointed out.

Poirot was forced to admit that perhaps that was so.

It was a few minutes past nine when I entered the sitting-room the next morning. Poirot was at the breakfast-table—as usual neatly slitting open his letters.

The telephone rang and I answered it.

A heavy-breathing female voice spoke:

"Is that M. Poirot? Oh, it's you, Captain Hastings."

There was a sort of gasp and a sob.

"Is that Miss Lawson?" I asked.

"Yes, yes, such a terrible thing has happened!"

I grasped the receiver tightly.

"What is it?"

"She left the Wellington, you know—Bella, I mean. I went there late in the afternoon yesterday and they said she'd left. Without a word to me, either! *Most* extraordinary! It makes me feel that perhaps, after all, Dr. Tanios was *right*. He spoke so *nicely* about her and seemed so *distressed*, and now it really looks as though he were right after all."

"But what's happened, Miss Lawson? Is it just that Mrs. Tanios left the hotel without telling you?"

"Oh, no, it's not *that*! Oh, dear me, no. If that were all it would be *quite* all right. Though I do think it was *odd*, you know. Dr. Tanios did say that he was afraid she wasn't quite—not *quite*—if you know what I mean. Persecution mania, he called it."

"Yes." (Damn the woman!) "But what's *happened*?"

"Oh, dear—it is terrible. Died in her sleep. An overdose of some sleeping stuff! And those *poor* little children! It all seems so dreadfully *sad*! I've done nothing but cry since I heard."

"How did you hear? Tell me all about it."

Out of the tail of my eye I noticed that Poirot had stopped opening his letters. He was listening to my side of the conversation. I did not like to cede my place to him. If I did it seemed highly probable that Miss Lawson would start with lamentations all over again.

"They rang me up. From the hotel. The Coniston it's called. It seems they found my name and address in her bag. Oh, dear, M. Poirot—Captain Hastings, I mean—*isn't it terrible*? Those poor little children left motherless.''

''Look here,'' I said. ''Are you sure it's an accident? They didn't think it could be suicide?''

''Oh, what a *dreadful* idea, Captain Hastings! Oh, dear, I don't know, I'm sure. Do you think it could be? That would be *dreadful*! Of course she *did* seem very depressed. But she needn't have been. I mean there wouldn't have been any difficulty about *money*. I was going to *share* with her—indeed I was! Dear Miss Arundell would have wished it. I'm sure of that! It seems so awful to think of her taking her own life—but perhaps she didn't. . . . The hotel people seemed to think it was an accident.''

''What did she take?''

''One of those sleeping things. Veronal, I think. No, chloral. Yes, that was it. Chloral. Oh, dear, Captain Hastings, do you think—''

Unceremoniously I banged down the receiver. I turned to Poirot.

''Mrs. Tanios—''

He raised a hand.

''Yes, yes, I know what you are going to say. She is dead, is she not?''

''Yes. Overdose of sleeping-draught. Chloral.''

Poirot got up.

''Come, Hastings, we must go there at once.''

''Is this what you feared—last night? When you said you were always nervous towards the end of a case?''

''I feared another death—yes.''

Poirot's face was set and stern. We said very little as we drove towards Euston. Once or twice Poirot shook his head.

I said timidly:

''You don't think—? Could it be an accident?''

''No, Hastings—no. It was not an accident.''

''How on earth did he find out where she had gone?''

Poirot only shook his head without replying.

The Coniston was an unsavoury-looking place quite near Euston station. Poirot, with his card, and a suddenly bullying manner, soon fought his way into the manager's office.

The facts were quite simple.

Mrs. Peters, as she had called herself, and her two children had arrived about half-past twelve. They had had lunch at one o'clock.

At four o'clock a man had arrived with a note for Mrs. Peters. The note had been sent up to her. A few minutes later she had come down with the two children and a suitcase. The children had then left with the visitor.

Mrs. Peters had gone to the office and explained that she should only want the one room after all.

She had not appeared exceptionally distressed or upset, indeed she had seemed quite calm and collected. She had had dinner about seven-thirty and had gone to her room soon afterwards.

On calling her in the morning the chambermaid had found her dead.

A doctor had been sent for and had pronounced her to have been dead for some hours. An empty glass was found on the table by the bed. It seemed fairly obvious that she had taken a sleeping-draught, and, by mistake, taken an overdose. Chloral hydrate, the doctor said, was a somewhat uncertain drug. There were no indications of suicide. No letter had been left. Searching for means of notifying her relations, Miss Lawson's name and address had been found and she had been communicated with by telephone.

Poirot asked if anything had been found in the way of letters or papers. The letter, for instance, brought by the man who had called for the children.

No papers of any kind had been found, the man said, but there was a pile of charred paper on the hearth.

Poirot nodded thoughtfully.

As far as any one could say, Mrs. Peters had had no visitors and no one had come to her room—with the solitary exception of the man who had called for the two children.

I questioned the porter myself as to his appearance, but the man was very vague. A man of medium height—he thought fair-haired—rather military build—of somewhat nondescript appearance. No, he was positive the man had no beard.

"It wasn't Tanios," I murmured to Poirot.

"My dear Hastings! Do you really believe that Mrs. Tanios, after all the trouble she was taking to get the children away from their father, would quite meekly hand them over to him without the least fuss or protest? Ah, that, no!"

"Then who was the man?"

"Clearly it was some one in whom Mrs. Tanios had confidence or rather it was some one sent by a third person in whom Mrs. Tanios had confidence."

"A man of medium height," I mused.

"You need hardly trouble yourself about his appearance, Hastings. I am quite sure that the man who actually called for the children was some quite unimportant personage. The real agent kept himself in the background!"

"And the note was from this third person?"

"Yes."

"Some one in whom Mrs. Tanios had confidence?"

"Obviously."

"And the note is now burnt?"

"Yes, she was instructed to burn it."

"What about that résumé of the case that you gave her?"

Poirot's face looked unusually grim.

"That, too, is burned. But that does not matter!"

"No?"

"No. For you see—it is all in the head of Hercule Poirot."

He took me by the arm.

"Come, Hastings, let us leave here. Our concern is not with the dead but with the living. It is with them I have to deal."

29

Inquest at Littlegreen House

IT WAS ELEVEN o'clock the following morning.

Seven people were assembled at Littlegreen House. Hercule Poirot stood by the mantelpiece. Charles and Theresa Arundell were on the sofa, Charles on the arm of it with his hand on Theresa's shoulder. Dr. Tanios sat in a grandfather chair. His eyes were red-rimmed and he wore a black band round his arm.

On an upright chair by a round table sat the owner of the house, Miss Lawson. She, too, had red eyes. Her hair was even untidier than usual. Dr. Donaldson sat directly facing Poirot. His face was quite expressionless.

My interest quickened as I looked at each face in turn.

In the course of my association with Poirot I had assisted at many such a scene. A little company of people, all outwardly composed with well-bred masks for faces. And I had seen Poirot strip the mask from one face and show it for what it was—*the face of a killer*!

Yes, there was no doubt of it. *One of these people was a murderer!* But which? Even now I was not *sure*.

Poirot cleared his throat—a little pompously as was his habit—and began to speak.

"We are assembled here, ladies and gentlemen, to inquire into the death of Emily Arundell on the first of May last. There are four possibilities—

that she died naturally—that she died as the result of an accident—that she took her own life—or lastly that she met her death at the hands of some person known or unknown.

"No inquest was held at the time of her death, since it was assumed that she died from natural causes and a medical certificate to that effect was given by Dr. Grainger.

"In a case where suspicion arises after burial has taken place it is usual to exhume the body of the person in question. There are reasons why I have not advocated that course. The chief of them is that my client would not have liked it."

It was Dr. Donaldson who interrupted. He said:

"Your client?"

Poirot turned to him.

"My client is Miss Emily Arundell. I am acting for her. Her greatest desire was that there should be no scandal."

I will pass over the next ten minutes, since it would involve much needless repetition. Poirot told of the letter he had received, and producing it he read it aloud. He went on to explain the steps he had taken on coming to Market Basing, and of his discovery of the means taken to bring about the accident.

Then he paused, cleared his throat once more, and went on:

"I am now going to take you over the ground I travelled to get at the truth. I am going to show you what I believe to be a true reconstruction of the facts of the case.

"To begin with it is necessary to picture exactly what passed in Miss Arundell's mind. That, I think, is fairly easy. She has a fall, her fall is supposed to be occasioned by a dog's ball, but *she herself knows better*. Lying there on her bed her active and shrewd mind goes over the circumstances of her fall and she comes to a very definite conclusion about it. Some one has deliberately tried to injure—perhaps to kill her.

"From that conclusion she passes to a consideration of who that person can be. There were *seven* people in the house—four guests, her companion and two servants. Of these seven people only one can be entirely exonerated—since to that one person no advantage could accrue. She does not seriously suspect the two servants, both of whom have been with her for many years and whom she knows to be devoted to her. There remain then, *four* persons, three of them members of her family, and one of them a connection by marriage. *Each of those four persons benefit, three directly, one indirectly, by her death.*

"She is in a difficult position, since she is a woman with a strong sense of family feeling. Essentially she is not one who wishes to wash the dirty linen in public, as the saying goes. On the other hand, she is not one to submit tamely to attempted murder!

"She takes her decision and writes to me. She also takes a further step. That further step was, I believe, actuated by two motives. One, I think, was a distant feeling of *spite* against her entire family! She suspected them all impartially, and she determined at all costs to score off them! The second and more reasoned motive was a wish to protect herself and a realization of how this could be accomplished. As you know, she wrote to her lawyer, Mr. Purvis, and directed him to draw up a will in favour of the one person in the house whom, she felt convinced, could have had no hand in her accident.

"Now I may say that, from the terms of her letter to me and from her subsequent actions, I am quite sure that Miss Arundell passed from *indefinite* suspicion of four people to *definite* suspicion of *one* of those four. The whole tenor of her letter to me is an insistence that this business must be kept strictly private, since the honour of the family is involved.

"I think that, from a Victorian point of view, this means that a person of *her own name* was indicated—and preferably a *man*.

"If she had suspected Mrs. Tanios she would have been quite as anxious to secure her own safety, but not quite as concerned for the family honour. She might have felt much the same about Theresa Arundell, but not nearly as intensely as she would feel about Charles.

"Charles was an *Arundell*. He bore the family *name*! Her reasons for suspecting him seem quite clear. To begin with, she had no illusions about Charles. He had come near to disgracing the family once before. That is, she knew him to be not only a *potential* but an *actual* criminal! He had already forged her name to a cheque. After forgery—a step further—murder!

"Also she had had a somewhat suggestive conversation with him only two days before her accident. He had asked her for money and she had refused and he had thereupon remarked—oh, lightly enough—that she was going the right way to get herself bumped off. To this she had responded that she could take care of herself! To this, we are told, her nephew responded, 'Don't be too sure.' *And two days later this sinister accident takes place.*

"It is hardly to be wondered at that lying there and brooding over the occurrence, Miss Arundell came definitely to the conclusion that it was *Charles Arundell* who had made an attempt upon her life.

"The sequence of events is perfectly clear. The conversation with Charles. The accident. The letter written to me in great distress of mind. The letter to the lawyer. On the following Tuesday, the 21st, Mr. Purvis brings the will and she signs it.

"Charles and Theresa Arundell come down the following week-end and Miss Arundell at once takes the necessary steps to safeguard herself. *She tells Charles about the will.* She not only *tells* him but she actually *shows* it to him! That, to my mind, is *absolutely conclusive. She is making it quite clear to a would-be murderer that murder would bring him nothing whatever*!

"She probably thought that Charles would pass on that information to his sister. But he did not do so. Why? I fancy that he had a very good reason—he felt guilty! He believed that it was *his* doing that the will had been made. But *why* did he feel guilty? Because he had really attempted murder? Or merely because he had helped himself to a small sum of ready cash? Either the serious crime or the petty one might account for his reluctance. He said nothing, hoping that his aunt would relent and change her mind.

"As far as Miss Arundell's state of mind was concerned I felt that I had reconstructed events with a fair amount of correctness. I had next to make up my mind if her suspicions were, in actual fact, justified.

"Just as she had done, I realized that my suspicions were limited to a narrow circle—seven people to be exact. Charles and Theresa Arundell, Dr. Tanios and Mrs. Tanios, the two servants, and Miss Lawson. There was an eighth person who had to be taken into account—namely, Dr. Donaldson, who dined there that night, but I did not learn of his presence until later.

"These seven persons that I was considering fell easily into two categories. Six of them stood to benefit in a greater or lesser degree by Miss Arundell's death. If any one of those six had committed the crime the reason was probably a plain matter of *gain*. The second category contained one person only—Miss Lawson. Miss Lawson did *not* stand to gain by Miss Arundell's death, but *as a result of the accident*, she did benefit considerably *later*!

"That meant that if Miss Lawson staged the so-called accident—"

"I never did anything of the kind!" Miss Lawson interrupted. "It's disgraceful! Standing up there and saying such things!"

"A little patience, mademoiselle. And be kind enough not to interrupt," said Poirot.

Miss Lawson tossed her head angrily.

"I insist on making my protest! Disgraceful, that's what it is! Disgraceful!"

Poirot went on, unheeding.

"I was saying that *if* Miss Lawson staged that accident she did so for an entirely *different* reason—that is, she engineered it so that Miss Arundell *would naturally suspect her own family and become alienated from them.*

That *was* a possibility! I searched to see if there were any confirmation or otherwise and I unearthed one very definite fact. If Miss Lawson wanted Miss Arundell to suspect her own family, she would have stressed the fact of the dog, Bob, being *out* that night. But on the contrary Miss Lawson took the utmost pains to *prevent* Miss Arundell hearing of that. Therefore, I argued, Miss Lawson *must* be innocent.''

Miss Lawson said sharply:

''I should hope so!''

''I next considered the problem of Miss Arundell's death. If one attempt to murder a person is made, a second attempt usually follows. It seemed to me significant that within a fortnight of the first attempt Miss Arundell should have died. I began to make inquiries.

''Dr. Grainger did not seem to think there was anything unusual about his patient's death. That was a little damping to my theory. But, inquiring into the happenings of the last evening before she was taken ill, I came across a rather significant fact. Miss Isabel Tripp mentioned a halo of light that had appeared round Miss Arundell's head. Her sister confirmed her statement. They might, of course, be inventing—in a romantic spirit—but I did not think that the incident was quite a likely one to occur to them unprompted. When questioning Miss Lawson she also gave me an interesting piece of information. She referred to a luminous ribbon issuing from Miss Arundell's mouth and forming a luminous haze round her head.

''Obviously, though described somewhat differently by two different observers, the actual *fact* was the same. What it amounted to, shorn of spirtualistic significance, was this: *On the night in question Miss Arundell's breath was phosphorescent!*''

Dr. Donaldson moved a little in his chair.

Poirot nodded to him.

''Yes, you begin to see. There are not very many phosphorescent substances. The first and most common one gave me exactly what I was looking for. I will read you a short extract from an article on phosphorus poisoning.

''*The person's breath may be phosphorescent before he feels in any way affected*. That is what Miss Lawson and the Misses Tripp saw in the dark—Miss Arundell's phosphorescent breath—'a luminous haze.' And here I will read you again. *The jaundice having thoroughly pronounced itself, the system may be considered as not only under the influence of the toxic action of phosphorus, but as suffering in addition from all the accidents incidental to the retention of the biliary secretion in the blood, nor is there from this point any special difference between phosphorus poisoning and certain affections of the liver—such for example as yellow atrophy.*

"You see the cleverness of that? Miss Arundell has suffered for years from liver trouble. The symptoms of phosphorus poisoning would only look like *another attack of the same complaint*. There will be nothing new, nothing startling about it.

"Oh! it was well planned! Foreign matches—vermin paste? It is not difficult to get hold of phosphorus, and a very small dose will kill. The medicinal dose is from 1/100 to 1/30 grain.

"*Voilà*. How clear—how marvellously clear the whole business becomes! Naturally, the doctor is deceived—especially as I find his sense of smell is affected—the garlic odour of the breath is a distinct symptom of phosphorus poisoning. He had no suspicions—why should he have? There were no suspicious circumstances and the one thing that might have given him a hint was the one thing he would never hear—or if he did hear it he would only class it as spiritualistic nonsense.

"I was now sure (from the evidence of Miss Lawson and the Misses Tripp) that murder had been committed. The question still was by *whom*? I eliminated the servants—their mentality was obviously not adapted to such a crime. I eliminated Miss Lawson, since she would hardly have prattled on about luminous ectoplasm if she had been connected with the crime. I eliminated Charles Arundell, *since he knew, having seen the will, that he would gain nothing by his aunt's death*.

"There remained his sister Theresa, Dr. Tanios, Mrs. Tanios and Dr. Donaldson, who I discovered to have been dining in the house on the evening of the dog's ball incident.

"At this point I had very little to help me. I had to fall back upon the psychology of the crime and the *personality* of the murderer! Both crimes had roughly *the same outline*. They were both *simple*. They were cunning, and carried out with efficiency. They required a certain amount of knowledge but not a great deal. The facts about phosphorus poisoning are easily learned, and the stuff itself, as I say, is quite easily obtained, especially abroad.

"I considered first the two men. Both of them were doctors, and both were clever men. Either of them might have thought of phosphorus and its suitability in this particular case, but the incident of the dog's ball did not seem to fit a masculine mind. The incident of the ball seemed to me essentially a *woman's* idea.

"I considered first of all Theresa Arundell. She had certain potentialities. She was bold, ruthless, and not overscrupulous. She had led a selfish and greedy life. She had always had everything she wanted and she had reached a point where she was desperate for money—both for herself and for the man she loved. Her manner, also, showed plainly that she knew her aunt had been murdered.

"There was an interesting little passage between her and her brother. I conceived the idea that *each suspected the other of the crime*. Charles endeavoured to make her say that *she knew of the existence of the new will*. Why? Clearly because if she knew of it she could not be suspected of the murder. She, on the other hand, clearly did not believe Charles's statement that Miss Arundell had shown it to him! She regarded it as a singularly clumsy attempt on his part to divert suspicion from himself.

"There was another significant point. Charles displayed a reluctance to use the word arsenic. Later I found that he had questioned the old gardener at length upon the strength of some weed-killer. It was clear what had been in his mind."

Charles Arundell shifted his position a little.

"I thought of it," he said. "But—well, I suppose I hadn't got the nerve."

Poirot nodded at him.

"Precisely, *it is not in your psychology*. Your crimes will always be the crimes of weakness. To steal, to forge—yes, it is the easiest way—but to kill—*no*! To kill one needs the type of mind that can be obsessed by an idea."

He resumed his lecturing manner.

"Theresa Arundell, I decided, had quite sufficient strength of mind to carry such a design through, but there were other facts to take into consideration. She had never been thwarted, she had lived fully and selfishly—but that type of person is *not the type that kills*—except perhaps in sudden anger. And yet—I felt sure—*it was Theresa Arundell who had taken the weed-killer from the tin*."

Theresa spoke suddenly:

"I'll tell you the truth. I thought of it. I actually took some weed-killer from a tin down at Littlegreen House. But I couldn't do it! I'm too fond of living—of being alive—I couldn't do that to any one—take life from them. . . . I may be bad and selfish, but there are things I can't do! I couldn't kill a living, breathing, human creature!"

Poirot nodded.

"No, that is true. And you are not as bad as you paint yourself, mademoiselle. You are only young—and reckless."

He went on:

"There remained Mrs. Tanios. As soon as I saw her I realized that she was afraid. She saw that I realized that and she very quickly made capital out of that momentary betrayal. She gave a very convincing portrait of a woman *who is afraid for her husband*. A little later she changed her tactics. It was very cleverly done—but the change did not deceive me. A woman can be afraid *for* her husband or she can be afraid *of* her husband—but she can hardly be *both*. Mrs. Tanios decided on the latter rôle—and she played her part cleverly—even to coming out after me into the hall of the hotel and pretending that there was something she wanted to tell me. When her husband followed her as she knew he would, she pretended that she could not speak before him.

"I realized at once, not that she feared her husband, but that she disliked him. And at once, summing the matter up, I felt convinced that here was the exact character I had been looking for. Here was—not a self-indulgent woman—but a thwarted one. A plain girl, leading a dull existence, unable to attract the men she would like to attract, finally accepting a man she did not care for rather than be left an old maid. I could trace her growing dissatisfaction with life, her life in Smyrna exiled from all she cared for in life. Then the birth of her children and her passionate attachment to them.

"Her husband was devoted to her, but she came secretly to dislike him more and more. He had speculated with her money and lost it—another grudge against him.

"There was only one thing that illumined her drab life, the expectation of her aunt Emily's death. Then she would have money, independence, the means to educate her children as she wished—and remember education meant a lot to her—she was a professor's daughter!

"She may have already planned the crime, or had the idea of it in her mind, before she came to England. She had a certain knowledge of chemistry, having assisted her father in the laboratory. She knew the nature of Miss Arundell's complaint and she was well aware that phosphorus would be an ideal substance for her purpose.

"Then, when she came to Littlegreen House, a simpler method presented itself to her. The dog's ball—a thread or string across the top of the stairs. A simple, ingenious woman's idea.

"She made her attempt—and failed. I do not think that she had any idea that Miss Arundell was aware of the true facts of the matter. Miss Arundell's suspicions were directed entirely against Charles. I doubt if her manner to Bella showed any alteration. And so, quietly and determinedly, this self-contained, unhappy, ambitious woman put her original plan into execution. She found an excellent vehicle for the poison, some patent capsules that Miss Arundell was in the habit of taking after meals. To open a capsule, place the phosphorus inside and close it again, was child's play. The capsule was replaced among the others. Sooner or later Miss Arundell would swallow it. Poison was not likely to be suspected. Even if, by some unlikely chance it was, she herself would be nowhere near Market Basing at the time.

"Yet she took one precaution. She obtained a double supply of chloral hydrate at the druggist's, forging her husband's name to the prescription. I have no doubt of what that was for—to keep by her in case anything went wrong.

"As I say, I was convinced from the first moment I saw her that Mrs. Tanios was the person I was looking for, but I had absolutely no *proof* of the fact. I had to proceed carefully. If Mrs. Tanios had any idea I suspected her, I was afraid that she might proceed to a further crime. Furthermore, I believed that the idea of that crime had already occurred to her. Her one wish in life was to shake herself free of her husband.

"Her original murder had proved a bitter disappointment. The money, the wonderful all-intoxicating money, had all gone to Miss Lawson! It was a blow, but she set to work most intelligently. She began to work on Miss Lawson's conscience which, I suspect, was already not too comfortable."

There was a sudden outburst of sobs. Miss Lawson took out her handkerchief and cried into it.

"It's been dreadful," she sobbed. "I've been wicked! Very wicked. You see, I was very curious about the will—why Miss Arundell had made a new one, I mean. And one day, when Miss Arundell was resting, I managed to unlock the drawer in the desk. And then I found she'd left it all to *me*! Of course, I never dreamed it was so *much*. Just a few thousands—that's all I thought it was. And why not? After all, her own relations didn't really *care* for her! But then, when she was so ill, she asked for the will. I could see—I felt sure—she was going to destroy it. . . . And that's when I was so wicked. I told her she'd sent it back to Mr. Purvis. Poor dear, she was so forgetful. She never remembered what she'd done with things. She believed me. Said I must write for it and I said I would.

"Oh, dear—oh, dear—and then she got worse and couldn't think of anything. And she died. And when the will was read and it was all that money I felt *dreadful*. Three hundred and seventy-five thousand pounds. I'd never dreamed for a minute it was anything like that or I wouldn't have done it.

"I felt just as though I'd *embezzled* the money—and I didn't know what to do. The other day, when Bella came to me, I told her that she should have half of it. I felt sure that then I would feel happy again."

"You see?" said Poirot. "Mrs. Tanios was succeeding in her object. That is why she was so averse to any attempt to contest the will. She had her own plans and the last thing she wanted to do was to antagonize Miss Lawson. She pretended, of course, to fall in at once with her husband's wishes, but she made it quite clear what her real feelings were.

"She had at that time two objects: to detach herself and her children from Dr. Tanios and to obtain her share of the money. Then she would have what she wanted—a rich contented life in England with her children.

"As time went on she could no longer conceal her dislike from her husband. In fact, she did not try to. He, poor man, was seriously upset and distressed. Her actions must have seemed quite incomprehensible to him. Really, they were logical enough. She was playing the part of the terrorized woman. If I had suspicions—and she was fairly sure that that must be the case—she wished me to believe that her husband had committed the murder. And at any moment that second murder which I am convinced was already planned in her mind might occur. I knew that she had a lethal dose of chloral in her possession. I feared that she would stage a pretended suicide and confession on his part.

"And still I had no evidence against her! And then, when I was quite in despair, I got something at last! Miss Lawson told me that she had seen Theresa Arundell kneeling on the stairs on the night of Easter Monday. I soon discovered that Miss Lawson could not have seen Theresa at all clearly—not nearly clearly enough to recognize her *features*. Yet she was quite positive in her identification. On being pressed she mentioned a brooch with Theresa's initials—T.A.

"On my request Miss Theresa Arundell showed me the brooch in question. At the same time she absolutely denied having been on the stairs at the time stated. At first I fancied some one else had borrowed her brooch, but when I looked at the brooch in the glass the truth leaped at me. Miss Lawson, waking up, had seen a dim figure with the initials T.A. flashing in the light. She had leapt to the conclusion that it was Theresa.

"But if in the glass she had seen the initials T.A.—then the real initials must have been A. T., since the glass naturally reversed the order.

"Of course! Mrs. Tanios's mother was Arabella Arundell. Bella is only a contraction. A. T. stood for Arabella Tanios. There was nothing odd in Mrs. Tanios possessing a similar type of brooch. It had been exclusive last Christmas, but by the spring they were all the rage, and I had already observed that Mrs. Tanios copied her cousin Theresa's hats and clothes as far as she was able with her limited means.

"In my own mind, at any rate, my case was proved.

"Now—what was I to do? Obtain a Home Office order for the exhumation of the body? That could doubtless be managed. I *might* prove that Miss Arundell had been poisoned with phosphorus, though there was a little doubt about that. The body had been buried two months, and I understand that there have been cases of phosphorus poisoning where no lesions have been found and where the post mortem appearances are very indecisive. Even then, could I connect Mrs. Tanios with the purchase or possession of phosphorus? Very doubtful, since she had probably obtained it abroad.

"At this juncture Mrs. Tanios took a decisive action. She left her husband, throwing herself on the pity of Miss Lawson. She also definitely accused her husband of the murder.

"Unless I acted I felt convinced that he would be her next victim. I took steps to isolate them one from the other on the pretext that it was for her safety. She could not very well contradict that. Really, it was *his* safety I had in mind. And then—and then—"

He paused—a long pause. His face had gone rather white.

"But that was only a temporary measure. I had to make sure that the killer would kill no more. I had to assure the safety of the innocent.

"So I wrote out my construction of the case and gave it to Mrs. Tanios."

There was a long silence.

Dr. Tanios cried out:

"Oh, my God, so that's why she killed herself."

Poirot said gently:

"Was it not the best way? She thought so. There were, you see, the children to consider."

Dr. Tanios buried his face in his hands.

Poirot came forward and laid a hand on his shoulder.

"It had to be. Believe me it was necessary. There would have been more deaths. First yours—then possibly, under certain circumstances, Miss Lawson's. And so it goes on."

He paused.

In a broken voice Tanios said:

"She wanted me—to take a sleeping-draught one night. . . . There was something in her face—I threw it away. That was when I began to believe her mind was going. . . ."

"Think of it that way. It is indeed partly true. But not in the legal meaning of the term. She knew the meaning of her action. . . ."

Dr. Tanios said wistfully:

"She was much too good for me—always."

A strange epitaph on a self-confessed murderess!

30
The Last Word

THERE IS VERY little more to tell.

Theresa married her doctor shortly afterwards. I know them fairly well now and I have learnt to appreciate Donaldson—his clarity of vision and the deep, underlying force and humanity of the man. His manner, I may say, is just as dry and precise as ever; Theresa often mimics him to his face. She is, I think, amazingly happy and absolutely wrapped up in her husband's career. He is already making a big name for himself and is an authority on the functions of ductless glands.

Miss Lawson, in an acute attack of conscience, had to be restrained forcibly from denuding herself of every penny. A settlement agreeable to all parties was drawn up by Mr. Purvis whereby Miss Arundell's fortune was shared out between Miss Lawson, the two Arundells and the Tanios children.

Charles went through his share in a little over a year and is now, I believe, in British Columbia.

Just two incidents.

"You're a downy fellow, ain't you?" said Miss Peabody, stopping us as we emerged from the gate of Littlegreen House one day. "Managed to hush everything up! No exhumation. Everything done decently."

"There seems to be no doubt that Miss Arundell died of yellow atrophy of the liver," said Poirot gently.

"That's very satisfactory," said Miss Peabody. "Bella Tanios took an overdose of sleeping stuff, I hear."

"Yes, it was very sad."

"She was a miserable kind of woman—always wanting what she hadn't got. People go a bit queer sometimes when they're like that. Had a kitchen maid once. Same thing. Plain girl. Felt it. Started writing anonymous letters. Queer kinks people get. Ah, well, I dare say it's all for the best."

"One hopes so, madame. One hopes so."

"Well," said Miss Peabody, preparing to resume her walk, "I'll say this for you. You've hushed things up nicely. Very nicely indeed."

She walked on.

There was a plaintive "Wuff" behind me.

I turned and opened the gate.

"Come on, old man."

Bob bounced through. There was a ball in his mouth.

"You can't take that for a walk."

Bob sighed, turned and slowly ejected the ball inside the gate. He looked at it anxiously, then passed through.

He looked up at me.

"If you say so, master, I suppose it's all right."

I drew a long breath.

"My word, Poirot, it's good to have a dog again."

"The spoils of war," said Poirot. "But I would remind you, my friend, that it was to *me* that Miss Lawson presented Bob, not to *you*."

"Possibly," I said. "But you're not really any good with a dog, Poirot. You don't understand dog psychology! Now Bob and I understand each other perfectly, don't we?"

"Woof," said Bob in energetic assent.

Funerals Are Fatal

FOR JAMES

In memory of happy days at Abney

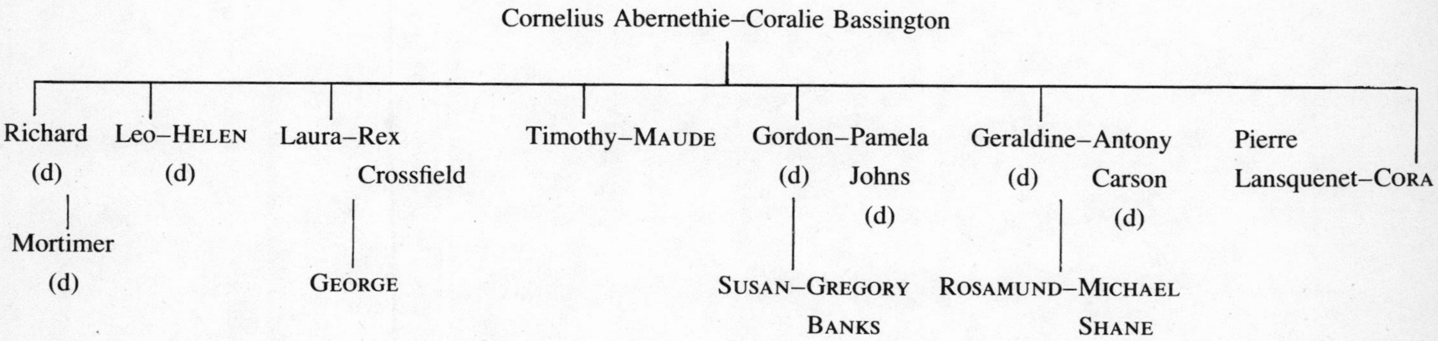

THE ABERNETHIE FAMILY.

Those designated in Capital and Small Cap letters were present at the funeral of RICHARD ABERNETHIE.

I

OLD LANSCOMBE moved totteringly from room to room, pulling up the blinds. Now and then he peered with screwed up rheumy eyes through the windows.

Soon they would be coming back from the funeral. He shuffled along a little faster. There were so many windows.

Enderby Hall was a vast Victorian house built in the Gothic style. In every room the curtains were of rich faded brocade or velvet. Some of the walls were still hung with faded silk. In the green drawing room, the old butler glanced up at the portrait above the mantelpiece of old Cornelius Abernethie for whom Enderby Hall had been built. Cornelius Abernethie's brown beard stuck forward aggressively, his hand rested on a terrestrial globe, whether by desire of the sitter, or as a symbolic conceit on the part of the artist, no one could tell.

A very forceful looking gentleman, so old Lanscombe had always thought, and was glad that he himself had never known him personally. Mr. Richard had been *his* gentleman. A good master, Mr. Richard. And taken very sudden, he'd been, though of course the doctor had been attending him for some little time. Ah, but the master had never recovered from the shock of young Mr. Mortimer's death. The old man shook his head as he hurried through a connecting door into the White Boudoir. Terrible, that had been, a real catastrophe. Such a fine upstanding young gentleman, so strong and healthy. You'd never have thought such a thing likely to happen to him. Pitiful, it had been, quite pitiful. And Mr. Gordon killed in the war. One thing on top of another. That was the way things went nowadays. Too much for the master, it had been. And yet he'd seemed almost himself a week ago.

The third blind in the White Boudoir refused to go up as it should. It went up a little way and stuck. The springs were weak—that's what it was—very old, these blinds were, like everything else in the house. And you couldn't get these old things mended nowadays. Too old fashioned, that's what they'd say, shaking their heads in that silly superior way—as if the old things weren't a great deal better than the new ones! *He* could tell them that! Gimcrack, half the new stuff was—came to pieces in your hand. The material wasn't good, or the craftsmanship either. Oh yes, *he* could tell them.

Couldn't do anything about this blind unless he got the steps. He didn't like climbing up the steps much, these days, made him come over giddy. Anyway, he'd leave the blind for now. It didn't matter since the White Boudoir didn't face the front of the house where it would be seen as the cars came back from the funeral—and it wasn't as though the room was ever used nowadays. It was a lady's room, this, and there hadn't been a lady at Enderby for a long while now. A pity Mr. Mortimer hadn't married. Always going off to Norway for fishing and to Scotland for shooting and to Switzerland for those winter sports, instead of marrying some nice young lady and settling down at home with children running about the house. It was a long time since there had been any children in the house.

And Lanscombe's mind went ranging back to a time that stood out clearly and distinctly—much more distinctly than the last twenty years or so, which were all blurred and confused and he couldn't really remember who had come and gone or indeed what they looked like. But he could remember the old days well enough.

More like a father to those young brothers and sisters of his, Mr. Richard had been. Twenty-four when his father had died, and he'd pitched in right away to the business, going off every day as punctual as clockwork, and keeping the house running and everything as lavish as it could be. A very happy household with all those young ladies and gentlemen growing up. Fights and quarrels now and again, of course, and those governesses had had a bad time of it! Poor spirited creatures, governesses, Lanscombe had always despised them. Very spirited the young ladies had been. Miss Geraldine in particular. Miss Cora, too, although she was so much younger. And now Mr. Leo was dead, and Miss Laura gone too. And Mr. Timothy such a sad invalid. And Miss Geraldine dying somewhere abroad. And Mr. Gordon killed in the war. Although he was the eldest, Mr. Richard himself turned out the strongest of the lot. Outlived them all, he had—at least not quite because Mr. Timothy was still alive and little Miss Cora who'd married that unpleasant artist chap. Twenty five years since he'd seen her and she'd been a pretty young girl when she went off with that chap, and now he'd hardly have known her, grown so stout—and so arty crafty in her dress! A Frenchman her husband had been, or nearly a Frenchman—and no good ever came of marrying one of *them!* But Miss Cora had always been a bit—well, *simple like* you'd call it if she'd lived in a village. Always one of them in a family.

She'd remembered *him* all right. "Why, it's Lanscombe!" she'd said and seemed ever so pleased to see him. Ah, they'd all been fond of him in the old days and when there was a dinner party they'd crept down to the pantry and he'd given them jelly and Charlotte Russe when it came out of the dining room. They'd all known old Lanscombe, and now there was hardly anyone who remembered. Just the younger lot whom he could never keep clear in his mind and who just thought of him as a butler who'd been there a long time. A lot of strangers, he had thought, when they all arrived for the funeral—and a seedy lot of strangers at that!

Not Mrs. Leo—she was different. She and Mr. Leo had come here off and on ever since Mr. Leo married. She was a nice lady, Mrs. Leo—a *real* lady. Wore proper clothes and did her hair well and looked what she was. And the master had always been fond of her. A pity that she and Mr. Leo had never had any children . . .

Lanscombe roused himself; what was he doing standing here and dreaming about old days with so much to be done? The blinds were all attended to on the ground floor now, and he'd told Jane to go upstairs and do the bedrooms. He and Janet and the cook had gone to the funeral service in the church but instead of going on to the Crematorium they'd driven back to the house to get the blinds up and the lunch ready. Cold lunch, of course, it had to be. Ham and chicken and tongue and salad. With cold lemon soufflé and apple tart to follow. Hot soup first—and he'd better go along and see that Marjorie had got it on ready to serve, for they'd be back in a minute or two now for certain.

Lanscombe broke into a shuffling trot across the room. His gaze, abstracted and uncurious, just swept up to the picture over this mantelpiece—the companion portrait to the one in the green drawing room. It was a nice painting of white satin and pearls. The human being round whom they were draped and clasped was not nearly so impressive. Meek features, a rosebud mouth, hair parted in the middle. A woman both modest and unassuming. The only thing really worthy of note about Mrs. Cornelius Abernethie had been her name—Coralie.

For over sixty years after their original appearance, Coral Cornplasters and the allied "Coral" foot preparations still held their own. Whether there had ever been anything outstanding about Coral Cornplasters nobody could say—but they had appealed to the public fancy. On a foundation of Coral Cornplasters there had arisen this neo Gothic palace, its acres of gardens, and the money that had paid out an income to seven sons and daughters and had allowed Richard Abernethie to die three days ago a very rich man.

II

Looking into the kitchen with a word of admonition, Lanscombe was snapped at by Marjorie, the cook. Marjorie was young, only twenty seven, and was a constant irritation to Lanscombe as being so far removed from what his conception of a proper cook should be. She had no dignity and no proper appreciation of his, Lanscombe's, position. She frequently called the house "a proper old mausoleum" and complained of the immense area of the kitchen, scullery and larder, saying that it was a "day's walk to get round them all." She had been at Enderby two years and only stayed because, in the first place the money was good, and in the second because Mr. Abernethie had really appreciated her cooking. She cooked very well. Janet, who stood by the kitchen table, refreshing herself with a cup of tea, was an elderly housemaid who, although enjoying frequent acid disputes with Lanscombe, was nevertheless usually in alliance with him against the younger generation as represented by Marjorie. The fourth person in the kitchen was Mrs. Jacks who "came in" to lend assistance where it was wanted and who had much enjoyed the funeral.

"Beautiful it was," she said with a decorous sniff as she replenished her cup. "Nineteen cars and the church quite full and the Canon read the service beautiful, I thought. A nice fine day for it, too. Ah, poor dear Mr. Abernethie, there's not many like him left in the world. Respected by all, he was."

There was the note of a horn and the sound of a car coming up the drive, and Mrs. Jacks put down her cup and exclaimed: "Here they are."

Marjorie turned up the gas under her large saucepan of creamy chicken soup. The large kitchen range of the days of Victorian grandeur stood cold and unused, like an altar to the past.

The cars drove up one after the other and the people issuing from them in their black clothes moved rather uncertainly across the hall and into the big green drawing room. In the big steel grate a fire was burning, tribute to the first chill of the Autumn days and calculated to counteract the further chill of standing about at a funeral.

Lanscombe entered the room, offering glasses of sherry on a silver tray.

Mr. Entwhistle, senior partner of the old and respected firm of Bollard, Entwhistle, Entwhistle and Bollard, stood with his back to the fireplace warming himself. He accepted a glass of sherry, and surveyed the company with his shrewd lawyer's gaze. Not all of them were personally known to him, and he was under the necessity of sorting them out, so to speak. Introductions before the departure for the funeral had been hushed and perfunctory.

Appraising old Lanscombe first, Mr. Entwhistle thought to himself, "Getting very shaky, poor old chap—going on for ninety I shouldn't wonder. Well, he'll have that nice little annuity. Nothing for *him* to worry about. Faithful soul. No such thing as old fashioned service nowadays.

Household helps and baby sitters, God help us all! A sad world. Just as well, perhaps, poor Richard didn't last his full time. He hadn't much to live for."

To Mr. Entwhistle who was seventy two, Richard Abernethie's death at sixty eight was definitely that of a man dead before his time. Mr. Entwhistle had retired from active business two years ago, but as executor of Richard Abernethie's will and in respect for one of his oldest clients who was also a personal friend, he had made the journey to the North.

Reflecting in his own mind on the provisions of the will, he mentally appraised the family.

Mrs. Leo, Helen, he knew well, of course. A very charming woman for whom he had both liking and respect. His eyes dwelt approvingly on her now as she stood near one of the windows. Black suited her. She had kept her figure well. He liked the clear cut features, the springing line of grey hair back from her temples and the eyes that had once been likened to cornflowers and which were still quite vividly blue.

How old was Helen now? About fifty one or two, he supposed. Strange that she had never married again after Leo's death. An attractive woman. Ah, but they had been very devoted, those two.

His eyes went on to Mrs. Timothy. He had never known her very well. Black didn't suit her—country tweeds were her wear. A big sensible capable-looking woman. She'd always been a good devoted wife to Timothy. Looking after his health, fussing over him—fussing over him a bit too much, probably. Was there really anything the matter with Timothy? Just a hypochondriac, Mr. Entwhistle suspected. Richard Abernethie had suspected so, too. "Weak chest, of course, when he was a boy," he had said. "But blest if I think there's much wrong with him now." Oh well, everybody had to have some hobby. Timothy's hobby was the all absorbing one of his own health. Was Mrs. Tim taken in? Probably not—but women never admitted that sort of thing. Timothy must be quite comfortably off. He'd never been a spendthrift. However, the extra would not come amiss—not in these days of taxation. He'd probably had to retrench his scale of living a good deal since the war.

Mr. Entwhistle transferred his attention to George Crossfield, Laura's son. Dubious sort of fellow Laura had married. Nobody had ever known much about him. A stockbroker he had called himself. Young George was in a solicitor's office—not a very reputable firm. Good looking young fellow—but something a little shifty about him. He couldn't have too much to live on. Laura had been a complete fool over her investments. She'd left next to nothing when she died five years ago. A handsome romantic girl, she'd been, but no money sense.

Mr. Entwhistle's eyes went on from George Crossfield. Which of the two girls was which? Ah yes, that was Rosamund, Geraldine's daughter, looking at the wax flowers on the malachite table. Pretty girl, beautiful, in fact—rather a silly face. On the stage. Repertory companies or some nonsense like that. Had married an actor, too. Good looking fellow. "*And* knows he is," thought Mr. Entwhistle who was prejudiced against the stage as a profession. "Wonder what sort of a background *he* has and where he comes from."

He looked disapprovingly at Michael Shane with his fair hair and his haggard charm.

Now Susan, Gordon's daughter, would do much better on the stage than Rosamund. More personality. A little too much personality for everyday life, perhaps. She was quite near him and Mr. Entwhistle studied her covertly. Dark hair, hazel—almost golden—eyes, a sulky attractive mouth. Beside her was the husband she had just married—a chemist's assistant, he understood. Really, a chemist's assistant! In Mr. Entwhistle's creed girls did not marry young men who served behind a counter. But now of course, they married *anybody!* The young man who had a pale nondescript face and sandy hair seemed very ill at ease. Mr. Entwhistle wondered why, but decided charitably that it was the strain of meeting so many of his wife's relations.

Last in his survey Mr. Entwhistle came to Cora Lansquenet. There was a certain justice in that, for Cora had decidedly been an afterthought in the family. Richard's youngest sister, she had been born when her mother was just on fifty, and that meek woman had not survived her tenth pregnancy (three children had died in infancy). Poor little Cora! All her life, Cora had been rather an embarrassment—growing up tall and gawky, and given to blurting out remarks that had always better have remained unsaid. All her elder brothers and sisters had been very kind to Cora, atoning for her deficiencies and covering her social mistakes. It had never really occurred to anyone that Cora would marry. She had not been a very attractive girl, and her rather obvious advances to visiting young men had usually caused the latter to retreat in some alarm. And then, Mr. Entwhistle mused, there had come the Lansquenet business—Pierre Lansquenet, half French, whom she had come across in an Art school where she had been having very correct lessons in painting flowers in water colours. But somehow she had got into the Life class and there she had met Pierre Lansquenet and had come home and announced her intention of marrying him. Richard Abernethie had put his foot down—he hadn't liked what he saw of Pierre Lansquenet and suspected that the young man was really in search of a rich wife. But whilst he was making a few researches into Lansquenet's antecedents, Cora had bolted with the fellow and married him out of hand. They had spent most of their married life in Brittany and Cornwall and other painters' conventional haunts. Lansquenet had been a very bad painter and not, by all accounts, a very nice man, but Cora had remained devoted to him and had never forgiven her family for their attitude to him. Richard had generously made his young sister an allowance and on that they had, so Mr. Entwhistle believed, lived. He doubted if Lansquenet had ever earned any money at all. He must have been dead now twelve years or more, thought Mr. Entwhistle. And now here was his widow, rather cushion-like in shape and dressed in wispy artistic black with festoons of jet beads, back in the home of her girlhood, moving about and touching things and exclaiming with pleasure when she recalled some childish memory. She made very little pretence of grief at her brother's death. But then, Mr. Entwhistle reflected, Cora had never pretended.

Re-entering the room Lanscombe murmured in muted tones suitable to the occasion:

"Luncheon is served."

2

AFTER THE DELICIOUS chicken soup, and plenty of cold viands accompanied by an excellent *chablis*, the funeral atmosphere lightened. Nobody had really felt any deep grief for Richard Abernethie's death since none of them had had any close ties with him. Their behaviour had been suitably decorous and subdued (with the exception of the uninhibited Cora who was clearly enjoying herself) but it was now felt that the decencies had been observed and that normal conversation could be resumed. Mr. Entwhistle encouraged this attitude. He was experienced in funerals and knew exactly how to set correct funeral timing.

After the meal was over, Lanscombe indicated the library for coffee. This was his feeling for niceties. The time had come when business—in other words, The Will—would be discussed. The library had the proper atmosphere for that with its bookshelves and its heavy red velvet curtains. He served coffee to them there and then withdrew closing the door.

After a few desultory remarks, everyone began to look tentatively at Mr. Entwhistle. He responded promptly after glancing at his watch.

"I have to catch the 3.30 train," he began.

Others, it seemed, also had to catch that train.

"As you know," said Mr. Entwhistle, "I am the executor of Richard Abernethie's will—"

He was interrupted.

"*I* didn't know," said Cora Lansquenet brightly. "Are you? Did he leave me anything?"

Not for the first time, Mr. Entwhistle felt that Cora was too apt to speak out of turn.

Bending a repressive glance at her he continued:

"Up to a year ago, Richard Abernethie's will was very simple. Subject to certain legacies he left everything to his son Mortimer."

"Poor Mortimer," said Cora. "I do think all this infantile paralysis is *dreadful*."

"Mortimer's death, coming so suddenly and tragically, was a great blow to Richard. It took him some months to rally from it. I pointed out to him that it might be advisable for him to make new testamentary dispositions."

Maude Abernethie asked in her deep voice:

"What would have happened if he *hadn't* made a new will? Would it—would it all have gone to Timothy—as the next of kin, I mean?"

Mr. Entwhistle opened his mouth to give a disquisition on the subject of next of kin, thought better of it, and said crisply:

"On my advice, Richard decided to make a new will. First of all, however, he decided to get better acquainted with the younger generation."

"He had us up on appro," said Susan with a sudden rich laugh. "First George and then Greg and I, and then Rosamund and Michael."

Gregory Banks said sharply, his thin face flushing:

"I don't think you ought to put it like that, Susan. On appro, indeed!"

"But that was what it was, wasn't it, Mr. Entwhistle?"

"Did he leave *me* anything?" repeated Cora.

Mr. Entwhistle coughed and spoke rather coldly:

"I propose to send you all copies of the will. I can read it to you in full now if you like but its legal phraseology may seem to you rather obscure. Briefly it amounts to this: After certain small bequests and a substantial legacy to Lanscombe to purchase an annuity, the bulk of the estate—a very considerable one—is to be divided into six equal portions. Four of these, after all duties are paid, are to go to Richard's brother Timothy, his nephew George Crossfield, his niece Susan Banks, and his niece Rosamund Shane. The other two portions are to be held upon trust and the income from them paid to Mrs. Helen Abernethie, the widow of his brother Leo; and to his sister Mrs. Cora Lansquenet, during their lifetime. The capital after their death to be divided between the other four beneficiaries or their issue."

"That's *very* nice!" said Cora Lansquenet with real appreciation. "An income! How much?"

"I—er—can't say exactly at present. Death duties of course will be heavy and—"

"Can't you give me any idea?"

Mr. Entwhistle realised that Cora must be appeased.

"Possibly somewhere in the neighbourhood of three to four thousand a year."

"Goody!" said Cora. "I shall go to Capri."

Helen Abernethie said softly:

"How very kind and generous of Richard. I do appreciate his affection towards me."

"He was very fond of you," said Mr. Entwhistle. "Leo was his favourite brother and your visits to him were always much appreciated after Leo died."

Helen said regretfully:

"I wish I had realised how ill he was—I came up to see him not long before he died, but although I knew he *had* been ill, I did not think it was serious."

"It was always serious," said Mr. Entwhistle. "But he did not want it talked about and I do not believe that anybody expected the end to come as soon as it did. The doctor was quite surprised, I know."

" '*Suddenly, at his residence*,' that's what it said in the paper," said Cora nodding her head. "I wondered, then."

"It was a shock to all of us," said Maude Abernethie. "It upset poor Timothy dreadfully. So sudden, he kept saying. So *sudden*."

"Still it's been hushed up very nicely, hasn't it?" said Cora.

Everybody stared at her and she seemed a little flustered.

"I think you're all quite right," she said hurriedly. "*Quite* right. I mean—it can't do any good—making it public. Very unpleasant for everybody. It should be kept strictly in the family."

The faces turned towards her looked even more blank.

Mr. Entwhistle leaned forward:

"Really, Cora, I'm afraid I don't quite understand what you mean."

Cora Lansquenet looked around at the family in wide-eyed surprise. She tilted her head on one side with a birdlike movement.

"But he *was* murdered, wasn't he?" she said.

3

TRAVELLING TO London in the corner of a first class carriage Mr. Entwhistle gave himself up to somewhat uneasy thought over that extraordinary remark made by Cora Lansquenet. Of course Cora was a rather unbalanced and excessively stupid woman, and she had been noted, even as a girl, for the embarrassing manner in which she had blurted out unwelcome truths. At least, he didn't mean *truths*—that was *quite* the wrong word to use. Awkward statements—that was a much better term.

In his mind he went back over the immediate sequence to that unfortunate remark. The combined stare of many startled and disapproving eyes had roused Cora to a sense of the enormity of what she had said.

Maude had exclaimed, "*Really*, Cora!" George had said, "My dear Aunt Cora." Somebody else had said, "What *do* you mean?"

And at once Cora Lansquenet, abashed, and convicted of enormity, had burst into fluttering phrases.

"Oh I'm sorry—I didn't mean—oh, of course, it was very stupid of me, but I did think from what he said—Oh, of course I know it's quite all right, but his death was so *sudden*—Please forget that I said anything at all—I didn't mean to be so stupid—I know I'm always saying the wrong thing. . . ."

And then the momentary upset had died down and there had been a practical discussion about the disposition of the late Richard Abernethie's personal effects. The house and its contents, Mr. Entwhistle supplemented, would be put up for sale.

Cora's unfortunate *gaffe* had been forgotten. After all, Cora had always been, if not subnormal, at any rate embarrassingly *naive*. She had never had any idea of what should or should not be said. At nineteen it had not mattered so much. The mannerisms of an *enfant terrible* can persist to then, but an *enfant terrible* of nearly fifty is decidedly disconcerting. To blurt out unwelcome truths—

Mr. Entwhistle's train of thought came to an abrupt check. It was the second time that that disturbing word had occurred. *Truths*. And why was it so disturbing? Because, of course, that had always been at the bottom of the embarrassment that Cora's outspoken comments had caused. It was because her *naive* statements had been either true or had contained some grain of truth that they had been so embarrassing!

Although in the plump woman of forty nine, Mr. Entwhistle had been able to see little resemblance to the gawky girl of earlier days, certain of Cora's mannerisms had persisted—the slight birdlike twist of the head as she brought out a particularly outrageous remark—a kind of air of pleased expectancy. In just such a way had Cora once commented on the figure of the kitchenmaid. "Mollie can hardly get near the kitchen table, her stomach sticks out so. It's only been like that the last month or two. I wonder *why* she's getting so fat?"

Cora had been quickly hushed. The Abernethie household was Victorian in tone. The kitchenmaid had disappeared from the premises the next day, and after due inquiry the second gardener had been ordered to make an honest woman of her and had been presented with a cottage in which to do so.

Far off memories—but they had their point. . . .

Mr. Entwhistle examined his uneasiness more closely. What was there in Cora's ridiculous remarks that had remained to tease his subconscious in this manner? Presently he isolated two phrases. "I did think from what he said—" and "his death was so sudden . . ."

Mr. Entwhistle examined that last remark first. Yes, Richard's death could, in a fashion, be considered sudden. Mr. Entwhistle had discussed Richard's health both with Richard himself and with his doctor. The latter had indicated plainly that a long life could not be expected. If Mr. Abernethie took reasonable care of himself he might live two or even three years. Perhaps longer—but that was unlikely. In any case the doctor had anticipated no collapse in the near future.

Well, the doctor had been wrong—but doctors, as they were the first to admit themselves, could never be sure about the individual reaction of a patient to disease. Cases given up, unexpectedly recovered. Patients on the way to recovery, relapsed and died. So much depended on the vitality of the patient. On his own inner urge to live.

And Richard Abernethie, though a strong and vigorous man, had had no great incentive to live.

For six months previously his only surviving son, Mortimer, had contracted infantile paralysis and had died within a week. His death had been a shock greatly augmented by the fact that he had been such a particularly strong and vital young man. A keen sportsman, he was also a good athlete and was one of those people of whom it was said that he had never had a day's illness in his life. He was on the point of becoming engaged to a very charming girl and his father's hopes for the future were centered in this dearly loved and thoroughly satisfactory son of his.

Instead had come tragedy. And besides the sense of personal loss, the future had had little to hold Richard Abernethie's interest. One son had died in infancy, the second without issue. He had no grandchildren. There was, in fact, no one of the Abernethie name to come after him, and he was the holder of a vast fortune with wide business interests which he himself still controlled to a certain extent. Who was to succeed to that fortune and to the control of those interests?

That this had worried the old man deeply, Entwhistle knew. His only surviving brother was very much of an invalid. There remained the younger generation. It had been in Richard's mind, the lawyer thought, though his friend had not actually said so, to choose one definite successor, though minor legacies would probably have been made. Anyway, as Entwhistle knew, within the last six months Richard Abernethie had invited to stay with him, in succession, his nephew George, his niece Susan and her husband, his niece Rosamund and her husband, and his sister-in-law, Mrs. Leo Abernethie. It was amongst the first three so the lawyer thought, that Abernethie had looked for his successor. Helen Abernethie, he thought, had been asked out of personal affection and even possibly as someone to consult, for Richard had always held a high opinion of her good sense and practical judgment. Mr. Entwhistle also remembered that sometime during that six months' period Richard had paid a short visit to his brother Timothy.

The net result had been the will which the lawyer now carried in his brief case. An equable distribution of property. The only conclusion that could be drawn, therefore, was that he had been disappointed both in his nephew, and in his nieces—or perhaps in his nieces' husbands.

As far as Mr. Entwhistle knew, he had not invited his sister, Cora Lansquenet, to visit him—and that brought the lawyer back to that first disturbing phrase that Cora had let slip so incoherently—"but I did think from what he *said*—"

What had Richard Abernethie said? And when had he said it? If Cora had not been to Enderby, then Richard Abernethie must have visited her at the artistic village in Berkshire where she had a cottage. Or was it something that Richard had said in a letter?

Mr. Entwhistle frowned. Cora, of course, was a very stupid woman. She could easily have misinterpreted a phrase, and twisted its meaning. But he did wonder what the phrase could have been. . . .

There was enough uneasiness in him to make him consider the possibility of approaching Mrs. Lansquenet on the subject. Not too soon. Better not make it seem of importance. But he *would* like to know just what it was that Richard Abernethie had said to her which had led her to pipe up so briskly with that outrageous question:

"But he was murdered, wasn't he?"

II

In a third class carriage, further along the train, Gregory Banks said to his wife:

"That aunt of yours must be completely bats!"

"Aunt Cora?" Susan was vague. "Oh, yes, I believe she was always a bit simple or something."

George Crossfield, sitting opposite, said sharply:

"She really ought to be stopped from going about saying things like that. It might put ideas into people's heads."

Rosamund Shane, intent on outlining the cupid's bow of her mouth with lipstick, murmured vaguely:

"I don't suppose anyone would pay any attention to what a frump like that says. The most peculiar clothes and lashings and lashings of jet—"

"Well, I think it ought to be stopped," said George.

"All right, darling," laughed Rosamund, putting away her lipstick and contemplating her image with satisfaction in the mirror. "You stop it."

Her husband said unexpectedly:

"I think George is right. It's so easy to set people talking."

"Well, would it matter?" Rosamund contemplated the question. The cupid's bow lifted at the corners in a smile. "It might really be rather fun."

"Fun?" Four voices spoke.

"Having a murder in the family," said Rosamund. "Thrilling, you know!"

It occurred to that nervous and unhappy young man Gregory Banks that Susan's cousin, setting aside her attractive exterior, might have some faint points of resemblance to her Aunt Cora. Her next words rather confirmed his impression.

"If he was murdered," said Rosamund, "who do you think did it?"

Her gaze travelled thoughtfully round the carriage.

"His death has been awfully convenient for all of us," she said thoughtfully. "Michael and I are absolutely on our beam ends. Mick's had a really good part offered to him in the Sandborne show if he can afford to wait for it. Now we'll be in clover. We'll be able to back our own show if we want to. As a matter of fact there's a play with a simply wonderful part—"

Nobody listened to Rosamund's ecstatic disquisition. Their attention had shifted to their own immediate future.

"Touch and go," thought George to himself. "Now I can put that money back and nobody will ever know. . . . But it's been a near shave."

Gregory closed his eyes as he lay back against the seat. Escape from bondage.

Susan said in her clear rather hard voice, "I'm very sorry, of course, for poor old Uncle Richard. But then he *was* very old, and Mortimer had died, and he'd nothing to live for and it would have been awful for him to go on as an invalid year after year. *Much* better for him to pop off suddenly like this with no fuss."

Her hard confident young eyes softened as they watched her husband's absorbed face. She adored Greg. She sensed vaguely that Greg cared for her less than she cared for him—but that only strengthened her passion. Greg was hers, she'd do anything for him. Anything at all. . . .

III

Maude Abernethie, changing her dress for dinner at Enderby (for she was staying the night), wondered if she ought to have offered to stay longer to help Helen out with the sorting and clearing of the house—There would be all Richard's personal things. . . . There might be letters. . . . All important papers, she supposed, had already been taken possession of by Mr. Entwhistle. And it really was necessary for her to get back to Timothy as soon as possible. He fretted so when she was not there to look after him. She hoped he would be pleased about the will and not annoyed. He had expected, she knew, that most of Richard's fortune would come to *him*. After all, he was the only surviving Abernethie. Richard could surely have trusted *him* to look after the younger generation. Yes, she was afraid Timothy *would* be annoyed. . . . And that was so bad for his digestion. And really, when he was annoyed, Timothy could become quite unreasonable. There were times when he seemed to lose his sense of proportion. . . . She wondered if she ought to speak to Dr. Barton about it. . . . Those sleeping pills—Timothy had been taking far too many of them lately—he got so angry when she wanted to keep the bottle for him. But they could be dangerous—Dr. Barton had said so—you could get drowsy and forget you'd taken them—and then take more. And then anything might happen! There certainly weren't as many left in the bottle as there ought to be. . . . Timothy was really very naughty about medicines. He wouldn't listen to her. . . . He was very difficult sometimes.

She sighed—then brightened—Things were going to be much easier now. The garden, for instance—

IV

Helen Abernethie sat by the fire in the green drawing room waiting for Maude to come down to dinner.

She looked round her, remembering old days here with Leo and the others. It had been a happy house. But a house like this needed *people*. It needed children and servants and big meals and plenty of roaring fires in winter. It had been a sad house when it had been lived in by one old man who had lost his son. . . .

Who would buy it, she wondered? Would it be turned into a Hotel, or an Institute, or perhaps one of those Hostels for young people? That was what happened to these vast houses nowadays. No one would buy them to live in. It would be pulled down, perhaps, and the whole estate built over. It made her sad to think of that, but she pushed the sadness aside resolutely. It did one no good to dwell on the past. This house, and happy days here, and Richard, and Leo, all that was good, but it was over. She had her own activities and friends and interests. Yes, her interests. . . . And now, with the income Richard had left her, she would be able to keep on the villa in Cyprus and do all the things she had planned to do.

How worried she had been lately over money—taxation—all those investments going wrong. . . . Now, thanks to Richard's money, all that was over. . . .

Poor Richard. To die in his sleep like that had been really a great mercy. . . . *Suddenly on the 22nd*—she supposed that that was what had put the idea into Cora's head. Really Cora was outrageous! She always had been. Helen remembered meeting her once abroad, soon after her marriage to Pierre Lansquenet. She had been particularly foolish and fatuous that day, twisting her head sideways and making dogmatic statements about painting, and particularly about her husband's painting, which must have been most uncomfortable for him. No man could like his wife appearing such a fool. And Cora was a fool! Oh, well, poor thing, she couldn't help it, and that husband of hers hadn't treated her too well.

Helen's gaze rested absently on a bouquet of wax flowers that stood on a round malachite table. Cora had been sitting beside it when they had all been sitting round waiting to start for the church. She had been full of reminiscences and delighted recognitions of various things and was clearly so pleased at being back in her old home that she had completely lost sight of the reason for which they were assembled.

"But perhaps," thought Helen, "she was just less of a hypocrite than the rest of us. . . ."

Cora had never been one for observing the conventions. Look at the way she had plumped out that question: "But he *was* murdered, wasn't he?"

The faces all round, startled, shocked, staring at her! Such a variety of expressions there must have been on those faces. . . .

And suddenly, seeing the picture clearly in her mind, Helen frowned. . . . There was something wrong with that picture . . .

Something . . . ?

Somebody . . . ?

Was it an expression on someone's face? Was that it? Something that —how could she put it?—ought not to have been there . . . ?

She didn't know . . . she couldn't place it . . . but there had been something—somewhere—*wrong*.

V

Meanwhile, in the buffet at Swindon, a lady in wispy mourning and festoons of jet was eating bath buns and drinking tea and looking forward to the future. She had no premonitions of disaster. She was happy.

These cross country journeys were certainly tiring. It would have been easier to get back to Lytchett St. Mary via London—and not so very much more expensive. Ah, but expense didn't matter now. Still, she would have had to travel with the family—probably having to talk all the way. Too much of an effort.

No, better to go home cross country. These bath buns were really excellent. Extraordinary how hungry a funeral made you feel. The soup at Enderby had been delicious—and so was the cold soufflé.

How smug people were—and what hypocrites! All those faces—when she'd said that about murder! The way they'd all looked at her!

Well, it had been the right thing to say. She nodded her head in satisfied approval of herself. Yes, it had been the right thing to do.

She glanced up at the clock. Five minutes before her train went. She drank up her tea. Not very good tea. She made a grimace.

For a moment or two she sat dreaming. Dreaming of the future unfolding before her. . . . She smiled like a happy child.

She was really going to enjoy herself at last. . . . She went out to the small branch line train busily making plans. . . .

4

MR. ENTWHISTLE passed a very restless night. He felt so tired and so unwell in the morning that he did not get up.

His sister, who kept house for him, brought up his breakfast on a tray and explained to him severely how wrong he had been to go gadding off to the North of England at his age and in his frail state of health.

Mr. Entwhistle contented himself with saying that Richard Abernethie had been a very old friend.

"Funerals!" said his sister with deep disapproval. "Funerals are absolutely fatal for a man of your age! You'll be taken off as suddenly as your precious Mr. Abernethie was if you don't take more care of yourself."

The word "suddenly" made Mr. Entwhistle wince. It also silenced him. He did not argue.

He was well aware of what had made him flinch at the word *suddenly*.

Cora Lansquenet! What she had suggested was definitely quite impossible, but all the same he would like to find out exactly why she had suggested it. Yes, he would go down to Lytchett St. Mary and see her. He could pretend that it was business connected with probate, that he needed her signature. No need to let her guess that he had paid any attention to her silly remark. But he would go down and see her—and he would do it soon.

He finished his breakfast and lay back on his pillows and read the *Times*. He found the *Times* very soothing.

It was about a quarter to six that evening when his telephone rang.

He picked it up. The voice at the other end of the wire was that of Mr. James Parrott, the present second partner of Bollard, Entwhistle, Entwhistle and Bollard.

"Look here, Entwhistle," said Mr. Parrott, "I've just been rung up by the police from a place called Lytchett St. Mary."

"Lytchett St. Mary?"

"Yes. It seems—" Mr. Parrott paused a moment. He seemed embarrassed. "It's about a Mrs. Cora Lansquenet. Wasn't she one of the heirs of the Abernethie estate?"

"Yes, of course. I saw her at the funeral yesterday."

"Oh? She was at the funeral, was she?"

"Yes. What about her?"

"Well," Mr. Parrott sounded apologetic. "She's—it's really *most* extraordinary—she's been—well—*murdered.*"

Mr. Parrott said the last word with the uttermost deprecation. It was not the sort of word, he suggested, that ought to mean anything to the firm of Bollard, Entwhistle, Entwhistle and Bollard.

"Murdered?"

"Yes—yes—I'm afraid so. Well, I mean, there's no doubt about it."

"How did the police get on to us?"

"Her companion, or housekeeper, or whatever she is—a Miss Gilchrist. The police asked for the name of her nearest relative or of her solicitors. And this Miss Gilchrist seemed rather doubtful about relatives and their addresses, but she knew about us. So they got through at once."

"What makes them think she was murdered?" demanded Mr. Entwhistle.

Mr. Parrott sounded apologetic again.

"Oh well, it seems there can't be any doubt about *that*—I mean it was a hatchet or something of that kind—a very violent sort of crime."

"Robbery?"

"That's the idea. A window was smashed and there are some trinkets missing and drawers pulled out and all that, but the police seem to think there might be something—well—phony about it."

"What time did it happen?"

"Sometime between two and four this afternoon."

"Where was the housekeeper?"

"Changing library books in Reading. She got back about five o'clock and found Mrs. Lansquenet dead. The police want to know if we've any idea of who could have been likely to attack her. I said," Mr. Parrott's voice sounded outraged, "that I thought it was a most unlikely thing to happen."

"Yes, of course."

"It *must* be some half-witted local oaf—who thought there might be something to steal and then lost his head and attacked her. That must be it—eh, don't you think so, Entwhistle?"

"Yes, yes . . ." Mr. Entwhistle spoke absentmindedly.

Parrott was right, he told himself. That was what must have happened. . . .

But uncomfortably he heard Cora's voice saying brightly:

"But he *was* murdered, wasn't he?"

Such a fool, Cora. Always had been. Rushing in where angels fear to tread. . . . Blurting out unpleasant truths. . . .

Truths!

That blasted word again . . .

II

Mr. Entwhistle and Inspector Morton looked at each other appraisingly.

In his neat precise manner Mr. Entwhistle had placed at the Inspector's disposal all the relevant facts about Cora Lansquenet. Her upbringing, her marriage, her widowhood, her financial position, her relatives.

"Mr. Timothy Abernethie is her only surviving brother and her next of kin, but he is a recluse and an invalid, and is quite unable to leave home. He has empowered me to act for him and to make all such arrangements as may be necessary."

The Inspector nodded. It was a relief for him to have this shrewd elderly solicitor to deal with. Moreover he hoped that the lawyer might be able to give him some assistance in solving what was beginning to look like a rather puzzling problem.

He said:

"I understand from Miss Gilchrist that Mrs. Lansquenet had been North, to the funeral of an elder brother, on the day before her death?"

"That is so, Inspector. I myself was there."

"There was nothing unusual in her manner—nothing strange—or apprehensive?"

Mr. Entwhistle raised his eyebrows in well simulated surprise.

"Is it customary for there to be something strange in the manner of a person who is shortly to be murdered?" he asked.

The Inspector smiled rather ruefully.

"I'm not thinking of her being 'fey' or having a premonition. No, I'm just hunting around for something—well, something out of the ordinary."

"I don't think I quite understand you, Inspector," said Mr. Entwhistle.

"It's not a very easy case to understand, Mr. Entwhistle. Say someone watched the Gilchrist woman come out of the house at about two o'clock and go along to the village and the bus stop. This someone then deliberately takes the hatchet that was lying by the woodshed, smashes the kitchen window with it, gets into the house, goes upstairs, attacks Mrs. Lansquenet with the hatchet—and attacks her savagely. Six or eight blows were struck." Mr. Entwhistle flinched—"Oh, yes, quite a brutal crime. Then the intruder pulls out a few drawers, scoops up a few trinkets—worth perhaps a tenner in all, and clears off."

"She was in bed?"

"Yes. It seems she returned late from the North the night before, exhausted and very excited. She'd come into some legacy as I understand?"

"Yes."

"She slept very badly and woke with a terrible headache. She had several cups of tea and took some dope for her head and then told Miss Gilchrist not to disturb her till lunch-time. She felt no better and decided to take two sleeping pills. She then sent Miss Gilchrist into Reading by the bus to change some library books. She'd have been drowsy, if not already asleep, when this man broke in. He could have taken what he wanted by means of threats, or he could easily have gagged her. A hatchet, deliberately taken up with him from the outside, seems excessive."

"He may just have meant to threaten her with it," Mr. Entwhistle suggested. "If she showed fight then—"

"According to the medical evidence there is no sign that she did. Everything seems to show that she was lying on her side sleeping peacefully when she was attacked."

Mr. Entwhistle shifted uneasily in his chair.

"One does hear of these brutal and rather senseless murders," he pointed out.

"Oh yes, yes, that's probably what it will turn out to be. There's an alert out, of course, for any suspicious character. Nobody local is concerned, we're pretty sure of that. The locals are all accounted for satisfactorily. Most people are at work at that time of day. Of course her cottage is up a lane outside the village proper. Anyone could get there easily without being seen. There's a maze of lanes all round the village. It was a fine morning and there has been no rain for some days so there aren't any distinctive car tracks to go by—in case anyone came by car."

"You think someone came by car?" Mr. Entwhistle asked sharply.

The Inspector shrugged his shoulders. "I don't know. All I'm saying is there are curious features about the case. These, for instance—" He shoved across his desk a handful of things—a trefoil-shaped brooch with small pearls, a brooch set with amethysts, a small string of seed pearls, and a garnet bracelet.

"Those are the things that were taken from her jewel box. They were found just outside the house shoved into a bush."

"Yes—yes, that *is* rather curious. Perhaps if her assailant was frightened at what he had done—"

"Quite. But he would probably then have left them upstairs in her room . . . Of course a panic may have come over him between the bedroom and the front gate."

Mr. Entwhistle said quietly:

"Or they may, as you are suggesting, have only been taken as a blind."

"Yes, several possibilities . . . Of course this Gilchrist woman may have done it. Two women living alone together—you never know what quarrels or resentments or passions may have been aroused. Oh yes, we're taking that possibility into consideration as well. But it doesn't seem very likely. From all accounts they seemed to be on quite amicable terms." He paused before going on. "According to you nobody stands to gain by Mrs. Lansquenet's death?"

The lawyer shifted uneasily.

"I didn't quite say that."

Inspector Morton looked up sharply.

"I thought you said that Mrs. Lansquenet's source of income was an allowance made to her by her brother and that as far as you knew she had no property or means of her own."

"That is so. Her husband died a bankrupt, and from what I knew of her as a girl and since, I should be surprised if she had ever saved or accumulated any money."

"The cottage itself is rented, not her own, and the few sticks of furniture aren't anything to write home about, even in these days. Some spurious 'cottage oak' and some arty painted stuff. Whoever she's left them to won't gain much—if she's made a will, that is to say."

Mr. Entwhistle shook his head.

"I know nothing about her will. I had not seen her for many years, you must understand."

"Then what exactly did you mean just now? You had something in mind, I think?"

"Yes. Yes, I did. I wished to be strictly accurate."

"Were you referring to the legacy you mentioned? The one that her brother left her? Had she the power to dispose of that by will?"

"No, not in the sense you mean. She had no power to dispose of the capital. Now that she is dead, it will be divided amongst the five other beneficiaries of Richard Abernethie's will. That is what I meant. All five of them will benefit automatically by her death."

The Inspector looked disappointed.

"Oh, I thought we were on to something. Well, there certainly seems no motive there for anyone to come and swipe her with a hatchet. Looks as though it's some chap with a screw loose—one of these adolescent criminals, perhaps—a lot of them about. And then he lost his nerve and bushed the trinkets and ran . . . Yes, it must be that. Unless it's the highly respectable Miss Gilchrist and I must say that seems unlikely."

"When did she find the body?"

"Not until just about five o'clock. She came back from Reading by the 4.50 bus. She arrived back at the cottage, let herself in by the front door, and went into the kitchen and put the kettle on for tea. There was no sound from Mrs. Lansquenet's room, but Miss Gilchrist assumed that she was still sleeping. Then Miss Gilchrist noticed the kitchen window, the glass was all over the floor. Even then, she thought at first it might have been done by a boy with a ball or a catapult. She went upstairs and peeped very gently into Mrs. Lansquenet's room to see if she were asleep or if she was ready for some tea. Then of course, she let loose, shrieked, and rushed down the lane to the nearest neighbour. Her story seems perfectly consistent and there was no trace of blood in her room or in the bathroom, or on her clothes. No, I don't think Miss Gilchrist had anything to do with it. The doctor got there at half past five. He puts the time of death not later than four o'clock—and probably much nearer to two o'clock, so it looks as though whoever it was, was hanging round waiting for Miss Gilchrist to leave the cottage."

The lawyer's face twitched slightly. Inspector Morton went on: "You'll be going to see Miss Gilchrist, I suppose?"

"I thought of doing so."

"I should be glad if you would. She's told us, I think, everything that she can, but you never know. Sometimes in conversation, some point or other may crop up. She's a trifle old-maidish—but quite a sensible practical woman—and she's really been most helpful and efficient."

He paused and then said:

"The body's at the mortuary. If you would like to see it—"

Mr. Entwhistle assented though with no enthusiasm.

Some few minutes later he stood looking down at the mortal remains of Cora Lansquenet. She had been savagely attacked and the henna dyed fringe was clotted and stiffened with blood. Mr. Entwhistle's lips tightened and he looked away queasily.

Poor little Cora. How eager she had been the day before yesterday to know whether her brother had left her anything. What rosy anticipations she must have had of the future. What a lot of silly things she could have done—and enjoyed doing—with the money.

Poor Cora. . . . How short a time those anticipations had lasted.

No one had gained by her death—not even the brutal assailant who had thrust away those trinkets as he fled. Five people had a few thousands more of capital—but the capital they had already received was probably more than sufficient for them. No, there could be no motive there.

Funny that murder should have been running in Cora's mind the very day before she herself was murdered.

"It was murder, wasn't it?"

Such a ridiculous thing to say. Ridiculous! Quite ridiculous! Much too ridiculous to mention to Inspector Morton.

Of course, after he had seen Miss Gilchrist . . .

Supposing that Miss Gilchrist, although it was unlikely, could throw any light on what Richard had said to Cora.

"*I thought from what he said—*" What *had* Richard said?

"I must see Miss Gilchrist at once," said Mr. Entwhistle to himself.

III

Miss Gilchrist was a spare faded-looking woman with short iron grey hair. She had one of those indeterminate faces that women around fifty so often acquire.

She greeted Mr. Entwhistle warmly.

"I'm *so* glad you have come, Mr. Entwhistle. I really know *so little* about Mrs. Lansquenet's family, and of course I've never never had anything to do with a *murder* before. It's too dreadful!"

Mr. Entwhistle felt quite sure that Miss Gilchrist had never before had anything to do with murder. Indeed, her reaction to it was very much that of his partner.

"One *reads* about them, of course," said Miss Gilchrist, relegating crimes to their proper sphere. "And even *that* I'm not very fond of doing. So *sordid*, most of them."

Following her into the sitting room Mr. Entwhistle was looking sharply about him. There was a strong smell of oil paint. The cottage was overcrowded, less by furniture, which was much as Inspector Morton had described it, than by pictures. The walls were covered with pictures, mostly very dark and dirty oil paintings. But there were water colour sketches as well, and one or two still lifes. Smaller pictures were stacked on the window seat.

"Mrs. Lansquenet used to buy them at sales," Miss Gilchrist explained. "It was a great interest to her, poor dear. She went to all the sales round about. Pictures go so cheap, nowadays, a mere song. She never paid more than a pound for any of them, sometimes only a few shillings and there was a wonderful chance, she always said, of picking up something worthwhile. She used to say that this was an Italian Primitive that might be worth a lot of money."

Mr. Entwhistle looked at the Italian Primitive pointed out to him dubiously. Cora, he reflected, had never really known anything about pictures. He'd eat his hat if any of these daubs were worth a five pound note!

"Of course," said Miss Gilchrist, noticing his expression, and quick to sense his reaction. "I don't know much myself, though my father was a painter—not a very successful one, I'm afraid. But I used to do water colours myself as a girl and I heard a lot of talk about painting and that made it nice for Mrs. Lansquenet to have someone she could talk to about painting and who'd understand. Poor dear soul, she cared so much about artistic things."

"You were fond of her?"

A foolish question, he told himself. Could she possibly answer "no"? Cora, he thought, must have been a tiresome woman to live with.

"Oh *yes*," said Miss Gilchrist. "We got on *very* well together. In some ways, you know, Mrs. Lansquenet was just like a child. She said anything that came into her head. I don't know that her *judgement* was always very good—"

One does not say of the dead—"She was a thoroughly silly woman"—Mr. Entwhistle said, "She was not in any sense an intellectual woman."

"No—no—perhaps not. But she was very shrewd, Mr. Entwhistle. Really very shrewd. It quite surprised me sometimes—how she managed to hit the nail on the head."

Mr. Entwhistle looked at Miss Gilchrist with more interest. He thought that she was no fool herself.

"You were with Mrs. Lansquenet for some years, I think?"

"Three and a half."

"You—er—acted as companion and also did the—er—well—looked after the house?"

It was evident that he had touched on a delicate subject. Miss Gilchrist flushed a little.

"Oh yes, indeed. I did most of the cooking—I *quite* enjoy cooking—and did some dusting and light housework. None of the *rough*, of course." Miss Gilchrist's tone expressed a firm principle. Mr. Entwhistle, who had no idea what "the rough" was, made a soothing murmur.

"Mrs. Panter from the village came in for that. Twice a week regularly. You see, Mr. Entwhistle, I could not have contemplated being in any way a *servant*. When my little teashop failed—such a disaster—it was the war, you know. A delightful place. I called it the Willow Tree and all the china was blue willow pattern—sweetly pretty—and the cakes *really* good—I've always had a hand with cakes and scones. Yes I was doing really well and then the war came and supplies were cut down and the whole thing went bankrupt—a war casualty, that is what I always say, and I try to think of it like that. I lost the little money my father left me that I had invested in it, and of course I had to look round for something to do. I'd never been trained for anything. So I went to one lady but it didn't answer at all—she was so rude and overbearing and then I did some office work—but I didn't like that at all, and then I came to Mrs. Lansquenet and we suited each other from the start—her husband being an artist and everything.'' Miss Gilchrist came to a breathless stop and added mournfully: ''But how I loved my dear dear little teashop. Such *nice* people used to come to it!''

Looking at Miss Gilchrist, Mr. Entwhistle felt a sudden stab of recognition—a composite picture of hundreds of ladylike figures approaching him in numerous Bay Trees, Ginger Cats, Blue Parrots, Willow Trees and Cosy Corners, all chastely encased in blue or pink or orange overalls and taking orders for pots of china tea and cakes. Miss Gilchrist had a Spiritual Home—a ladylike teashop of Ye Olde Worlde variety with a suitable genteel clientele. There must, he thought, be large numbers of Miss Gilchrists all over the country, all looking much alike with mild patient faces and obstinate upper lips and slightly wispy grey hair.

Miss Gilchrist went on:

''But really I must not talk about myself. The police have been very kind and considerate. Very kind indeed. An Inspector Morton came over from headquarters and he was *most* understanding. He even arranged for me to go and spend the night at Mrs. Lake's down the lane but I said 'No.' I felt it my duty to stay here with all Mrs. Lansquenet's nice things in the house. They took the—the—'' Miss Gilchrist gulped a little—''the body away, of course, and locked up the room, and the Inspector told me there would be a constable on duty in the kitchen all night—because of the broken window—it has been reglazed this morning, I am glad to say—where was I?—Oh yes, so I said I should be *quite* all right in my own room, though I must confess I *did* pull the chest of drawers across the door and put a big jug of water on the window-sill. One never knows—and if by any chance it *was* a maniac—one does hear of such things . . .''

Here Miss Gilchrist ran down. Mr. Entwhistle said quickly:

''I am in possession of all the main facts. Inspector Morton gave them to me. But if it would not distress you too much to give me your own account—?''

''Of course, Mr. Entwhistle. I know *just* what you feel. The police are so impersonal, are they not? Rightly so, of course.''

''Mrs. Lansquenet got back from the funeral the night before last,'' Mr. Entwhistle prompted.

''Yes, her train didn't get in until quite late. I had ordered a taxi to meet it as she told me to. She was very tired, poor dear—as was only natural—but on the whole she was in quite good spirits.''

''Yes, yes. Did she talk about the funeral at all?''

''Just a little. I made her a cup of Ovaltine—she didn't want anything else—and she told me that the church had been quite full and lots of flowers—oh! and she said that she was sorry not to have seen her other brother—Timothy—was it?''

''Yes, Timothy.''

''She said it was over twenty years since she had seen him and that she hoped he would have been there, but she quite realised he would have thought it better not to come under the circumstances, but that his wife was there and that she'd never been able to stand Maude—oh dear, I *do* beg your pardon, Mr. Entwhistle—it just slipped out—I never meant—''

''Not at all. Not at all,'' said Mr. Entwhistle encouragingly. ''I am no relation, you know. And I believe that Cora and her sister-in-law never hit it off very well.''

''Well, she almost said as much. 'I always knew Maude would grow into one of those bossy interfering women,' is what she said. And then she was very tired and said she'd go to bed at once—I'd got her hot water bottle in all ready—and she went up.''

''She said nothing else that you can remember specially?''

''She had no *premonition*, Mr. Entwhistle, if that is what you mean. I'm sure of that. She was really, you know, in remarkably good spirits—apart from tiredness and the—the sad occasion. She asked me how I'd like to go to Capri. To Capri! Of course I said it would be too wonderful—it's a thing I'd never dreamed I'd ever do—and she said, 'We'll go!' Just like that. I gathered—of course it wasn't actually *mentioned*—that her brother had left her an annuity or something of the kind.''

Mr. Entwhistle nodded.

''Poor dear. Well, I'm glad she had the pleasure of planning—at all events.'' Miss Gilchrist sighed and murmured wistfully, ''I don't suppose I shall ever go to Capri now. . . .''

''And the next morning?'' Mr. Entwhistle prompted, oblivious of Miss Gilchrist's disappointments.

''The next morning Mrs. Lansquenet wasn't at all well. Really, she looked dreadful. She'd hardly slept at all, she told me. Nightmares. 'It's because you were overtired yesterday,' I told her, and she said maybe it was. She had her breakfast in bed, and she didn't get up all the morning, but at lunchtime she told me that she still hadn't been able to sleep. 'I feel so restless,' she said. 'I keep thinking of things and wondering.' And then she said she'd take some sleeping tablets and try and get a good sleep in the afternoon. And she wanted me to go over by bus to Reading and change her two library books, because she'd finished them both on the train journey and she hadn't got anything to read. Usually two books lasted her nearly a week. So I went off just after two and that—and that—was the last time—" Miss Gilchrist began to sniff. "She must have been asleep, you know. She wouldn't have heard anything and the Inspector assures me that she didn't suffer. . . . He thinks the first blow killed her. Oh dear, it makes me quite sick even to *think* of it!"

"Please, please. I've no wish to take you any further over what happened. All I wanted was to hear what you could tell me about Mrs. Lansquenet before the tragedy."

"Very natural, I'm sure. Do tell her relations that apart from having such a bad night she was really very happy and looking forward to the future."

Mr. Entwhistle paused before asking his next question. He wanted to be careful not to lead the witness.

"She did not mention any of her relations in particular?"

"No, no, I don't think so." Miss Gilchrist considered. "Except what she said about being sorry not to see her brother Timothy."

"She did not speak at all about her brother's decease? The—er—cause of it? Anything like that?"

"No."

There was no sign of alertness in Miss Gilchrist's face. Mr. Entwhistle felt certain there would have been if Cora had plumped out her verdict of murder.

"He'd been ill for some time, I think," said Miss Gilchrist vaguely, "though I must say I was surprised to hear it. He looked so very vigorous."

Mr. Entwhistle said quickly:

"You saw him—when?"

"When he came down here to see Mrs. Lansquenet. Let me see—that was about three weeks ago."

"Did he stay here?"

"Oh—no—just came for luncheon. It was quite a surprise. Mrs. Lansquenet hadn't expected him. I gather there had been some family disagreement. She hadn't seen him for years, she told me."

"Yes, that is so."

"It quite upset her—seeing him again—and probably realizing how ill he was—"

"She knew that he was ill?"

"Oh yes, I remember quite well. Because I wondered—only in my own mind, you understand—if perhaps Mr. Abernethie might be suffering from softening of the brain. An aunt of mine—"

Mr. Entwhistle deftly sidetracked the aunt.

"Something Mrs. Lansquenet said caused you to think of softening of the brain?"

"Yes. Mrs. Lansquenet said something like 'Poor Richard. Mortimer's death must have aged him a lot. He sounds quite senile. All these fancies about persecution and that someone is poisoning him. Old people get like that.' And of course, as I knew, that is only too *true*. This aunt that I was telling you about—convinced the servants were trying to poison her in her food and at last would eat only boiled eggs—because, she said, you couldn't get inside a boiled egg to poison it. We humoured her, but if it had been nowadays I don't know *what* we should have done. With eggs so scarce and mostly foreign at that, so that boiling is always risky."

Mr. Entwhistle listened to the saga of Miss Gilchrist's aunt with deaf ears. He was very much disturbed.

He said at last, when Miss Gilchrist had twittered into silence:

"I suppose Mrs. Lansquenet didn't take all this too seriously?"

"Oh no, Mr. Entwhistle, she *quite* understood."

Mr. Entwhistle found that remark disturbing too, though not quite in the sense in which Miss Gilchrist had used it.

Had Cora Lansquenet understood? Not then, perhaps, but later. Had she understood only too well?

Mr. Entwhistle knew that there had been no senility about Richard Abernethie. Richard had been in full possession of his faculties. He was not the man to have persecution mania in any form. He was, as he always had been, a hard-headed business man—and his illness made no difference in that respect.

It seemed extraordinary that he should have spoken to his sister in the terms that he had. But perhaps Cora, with her odd childlike shrewdness, had read between the lines, and had crossed the t's and dotted the i's of what Richard Abernethie had actually said.

In most ways, thought Mr. Entwhistle, Cora had been a complete fool. She had no judgment, no balance, and a crude childish point of view, but she had also the child's uncanny knack of sometimes hitting the nail on the head in a way that seemed quite startling.

Mr. Entwhistle left it at that. Miss Gilchrist, he thought, knew no more than she had told him. He asked whether she knew if Cora Lansquenet had left a will. Miss Gilchrist replied promptly that Mrs. Lansquenet's will was at the Bank.

With that and after making certain further arrangements he took his leave. He insisted on Miss Gilchrist's accepting a small sum in cash to defray present expenses and told her he would communicate with her again, and in the meantime he would be grateful if she would stay on at the cottage while she was looking about for a new post. That would be, Miss Gilchrist said, a great convenience and really she was not at all nervous.

He was unable to escape without being shown round the cottage by Miss Gilchrist, and introduced to various pictures by the late Pierre Lansquenet which were crowded into the small dining room and which made Mr. Entwhistle flinch—they were mostly nudes executed with a singular lack of draughtsmanship but with much fidelity to detail. He was also made to admire various small oil sketches of picturesque fishing ports done by Cora herself.

"Polperro," said Miss Gilchrist proudly. "We were there last year and Mrs. Lansquenet was delighted with its picturesqueness."

Mr. Entwhistle, viewing Polperro from the southwest, from the northwest, and presumably from the several other points of the compass, agreed that Mrs. Lansquenet had certainly been enthusiastic.

"Mrs. Lansquenet promised to leave me her sketches," said Miss Gilchrist wistfully. "I admired them so much. One can really see the waves breaking in this one, can't one? Even if she forgot, I might perhaps have just *one* as a souvenir, do you think?"

"I'm sure that could be arranged," said Mr. Entwhistle graciously.

He made a few further arrangements and then left to interview the Bank Manager and to have a further consultation with Inspector Morton.

5

"WORN OUT, that's what you are," said Miss Entwhistle in the indignant and bullying tones adopted by devoted sisters towards brothers for whom they keep house. "You shouldn't do it, at your age. What's it all got to do with you, I'd like to know? You've retired, haven't you?"

Mr. Entwhistle said mildly that Richard Abernethie had been one of his oldest friends.

"I daresay. But Richard Abernethie's dead, isn't he? So I see no reason for you to go mixing yourself up in things that are no concern of yours and catching your death of cold in these nasty draughty railway trains. And murder, too! *I* can't see why they sent for you at all."

"They communicated with me because there was a letter in the cottage signed by me, telling Cora the arrangements for the funeral."

"Funerals! One funeral after another, and that reminds me. Another of these precious Abernethies has been ringing you up—Timothy, I think he said. From somewhere in Yorkshire—and *that's* about a funeral, too! Said he'd ring again later."

A personal call for Mr. Entwhistle came through that evening. Taking it, he heard Maude Abernethie's voice at the other end.

"Thank goodness I've got hold of you at last! Timothy has been in the most terrible state. This news about Cora has upset him dreadfully."

"Quite understandable," said Mr. Entwhistle.

"What did you say?"

"I said it was quite understandable."

"I suppose so." Maude sounded more than doubtful. "Do you mean to say it was really murder?"

(*"It was murder, wasn't it?"* Cora had said. But this time there was no hesitation about the answer.)

"Yes, it was murder," said Mr. Entwhistle.

"And with a hatchet, so the papers say?"

"Yes."

"It seems *quite* incredible to me," said Maude, "that Timothy's sister—his own sister—can have been murdered with a *hatchet!*"

It seemed no less incredible to Mr. Entwhistle. Timothy's life was so remote from violence that even his relations, one felt, ought to be equally exempt.

"I'm afraid one has to face the fact," said Mr. Entwhistle mildly.

"I am really *very* worried about Timothy. It's so bad for him, all this! I've got him to bed now but he insists on my persuading you to come up and see him. He wants to know a hundred things—whether there will be an inquest, and who ought to attend, and how soon after that the funeral can take place, and where, and what funds there are, and if Cora expressed any wishes about being cremated or what, and if she left a will—"

Mr. Entwhistle interrupted before the catalogue got too long.

"There is a will, yes. She left Timothy her executor."

"Oh dear, I'm afraid Timothy can't undertake anything—"

"The firm will attend to all the necessary business. The will's very simple. She left her own sketches and an amethyst brooch to her companion, Miss Gilchrist, and everything else to Susan."

"To Susan? Now I wonder why Susan? I don't believe she ever saw Susan—not since she was a baby anyway."

"I imagine that it was because Susan was reported to have made a marriage not wholly pleasing to the family."

Maude snorted.

"Even Gregory is a great deal better than Pierre Lansquenet ever was! Of course marrying a man who serves in a shop would have been unheard of in my day—but a chemist's shop is much better than a haberdasher's—and at least Gregory seems quite respectable." She paused and added: "Does this mean that Susan gets the income Richard left to Cora?"

"Oh no. The capital of that will be divided according to the instructions of Richard's will. No, poor Cora had only a few hundred pounds and the furniture of her cottage to leave. When outstanding debts are paid and the furniture sold I doubt if the whole thing will amount to more than at most five hundred pounds." He went on: "There will have to be an inquest, of course. That is fixed for next Thursday. If Timothy is agreeable, we'll send down young Lloyd to watch the proceedings on behalf of the family." He added apologetically: "I'm afraid it may attract some notoriety owing to the—er—circumstances."

"How very unpleasant! Have they caught the wretch who did it?"

"Not yet."

"One of these dreadful half baked young men who go about the country roving and murdering, I suppose. The police are so incompetent."

"No, no," said Mr. Entwhistle. "The police are by no means incompetent. Don't imagine that, for a moment."

"Well, it all seems to me quite extraordinary. And *so* bad for Timothy. I suppose you couldn't possibly come down here, Mr. Entwhistle? I should be *most* grateful if you could. I think Timothy's mind might be set at rest if you were here to reassure him."

Mr. Entwhistle was silent for a moment. The invitation was not unwelcome.

"There is something in what you say," he admitted. "And I shall need Timothy's signature as executor to certain documents. Yes, I think it might be quite a good thing."

"That is splendid. I am so relieved. Tomorrow? And you'll stay the night? The best train is the 11.20 from St. Pancras."

"It will have to be an afternoon train, I'm afraid. I have—" said Mr. Entwhistle, "other business in the morning . . ."

II

George Crossfield greeted Mr. Entwhistle heartily but with, perhaps, just a shade of surprise.

Mr. Entwhistle said, in an explanatory way, although it really explained nothing:

"I've just come up from Lytchett St. Mary."

"Then it really was Aunt Cora? I read about it in the papers and I just couldn't believe it. I thought it must be someone of the same name."

"Lansquenet is not a common name."

"No, of course it isn't. I suppose there is a natural aversion to believing that anyone of one's own family can be murdered. Sounds to me rather like that case last month on Dartmoor."

"Does it?"

"Yes. Same circumstances. Cottage in a lonely position. Two elderly women living together. Amount of cash taken really quite pitifully inadequate one would think."

"The value of money is always relative," said Mr. Entwhistle. "It is the need that counts."

"Yes—yes, I suppose you're right."

"If you need ten pounds desperately—then fifteen is more than adequate. And inversely also. If your need is for a hundred pounds, forty five would be worse than useless. And if it's thousands you need, then hundreds are not enough."

George said with a sudden flicker of the eyes: "I'd say *any* money came in useful these days. Everyone's hard up."

"But not *desperate*," Mr. Entwhistle pointed out. "It's the desperation that counts."

"Are you thinking of something in particular?"

"Oh no, not at all." He paused, then went on. "It will be a little time before the estate is settled, would it be convenient for you to have an advance?"

"As a matter of fact, I *was* going to raise the subject. However, I saw the Bank this morning and referred them to you and they were quite obliging about an overdraft."

Again there came that flicker in George's eyes, and Mr. Entwhistle, from the depths of his experience, recognised it. George, he felt certain, had been, if not desperate, then in very sore straits for money. He knew at that moment, what he had felt sub-consciously all along, that in money matters he would not trust George. He wondered if old Richard Abernethie, who also had had great experience in judging men, had felt that. Mr. Entwhistle was almost sure that after Mortimer's death, Richard Abernethie had formed the intention of making George his heir. George was not an Abernethie, but he was the only male of the younger generation. He was the natural successor to Mortimer. Richard Abernethie had sent for George, had had him staying in the house for some days. It seemed probable that at the end of the visit the older man had not found George satisfactory. Had he felt instinctively, as Mr. Entwhistle felt, that George was not straight? George's father, so the family had thought, had been a poor choice on Laura's part. A stockbroker who had had other rather mysterious activities. George took after his father rather than after the Abernethies.

Perhaps misinterpreting the old lawyer's silence, George said with an uneasy laugh:

"Truth is, I've not been very lucky with my investments lately. I took a bit of a risk and it didn't come off. More or less cleaned me out. But I'll be able to recoup myself now. All one needs is a bit of capital. Ardens Consolidated are pretty good, don't you think?"

Mr. Entwhistle neither agreed nor dissented. He was wondering if by any chance George had been speculating with money that belonged to clients and not with his own? If George had been in danger of criminal prosecution—

Mr. Entwhistle said precisely:

"I tried to reach you the day after the funeral, but I suppose you weren't in the office."

"Did you? They never told me. As a matter of fact, I thought I was entitled to a day off after the good news!"

"The good news?"

George reddened.

"Oh look here, I didn't mean Uncle Richard's death. But knowing you've come into money does give one a bit of a kick. One feels one must celebrate. As a matter of fact I went to Hurst Park. Backed two winners. It never rains but it pours! If your luck's in, it's in! Only a matter of fifty quid, but it all helps."

"Oh yes," said Mr. Entwhistle. "It all helps. And there will now be an additional sum coming to you as a result of your Aunt Cora's death."

George looked concerned.

"Poor old girl," he said. "It does seem rotten luck, doesn't it? Probably just when she was all set to enjoy herself."

"Let us hope the police will find the person responsible for her death," said Mr. Entwhistle.

"I expect they'll get him all right. They're good, our police. They round up all the undesirables in the neighbourhood and go through 'em with a tooth comb—make them account for their actions at the time it happened."

"Not so easy if a little time has elapsed," said Mr. Entwhistle. He gave a wintry little smile that indicated he was about to make a joke. "I myself was in Hatchard's bookshop at 3.30 on the day in question. Should I remember that if I were questioned by the police in ten days' time? I very much doubt it. And you, George, you were at Hurst Park. Would you remember which day you went to the races in—say—a month's time?"

"Oh I could fix it by the funeral—the day after."

"True—true. And then you backed a couple of winners. Another aid to memory. One seldom forgets the name of a horse on which one has won money. Which were they, by the way?"

"Let me see. Gaymarck and Frogg II. Yes, I shan't forget them in a hurry."

Mr. Entwhistle gave his dry little cackle of laughter and took his leave.

III

"It's lovely to see you, of course," said Rosamund without any marked enthusiasm. "But it's frightfully early in the morning."

She yawned heavily.

"It's eleven o'clock," said Mr. Entwhistle.

Rosamund yawned again. She said apologetically:

"We had the hell of a party last night. Far too much to drink. Michael's got a terrible hangover still."

Michael appeared at this moment, also yawning. He had a cup of black coffee in his hand and was wearing a very smart dressing gown. He looked haggard and attractive—and his smile had the usual charm. Rosamund was wearing a black skirt, a rather dirty yellow pullover, and nothing else as far as Mr. Entwhistle could judge.

The precise and fastidious lawyer did not approve at all of the young Shanes' way of living. The rather ramshackle flat on the first floor of a Chelsea house—the bottles and glasses and cigarette ends that lay about in profusion—the stale air, and the general air of dust and dishevelment.

In the midst of this discouraging setting Rosamund and Michael bloomed with their wonderful good looks. They were certainly a very handsome couple and they seemed, Mr. Entwhistle thought, very fond of each other. Rosamund was certainly adoringly fond of Michael.

"Darling," she said. "Do you think just a teeny sip of champagne? Just to pull us together and toast the future. Oh, Mr. Entwhistle, it really is the most marvellous luck Uncle Richard leaving us all that lovely money just now—"

Mr. Entwhistle noted the quick, almost scowling frown that Michael gave, but Rosamund went on serenely:

"Because there's the most wonderful chance of a play. Michael's got an option on it. It's a most wonderful part for him and even a small part for me, too. It's about one of these young criminals, you know, that are really saints—it's absolutely full of the latest modern ideas."

"So it would seem," said Mr. Entwhistle stiffly.

"He robs, you know, and he kills, and he's hounded by the police and by society—and then in the end, he does a miracle."

Mr. Entwhistle sat in outraged silence. Pernicious nonsense these young fools talked! *And* wrote.

Not that Michael Shane was talking much. There was still a faint scowl on his face.

"Mr. Entwhistle doesn't want to hear all our rhapsodies, Rosamund," he said. "Shut up for a bit and let him tell us why he's come to see us."

"There are just one or two little matters to straighten out," said Mr. Entwhistle. "I have just come back from Lytchett St. Mary."

"Then it *was* Aunt Cora who was murdered? We saw it in the paper. And I said it must be because it's a very uncommon name. Poor old Aunt Cora. I was looking at her at the funeral that day and thinking what a frump she was and that really one might as well be dead if one looked like that—and now she *is* dead. They absolutely wouldn't *believe* it last night when I told then that that murder with the hatchet in the paper was actually *my aunt!* They just laughed, didn't they, Michael?"

Michael Shane did not reply and Rosamund with every appearance of enjoyment said:

"Two murders one after another. It's almost too much, isn't it?"

"Don't be a fool, Rosamund, your Uncle Richard wasn't murdered."

"Well, Cora thought he was."

Mr. Entwhistle intervened to ask:

"You came back to London after the funeral, didn't you?"

"Yes, we came by the same train as you did."

"Of course . . . of course. I ask because I tried to get hold of you," he shot a quick glance at the telephone—"on the following day—several times in fact, and couldn't get an answer."

"Oh dear—I'm so sorry. What were we doing that day? The day before yesterday. We were here until about twelve, weren't we? And then you went round to try and get hold of Rosenheim and you went on to lunch with Oscar and I went out to see if I could get some nylons and round the shops. I was to meet Janet but we missed each other. Yes, I had a lovely afternoon shopping—and then we dined at the *Castile*. We got back here about ten o'clock, I suppose."

"About that," said Michael. He was looking thoughtfully at Mr. Entwhistle. "What did you want to get hold of us for, sir?"

"Oh! Just some points that had arisen about Richard Abernethie's estate—papers to sign—all that."

Rosamund asked: "Do we get the money now, or not for ages?"

"I'm afraid," said Mr. Entwhistle, "that the law is prone to delays."

"But we can get an advance, can't we?" Rosamund looked alarmed. "Michael said we could. Actually it's terribly important. Because of the play."

Michael said pleasantly:

"Oh, there's no real hurry. It's just a question of deciding whether or not to take up the option."

"It will be quite easy to advance you some money," said Mr. Entwhistle. "As much as you need."

"Then that's all right." Rosamund gave a sigh of relief. She added as an afterthought: "Did Aunt Cora leave any money?"

"A little. She left it to your Cousin Susan."

"Why Susan, I should like to know! Is it much?"

"A few hundred pounds and some furniture."

"Nice furniture?"

"No," said Mr. Entwhistle.

Rosamund lost interest. "It's all very odd, isn't it?" she said. "There was Cora, after the funeral, suddenly coming out with 'He *was* murdered!' and then, the very next day, *she* goes and gets *herself* murdered! I mean, it is *odd*, isn't it?"

There was a moment's rather uncomfortable silence before Mr. Entwhistle said quietly:

"Yes, it is indeed very odd. . . ."

IV

Mr. Entwhistle studied Susan Banks as she leant forward across the table talking in her animated manner.

None of the loveliness of Rosamund here. But it was an attractive face and its attraction lay, Mr. Entwhistle decided, in its vitality. The curves of the mouth were rich and full. It was a woman's mouth and her body was very decidedly a woman's—emphatically so. Yet in many ways Susan reminded him of her uncle, Richard Abernethie. The shape of her head, the line of her jaw, the deep set reflective eyes. She had the same kind of dominant personality that Richard had had, the same driving energy, the same foresightedness and forthright judgment. Of the three members of the younger generation she alone seemed to be made of the mettle that had raised up the vast Abernethie fortunes. Had Richard recognised in this niece a kindred spirit to his own? Mr. Entwhistle thought he must have done. Richard had always had a keen appreciation of character. Here, surely, were exactly the qualities of which he was in search. And yet, in his will, Richard Abernethie had made no distinction in her favour. Distrustful, as Mr. Entwhistle believed, of George, passing over that lovely dimwit, Rosamund—could he not have found in Susan what he was seeking—an heir of his own mettle?

If not, the cause must be—yes, it followed logically—the husband. . . .

Mr. Entwhistle's eyes slid gently over Susan's shoulder to where Gregory Banks stood absently whittling at a pencil.

A thin pale nondescript young man with reddish sandy hair. So overshadowed by Susan's colourful personality that it was difficult to realise what he himself was really like. Nothing to take hold of in the fellow—quite pleasant, ready to be agreeable—a yes man, as the modern term went. And yet that did not seem to describe him satisfactorily. There was something vaguely disquieting about the unobtrusiveness of Gregory Banks. He had been an unsuitable match—yet Susan had insisted on marrying him—had overborne all opposition—why? What had she seen in him?

And now, six months after the marriage—"She's crazy about the fellow," Mr. Entwhistle said to himself. He knew the signs. A large number of wives with matrimonial troubles had passed through the office of Bollard, Entwhistle, Entwhistle and Bollard. Wives madly devoted to unsatisfactory and often what appeared quite unprepossessing husbands, wives contemptuous of, and bored by, apparently attractive and impeccable husbands. What any woman saw in some particular man was beyond the comprehension of the average intelligent male. It just was so. A woman who could be intelligent about everything else in the world could be a complete fool when it came to some particular man. Susan, thought Mr. Entwhistle, was one of those women. For her the world revolved around Greg. And that had its dangers in more ways than one.

Susan was talking with emphasis and indignation.

"—because it *is* disgraceful. You remember that woman who was murdered in Yorkshire last year? Nobody was ever arrested. And the old woman in the sweet shop who was killed with a crowbar. They detained some man, and then they let him go!"

"There has to be evidence, my dear," said Mr. Entwhistle.

Susan paid no attention.

"And that other case—a retired Nurse—that was a hatchet or an axe—just like Aunt Cora."

"Dear me, you appear to have made quite a study of these crimes, Susan," said Mr. Entwhistle mildly.

"Naturally one remembers these things—and when someone in one's own family is killed—and in very much the same way—well, it shows that there must be a lot of these sort of people going round the countryside, breaking into places and attacking lonely women—and that the police just don't *bother!*"

Mr. Entwhistle shook his head.

"Don't belittle the police, Susan. They are a very shrewd and patient body of men—persistent, too. Just because it isn't still mentioned in the newspapers doesn't mean that a case is closed. Far from it."

"And yet there are hundreds of unsolved crimes every year."

"Hundreds?" Mr. Entwhistle looked dubious. "A certain number, yes. But there are many occasions when the police know who has committed a crime but where the evidence is insufficient for a prosecution."

"I don't believe it," said Susan. "I believe if you knew definitely *who* committed a crime you could always get the evidence."

"I wonder now." Mr. Entwhistle sounded thoughtful. "I very much wonder. . . ."

"Have they any idea *at all*—in Aunt Cora's case—of who it might be?"

"That I couldn't say. Not as far as I know. But they would hardly confide in me—and it's early days yet—the murder took place only the day before yesterday, remember."

"It's definitely got to be a certain kind of person," Susan mused. "A brutal, perhaps slightly half witted type—a discharged soldier or a gaol bird. I mean, using a hatchet like that."

Looking slightly quizzical, Mr. Entwhistle raised his eyebrows and murmured:

> "*Lizzie Borden with an axe*
> *Gave her father forty whacks*
> *When she saw what she had done*
> *She gave her mother forty one.*"

"Oh," Susan flushed angrily, "Cora hadn't got any relations living with her—unless you mean the companion. And anyway Lizzie Borden was acquitted. Nobody knows for certain she killed her father and stepmother."

"The rhyme is quite definitely libellous," Mr. Entwhistle agreed.

"You mean the companion *did* do it? Did Cora leave her anything?"

"An amethyst brooch of no great value and some sketches of fishing villages of sentimental value only."

"One has to have a motive for murder—unless one is half witted."

Mr. Entwhistle gave a little chuckle.

"As far as one can see, the only person who had a motive is *you*, my dear Susan."

"What's that?" Greg moved forward suddenly. He was like a sleeper coming awake. An ugly light showed in his eyes. He was suddenly no longer a negligible feature in the background. "What's Sue got to do with it? What do you mean—saying things like that?"

Susan said sharply:

"Shut up, Greg. Mr. Entwhistle doesn't mean anything—"

"Just my little joke," said Mr. Entwhistle apologetically. "Not in the best taste, I'm afraid. Cora left her estate, such as it was, to you, Susan. But to a young lady who has just inherited several hundred thousand pounds, an estate, amounting at the most to a few hundreds, can hardly be said to represent a motive for murder."

"She left her money to me?" Susan sounded surprised. "How extraordinary. She didn't even know me. Why did she do it, do you think?"

"I think she had heard rumours that there had been a little difficulty—er—over your marriage." Greg, back again at sharpening his pencil, scowled. "There had been a certain amount of trouble over her own marriage—and I think she experienced a fellow feeling."

Susan asked with a certain amount of interest:

"She married an artist, didn't she, whom none of the family liked? Was he a good artist?"

Mr. Entwhistle shook his head very decidedly.

"Are there any of his paintings in the cottage?"

"Yes."

"Then I shall judge for myself," said Susan.

Mr. Entwhistle smiled at the resolute tilt of Susan's chin.

"So be it. Doubtless I am on old fogey and hopelessly old fashioned in matters of art, but I really don't think you will dispute my verdict."

"I suppose I ought to go down there, anyway? And look over what there is. Is there anybody there now?"

"I have arranged with Miss Gilchrist to remain there until further notice."

Greg said: "She must have a pretty good nerve—to stay in a cottage where a murder's been committed."

"Miss Gilchrist is quite a sensible woman, I should say. Besides," added the lawyer drily, "I don't think she has anywhere else to go until she gets another situation."

"So Aunt Cora's death left her high and dry? Did she—were she and Aunt Cora—on intimate terms—"

Mr. Entwhistle looked at her rather curiously, wondering just exactly what was in her mind.

"Moderately so, I imagine," he said. "She never treated Miss Gilchrist as a servant."

"Treated her a damned sight worse, I daresay," said Susan. "These wretched so called 'ladies' are the ones who get it taken out of them nowadays. I'll try and find her a decent post somewhere. It won't be difficult. Anyone who's willing to do a bit of housework and cook is worth their weight in gold—she does cook, doesn't she?"

"Oh yes. I gather it is something she called—er—*the rough* that she objected to. I'm afraid I don't quite know what 'the rough' is."

Susan appeared to be a good deal amused.

Mr. Entwhistle, glancing at his watch, said:

"Your aunt left Timothy her executor."

"Timothy," said Susan with scorn. "Uncle Timothy is practically a myth. Nobody ever sees him."

"Quite." Mr. Entwhistle glanced at his watch. "I am travelling up to see him this afternoon. I will acquaint him with your decision to go down to the cottage."

"It will only take me a day or two, I imagine. I don't want to be long away from London. I've got various schemes in hand. I'm going into business."

Mr. Entwhistle looked round him at the cramped sitting room of the tiny flat. Greg and Susan were evidently hard up. Her father, he knew, had run through most of his money. He had left his daughter badly off.

"What are your plans for the future, if I may ask?"

"I've got my eye on some premises in Cardigan Street. I suppose, if necessary, you can advance me some money? I may have to pay a deposit."

"That can be managed," said Mr. Entwhistle. "I rang you up the day after the funeral several times—but could get no answer. I thought perhaps you might care for an advance. I wondered whether you might perhaps have gone out of town."

"Oh no," said Susan quickly. "We were in all day. Both of us. We didn't go out at all."

Greg said gently:

"You know, Susan, I think our telephone must have been out of order that day. You remember how I couldn't get through to Hard and Co. in the afternoon? I meant to report it, but it was all right the next morning."

"Telephones," said Mr. Entwhistle, "can be very unreliable sometimes."

Susan said suddenly:

"How did Aunt Cora know about our marriage? It was at a Registry Office and we didn't tell anyone until afterwards—"

"I fancy Richard may have told her about it. She remade her will about three weeks ago. (It was formerly in favour of the Theosophical Society)—just about the time he had been down to see her."

Susan looked startled.

"Did Uncle Richard go down to see her? I'd no idea of that."

"I hadn't any idea of it myself," said Mr. Entwhistle.

"So that was when—"

"When what?"

"Nothing," said Susan.

6

"VERY GOOD of you to come along," said Maude gruffly, as she greeted Mr. Entwhistle on the platform of Bayham Compton station. "I can assure you that both Timothy and I much appreciate it. Of course the truth is that Richard's death was the worst thing possible for Timothy."

Mr. Entwhistle had not yet considered his friend's death from this particular angle. But it was, he saw, the only angle from which Mrs. Timothy Abernethie was likely to regard it.

As they proceeded towards the exit, Maude developed the theme.

"To begin with, it was a *shock*—Timothy was really very attached to Richard. And then unfortunately it put the idea of death into Timothy's head. Being such an invalid has made him rather nervous about himself. He realised that he was the only one of the brothers left alive—and he started saying that he'd be the next to go—and that it wouldn't be long now—all very morbid talk, as I told him."

They emerged from the station and Maude led the way to a dilapidated car of almost fabulous antiquity.

"Sorry about our old rattletrap," she said. "We've wanted a new car for years, but really we couldn't afford it. This has had a new engine twice—and these old cars really stand up to a lot of hard work—

"I hope it will start," she added. "Sometimes one has to wind it."

She pressed the starter several times but only a meaningless whirr resulted. Mr. Entwhistle, who had never cranked a car in his life, felt rather apprehensive, but Maude herself descended, inserted the starting handle and with a vigorous couple of turns woke the motor to life. It was fortunate, Mr. Entwhistle reflected, that Maude was such a powerfully built woman.

"That's that," she said. "The old brute's been playing me up lately. Did it when I was coming back after the funeral. Had to walk a couple of miles to the nearest garage and they weren't good for much—just a village affair. I had to put up at the local Inn while they tinkered at it. Of course *that* upset Timothy too. I had to phone through to him and tell him I couldn't be back till the next day. Fussed him terribly. One tries to keep things from him as much as possible—but some things one can't do anything about—Cora's murder, for instance. I had to send for Dr. Barton to give him a sedative. Things like murder are too much for a man in Timothy's state of health. I gather Cora was always a fool."

Mr. Entwhistle digested this remark in silence. The inference was not quite clear to him.

"I don't think I'd seen Cora since our marriage," said Maude. "I didn't like to say to Timothy at the time: 'Your youngest sister's batty,' not just like that. But it's what I *thought*. There she was saying the most extraordinary things! One didn't know whether to resent them or whether to laugh. I suppose the truth is she lived in a kind of imaginary world of her own—full of melodrama and fantastic ideas about other people. Well, poor soul, she's paid for it now. She didn't have any protégés, did she?"

"Protégés? What do you mean?"

"I just wondered. Some young cadging artist, or musician—or something of that kind. Someone she might have let in that day, and who killed her for her loose cash. Perhaps an adolescent—they're so queer at that age sometimes—especially if they're the neurotic arty type. I mean, it seems so odd to break in and murder her in the middle of the afternoon. If you break into a house surely you'd do it at night."

"There would have been two women there then."

"Oh yes, the companion. But really I can't believe that anyone would deliberately wait until she was out of the way and then break in and attack Cora. What for? He can't have expected she'd have any cash or stuff to speak of, and there must have been times when both the women were out and the house was empty. That would have been much safer. It seems so stupid to go and commit a murder unless it's absolutely necessary."

"And Cora's murder, you feel, was unnecessary?"

"It all seems so stupid."

Should murder make sense? Mr. Entwhistle wondered. Academically the answer was yes. But many pointless crimes were on record. It depended, Mr. Entwhistle reflected, on the mentality of the murderer.

What did he really know about murderers and their mental processes? Very little. His firm had never had a criminal practice. He was no student of criminology himself. Murderers, as far as he could judge, seemed to be of all sorts and kinds. Some had had over-weening vanity, some had had a lust for power, some, like Seddon, had been mean and avaricious, others, like Smith and Rowse, had had an incredible fascination for women; some, like Armstrong, had been pleasant fellows to meet. Edith Thompson had lived in a world of violent unreality, Nurse Waddington had put her elderly patients out of the way with business-like cheerfulness.

Maude's voice broke into his meditations.

"If I could only keep the newspapers from Timothy! But he will insist on reading them—and then, of course, it upsets him. You do understand, don't you, Mr. Entwhistle, that there can be *no question* of Timothy's attending the inquest? If necessary, Dr. Barton can write out a certificate or whatever it is."

"You can set your mind at rest about that."

"Thank goodness!"

They turned in through the gates of Stansfield Grange, and up a neglected drive. It had been an attractive small property once—but had now a doleful and neglected appearance. Maude sighed as she said:

"We had to let this go to seed during the war. Both gardeners called up. And now we've only got one old man—and he's not much good. Wages have gone up so terribly. I must say it's a blessing to realise that we'll be able to spend a little money on the place now. We're both so fond of it. I was really afraid that we might have to sell it. . . . Not that I suggested anything of the kind to Timothy. It would have upset him—dreadfully."

They drew up before the portico of a very lovely old Georgian house which badly needed a coat of paint.

"No servants," said Maude bitterly, as she led the way in. "Just a couple of women who come in. We had a resident maid until a month ago—slightly hunchbacked and terribly adenoidal and in many ways not too bright, but she was *there* which was such a comfort—and quite good at plain cooking. And would you believe it, she gave notice and went to a fool of a woman who keeps six Pekinese dogs (it's a larger house than this and more work) because she was 'so fond of little doggies,' she said. Dogs, indeed! Being sick and making messes all the time I've no doubt! Really, these girls are *mental!* So there we are, and if I have to go out any afternoon, Timothy is left quite alone in the house and if anything should happen, how could he get help? Though I do leave the telephone close by his chair so that if he felt faint he could dial Dr. Barton immediately."

Maude led the way into the drawing room where tea was laid ready by the fireplace, and establishing Mr. Entwhistle there, disappeared, presumably to the back regions. She returned in a few minutes' time with a teapot and silver kettle, and proceeded to minister to Mr. Entwhistle's needs. It was a good tea with homemade cake and fresh buns. Mr. Entwhistle murmured:

"What about Timothy?" and Maude explained briskly that she had taken Timothy his tray before she set out for the station.

"And now," said Maude, "he will have had his little nap and it will be the best time for him to see you. Do try and not let him excite himself too much."

Mr. Entwhistle assured her that he would exercise every precaution.

Studying her in the flickering firelight, he was seized by a feeling of compassion. This big stalwart matter of fact woman, so healthy, so vigorous, so full of common sense, and yet so strangely, almost pitifully, vulnerable in one spot. Her love for her husband was maternal love, Mr. Entwhistle decided. Maude Abernethie had borne no child and she was a woman built for motherhood. Her invalid husband had become her child, to be shielded, guarded, watched over. And perhaps, being the stronger character of the two, she had unconsciously imposed on him a state of invalidism greater than might otherwise have been the case.

"Poor Mrs. Tim," thought Mr. Entwhistle to himself.

II

"Good of you to come, Entwhistle."

Timothy raised himself up in his chair as he held out a hand.

He was a big man with a marked resemblance to his brother Richard. But what was strength in Richard, in Timothy was weakness. The mouth was irresolute, the chin very slightly receding, the eyes less deepset. Lines of peevish irritability showed on his forehead.

His invalid status was emphasised by the rug across his knees and a positive pharmacopeia of little bottles and boxes on a table at his right hand.

"I mustn't exert myself," he said warningly. "Doctor's forbidden it. Keeps telling me not to worry! Worry! If *he'd* had a murder in his family *he'd* do a bit of worrying, I bet! It's too much for a man—first Richard's death—then hearing all about his funeral and his will—what a will!—and on top of that poor little Cora killed with a hatchet. Hatchet! Ugh! This country's full of gangsters nowadays—thugs—left over from the war! Going about killing defenseless women. Nobody's got the guts to put these things down—to take a strong hand. What's the country coming to, I'd like to know? What's the damned country coming to?"

Mr. Entwhistle was familiar with this gambit. It was a question almost invariably asked sooner or later by his clients for the last twenty years and he had his routine for answering it. The non-committal words he uttered could have been classified under the heading of soothing noises.

"It all began with that damned Labour Government," said Timothy. "Sending the whole Country to blazes. And the Government we've got now is no better. Mealy mouthed milk and water socialists! Look at the state *we*'re in! Can't get a decent gardener, can't get servants—poor Maude here has to work herself to a shadow messing about in the kitchen—(by the way, I think a custard pudding would go well with the sole tonight, my dear—and perhaps a little clear soup first?) I've got to keep my strength up—Doctor Barton said so—let me see, where was I? Oh yes, *Cora*. It's a shock, I can tell you, to a man, when he hears his sister—his own sister—has been *murdered!* Why, I had palpitations for twenty minutes! You'll have to attend to everything for me, Entwhistle. *I* can't go to the inquest or be bothered by business of any kind connected with Cora's estate. I want to forget the whole thing. What happens, by the way, to Cora's share of Richard's money? Comes to me, I suppose?"

Murmuring something about clearing away tea, Maude left the room.

Timothy lay back in his chair and said:

"Good thing to get rid of the women. Now we can talk business without any silly interruptions."

"The sum left in trust for Cora," said Mr. Entwhistle, "goes equally to you and the nieces and nephew."

"But look here," Timothy's cheeks assumed a purplish hue of indignation. "Surely I'm her next of kin? Only surviving brother."

Mr. Entwhistle explained with some care the exact provisions of Richard Abernethie's will, reminding Timothy gently that he had had a copy sent him.

"Don't expect me to understand all that legal jargon, do you?" said Timothy ungratefully. "You lawyers! Matter of fact, I couldn't believe it when Maude came home and told me the gist of it. Thought she'd got it wrong. Women are never clear headed. Best woman in the world, Maude—but women don't understand finance. I don't believe Maude even realises that if Richard hadn't died when he did, we might have had to clear out of here. Fact!"

"Surely if you had applied to Richard—"

Timothy gave a short bark of harsh laughter.

"That's not my style. Our father left us all a perfectly reasonable share of his money—that is, if we didn't want to go into the family concern. I didn't. I've a soul above cornplasters, Entwhistle! Richard took my attitude a bit hard. Well, what with taxes, depreciation of income, one thing and another—it hasn't been easy to keep things going. I've had to realise a good deal of capital. Best thing to do these days. I did hint once to Richard that this place was getting a bit hard to run. He took the attitude that we'd be much better off in a smaller place altogether. Easier for Maude, he said, more labour saving—labour saving, what a term! Oh no, I wouldn't have asked Richard for help. But I can tell you, Entwhistle, that the worry affected my health most unfavourably. A man in my state of health oughtn't to have to worry. Then Richard died and though of course naturally I was cut up about it—my brother and all that—I couldn't help feeling relieved about future prospects. Yes, it's all plain sailing now—and a great relief. Get the house painted—get a couple of really good men on the garden—you can get them at a price. Restock the rose garden completely. And—where was I—"

"Detailing your future plans."

"Yes, yes—but I mustn't bother you with all that. What did hurt me—and hurt me cruelly—were the terms of Richard's will."

"Indeed?" Mr. Entwhistle looked enquiring. "They were not—as you expected?"

"I should say they weren't! Naturally, after Mortimer's death, I assumed that Richard would leave everything to *me*."

"Ah—did he—ever—indicate that to you?"

"He never said so—not in so many words. Reticent sort of chap, Richard. But he asked himself here—not long after Mortimer's death. Wanted to talk over family affairs generally. We discussed young George—and the girls and their husbands. Wanted to know my views—not that I could tell him much. I'm an invalid and I don't get about, and Maude and I live out of the world. Rotten silly marriages both of those girls made, if you ask me. Well, I ask you, Entwhistle, naturally I thought he was consulting me as the head of the family after he was gone and naturally I thought the control of the money would be mine. Richard could surely trust me to do the right thing by the younger generation. And to look after poor old Cora. Dash it all, Entwhistle, I'm an Abernethie—the last Abernethie. Full control should have been left in my hands."

In his excitement Timothy had kicked aside his rug and had sat up in his chair. There were no signs of weakness or fragility about him. He looked, Mr. Entwhistle thought, a perfectly healthy man, even if a slightly excitable one. Moreover the old lawyer realised very clearly that Timothy Abernethie had probably always been secretly jealous of his brother Richard. They had been sufficiently alike for Timothy to resent his brother's strength of character and firm grasp of affairs. When Richard had died, Timothy had exulted in the prospect of succeeding at this late date to the power to control the destinies of others.

Richard Abernethie had not given him that power. Had he thought of doing so and then decided against it?

A sudden squalling of cats in the garden brought Timothy up out of his chair. Rushing to the window he threw up the sash, bawled out "Stop it, you!" and picking up a large book hurled it out at the marauders.

"Beastly cats," he grumbled, returning to his visitor. "Ruin the flower beds and I can't stand that damned yowling."

He sat down again and asked:

"Have a drink, Entwhistle?"

"Not quite so soon. Maude has just given me an excellent tea."

Timothy grunted.

"Capable woman, Maude. But she does too much. Even has to muck about with the inside of that old car of ours—she's quite a mechanic in her way, you know."

"I hear she had a breakdown coming back from the funeral?"

"Yes. Car conked out. She had the sense to telephone through about it, in case I should be anxious, but that ass of a daily woman of ours wrote down the message in a way that didn't make sense. I was out getting a bit of fresh air—I'm advised by the doctor to take what exercise I can if I feel like it—I got back from my walk to find scrawled on a bit of paper: 'Madam's sorry car gone wrong got to stay night.' Naturally I thought she was still at Enderby. Put a call through and found Maude had left that morning. Might have had the breakdown *anywhere!* Pretty kettle of fish! Fool of a daily woman only left me a lumpy macaroni cheese for supper. I had to go down to the kitchen and warm it up *myself—and* make myself a cup of tea—to say nothing of stoking the boiler. I might have had a heart attack—but does that class of woman care? Not she. With any decent feelings she'd have come back that evening and looked after me properly. No loyalty any more in the lower classes—"

He brooded sadly.

"I don't know how much Maude told you about the funeral and the relatives," said Mr. Entwhistle. "Cora produced rather an awkward moment. Said brightly that Richard had been murdered, hadn't he? Perhaps Maude told you."

Timothy chuckled easily.

"Oh yes, I heard about that. Everybody looked down their noses and pretended to be shocked. Just the sort of thing Cora would say! You know how she always managed to put her foot in it when she was a girl, Entwhistle? Said something at our wedding that upset Maude, I remember. Maude never cared for her very much. Yes, Maude rang me up that evening after the funeral to know if I was all right and if Mrs. Jones had come in to give me my evening meal and then she told me it had all gone off very well, and I said 'What about the will?' and she tried to hedge a bit, but of course I had the truth out of her. I couldn't believe it, and I said she must have made a mistake, but she stuck to it. It hurt me, Entwhistle—it really *wounded* me, if you know what I mean. If you ask me, it was just *spite* on Richard's part. I know one shouldn't speak ill of the dead, but, upon my word—"

Timothy continued on this theme for some time.

Then Maude came back into the room and said firmly:

"I think, dear, Mr. Entwhistle has been with you quite long enough. You really *must* rest. If you have settled everything—"

"Oh, we've settled things. I leave it all to you, Entwhistle. Let me know when they catch the fellow—if they ever do. I've no faith in the police nowadays—the Chief Constables aren't the right type. You'll see to the er—interment—won't you? We shan't be able to come I'm afraid. But order an expensive wreath—and there must be a proper stone put up in due course—she'll be buried locally, I suppose? No point in bringing her North and I've no idea where Lansquenet is buried, somewhere in France I believe. I don't know what one puts on a stone when it's murder. . . . Can't very well say 'entered into rest' or anything like that. One will have to choose a text—something appropriate. R.I.P.? No, that's only for Catholics."

"O Lord thou hast seen my wrong. Judge thou my case," murmured Mr. Entwhistle.

The startled glance Timothy bent on him made Mr. Entwhistle smile faintly.

"From Lamentations," he said. "It seemed appropriate if somewhat melodramatic. However, it will be some time before the question of the Memorial stone comes up. The—er—ground has to settle, you know. Now don't worry about anything. We will deal with things and keep you fully informed."

Mr. Entwhistle left for London by the breakfast train on the following morning.

When he got home, after a little hesitation, he rang up a friend of his.

7

"I CAN'T TELL you how much I appreciate your invitation."

Mr. Entwhistle pressed his host's hand warmly.

Hercule Poirot gestured hospitably to a chair by the fire.

Mr. Entwhistle sighed as he sat down.

On one side of the room a table was laid for two.

"I returned from the country this morning," he said.

"And you have a matter on which you wish to consult me?"

"Yes. It's a long rambling story, I'm afraid."

"Then we will not have it until after we have dined. *Georges?*"

The efficient Georges materialised with some *Pâté de Foie Gras* accompanied by hot toast in a napkin.

"We will have our *Pâté* by the fire," said Poirot. "Afterwards we will move to the table."

It was an hour and a half later that Mr. Entwhistle stretched himself comfortably out in his chair and sighed a contented sigh.

"You certainly know how to do yourself well, Poirot. Trust a Frenchman."

"I am a Belgian. But the rest of your remark applies. At my age the chief pleasure, almost the *only* pleasure that still remains, is the pleasure of the table. Mercifully I have an excellent stomach."

"Ah," murmured Mr. Entwhistle.

They had dined off a *Sole Véronique*, followed by *Escalope de Veau Milanaise*, proceeding to *Poire Flambée* with ice cream.

They had drunk a *Pouilly Fuissé* followed by a *Corton* and a very good port now reposed at Mr. Entwhistle's elbow. Poirot, who did not care for port, was sipping *Crème de Cacao*.

"I don't know," murmured Mr. Entwhistle reminiscently, "how you manage to get hold of an escalope like that! It melted in the mouth!"

"I have a friend who is a Continental butcher. For him I solve a small domestic problem. He is appreciative—and ever since then he is most sympathetic to me in the matters of the stomach."

"A domestic problem." Mr. Entwhistle sighed. "I wish you had not reminded me. . . . This is such a perfect moment. . . ."

"Prolong it, my friend. We will have presently the *demi tasse* and the fine brandy, and then, when digestion is peacefully under way, *then* you shall tell why you need my advice.''

The clock struck the half hour after nine before Mr. Entwhistle stirred in his chair. The psychological moment had come. He no longer felt reluctant to bring forth his perplexities—he was eager to do so.

''I don't know,'' he said, ''whether I'm making the most colossal fool of myself. In any case I don't see that there's anything that can possibly be done. But I'd like to put the facts before you, and I'd like to know what you think.''

He paused for a moment or two, then in his dry meticulous way, he told his story. His trained legal brain enabled him to put the facts clearly, to leave nothing out, and to add nothing extraneous. It was a clear succinct account, and as such appreciated by the little elderly man with the egg shaped head who sat listening to him.

When he had finished there was a pause. Mr. Entwhistle was prepared to answer questions, but for some few moments no question came. Hercule Poirot was reviewing the evidence.

He said at last:

''It seems very clear. You have in your mind the suspicion that your friend, Richard Abernethie, may have been murdered? That suspicion, or assumption, rests on the basis of one thing only—*the words spoken by Cora Lansquenet at Richard Abernethie's funeral*. Take those away—and there is nothing left. The fact that she herself was murdered the day afterwards *may* be the purest coincidence. It is true that Richard Abernethie died suddenly, but he was attended by a reputable doctor who knew him well, and that doctor had no suspicions and gave a death certificate. Was Richard buried or cremated?''

''Cremated—according to his own request.''

''Yes, that is the law. And it means that a second doctor signed the certificate—but there would be no difficulty about that. So we come back to the essential point, *what Cora Lansquenet said*. You were there and you heard her. She said: 'But he *was* murdered, wasn't he?' ''

''Yes.''

''And the real point is—that you believe she was speaking the truth.''

The lawyer hesitated for a moment, then he said:

''Yes, I do.''

''Why?''

''Why?'' Entwhistle repeated the word, slightly puzzled.

''But yes, *why?* Is it because, already, deep down, you had an uneasiness about the manner of Richard's death?''

The lawyer shook his head. ''No, no, not in the least.''

"Then it is because of *her*—of Cora herself. You knew her well?"

"I had not seen her for—oh—over twenty years."

"Would you have known her if you had met her in the street?"

Mr. Entwhistle reflected.

"I might have passed her by in the street without recognising her. She was a thin slip of a girl when I saw her last and she had turned into a stout shabby middle-aged woman. But I think that the moment I spoke to her face to face I should have recognised her. She wore her hair in the same way, a bang cut straight across the forehead and she had a trick of peering up at you through her fringe like a rather shy animal, and she had a very characteristic abrupt way of talking, and a way of putting her head on one side and then coming out with something quite outrageous. She had *character*, you see, and character is always highly individual."

"She was, in fact, the same Cora you had known years ago. And she still said outrageous things! The things, the outrageous things, she had said in the past—were they usually—justified?"

"That was always the awkward thing about Cora. When truth would have been better left unspoken, she spoke it."

"And that characteristic remained unchanged. Richard Abernethie was murdered—so Cora at once mentioned the fact."

Mr. Entwhistle stirred.

"You think he *was* murdered?"

"Oh, no, no, my friend, we cannot go so fast. We agree on this—Cora *thought* he had been murdered. She was quite sure he had been murdered. It was, to her, more a certainty than a surmise. And so, we come to this, *she must have had some reason for the belief*. We agree, by your knowledge of her, that it was not just a bit of mischief making. Now tell me—when she said what she did, there was, at once, a kind of chorus of protest—that is right?"

"Quite right."

"And she then became confused, abashed, and retreated from the position—saying—as far as you can remember, something like 'But I thought—from what he told me—' "

The lawyer nodded.

"I wish I could remember more clearly. But I am fairly sure of that. She used the words 'he told me' or 'he said'—"

"And the matter was then smoothed over and everyone spoke of something else. You can remember, looking back, no special expression on anyone's face? Anything that remains in your memory as—shall we say —*unusual?*"

"No."

''And the very next day, *Cora is killed*—and you ask yourself: 'Can it be cause and effect?' ''

The lawyer stirred.

''I suppose that seems to you quite fantastic?''

''Not at all,'' said Poirot. ''Given that the original assumption is correct, it is logical. The perfect murder, the murder of Richard Abernethie, had been committed, all has gone off smoothly—and suddenly it appears that there is one person who has a knowledge of the truth! Clearly that person must be silenced *as quickly as possible*.''

''Then you do think that—it was murder?''

Poirot said gravely:

''I think, *mon cher*, exactly as you thought—that there is a case for investigation. Have you taken any steps? You have spoken of these matters to the police?''

''No.'' Mr. Entwhistle shook his head. ''It did not seem to me that any good purpose could be achieved. My position is that I represent the family. If Richard Abernethie was murdered, there seems only one method by which it could be done.''

''By poison?''

''Exactly. *And the body has been cremated*. There is now no evidence available. But I decided that I, myself, *must* be satisfied on the point. That is why, Poirot, I have come to *you*.''

''Who was in the house at the time of his death?''

''An old butler who has been with him for years, a cook and a housemaid. It would seem, perhaps, as though it must necessarily be one of them—''

''Ah! do not try to pull the wool upon my eyes. This Cora, she knows Richard Abernethie was killed, yet she acquiesces in the hushing up. She says 'I think you are all quite right.' Therefore it *must* be one of the family who is concerned, someone whom the victim himself might prefer not to have openly accused. Otherwise, since Cora was fond of her brother, she would not agree to let the sleeping murderer lie. You agree to that, yes?''

''It was the way I reasoned—yes,'' confessed Mr. Entwhistle. ''Though how any of the family could possibly—''

Poirot cut him short.

''Where poison is concerned there are all sorts of possibilities. It must, presumably, have been a narcotic of some sort if he died in his sleep and if there were no suspicious appearances. Possibly he was already having some narcotic administered to him.''

''In any case,'' said Mr. Entwhistle, ''the *how* hardly matters. We shall never be able to prove anything.''

''In the case of Richard Abernethie, no. But the murder of Cora Lansquenet is different. Once we know 'who' then evidence ought to be possible to get." He added with a sharp glance, "You have, perhaps, already done something."

"Very little. My purpose was mainly, I think, *elimination*. It is distasteful to me to think that one of the Abernethie family is a murderer. I still can't quite believe it. I hoped that by a few apparently idle questions I could exonerate certain members of the family beyond question. Perhaps, who knows, *all* of them? In which case, Cora would have been wrong in her assumption and her own death could be ascribed to some casual prowler who broke in. After all, the issue is very simple. What were the members of the Abernethie family doing on the afternoon that Cora Lansquenet was killed?"

"*Eh bien,*" said Poirot, "what were they doing?"

"George Crossfield was at Hurst Park races. Rosamund Shane was out shopping in London. Her husband—for one must include husbands—"

"Assuredly."

"Her husband was fixing up a deal about an option on a play, Susan and Gregory Banks were at home all day. Timothy Abernethie who is an invalid was at his home in Yorkshire, and his wife was driving herself home from Enderby."

He stopped.

Hercule Poirot looked at him and nodded comprehendingly.

"Yes, that is what they *say*. And is it all true?"

"I simply don't know, Poirot. Some of the statements are capable of proof or disproof—but it would be difficult to do so without showing one's hand pretty plainly. In fact to do so would be tantamount to an accusation. I will simply tell you certain conclusions of my own. George *may* have been at Hurst Park races, but I do not think he was. He was rash enough to boast that he had backed a couple of winners. It is my experience that so many offenders against the law ruin their own case by saying too much. I asked him the name of the winners, and he gave the names of two horses without any apparent hesitation. Both of them, I found, had been heavily tipped on the day in question and one had duly won. The other, though an odds on favourite, had unaccountably failed even to get a place."

"Interesting. Had this George any urgent need for money at the time of his uncle's death?"

"It is my impression that his need was very urgent. I have no evidence for saying so, but I strongly suspect that he has been speculating with his clients' funds and that he was in danger of prosecution. It is only my impression but I have some experience in these matters. Defaulting solicitors, I regret to say, are not entirely uncommon. I can only tell you that

I would not have cared to entrust my own funds to George, and I suspect that Richard Abernethie, a very shrewd judge of men, was dissatisfied with his nephew and placed no reliance on him.

"His mother," the lawyer continued, "was a good-looking rather foolish girl and she married a man of what I should call dubious character." He sighed. "The Abernethie girls were not good choosers."

He paused and then went on.

"As for Rosamund she is a lovely nit-wit. I really cannot see her smashing Cora's head in with a hatchet! Her husband, Michael Shane, is something of a dark horse—he's a man with ambition and also a man of overweening vanity I should say—But really I know very little about him. I have no reason to suspect him of a brutal crime or of a carefully planned poisoning, but until I know that he really was doing what he says he was doing I cannot rule him out."

"But you have no doubts about the wife?"

"No—no—there is a certain rather startling callousness . . . but no, I really cannot envisage the hatchet. She is a fragile looking creature."

"And beautiful!" said Poirot with a faint cynical smile. "And the other niece?"

"Susan? She is a very different type from Rosamund—a girl of remarkable ability, I should say. She and her husband were at home together that day. I said (falsely) that I had tried to get them on the telephone on the afternoon in question. Greg said very quickly that the telephone had been out of order all day. He had tried to get someone and failed."

"So again it is not conclusive. . . . You cannot eliminate as you hoped to do. . . . What is the husband like?"

"I find him hard to make out. He has a somewhat unpleasing personality though one cannot say exactly why he makes this impression. As for Susan—"

"Yes?"

"Susan reminds me of her uncle. She has the vigour, the drive, the mental capacity of Richard Abernethie. It may be my fancy that she lacks some of the kindliness and the warmth of my old friend."

"Women are never kind," remarked Poirot. "Though they can sometimes be tender. She loves her husband?"

"Devotedly, I should say. But really, Poirot, I can't believe—I *won't* believe for one moment that Susan—"

"You prefer George?" said Poirot. "It is natural! As for me, I am not so sentimental about beautiful young ladies. Now tell me about your visit to the older generation?"

Mr. Entwhistle described his visit to Timothy and Maude at some length. Poirot summarised the result.

"So Mrs. Abernethie is a good mechanic. She knows all about the inside of a car. And Mr. Abernethie is not the invalid he likes to think himself. He goes out for walks and is, according to you, capable of vigorous action. He is also a bit of an ego maniac and he resented his brother's success and superior character."

"He spoke very affectionately of Cora."

"And ridiculed her silly remark after the funeral. What of the sixth beneficiary?"

"Helen? Mrs. Leo? I do not suspect her for a moment. In any case, her innocence will be easy to prove. She was at Enderby. With three servants in the house."

"*Eh bien*, my friend," said Poirot. "Let us be practical. What do you want me to do?"

"I want to know the truth, Poirot."

"Yes. Yes, I should feel the same in your place."

"And you're the man to find it out for me. I know you don't take cases any more, but I ask you to take this one. This is a matter of business. I will be responsible for your fees. Come now, money is always useful."

Poirot grinned.

"Not if it all goes in the taxes! But I will admit, your problem interests me! Because it is not easy. . . . It is all so nebulous. . . . One thing, my friend, had better be done by you. After that, I will occupy myself of everything. But I think it will be best if you yourself seek out the doctor who attended Mr. Richard Abernethie. You know him?"

"Slightly."

"What is he like?"

"Middle-aged G.P. Quite competent. On very friendly terms with Richard. A thoroughly good fellow."

"Then seek him out. He will speak more freely to you than to me. Ask him about Mr. Abernethie's illness. Find out what medicines Mr. Abernethie was taking at the time of his death and before. Find out if Richard Abernethie ever said anything to his doctor about fancying himself being poisoned. By the way, this Miss Gilchrist is sure that he used the term *poisoned* in talking to his sister?"

Mr. Entwhistle reflected.

"It was the word she used—but she is the type of witness who often changes the actual words used, because she is convinced she is keeping to the sense of them. If Richard had said he was afraid someone wanted to kill him, Miss Gilchrist might have assumed poison because she connected his fears with those of an aunt of hers who thought her food was being tampered with. I can take up the point with her again some time."

"Yes. Or I will do so." He paused and then said in a different voice:

"Has it occurred to you, my friend, that your Miss Gilchrist may be in some danger herself ?"

Mr. Entwhistle looked surprised.

"I can't say that it had."

"But, yes. Cora voiced her suspicions on the day of the funeral. The question in the murderer's mind will be, did she voice them to anybody when she first heard of Richard's death? And the most likely person for her to have spoken to about them will be Miss Gilchrist. I think, *mon cher*, that she had better not remain alone in that cottage."

"I believe Susan is going down."

"Ah, so Mrs. Banks is going down?"

"She wants to look through Cora's things."

"I see. . . . I see. . . . Well, my friend, do what I have asked of you. You might also prepare Mrs. Abernethie—Mrs. Leo Abernethie, for the possibility that I may arrive in the house. We will see. From now on I occupy myself of everything."

And Poirot twirled his moustaches with enormous energy.

8

MR. ENTWHISTLE looked at Dr. Larraby thoughtfully.

He had had a lifetime of experience in summing people up. There had been frequent occasions on which it had been necessary to tackle a difficult situation or a delicate subject. Mr. Entwhistle was an adept by now in the art of how exactly to make the proper approach. How would it be best to tackle Dr. Larraby on what was certainly a very difficult subject and one which the doctor might very well resent as reflecting upon his own professional skill?

Frankness, Mr. Entwhistle thought—or at least a modified frankness. To say that suspicions had arisen because of a haphazard suggestion thrown out by a silly woman would be ill-advised. Dr. Larraby had not known Cora.

Mr. Entwhistle cleared his throat and plunged bravely.

"I want to consult you on a very delicate matter," he said. "You may be offended, but I sincerely hope not. You are a sensible man and you will realise, I'm sure, that a—er—preposterous suggestion is best dealt with by finding a reasonable answer and not by condemning it out of hand. It concerns my client, the late Mr. Abernethie. I'll ask you my question flat out. Are you certain, *absolutely certain*, that he died what is termed a natural death?''

Dr. Larraby's good humoured rubicund middle-aged face turned in astonishment on his questioner.

''What on earth—Of course he did. I gave a certificate, didn't I? If I hadn't been satisfied—''

Mr. Entwhistle cut in adroitly:

''Naturally, naturally. I assure you that I am not assuming anything to the contrary. But I would be glad to have your positive assurance—in face of the—er—rumours that are flying around.''

''Rumours? What rumours?''

''One doesn't know quite how these things start,'' said Mr. Entwhistle mendaciously. ''But my feeling is that they should be stopped—authoritatively, if possible.''

''Abernethie was a sick man. He was suffering from a disease that would have proved fatal within, I should say, at the earliest, two years. It might have come much sooner. His son's death had weakened his will to live, and his powers of resistance. I admit that I did not expect his death to come so soon, or indeed so suddenly, but there are precedents—plenty of precedents. Any medical man who predicts exactly when a patient will die, or exactly how long he will live, is bound to make a fool of himself. The human factor is always incalculable. The weak have often unexpected powers of resistance, the strong sometimes succumb.''

''I understand all that. I am not doubting your diagnosis. Mr. Abernethie was, shall we say—(rather melodramatically, I'm afraid)—under sentence of death. All I'm asking you is, is it quite impossible that a man, knowing or suspecting that he is doomed, might of his own accord shorten that period of life? Or that someone else might do it for him?''

Dr. Larraby frowned.

''Suicide, you mean? Abernethie wasn't a suicidal type.''

''I see. You can assure me, medically speaking, that such a suggestion is impossible.''

The doctor stirred uneasily.

''I wouldn't use the word impossible. After his son's death life no longer held the interest for Abernethie that it had done. I certainly don't feel that suicide is likely—but I can't say that it's *impossible*.''

''You are speaking from the psychological angle. When I said *medically*, I really meant; do the circumstances of his death make such a suggestion impossible?''

"No, oh no. No, I can't say that. He died in his sleep, as people often do. There was no reason to suspect suicide, no evidence of his state of mind. If one were to demand an autopsy every time a man who is seriously ill died in his sleep—"

The doctor's face was getting redder and redder. Mr. Entwhistle hastened to interpose.

"Of course. Of course. But if there *had* been evidence—evidence of which you yourself were not aware? If, for instance, he had said something to someone—"

"Indicating that he was contemplating suicide? Did he? I must say it surprises me."

"But if it *were* so—my case is purely hypothetical—could you rule out the possibility?"

Dr. Larraby said slowly:

"No—no—I could not do that. But I say again, I should be very much surprised."

Mr. Entwhistle hastened to follow up his advantage.

"If, then, we assume that his death was *not* natural—(all this is *purely* hypothetical)—what could have caused it? What kind of a drug, I mean?"

"Several. Some kind of a narcotic would be indicated. There was no sign of cyanosis, the attitude was quite peaceful."

"He had sleeping draughts or pills? Something of that kind."

"Yes. I had prescribed Slumberyl—a very safe and dependable hypnotic. He did not take it every night. And he only had a small bottle of tablets at a time. Three or even four times the prescribed dose would not have caused death. In fact, I remember seeing the bottle on his washstand after his death still nearly full."

"What else had you prescribed for him?"

"Various things—a medicine containing a small quantity of morphia to be taken when he had an attack of pain. Some vitamin capsules. An indigestion mixture."

Mr. Entwhistle interrupted.

"Vitamin capsules? I think I was once prescribed a course of those. Small round capsules of gelatine."

"Yes. Containing adexoline."

"Could anything else have been introduced into—say—one of those capsules?"

"Something lethal, you mean?" The doctor was looking more and more surprised. "But surely no man would ever—look here, Entwhistle, what are you getting at? My God, man, are you suggesting *murder?*"

"I don't quite know what I'm suggesting. . . . I just want to know what would be *possible*."

"But what evidence have you for even suggesting such a thing?"

"I haven't any evidence," said Mr. Entwhistle in a tired voice. "Mr. Abernethie is dead—and the person to whom he spoke is also dead. The whole thing is rumour—vague, unsatisfactory rumour, and I want to scotch it if I can. If you tell me that no one could possibly have poisoned Abernethie in any way whatsoever, I'll be delighted! It would be a big weight off my mind, I can assure you."

Dr. Larraby got up and walked up and down.

"I can't tell you what you want me to tell you," he said at last. "I wish I could. Of course it could have been done. Anybody could have extracted the oil from a capsule and replaced it with—say—pure nicotine or half a dozen other things. Or something could have been put in his food or drink? Isn't that more likely?"

"Possibly. But you see there were only the servants in the house when he died—and I don't think it was any of them—in fact I'm quite sure it wasn't. So I'm looking for some delayed action possibility. There's no drug, I suppose, that you can administer and then the person dies weeks later?"

"A convenient idea—but untenable, I'm afraid," said the doctor drily. "I know you're a responsible person, Entwhistle, but who *is* making this suggestion? It seems to me wildly farfetched."

"Abernethie never said anything to you? Never hinted that one of his relations might be wanting him out of the way?"

The doctor looked at him curiously.

"No, he never said anything to me. Are you sure, Entwhistle, that somebody hasn't been—well, playing up the sensational? Some hysterical subjects can give an appearance of being quite reasonable and normal, you know."

"I hope it was like that. It might well be."

"Let me understand. Someone claims that Abernethie told her—it was a woman, I suppose?"

"Oh yes, it was a woman."

"—told her that someone was trying to kill him?"

Cornered, Mr. Entwhistle reluctantly told the tale of Cora's remark at the funeral. Dr. Larraby's face lightened.

"My dear fellow. I shouldn't pay any attention! The explanation is quite simple. The woman's at a certain time of life—craving for sensation, unbalanced, unreliable—might say anything. They do, you know!"

Mr. Entwhistle resented the doctor's easy assumption. He himself had had to deal with plenty of sensation-hunting and hysterical women.

"You may be quite right," he said, rising. "Unfortunately we can't tackle her on the subject, as she's been murdered herself."

''What's that—murdered?'' Dr. Larraby looked as though he had grave suspicions of Mr. Entwhistle's own stability of mind.

''You've probably read about it in the paper. Mrs. Lansquenet at Lytchett St. Mary in Berkshire.''

''Of course—I'd no idea she was a relation of Richard Abernethie's!'' Dr. Larraby was looking quite shaken.

Feeling that he had revenged himself for the doctor's professional superiority, and unhappily conscious that his own suspicions had not been assuaged as a result of the visit, Mr. Entwhistle took his leave.

II

Back at Enderby, Mr. Entwhistle decided to talk to Lanscombe.

He started by asking the old butler what his plans were.

''Mrs. Leo has asked me to stay on here until the house is sold, sir, and I'm sure I shall be very pleased to oblige her. We are all very fond of Mrs. Leo.'' He sighed. ''I feel it very much, sir, if you will excuse me mentioning it, that the house has to be sold. I've known it for so very many years, and seen all the young ladies and gentlemen grow up in it. I always thought that Mr. Mortimer would come after his father and perhaps bring up a family here, too. It was arranged, sir, that I should go to the North Lodge when I got past doing my work here. A very nice little place, the North Lodge—and I looked forward to having it very spick and span. But I suppose that's all over now.''

''I'm afraid so, Lanscombe. The estate will all have to be sold together. But with your legacy—''

''Oh I'm not complaining, sir, and I'm very sensible of Mr. Abernethie's generosity. I'm well provided for, but it's not so easy to find a little place to buy nowadays and though my married niece has asked me to make my home with them, well, it won't be quite the same thing as living on the estate.''

''I know,'' said Mr. Entwhistle. ''It's a hard new world for us old fellows. I wish I'd seen more of my old friend before he went. How did he seem those last few months?''

''Well, he wasn't himself, sir. Not since Mr. Mortimer's death.''

''No, it broke him up. And then he was a sick man—sick men have strange fancies sometimes. I imagine Mr. Abernethie suffered from that sort of thing in his last days. He spoke of enemies sometimes, of somebody wishing to do him harm—perhaps? He may even have thought his food was being tampered with?''

Old Lanscombe looked surprised—surprised and offended.

"I cannot recall anything of that kind, sir."

Entwhistle looked at him keenly.

"You're a very loyal servant, Lanscombe, I know that. But such fancies on Mr. Abernethie's part would be quite—er—unimportant—a natural symptom in some—er—diseases."

"Indeed, sir? I can only say Mr. Abernethie never said anything like that to me, or in my hearing."

Mr. Entwhistle slid gently to another subject.

"He had some of his family down to stay with him, didn't he, before he died. His nephew and his two nieces and their husbands?"

"Yes, sir, that is so."

"Was he satisfied with those visits? Or was he disappointed?"

Lanscombe's eyes became remote, his old back stiffened.

"I really could not say, sir."

"I think you could, you know," said Mr. Entwhistle gently. "It's not your place to say anything of that kind—that's what you really mean. But there are times when one has to do violence to one's sense of what is fitting. I was one of your master's oldest friends. I care for him very much. So did you. That's why I'm asking you for your opinion as a *man*, not as a butler."

Lanscombe was silent for a moment, then he said in a colourless voice:

"Is there anything—wrong, sir?"

Mr. Entwhistle replied truthfully.

"I don't know," he said. "I hope not. I would like to make sure. Have you yourself felt that something was—wrong?"

"Only since the funeral, sir. And I couldn't say exactly what it is. But Mrs. Leo and Mrs. Timothy, too, they didn't seem quite themselves that evening after the others had gone."

"You know the contents of the will?"

"Yes, sir. Mrs. Leo thought I would like to know. It seemed to me, if I may permit myself to comment, a very fair will."

"Yes, it was a fair will. Equal benefits. But it is not, I think, the will that Mr. Abernethie originally intended to make after his son died. Will you answer now the question that I asked you just now?"

"As a matter of personal opinion—"

"Yes, yes, that is understood."

"The master, sir, was very much disappointed after Mr. George had been here. . . . He had hoped, I think, that Mr. George might resemble Mr. Mortimer. Mr. George, if I may say so, did not come up to standard. Miss Laura's husband was always considered unsatisfactory, and I'm afraid Mr. George took after him." Lanscombe paused and then went on, "Then the young ladies came with their husbands. Miss Susan he took to at once—a very spirited and handsome young lady, but it's my opinion he couldn't abide her husband. Young ladies make funny choices nowadays, sir."

"And the other couple?"

"I couldn't say much about that. A very pleasant and good-looking young pair. I think the master enjoyed having them here—but I don't think—" the old man hesitated.

"Yes, Lanscombe?"

"Well, the master had never had much truck with the stage. He said to me one day, 'I can't understand why anyone gets stagestruck. It's a foolish kind of life. Seems to deprive people of what little sense they have. I don't know what it does to your moral sense. You certainly lose your sense of proportion.' Of course he wasn't referring directly—"

"No, no, I quite understand. Now after these visits, Mr. Abernethie himself went away—first to his brother, and afterwards to his sister Mrs. Lansquenet."

"That I did not know, sir. I mean he mentioned to me that he was going to Mr. Timothy and afterwards to Something St. Mary."

"That is right. Can you remember anything he said on his return in regard to those visits?"

Lanscombe reflected.

"I really don't know—nothing direct. He was glad to be back. Travelling and staying in strange houses tired him very much—that I do remember his saying."

"Nothing else? Nothing about either of them?"

Lanscombe frowned.

"The master used to—well, to *murmur*, if you get my meaning—speaking to me and yet more to himself—hardly noticing I was there—because he knew me so well. . . ."

"Knew you and trusted you, yes."

"But my recollection is very vague as to what he said—something about he couldn't think what he'd done with his money—that was Mr. Timothy, I take it. And then he said something about 'Women can be fools in ninety nine different ways but be pretty shrewd in the hundredth.' Oh yes, and he said, 'You can only say what you really think to some of your own generation. They don't think you're fancying things as the younger ones do.' And later he said—but I don't know in what connection—'It's not very nice to have to set traps for people, but I don't see what else I can do.' But I think it possible, sir, that he may have been thinking of the second gardener—a question of the peaches being taken."

But Mr. Entwhistle did not think that it was the second gardener who had been in Richard Abernethie's mind. After a few more questions he let Lanscombe go and reflected on what he had learned. Nothing, really —nothing, that is, that he had not deduced before. Yet there were suggestive points. It was not his sister-in-law, Maude, but his sister Cora of whom he had been thinking when he made the remark about women who were fools and yet shrewd. And it was to her he had confided his "fancies." And he had spoken of setting a trap. For whom?

III

Mr. Entwhistle had meditated a good deal over how much he should tell Helen. In the end he decided to take her wholly into his confidence.

First he thanked her for sorting out Richard's things and for making various household arrangements. The house had been advertised for sale and there were one or two prospective buyers who would be shortly coming to look over it.

"Private buyers?"

"I'm afraid not. The Y.W.C.A. are considering it, and there is a young people's club, and the Trustees of the Jefferson Trust are looking for a suitable place to house their Collection.

"It seems sad that the house will not be lived in, but of course it is not a practicable proposition nowadays."

"I am going to ask you if it would be possible for you to remain here until the house is sold. Or would it be a great inconvenience?"

"No—actually it would suit me very well. I don't want to go to Cyprus until May, and I much prefer being here than to being in London as I had planned. I love this house, you know, Leo loved it, and we were always happy when we were here together."

"There is another reason why I should be grateful if you would stay on. There is a friend of mine, a man called Hercule Poirot—"

Helen said sharply: "Hercule Poirot? Then you think—"

"You know of him?"

"Yes. Some friends of mine—but I imagined that he was dead long ago."

"He is very much alive. Not young, of course."

"No, he could hardly be young."

She spoke mechanically. Her face was white and strained. She said with an effort:

"You think—that Cora was right? That Richard was—*murdered?*"

Mr. Entwhistle unburdened himself. It was a pleasure to unburden himself to Helen with her clear calm mind.

When he had finished she said:

"One ought to feel it's fantastic—but one doesn't. Maude and I, that night after the funeral—it was in both our minds, I'm sure. Saying to ourselves what a silly woman Cora was—and yet being uneasy. And then—Cora was killed—and I told myself it was just coincidence—and of course it may be—but oh! if one can only be sure. It's all so difficult."

"Yes, it's difficult. But Poirot is a man of great originality and he has something really approaching genius. He understands perfectly what we need—assurance that the whole thing is a mare's nest."

"And suppose it isn't?"

"What makes you say that?" asked Mr. Entwhistle sharply.

"I don't know. I've been uneasy. . . . Not just about what Cora said that day—something else. Something that I felt at the time to be wrong."

"Wrong? In what way?"

"That's just it. I don't know."

"You mean it was something about one of the people in the room?"

"Yes—yes—something of that kind. But I don't know who or what. . . . Oh, that sounds absurd—"

"Not at all. It is interesting—very interesting. You are not a fool, Helen. If you noticed something that something had significance."

"Yes, but I can't remember what it *was*. The more I think—"

"Don't think. That is the wrong way to bring anything back. Let it go. Sooner or later it will flash into your mind. And when it does—let me know—at once."

"I will."

9

MISS GILCHRIST pulled her black felt hat down firmly on her head and tucked in a wisp of grey hair. The inquest was set for twelve o'clock and it was not quite twenty past eleven. Her grey coat and skirt looked quite nice, she thought, and she had bought herself a black blouse. She wished she could have been all in black, but that would have been far beyond her means. She looked round the small neat bedroom and at the walls hung with representations of Brixham harbour, Cockington Forge, Anstey's Cove, Kynance Cove, Polflexan harbour, Babbacombe Bay, etc., all signed in a dashing way, Cora Lansquenet. Her eyes rested with particular fondness on Polflexan harbour. On the chest of drawers, a faded photograph, carefully framed, represented the Willow Teashop. Miss Gilchrist looked at it lovingly and sighed.

She was disturbed from her reverie by the sound of the door bell below.

"Dear me," murmured Miss Gilchrist, "I wonder who—"

She went out of her room and down the rather rickety stairs. The bell sounded again and there was a sharp knock.

For some reason Miss Gilchrist felt nervous. For a moment or two her steps slowed up, then she went rather unwillingly to the door, adjuring herself not to be so silly.

A young woman dressed smartly in black and carrying a small suitcase was standing on the step. She noticed the alarmed look on Miss Gilchrist's face and said quickly:

"Miss Gilchrist? I am Mrs. Lansquenet's niece—Susan Banks."

"Oh dear, yes, of course. I didn't know. Do come in, Mrs. Banks. Mind the hall stand—it sticks out a little. In here, yes. I didn't know you were coming down for the inquest. I'd have had something ready—some coffee or something."

Susan Banks said briskly:

"I don't want anything. I'm so sorry if I startled you."

"Well, you know you *did*, in a way. It's very silly of me. I'm not usually nervous. In fact, I told the lawyer that I wasn't nervous, and that I wouldn't be nervous staying on here alone, and really I'm not nervous. Only—perhaps it's just the inquest and—and thinking of things, but I have been jumpy all this morning. Just about half an hour ago the bell rang and I could hardly bring myself to open the door—which was really very stupid and so untimely that a murderer would come back—and why should he?—and actually it was only a nun, collecting for an orphanage—and I was so relieved I gave her two shillings although I'm *not* a Roman Catholic, though I believe the Little Sisters of the Poor do really do good work. But do please sit down, Mrs.—Mrs.—"

"Banks."

"Yes, of course, Banks. Did you come down by train?"

"No, I drove down. The lane seemed so narrow I ran the car on a little way and found a sort of old quarry I backed it into."

"This lane is very narrow, but there's hardly ever any traffic along here. It's rather a lonely road."

Miss Gilchrist gave a little shiver as she said those last words.

Susan Banks was looking round the room.

"Poor old Aunt Cora," she said. "She left what she had to me, you know."

"Yes, I know. Mr. Entwhistle told me. I expect you'll be glad of the furniture. You're newly married, I understand, and furnishing is such an expense nowadays. Mrs. Lansquenet had some very nice things."

Susan did not agree. Cora had had no taste for the antique. The contents varied between "modernistic" pieces and the "arty" type.

"I shan't want any of the furniture," she said. "I've got my own, you know. I shall put it up for auction. Unless—is there any of it you would like? I'd be very glad . . ."

She stopped, a little embarrassed. But Miss Gilchrist was not at all embarrassed. She beamed.

"Now really, that's *very* kind of you, Mrs. Banks—yes, very kind indeed. I really do appreciate it. But actually, you know, I have my own things. I put them in store in case—someday—I should need them. There are some pictures my father left, too. I had a small teashop at one time, you know—but then the war came—it was all very unfortunate. But I didn't sell up everything, because I did hope to have my own little home again one day, so I put the best things in store with my father's pictures and some relics of our old home. But I *would* like very much, if you *really* wouldn't mind, to have that little painted tea table of dear Mrs. Lansquenet's. Such a pretty thing and we always had tea on it."

Susan, looking with a slight shudder at a small green table painted with large purple clematis, said quickly that she would be delighted for Miss Gilchrist to have it.

"Thank you *very* much, Mrs. Banks. I feel a little greedy. I've got all her beautiful pictures, you know, and a lovely amethyst brooch, but I feel that perhaps I ought to give *that* back to you."

"No, no, indeed."

"You'll want to go through her things? After the inquest, perhaps?"

"I thought I'd stay here a couple of days, go through things, and clear everything up."

"Sleep here, you mean?"

"Yes. Is there any difficulty?"

"Oh no, Mrs. Banks, of course not. I'll put fresh sheets on my bed, and I can doss down here on the couch quite well."

"But there's Aunt Cora's room, isn't there? I can sleep in that."

"You—you wouldn't mind?"

"You mean because she was murdered there? Oh no, I wouldn't mind. I'm very tough, Miss Gilchrist. It's been—I mean—it's all right again?"

Miss Gilchrist understood the question.

"Oh *yes*, Mrs. Banks. All the blankets sent away to the cleaners and Mrs. Panter and I scrubbed the whole room out thoroughly. And there are plenty of spare blankets. But come up and see for yourself."

She led the way upstairs and Susan followed her.

The room where Cora Lansquenet had died was clean and fresh and curiously devoid of any sinister atmosphere. Like the sitting room it contained a mixture of modern utility and elaborately painted furniture. It represented Cora's cheerful tasteless personality. Over the mantelpiece an oil painting showed a buxom young woman about to enter her bath.

Susan gave a slight shudder as she looked at it and Miss Gilchrist said:

"That was painted by Mrs. Lansquenet's husband. There are a lot more of his pictures in the dining room downstairs."

"How terrible."

"Well, I don't care very much for that style of painting *myself*—but Mrs. Lansquenet was very proud of her husband as an artist and thought that his work was sadly unappreciated."

"Where are Aunt Cora's own pictures?"

"In my room. Would you like to see them?"

Miss Gilchrist displayed her treasures proudly.

Susan remarked that Aunt Cora seemed to have been fond of sea coast resorts.

"Oh yes. You see, she lived for many years with Mr. Lansquenet at a small fishing village in Brittany. Fishing boats are always so picturesque, are they not?"

"Obviously," Susan murmured. A whole series of picture postcards could, she thought, have been made from Cora Lansquenet's paintings which were faithful to detail and very highly coloured. They gave rise to the suspicion that they might actually have been painted from picture postcards.

But when she hazarded this opinion Miss Gilchrist was indignant. Mrs. Lansquenet *always* painted from Nature! Indeed once she had had a touch of the sun from reluctance to leave a subject when the light was just right.

"Mrs. Lansquenet was a real artist," said Miss Gilchrist reproachfully.

She glanced at her watch and Susan said quickly:

"Yes, we ought to start for the inquest. Is it far? Shall I get the car?"

It was only five minutes' walk, Miss Gilchrist assured her. So they set out together on foot. Mr. Entwhistle, who had come down by train, met them and shepherded them into the Village Hall.

There seemed to be a large number of strangers present. The inquest was not sensational. There was evidence of identification of the deceased. Medical evidence as to the nature of the wounds that had killed her. There were no signs of a struggle. Deceased was probably under a narcotic at the time she was attacked and would have been taken quite unawares. Death was unlikely to have occurred later than four thirty. Between two and four thirty was the nearest approximation. Miss Gilchrist testified to finding the body. A police constable and Inspector Morton gave their evidence. The Coroner summed up briefly. The jury made no bones about the verdict *"Murder by some person or persons unknown."*

It was over. They came out again into the sunlight. Half a dozen cameras clicked. Mr. Entwhistle shepherded Susan and Miss Gilchrist into the King's Arms where he had taken the precaution to arrange for lunch to be served in a private room behind the bar.

"Not a very good lunch, I am afraid," he said apologetically.

But the lunch was not at all bad. Miss Gilchrist sniffed a little and murmured that "it was all so dreadful" but cheered up and tackled the Irish stew with appetite after Mr. Entwhistle had insisted on her drinking a glass of sherry. He said to Susan:

"I'd no idea you were coming down today, Susan. We could have come together."

"I know I said I wouldn't. But it seemed rather mean for none of the family to be there. I rang up George but he said he was very busy and couldn't possibly make it, and Rosamund had an audition and Uncle Timothy, of course, is a crock. So it had to be me."

"Your husband didn't come with you?"

"Greg had to settle up with his tiresome shop."

Seeing a startled look in Miss Gilchrist's eye, Susan said: "My husband works in a chemist's shop."

A husband in retail trade did not quite square with Miss Gilchrist's impression of Susan's smartness, but she said valiantly:

"Oh yes, just like Keats."

"Greg's no poet," said Susan.

She added:

"We've got great plans for the future—a double barrelled establishment—Cosmetics and Beauty parlour and a laboratory for special preparations."

"That will be much nicer," said Miss Gilchrist approvingly. "Something like Elizabeth Arden who is really a Countess, so I have been told —or is that Helena Rubinstein? In any case," she added kindly, "a pharmacist's is not in the least like an ordinary shop—a *draper*, for instance, or a *grocer*."

"You kept a teashop, you said, didn't you?"

"Yes, indeed," Miss Gilchrist's face lit up. That the Willow Tree had ever been "trade" in the sense that a shop was trade, would never have occurred to her. To keep a teashop was in her mind the essence of gentility. She started telling Susan about the Willow Tree.

Mr. Entwhistle who had heard about it before let his mind drift to other matters. When Susan had spoken to him twice without his answering he hurriedly apologised.

"Forgive me, my dear, I was thinking, as a matter of fact, about your uncle Timothy. I am a little worried."

"About Uncle Timothy? I shouldn't be. I don't believe really there's anything the matter with him. He's just a hypochondriac."

"Yes—yes, you may be right. I confess it was not his health that was worrying me. It's Mrs. Timothy. Apparently she's fallen downstairs and twisted her ankle. She's laid up and your uncle is in a terrible state."

"Because he'll have to look after her instead of the other way about? Do him a lot of good," said Susan.

"Yes—yes, I daresay. But will your poor aunt *get* any looking after? That is really the question. With no servants in the house."

"Life is really Hell for elderly people," said Susan. "They live in a kind of Georgian Manor house, don't they?"

Mr. Entwhistle nodded.

They came rather warily out of the King's Arms, but the Press seemed to have dispersed.

A couple of reporters were lying in wait for Susan by the cottage door. Shepherded by Mr. Entwhistle she said a few necessary and non-committal words. Then she and Miss Gilchrist went into the cottage and Mr. Entwhistle returned to the King's Arms where he had booked a room. The funeral was to be on the following day.

"My car's still in the quarry," said Susan. "I'd forgotten about it. I'll drive it along to the village later."

Miss Gilchrist said anxiously:

"Not too late. You won't go out after dark, will you?"

Susan looked at her and laughed.

"You don't think there's a murderer still hanging about, do you?"

"No—no, I suppose not." Miss Gilchrist looked embarrassed.

"But it's exactly what she does think," thought Susan. "How amazing!"

Miss Gilchrist had vanished towards the kitchen.

"I'm sure you'd like tea early. In about half an hour, do you think, Mrs. Banks?"

Susan thought that tea at half past three was overdoing it, but she was charitable enough to realise that "a nice cup of tea" was Miss Gilchrist's idea of restoration for the nerves and she had her own reasons for wishing to please Miss Gilchrist, so she said:

"Whenever you like, Miss Gilchrist."

A happy clatter of kitchen implements began and Susan went into the sitting room. She had only been there a few minutes when the bell sounded and was succeeded by a very precise little rat-tat-tat.

Susan came out into the hall and Miss Gilchrist appeared at the kitchen door wearing an apron and wiping floury hands on it.

"Oh dear, who do you think that can be?"

"More reporters, I expect," said Susan.

"Oh dear, how annoying for you, Mrs. Banks."

"Oh well, never mind, I'll attend to it."

"I was just going to make a few scones for tea."

Susan went towards the front door and Miss Gilchrist hovered uncertainly. Susan wondered whether she thought a man with a hatchet was waiting outside.

The visitor, however, proved to be an elderly gentleman who raised his hat when Susan opened the door and said, beaming at her in avuncular style,

"Mrs. Banks, I think?"

"Yes."

"My name is Guthrie—Alexander Guthrie. I was a friend—a very old friend, of Mrs. Lansquenet's. You, I think, are her niece, formerly Miss Susan Abernethie?"

"That's quite right."

"Then since we know who we are, I may come in?"

"Of course."

Mr. Guthrie wiped his feet carefully on the mat, stepped inside, divested himself of his overcoat, laid it down with his hat on a small oak chest and followed Susan into the sitting room.

"This is a melancholy occasion," said Mr. Guthrie to whom melancholy did not seem to come naturally, his own inclination being to beam. "Yes, a very melancholy occasion. I was in this part of the world and I felt the least I could do was to attend the inquest—and of course the funeral. Poor Cora—poor foolish Cora. I have known her, my dear Mrs. Banks, since the early days of her marriage. A high-spirited girl—and she took art very seriously—took Pierre Lansquenet seriously, too—as an artist, I mean. All things considered, he didn't make her too bad a husband. He strayed, if you know what I mean, yes, he strayed—but fortunately Cora took it as part of the artistic temperament. He was an artist and therefore immoral! In fact, I'm not sure she didn't go further: he was immoral and therefore he must be an artist! No kind of sense in artistic matters, poor Cora—though in other ways, mind you, Cora had a lot of sense—yes, a surprising lot of sense."

"That's what everybody seems to say," said Susan. "I didn't really know her."

"No, no, cut herself off from her family because they didn't appreciate her precious Pierre. She was never a pretty girl—but she had *something*. She was good company! You never knew what she'd say next and you never knew if her *naiveté* was genuine or whether she was doing it deliberately. She made us all laugh a good deal. The eternal child—that's what we always felt about her. And really the last time I saw her (I have seen her from time to time since Pierre died) she struck me as still behaving very much like a child."

Susan offered Mr. Guthrie a cigarette, but the old gentleman shook his head.

"No thank you, my dear. I don't smoke. You must wonder why I've come? To tell you the truth I was feeling rather conscience-stricken. I promised Cora to come and see her some weeks ago. I usually called upon her once a year, and just lately she'd taken up the hobby of buying pictures at local sales, and wanted me to look at some of them. My profession is that of art critic, you know. Of course most of Cora's purchases were horrible daubs, but take it all in all, it isn't such a bad speculation. Pictures go for next to nothing at these country sales and the frames alone are worth more than you pay for the picture. Naturally any important sale is attended by dealers and one isn't likely to get hold of masterpieces. But only the other day, a small Cuyp was knocked down for a few pounds at a farmhouse sale. The history of it was quite interesting. It had been given to an old nurse by the family she had served faithfully for many years—they had no idea of its value. Old nurse gave it to farmer nephew who liked the horse in it but thought it was a dirty old thing! Yes, yes, these things sometimes happen, and Cora was convinced that she had an eye for pictures. She hadn't, of course. Wanted me to come and look at a Rembrandt she had picked up last year. A Rembrandt! Not even a respectable copy of one! But she had got hold of a quite nice Bartolozzi engraving—damp spotted unfortunately. I sold it for her for thirty pounds and of course that spurred her on. She wrote to me with great gusto about an Italian Primitive she had bought at some sale and I promised I'd come along and see it."

"That's it over there, I expect," said Susan, gesturing to the wall behind him.

Mr. Guthrie got up, put on a pair of spectacles, and went over to study the picture.

"Poor dear Cora," he said at last.

"There are a lot more," said Susan.

Mr. Guthrie proceeded to a leisurely inspection of the art treasures acquired by the hopeful Mrs. Lansquenet. Occasionally he said, "Tchk tchk," occasionally he sighed.

Finally he removed his spectacles.

"Dirt," he said, "is a wonderful thing, Mrs. Banks! It gives a patina of romance to the most horrible examples of the painter's art. I'm afraid that Bartolozzi was beginner's luck. Poor Cora. Still it gave her an interest in life. I am really thankful that I did not have to disillusion her."

"There are some pictures in the dining room," said Susan, "but I think they are all her husband's work."

Mr. Guthrie shuddered slightly and held up a protesting hand.

"Do not force me to look at those again. Life classes have much to answer for! I always tried to spare Cora's feelings. A devoted wife—a very devoted wife. Well, dear Mrs. Banks, I must not take up more of your time."

"Oh, do stay and have some tea. I think it's nearly ready."

"That is very kind of you." Mr. Guthrie sat down again promptly.

"I'll just go and see."

In the kitchen, Miss Gilchrist was just lifting a last batch of scones from the oven. The teatray stood ready and the kettle was just gently rattling its lid.

"There's a Mr. Guthrie here, and I've asked him to stay for tea."

"Mr. Guthrie? Oh yes, he was a great friend of dear Mrs. Lansquenet's. He's the celebrated art critic. How fortunate; I've made a nice lot of scones and that's some home made strawberry jam, and I just whipped up some little drop cakes. I'll just make the tea—I've warmed the pot. Oh please, Mrs. Banks, don't carry that heavy tray. I can manage *everything*."

However Susan took in the tray and Miss Gilchrist followed with teapot and kettle, greeted Mr. Guthrie, and they set to.

"Hot scones, that *is* a treat," said Mr. Guthrie, "and what delicious jam! Really, the stuff one buys nowadays."

Miss Gilchrist was flushed and delighted. The little cakes were excellent and so were the scones, and everyone did justice to them. The ghost of the Willow Tree hung over the party. Here, it was clear, Miss Gilchrist was in her element.

"Well, thank you, perhaps I will," said Mr. Guthrie as he accepted the last cake, pressed upon him by Miss Gilchrist. "I do feel rather guilty, though—enjoying my tea, here, where poor Cora was so brutally murdered."

Miss Gilchrist displayed an unexpected Victorian reaction to this.

"Oh but Mrs. Lansquenet would have wished you to make a good tea. You've got to keep your strength up."

"Yes, yes, perhaps you are right. The fact is, you know, that one cannot really bring oneself to believe that someone you knew—actually knew—*can* have been murdered!"

"I agree," said Susan. "It just seems—fantastic."

"And certainly not by some casual tramp who broke in and attacked her. I *can* imagine, you know, reasons why Cora might have been murdered—"

Susan said quickly, "Can you? What reasons?"

"Well, she wasn't discreet," said Mr. Guthrie. "Cora was never discreet. And she enjoyed—how shall I put it—showing how sharp she could be? Like a child who's got hold of somebody's secret. If Cora got hold of a secret she'd want to talk about it. Even if she promised not to, she'd still do it. She wouldn't be able to help herself."

Susan did not speak. Miss Gilchrist did not either. She looked worried. Mr. Guthrie went on.

"Yes, a little dose of arsenic in a cup of tea—*that* would not have surprised me, or a box of chocolates by post. But sordid robbery and assault—that seems highly incongruous. I may be wrong but I should have thought she had very little to take that would be worth a burglar's while. She didn't keep much money in the house, did she?"

Miss Gilchrist said, "Very little."

Mr. Guthrie sighed and rose to his feet.

"Ah! well, there's a lot of lawlessness about since the war. Times have changed."

Thanking them for tea, he took a polite farewell of the two women. Miss Gilchrist saw him out and helped him on with his overcoat. From the window of the sitting room, Susan watched him trot briskly down the front path to the gate.

Miss Gilchrist came back into the room with a small parcel in her hand.

"The postman must have been while we were at the inquest. He pushed it through the letter box and it had fallen in the corner behind the door. Now I wonder—why, of course, it must be wedding cake."

Happily Miss Gilchrist ripped off the paper. Inside was a small white box tied with silver ribbon.

"It is!" She pulled off the ribbon; inside was a modest wedge of rich cake with almond paste and white icing. "How nice! Now who—" she consulted the card attached. "*John and Mary*—Now who *can* that be? How silly to put no surname."

Susan, rousing herself from contemplation, said vaguely,

"It's quite difficult sometimes with people just using Christian names. I got a postcard the other day signed Joan. I counted up I knew eight Joans—and with telephoning so much, one often doesn't know their handwriting."

Miss Gilchrist was happily going over the possible Johns or Marys of her acquaintance.

"It might be Dorothy's daughter—*her* name was Mary, but I hadn't heard of an engagement, still less of a marriage. Then there's little John Banfield—I suppose he's grown up and old enough to be married—or the Enfield girl—no, her name was Margaret. No address or anything. Oh well, I daresay it will come to me . . ."

She picked up the tray and went out to the kitchen.

Susan roused herself and said:

"Well—I suppose I'd better go and put the car somewhere."

IO

SUSAN RETRIEVED the car from the quarry where she had left it and drove it into the village. There was a petrol pump but no garage and she was advised to take it to the King's Arms. They had room for it there and she left it by a big Daimler which was preparing to go out. It was chauffeur driven and inside it, very much muffled up, was an elderly foreign gentleman with a large moustache.

The boy to whom Susan was talking about the car was staring at her with such rapt attention that he did not seem to be taking in half of what she said.

Finally he said in an awestricken voice:

"You're her niece, aren't you?"

"What?"

"You're the victim's niece," the boy repeated with relish.

"Oh—yes—yes, I am."

"Ar! Wondered where I'd seen you before."

"Ghoul," thought Susan as she retraced her steps to the cottage.

Miss Gilchrist greeted her with:

"Oh you're safely back," in tones of relief which further annoyed her. Miss Gilchrist added anxiously:

"You *can* eat spaghetti, can't you? I thought for tonight—"

"Oh yes, anything. I don't want much."

"I really flatter myself that I can make a very tasty spaghetti *au gratin*."

The boast was not an idle one. Miss Gilchrist, Susan reflected, was really an excellent cook. Susan offered to help wash up but Miss Gilchrist, though clearly gratified by the offer, assured Susan that there was very little to do.

She came in a little while later with coffee. The coffee was less excellent, being decidedly weak. Miss Gilchrist offered Susan a piece of the wedding cake which Susan refused.

"It's really very good cake," Miss Gilchrist insisted, tasting it. She had settled to her own satisfaction that it must have been sent by someone whom she alluded to as "dear Ellen's daughter who I know was engaged to be married but I can't remember her name."

Susan let Miss Gilchrist chirrup away into silence before starting her own subject of conversation. This moment, after supper, sitting before the fire, was a companionable one.

She said at last:

"My uncle Richard came down here before he died, didn't he?"

"Yes, he did."

"When was that exactly?"

"Let me see—it must have been one, two—nearly three weeks before his death was announced."

"Did he seem—ill?"

"Well, no, I wouldn't say he seemed exactly ill. He had a very hearty vigorous manner. Mrs. Lansquenet was very surprised to see him. She said, 'Well, really, Richard, after all these years!' And he said, 'I came to see for myself exactly how things are with you.' And Mrs. Lansquenet said, '*I*'m all right.' I think, you know, she was a teeny bit offended by his turning up so casually—after the long break. Anyway Mr. Abernethie said, 'No use keeping up old grievances. You and I and Timothy are the only ones left—and nobody can talk to Timothy except about his own health.' And he said, 'Pierre seems to have made you happy, so it seems I was in the wrong. There, will that content you?' Very nicely he said it. A handsome man, though elderly, of course."

"How long was he here?"

"He stayed for lunch. Beef olives, I made. Fortunately it was the day the butcher called."

Miss Gilchrist's memory seemed to be almost wholly culinary.

"They seemed to be getting on well together?"

"Oh yes."

Susan paused and then said:

"Was Aunt Cora surprised when—he died?"

"Oh yes, it was quite sudden, wasn't it?"

"Yes, it was sudden . . . I meant—she *was* surprised. He hadn't given her any indication how ill he was."

"Oh—I see what you mean." Miss Gilchrist paused a moment. "No, no, I think perhaps you are right. She did say that he had got very old—I think she said senile . . ."

"But *you* didn't think he was senile?"

"Well, not to *look* at. But I didn't talk to him much. Naturally, I left them alone together."

Susan looked at Miss Gilchrist speculatively. Was Miss Gilchrist the kind of woman who listened at doors? She was honest, Susan felt sure, she wouldn't ever pilfer, or cheat over the house-keeping, or open letters. But inquisitiveness can drape itself in a mantle of rectitude. Miss Gilchrist might have found it necessary to garden near an open window, or to dust the hall . . . That would be within the permitted lengths. And then, of course, she could not have helped hearing something . . .

"You didn't hear any of their conversation?" Susan asked.

Too abrupt. Miss Gilchrist flushed angrily.

"No, indeed, Mrs. Banks. It has never been my custom to listen at doors!"

That means she does, thought Susan, otherwise she'd just say "No."

Aloud she said: "I'm so sorry, Miss Gilchrist. I didn't mean it that way. But sometimes, in these small flimsily built cottages, one simply can't help hearing everything that goes on, and now that they are both dead, it's really rather important to the family to know just what was said at that meeting between them."

The cottage was anything but flimsily built—it dated from a sturdier era of building, but Miss Gilchrist accepted the bait, and rose to the suggestion held out.

"Of course what you say is quite true, Mrs. Banks—this *is* a very small place and I do appreciate that you would want to know what passed between them, but really I'm afraid I can't help very much. I think they were talking about Mr. Abernethie's health—and certain—well, *fancies* he had. He didn't look it, but he must have been a sick man and as is so often the case, he put his ill health down to *outside agencies*. A common symptom, I believe. My aunt—"

Miss Gilchrist described her aunt.

Susan, like Mr. Entwhistle, sidetracked the aunt.

"Yes," she said. "That is just what we thought. My uncle's servants were all very attached to him and naturally they are upset by his thinking—" She paused.

"Oh of course! Servants are *very* touchy about anything of that kind. I remember that my aunt—"

Again Susan interrupted.

"It *was* the servants he suspected, I suppose? Of poisoning him, I mean?"

"I don't know . . . I—really—"

Susan noted her confusion.

"It wasn't the servants. Was it one particular person?"

"I don't know, Mrs. Banks. Really I don't know—"

But her eye avoided Susan's. Susan thought to herself that Miss Gilchrist knew more than she was willing to admit.

It was possible that Miss Gilchrist knew a good deal. . . .

Deciding not to press the point for the moment, Susan said:

"What are your own plans for the future, Miss Gilchrist?"

"Well, really, I was going to speak to you about that, Mrs. Banks. I told Mr. Entwhistle I would be willing to stay on until everything here was cleared up."

"I know. I'm very grateful."

"And I wanted to ask you how long that was likely to be, because, of course, I must start looking about for another post."

Susan considered.

"There's really not very much to be done here. In a couple of days I can get things sorted and notify the auctioneer."

"You have decided to sell up everything, then?"

"Yes. I don't suppose there will be any difficulty in letting the cottage?"

"*Oh no*—people will queue up for it, I'm sure. There are so few cottages to rent. One nearly always has to buy."

"So it's all very simple, you see." Susan hesitated a moment before saying, "I wanted to tell you—that I hope you'll accept three months' salary."

"That's very generous of you, I'm sure, Mrs. Banks. I do appreciate it. And you would be prepared to—I mean I could ask you—if necessary—to—to recommend me? To say that I had been with a relation of yours and that I had—proved satisfactory?"

"Oh, of course."

"I don't know whether I ought to ask it." Miss Gilchrist's hands began to shake and she tried to steady her voice. "But would it be possible not to—to mention the circumstances—or even the *name*?"

Susan stared.

"I don't understand."

"That's because you haven't thought, Mrs. Banks. It's *murder*. A murder that's been in the papers and that everybody has read about. Don't you see? People might think. 'Two women living together, and one of them is killed—and *perhaps the companion did it*.' Don't you see, Mrs. Banks? I'm sure that if *I* was looking for someone, I'd—well, I'd think twice before engaging myself —if you understand what I mean. Because one never *knows!* It's been worrying me dreadfully, Mrs. Banks; I've been lying awake at night thinking that perhaps I'll never get another job—not of this kind. And what else is there that I can do?"

The question came out with unconscious pathos. Susan felt suddenly stricken. She realised the desperation of this pleasant-spoken commonplace woman who was dependent for existence on the fears and whims of employers. And there was a lot of truth in what Miss Gilchrist had said. You wouldn't, if you could help it, engage a woman to share domestic intimacy who had figured, however innocently, in a murder case.

Susan said: "But if they find the man who did it—"

"Oh *then*, of course, it will be quite all right. But will they find him? I don't think, myself, the police have the *least idea*. And if he's *not* caught—well, that leaves me as—as not quite the most likely person, but as a person who *could* have done it."

Susan nodded thoughtfully. It was true that Miss Gilchrist did not benefit from Cora Lansquenet's death—but who was to know that? And besides there were so many tales—ugly tales—of animosity arising between women who lived together—strange pathological motives for sudden violence. Someone who had not known them might imagine that Cora Lansquenet and Miss Gilchrist had lived on those terms. . . .

Susan spoke with her usual decision.

"Don't worry, Miss Gilchrist," she said, speaking briskly and cheerfully. "I'm sure I can find you a post amongst my friends. There won't be the least difficulty."

"I'm afraid," said Miss Gilchrist, regaining some of her customary manner, "that I couldn't undertake any really *rough* work. Just a little plain cooking and housework—"

The telephone rang and Miss Gilchrist jumped.

"Dear me, I wonder who *that* can be."

"I expect it's my husband," said Susan, jumping up. "He said he'd ring me tonight."

She went to the telephone.

"Yes?—yes, this is Mrs. Banks speaking personally . . ." There was a pause and then her voice changed. It became soft and warm. "Hullo, darling—yes, it's me. . . . Oh, quite well . . . Murder by someone unknown . . . the usual thing. . . . Only Mr. Entwhistle. . . . What? . . . It's difficult to say, but I think so. . . . Yes, just as we thought. . . . Absolutely according to plan. . . . I shall sell the stuff. There's nothing *we'd* want. . . . Not for a day or two. . . . Absolutely frightful. . . . Don't fuss. I know what I'm doing. . . . Greg, you didn't . . . You were careful to . . . No, it's nothing. Nothing at all. Good night, darling."

She rang off. The nearness of Miss Gilchrist had hampered her a little. Miss Gilchrist could probably hear from the kitchen, where she had tactfully retired, exactly what went on. There were things she had wanted to ask Greg, but she hadn't liked to.

She stood by the telephone, frowning abstractedly. Then suddenly an idea came to her.

"Of course," she murmured. "Just the thing."

Lifting the receiver she asked for Trunk Enquiry.

Some quarter of an hour later a weary voice from the exchange was saying:

"I'm afraid there's no reply."

"Please go on ringing them."

Susan spoke autocratically. She listened to the far off buzzing of a telephone bell. Then, suddenly it was interrupted and a man's voice, peevish and slightly indignant, said:

"Yes, yes, what is it?"

"Uncle Timothy?"

"What's that? I can't hear you."

"Uncle Timothy? I'm Susan Banks."

"Susan who?"

"Banks. Formerly Abernethie. Your niece Susan."

"Oh, you're Susan, are you? What's the matter? What are you ringing up for at this time of night?"

"It's quite early still."

"It isn't. I was in bed."

"You must go to bed very early. How's Aunt Maude?"

"Is that all you rang up to ask? Your aunt's in a good deal of pain and she can't do a thing. Not a thing. She's helpless. We're in a nice mess, I can tell you. That fool of a doctor says he can't even get a nurse. He wanted to cart Maude off to hospital. I stood out against *that*. He's trying to get hold of someone for us. *I* can't do anything—I daren't even try. There's a fool from the village staying in the house tonight—but she's murmuring about getting back to her husband. Don't know *what* we're going to do."

"That's what I rang up about. Would you like Miss Gilchrist?"

"Who's she? Never heard of her."

"Aunt Cora's companion. She's very nice and capable."

"Can she cook?"

"Yes, she cooks very well, and she could look after Aunt Maude."

"That's all very well, but when could she come? Here I am, all on my own, with only these idiots of village women popping in and out at odd hours, and it's not good for me. My heart's playing me up."

"I'll arrange for her to get off to you as soon as possible. The day after tomorrow, perhaps?"

"Well, thanks very much," said the voice rather grudgingly. "You're a good girl, Susan—er—thank you."

Susan rang off and went into the kitchen.

"Would you be willing to go up to Yorkshire and look after my aunt? She fell and broke her ankle and my uncle is quite useless. He's a bit of a pest but Aunt Maude is a very good sort. They have help in from the village, but you could cook and look after Aunt Maude."

Miss Gilchrist dropped the coffee pot in her agitation.

"Oh thank you, thank you—that really is kind. I think I can say of myself that I am really good in the sickroom, and I'm sure I can manage your uncle and cook him nice little meals. It's really very kind of you, Mrs. Banks, and I *do* appreciate it."

II

SUSAN LAY IN BED and waited for sleep to come. It had been a long day and she was tired. She had been quite sure that she would go to sleep at once. She never had any difficulty in going to sleep. And yet here she lay, hour after hour, wide awake, her mind racing.

She had said she did not mind sleeping in this room, in this bed. This bed where Cora Abernethie—

No, no, she must put all that out of her mind. She had always prided herself on having no nerves. Why think of that afternoon less than a week ago? Think ahead—the future. Her future and Greg's. Those premises in Cardigan Street—just what they wanted. The business on the ground floor and a charming flat upstairs. The room out at the back a laboratory for Greg. For purposes of income tax it would be an excellent set up. Greg would get calm and well again. There would be no more of those alarming brain storms. The times when he looked at her without seeming to know who she was. Once or twice she'd been quite frightened . . . And old Mr. Cole—he'd hinted—threatened: "If this happens again . . ." And it might have happened again—it *would* have happened again. If Uncle Richard hadn't died just when he did . . .

Uncle Richard—but really why look at it like that? He'd nothing to live for. Old and tired and ill. His son dead. It was a mercy really. To die in his sleep quietly like that. Quietly . . . in his sleep. . . . If only she could sleep. It was so stupid lying awake hour after hour . . . hearing the furniture creak, and the rustling of trees and bushes outside the window and the occasional queer melancholy hoot—an owl, she supposed. How sinister the country was, somehow. So different from the big noisy indifferent town. One felt so safe there—surrounded by people—never alone. Whereas here . . .

Houses where a murder had been committed were sometimes haunted. Perhaps this cottage would come to be known as the haunted cottage. Haunted by the spirit of Cora Lansquenet . . . Aunt Cora. Odd, really, how ever since she had arrived she had felt as though Aunt Cora were quite close to her . . . within reach. All nerves and fancy. Cora Lansquenet was dead, tomorrow she would be buried. There was no one in the cottage except Susan herself and Miss Gilchrist. Then why did she feel that there was someone in this room, someone close beside her. . . .

She had lain on this bed when the hatchet fell . . . Lying there trustingly asleep . . . Knowing nothing till the hatchet fell . . . And now she wouldn't let Susan sleep. . . .

The furniture creaked again . . . was that a stealthy step? . . . Susan switched on the light. Nothing. Nerves, nothing but nerves. Relax . . . close your eyes. . . .

Surely that was a groan—a groan or a faint moan . . . Someone in pain—someone dying. . . .

"I mustn't imagine things, I mustn't, I mustn't," Susan whispered to herself.

Death was the end—there was no existence after death. Under no circumstances could anyone come back. Or was she re-living a scene from the past—a dying woman groaning. . . .

There it was again . . . stronger . . . someone groaning in acute pain. . . .

But—this was real. Once again Susan switched on the light, sat up in bed and listened. The groans were real groans and she was hearing them through the wall. They came from the room next door.

Susan jumped out of bed, flung on a dressing gown and crossed to the door. She went out onto the landing, tapped for a moment on Miss Gilchrist's door and then went in. Miss Gilchrist's light was on. She was sitting up in bed. She looked ghastly. Her face was distorted with pain.

"Miss Gilchrist, what's the matter? Are you ill?"

"Yes. I don't know what—I—" she tried to get out of bed, was seized with a fit of vomiting and then collapsed back on the pillows.

She murmured: "Please—ring up doctor. Must have eaten something. . . ."

"I'll get you some bicarbonate. We can get the doctor in the morning if you're not better."

Miss Gilchrist shook her head.

"No, get doctor now. I—I feel dreadful."

"Do you know his number? Or shall I look in the book?"

Miss Gilchrist gave her the number. She was interrupted by another fit of retching.

Susan's call was answered by a sleepy male voice.

"Who? Gilchrist? In Mead's Lane. Yes, I know. I'll be right along."

He was as good as his word. Ten minutes later Susan heard his car draw up outside and she went to open the door to him.

She explained the case as she took him upstairs. "I think," she said, "she must have eaten something that disagreed with her. But she seems pretty bad."

The doctor had had the air of one keeping his temper in leash and who has had some experience of being called out unnecessarily on more than one occasion. But as soon as he examined the moaning woman his manner changed. He gave various curt orders to Susan and presently came down and telephoned. Then he joined Susan in the sitting room.

"I've sent for an ambulance. Must get her into hospital."

"She's really bad then?"

"Yes. I've given her a shot of morphia to ease the pain. But it looks—" he broke off. "What's she eaten?"

"We had macaroni *au gratin* for supper and a custard pudding. Coffee afterwards."

"You have the same things?"

"Yes."

"And you're all right? No pain or discomfort?"

"No."

"She's taken nothing else? No tinned fish? Or sausages?"

"No. We had lunch at the King's Arms—after the inquest."

"Yes, of course. You're Mrs. Lansquenet's niece?"

"Yes."

"That was a nasty business. Hope they catch the man who did it."

"Yes, indeed."

The ambulance came. Miss Gilchrist was taken away and the doctor went with her. He told Susan he would ring her up in the morning. When he had left she went upstairs to bed.

This time she fell asleep as soon as her head touched the pillow.

II

The funeral was well attended. Most of the village had turned out. Susan and Mr. Entwhistle were the only mourners, but various wreaths had been sent by the other members of the family. Mr. Entwhistle asked where Miss Gilchrist was, and Susan explained the circumstances in a hurried whisper. Mr. Entwhistle raised his eyebrows.

"Rather an odd occurrence?"

"Oh, she's better this morning. They rang up from the hospital. People do get these bilious turns. Some make more fuss than others."

Mr. Entwhistle said no more. He was returning to London immediately after the funeral.

Susan went back to the cottage. She found some eggs and made herself an omelette. Then she went up to Cora's room and started to sort through the dead woman's things.

She was interrupted by the arrival of the doctor.

The doctor was looking worried. He replied to Susan's inquiry by saying that Miss Gilchrist was much better.

"She'll be out and around in a couple of days," he said. "But it was lucky I got called in so promptly. Otherwise—it might have been a near thing."

Susan stared. "Was she really so bad?"

"Mrs. Banks, will you tell me again exactly what Miss Gilchrist had to eat and drink yesterday. Everything."

Susan reflected and gave a meticulous account. The doctor shook his head in a dissatisfied manner.

"There must have been something she had and you didn't?"

"I don't think so . . . Cakes, scones, jam, tea—and then supper. No, I can't remember anything."

The doctor rubbed his nose. He walked up and down the room.

"Was it definitely something she ate? Definitely food poisoning?"

The doctor threw her a sharp glance. Then he seemed to come to a decision.

"It was arsenic," he said.

"Arsenic?" Susan stared. "You mean somebody gave her arsenic?"

"That's what it looks like."

"Could she have taken it herself? Deliberately, I mean?"

"Suicide? She says not and she should know. Besides if she wanted to commit suicide she wouldn't be likely to choose arsenic. There are sleeping pills in this house. She could have taken an overdose of them."

"Could the arsenic have got into something by accident?"

"That's what I am wondering. It seems very unlikely, but such things have been known. But if you and she ate the same things—"

Susan nodded. She said, "It all seems impossible—" then she gave a sudden gasp. "Why, of course, the wedding cake!"

"What's that? Wedding cake?"

Susan explained. The doctor listened with close attention.

"Odd. And you say she wasn't sure who sent it? Any of it left? Or is the box it came in lying around?"

"I don't know. I'll look."

They searched together and finally found the white cardboard box with a few crumbs of cake still in it lying on the kitchen dresser. The doctor packed it away with some care.

"I'll take charge of this. Any idea where the wrapping paper it came in might be?"

Here they were not successful and Susan said that it had probably gone into the Ideal boiler.

"You won't be leaving here just yet, Mrs. Banks?"

His tone was genial, but it made Susan feel a little uncomfortable.

"No, I have to go through my aunt's things. I shall be here for a few days."

"Good. You understand the police will probably want to ask some questions. You don't know of anyone who—well, might have had it in for Miss Gilchrist?"

Susan shook her head.

"I don't really know much about her. She was with my aunt for some years—that's all I know."

"Quite, quite. Always seemed a pleasant unassuming woman—quite ordinary. Not the kind, you'd say, to have enemies or anything melodramatic of that kind. Wedding cake through the post. Sounds like some jealous woman—but who'd be jealous of Miss Gilchrist? Doesn't seem to fit."

"No."

"Well, I must be on my way. I don't know what's happening to us in quiet little Lytchett St. Mary. First a brutal murder and now attempted poisoning through the post. Odd, the one following the other."

He went down the path to his car. The cottage felt stuffy and Susan left the door standing open as she went slowly upstairs to resume her task.

Cora Lansquenet had not been a tidy or methodical woman. Her drawers held a miscellaneous assortment of things. There were toilet accessories and letters and old handkerchiefs and paint brushes mixed up together in one drawer. There were a few old letters and bills thrust in amongst a bulging drawer of underclothes. In another drawer under some woollen jumpers was a cardboard box holding two false fringes. There was another drawer full of old photographs and sketching books. Susan lingered over a group taken evidently at some French place many years ago and which showed a younger thinner Cora clinging to the arm of a tall lanky man with a straggling beard dressed in what seemed to be a velveteen coat and whom Susan took to be the late Pierre Lansquenet.

The photographs interested Susan, but she laid them aside, sorted all the papers she had found into a heap and began to go through them methodically. About a quarter way through she came on a letter. She read it through twice and was still staring at it when a voice speaking behind her caused her to give a cry of alarm.

"And what may you have got hold of there, Susan? Hullo, what's the matter?"

Susan reddened with annoyance. Her cry of alarm had been quite involuntary and she felt ashamed and anxious to explain.

"George! How you startled me!"

Her cousin smiled lazily.

"So it seems."

"How did you get here?"

"Well, the door downstairs was open, so I walked in. There seemed to be nobody about on the ground floor, so I came up here. If you mean how did I get to this part of the world, I started down this morning to come to the funeral."

"I didn't see you there?"

"The old bus played me up. The petrol feed seemed choked. I tinkered with it for some time and finally it seemed to clear itself. I was too late for the funeral by then, but I thought I might as well come on down. I knew you were here."

He paused and then went on:

"I rang you up, as a matter of fact—and Greg told me you'd come down to take possession, as it were. I thought I might give you a hand."

Susan said, "Aren't you needed in the office? Or can you take days off whenever you like?"

"A funeral has always been a recognised excuse for absenteeism. And this funeral is indubitably genuine. Besides a murder always fascinates people. Anyway, I shan't be going much to the office in future—not now that I'm a man of means. I shall have better things to do."

He paused and grinned. "Same as Greg," he said.

Susan looked at George thoughtfully. She had never seen much of this cousin of hers and when they did meet she had always found him rather difficult to make out.

She asked, "Why did you really come down here, George?"

"I'm not sure it wasn't to do a little detective work. I've been thinking a good deal about the last funeral we attended. Aunt Cora certainly threw a spanner into the works that day. I've wondered whether it was sheer irresponsibility and auntly *joie de vivre* that prompted her words, or whether she really had something to go upon. What actually is in that letter that you were reading so attentively when I came in?"

Susan said slowly, "It's a letter that Uncle Richard wrote to Cora after he'd been down here to see her."

How very black George's eyes were. She'd thought of them as brown but they were black, and there was something curiously impenetrable about black eyes. They concealed the thoughts that lay behind them.

George drawled slowly, "Anything interesting in it?"

"No, not exactly . . ."

"Can I see?"

She hesitated for a moment, then put the letter into his outstretched hand.

He read it, skimming over the contents in a low monotone.

"Glad to have seen you again after all these years . . . looking very well . . . had a good journey home and arrived back not too tired. . . ."

His voice changed suddenly, sharpened:

"Please don't say anything to anyone about what I told you. It may be a mistake. Your loving brother, Richard."

He looked up at Susan. "What does that mean?"

"It might mean anything. . . . It might be just about his health. Or it might be some gossip about a mutual friend."

"Oh yes, it might be a lot of things. It isn't conclusive—but it's suggestive. . . . What did he tell Cora? Does anyone know what he told her?"

"Miss Gilchrist might know," said Susan thoughtfully. "I think she listened."

"Oh yes, the companion help. Where is she, by the way?"

"In hospital, suffering from arsenic poisoning."

George stared.

"You don't mean it?"

"I do. Someone sent her some poisoned wedding cake."

George sat down on one of the bedroom chairs and whistled.

"It looks," he said, "as though Uncle Richard was not mistaken."

III

On the following morning Inspector Morton called at the cottage.

He was a quiet middle-aged man with a soft country burr in his voice. His manner was quiet and unhurried, but his eyes were shrewd.

"You realise what this is about, Mrs. Banks?" he said. "Dr. Proctor has already told you about Miss Gilchrist. The few crumbs of wedding cake that he took from here have been analysed and show traces of arsenic."

"So somebody deliberately wanted to poison her?"

"That's what it looks like. Miss Gilchrist herself doesn't seem able to help us. She keeps repeating that it's impossible—that nobody would do such a thing. But somebody did. *You* can't throw any light on the matter?"

Susan shook her head.

"I'm simply dumbfounded," she said. "Can't you find out anything from the postmark? Or the handwriting?"

"You've forgotten—the wrapping paper was presumably burnt. And there's a little doubt whether it came through the post at all. Young Andrews, the driver of the postal van, doesn't seem able to remember delivering it. He's got a big round, and he can't be sure—but there it is—there's a doubt about it."

"But—what's the alternative?"

"The alternative, Mrs. Banks, is that an old piece of brown paper was used that already had Miss Gilchrist's name and address on it and a cancelled stamp, and that the package was pushed through the letter box or deposited inside the door by hand to create the impression that it had come by post."

He added dispassionately:

"It's quite a clever idea, you know, to choose wedding cake. Lonely middle-aged women are sentimental about wedding cake, pleased at having been remembered. A box of sweets, or something of that kind *might* have awakened suspicion."

Susan said slowly:

"Miss Gilchrist speculated a good deal about who could have sent it, but she wasn't at all suspicious—as you say, she was pleased and yes—flattered."

She added: "Was there enough poison in it to—kill?"

"That's difficult to say until we get the quantitative analysis. It rather depends on whether Miss Gilchrist ate the whole of the wedge. She seems to think that she didn't. Can you remember?"

"No—no, I'm not sure. She offered me some and I refused and then she ate some and said it was a very good cake, but I don't remember if she finished it or not.''

''I'd like to go upstairs if you don't mind, Mrs. Banks.''

''Of course.''

She followed him up to Miss Gilchrist's room. She said apologetically:

''I'm afraid it's in a rather disgusting state. But I didn't have time to do anything about it with my aunt's funeral and everything, and then after Dr. Proctor came I thought perhaps I ought to leave it as it was.''

''That was very intelligent of you, Mrs. Banks. It's not everyone who would have been so intelligent.''

He went to the bed and slipping his hand under the pillow raised it carefully. A slow smile spread over his face.

''There you are,'' he said.

A piece of wedding cake lay on the sheet looking somewhat the worse for wear.

''How extraordinary,'' said Susan.

''Oh no, it's not. Perhaps your generation doesn't do it. Young ladies nowadays mayn't set so much store on getting married. But it's an old custom. Put a piece of wedding cake under your pillow and you'll dream of your future husband.''

''But surely Miss Gilchrist—''

''She didn't want to tell us about it because she felt foolish doing such a thing at her age. But I had a notion that's what it might be.'' His face sobered. ''And if it hadn't been for an old maid's foolishness, Miss Gilchrist mightn't be alive today.''

''But who could have possibly wanted to kill her?''

His eyes met hers, a curious speculative look in them that made Susan feel uncomfortable.

''You don't know?'' he asked.

''No—of course I don't.''

''It seems then as though we shall have to find out,'' said Inspector Morton.

12

TWO ELDERLY MEN sat together in a room whose furnishings were of the most modern kind. There were no curves in the room. Everything was square. Almost the only exception was Hercule Poirot himself who was full of curves. His stomach was pleasantly rounded, his head resembled an egg in shape, and his moustaches curved upwards in a flamboyant flourish.

He was sipping a glass of *sirop* and looking thoughtfully at Mr. Goby.

Mr. Goby was small and spare and shrunken. He had always been refreshingly nondescript in appearance and he was now so nondescript as practically not to be there at all. He was not looking at Poirot because Mr. Goby never looked at anybody.

Such remarks as he was now making seemed to be addressed to the left hand corner of the chromium plated fireplace curb.

Mr. Goby was famous for the acquiring of information. Very few people knew about him and very few employed his services—but those few were usually extremely rich. They had to be, for Mr. Goby was very expensive. His speciality was the acquiring of information quickly. At the flick of Mr. Goby's double jointed thumb, hundreds of patient questioning plodding men and women, old and young, of all apparent stations in life, were despatched to question, and probe, and achieve results.

Mr. Goby had now practically retired from business. But he occasionally "obliged" a few old patrons. Hercule Poirot was one of these.

"I've got what I could for you," he told the fire curb in a soft confidential whisper. "I sent the boys out. They do what they can—good lads—good lads all of them, but not what they used to be in the old days. They don't come that way nowadays. Not willing to learn, that's what it is. Think they know everything after they've only been a couple of years on the job. And they work to time. Shocking the way they work to time."

He shook his head sadly and shifted his gaze to an electric plug socket.

"It's the Government," he told it. "And all this education racket. It gives them ideas. They come back and tell us what they think. They *can't* think, most of them, anyway. All they know is things out of books. That's no good in our business. Bring in the answers—that's all that's needed—no thinking."

Mr. Goby flung himself back in his chair and winked at a lampshade.

"Mustn't crab the Government, though! Don't know really what we'd do without it. I can tell you that nowadays you can walk in most anywhere with a notebook and pencil, dressed right, and speaking B.B.C., and ask people all the most intimate details of their daily lives and all their back history, and what they had for dinner on November 23rd because that was a test day for middle-class incomes—or whatever it happens to be, (making it a grade above to butter them up!)—ask 'em any mortal thing you can; and nine times out of ten they'll come across pat, and even the tenth time though they may cut up rough, they won't doubt for a minute that you're what you say you are—and that the Government really wants to know—for some completely unfathomable reason! I can tell you, M. Poirot,'' said Mr. Goby still talking to the lampshade, ''that it's the best line we've ever had; much better than taking the electric meter or tracing a fault in the telephone—yes, or than calling as nuns, or the Girl Guides or the Boy Scouts asking for subscriptions—though we use all those too. Yes, Government snooping is God's gift to investigators and long may it continue!''

Poirot did not speak. Mr. Goby had grown a little garrulous with advancing years, but he would come to the point in his own good time.

''Ar,'' said Mr. Goby and took out a very scrubby little notebook. He licked his finger and flicked over the pages. ''Here we are. Mr. George Crossfield. We'll take him first. Just the plain facts. You won't want to know how I got them. He's been in Queer Street for quite a while now. Horses, mostly, and gambling—he's not a great one for women. Goes over to France now and then, and Monte too. Spends a lot of time at the Casino. Too downy to cash cheques there, but gets hold of a lot more money than his travelling allowance would account for. I didn't go into that, because it wasn't what you want to know. But he's not scrupulous about evading the law—and being a lawyer he knows how to do it. Some reason to believe that he's been using trust funds entrusted to him to invest. Plunging pretty wildly of late—on the Stock Exchange *and* on the gee-gees! Bad judgement and bad luck. Been off his feed badly for three months. Worried, bad tempered and irritable in the office. *But* since his uncle's death that's all changed. He's like the breakfast eggs (if we had 'em). Sunny side up!

''Now, as to particular information asked for. Statement that he was at Hurst Park races on day in question almost certainly untrue. Almost invariably places bets with one or other of two bookies on the course. They didn't see him that day. Possible that he left Paddington by train for destination unknown. Taxi driver who took fare to Paddington made doubtful identification of his photograph. But I wouldn't bank on it. He's a very common type—nothing outstanding about him. No success with porters etc., at Paddington. Certainly didn't arrive at Cholsey Station—which is nearest for Lytchett St. Mary. Small station, strangers noticeable. Could have got out at Reading and taken bus. Buses there crowded, frequent and several routes go within a mile or so of Lytchett St. Mary as well as the bus service that goes right into the village. He wouldn't take that—not if he meant business. All in all, he's a downy card. Wasn't seen in Lytchett St. Mary but he needn't have been. Other ways of approach than through the village. Was in the OUDS at Oxford, by the way. If he went to the cottage that day he mayn't have looked quite like the usual George Crossfield. I'll keep him in my book, shall I? There's a black market angle I'd like to play up.''

''You may keep him in,'' said Hercule Poirot.

Mr. Goby licked his finger and turned another page of his notebook.

''Mr. Michael Shane. He's thought quite a lot of in the profession. Has an even better idea of himself than other people have. Wants to star and wants to star quickly. Fond of money and doing himself well. Very attractive to women. They fall for him right and left. He's partial to them himself—but business comes first, as you might say. He's been running around with Sorrel Dainton who was playing the lead in the last show he was in. He only had a minor part but made quite a hit in it, and Miss Dainton's husband doesn't like him. His wife doesn't know about him and Miss Dainton. Doesn't know much about anything, it seems. Not much of an actress, I gather, but easy on the eye. Crazy about her husband. Some rumour of a bust up likely between them not long ago, but that seems out now. Out since Mr. Richard Abernethie's death.''

Mr. Goby emphasised the last point by nodding his head significantly at a cushion on the sofa.

''On the day in question, Mr. Shane says he was meeting a Mr. Rosenheim and a Mr. Oscar Lewis to fix up some stage business. He didn't meet them. Sent them a wire to say he was terribly sorry he couldn't make it. What he *did* do was to go to the Emeraldo Car people, who hire out drive yourself cars. He hired a car about twelve o'clock and drove away in it. He returned it about six in the evening. According to the speedometer it had been driven just about the right number of miles for what we're after. No confirmation from Lytchett St. Mary. No strange car seems to have been observed there that day. Lots of places it could be left unnoticed a mile or so away. And there's even a disused quarry a few hundred yards down the lane from the cottage. Three market towns within walking distance where you can park in side streets, without the police bothering about you. All right, we keep Mr. Shane in?''

''Most certainly.''

''Now Mrs. Shane.'' Mr. Goby rubbed his nose and told his left cuff about Mrs. Shane. ''She says she was shopping. Just shopping . . .'' Mr. Goby raised his eyes to the ceiling. ''Women who are shopping—just scatty, that's what they are. And she'd heard she'd come into money the day before. Naturally there'd be no holding her. She has one or two charge accounts but they're overdrawn and they've been pressing her for payment and she didn't put any more on the sheet. It's quite on the cards that she went in here and there and everywhere, trying on clothes, looking at jewellery, pricing this, that, and the other—and as likely as not, not buying anything! She's easy to approach—I'll say that. I had one of my young ladies who's knowledgeable on the theatrical line do a hook up. Stopped by her table in a restaurant and exclaimed the way they do: "Darling, I haven't seen you since 'Way Down Under.' You were *wonderful* in that! Have you seen Hubert lately?" That was the producer and Mrs. Shane was a bit of a flop in the play—but that makes it go all the better. They're chatting theatrical stuff at once, and my girl throws the right names about, and then she says, 'I believe I caught a glimpse of you at so and so, on so and so,' giving the day—and most ladies fall for it and say, 'Oh no, I was—' whatever it may be. But not Mrs. Shane. Just looks vacant and says, 'Oh, I daresay.' What can you do with a lady like that?" Mr. Goby shook his head severely at the radiator.

"Nothing," said Hercule Poirot with feeling. "Do I not have cause to know it? Never shall I forget the killing of Lord Edgware. I was nearly defeated—yes, I, Hercule Poirot—by the extremely simple cunning of a vacant brain. The very simple minded have often the genius to commit an uncomplicated crime and then leave it alone. Let us hope that our murderer—if there is a murderer in this affair—is intelligent and superior and thoroughly pleased with himself and unable to resist painting the lily. *Enfin*—but continue."

Once more Mr. Goby applied himself to his little book.

"Mr. and Mrs. Banks—who said they were at home all day. *She* wasn't, anyway! Went around to the garage, got out her car, and drove off in it about 1 o'clock. Destination unknown. Back about five. Can't tell about mileage because she's had it out every day since and it's been nobody's business to check.

"As to Mr. Banks, we've dug up something curious. To begin with, I'll mention that on the day in question we don't know *what* he did. He didn't go to work. Seems he'd already asked for a couple of days off on account of the funeral. And since then he's chucked his job—with no consideration for the firm. Nice, well established pharmacy, it is. They're not too keen on Master Banks. Seems he used to get into rather queer excitable states.

"Well, as I say, we don't know what he was doing on the day of Mrs. L's death. He didn't go with his wife. It *could* be that he stopped in their little flat all day. There's no porter there, and nobody knows whether tenants are in or out. But his back history is interesting. Up till about four months ago—just before he met his wife, he was in a Mental Home. Not certified—just what they call a mental breakdown. Seems he made some slip up in dispensing a medicine. (He was working with a Mayfair firm then.) The woman recovered, and the firm were all over themselves apologising, and there was no prosecution. After all, these accidental slips do occur, and most decent people are sorry for a poor young chap who's done it—so long as there's no permanent harm done, that is. The firm didn't sack him, but he resigned—said it had shaken his nerve. But afterwards, it seems, he got into a very low state and told the doctor he was obsessed by guilt—that it had all been deliberate—the woman had been overbearing and rude to him when she came into the shop, had complained that her last prescription had been badly made up—and that he had resented this and had deliberately added a near lethal dose of some drug or other. He said 'She had to be punished for daring to speak to me like that!' And then wept and said he was too wicked to live and a lot of things like that. The medicos have a long word for that sort of thing—guilt complex or something—and don't believe it was deliberate at all, just carelessness, but that he wanted to make it important and serious."

"Ça se peut," said Hercule Poirot.

"Pardon? Anyway, he went into this Sanitorium and they treated him and discharged him as cured, and he met Miss Abernethie as she was then. And he got a job in this respectable but rather obscure little chemist's shop. Told them he'd been out of England for a year and a half, and gave them his former reference from some shop in Eastbourne. Nothing against him in that shop, but a fellow dispenser said he had a very queer temper and was odd in his manner sometimes. There's a story about a customer saying once as a joke, 'Wish you'd sell me something to poison my wife, ha ha!' And Banks says to him, very soft and quiet: 'I could . . . It would cost you two hundred pounds.' The man felt uneasy and laughed it off. *May* have been all a joke, but it doesn't seem to me that Banks is the joking kind."

"Mon ami," said Hercule Poirot. "It really amazes me how you get your information! Medical and highly confidential most of it!"

Mr. Goby's eyes swivelled right round the room and he murmured, looking expectantly at the door, that there were *ways*. . . .

"Now we come to the country department. Mr. and Mrs. Timothy Abernethie. Very nice place they've got, but sadly needing money spent on it. Very straitened they seem to be, very straitened. Taxation and unfortunate investments. Mr. Abernethie enjoys ill health and the emphasis is on the enjoyment. Complains a lot and has everyone running and fetching and carrying. Eats hearty meals, and seems quite strong physically if he likes to make the effort. There's no one in the house after the daily woman goes and no one's allowed into Mr. Abernethie's room unless he rings his bell. He was in a very bad temper the morning of the day after the funeral. Swore at Mrs. Jones. Ate only a little of his breakfast and said he wouldn't have any lunch—he'd had a bad night. He was in a worse temper still the next day and said the supper she had left out for him was unfit to eat and a good deal more. He was alone in the house and unseen by anybody from 9.30 that morning until the following morning."

"And Mrs. Abernethie?"

"She started off from Enderby by car at the time you mentioned. Arrived on foot at a small local garage in a place called Cathstone and explained her car had broken down a couple of miles away.

"A mechanic drove her out to it, made an investigation and said they'd have to tow it in and it would be a long job—couldn't promise to finish it that day. The lady was very put out, but went to a small Inn, arranged to stay the night, and asked for some sandwiches as she said she'd like to see something of the countryside—it's on the edge of the moorland country. She didn't come back to the Inn till quite late that evening. My informant said he didn't wonder. It's a sordid little place!"

"And the times?"

"She got the sandwiches at eleven. If she'd walked to the main road, a mile, she could have hitch-hiked into Wallcaster and caught a special South Coast express which stops at Reading West. I won't go into details of buses etcetera. It *could* just have been done if you could make the—er—attack fairly late in the afternoon."

"I understand the doctor stretched the time limit to possibly 4.30."

"Mind you," said Mr. Goby, "I shouldn't say it was likely. She seems to be a nice lady, liked by everybody. She's devoted to her husband, treats him like a child."

"Yes, yes, the maternal complex."

"She's strong and hefty, chops the wood and often hauls in great baskets of logs. Pretty good with the inside of a car, too."

"I was coming to that. What exactly *was* wrong with the car?"

"Do you want the exact details, M. Poirot?"

"Heaven forbid. I have no mechanical knowledge."

"It was a difficult thing to spot. And also to put right. And it *could* have been done maliciously by someone without very much trouble. By someone who was familiar with the insides of a car."

"*C'est magnifique!*" said Poirot with bitter enthusiasm. "All so convenient, all so possible. *Bon dieu*, can we eliminate *nobody?* And Mrs. Leo Abernethie?"

"She's a very nice lady, too. Mr. Abernethie deceased was very fond of her. She came there to stay about a fortnight before he died."

"After he had been to Lytchett St. Mary to see his sister?"

"No, just before. Her income is a good deal reduced since the war. She gave up her house in England and took a small flat in London. She has a villa in Cyprus and spends part of the year there. She has a young nephew whom she is helping to educate, and there seems to be one or two young artists whom she helps financially from time to time.''

''St. Helen of the blameless life,'' said Poirot shutting his eyes. ''And it was quite impossible for her to have left Enderby that day without the servants knowing? Say that that is so, I implore you!''

Mr. Goby brought his glance across to rest apologetically on Poirot's polished patent leather shoe, the nearest he had come to a direct encounter, and murmured:

''I'm afraid I can't say that, M. Poirot. Mrs. Abernethie went to London to fetch some extra clothes and belongings as she had agreed with Mr. Entwhistle to stay on and see to things.''

''Il ne manquait que ça!'' said Poirot with strong feeling.

13

WHEN THE CARD of Inspector Morton of the Berkshire County Police was brought to Hercule Poirot, his eyebrows went up.

''Show him in, Georges, show him in. And bring—what is it that the police prefer?''

''I would suggest beer, sir.''

''How horrible! But how British. Bring beer, then.''

Inspector Morton came straight to the point.

''I had to come to London,'' he said. ''And I got hold of your address, M. Poirot. I was interested to see you at the inquest on Thursday.''

''So you saw me there?''

''Yes. I was surprised—and, as I say, interested. You won't remember me but I remember you very well. In that Pangbourne Case.''

''Ah, you were connected with that?''

''Only in a very junior capacity. It's a long time ago but I've never forgotten you.''

''And you recognised me at once the other day?''

''That wasn't difficult, sir.'' Inspector Morton repressed a slight smile. ''Your appearance is—rather unusual.''

His gaze took in Poirot's sartorial perfection and rested finally on the curving moustaches.

''You stick out in a country place,'' he said.

"It is possible, it is possible," said Poirot with complacency.

"It interested me *why* you should be there. That sort of crime—robbery—assault—doesn't usually interest you."

"Was it the usual ordinary brutal type of crime?"

"That's what I've been wondering."

"You have wondered from the beginning, have you not?"

"Yes, M. Poirot. There were some unusual features. Since then we've worked along the routine lines. Pulled in one or two people for questioning, but everyone has been able to account quite satisfactorily for his time that afternoon. It wasn't what you'd call an 'ordinary' crime, M. Poirot—we're quite sure of that. The Chief Constable agrees. It was done by someone who wished to make it appear that way. It could have been the Gilchrist woman, but there doesn't seem to be any motive—and there wasn't any emotional background. Mrs. Lansquenet was perhaps a bit mental—or 'simple,' if you like to put it that way, but it was a household of mistress and dogsbody with no feverish feminine friendship about it. There are dozens of Miss Gilchrists about, and they're not usually the murdering type."

He paused.

"So it looks as though we'd have to look farther afield. I came to ask if you could help us at all. *Something* must have brought you down there, M. Poirot."

"Yes, yes, something did. An excellent Daimler car. But not only that."

"You had—information?"

"Hardly in your sense of the word. Nothing that could be used as evidence."

"But something that could be—a pointer?"

"Yes."

"You see, M. Poirot, there have been developments."

Meticulously, in detail, he told of the poisoned wedge of wedding cake.

Poirot took a deep hissing breath.

"Ingenious—yes, ingenious . . . I warned Mr. Entwhistle to look after Miss Gilchrist. An attack on her was always a possibility. But I must confess that I did *not* expect poison. I anticipated a repetition of the hatchet *motif*. I merely thought that it would be inadvisable for her to walk alone in unfrequented lanes after dark."

"But *why* did you anticipate an attack on her? I think, M. Poirot, you ought to tell me that."

Poirot nodded his head slowly.

"Yes, I will tell you. Mr. Entwhistle will not tell you, because he is a lawyer and lawyers do not like to speak of suppositions, of inferences made from the character of a dead woman, or from a few irresponsible words. But he will not be adverse to *my* telling you—no, he will be relieved. He does not wish to appear foolish or fanciful, but he wants you to know what may—only *may*—be the facts."

Poirot paused as George entered with a tall glass of beer.

"Some refreshment, Inspector. No, no, I insist."

"Won't you join me?"

"I do not drink the beer. But I will myself have a glass of *sirop de cassis*—the English they do not care for it, I have noticed."

Inspector Morton looked gratefully at his beer.

Poirot, sipping delicately from his glass of dark purple fluid, said:

"It begins, all this, at a funeral. Or rather, to be exact, *after* the funeral."

Graphically, with many gestures, he set forth the story as Mr. Entwhistle had told it to him, but with such embellishments as his exuberant nature suggested. One almost felt that Hercule Poirot had himself been an eye-witness of the scene.

Inspector Morton had an excellent clear cut brain. He seized at once on what were, for his purposes, the salient points.

"This Mr. Abernethie may have been poisoned?"

"It is a possibility."

"And the body has been cremated and there is no evidence?"

"Exactly."

Inspector Morton ruminated.

"Interesting. There's nothing in it for *us*. Nothing, that is, to make Richard Abernethie's death worth investigating. It would be waste of time."

"Yes."

"But there are the *people*—the people who were there—the people who heard Cora Lansquenet say what she did, and one of whom *may* have thought that she might say it again and with more detail."

"As she undoubtedly would have. There are, Inspector, as you say, *the people*. And now you see why I was at the inquest, why I interest myself in the case—because it is, always, *people* in whom I interest myself."

"Then the attack on Miss Gilchrist—"

"Was always indicated. Richard Abernethie had been down to the cottage. He had talked to Cora. He had, perhaps, actually mentioned a *name*. The only person who might possibly have known or overheard something was Miss Gilchrist. After Cora is silenced, the murderer might continue to be anxious. Does the other woman know something—anything? Of course, if the murderer is wise he will let well alone, but murderers, Inspector, are seldom wise. Fortunately for us. They brood, they feel uncertain, they desire to make sure—quite sure. They are pleased with their own cleverness. And so, in the end, they protrude their necks as you say."

Inspector Morton smiled faintly.

Poirot went on:

"This attempt to silence Miss Gilchrist, already it is a mistake. For now there are *two* occasions about which you make enquiry. There is the handwriting on the wedding label also. It is a pity the wrapping paper was burnt."

"Yes, I could have been certain, then, whether it came by post or whether it didn't."

"You have reason for thinking the latter, you say?"

"It's only what the postman thinks—he's not sure. If the parcel had gone through a village post office, it's ten to one the postmistress would have noticed it, but nowadays the mail is delivered by van from Market Keynes and of course the young chap does quite a round and delivers a lot of things. He thinks it was letters only and no parcel at the cottage—but he isn't sure. As a matter of fact he's having a bit of girl trouble and he can't think about anything else. I've tested his memory and he isn't reliable in any way. If he *did* deliver it, it seems to me odd that the parcel shouldn't have been noticed until after this Mr.—whatshisname—Guthrie—"

"Ah, Mr. Guthrie."

Inspector Morton smiled.

"Yes, M. Poirot. We're checking up on him. After all, it would be easy, wouldn't it, to come along with a plausible tale of having been a friend of Mrs. Lansquenet's. Mrs. Banks wasn't to know if he was or he wasn't. He could have dropped that little parcel, you know. It's easy to make a thing look as though it's been through the post. Lamp black a little smudged, makes quite a good postmark cancellation mark over a stamp."

He paused and then added:

"And there are other possibilities."

Poirot nodded.

"You think—?"

"Mr. George Crossfield was down in that part of the world—but not until the next day. Meant to attend the funeral, but had a little engine trouble on the way. Know anything about him, M. Poirot?"

"A little. But not as much as I would like to know."

"Like that, is it? Quite a little bunch interested in the late Mr. Abernethie's will, I understand. I hope it doesn't mean going after all of them."

"I have accumulated a little information. It is at your disposal. Naturally

I have no authority to ask these people questions. In fact it would not be wise for me to do so.''

''I shall go slowly myself. You don't want to fluster your bird too soon. But when you do fluster it, you want to fluster it well.''

''A very sound technique. For you then, my friend, the routine—with all the machinery you have at your disposal. It is slow—but sure. For myself—''

''Yes, M. Poirot?''

''For myself, I go North. As I have told you, it is *people* in whom I interest myself. Yes—a little preparatory *camouflage*—and I go North.

''I intend,'' added Hercule Poirot, ''to purchase a country mansion for foreign refugees. I represent U.N.A.R.C.O.''

''And what's U.N.A.R.C.O.?''

''United Nations Aid for Refugee Centres Old Age. It sounds well, do you not think?''

Inspector Morton grinned.

14

HERCULE POIROT said to a grim-faced Janet:

''Thank you very much. You have been most kind.''

Janet, her lips still fixed in a sour line, left the room. These foreigners! The questions they asked. Their impertinence! All very well to say that he was a specialist interested in unsuspected heart conditions such as Mr. Abernethie must have suffered from. That was very likely true—gone very sudden the master had, and the doctor had been surprised. But what business was it of some foreign doctor coming along and nosing in?

All very well for Mrs. Leo to say: ''Please answer Monsieur Pontarlier's questions. He has a good reason for asking.''

Questions. Always questions. Sheets of them sometimes to fill in as best you could—and what did the Government or anyone else want to know about your private affairs for? Asking your age at that census—downright impertinent and she hadn't told them, either! Cut off five years she had. Why not? If she only felt fifty four, she'd *call* herself fifty four!

At any rate Monsieur Pontarlier hadn't wanted to know her age. He'd had *some* decency. Just questions about the medicines the master had taken, and where they were kept, and if, perhaps, he might have taken too much of them if he was feeling not quite the thing—or if he'd been forgetful. As though she could remember all that rubbish—the master knew what he was doing! And asking if any of the medicines he took were still in the house. Naturally they'd all been thrown away. Heart condition —and some long word he'd used. Always thinking of something new they were, these doctors. Look at them telling old Rogers he had a disc or some such in his spine. Plain lumbago, that was all that was the matter with him. Her father had been a gardener and *he*'d suffered from lumbago. Doctors!

The self-appointed medical man sighed and went downstairs in search of Lanscombe. He had not got very much out of Janet but he had hardly expected to do so. All he had really wanted to do was to check such information as could unwillingly be extracted from her with that given him by Helen Abernethie and which had been obtained from the same source—but with much less difficulty, since Janet was ready to admit that Mrs. Leo had a perfect right to ask such questions and indeed Janet herself had enjoyed dwelling at length on the last few weeks of her master's life. Illness and death were congenial subjects to her.

Yes, Poirot thought, he could have relied on the information that Helen had got for him. He had done so really. But by nature and long habit he trusted nobody until he himself had tried and proved them.

In any case the evidence was slight and unsatisfactory. It boiled down to the fact that Richard Abernethie had been prescribed vitamin oil capsules. That these had been in a large bottle which had been nearly finished at the time of his death. Anybody who had wanted to, could have operated on one or more of those capsules with a hypodermic syringe and could have rearranged the bottle so that the fatal dose would only be taken some weeks after that somebody had left the house. Or someone might have slipped into the house on the day before Richard Abernethie died and have doctored a capsule then—or, which was more likely—have substituted something else for a sleeping tablet in the little bottle that stood beside the bed. Or again might have quite simply tampered with the food or drink.

Hercule Poirot had made his own experiments. The front door was kept locked, but there was a side door giving on the garden which was not locked until evening. At about quarter past one, when the gardeners had gone to lunch and when the household was in the dining room, Poirot had entered the grounds, come to the side door, and mounted the stairs to Richard Abernethie's bedroom without meeting anybody. As a variant he had pushed through a baize door and slipped into the larder. He had heard voices from the kitchen at the end of the passage but no one had seen him.

Yes, it could have been done. But had it been done? There was nothing to indicate that that was so. Not that Poirot was really looking for evidence—he wanted only to satisfy himself as to possibilities. The murder of Richard Abernethie could only be a hypothesis. It was Cora Lansquenet's murder for which evidence was needed. What he wanted was to study the people who had been assembled for the funeral that day, and to form his own conclusions about them. He already had his plan, but first he wanted a few more words with old Lanscombe.

Lanscombe was courteous but distant. Less resentful than Janet, he nevertheless regarded this upstart foreigner as the materialization of the Writing on the Wall. This was What We are Coming to!

He put down the leather with which he was lovingly polishing the Georgian teapot and straightened his back.

"Yes, sir?" he said politely.

Poirot sat down gingerly on a pantry stool.

"Mrs. Abernethie tells me that you hoped to reside in the lodge by the North gate when you retired from service here?"

"That is so, sir. Naturally all that is changed now. When the property is sold—"

Poirot interrupted deftly:

"It might still be possible. There are cottages for the gardeners. The lodge is not needed for the guests or their attendants. It might be possible to make an arrangement of some kind."

"Well, thank you, sir, for the suggestion. But I hardly think—The majority of the—guests would be foreigners, I presume?"

"Yes, they will be foreigners. Amongst those who fled from Europe to this country are several who are old and infirm. There can be no future for them if they return to their own countries, for these persons, you understand, are those whose relatives there have perished. They cannot earn their living here as an able-bodied man or woman can do. Funds have been raised and are being administered by the organisation which I represent to endow various country homes for them. This place is, I think, eminently suitable. The matter is practically settled."

Lanscombe sighed.

"You'll understand, sir, that it's sad for me to think that this won't be a private dwelling house any longer. But I know how things are nowadays. None of the family could afford to live here—and I don't think the young ladies and gentlemen would even want to do so. Domestic help is too difficult to obtain these days, and even if obtained is expensive and unsatisfactory. I quite realise that these fine mansions have served their turn." Lanscombe sighed again. "If it has to be an—an institution of some kind, I'll be glad to think that it's the kind you're mentioning. We were Spared in This Country, sir, owing to our Navy and Air Force and our brave young men and being fortunate enough to be an island. If Hitler had landed here we'd all have turned out and given him short shrift. My sight isn't good enough for shooting, but I could have used a pitchfork, sir, and I intended to do so if necessary. We've always welcomed the unfortunate in this country, sir, it's been our pride. We shall continue so to do."

"Thank you, Lanscombe," said Poirot gently. "Your master's death must have been a great blow to you."

"It was, sir. I'd been with the master since he was quite a young man. I've been very fortunate in my life, sir. No one could have had a better master."

"I have been conversing with my friend and—er—colleague, Dr. Larraby. We were wondering if your master could have had any extra worry—any unpleasant interview—on the day before he died? You do not remember if any visitors came to the house that day?"

"I think not, sir. I do not recall any."

"No one called at all just about that time?"

"The vicar was here to tea the day before. Otherwise—some nuns called for a subscription—and a young man came to the back door and wanted to sell Marjorie some brushes and saucepan cleaners. Very persistent he was. Nobody else."

A worried expression had appeared on Lanscombe's face. Poirot did not press him further. Lanscombe had already unburdened himself to Mr. Entwhistle. He would be far less forthcoming with Hercule Poirot.

With Marjorie, on the other hand, Poirot had had instant success. Marjorie had none of the conventions of "good service." Marjorie was a first class cook and the way to her heart lay through her cooking. Poirot had visited her in the kitchen, praised certain dishes with discernment, and Marjorie, realising that here was someone who knew what he was talking about, hailed him immediately as a fellow spirit. He had no difficulty in finding out exactly what had been served the night before Richard Abernethie had died. Marjorie, indeed, was inclined to view the matter as "It was the night I made that chocolate soufflé that Mr. Abernethie died. Six eggs I'd saved up for it. The dairyman he's a friend of mine. Got hold of some cream too. Better not ask how. Enjoyed it, Mr. Abernethie did." The rest of the meal was likewise detailed. What had come out from the dining room had been finished in the kitchen. Ready as Marjorie was to talk, Poirot had learned nothing of value from her.

He went now to fetch his overcoat and a couple of scarves, and thus padded against the North Country air he went out on the terrace and joined Helen Abernethie who was clipping some late roses.

"Have you found out anything fresh?" she asked.

"Nothing. But I hardly expected to do so."

"I know. Ever since Mr. Entwhistle told me you were coming, I've been ferreting round, but there's really been nothing."

She paused and said hopefully:

"Perhaps it *is* all a mare's nest?"

"To be attacked with a hatchet?"

"I wasn't thinking of Cora."

"But it is of Cora that I think. Why was it necessary for someone to kill her? Mr. Entwhistle has told me that on that day, at the moment that she came out suddenly with her *gaffe*, you yourself felt that something was wrong. That is so?"

"Well—yes, but I don't know—"

Poirot swept on.

"How 'wrong'? Unexpected? Surprising? Or—what shall we say—uneasy? Sinister?"

"Oh no, not sinister. Just something that wasn't—oh, I don't know. I can't remember and it wasn't important."

"But why cannot you remember—because something else put it out of your head—something more important?"

"Yes—yes—I think you're right there. It was the mention of murder, I suppose. That swept away everything else."

"It was, perhaps, the reaction of some particular person to the word 'murder'?"

"Perhaps . . . But I don't remember looking at anyone in particular. We were all staring at Cora."

"It may have been something you heard—something dropped perhaps . . . or broken . . ."

Helen frowned in an effort of remembrance.

"No . . . I don't think so. . . ."

"Ah well, someday it will come back. And it may be of no consequence. Now tell me, Madame, of those here, who knew Cora best?"

Helen considered.

"Lanscombe, I suppose. He remembers her from a child. The housemaid, Janet, only came after she had married and gone away."

"And next to Lanscombe?"

Helen said thoughtfully: "I suppose—*I* did. Maude hardly knew her at all."

"Then, taking you as the person who knew her best, why do you think she asked that question as she did?"

Helen smiled.

"It was very characteristic of Cora!"

"What I mean is, was it a *bêtise* pure and simple? Did she just blurt out what was in her mind without thinking? Or was she being malicious—amusing herself by upsetting everyone?"

Helen reflected.

"One can't ever be quite sure about a person, can you? I never have known whether Cora was just ingenuous—or whether she counted, childishly, on making an effect. That's what you mean, isn't it?"

"Yes. I was thinking: Suppose this Mrs. Cora says to herself, 'What fun it would be to ask if Richard was murdered and see how they all look!' That would be like her, yes?"

Helen looked doubtful.

"It might be. She certainly had an impish sense of humour as a child. But what difference does it make?"

"It would underline the point that it is unwise to make jokes about murder," said Poirot drily.

Helen shivered.

"Poor Cora."

Poirot changed the subject.

"Mrs. Timothy Abernethie stayed the night after the funeral?"

"Yes."

"Did she talk to you at all about what Cora had said?"

"Yes, she said it was outrageous and just like Cora!"

"She didn't take it seriously?"

"Oh no. No, I'm sure she didn't. . . ."

The second "no," Poirot thought, had sounded suddenly doubtful. But was not that almost always the case when you went back over something in your mind?

"And you, Madame, did you take it seriously?"

Helen Abernethie, her eyes looking very blue and strangely young under the sideways sweep of crisp grey hair, said thoughtfully:

"Yes, M. Poirot, I think I did."

"Because of your feeling that something was wrong?"

"Perhaps."

He waited—but as she said nothing more, he went on:

"There had been an estrangement, lasting many years, between Mrs. Lansquenet and her family?"

"Yes. None of us liked her husband and she was offended about it, and so the estrangement grew."

"And then, suddenly, your brother-in-law went to see her. Why?"

"I don't know—I suppose he knew, or guessed, that he hadn't very long to live and wanted to be reconciled—but I really don't know."

"He didn't tell you?"

"Tell *me?*"

"Yes. You were here, staying with him, just before he went there. He didn't even mention his intention to you?"

He thought a slight reserve came into her manner.

"He told me that he was going to see his brother Timothy—which he did. He never mentioned Cora at all. Shall we go in? It must be nearly lunchtime."

She walked beside him carrying the flowers she had picked. As they went in by the side door, Poirot said:

"You are sure, quite sure, that during your visit, Mr. Abernethie said nothing to you about any member of the family which might be relevant?"

A faint resentment in her manner, Helen said:

"You are speaking like a policeman."

"I *was* a policeman—once. I have no status—no right to question you. But you want the truth—or so I have been led to believe?"

They entered the green drawing room. Helen said with a sigh:

"Richard was disappointed in the younger generation. Old men usually are. He disparaged them in various ways—but there was nothing—*nothing*, do you understand—that could possibly suggest a motive for murder."

"Ah," said Poirot. She reached for a Chinese bowl and began to arrange the roses in it. When they were disposed to her satisfaction she looked round for a place to put it.

"You arrange flowers admirably, Madame," said Hercule. "I think that anything you undertook you would manage to do with perfection."

"Thank you. I am fond of flowers. I think this would look well on that green malachite table."

There was a bouquet of wax flowers under a glass shade on the malachite table. As she lifted it off, Poirot said casually:

"Did anyone tell Mr. Abernethie that his niece Susan's husband had come near to poisoning a customer when making up a prescription? Ah, *pardon!*"

He sprang forward.

The Victorian ornament had slipped from Helen's fingers. Poirot's spring forward was not quick enough. It dropped on the floor and the glass shade broke. Helen gave an expression of annoyance.

"How careless of me. However, the flowers are not damaged. I can get a new glass shade made for it. I'll put it away in the big cupboard under the stairs."

It was not until Poirot had helped her to lift it onto a shelf in the dark cupboard and had followed her back to the drawing room that he said:

"It was my fault. I should not have startled you."

"What was it that you asked me? I have forgotten."

"Oh, there is no need to repeat my question. Indeed—I have forgotten what it was."

Helen came up to him. She laid her hand on his arm.

"M. Poirot, is there anyone whose life would really bear close investigation? *Must* people's lives be dragged into this when they have nothing to do with—with—"

"With the death of Cora Lansquenet? Yes. Because one has to examine *everything*. Oh! it is true enough—it is an old maxim—*everyone has something to hide*. It is true of all of us—it is perhaps true of you, too, Madame. But I say to you, nothing can be ignored. That is why your friend, Mr. Entwhistle, he has come to me. For I am not the police. I am discreet and what I learn does not concern me. But I have to *know*. And since in this matter is not so much *evidence* as *people*—then it is *people* with whom I occupy myself. I need, Madame, to meet everyone who was here on the day of the funeral. And it would be a great convenience—yes, and it would be strategically satisfactory—if I could meet them *here*."

"I'm afraid," Helen said slowly, "that that would be too difficult—"

"Not so difficult as you think. Already I have devised a means. The house, it is sold. So Mr. Entwhistle will declare. (*Entendu*, sometimes these things fall through!) He will invite the various members of the family to assemble here and to choose what they will from the furnishings before it is all put up to auction. A suitable weekend can be selected for that purpose."

He paused and then said:

"You see, it is easy, is it not?"

Helen looked at him. The blue eyes were cold—almost frosty.

"Are you laying a trap for someone, M. Poirot?"

"Alas! I wish I knew enough. No, I have still the open mind.

"There may," Hercule Poirot added thoughtfully, "be certain tests . . ."

"Tests? What kind of tests?"

"I have not yet formulated them to myself. And in any case, Madame, it would be better that you should not know them."

"So that I can be tested too?"

"You, Madame, have been taken behind the scenes. Now there is one thing that is doubtful. The young people will, I think, come readily. But it may be difficult, may it not, to secure the presence here of Mr. Timothy Abernethie. I hear that he never leaves home."

Helen smiled suddenly.

"I believe you may be lucky there, M. Poirot. I heard from Maude yesterday. The workmen are in painting the house and Timothy is suffering terribly from the smell of the paint. He says that it is seriously affecting his health. I think that he and Maude would both be pleased to come here—perhaps for a week or two. Maude is still not able to get about very well—you know she broke her ankle?"

"I had not heard. How unfortunate."

"Luckily they have got Cora's companion, Miss Gilchrist. It seems that she has turned out a perfect treasure."

"What is that?" Poirot turned sharply on Helen. "Did *they* ask for Miss Gilchrist to go to them? Who suggested it?"

"I think Susan fixed it up. Susan Banks."

"Aha," said Poirot in a curious voice. "So it was the little Susan who suggested it. She is fond of making the arrangements."

"Susan struck me as being a very competent girl."

"Yes. She is competent. Did you hear that Miss Gilchrist had a narrow escape from death with a piece of poisoned wedding cake?"

"No!" Helen looked startled. "I do remember now that Maude said over the telephone that Miss Gilchrist had just come out of hospital but I'd no idea why she had been in hospital. Poisoned? But, M. Poirot—*why?*"

"Do you really ask that?"

Helen said with sudden vehemence:

"Oh! get them all here! Find out the truth! There mustn't be any more murders."

"So you will co-operate?"

"Yes—I will co-operate."

15

"THAT LINOLEUM does look nice, Mrs. Jones. What a hand you have with lino. The teapot's on the kitchen table, so go and help yourself. I'll be there as soon as I've taken up Mr. Abernethie's elevenses."

Miss Gilchrist trotted up the staircase, carrying a daintily set out tray. She tapped on Timothy's door, interpreted a growl from within as an invitation to enter, and tripped briskly in.

"Morning coffee and biscuits, Mr. Abernethie. I do hope you're feeling brighter today. Such a lovely day."

Timothy grunted and said suspiciously:

"Is there skim on that milk?"

"Oh no, Mr. Abernethie. I took it off very carefully, and anyway I've brought up the little strainer in case it should form again. Some people like it, you know, they say it's the *cream*—and so it is really."

"Idiots!" said Timothy. "What kind of biscuits are those?"

"They're those nice digestive biscuits."

"Digestive tripe. Ginger nuts are the only biscuits worth eating."

"I'm afraid the grocer hadn't got any this week. But these are really *very* nice. You try them and see."

"I know what they're like, thank you. Leave those curtains alone, can't you?"

"I thought you might like a little sunshine. It's such a nice sunny day."

"I want the room kept dark. My head's terrible. It's this paint. I've always been sensitive to paint. It's poisoning me."

Miss Gilchrist sniffed experimentally and said brightly:

"One really can't smell it much in here. The workmen are over on the other side."

"You're not sensitive like I am. Must I have *all* the books I'm reading taken out of my reach?"

"I'm so sorry, Mr. Abernethie, I didn't know you were reading all of them."

"Where's my wife? I haven't seen her for over an hour."

"Mrs. Abernethie's resting on the sofa."

"Tell her to come and rest up here."

"I'll tell her, Mr. Abernethie. But she may have dropped off to sleep. Shall we say in about a quarter of an hour?"

"No, tell her I want her now. Don't monkey about with that rug. It's arranged the way I like it."

"I'm so sorry. I thought it was slipping off the far side."

"I like it slipping off. Go and get Maude. I want her."

Miss Gilchrist departed downstairs and tiptoed into the drawing room where Maude Abernethie was sitting with her leg up reading a novel.

"I'm so sorry, Mrs. Abernethie," she said apologetically. "Mr. Abernethie is asking for you."

Maude thrust aside her novel with a guilty expression.

"Oh dear," she said, "I'll go up at once."

She reached for her stick.

Timothy burst out as soon as his wife entered the room:

"So there you are at last!"

"I'm so sorry, dear, I didn't know you wanted me."

"That woman you've got into the house will drive me mad. Twittering and fluttering round like a demented hen. Real typical old maid, that's what she is."

"I'm sorry she annoys you. She tries to be kind, that's all."

"I don't want anybody kind. I don't want a blasted old maid always chirruping over me. She's so damned arch, too—"

"Just a little, perhaps."

"Treats me as though I was a confounded kid! It's maddening."

"I'm sure it must be. But please, *please*, Timothy, do try not to be rude to her. I'm really very helpless still—and you yourself say she cooks well."

"Her cooking's all right," Mr. Abernethie admitted grudgingly. "Yes, she's a decent enough cook. But keep her in the kitchen, that's all I ask. Don't let her come fussing round me."

"No, dear, of course not. How are you feeling?"

"Not at all well. I think you'd better send for Barton to come and have a look at me. This paint affects my heart. Feel my pulse—the irregular way it's beating."

Maude felt it without comment.

"Timothy, shall we go to a hotel until the house painting is finished?"

"It would be a great waste of money."

"Does that matter so much—now?"

"You're just like all women—hopelessly extravagant! Just because we've come into a ridiculously small part of my brother's estate, you think we can go and live indefinitely at the Ritz."

"I didn't quite say that, dear."

"I can tell you that the difference Richard's money will make will be hardly appreciable. This bloodsucking Government will see to that. You mark my words, the whole lot will go in taxation."

Mrs. Abernethie shook her head sadly.

"This coffee's cold," said the invalid, looking with distaste at the cup which he had not as yet tasted. "Why can't I ever get a cup of really hot coffee?"

"I'll take it down and warm it up."

In the kitchen Miss Gilchrist was drinking tea and conversing affably, though with slight condescension, with Mrs. Jones.

"I'm so anxious to spare Mrs. Abernethie all I can," she said. "All this running up and down stairs is so painful for her."

"Waits on him hand and foot, she does," said Mrs. Jones stirring the sugar in her cup.

"It's very sad his being such an invalid."

"Not such an invalid either," Mrs. Jones said darkly. "Suits him very well to lie up and ring bells and have trays brought up and down. But he's well able to get up and go about. Even seen him out in the village, I have, when *she*'s been away. Walking as hearty as you please. Anything he *really* needs—like his tobacco or a stamp—he can come and get. And that's why when *she* was off at that funeral and got held up on the way back, and *he* told me I'd got to come in and stay the night again, I refused. 'I'm sorry, sir,' I said, 'but I've got my husband to think of. Going out to oblige in the mornings is all very well, but I've got to be there to see to him when he comes back from work.' Nor I wouldn't budge, I wouldn't. Do him good, I thought, to get about the house and look after himself for once. Might make him see what a lot he gets done for him. So I stood firm, I did. He didn't half create."

Mrs. Jones drew a deep breath and took a long satisfying drink of sweet inky tea.

"Ar," she said.

Though deeply suspicious of Miss Gilchrist, and considering her as a finicky thing, and a "regular fussy old maid" Mrs. Jones approved of the lavish way in which Miss Gilchrist dispensed her employer's tea and sugar ration.

She set down the cup and said affably:

"I'll give the kitchen floor a nice scrub down and then I'll be getting along. The potatoes is all ready peeled, dear, you'll find them by the sink."

Though slightly affronted by the "dear," Miss Gilchrist was appreciative of the good will which had divested an enormous quantity of potatoes of their outer coverings.

Before she could say anything the telephone rang and she hurried out in the hall to answer it. The telephone, in the style of fifty odd years ago, was situated inconveniently in a draughty passage behind the staircase.

Maude Abernethie appeared at the top of the stairs, while Miss Gilchrist was still speaking. The latter looked up and said:

"It's Mrs.—Leo—is it?—Abernethie speaking."

"Tell her I'm just coming."

Maude descended the stairs slowly and painfully.

Miss Gilchrist murmured, "I'm so sorry you've had to come down again, Mrs. Abernethie. Has Mr. Abernethie finished his elevenses? I'll just nip up and get the tray."

She trotted up the stairs as Mrs. Abernethie said into the receiver:

"Helen? This is Maude here."

The invalid received Miss Gilchrist with a baleful glare. As she picked up the tray he asked fretfully:

"Who's that on the telephone?"

"Mrs. Leo Abernethie."

"Oh? Suppose they'll go gossiping for about an hour. Women have no sense of time when they get on the phone. Never think of the money they're wasting."

Miss Gilchrist said brightly that it would be Mrs. Leo who had to pay, and Timothy grunted.

"Just pull that curtain aside, will you? No, not that one, the *other* one. I don't want the light slap in my eyes. That's better. No reason because I'm an invalid that I should have to sit in the dark all day."

He went on:

"And you might look in that book case over there for a green—What's the matter now? What are you rushing off for?"

"It's the front door, Mr. Abernethie."

"*I* didn't hear anything. You've got that woman downstairs, haven't you? Let her go and answer it."

"Yes, Mr. Abernethie. What was the book you wanted me to find?"

The invalid closed his eyes.

"I can't remember now. You've put it out of my head. You'd better go."

Miss Gilchrist seized the tray and hurriedly departed. Putting the tray on the pantry table she hurried into the front hall, passing Mrs. Abernethie who was still at the telephone.

She returned in a moment to ask in a muted voice:

"I'm so sorry to interrupt. It's a nun. Collecting. The Heart of Mary Fund, I think she said. She has a book. Half a crown or five shillings most people seem to have given."

Maude Abernethie said:

"Just a moment, Helen," into the telephone, and to Miss Gilchrist, "We have our own Church charities."

Miss Gilchrist hurried away again.

Maude terminated her conversation after a few minutes with the phrase, "I'll talk to Timothy about it."

She replaced the receiver and came into the front hall. Miss Gilchrist was standing quite still by the drawing room door. She was frowning in a puzzled way and jumped when Maude Abernethie spoke to her.

"There's nothing the matter, is there, Miss Gilchrist?"

"Oh no, Mrs. Abernethie, I'm afraid I was just wool gathering. So stupid of me when there's so much to be done."

Miss Gilchrist resumed her imitation of a busy ant and Maude Abernethie climbed the stairs slowly and painfully to her husband's room.

''That was Helen on the telephone. It seems that the place is definitely sold—some Institution for Foreign Refugees—''

She paused whilst Timothy expressed himself forcefully on the subject of Foreign Refugees, with side issues as to the house in which he had been born and brought up. ''No decent standards left in this country. My old home! I can hardly bear to think of it.''

Maude went on.

''Helen quite appreciates what you—we—will feel about it. She suggests that we might like to come there for a visit before it goes. She was very distressed about your health and the way the painting is affecting it. She thought you might prefer coming to Enderby to going to a hotel. The servants are there still, so you could be looked after comfortably.''

Timothy, whose mouth had been open in outraged protests half way through this, had closed it again. His eyes had become suddenly shrewd. He now nodded his head approvingly.

''Thoughtful of Helen,'' he said. ''Very thoughtful. I don't know, I'm sure, I'll have to think it over. . . . There's no doubt that this paint is poisoning me—there's arsenic in paint, I believe. I seem to have heard something of the kind. On the other hand the exertion of moving might be too much for me. It's difficult to know what would be the best.''

''Perhaps you'd prefer a hotel, dear,'' said Maude. ''A good hotel is very expensive, but where your health is concerned—''

Timothy interrupted.

''I wish I could make you understand, Maude, that we *are not millionaires*. Why go to a hotel when Helen has very kindly suggested that we should go to Enderby? Not that it's really for her to suggest! The house isn't hers. I don't understand legal subtleties, but I presume it belongs to us equally until it's sold and the proceeds divided. Foreign Refugees! It would have made old Cornelius turn in his grave. Yes,'' he sighed, ''I should like to see the old place again before I die.''

Maude played her last card adroitly.

''I understand that Mr. Entwhistle has suggested that the members of the family might like to choose certain pieces of furniture or china or something—before the contents are put up for auction.''

Timothy heaved himself briskly upright.

''We must certainly go. There must be a very exact valuation of what is chosen by each person. Those men the girls have married—I wouldn't trust either of them from what I've heard. There might be some sharp practice. Helen is far too amiable. As the head of the family, it is my duty to be present!''

He got up and walked up and down the room with a brisk vigorous tread.

"Yes, it is an excellent plan. Write to Helen and accept. What I am really thinking about is you, my dear. It will be a nice rest and change for you. You have been doing far too much lately. The decorators can get on with the painting while we are away and that Gillespie woman can stay here and look after the house."

"Gilchrist," said Maude.

Timothy waved a hand and said that it was all the same.

II

"I can't do it," said Miss Gilchrist.

Maude looked at her in surprise.

Miss Gilchrist was trembling. Her eyes looked pleadingly into Maude's.

"It's stupid of me, I know . . . But I simply can't. Not stay here all alone in the house. If there was anyone who could come and—and sleep here, too?"

She looked hopefully at the other woman, but Maude shook her head. Maude Abernethie knew only too well how difficult it was to get anyone in the neighbourhood to "live in."

Miss Gilchrist went on, a kind of desperation in her voice.

"I know you'll think it nervy and foolish—and I wouldn't have dreamed once that I'd ever feel like this. I've never been a nervous woman—or fanciful. But now it all seems different. I'd be terrified—yes, literally terrified—to be all alone here."

"Of course," said Maude. "It's stupid of me. After what happened at Lytchett St. Mary."

"I suppose that's it. . . . It's not logical, I know. And I didn't feel it at first. I didn't mind being alone in the cottage after—after it had happened. The feeling's grown up gradually. You'll have no opinion of me at all, Mrs. Abernethie, but even since I've been here I've been feeling it—*frightened*, you know. Not of anything in particular—but just *frightened* . . . It's so silly and I really am ashamed. It's just as though all the time I was expecting something awful to happen. . . . Even that nun coming to the door startled me. Oh dear, I *am* in a bad way. . . ."

"I suppose it's what they call delayed shock," said Maude vaguely.

"Is it? I don't know. Oh dear, I'm so sorry to appear so—so ungrateful, and after all your kindness. What you will think—"

Maude soothed her.

"We must think of some other arrangement," she said.

16

GEORGE CROSSFIELD paused irresolutely for a moment as he watched a particular feminine back disappear through a doorway. Then he nodded to himself and went in pursuit.

The doorway in question was that of a double fronted shop—a shop that had gone out of business. The plate glass windows showed a disconcerting emptiness within. The door was closed, but George rapped on it. A vacuous faced young man with spectacles opened it and stared at George.

"Excuse me," said George. "But I think my cousin just came in here."

The young man drew back and George walked in.

"Hullo, Susan," he said.

Susan, who was standing on a packing case and using a foot-rule, turned her head in some surprise.

"Hullo, George. Where did you spring from?"

"I saw your back. I was sure it was yours."

"How clever of you. I suppose backs are distinctive."

"Much more so than faces. Add a beard and pads in your cheeks and do a few things to your hair and nobody will know you when you come face to face with them—but beware of the moment when you walk away."

"I'll remember. Can you remember seven feet fifteen inches until I've got time to write it down?"

"Certainly. What is this, book shelves?"

"No, cubicle space. Eight feet nineteen—and three twelve . . ."

The young man with the spectacles, who had been fidgeting from one foot to the other, coughed apologetically.

"Excuse me, Mrs. Banks, but if you want to be here for some time—"

"I do, rather," said Susan. "If you leave the keys, I'll lock the door and return them to the office when I go past. Will that be all right?"

"Yes, thank you. If it weren't that we're short staffed this morning—"

Susan accepted the apologetic intent of the half finished sentence and the young man removed himself to the outer world of the street.

"I'm glad we've got rid of him," said Susan. "House agents are a bother. They will keep talking just when I want to do sums."

"Ah," said George. "Murder in an empty shop. How exciting it would be for the passers by to see the dead body of a beautiful young woman displayed behind plate glass. How they would goggle. Like goldfish."

"There wouldn't be any reason for you to murder me, George."

"Well, I should get a fourth part of your share of our esteemed uncle's estate. If one were sufficiently fond of money that should be a reason."

Susan stopped taking measurements and turned to look at him. Her eyes opened a little.

"You look a different person, George. It's really—extraordinary."

"Different? How different?"

"Like an advertisement. *This is the same man that you saw overleaf, but now he has taken Uppington's Health Salts.*"

She sat down on another packing case and lit a cigarette.

"You must have wanted your share of old Richard's money pretty badly, George?"

"Nobody could honestly say that money isn't welcome these days."

George's tone was light.

Susan said: "You were in a jam, weren't you?"

"Hardly your business, is it, Susan?"

"I was just interested."

"Are you renting this shop as a place of business?"

"I'm buying the whole house."

"With possession?"

"Yes. The two upper floors were flats. One's empty and went with the shop. The other I'm buying the people out."

"Nice to have money, isn't it, Susan?"

There was a malicious tone in George's voice. But Susan merely took a deep breath and said:

"As far as I'm concerned, it's wonderful. An answer to prayer."

"Does prayer kill off elderly relatives?"

Susan paid no attention.

"This place is exactly *right*. To begin with it's a very good piece of period architecture. I can make the living part upstairs something quite unique. There are two lovely moulded ceilings and the rooms are a beautiful shape. This part down here which has already been hacked about I shall have completely modern."

"What is this? A dress business?"

"No. Beauty culture. Herbal preparations. Face creams!"

"The full racket?"

"The racket as before. It pays. It always pays. What you need to put it over is personality. I can do it."

George looked at his cousin appreciatively. He admired the slanting planes of her face, the generous mouth, the radiant colouring. Altogether an unusual and vivid face. And he recognised in Susan that odd, indefinable quality, the quality of success.

"Yes," he said, "I think you've got what it takes, Susan. You'll get back your outlay on this scheme and you'll get places with it."

"It's the right neighbourhood, just off a main shopping street *and* you can park a car right in front of the door."

Again George nodded.

"Yes, Susan, you're going to succeed. Have you had this in mind for a long time?"

"Over a year."

"Why didn't you put it up to old Richard? He might have staked you."

"I did put it up to him."

"And he didn't see his way? I wonder why. I should have thought he'd have recognised the same mettle that he himself was made of."

Susan did not answer, and into George's mind there leapt a swift bird's eye view of another figure. A thin nervous suspicious eyed young man.

"Where does—what's his name—Greg—come in on all this?" he asked. "He'll give up dishing out pills and powders, I take it?"

"Of course. There will be a laboratory built out at the back. We shall have our own formulas for face creams and beauty preparations."

George suppressed a grin. He wanted to say: "So baby is to have his play pen," but he did not say it. As a cousin he did not mind being spiteful, but he had an uneasy sense that Susan's feeling for her husband was a thing to be treated with care. It had all the qualities of a dangerous explosive. He wondered, as he had wondered on the day of the funeral, about that queer fish, Gregory. Something odd about the fellow. So nondescript in appearance—and yet, in some way, not nondescript . . .

He looked again at Susan, calmly and radiantly triumphant.

"You've got the true Abernethie touch," he said. "The only one of the family who has. Pity as far as old Richard was concerned that you're a woman. If you'd been a boy, I bet he'd have left you the whole caboodle."

Susan said slowly: "Yes, I think he would."

She paused and then went on:

"He didn't like Greg, you know. . . ."

"Ah." George raised his eyebrows. "His mistake."

"Yes."

"Oh well. Anyway things are going well now—all going according to plan."

As he said the words he was struck by the fact that they seemed particularly applicable to Susan.

The idea made him, just for a moment, a shade uncomfortable.

He didn't really like a woman who was so cold bloodedly efficient.

Changing the subject he said:

"By the way, did you get a letter from Helen? About Enderby?"

"Yes, I did. This morning. Did you?"

"Yes. What are you going to do about it?"

"Greg and I thought of going up the weekend after next—if that suits everyone else. Helen seemed to want us all together."

George laughed shrewdly.

"Or somebody might choose a more valuable piece of furniture than somebody else?"

Susan laughed.

"Oh, I suppose there is a proper valuation. But a valuation for probate will be much lower than the things would be in the open market. And besides I'd quite like to have a few relics of the founder of the family fortunes. Then I think it would be amusing to have one or two really absurd and charming specimens of the Victorian age in this place. Make a kind of *thing* of them! That period's coming in now. There was a green malachite table in the drawing room. You could build quite a colour scheme around it. And perhaps a case of stuffed humming birds—or one of those crowns made of waxed flowers. Something like that—just as a key note can be very effective."

"I trust your judgement."

"You'll be there I suppose?"

"Oh, I shall be there—to see fair play if nothing else."

Susan laughed.

"What do you bet there will be a grand family row?" she asked.

"Rosamund will probably want your green malachite table for a stage set!"

Susan did not laugh. Instead she frowned.

"Have you seen Rosamund lately?"

"I have not seen beautiful Cousin Rosamund since we all came back third class from the funeral."

"I've seen her once or twice. . . . She—she seemed rather odd—"

"What was the matter with her? Trying to think?"

"No. She seemed—well—upset."

"Upset about coming into a lot of money and being able to put on some perfectly frightful play in which Michael can make an ass of himself?"

"Oh, that's going ahead. And it *does* sound frightful—but all the same it may be a success. Michael's good, you know. He can put himself across the footlights—or whatever the term is. He's not like Rosamund who's just beautiful and ham."

"Poor beautiful ham Rosamund."

"All the same Rosamund is not quite so dumb as one might think. She says things that are quite shrewd, sometimes. Things that you wouldn't have imagined she'd even noticed. It's—it's quite disconcerting.''

''Quite like our Aunt Cora—''

''Yes . . .''

A momentary uneasiness descended on them both—conjured up, it seemed, by the mention of Cora Lansquenet.

Then George said with a rather elaborate air of unconcern:

''Talking of Cora—what about that companion woman of hers? I rather think something ought to be done about her.''

''Done about her? What do you mean?''

''Well, it's up to the family so to speak. I mean I've been thinking Cora was our aunt—and it occurred to me that this woman mayn't find it easy to get another post.''

''That occurred to you, did it?''

''Yes. People are so careful of their skins. I don't say they'd actually think that this Gilchrist female would take a hatchet to them—but at the back of their minds they feel that it might be unlucky. People are superstitious.''

''How odd that you should have thought of all that, George? How would you know about things like that?''

George said drily:

''You forget that I'm a lawyer. I see a lot of the queer illogical side of people. What I'm getting at is, that I think we might do something about the woman, give her a small allowance or something, to tide her over, or find some office post for her if she's capable of that sort of thing. I feel rather as though we ought to keep in touch with her.''

''You needn't worry,'' said Susan. Her voice was dry and ironic. ''I've seen to things. She's gone to Timothy and Maude.''

George looked startled.

''I say, Susan—is that wise?''

''It was the best thing I could think of—at the moment.''

George looked at her curiously.

''You're very sure of yourself, aren't you, Susan? You know what you're doing and you don't have—regrets.''

Susan said lightly:

''It's a waste of time—having regrets.''

17

MICHAEL TOSSED the letter across the table to Rosamund.

"What about it?"

"Oh, we'll go. Don't you think so?"

Michael said slowly:

"It might be as well."

"There might be some jewellery . . . Of course all the things in the house are quite hideous—stuffed birds and wax flowers—ugh!"

"Yes. Bit of a mausoleum. As a matter of fact I'd like to make a sketch or two—particularly in that drawing room. The mantelpiece, for instance, and that very odd shaped couch. They'd be just right for 'The Baronet's Progress'—if we revive it."

He got up and looked at his watch.

"That reminds me. I must go round and see Rosenheim. Don't expect me until rather late this evening. I'm dining with Oscar and we're going into the question of taking up that option and how it fits in with the American offer."

"Darling Oscar. He'll be pleased to see you after all this time. Give him my love."

Michael looked at her sharply. He no longer smiled and his face had an alert predatory look.

"What do you mean—after all this time? Anyone would think I hadn't seen him for months."

"Well, you haven't, have you?" murmured Rosamund.

"Yes, I have. We lunched together only a week ago."

"How funny. He must have forgotten about it. He rang up yesterday and said he hadn't seen you since the first night of *Tilly Looks West*."

"The old fool must be off his head."

Michael laughed. Rosamund, her eyes wide and blue, looked at him without emotion.

"You think I'm a fool, don't you, Mick?"

Michael protested.

"Darling, of course I don't."

"Yes, you do. But I'm not an absolute nit-wit. You didn't go near Oscar that day. I know where you did go."

"Rosamund darling—what do you mean?"

"I mean I know where you really were. . . ."

Michael, his attractive face uncertain, stared at his wife. She stared back at him, placid, unruffled.

How very disconcerting, he suddenly thought, a really empty stare could be.

He said rather unsuccessfully:

"I don't know what you're driving at. . . ."

"I just meant it's rather silly telling me a lot of lies."

"Look here, Rosamund—"

He had started to bluster—but he stopped, taken aback, as his wife said softly:

"We do want to take up this option and put this play on, don't we?"

"Want to? It's the part I've always dreamed must exist somewhere."

"Yes—that's what I mean."

"Just what do you mean?"

"Well—it's worth a good deal, isn't it? But one mustn't take *too* many risks."

He stared at her and said slowly:

"It's your money—I know that. If you don't want to risk it—"

"It's *our* money, darling." Rosamund stressed it. "I think that's rather important."

"Listen, darling. The part of Eileen—it would bear writing up."

Rosamund smiled.

"I don't think—really—I want to play it."

"My dear girl." Michael was aghast. "What's come over you?"

"Nothing."

"Yes, there is, you've been different lately—moody—nervous, what is it?"

"Nothing. I only want you to be—careful, Mick."

"Careful about what? I'm always careful."

"No, I don't think you are. You always think you can get away with things and that everyone will believe whatever you want them to. You were stupid about Oscar that day."

Michael flushed angrily.

"And what about you? You said you were going shopping with Jane. You didn't. Jane's in America, has been for weeks."

"Yes," said Rosamund. "That was stupid, too. I really just went for a walk—in Regent's Park."

Michael looked at her curiously.

"Regent's Park? You never went for a walk in Regent's Park in your life. What's it all about? Have you got a boy friend? You may say what you like, Rosamund, you *have* been different lately. Why?''

''I've been—thinking about things. About what to do . . .''

Michael came round the table to her in a satisfying spontaneous rush. His voice held fervour as he cried:

''Darling—you know I love you madly!''

She responded satisfactorily to the embrace, but as they drew apart he was struck again disagreeably by the odd calculation in those beautiful eyes.

''Whatever I'd done, you'd always forgive me, wouldn't you?'' he demanded.

''I suppose so,'' said Rosamund vaguely. ''That's not the point. You see, it's all different now. We've got to think and plan.''

''Think and plan—what?''

Rosamund, frowning, said:

''Things aren't over when you've done them. It's really a sort of beginning and then one's got to arrange what to do next, and what's important and what is not.''

''Rosamund . . .''

She sat, her face perplexed, her wide gaze on a middle distance in which Michael, apparently, did not feature.

At the third repetition of her name, she started slightly and came out of her reverie.

''What did you say?''

''I asked you what you were thinking about. . . .''

''Oh? Oh yes, I was wondering if I'd go down to—what is it?—Lytchett St. Mary, and see that Miss Somebody—the one who was with Aunt Cora.''

''But why?''

''Well, she'll be going away soon, won't she? To relatives or someone. I don't think we ought to let her go away until we've asked her.''

''Asked her what?''

''Asked her who killed Aunt Cora.''

Michael stared.

''You mean—you think she *knows?*''

Rosamund said rather absently:

''Oh yes, I expect so. . . . She lived there, you see.''

''But she'd have told the police.''

''Oh, I don't mean she knows *that* way—I just mean that she's probably quite sure. Because of what Uncle Richard said when he went down there.''

''But she wouldn't have heard what he said.''

"Oh yes, she would, darling." Rosamund sounded like someone arguing with an unreasonable child.

"Nonsense, I can hardly see old Richard Abernethie discussing his suspicions of his family before an outsider."

"Well, of course. She'd have heard it through the door."

"Eavesdropping, you mean?"

"I expect so—in fact I'm sure. It must be so deadly dull shut up, two women in a cottage and nothing ever happening except washing up and the sink and putting the cat out and things like that. Of course she listened and read letters—anyone would."

Michael looked at her with something faintly approaching dismay.

"Would you?" he demanded bluntly.

"I wouldn't go and be a companion in the country." Rosamund shuddered. "I'd rather die."

"I meant—would you read letters and—and all that?"

Rosamund said calmly:

"If I wanted to know, yes. Everybody does, don't you think so?"

The limpid gaze met his.

"One just wants to know," said Rosamund. "One doesn't want to do anything about it. I expect that's how *she* feels—Miss Gilchrist, I mean. But I'm certain she *knows*."

Michael said in a stifled voice:

"Rosamund, who do you think killed Cora? And old Richard?"

Once again that limpid blue gaze met his.

"Darling—don't be absurd. . . . You know as well as I do. But it's much much better *never* to mention it. So we won't."

18

FROM HIS SEAT by the fireplace in the library, Hercule Poirot looked at the assembled company.

His eyes passed thoughtfully over Susan, sitting upright, looking vivid and animated, over her husband, sitting near her, his expression rather vacant and his fingers twisting a loop of string; they went on to George Crossfield, debonair and distinctly pleased with himself, talking about card sharpers on Atlantic Cruises to Rosamund, who said mechanically, "How extraordinary, darling. But why?" in a completely uninterested voice; went on to Michael with his very individual type of haggard good looks and his very apparent charm; to Helen, poised and slightly remote, to Timothy comfortably settled in the best armchair with an extra cushion at his back and Maude, sturdy and thick-set, in devoted attendance, and finally to the figure sitting with a tinge of apology just beyond the range of the family circle—the figure of Miss Gilchrist wearing a rather peculiar "dressy" blouse. Presently, he judged, she would get up, murmur an excuse and leave the family gathering and go up to her room. Miss Gilchrist, he thought, knew her place. She had learned it the hard way.

Hercule Poirot sipped his after dinner coffee and between half closed lids made his appraisal.

He had wanted them there—all together, and he had got them. And what, he thought to himself, was he going to do with them now? He felt a sudden weary distaste for going on with the business. Why was that, he wondered? Was it the influence of Helen Abernethie? There was a quality of passive resistance about her that seemed unexpectedly strong. Had she, while apparently graceful and unconcerned, managed to impress her own reluctance upon him? She was averse to this raking up of the details of old Richard's death, he knew that. She wanted it left alone, left to die out into oblivion. Poirot was not surprised by that. What did surprise him was his own disposition to agree with her.

Mr. Entwhistle's account of the family had, he realised, been admirable. He had described all these people shrewdly and well. With the old lawyer's knowledge and appraisal to guide him, Poirot had wanted to see for himself. He had fancied that, meeting these people intimately, he would have a very shrewd idea—not of *how* and *when*—(those were questions with which he did not propose to concern himself. Murder had been possible —that was all he needed to know!)—but of *who*. For Hercule Poirot had a lifetime of experience behind him, and as a man who deals with pictures can recognize the artist, so Poirot believed he could recognize a likely type of the amateur criminal who will—if his own particular need arises —be prepared to kill.

But it was not to be so easy.

Because he could visualise almost all of these people as a possible—though not a probable—murderer. George might kill—as the cornered rat kills. Susan calmly—efficiently—to further a plan. Gregory because he had that queer morbid streak which discounts and invites, almost craves, punishment. Michael because he was ambitious and had a murderer's cocksure vanity. Rosamund because she was frighteningly simple in outlook. Timothy because he had hated and resented his brother and had craved the power his brother's money would give. Maude because Timothy was her child and where her child was concerned she would be ruthless. Even Miss Gilchrist, he thought, might have contemplated murder if it could have restored to her the Willow Tree in its ladylike glory!

And Helen? He could not see Helen as committing murder. She was too civilised—too removed from violence. And she and her husband had surely loved Richard Abernethie.

Poirot sighed to himself. There were to be no short cuts to the truth. Instead he would have to adopt a longer, but a reasonably sure method. There would have to be conversation. Much conversation. For in the long run, either through a lie, or through truth, people were bound to give themselves away. . . .

He had been introduced by Helen to the gathering, and had set to work to overcome the almost universal annoyance caused by his presence—a foreign stranger!—in this family gathering. He had used his eyes and his ears. He had watched and listened—openly and behind doors! He had noticed affinities, antagonisms, the unguarded words that arose as always when property was to be divided. He had engineered adroitly tête-à-têtes, walks upon the terrace, and had made his deductions and observations. He had talked with Miss Gilchrist about the vanished glories of her teashop and about the correct composition of *brioches* and chocolate *éclairs* and had visited the kitchen garden with her to discuss the proper use of herbs in cooking. He had spent some long half hours listening to Timothy talking about his own health and about the effect upon it of paint.

Paint? Poirot frowned. Somebody else had said something about paint —Mr. Entwhistle?

There had also been discussion of a different kind of painting. Pierre Lansquenet as a painter. Cora Lansquenet's paintings, rapturized over by Miss Gilchrist, dismissed scornfully by Susan. "Just like picture postcards," she had said. "She did them from postcards, too."

Miss Gilchrist had been quite upset by that and had said sharply that dear Mrs. Lansquenet always painted from Nature.

"But I bet she cheated," said Susan to Poirot when Miss Gilchrist had gone out of the room. "In fact I know she did, though I won't upset the old pussy by saying so."

"And how do you know?"

Poirot watched the strong confident line of Susan's chin.

"She will always be sure, this one," he thought. "And perhaps sometime, she will be too sure. . . ."

Susan was going on.

"I'll tell you, but don't pass it on to the Gilchrist. One picture is of

Polflexan, the cove and the lighthouse and the pier—the usual aspect that all amateur artists sit down and sketch. But the pier was blown up in the war, and since Aunt Cora's sketch was done a couple of years ago, it can't very well be from Nature, can it? But the postcards they sell there still show the pier as it used to be. There was one in her bedroom drawer. So Aunt Cora started her 'rough sketch' down there, I expect, and then finished it surreptitiously later at home from a postcard! It's funny, isn't it, the way people get caught out?"

"Yes, it is, as you say, funny." He paused, and then thought that the opening was a good one.

"You do not remember me, Madame," he said, "but I remember you. This is not the first time that I have seen you."

She stared at him. Poirot nodded with great gusto.

"Yes, yes, it is so. I was inside an automobile, well wrapped up, and from the window I saw you. You were talking to one of the mechanics in the garage. You do not notice me—it is natural—I am inside the car—an elderly muffled-up foreigner! But *I* notice *you*, for you are young and agreeable to look at and you stand there in the sun. So when I arrive here, I say to myself, '*Tiens!* what a coincidence!' "

"A garage? Where? When was this?"

"Oh a little time ago—a week—no, more. For the moment," said Poirot disingenuously and with a full recollection of the King's Arms Garage in his mind, "I cannot remember where. I travel so much all over this country."

"Looking for a suitable house to buy for your refugees?"

"Yes. There is so much to take into consideration, you see. Price—neighbourhood—suitability for conversion."

"I suppose you'll have to pull the house about a lot? Lots of horrible partitions."

"In the bedrooms, yes, certainly. But most of the ground floor rooms we shall not touch." He paused before going on. "Does it sadden you, Madame, that this old family mansion of yours should go this way—to strangers?"

"Of course not." Susan looked amused. "I think it's an excellent idea. It's an impossible place for anybody to think of living in as it is. And I've nothing to be sentimental about. It's not *my* old home. My mother and father lived in London. We just came here for Christmas sometimes. Actually I've always thought it quite hideous—an almost indecent temple to wealth."

"The altars are different now. There is the building in, and the concealed lighting and the expensive simplicity. But wealth still has its temples,

Madame. I understand—I am not, I hope, indiscreet—that you yourself are planning such an edifice? Everything *de luxe*—and no expense spared.''

Susan laughed.

''Hardly a temple—it's just a place of business.''

''Perhaps the name does not matter. . . . But it will cost much money —that is true, is it not?''

''Everything's wickedly expensive nowadays. But the initial outlay will be worthwhile, I think.''

''Tell me something about these plans of yours. It amazes me to find a beautiful young woman so practical, so competent. In my young days—a long time ago, I admit—beautiful women thought only of their pleasures, of cosmetics, of *la toilette*.''

''Women still think a great deal about their faces—that's where I come in.''

''Tell me.''

And she had told him. Told him with a wealth of detail and with a great deal of unconscious self-revelation. He appreciated her business acumen, her boldness of planning and her grasp of detail. A good bold planner, sweeping all side issues away. Perhaps a little ruthless as all those who plan boldly must be. . . .

Watching her, he had said:

''Yes, you will succeed. You will go ahead. How fortunate that you are not restricted, as so many are, by poverty. One cannot go far without the capital outlay. To have had these creative ideas and to have been frustrated by lack of means—that would have been unbearable.''

''I couldn't have borne it! But I'd have raised money somehow or other—got someone to back me.''

''Ah! of course. Your uncle, whose house this was, was rich. Even if he had not died, he would, as you express it, have 'staked' you.''

''Oh no, he wouldn't. Uncle Richard was a bit of a stick-in-the-mud where women were concerned. If I'd been a man—'' A quick flash of anger swept across her face. ''He made me very angry.''

''I see—yes, I see. . . .''

''The old shouldn't stand in the way of the young. I—oh, I beg your pardon.''

Hercule Poirot laughed easily and twirled his moustache.

''I am old, yes. But I do not impede youth. There is no one who needs to wait for my death.''

''What a horrid idea.''

''But you are a realist, Madame. Let us admit without more ado that the world is full of the young—or even the middle-aged—who wait, patiently or impatiently, for the death of someone whose decease will give them, if not affluence—then opportunity."

"Opportunity!" Susan said, taking a deep breath. "That's what one needs."

Poirot, who had been looking beyond her, said gaily:

"And here is your husband come to join our little discussion. . . . We talk, Mr. Banks, of opportunity. Opportunity the golden—opportunity who must be grasped with both hands. How far in conscience can one go? Let us hear your views?"

But he was not destined to hear the views of Gregory Banks on opportunity or on anything else. In fact he had found it next to impossible to talk to Gregory Banks at all. Banks had a curious fluid quality. Whether by his own wish, or by that of his wife, he seemed to have no liking for tête-à-têtes or quiet discussions. No, "conversation" with Gregory had failed.

Poirot had talked with Maude Abernethie—also about paint (the smell of) and how fortunate it had been that Timothy had been able to come to Enderby, and how kind it had been of Helen to extend an invitation to Miss Gilchrist also.

"For really she is *most* useful. Timothy so often feels like a snack—and one cannot ask too much of other people's servants but there is a gas ring in a little room off the pantry, so that Miss Gilchrist can warm up Ovaltine or Benger's there without disturbing anybody. And she's so willing about fetching things, she's quite willing to run up and down stairs a dozen times a day. Oh yes, I feel that it was really quite Providential that she should have lost her nerve about staying alone in the house as she did, though I admit it vexed me at the time."

"Lost her nerve?" Poirot was interested.

He listened whilst Maude gave him an account of Miss Gilchrist's sudden collapse.

"She was frightened, you say? And yet could not exactly say why? That is interesting. Very interesting."

"I put it down myself to delayed shock."

"Perhaps."

"Once, during the war, when a bomb dropped about a mile away from us, I remember Timothy—"

Poirot abstracted his mind from Timothy.

"Had anything particular happened that day?" he asked.

"On what day?" Maude looked blank.

"The day that Miss Gilchrist was upset."

"Oh, *that*—no, I don't think so. It seems to have been coming on ever since she left Lychett St. Mary, or so she said. She didn't seem to mind when she was there.''

And the result, Poirot thought, had been a piece of poisoned wedding cake. Not so very surprising that Miss Gilchrist was frightened after that. . . . And even when she had removed herself to the peaceful country round Stansfield Grange, the fear had lingered. More than lingered. Grown. Why grown? Surely attending on an exacting hypochondriac like Timothy must be so exhausting that nervous fears would be likely to be swallowed up in exasperation?

But something in that house had made Miss Gilchrist afraid. What? Did she know herself?

Finding himself alone with Miss Gilchrist for a brief space before dinner, Poirot had sailed into the subject with an exaggerated foreign curiosity.

''Impossible, you comprehend, for me to mention the matter of murder to members of the family. But I am intrigued. Who would not be? A brutal crime—a sensitive artist attacked in a lonely cottage. Terrible for her family. But terrible, also, I imagine, for *you*. Since Mrs. Timothy Abernethie gives me to understand that you were there at the time?''

''Yes, I was. And if you'll excuse me, M. Pontarlier, I don't want to talk about it.''

''I understand—oh yes, I completely understand.''

Having said this, Poirot waited. And, as he had thought, Miss Gilchrist immediately *did* begin to talk about it.

He heard nothing from her that he had not heard before, but he played his part with perfect sympathy, uttering little cries of comprehension and listening with an absorbed interest which Miss Gilchrist could not but help enjoy.

Not until she had exhausted the subject of what she herself had felt, and what the doctor had said, and how kind Mr. Entwhistle had been, did Poirot proceed cautiously to the next point.

''You were wise, I think, not to remain alone down in that cottage.''

''I couldn't have done it, M. Pontarlier. I really couldn't have done it.''

''No. I understand even that you were afraid to remain alone in the house of Mr. Timothy Abernethie whilst they came here?''

Miss Gilchrist looked guilty.

''I'm terribly ashamed about that. So foolish really. It was just a kind of panic I had—I really don't know *why*.''

''But of course one knows why. You had just recovered from a dastardly attempt to poison you—''

Miss Gilchrist here sighed and said she simply couldn't understand it. Why should anyone try to poison her?

"But obviously, my dear lady, because this criminal, this assassin, thought that you knew something that might lead to his apprehension by the police."

"But what could *I* know? Some dreadful tramp, or semi-crazed creature."

"If it *was* a tramp. It seems to me unlikely—"

"Oh please, M. Pontarlier—" Miss Gilchrist became suddenly very upset. "Don't suggest such things. I don't want to believe it."

"You do not want to believe what?"

"I don't want to believe that it wasn't—I mean—that it was—"

She paused, confused.

"And yet," said Poirot shrewdly, "you *do* believe."

"Oh I don't. I *don't!*"

"But I think you do. That is why you are frightened. . . . You are still frightened, are you not?"

"Oh no, not since I came here. So many people. And such a nice family atmosphere. Oh no, everything seems quite all right here."

"It seems to me—you must excuse my interest—I am an old man, somewhat infirm, and a great part of my time is given to idle speculation on matters which interest me—it seems to me that there must have been some definite occurrence at Stansfield Grange which, so to speak, brought your fears to a *head*. Doctors recognize nowadays how much takes place in our subconscious."

"Yes, yes—I know they say so."

"And I think your subconscious fears might have been brought to a point by some small concrete happening, something, perhaps, quite extraneous, serving, shall we say, as a focal point."

Miss Gilchrist seemed to lap this up eagerly.

"I'm sure you are right," she said.

"Now what, should you think, was this—er—extraneous circumstance?"

Miss Gilchrist pondered a moment, and then said, unexpectedly:

"I think, you know, M. Pontarlier, it was the *nun*."

Before Poirot could take this up, Susan and her husband came in, closely followed by Helen.

"A nun," thought Poirot. . . . "Now where, in all this, have I heard something about a nun?"

He resolved to lead the conversation to nuns sometime in the course of the evening.

19

THE FAMILY had all been polite to M. Pontarlier, the representative of N.A.R.C.O. And how right he had been to have chosen to designate himself by initials. Everyone had accepted N.A.R.C.O. as a matter of course—had even pretended to know all about it! How averse human beings were ever to admit ignorance! An exception had been Rosamund who had asked him wonderingly: "But what *is* it? I never heard of it?" Fortunately no one else had been there at the time. Poirot had explained the organisation in such a way that anyone but Rosamund would have felt abashed at having displayed ignorance of such a well-known, world wide institution. Rosamund, however, had only said vaguely, "Oh! refugees all over *again*. I'm so *tired* of refugees." Thus voicing the unspoken reaction of many, who were usually too conventional to express themselves so frankly.

M. Pontarlier was, therefore, now accepted—as a nuisance but also as a nonentity. He had become, as it were, a piece of foreign *décor*. The general opinion was that Helen should have avoided having him here this particular weekend, but as he was here they must make the best of it. Fortunately this queer little foreigner did not seem to know much English. Quite often he did not understand what you said to him, and when everyone was speaking more or less at once he seemed completely at sea. He appeared to be interested only in refugees and post war conditions, and his vocabulary only included those subjects. Ordinary chit chat appeared to bewilder him. More or less forgotten by all, Hercule Poirot leant back in his chair, sipped his coffee and observed, as a cat may observe, the twitterings, and comings and goings of a flock of birds. The cat is not ready yet to make its spring.

After twenty four hours of prowling round the house and examining its contents, the heirs of Richard Abernethie were ready to state their preferences, and, if need be, to fight for them.

The subject of conversation was, first, a certain Spode dinner dessert service off which they had just been eating dessert.

"I don't suppose I have long to live," said Timothy in a faint melancholy voice. "And Maude and I have no children. It is hardly worth while our burdening ourselves with useless possessions. But for sentiment's sake I *should* like to have the old dessert service. I remember it in the dear old days. It's out of fashion, of course, and I understand dessert services have very little value nowadays—but there it is. I shall be *quite* content with that—and perhaps the Boule Cabinet in the White Boudoir."

"You're too late, Uncle," George spoke with debonair insouciance. "I asked Helen to mark off the Spode service to me this morning."

Timothy became purple in the face.

"Mark it off—mark it off? What do you mean? Nothing's been settled yet. And what do *you* want with a dessert service? You're not married."

"As a matter of fact I collect Spode. And this is really a splendid specimen. But it's quite all right about the Boule Cabinet, Uncle. I wouldn't have that as a gift."

Timothy waved aside the Boule Cabinet.

"Now look here, young George. You can't go butting in, in this way. I'm an older man than you are—and I'm Richard's only surviving brother. That dessert service is *mine*."

"Why not take the Dresden service, Uncle? A very fine example and I'm sure just as full of sentimental memories. Anyway, the Spode's mine. First come, first served."

"Nonsense—nothing of the kind!" Timothy spluttered.

Maude said sharply:

"Please don't upset your uncle, George. It's very bad for him. Naturally he will take the Spode if he wants to! The first choice is *his*, and you young people must come afterwards. He was Richard's brother, as he says, and you are only a nephew."

"And I can tell you this, young man." Timothy was seething with fury. "If Richard had made a proper will, the disposal of the contents of this place would have been entirely in my hands. That's the way the property *should* have been left, and if it wasn't, I can only suspect *undue influence*. Yes—and I repeat it—*undue influence*."

Timothy glared at his nephew.

"A preposterous will," he said. "Preposterous!"

He leant back, placed a hand to his heart, and groaned:

"This is very bad for me. If I could have—a little brandy."

Miss Gilchrist hurried to get it and returned with the restorative in a small glass.

"Here you are, Mr. Abernethie. Please—please don't excite yourself. Are you sure you oughtn't to go up to bed?"

"Don't be a fool." Timothy swallowed the brandy. "Go to bed? I intend to protect my interests."

"Really, George, I'm surprised at you," said Maude. "What your uncle says is perfectly true. His wishes come first. If he wants the Spode dessert service he shall have it!"

''It's quite hideous anyway,'' said Susan.

''Hold your tongue, Susan,'' said Timothy.

The thin young man who sat beside Susan raised his head. In a voice that was a little shriller than his ordinary tones, he said:

''Don't speak like that to my wife!''

He half rose from his seat.

Susan said quickly: ''It's all right, Greg. I don't mind.''

''But *I* do.''

Helen said: ''I think it would be graceful on your part, George, to let your uncle have the dessert service.''

Timothy spluttered indignantly: ''There's no 'letting' about it!''

But George, with a slight bow to Helen said, ''Your wish is law, Aunt Helen. I abandon my claim.''

''You didn't really want it, anyway, did you?'' said Helen.

He cast a sharp glance at her, then grinned:

''The trouble with you, Aunt Helen, is that you're too sharp by half! You see more than you're meant to see. Don't worry, Uncle Timothy, the Spode is yours. Just my idea of fun.''

''Fun, indeed.'' Maude Abernethie was indignant. ''Your uncle might have had a heart attack!''

''Don't you believe it,'' said George cheerfully. ''Uncle Timothy will probably outlive us all. He's what is known as a creaking gate.''

Timothy leaned forward balefully.

''I don't wonder,'' he said, ''that Richard was disappointed in *you*.''

''What's that?'' The good humour went out of George's face.

''You came up here after Mortimer died, expecting to step into his shoes—expecting that Richard would make you his heir, didn't you? But my poor brother soon took *your* measure. He knew where the money would go if you had control of it. I'm surprised that he even left you a part of his fortune. He knew where it would go. Horses, Gambling, Monte Carlo, foreign Casinos. Perhaps worse. He suspected you of not being straight, didn't he?''

George, a white dint appearing each side of his nose, said quietly:

''Hadn't you better be careful of what you are saying?''

''I wasn't well enough to come here for the funeral,'' said Timothy slowly, ''but Maude told me what *Cora said*. Cora always was a fool—but there *may* have been something in it! And if so, I know who *I'd* suspect—''

''Timothy!'' Maude stood up, solid, calm, a tower of forcefulness. ''You have had a very trying evening. You must consider your health. I can't have you getting ill again. Come up with me. You must take a sedative and go straight to bed. Timothy and I, Helen, will take the Spode dessert service and the Boule Cabinet as mementos of Richard. There is no objection to that, I hope?''

Her glance swept round the company. Nobody spoke, and she marched out of the room supporting Timothy with a hand under his elbow, waving aside Miss Gilchrist who was hovering half heartedly by the door.

George broke the silence after they had departed.

''Femme formidable!'' he said. ''That describes Aunt Maude exactly. I should hate ever to impede her triumphal progress.''

Miss Gilchrist sat down again rather uncomfortably and murmured:

''Mrs. Abernethie is always so kind.''

The remark fell rather flat.

Michael Shane laughed suddenly and said: ''You know, I'm enjoying all this! 'The Voysey Inheritance' to the life. By the way, Rosamund and I want that malachite table in the drawing room.''

''Oh no,'' cried Susan. ''*I* want that.''

''Here we go again,'' said George, raising his eyes to the ceiling.

''Well, we needn't get angry about it,'' said Susan. ''The reason I want it is for my new Beauty shop. Just a note of colour—and I shall put a great bouquet of wax flowers on it. It would look wonderful. I can find wax flowers easily enough, but a green malachite table isn't so common.''

''But, darling,'' said Rosamund, ''that's just why *we* want it. For the new set. As you say, a note of colour—and so *absolutely* period. And either wax flowers or stuffed humming birds. It will be absolutely *right*.''

''I see what you mean, Rosamund,'' said Susan. ''But I don't think you've got as good a case as I have. You could easily have a painted malachite table for the stage—it would look just the same. But for my *salon* I've *got* to have the genuine thing.''

''Now, ladies,'' said George. ''What about a sporting decision? Why not toss for it? Or cut the cards? All quite in keeping with the period of the table.''

Susan smiled pleasantly.

''Rosamund and I will talk about it tomorrow,'' she said.

She seemed, as usual, quite sure of herself. George looked with some interest from her face to that of Rosamund. Rosamund's face had a vague, rather far away expression.

''Which one will you back, Aunt Helen?'' he asked. ''An even money chance, I'd say. Susan has determination, but Rosamund is so wonderfully single minded.''

''Or perhaps *not* humming birds,'' said Rosamund. ''One of those big Chinese vases would make a lovely lamp, with a gold shade.''

Miss Gilchrist hurried into placating speech.

"This house is full of so many beautiful things," she said. "That green table would look wonderful in your new establishment, I'm sure, Mrs. Banks. I've never seen one like it. It must be worth a lot of money."

"It will be deducted from my share of the estate, of course," said Susan.

"I'm so sorry—I didn't mean—" Miss Gilchrist was covered with confusion.

"It may be deducted from *our* share of the estate," Michael pointed out. "With the wax flowers thrown in."

"They look so right on that table," Miss Gilchrist murmured. "Really artistic. Sweetly pretty."

But nobody was paying any attention to Miss Gilchrist's well meant trivialities.

Greg said, speaking again in that high nervous voice:

"Susan *wants* that table."

There was a momentary stir of unease, as though, by his words, Greg had set a different musical key.

Helen said quickly:

"And what do you really want, George? Leaving out the Spode service."

George grinned and the tension relaxed.

"Rather a shame to bait old Timothy," he said. "But he really is quite unbelievable. He's had his own way in everything so long that he's become quite pathological about it."

"You have to humour an invalid, Mr. Crossfield," said Miss Gilchrist.

"Ruddy old hypochondriac, that's what he is," said George.

"Of course he is," Susan agreed. "I don't believe there's anything whatever the matter with him, do you, Rosamund?"

"What?"

"Anything the matter with Uncle Timothy."

"No—no, I shouldn't think so." Rosamund was vague. She apologised. "I'm sorry. I was thinking about what lighting would be right for the table."

"You see?" said George. "A woman of one idea. Your wife's a dangerous woman, Michael. I hope you realise it."

"I realise it," said Michael rather grimly.

George went on with every appearance of enjoyment.

"The Battle of the Table! To be fought tomorrow—politely—but with grim determination. We ought all to take sides. I back Rosamund who looks so sweet and yielding and isn't. Husbands presumably back their own wives. Miss Gilchrist? On Susan's side, obviously."

"Oh really, Mr. Crossfield, I wouldn't venture to—"

"Aunt Helen?" George paid no attention to Miss Gilchrist's flutterings. "You have the casting vote. Oh er—I forgot. M. Pontarlier?"

"Pardon?" Hercule Poirot looked blank.

George considered explanations, but decided against it. The poor old boy hadn't understood a word of what was going on. He said: "Just a family joke."

"Yes, yes, I comprehend." Poirot smiled amiably.

"So yours is the casting vote, Aunt Helen. Whose side are you on?"

Helen smiled.

"Perhaps I want it myself, George."

She changed the subject deliberately, turning to her foreign guest.

"I'm afraid this is all very dull for you, M. Pontarlier?"

"Not at all, Madame. I consider myself privileged to be admitted to your family life—" he bowed. "I would like to say—I cannot quite express my meaning—my regret that this house has to pass out of your hands into the hands of strangers. It is, without doubt—a great sorrow."

"No, indeed, we don't regret at all," Susan assured him.

"You are very amiable, Madame. It will be, let me tell you, perfection here for my elderly sufferers of persecution. What a haven! What peace! I beg you to remember that, when the harsh feelings come to you as assuredly they must. I hear that there was also the question of a school coming here—not a regular school, a convent—run by *religieuses*—by 'nuns,' I think you say? You would have preferred that, perhaps?"

"Not at all," said George.

"The Sacred Heart of Mary," continued Poirot. "Fortunately, owing to the kindness of an unknown benefactor we were able to make a slightly higher offer." He addressed Miss Gilchrist directly. "You do not like nuns, I think?"

Miss Gilchrist flushed and looked embarrassed.

"Oh really, Mr. Pontarlier, you mustn't—I mean, it's nothing *personal*. But I never do see that it's right to shut yourself up from the world in that way—not necessary, I mean, and really almost selfish, though not teaching ones, of course, or the ones that go about amongst the poor—because I'm sure they're thoroughly unselfish women and do a lot of good."

"I simply can't imagine wanting to be a nun," said Susan.

"It's very becoming," said Rosamund. "You remember—when they revived 'The Miracle' last year. Sonia Wells looked absolutely too glamorous for *words*."

"What beats me," said George, "is why it should be pleasing to the Almighty to dress oneself up in mediaeval dress. For after all, that's all a nun's dress is. Thoroughly cumbersome, unhygienic and impractical."

"And it makes them look so alike, doesn't it?" said Miss Gilchrist. "It's silly, you know, but I got quite a turn when I was at Mrs. Abernethie's and a nun came to the door, collecting. I got it into my head she was the same as a nun who came to the door on the day of the inquest on poor Mrs. Lansquenet at Lytchett St. Mary. I felt, you know, almost as though she had been following me round!"

"I thought nuns always collected in couples," said George. "Surely a detective story hinged on that point once?"

"There was only one this time," said Miss Gilchrist. "Perhaps they've got to economise," she added vaguely. "And anyway it couldn't have been the same nun, for the other one was collecting for an organ for St. —Barnabas, I think—and this one was for something quite different—something to do with children."

"But they both had the same type of features?" Hercule Poirot asked. He sounded interested. Miss Gilchrist turned to him.

"I suppose that must be it. . . . The upper lip—almost as though she had a moustache. I think, you know, that *that* is really what alarmed me —being in a rather nervous state at the time, and remembering those stories during the war of nuns who were really men and in the Fifth Column and landed by parachute. Of course it was very foolish of me. I knew that afterwards."

"A nun would be a good disguise," said Susan thoughtfully. "It hides your feet."

"The truth is," said George, "that one very seldom looks properly at anyone. That's why one gets such wildly differing accounts of a person from different witnesses in court. You'd be surprised. A man is often described as tall—short; thin—stout; fair—dark; dressed in a dark—light—suit; and so on. There's usually *one* reliable observer, but one has to make up one's mind who that is."

"Another queer thing," said Susan, "is that you sometimes catch sight of yourself in a mirror unexpectedly and don't know who it is. It just looks vaguely familiar. And you say to yourself, 'That's somebody I know quite well. . . .' and then suddenly realise it's yourself!"

George said: "It would be more difficult still if you could really see yourself—and not a mirror image."

"Why?" asked Rosamund, looking puzzled.

"Because, don't you see, nobody ever sees themselves—*as they appear to other people*. They always see themselves in a *glass*—that is—as a reversed image."

"But does that look any different?"

"Oh yes," said Susan quickly. "It must. Because people's faces aren't the same both sides. Their eyebrows are different, and their mouths go up one side, and their noses aren't really straight. You can see with a pencil—who's got a pencil?''

Somebody produced a pencil, and they experimented, holding a pencil each side of the nose and laughing to see the ridiculous variation in angle.

The atmosphere now had lightened a good deal. Everybody was in a good humour. They were no longer the heirs of Richard Abernethie gathered together for a division of property. They were a cheerful and normal set of people gathered together for a weekend in the country.

Only Helen Abernethie remained silent and abstracted.

With a sigh, Hercule Poirot rose to his feet and bade his hostess a polite good night.

''And perhaps, Madame, I had better say goodbye. My train departs itself at nine o'clock tomorrow morning. That is very early. So I will thank you now for all your kindness and hospitality. The date of possession—that will be arranged with the good Mr. Entwhistle. To suit your convenience, of course.''

''It can be any time you please, Mr. Pontarlier. I—I have finished all that I came here to do.''

''You will return now to your villa at Cyprus?''

''Yes.'' A little smile curved Helen Abernethie's lips.

Poirot said:

''You are glad, yes. You have no regrets?''

''At leaving England? Or leaving here, do you mean?''

''I meant—leaving here?''

''No—no. It's no good, is it, to cling on to the past? One must leave that behind one.''

''If one can.'' Blinking his eyes innocently Poirot smiled apologetically round on the group of polite faces that surrounded him.

''Sometimes, is it not, the past will not be left, will not suffer itself to pass into oblivion? It stands at one's elbow—it says *'I am not done with yet.'* ''

Susan gave a rather doubtful laugh. Poirot said:

''But I am serious—yes.''

''You mean,'' said Michael, ''that your refugees when they come here will not be able to put their past sufferings completely behind them?''

''I did not mean my refugees.''

''He meant us, darling,'' said Rosamund. ''He means Uncle Richard and Aunt Cora and the hatchet, and all that.''

She turned to Poirot.

''Didn't you?''

Poirot looked at her with a blank face. Then he said:

"Why do you think that, Madame?"

"Because you're a detective, aren't you? That's why you're here. N.A.R.C.O., or whatever you call it, is just nonsense, isn't it?"

20

THERE WAS A MOMENT of extraordinary tenseness. Poirot felt it, though he himself did not remove his eyes from Rosamund's lovely placid face.

He said with a little bow, "You have great perspicacity, Madame."

"Not really," said Rosamund. "You were pointed out to me once in a Restaurant. I remembered."

"But you have not mentioned it—until now?"

"I thought it would be more fun not to," said Rosamund.

Michael said in an imperfectly controlled voice:

"My—dear girl."

Poirot shifted his gaze then to look at him.

Michael was angry. Angry and something else—apprehensive?

Poirot's eyes went slowly round all the faces. Susan's, angry and watchful; Gregory's, dead and shut in; Miss Gilchrist's, foolish, her mouth wide open; George, wary; Helen, dismayed and nervous. . . .

All those expressions were normal ones under the circumstances. He wished he could have seen their faces a split second earlier, when the words "a detective" fell from Rosamund's lips. For now, inevitably, it could not be quite the same. . . .

He squared his shoulders and bowed to them. His language and his accent became less foreign.

"Yes," he said. "I am a detective."

George Crossfield said, the white dints showing once more each side of his nose:

"Who sent you here?"

"I was commissioned to enquire into the circumstances of Richard Abernethie's death."

"By whom?"

"For the moment, that does not concern you. But it would be an advantage, would it not, if you could be assured *beyond any possible doubt* that Richard Abernethie died a natural death?''

''Of course he died a natural death. Who says anything else?''

''Cora Lansquenet said so. And Cora Lansquenet is dead herself.''

A little wave of uneasiness seemed to sigh through the room like an evil breeze.

''She said it here—in this room,'' said Susan. ''But I didn't really think—''

''Didn't you, Susan?'' George Crossfield turned his sardonic glance upon her. ''Why pretend any more? You won't take M. Pontarlier in?''

''We all thought so really,'' said Rosamund. ''And his name isn't Pontarlier—it's Hercules something.''

''Hercule Poirot—at your service.''

Poirot bowed.

There were no gasps of astonishment or of apprehension. His name seemed to mean nothing at all to them.

They were less alarmed by it than they had been by the single word *'detective.'*

''May I ask what conclusions you have come to?'' asked George.

''He won't tell you, darling,'' said Rosamund. ''Or if he does tell you, what he says won't be true.''

Alone of the company she appeared to be amused.

Hercule Poirot looked at her thoughtfully.

II

Hercule Poirot did not sleep well that night. He was perturbed, and he was not quite sure *why* he was perturbed. Elusive snatches of conversation, various glances, odd movements—all seemed fraught with a tantalising significance in the loneliness of the night. He was on the threshold of sleep, but sleep would not come. Just as he was about to drop off, something flashed into his mind and woke him up again. Paint—Timothy and paint. Oil paint—the smell of oil paint—connected somehow with Mr. Entwhistle. Paint and Cora. Cora's paintings—picture postcards . . . Cora was deceitful about her painting. . . . No, back to Mr. Entwhistle—something Mr. Entwhistle had said—or was it Lanscombe? A nun who came to the house on the day that Richard Abernethie died. A nun with a moustache. A nun at Stansfield Grange—and at Lytchett St. Mary. Altogether too many nuns! Rosamund looking glamorous as a nun on the stage. Rosamund—saying that he was a detective—and everyone staring at her when she said it. That was the way they must all have stared at Cora that day when she said, "But he was murdered, wasn't he?" What was it Helen Abernethie had felt to be "wrong" on that occasion? Helen Abernethie—leaving the past behind—going to Cyprus . . . Helen dropping the wax flowers with a crash when he had said—*what* was it he had said? He couldn't quite remember. . . .

He slept then, and as he slept he dreamed. . . .

He dreamed of the green malachite table. On it was the glass covered stand of wax flowers—only the whole thing had been painted over with thick crimson oil paint. Paint the colour of blood. He could smell the paint, and Timothy was groaning, was saying "I'm dying—dying . . . this is the end." And Maude, standing by, tall and stern, with a large knife in her hand was echoing him, saying "Yes, it's the end. . . ." The end—a deathbed, with candles and a nun praying. If he could just see the nun's face, he would know. . . .

Hercule Poirot woke up—and he did know!

Yes, it *was* the end. . . .

Though there was still a long way to go.

He sorted out the various bits of the mosaic.

Mr. Entwhistle, the smell of paint, Timothy's house and something that must be in it—or might be in it . . . the wax flowers . . . Helen . . . Broken glass . . .

III

Helen Abernethie, in her room, took some time in going to bed. She was thinking.

Sitting in front of her dressing table, she stared at herself unseeingly in the glass.

She had been forced into having Hercule Poirot in the house. She had not wanted it. But Mr. Entwhistle had made it hard for her to refuse. And now the whole thing had come out into the open. No question any more of letting Richard Abernethie lie quiet in his grave. All started by those few words of Cora's. . . .

That day after the funeral . . . How had they all looked, she wondered? How had they looked to Cora? How had she herself looked?

What was it George had said? About seeing oneself?

There was some quotation, too. *To see ourselves as others see us* . . . As others see us.

The eyes that were staring into the glass unseeingly suddenly focussed. She was seeing herself—but not really herself—not herself as others saw her—not as Cora had seen her that day.

Her right—no, her left eyebrow was arched a little higher than the right. The mouth? No, the curve of the mouth was symmetrical. If she met herself she would surely not see much difference from this mirror image. Not like Cora.

Cora—the picture came quite clearly . . . Cora, on the day of the funeral, her head tilted sideways—asking her question—looking at Helen . . .

Suddenly Helen raised her hands to her face. She said to herself, "*It doesn't make sense . . . it can't make sense . . .*"

IV

Miss Entwhistle was aroused from a delightful dream, in which she was playing Piquet with Queen Mary, by the ringing of the telephone.

She tried to ignore it—but it persisted. Sleepily she raised her head from the pillow and looked at the watch beside her bed. Five minutes to seven—who on earth could be ringing up at that hour? It must be a wrong number.

The irritating ding-ding continued. Miss Entwhistle sighed, snatched up a dressing gown and marched into the sitting room.

"This is Kensington 675498," she said with asperity as she picked up the receiver.

"This is Mrs. Abernethie speaking. Mrs. *Leo* Abernethie. Can I speak to Mr. Entwhistle?"

"Oh, good morning, Mrs. Abernethie." The 'good morning' was not cordial. "This is Miss Entwhistle. My brother is still asleep I'm afraid. I was asleep myself."

"I'm so sorry," Helen was forced to the apology. "But it's very important that I should speak to your brother at once."

"Wouldn't it do later?"

"I'm afraid not."

"Oh, very well then."

Miss Entwhistle was tart.

She tapped at her brother's door and went in.

"Those Abernethies again!" she said bitterly.

"Eh! The Abernethies?"

"Mrs. Leo Abernethie. Ringing up before seven in the morning! Really!"

"Mrs. Leo is it? Dear me. How remarkable. Where is my dressing gown? Ah, thank you."

Presently he was saying:

"Entwhistle speaking. Is that you, Helen?"

"Yes. I'm terribly sorry to get you out of bed like this. But you did tell me once to ring you up at once if I remembered what it was that struck me as having been wrong somehow on the day of the funeral when Cora electrified us all by suggesting that Richard had been murdered."

"Ah! You *have* remembered?"

Helen said in a puzzled voice:

"Yes, but it doesn't make sense."

"You must allow me to be the judge of that. Was it something you noticed about one of the people?"

"Yes."

"Tell me."

"It seems absurd." Helen's voice sounded apologetic. "But I'm quite sure of it. It came to me when I was looking at myself in the glass last night. Oh . . ."

The little startled half cry was succeeded by a sound that came oddly through the wires—a dull heavy sound that Mr. Entwhistle couldn't place at all—

He said urgently:

"Hullo—hullo—are you there? Helen, are you there? . . . Helen . . ."

21

IT WAS NOT until nearly an hour later that Mr. Entwhistle after a great deal of conversation with supervisors and others found himself at last speaking to Hercule Poirot.

"Thank heaven!" said Mr. Entwhistle with pardonable exasperation. "The Exchange seems to have had the greatest difficulty in getting the number."

"That is not surprising. The receiver was off the hook."

There was a grim quality in Poirot's voice which carried through to the listener.

Mr. Entwhistle said sharply:

"Has something happened?"

"Yes. Mrs. Leo Abernethie was found by the housemaid about twenty minutes ago lying by the telephone extension in the study. She was unconscious. A serious concussion."

"Do you mean she was struck on the head?"

"I think so. It is *just* possible that she fell and struck her head on a marble doorstop, but me I do not think so, and the doctor, he does not think so either."

"She was telephoning to me at the time. I wondered when we were cut off so suddenly."

"So it was to you she was telephoning. What did she say?"

"She mentioned to me some time ago that on the occasion when Cora Lansquenet suggested her brother had been murdered, she herself had a feeling of something being wrong—odd—she did not quite know how to put it—unfortunately she could not remember *why* she had that impression."

"And suddenly, she did remember?"

"Yes."

"And rang you up to tell you?"

"Yes."

"Eh bien?"

"There's no *eh bien* about it," said Mr. Entwhistle testily. "She started to tell me, but was interrupted."

"How much had she said?"

"Nothing pertinent."

"You will excuse me, *mon ami*, but *I* am the judge of that, not you. What exactly did she say?"

"She reminded me that I had asked her to let me know at once if she remembered what it was that had struck her as peculiar. She said she had remembered—but that it 'didn't make sense.'

"I asked her if it was something about one of the people who were there that day, and she said, yes, it was. She said it had come to her when she was looking in the glass—"

"Yes?"

"That was all."

"She gave no hint as to—which of the people concerned it was?"

"I should hardly fail to let you know if she had told me *that*," said Mr. Entwhistle acidly.

"I apologise, *mon ami*. Of course you would have told me."

Mr. Entwhistle said:

"We shall have to wait until she recovers consciousness before we know."

Poirot said gravely:

"That may not be for a very long time. Perhaps—never."

"Is it as bad as that?" Mr. Entwhistle's voice shook a little.

"Yes, it is as bad as that."

"But—that's terrible, Poirot."

"Yes, it is terrible. And it is why we cannot afford to wait! For it shows that we have to deal with someone who is either completely ruthless or so frightened that it comes to the same thing."

"But look here, Poirot, what about Helen? I feel worried. Are you sure she will be safe at Enderby?"

"No, she would not be safe. So she is not at Enderby. Already the ambulance has come and is taking her to a nursing home where she will have special nurses and where *no one*, family or otherwise, will be allowed in to see her."

Mr. Entwhistle sighed.

"You relieve my mind. She might have been in danger."

"She assuredly would have been in danger!"

Mr. Entwhistle's voice sounded deeply moved.

"I have a great regard for Helen Abernethie. I always have had. A woman of very exceptional character. She may have had certain—what shall I say?—reticences in her life?"

"Ah, there were reticences?"

"I have always had an idea that such was the case."

"Hence the villa in Cyprus. Yes, that explains a good deal. . . ."

"I don't want you to begin thinking—"

"You cannot stop me thinking. But now, there is a little commission that I have for you. One moment."

There was a pause, then Poirot's voice spoke again.

"I had to make sure that nobody was listening. All is well. Now here is what I want you to do for me. You must prepare to make a journey."

"A journey?" Mr. Entwhistle sounded faintly dismayed. "Oh, I see—you want me to come down to Enderby?"

"Not at all. *I* am in charge here. No, you will not have to travel so far. Your journey will not take you very far from London. You will travel to Bury St. Edmunds—(*Ma foi!* what names your English towns have!) and there you will hire a car and drive to Forsdyke House. It is a Mental Home. Ask for Dr. Penrith and inquire of him particulars about a patient who was recently discharged."

"What patient? Anyway, surely—"

Poirot broke in:

"The name of the patient is Gregory Banks. Find out for what form of insanity he was being treated."

"Do you mean that Gregory Banks is insane?"

"Sh. Be careful what you say. And now—I have not yet breakfasted and you, too, I suspect have not breakfasted?"

"Not yet. I was too anxious—"

"Quite so. Then, I pray you, eat your breakfast, repose yourself. There is a good train to Bury St. Edmunds at twelve o'clock. If I have any more news I will telephone you before you start."

"Be careful of *yourself*, Poirot," said Mr. Entwhistle with some concern.

"Ah that, yes! Me, I do not want to be hit on the head with a marble doorstop. You may be assured that I will take every precaution. And now—for the moment—goodbye."

Poirot heard the sound of the receiver being replaced at the other end, then he heard a very faint second click—and smiled to himself. Somebody had replaced the receiver on the telephone in the hall.

He went out there. There was no one about. He tiptoed to the cupboard at the back of the stairs and looked inside. At that moment Lanscombe came through the service door carrying a tray with toast and a silver coffee pot. He looked slightly surprised to see Poirot emerge from the cupboard.

"Breakfast is ready in the dining room, sir," he said.

Poirot surveyed him thoughtfully.

The old butler looked white and shaken.

"Courage," said Poirot, clapping him on the shoulder. "All will yet be well. Would it be too much trouble to serve me a cup of coffee in my bedroom?"

"Certainly, sir. I will send Janet up with it, sir."

Lanscombe looked disapprovingly at Hercule Poirot's back as the latter climbed the stairs. Poirot was attired in an exotic silk dressing gown with a pattern of triangles and squares.

"Foreigners!" thought Lanscombe bitterly. "Foreigners in the house! And Mrs. Leo with concussion! I don't know what we're coming to. Nothing's the same since Mr. Richard died."

Hercule Poirot was dressed by the time he received his coffee from Janet. His murmurs of sympathy were well received, since he stressed the shock her discovery must have given her.

"Yes, indeed, sir, what I felt when I opened the door of the study and came in with the Hoover and saw Mrs. Leo lying there I never shall forget. There she lay—and I made sure she was dead. She must have been taken faint as she stood at the phone—and fancy her being up at that time in the morning! I've never known her do such a thing before."

"Fancy, indeed!" He added casually: "No one else was up, I suppose?"

"As it happens, sir, Mrs. Timothy was up and about. She's a very early riser always—often goes for a walk before breakfast."

"She is of the generation that rises early," said Poirot nodding his head. "The younger ones, now—*they* do not get up so early?"

"No, indeed, sir, all fast asleep when I brought them their tea—and very late I was, too, what with the shock and getting the doctor to come and having to have a cup first to steady myself."

She went off and Poirot reflected on what she had said.

Maude Abernethie had been up and about, and the younger generation had been in bed—but that, Poirot reflected, meant nothing at all. Anyone could have heard Helen's door open and close, and have followed her down to listen—and would afterwards have made a point of being fast asleep in bed.

"But if I am right," thought Poirot. "And after all, it is natural to me to be right—it is a habit I have!—then there is no need to go into who was here and who was there. First, I must seek a proof where I have deduced the proof may be. And then—I make my little speech. And I sit back and see what happens . . ."

As soon as Janet had left the room, Poirot drained his coffee cup, put on his overcoat and his hat, left his room, ran nimbly down the back stairs and left the house by the side door. He walked briskly the quarter mile to the post office where he demanded a trunk call. Presently he was once more speaking to Mr. Entwhistle.

"Yes, it is I yet again! Pay no attention to the commission with which I entrusted you. *C'était une blague!* Someone was listening. Now, *mon vieux*, to the real commission. You must, as I said, take a train. But not to Bury St. Edmunds. I want you to proceed to the house of Mr. Timothy Abernethie."

"But Timothy and Maude are at Enderby."

"Exactly. There is no one in the house but a woman by the name of Jones who has been persuaded by the offer of considerable *largesse* to guard the house whilst they are absent. What I want you to do is to take something out of that house!"

"My dear Poirot! I really can't stoop to burglary!"

"It will not seem like burglary. You will say to the excellent Mrs. Jones, who knows you, that you have been asked by Mr. or Mrs. Abernethie to fetch this particular object and take it to London. She will not suspect anything amiss."

"No, no, probably not. But I don't like it." Mr. Entwhistle sounded most reluctant. "Why can't you go and get whatever it is yourself?"

"Because, my friend, I should be a stranger of foreign appearance and as such a suspicious character, and Mrs. Jones would at once raise the difficulties! With you, she will not."

"No, no—I see that. But what on earth are Timothy and Maude going to think when they hear about it? I have known them for forty odd years."

"And you knew Richard Abernethie for that time also! And you knew Cora Lansquenet when she was a little girl!"

In a martyred voice Mr. Entwhistle asked:

"You're sure this is really *necessary*, Poirot?"

"The old question they asked in the war time on the posters. *Is your journey really necessary?* I say to you, it *is* necessary. It is vital!"

"And what is this object I've got to get hold of?"

Poirot told him.

"But really, Poirot, I don't see—"

"It is not necessary for *you* to see. *I* am doing the seeing."

"And what do you want me to do with the damned thing?"

"You will take it to London, to an address in Elm Park Gardens. If you have a pencil, note it down."

Having done so, Mr. Entwhistle said, still in his martyred voice:

"I hope you know what you are doing, Poirot?"

He sounded very doubtful—but Poirot's reply was not doubtful at all.

"Of course I know what I am doing. We are nearing the end."

Mr. Entwhistle sighed.

"If we could only guess what Helen was going to tell me."

"No need to guess. I *know*."

"You know? But my dear Poirot—"

"Explanations must wait. But let me assure you of this. *I know what Helen Abernethie saw when she looked in her mirror*."

II

Breakfast had been an uneasy meal. Neither Rosamund nor Timothy had appeared, but the others were there and had talked in rather subdued tones, and eaten a little less than they normally would have done.

George was the first one to recover his spirits. His temperament was mercurial and optimistic.

"I expect Aunt Helen will be all right," he said. "Doctors always like to pull a long face. After all, what's concussion? Often clears up completely in a couple of days."

"A woman I knew had concussion during the war," said Miss Gilchrist conversationally. "A brick or something hit her as she was walking down Tottenham Court Road—it was during fly bomb time—and she never felt *anything* at all. Just went on with what she was doing—and collapsed in a train to Liverpool twelve hours later. And would you believe it, she had no recollection at all of going to the station and catching the train or *anything*. She just couldn't understand it when she woke up in hospital. She was there for nearly three weeks."

"What I can't make out," said Susan, "is what Helen was doing telephoning at that unearthly hour, and who she was telephoning to?"

"Felt ill," said Maude with decision. "Probably woke up feeling queer and came down to ring up the doctor. Then had a giddy fit and fell. That's the only thing that makes sense."

"Bad luck hitting her head on that doorstop," said Michael. "If she'd just pitched over onto that thick pile carpet she'd have been all right."

The door opened and Rosamund came in, frowning.

"I can't find those wax flowers," she said. "I mean the ones that were standing on the malachite table the day of Uncle Richard's funeral." She looked accusingly at Susan. "*You* haven't taken them?"

"Of course I haven't! Really, Rosamund, you're not *still* thinking about malachite tables with poor old Helen carted off to hospital with concussion?"

"I don't see why I shouldn't think about them. If you've got concussion you don't know what's happening and it doesn't matter to you. We can't do anything for Aunt Helen, and Michael and I have got to get back to London by tomorrow lunch-time because we're seeing Jackie Lygo about opening dates for 'The Baronet's Progress.' So I'd like to fix up definitely about the table. But I'd like to have a look at those wax flowers again. There's a kind of Chinese vase on the table now—nice—but not nearly so period. I do wonder where they are—perhaps Lanscombe knows."

Lanscombe had just looked in to see if they had finished breakfast.

"We're all through, Lanscombe," said George getting up. "What's happened to our foreign friend?"

"He is having his coffee and toast served upstairs."

"*Petit déjeuner* for N.A.R.C.O."

"Lanscombe, do you know where those wax flowers are that used to be on that green table in the drawing room?" asked Rosamund.

"I understand Mrs. Leo had an accident with them, m'am. She was going to have a new glass shade made, but I don't think she has seen about it yet."

"Then where is the thing?"

"It would probably be in the cupboard behind the staircase, m'am. That is where things are usually placed when awaiting repair. Shall I ascertain for you?"

"I'll go and look myself. Come with me, Michael sweetie. It's dark there, and I'm not going in any dark corners by myself after what happened to Aunt Helen."

Everybody showed a sharp reaction. Maude demanded in her deep voice:

"What *do* you mean, Rosamund?"

"Well, she was coshed by someone, wasn't she?"

Gregory Banks said sharply:

"She was taken suddenly faint and fell."

Rosamund laughed.

"Did she tell you so? Don't be silly, Greg, of course she was coshed."

George said sharply:

"You shouldn't say things like that, Rosamund."

"Nonsense," said Rosamund. "She *must* have been. I mean, it all adds up. A detective in the house looking for clues, and Uncle Richard poisoned, and Aunt Cora killed with a hatchet, and Miss Gilchrist given poisoned wedding cake, and now Aunt Helen struck down with a blunt instrument. You'll see, it will go on like that. One after another of us will be killed and the one that's left will be It—the murderer, I mean. But it's not going to be *me*—who's killed, I mean."

"And why should anyone want to kill you, beautiful Rosamund?" asked George lightly.

Rosamund opened her eyes very wide.

"Oh," she said. "Because I know too much, of course."

"What do you know?" Maude Abernethie and Gregory Banks spoke almost in unison.

Rosamund gave her vacant and angelic smile.

"Wouldn't you all like to know?" she said agreeably. "Come on, Michael."

22

AT ELEVEN O'CLOCK, Hercule Poirot called an informal meeting in the library. Everyone was there and Poirot looked thoughtfully round the semi-circle of faces.

"Last night," he said, "Mrs. Shane announced to you that I was a private detective. For myself, I hoped to retain my—*camouflage*, shall we say?—a little longer. But no matter! Today—or at most the day after—I would have told you the truth. Please listen carefully now to what I have to say.

"I am in my own line a celebrated person—I may say a *most* celebrated person. My gifts, in fact, are unequalled!"

George Crossfield grinned and said:

"That's the stuff, M. Pont—no, it's M. Poirot, isn't it? Funny, isn't it, that I've never even heard of you?"

"It is not funny," said Poirot severely. "It is lamentable! Alas, there is no proper education nowadays. Apparently one learns nothing but economics—and how to set Intelligence Tests! But to continue. I have been a friend for many years of Mr. Entwhistle's—"

"So *he*'s the nigger in the wood pile!"

"If you like to put it that way, Mr. Crossfield. Mr. Entwhistle was greatly upset by the death of his old friend, Mr. Richard Abernethie. He was particularly perturbed by some words spoken on the day of the funeral by Mr. Abernethie's sister, Mrs. Lansquenet. Words spoken in this very room."

"Very silly—and just like Cora," said Maude. "Mr. Entwhistle should have had more sense than to pay attention to them!"

Poirot went on:

"Mr. Entwhistle was even more perturbed after the—the coincidence, shall I say?—of Mrs. Lansquenet's death. He wanted one thing only—to be assured that that death *was* a coincidence. In other words he wanted to feel assured that Richard Abernethie had died a natural death. To that end he commissioned me to make the necessary investigations."

There was a pause.

"I have made them. . . ."

Again there was a pause. No one spoke.

Poirot threw back his head.

"*Eh bien*, you will all be delighted to hear that as a result of my investigations—*there is absolutely no reason to believe that Mr. Abernethie died anything but a natural death*. There is no reason *at all* to believe that he was murdered!" He smiled. He threw out his hands in a triumphant gesture.

"That is good news, is it not?"

It hardly seemed to be, the way they took it. They stared at him and in all but the eyes of one person there still seemed to be doubt and suspicion.

The exception was Timothy Abernethie who was nodding his head in violent agreement.

"Of course Richard wasn't murdered," he said angrily. "Never could understand why anybody ever even thought of such a thing for a moment! Just Cora up to her tricks, that was all. Wanting to give you all a scare. Her idea of being funny. Truth is that although she was my own sister, she was always a bit mental, poor girl. Well, Mr. whatever your name is, I'm glad you've had the sense to come to the right conclusion, though if you ask me, I call it damned cheek of Entwhistle to go commissioning you to come prying and poking about. And if he thinks he's going to charge the estate with your fee, I can tell you he won't get away with it! Damned cheek, and most uncalled for! Who's Entwhistle to set himself up? If the family's satisfied—"

"But the family wasn't, Uncle Timothy," said Rosamund.

"Hey—what's that?"

Timothy peered at her under beetling brows of displeasure.

"We weren't satisfied. And what about Aunt Helen this morning?"

Maude said sharply:

"Helen's just the age when you're liable to get a stroke. That's all there is to that."

"I see," said Rosamund. "Another coincidence, you think?"

She looked at Poirot.

"Aren't there rather too many coincidences?"

"Coincidences," said Hercule Poirot, "do happen."

"Nonsense," said Maude. "Helen felt ill, came down and rang up the doctor, and then—"

"But she didn't ring up the doctor," said Rosamund. "I asked him—"

Susan said sharply:

"Who did she ring up?"

"I don't know," said Rosamund, a shade of vexation passing over her face. "But I daresay I can find out," she added hopefully.

II

Hercule Poirot was sitting in the Victorian summerhouse. He drew his large watch from his pocket and laid it on the table in front of him.

He had announced that he was leaving by the twelve o'clock train. There was still half an hour to go. Half an hour for someone to make up their minds and come to him. Perhaps more than one person . . .

The summerhouse was clearly visible from most of the windows of the house. Surely, soon, someone would come?

If not, his knowledge of human nature was deficient, and his main premises incorrect.

He waited—and above his head a spider in its web waited for a fly.

It was Miss Gilchrist who came first. She was flustered and upset and rather incoherent.

"Oh, Mr. Pontarlier—I can't remember your other name," she said.

"I had to come and speak to you although I *don't* like doing it—but really I feel I *ought* to. I mean, after what happened to poor Mrs. Leo this morning—and I think myself Mrs. Shane was *quite right*—and *not* coincidence, and certainly not a *stroke*—as Mrs. Timothy suggested, because my own father had a stroke and it was quite a different appearance, and anyway the doctor *said* concussion quite clearly!"

She paused, took breath and looked at Poirot with appealing eyes.

"Yes," said Poirot gently and encouragingly. "You want to tell me something?"

"As I say, I don't like doing it—because she's been so kind. She found me the position with Mrs. Timothy and everything. She's been really *very* kind. That's why I feel so ungrateful. And even gave me Mrs. Lansquenet's musquash jacket which is really *most* handsome and fits beautifully because it never matters if fur is a little on the large side. And when I wanted to return her the amethyst brooch she wouldn't *hear* of it—"

"You are referring," said Poirot gently, "to Mrs. Banks?"

"Yes, you see—" Miss Gilchrist looked down, twisting her fingers unhappily. She looked up and said with a sudden gulp:

"You see, I *listened!*"

"You mean you happened to overhear a conversation—"

"No." Miss Gilchrist shook her head with an air of heroic determination. "I'd rather speak the truth. And it's not so bad telling you because you're not English."

Hercule Poirot understood her without taking offence.

"You mean that to a foreigner it is natural that people should listen at doors and open letters, or read letters that are left about?"

"Oh, I'd never open anybody else's letters," said Miss Gilchrist in a shocked tone. "Not *that*. But I *did* listen that day—the day that Mr. Richard Abernethie came down to see his sister. I was curious, you know, about his turning up suddenly after all those years. And I did wonder why—and—and—you see when you haven't much life of your own or very many friends, you do tend to get interested—when you're living *with* anybody, I mean."

"Most natural," said Poirot.

"Yes, I do think it was natural. . . . Though not, of course, at all *right*. But I did it! And I heard what he said!"

"You heard what Mr. Abernethie said to Mrs. Lansquenet?"

"Yes. He said something like—'It's no good talking to Timothy. He poohs-poohs everything. Simply won't listen. But I thought I'd like to get it off my chest to you, Cora. We three are the only ones left. And though you've always liked to play the simpleton you've got a lot of common sense. So what would *you* do about it, if you were me?'

"I couldn't quite hear what Mrs. Lansquenet said, but I caught the word *police*—and then Mr. Abernethie burst out quite loud, and said, 'I can't do that. Not when it's a question of *my own niece*.' And then I had to run in the kitchen for something boiling over and when I got back Mr. Abernethie was saying, 'Even if I die an unnatural death I don't want the police called in, if it can possibly be avoided. You understand that, don't you, my dear girl? But don't worry. Now that I *know*, I shall take all possible precautions.' And he went on, saying he'd made a new will, and that she, Cora, would be quite all right. And then he said about her having been happy with her husband and how perhaps he'd made a mistake over that in the past."

Miss Gilchrist stopped.

Poirot said: "I see—I see . . ."

"But I never wanted to say—to tell. I didn't think Mrs. Lansquenet would have wanted me to. . . . But now—after Mrs. Leo being attacked this morning—and then you saying so calmly it was coincidence. But, oh, M. Pontarlier, it *wasn't* coincidence!"

Poirot smiled. He said:

"No, it wasn't coincidence. . . . Thank you, Miss Gilchrist, for coming to me. It was very necessary that you should."

III

He had a little difficulty in getting rid of Miss Gilchrist, and it was urgent that he should, for he hoped for further confidences.

His instinct was right. Miss Gilchrist had hardly gone before Gregory Banks, striding across the lawn, came impetuously into the summerhouse. His face was pale and there were beads of perspiration on his forehead. His eyes were curiously excited.

"At last!" he said. "I thought that stupid woman would never go. You're all wrong in what you said this morning. You're wrong about everything. Richard Abernethie *was* killed. *I* killed him."

Hercule Poirot let his eyes move up and down over the excited young man. He showed no surprise.

"So you killed him, did you? How?"

Gregory Banks smiled.

"It wasn't difficult for *me*. You can surely realise that. There were fifteen or twenty different drugs I could lay my hands on that would do it. The method of administration took rather more thinking out, but I hit on a very ingenious idea in the end. The beauty of it was that *I* didn't need to be anywhere near at the time."

"Clever," said Poirot.

"Yes." Gregory Banks cast his eyes down modestly. He seemed pleased. "Yes—I *do* think it was ingenious."

Poirot asked with interest:

"Why did you kill him? For the money that would come to your wife?"

"No. No, of course not." Greg was suddenly excitedly indignant. "I'm not a money grubber. I didn't marry Susan for her *money!*"

"Didn't you, Mr. Banks?"

"That's what *he* thought," Greg said with sudden venom. "Richard Abernethie! He liked Susan, he admired her, he was proud of her as an example of Abernethie blood! But he thought she'd married beneath her—he thought *I* was no good—he despised me! I daresay I hadn't the right accent—I didn't wear my clothes the right way. He was a snob—a filthy snob!"

"I don't think so," said Poirot mildly. "From all I have heard, Richard Abernethie was no snob."

"He was. He was." The young man spoke with something approaching hysteria. "He thought nothing of me. He sneered at me—always very polite but underneath I could *see* that he didn't like me!"

"Possibly."

"People can't treat me like that and get away with it! They've tried it before! A woman who used to come and have her medicines made up. She was rude to me. Do you know what I did?"

"Yes," said Poirot.

Gregory looked startled.

"So you know that?"

"Yes."

"She nearly died." He spoke in a satisfied manner. "That shows you I'm not the sort of person to be trifled with! Richard Abernethie despised me—and what happened to him? He died."

"A most successful murder," said Poirot with grave congratulation.

He added: "But why come and give yourself away—to me?"

"Because you said you were through with it all! You said he *hadn't* been murdered. I had to show you that you're not as clever as you think you are—and besides—besides—"

"Yes," said Poirot. "And besides?"

Greg collapsed suddenly onto the bench. His face changed. It took on a sudden ecstatic quality.

"It was wrong—wicked. . . . I must be punished. . . . I must go back there—to the place of punishment . . . to atone . . . Yes, to *atone!* Repentance! Retribution!"

His face was alight now with a kind of glowing ecstasy. Poirot studied him for a moment or two curiously.

Then he asked:

"How badly do you want to get away from your wife?"

Gregory's face changed.

"Susan? Susan is wonderful—wonderful!"

"Yes. Susan is wonderful. That is a grave burden. Susan loves you devotedly. That is a burden, too?"

Gregory sat looking in front of him. Then he said, rather in the manner of a sulky child:

"Why couldn't she let me alone?"

He sprang up.

"She's coming now—across the lawn. I'll go now. But you'll tell her what I told you? Tell her I've gone to the police station. To confess."

IV

Susan came in breathlessly.

"Where's Greg? He was here! I saw him."

"Yes." Poirot paused a moment—before saying: "He came to tell me that it was he who poisoned Richard Abernethie . . ."

"What absolute *nonsense!* You didn't believe him, I hope?"

"Why should I not believe him?"

"He wasn't even near this place when Uncle Richard died!"

"Perhaps not. Where was he when Cora Lansquenet died?"

"In London. We both were."

Hercule Poirot shook his head.

"No, no, that will not do. You, for instance, took out your car that day and were away all afternoon. I think I know where you went. You went to Lytchett St. Mary."

"I did no such thing!"

Poirot smiled.

"When I met you here, Madame, it was not, as I told you, the first time I had seen you. After the inquest on Mrs. Lansquenet you were in the garage of the King's Arms. You talk there to a mechanic and close by you is a car containing an elderly foreign gentleman. You did not notice him, but he noticed you."

"I don't see what you mean. That was the day of the inquest."

"Ah, but remember what that mechanic said to you! He asked you if you were a relative of the victim, and you said you were her niece."

"He was just being a ghoul. They're all ghouls."

"And his next words were, 'Ah, wondered where I'd seen you before.' Where did he see you before, Madame? It must have been in Lytchett St. Mary, since in his mind his seeing you before was accounted for by your being Mrs. Lansquenet's niece. Had he seen you near her cottage? And when? It was a matter, was it not, that demands inquiry. And the result of the inquiry is, that you were there—in Lytchett St. Mary—on the afternoon Cora Lansquenet died. You parked your car in the same quarry where you left it the morning of the inquest. The car was seen and the number was noted. By this time Inspector Morton knows whose car it was."

Susan stared at him. Her breath came rather fast, but she showed no signs of discomposure.

"You're talking nonsense, M. Poirot. And you're making me forget what I came here to say—I wanted to try and find you alone—"

"To confess to me that it was you and not your husband who committed the murder?"

"No, of course not. What kind of fool do you think I am? And I've already told you that Gregory never left London that day."

"A fact which you cannot possibly know since you were away yourself. Why did you go down to Lytchett St. Mary, Mrs. Banks?"

Susan drew a deep breath.

"All right, if you must have it! What Cora said at the funeral worried me. I kept on thinking about it. Finally I decided to run down in the car and see her, and ask her what had put the idea into her head. Greg thought it a silly idea, so I didn't even tell him where I was going. I got there about three o'clock, knocked and rang, but there was no answer, so I thought she must be out or gone away. That's all there is to it. I didn't go round to the back of the cottage. If I had, I might have seen the broken window. I just went back to London without the faintest idea there was anything wrong."

Poirot's face was non-committal. He said:

"Why does your husband accuse himself of the crime?"

"Because he's—" a word trembled on Susan's tongue and was rejected. Poirot seized on it.

"You were going to say 'because he is batty' speaking in jest—but the jest was too near the truth, was it not?"

"Greg's all right. He is. He *is*."

"I know something of his history," said Poirot. "He was for some months in Forsdyke House Mental Home before you met him."

"He was never certified. He was a voluntary patient."

"That is true. He is not, I agree, to be classed as insane. But he is, very definitely, unbalanced. He has a punishment complex—has had it, I suspect, since infancy."

Susan spoke quickly and eagerly:

"You don't understand, M. Poirot. Greg has never had a *chance*. That's why I wanted Uncle Richard's money so badly. Uncle Richard was so matter of fact. He couldn't understand. I knew Greg had got to set up for himself. He had got to feel he was *someone*—not just a chemist's assistant, being pushed around. Everything will be different now. He will have his own laboratory. He can work out his own formulas."

"Yes, yes—you will give him the earth—because you love him. Love him too much for safety or for happiness. But you cannot give to people what they are incapable of receiving. At the end of it all, he will still be something that he does not want to be. . . ."

"What's that?"

"Susan's husband."

"How cruel you are! And what nonsense you talk!"

"Where Gregory Banks is concerned you are unscrupulous. You wanted your uncle's money—not for yourself—but for your husband. *How badly did you want it?"*

Angrily, Susan turned and dashed away.

V

"I thought," said Michael Shane lightly, "that I'd just come along and say goodbye."

He smiled, and his smile had a singularly intoxicating quality.

Poirot was aware of the man's vital charm.

He studied Michael Shane for some moments in silence. He felt as though he knew this man least well of all the house party, for Michael Shane only showed the side of himself that he wanted to show.

"Your wife," said Poirot conversationally, "is a very unusual woman."

Michael raised his eyebrows.

"Do you think so? She's lovely, I agree. But not, or so I've found, conspicuous for brains."

"She will never try to be too clever," Poirot agreed. "But she knows what she wants." He sighed. "So few people do."

"Ah!" Michael's smile broke out again. "Thinking of the malachite table?"

"Perhaps," Poirot paused and added: *"And of what was on it."*

"The wax flowers, you mean?"

"The wax flowers."

Michael frowned.

"I don't always quite understand you, M. Poirot. However," the smile was switched on again, "I'm more thankful than I can say that we're all out of the wood. It's unpleasant, to say the least of it, to go around with the suspicion that somehow or other one of us murdered poor old Uncle Richard."

"That is how he seemed to you when you met him?" Poirot inquired. "Poor old Uncle Richard?"

"Of course he was very well preserved and all that—"

"And in full possession of his faculties—"

"Oh yes."

"And, in fact, quite *shrewd?*"

"I daresay."

"A shrewd judge of character."

The smile remained unaltered.

"You can't expect me to agree with *that*, M. Poirot. He didn't approve of *me*."

"He thought you, perhaps, the unfaithful type?" Poirot suggested.

Michael laughed.

"What an old-fashioned idea!"

"But it is true, isn't it?"

"Now I wonder what you mean by *that?*"

Poirot placed the tips of his fingers together.

"There have been inquiries made, you know," he murmured.

"By you?"

"Not only by me."

Michael Shane gave him a quick searching glance. His reactions, Poirot noted, were quick. Michael Shane was no fool.

"You mean—the police are interested?"

"They have never been quite satisfied, you know, to regard the murder of Cora Lansquenet as a casual crime."

"And they've been making inquiries about me?"

Poirot said primly:

"They are interested in the movements of Mrs. Lansquenet's relations on the day that she was killed."

"That's extremely awkward." Michael spoke with a charming, confidential, rueful air.

"Is it, Mr. Shane?"

"More so than you can imagine! I told Rosamund, you see, that I was lunching with a certain Oscar Lewis on that day."

"When, in actual fact, you were not?"

"No. Actually I motored down to see a woman called Sorrel Dainton—quite a well-known actress. I was with her in her last show. Rather awkward, you see—for though it's quite satisfactory as far as the police are concerned, it won't go down very well with Rosamund."

"Ah!" Poirot looked discreet. "There has been a little trouble over this friendship of yours?"

"Yes . . . In fact—Rosamund made me promise I wouldn't see her any more."

"Yes, I can see that may be awkward. . . . *Entre nous*, you had an affair with the lady?"

"Oh, just one of those things! It's not as though I cared for the woman at all."

"But she cares for you?"

"Well, she's been rather tiresome. . . . Women do cling so. However, as you say, the police at any rate will be satisfied."

"You think so?"

"Well, I could hardly be taking a hatchet to Cora if I was dallying with Sorrel miles and miles away. She's got a cottage in Kent."

"I see—I see—and this Miss Dainton, she will testify for you?"

"She won't like it—but as it's murder, I suppose she'll have to do it."

"She will do it, perhaps, even if you were *not* dallying with her."

"What do you mean?" Michael looked suddenly black as thunder.

"The lady is fond of you. When they are fond, women will swear to what is true—and also to what is untrue."

"Do you mean to say that you don't believe me?"

"It does not matter if *I* believe you or not. It is not *I* you have to satisfy."

"Who then?"

Poirot smiled.

"Inspector Morton—who has just come out on the terrace through the side door."

Michael Shane wheeled round sharply.

23

"I HEARD YOU were here, M. Poirot," said Inspector Morton.

The two men were pacing the terrace together.

"I came over with Superintendent Parwell from Matchfield. Dr. Larraby rang him up about Mrs. Leo Abernethie and he's come over here to make a few inquiries. The doctor wasn't satisfied."

"And you, my friend," inquired Poirot, "where do you come in? You are a long way from your native Berkshire."

"I wanted to ask a few questions—and the people I wanted to ask them of seemed very conveniently assembled here." He paused before adding, "Your doing?"

"Yes, my doing."

"And as a result Mrs. Leo Abernethie gets knocked out."

"You must not blame me for that. If she had come to *me* . . . But she did not. Instead she rang up her lawyer in London."

"And was in process of spilling the beans to him when—Wonk!"

"When—as you say—Wonk!"

"And what had she managed to tell him?"

"Very little. She had only got as far as telling him that she was looking at herself in the glass."

"Ah! well," said Inspector Morton philosophically. "Women will do it." He looked sharply at Poirot. "That suggests something to you?"

"Yes, I think I know what it was she was going to tell him."

"Wonderful guesser, aren't you? You always were. Well, what was it?"

"Excuse me, are you inquiring into the death of Richard Abernethie?"

"Officially, no. Actually, of course, if it has a bearing on the murder of Mrs. Lansquenet—"

"It has a bearing on that, yes. But I will ask you, my friend, to give me a few more hours. I shall know by then if what I have imagined—imagined only, you comprehend—is correct. If it *is*—"

"Well, if it is?"

"Then I may be able to place in your hands a piece of concrete evidence."

"We could certainly do with it," said Inspector Morton with feeling. He looked askance at Poirot. "What have you been holding back?"

"Nothing. Absolutely nothing. Since the piece of evidence I have imagined may not in fact exist. I have only deduced its existence from various scraps of conversation. I may," said Poirot in a completely unconvinced tone, "be wrong."

Morton smiled.

"But that doesn't often happen to you?"

"No. Though I will admit—yes, I am forced to admit—that it *has* happened to me."

"I must say I'm glad to hear it! To be always right must be sometimes monotonous."

"I do not find it so," Poirot assured him.

Inspector Morton laughed.

"And you're asking me to hold off with my questioning?"

"No, no, not at all. Proceed as you had planned to do. I suppose you were not actually contemplating an arrest?"

Morton shook his head.

"Much too flimsy for that. We'd have to get a decision from the Public Prosecutor first—and we're a long way from that. No, just statements from certain parties of their movements on the day in question—in one case with a caution, perhaps."

"I see. Mrs. Banks?"

"Smart, aren't you? Yes. She was there that day. Her car was parked in that quarry."

"She was not seen actually *driving* the car?"

"No."

The Inspector added, "It's bad, you know, that she's never said a word about being down there that day. She's got to explain that satisfactorily."

"She is quite skilful at explanations," said Poirot drily.

"Yes. Clever young lady. Perhaps a thought too clever."

"It is never wise to be too clever. That is how murderers get caught. Has anything more come up about George Crossfield?"

"Nothing definite. He's a very ordinary type. There are a lot of young men like him going about the country in trains and buses or on bicycles. People find it hard to remember when a week or so has gone by if it was Wednesday or Thursday when they were at a certain place or noticed a certain person."

He paused and went on: "We've had one piece of rather curious information—from the Mother Superior of some convent or other. Two of her nuns had been out collecting from door to door. It seems that they went to Mrs. Lansquenet's cottage on the day *before* she was murdered, but couldn't make anyone hear when they knocked and rang. That's natural enough—she was up North at the Abernethie funeral and Gilchrist had been given the day off and had gone on an excursion to Bournemouth. The point is that they say *there was someone in the cottage*. They say they heard sighs and groans. I've queried whether it wasn't a day later but the Mother Superior is quite definite that that couldn't be so. It's all entered up in some book. Was there someone searching for something in the cottage that day, who seized the opportunity of both the women being away? And did that somebody not find what he or she was looking for and come back the next day? I don't set much store on the sighs and still less on the groans. Even nuns are suggestible and a cottage where murder has occurred positively *asks* for groans. The point is, was there someone in the cottage who shouldn't have been there? And if so, who was it? All the Abernethie crowd were at the funeral."

Poirot asked a seemingly irrelevant question:

"These nuns who were collecting in that district, did they return at all at a later date to try again?"

"As a matter of fact they did come again—about a week later. Actually on the day of the inquest, I believe."

"That fits," said Hercule Poirot. "That fits very well."

Inspector Morton looked at him.

"Why this interest in nuns?"

"They have been forced on my attention whether I will or no. It will not have escaped your attention, Inspector, that the visit of the nuns was the same day that poisoned wedding cake found its way into that cottage."

"You don't think—Surely that's a ridiculous idea?"

"My ideas are never ridiculous," said Hercule Poirot severely. "And now, *mon cher*, I must leave you to your questions and to the inquiries into the attack on Mrs. Abernethie. I myself must go in search of the late Richard Abernethie's niece."

"Now be careful what you go saying to Mrs. Banks."

"I do not mean Mrs. Banks. I mean Richard Abernethie's other niece."

II

Poirot found Rosamund sitting on a bench overlooking a little stream that cascaded down in a waterfall and then flowed through rhododendron thickets. She was staring into the water.

"I do not, I trust, disturb an Ophelia," said Poirot as he took his seat beside her. "You are, perhaps, studying the *rôle?*"

"I've never played in Shakespeare," said Rosamund. "Except once in Rep. I was Jessica in 'The Merchant.' A lousy part."

"Yet not without pathos. *'I am never merry when I hear sweet music.'* What a load she carried, poor Jessica, the daughter of the hated and despised Jew. What doubts of herself she must have had when she brought with her her father's ducats when she ran away to her lover. Jessica with gold was one thing—Jessica without gold might have been another."

Rosamund turned her head to look at him.

"I thought you'd gone," she said with a touch of reproach. She glanced down at her wrist-watch. "It's past twelve o'clock."

"I have missed my train," said Poirot.

"Why?"

"You think I missed it for a reason?"

"I suppose so. You're rather precise, aren't you? If you wanted to catch a train, I think you'd catch it."

"Your judgement is admirable. Do you know, Madame, I have been sitting in the little summerhouse hoping that you would, perhaps, pay me a visit there?"

Rosamund stared at him.

"Why should I? You more or less said goodbye to us all in the library."

"Quite so. And there was nothing—*you* wanted to say to *me?*"

"No." Rosamund shook her head. "I had a lot I wanted to think about. Important things."

"I see."

"I don't often do much thinking," said Rosamund. "It seems a waste of time. But this *is* important. I think one ought to plan one's life just as one wants it to be."

"And that is what you are doing?"

"Well, yes . . . I was trying to make a decision about something."

"About your husband?"

"In a way."

Poirot waited a moment, then he said:

"Inspector Morton has just arrived here." He anticipated Rosamund's question by going on: "He is the police officer in charge of the inquiries about Mrs. Lansquenet's death. He has come here to get statements from you all about what you were doing on the day she was murdered."

"I see. *Alibis*," said Rosamund cheerfully.

Her beautiful face relaxed into an impish glee.

"That will be hell for Michael," she said. "He thinks I don't really know he went off to be with that woman that day."

"How did you know?"

"It was obvious from the *way* he said he was going to lunch with Oscar. So frightfully casually, you know, and his nose twitching just a tiny bit like it always does when he tells lies."

"How devoutly thankful I am I am not married to you, Madame!"

"And then, of course, I made sure by ringing up Oscar," continued Rosamund. "Men always tell such silly lies."

"He is not, I fear, a very faithful husband?" Poirot hazarded.

Rosamund, however, did not reject the statement.

"No."

"But you do not mind?"

"Well, it's rather fun in a way," said Rosamund. "I mean, having a husband that all the other women want to snatch away from you. I should hate to be married to a man that nobody wanted—like poor Susan. Really Greg is so completely wet!''

Poirot was studying her.

''And suppose someone did succeed—in snatching your husband away from you?''

''They won't,'' said Rosamund. ''Not now,'' she added.

''You mean—''

''Not now that there's Uncle Richard's money. Michael falls for these creatures in a way—that Sorrel Dainton woman nearly got her hooks into him—wanted him for keeps—but with Michael the show will always come first. He can launch out now in a big way—put his own shows on. Do some production as well as acting. He's ambitious, you know, and he really is good. Not like me. I adore acting—but I'm ham, though I look nice. No, I'm not worried about Michael any more. Because it's my money, you see.''

Her eyes met Poirot's calmly. He thought how strange it was that both Richard Abernethie's nieces should have fallen deeply in love with men who were incapable of returning that love. And yet Rosamund was unusually beautiful and Susan was attractive and full of sex appeal. Susan needed and clung to the illusion that Gregory loved her. Rosamund, clear-sighted, had no illusions at all, but knew what she wanted.

''The point is,'' said Rosamund, ''that I've got to make a big decision—about the future. Michael doesn't know yet.'' Her face curved into a smile. ''He found out that I wasn't shopping that day and he's madly suspicious about Regent's Park.''

''What is this about Regent's Park?'' Poirot looked puzzled.

''I went there, you see, after Harley Street. Just to walk about and think. Naturally Michael thinks that if I went there at all, I went to meet some man!''

Rosamund smiled beatifically and added:

''He didn't like that *at all!*''

''But why should you not go to Regent's Park?'' asked Poirot.

''Just to walk there, you mean?''

''Yes. Have you never done it before?''

''Never. Why should I? What is there to go to Regent's Park *for?*''

Poirot looked at her and said:

''For you—nothing.''

He added:

''I think, Madame, that you must cede the green malachite table to your cousin Susan.''

Rosamund's eyes opened very wide.

"Why should I? I *want* it."

"I know. I know. But you—you will keep your husband. And the poor Susan, she will lose hers."

"Lose him? Do you mean Greg's going off with someone? I wouldn't have believed it of him. He looks so *wet*."

"Infidelity is not the only way of losing a husband, Madame."

"You don't mean—?" Rosamund stared at him. "You're not thinking that Greg poisoned Uncle Richard and killed Aunt Cora and conked Aunt Helen on the head? That's ridiculous. Even *I* know better than that."

"Who did, then?"

"George, of course. George is a wrong un, you know, he's mixed up in some sort of currency swindle—I heard about it from some friends of mine who were in Monte. I expect Uncle Richard got to know about it and was just going to cut him out of his will."

Rosamund added complacently:

"I've always known it was George."

24

THE TELEGRAM came about six o'clock that evening.

As specially requested it was delivered by hand, not telephoned, and Hercule Poirot, who had been hovering for some time in the neighbourhood of the front door, was at hand to receive it from Lanscombe as the latter took it from the telegraph boy.

He tore it open with somewhat less than his usual precision. It consisted of three words and a signature.

Poirot gave vent to an enormous sigh of relief.

Then he took a pound note from his pocket and handed it to the dumbfounded boy.

"There are moments," he said to Lanscombe, "when economy should be abandoned."

"Very possibly, sir," said Lanscombe politely.

"Where is Inspector Morton?" asked Poirot.

"One of the police gentlemen," Lanscombe spoke with distaste—and indicated subtly that such things as names for police officers were impossible to remember—"has left. The other is, I believe, in the study."

"Splendid," said Poirot. "I join him immediately."

He once more clapped Lanscombe on the shoulder and said:

"Courage, we are on the point of arriving!"

Lanscombe looked slightly bewildered since departures, and not arrivals, had been in his mind.

He said:

"You do not, then, propose to leave by the nine thirty train after all, sir?"

"Do not lose hope," Poirot told him.

Poirot moved away, then wheeling round, he asked:

"I wonder, can you remember what were the first words Mrs. Lansquenet said to you when she arrived here on the day of your master's funeral?"

"I remember very well, sir," said Lanscombe, his face lighting up. "Miss Cora—I beg pardon, Mrs. Lansquenet—I always think of her as Miss Cora, somehow—"

"Very naturally."

"—She said to me: 'Hullo, Lanscombe. It's a long time since you used to bring us out meringues to the huts.' All the children used to have a hut of their own—down by the fence in the Park. In summer, when there was going to be a dinner party, I used to take the young ladies and gentlemen—the younger ones, you understand, sir—some meringues. Miss Cora, sir, was always very fond of her food."

Poirot nodded.

"Yes," he said, "that was as I thought. Yes, it was very typical, that."

He went into the study to find Inspector Morton and without a word handed him the telegram.

Morton read it blankly.

"I don't understand a word of this."

"The time has come to tell you all."

Inspector Morton grinned.

"You sound like a young lady in a Victorian melodrama. But it's about time you came across with something. I can't hold out on this set-up much longer. That Banks fellow is still insisting that he poisoned Richard Abernethie and boasting that we can't find out how. What beats me is why there's always somebody who comes forward when there's a murder and yells out that they did it! What do they think there is in it for them? I've never been able to fathom that."

"In this case, probably shelter from the difficulties of being responsible for oneself—in other words—Forsdyke Sanatorium."

"More likely to be Broadmoor."

"That might be equally satisfactory."

"*Did* he do it, Poirot? The Gilchrist woman came out with the story she'd already told you and it would fit with what Richard Abernethie said about his niece. If her husband did it, it would involve her. Somehow, you know, I can't visualize that girl committing a lot of crimes. But there's nothing she wouldn't do to try and cover *him*."

"I will tell you all—"

"Yes, yes, tell me all! And for the Lord's sake hurry up and do it!"

II

This time it was in the big drawing room that Hercule Poirot assembled his audience.

There was amusement rather than tension in the faces that were turned towards him. Menace had materialised in the shape of Inspector Morton and Superintendent Parwell. With the police in charge, questioning, asking for statements, Hercule Poirot, private detective, had receded into something closely resembling a joke.

Timothy was not far from voicing the general feeling when he remarked in an audible *sotto voce* to his wife:

"Damned little mountebank! Entwhistle must be *gaga!*—that's all I can say."

It looked as though Hercule Poirot would have to work hard to make his proper effect.

He began in a slightly pompous manner.

"For the second time, I announce my departure! This morning I announced it for the twelve o'clock train. This evening I announce it for the nine thirty—immediately, that is, after dinner. I go because there is nothing more here for me to do."

"Could have told him that all along." Timothy's commentary was still in evidence. "Never was anything for him to do. The cheek of these fellows!"

"I came here originally to solve a riddle. The riddle is solved. Let me, first, go over the various points which were brought to my attention by the excellent Mr. Entwhistle.

"First, Mr. Richard Abernethie dies suddenly. Secondly, after his funeral, his sister Cora Lansquenet says, 'He was murdered, wasn't he?' Thirdly, Mrs. Lansquenet is killed. The question is, are those three things part of a *sequence?* Let us observe what happens next? Miss Gilchrist, the dead woman's companion, is taken ill after eating a piece of wedding cake which contains arsenic. That, then, is the *next* step in the sequence.

"Now, as I told you this morning, in the course of my inquiries I have come across nothing—nothing at all, to substantiate the belief that Mr. Abernethie was poisoned. Equally, I may say, I have found nothing to prove conclusively that he was *not* poisoned. But as we proceed, things become easier. Cora Lansquenet undoubtedly asked that sensational question at the funeral. Everyone agrees upon *that*. And undoubtedly, on the following day, Mrs. Lansquenet was murdered—a hatchet being the instrument employed. Now let us examine the fourth happening. The local post van driver is strongly of the belief—though he will not definitely swear to it—that he did not deliver that parcel of wedding cake in the usual way. And if that is so, then the parcel was left by hand and though we cannot exclude a 'person unknown'—we must take particular notice of those people who were actually on the spot and in a position to put the parcel where it was subsequently found. Those were: Miss Gilchrist herself, of course; Susan Banks, who came down that day for the inquest; Mr. Entwhistle (but yes, we must consider Mr. Entwhistle; he was present, remember, when Cora made her disquieting remark!). And there were two other people. An old gentleman who represented himself to be a Mr. Guthrie, an art critic, and a nun or nuns who called early that morning to collect a subscription.

''Now I decided that I would start on the assumption that the postal van driver's recollection was correct. Therefore the little group of people under suspicion must be very carefully studied. Miss Gilchrist did not benefit in any way by Richard Abernethie's death and in only a very minute degree by Mrs. Lansquenet's—in actual fact the death of the latter put her out of employment and left her with the possibility of finding it difficult to get new employment. Also Miss Gilchrist was taken to hospital definitely suffering from arsenical poisoning.

''Susan Banks *did* benefit from Richard Abernethie's death, and in a small degree from Mrs. Lansquenet's—though here her motive must almost certainly have been security. She might have very good reason to believe that Miss Gilchrist had overheard a conversation between Cora Lansquenet and her brother which referred to her, and she might therefore decide that Miss Gilchrist must be eliminated. She herself, remember, refused to partake of the wedding cake and also suggested not calling in a doctor until the morning, when Miss Gilchrist was taken ill in the night.

''Mr. Entwhistle did *not* benefit by either of the deaths—but he had had considerable control over Mr. Abernethie's affairs, and the trust funds, and there might well be some reason why Richard Abernethie should not live too long. But—you will say—if it is Mr. Entwhistle who was concerned, why should he come to *me?*

''And to that I will answer—it is not the first time that a murderer has been too sure of himself.

"We now come to what I may call the two outsiders. Mr. Guthrie and a nun. If Mr. Guthrie is really Mr. Guthrie, the art critic, then that clears him. The same applies to the nun, if she is really a nun. The question is, are these people themselves, or are they somebody else?

"And I may say that there seems to be a curious—*motif*—one might call it—of a nun running through this business. A nun comes to the door at Mr. Timothy Abernethie's house and Miss Gilchrist believes it is the same nun she has seen at Lytchett St. Mary. Also a nun, or nuns, called here the day before Mr. Abernethie died . . ."

George Crossfield murmured, "Three to one, the nun."

Poirot went on:

"So here we have certain pieces of our pattern—the death of Mr. Abernethie, the murder of Cora Lansquenet, the poisoned wedding cake, the '*motif*' of the 'Nun.'

"I will add some other features of the case that engaged my attention:

"The visit of an art critic, a smell of oil paint, a picture postcard of Polflexan harbour, and finally a bouquet of wax flowers standing on that malachite table where a Chinese vase stands now.

"It was reflecting on these things that led me to the truth—and I am now about to tell you the truth.

"The first part of it I told you this morning. Richard Abernethie died suddenly—but there would have been no reason at all to suspect foul play—had it not been for the words uttered by his sister Cora at his funeral. *The whole case for the murder of Richard Abernethie rests upon those words*. As a result of them, you all believed that murder had taken place, and you believed it, not really because of the words themselves but because of *the character of Cora Lansquenet herself*. For Cora Lansquenet had always been famous for speaking the truth at awkward moments. So the case for Richard's murder rested not only upon what Cora had *said* but upon Cora herself.

"And now I come to the question that I suddenly asked myself:

"*How well did you all know Cora Lansquenet?*"

He was silent for a moment, and Susan asked sharply, "What do you mean?"

Poirot went on:

"*Not well at all*—that is the answer! The younger generation had never seen her at all, or if so, only when they were very young children. There were actually only three people present that day who actually *knew* Cora. Lanscombe, the butler, who is old and very blind; Mrs. Timothy Abernethie, who had only seen her a few times round about the date of her own wedding, and Mrs. Leo Abernethie, who had known her quite well, but who had not seen her for over twenty years.

"So I said to myself: 'Supposing it was *not* Cora Lansquenet who came to the funeral that day?' "

"Do you mean that Aunt Cora—*wasn't* Aunt Cora?" Susan demanded incredulously. "Do you mean that it wasn't Aunt Cora who was murdered, but someone else?"

"No, no, it was Cora Lansquenet who was murdered. *But it was not Cora Lansquenet* who came the day before to her brother's funeral. The woman who came that day came for one purpose only—to exploit, one may say, the fact that Richard died suddenly. And to create in the minds of his relations the belief that he had been murdered. Which she managed to do most successfully!"

"Nonsense! Why? What was the point of it?" Maude spoke bluffly.

"Why? *To draw attention away from the other murder*. From the murder of Cora Lansquenet herself. For if Cora says that Richard has been murdered and the next day *she herself is killed*, the two deaths are bound to be at least considered as possible cause and effect. But if Cora is murdered and her cottage is broken into, and if the apparent robbery does not convince the police, then they will look—where? Close at home, will they not? Suspicion will tend to fall on the woman who shares the house with her."

Miss Gilchrist protested in a tone that was almost bright:

"Oh come—really—Mr. Pontarlier—you don't suggest I'd commit a murder for an amethyst brooch and a few worthless sketches?"

"No," said Poirot. "For a little more than that. There was one of those sketches, Miss Gilchrist, that represented Polflexan harbour and which, as Mrs. Banks was clever enough to realise, had been copied from a picture postcard which showed the old pier still in position. But Mrs. Lansquenet painted always from life. I remembered then that Mr. Entwhistle had mentioned there being *a smell of oil paint* in the cottage when he first got there. You can paint, can't you, Miss Gilchrist? Your father was an artist and you know a good deal about pictures. Supposing that one of the pictures that Cora picked up cheaply at a sale was a valuable picture. Supposing that she herself did not recognise it for what it was, but that you did. You knew she was expecting, very shortly, a visit from an old friend of hers who was a well known art critic. Then her brother dies suddenly—and a plan leaps into your head. Easy to administer a sedative to her in her early cup of tea that will keep her unconscious for the whole of the day of the funeral whilst you yourself are playing her part at Enderby. You know Enderby well from listening to her talk about it. She has talked, as people do when they get on in life, a great deal about her childhood days. Easy for you to start off by a remark to old Lanscombe about meringues and huts which will make him quite sure of your identity in case he was inclined to doubt. Yes, you used your knowledge of Enderby well that day, with allusions to this and that, and recalling memories. None of them suspected you were not Cora. You were wearing her clothes, slightly padded, and since she wore a false front of hair, it was easy for you to assume that. Nobody had seen Cora for twenty years—and in twenty years people change so much that one often hears the remark: 'I would never have known her!' But mannerisms are remembered, and Cora had certain very definite mannerisms, all of which you had practised carefully before the glass.

"And it was there, strangely enough, that you made your first mistake. *You forgot that a mirror image is reversed.* When you saw in the glass the perfect reproduction of Cora's birdlike sidewise tilt of the head, you didn't realise that it was actually the *wrong way round.* You saw, let us say, Cora inclining her head to the *right*—but you forgot that actually your own head was inclined to the *left* to produce that effect *in the glass.*

"That was what puzzled and worried Helen Abernethie at the moment when you made your famous insinuation. Something seemed to her 'wrong.' I realised myself the other night when Rosamund Shane made an unexpected remark about what happens on such an occasion. Everybody inevitably looks at the *speaker.* Therefore, when Mrs. Leo felt something was 'wrong,' it must be that something was wrong with *Cora Lansquenet.* The other evening, after talk about mirror images and 'seeing oneself' I think Mrs. Leo experimented before a looking glass. Her own face is not particularly asymmetrical. She probably thought of Cora, remembered how Cora used to incline her head to the right, did so, and looked in the glass—when, of course, the image seemed to her 'wrong' and she realised, in a flash, just what had been wrong on the day of the funeral. She puzzled it out—either Cora had taken to inclining her head in the opposite direction—most unlikely—or else *Cora had not been Cora.* Neither way seemed to her to make sense. But she determined to tell Mr. Entwhistle of her discovery at once. Someone who was used to getting up early was already about, and followed her down, and fearful of what revelations she might be about to make struck her down with a heavy doorstop."

Poirot paused and added:

"I may as well tell you now, Miss Gilchrist, that Mrs. Abernethie's concussion is not serious. She will soon be able to tell us her own story."

"I never did anything of the sort," said Miss Gilchrist. "The whole thing is a wicked lie."

"It *was* you that day," said Michael Shane suddenly. He had been studying Miss Gilchrist's face. "I ought to have seen it sooner—I felt in a vague kind of way I had seen you before somewhere—but of course one never looks much at—" he stopped.

"No, one doesn't bother to look at a mere companion help," said Miss

Gilchrist. Her voice shook a little. ''A drudge, a domestic drudge! Almost a servant! But go on, M. Poirot. Go on with this fantastic piece of nonsense!''

''The suggestion of murder thrown out at the funeral was only the first step, of course,'' said Poirot. ''You had more in reserve. At any moment you were prepared to admit to having listened to a conversation between Richard and his sister. What he actually told her, no doubt, was the fact that he had not long to live, and that explains a cryptic phrase in the letter he wrote her after getting home. The 'Nun' was another of your suggestions. The nun—or rather nuns—who called at the cottage on the day of the inquest suggested to you a mention of a nun who was 'following you round,' and you used that when you were anxious to hear what Mrs. Timothy was saying to her sister-in-law at Enderby. And also because you wished to accompany her there and find out for yourself just how suspicions were going. Actually to poison *yourself*, badly but not fatally, with arsenic, is a very old device—and I may say that it served to awaken Inspector Morton's suspicions of you.''

''But the picture?'' said Rosamund. ''What kind of a picture was it?''

Poirot slowly unfolded a telegram.

''This morning I rang up Mr. Entwhistle, a responsible person, to go to Stansfield Grange and, acting on authority from Mr. Abernethie himself'' (here Poirot gave a hard stare at Timothy) ''to look amongst the pictures in Miss Gilchrist's room and select the one of Polflexan Harbour on pretext of having it reframed as a surprise for Miss Gilchrist. He was to take it back to London and call upon Mr. Guthrie whom I had warned by telegram. The hastily painted sketch of Polflexan Harbour was removed and the original picture exposed.''

He held up the telegram and read:

''Definitely a Vermeer. Guthrie.''

Suddenly, with electrifying effect, Miss Gilchrist burst into speech.

''I knew it was a Vermeer. I *knew* it! *She* didn't know! Talking about Rembrandts and Italian Primitives and unable to recognise a Vermeer when it was under her nose! Always prating about Art—and really knowing nothing about it! She was a thoroughly stupid woman. Always maundering on about this place—about Enderby, and what they did there as children, and about Richard and Timothy and Laura and all the rest of them. Rolling in money always! Always the best of everything those children had. You don't know how boring it is listening to somebody going on about the same things, hour after hour and day after day. And saying 'Oh yes, Mrs. Lansquenet' and 'Really, Mrs. Lansquenet?' Pretending to be interested. And really bored—bored—*bored*. . . . And nothing to look forward to. . . . And then—a Vermeer! I saw in the papers that a Vermeer sold the other day for over two thousand pounds!''

''You killed her—in that brutal way—for two thousand pounds?'' Susan's voice was incredulous.

''Two thousand pounds,'' said Poirot, ''would have rented and equipped a teashop. . . .''

Miss Gilchrist turned to him.

''At least,'' she said. ''You *do* understand. It was the only chance I'd ever get. I *had* to have a capital sum.'' Her voice vibrated with the force and obsession of her dream. ''I was going to call it the Palm Tree. And have little camels as menu holders. One can occasionally get quite nice china—export rejects—not that awful white utility stuff. I meant to start it in some nice neighbourhood where nice people would come in. I had thought of Rye. . . . Or perhaps Chichester . . . I'm sure I could have made a success of it.'' She paused a minute, then added musingly, ''Oak tables—and little basket chairs with striped red and white cushions. . . .''

For a few moments the teashop that would never be, seemed more real than the Victorian solidity of the drawing room at Enderby. . . .

It was Inspector Morton who broke the spell.

Miss Gilchrist turned to him quite politely.

''Oh, certainly,'' she said. ''At once. I don't want to give any trouble, I'm sure. After all, if I can't have the Palm Tree, nothing really seems to matter very much. . . .''

She went out of the room with him and Susan said, her voice still shaken:

''I've never imagined a—*ladylike* murderer. It's horrible.''

25

''BUT I DON'T understand about the wax flowers,'' said Rosamund.

She fixed Poirot with large reproachful blue eyes.

They were at Helen's flat in London. Helen herself was resting on the sofa and Rosamund and Poirot were having tea with her.

''I don't see that *wax flowers* had anything to *do* with it,'' said Rosamund. ''Or the malachite table.''

''The malachite table, no. But the wax flowers were Miss Gilchrist's second mistake. She said how nice they looked on the malachite table. And you see, Madame, *she* could not have seen them there. Because they had been broken and put away before she arrived with the Timothy Abernethies. *So she could only have seen them when she was there as Cora Lansquenet.*''

''That *was* stupid of her, wasn't it?'' said Rosamund.

Poirot shook a forefinger at her.

''It shows you, Madame, the dangers of *conversation*. It is a profound belief of mine that if you can induce a person to talk to you for long enough, *on any subject whatever*, sooner or later they will give themselves away. Miss Gilchrist did.''

''I shall have to be careful,'' said Rosamund thoughtfully.

Then she brightened up.

''Did you know? I'm going to have a baby.''

''Aha! So that is the meaning of Harley Street and Regent's Park?''

''Yes. I was so upset, you know, and so surprised—that I just had to go somewhere and *think*.''

''You said, I remember, that that does not very often happen.''

''Well, it's much easier not to. But this time I had to decide about the future. And I've decided to leave the stage and just be a mother.''

''A *rôle* that will suit you admirably. Already I foresee delightful pictures in the Sketch and the Tatler.''

Rosamund smiled happily.

''Yes, it's wonderful. Do you know, Michael is *delighted*. I didn't really think he would be.''

She paused and added:

''Susan's got the malachite table. I thought, as I was having a baby—''

She left the sentence unfinished.

''Susan's cosmetic business promises well,'' said Helen. ''I think she is all set for a big success.''

''Yes, she was born to succeed,'' said Poirot. ''She is like her uncle.''

''You mean Richard, I suppose,'' said Rosamund. ''Not Timothy?''

''Assuredly not like Timothy,'' said Poirot.

They laughed.

''Greg's away somewhere,'' said Rosamund. ''Having a rest cure Susan *says?*''

She looked inquiringly at Poirot who said nothing.

''I can't think why he kept on saying he'd killed Uncle Richard,'' said Rosamund. ''Do you think it was a form of Exhibitionism?''

Poirot reverted to the previous topic.

''I received a very amiable letter from Mr. Timothy Abernethie,'' he said. "He expressed himself as highly satisfied with the services I had rendered the family."

"I do think Uncle Timothy is quite awful," said Rosamund.

"I am going to stay with them next week," said Helen. "They seem to be getting the gardens into order, but domestic help is still difficult."

"They miss the awful Gilchrist, I suppose," said Rosamund. "But I daresay in the end, she'd have killed Uncle Timothy, too. What fun if she had!"

"Murder has always seemed fun to you, Madame."

"Oh! not really," said Rosamund, vaguely. "But I *did* think it was George." She brightened up. "Perhaps he will do one some day."

"And that will be fun," said Poirot sarcastically.

"Yes, won't it?" Rosamund agreed.

She ate another éclair from the plate in front of her.

Poirot turned to Helen.

"And you, Madame, are off to Cyprus?"

"Yes, in a fortnight's time."

"Then let me wish you a happy journey."

He bowed over her hand. She came with him to the door, leaving Rosamund dreamily stuffing herself with cream pastries.

Helen said abruptly:

"I should like you to know, M. Poirot, that the legacy Richard left me meant more to me than theirs did to any of the others."

"As much as that, Madame?"

"Yes. You see—there is a child in Cyprus. . . . My husband and I were very devoted—it was a great sorrow to us to have no children. After he died my loneliness was unbelievable. When I was nursing in London at the end of the war, I met someone . . . He was younger than I was and married, though not very happily. We came together for a little while. That was all. He went back to Canada—to his wife and his children. He never knew about—our child. He would not have wanted it. I did. It seemed like a miracle to me—a middle-aged woman with everything behind her. With Richard's money I can educate my so-called nephew, and give him a start in life." She paused, then added, "I never told Richard. He was fond of me and I of him—but he would not have understood. You know so much about us all that I thought I would like you to know this about me."

Once again Poirot bowed over her hand.

He got home to find the armchair on the left of the fireplace occupied.

"Hullo, Poirot," said Mr. Entwhistle. "I've just come back from the Assizes. They brought in a verdict of Guilty, of course. But I shouldn't be surprised if she ends up in Broadmoor. She's gone definitely over the edge since she's been in prison. Quite happy you know, and *most* gracious. She spends her time making the most elaborate plans to run a chain of tea shops. Her newest establishment is to be the Lilac Bush. She's opening it in Cromer."

"One wonders if she was always a little mad? But me, I think not."

"Good Lord, no! Sane as you and I when she planned that murder. Carried it out in cold blood. She's got a good head on her, you know, underneath the fluffy manner."

Poirot gave a little shiver.

"I am thinking," he said, "of some words that Susan Banks said—that she had never imagined a *ladylike* murderer."

"Why not?" said Mr. Entwhistle. "It takes all sorts."

They were silent—and Poirot thought of murderers he had known. . . .